The Burning Stone

VOLUME THREE
OF
CROWN OF STARS

Kate Elliott

DAW BOOKS, INC.

DONALD A. WOLLHEIM, FOUNDER
375 Hudson Street, New York, NY 10014
ELIZABETH R. WOLLHEIM
SHEILA E. GILBERT
PUBLISHERS
www.dawbooks.com

AUTHOR'S NOTE

My thanks to my parents, Katharine Kerr, Blanca Maldonado, and Dorothy Hosler, for keeping me sane when it most mattered. More thanks go to Jeanne Reames Zimmerman, Howard Kerr, Michelle Sagara, and Sherwood Smith for taking the time to read the manuscript in its various stages of dishabille. Ann Marie Rasmussen, Ingrid Baber, and Morten Stokholm offered up details or insights when they were most needed (sometimes right at deadline). Jay Silverstein, as usual, solved the most dastardly of plot problems; I couldn't have done it without him, as he well knows. My editor, Sheila Gilbert, was always available, as long as I had access to a phone.

The Bibliographic Note at the end of *Prince of Dogs* still holds true for this volume, and although I was tempted to add another one here because of the many wonderful works I have consulted during the writing of this series and without which the landscape would, as I have said elsewhere, been immeasurably less rich, I will only mention here three translations of old texts: the always entertaining, not to mention often gleefully lurid, writings of Liudprand of Cremona, translated by F. A. Wright and edited by John Julius Norwich in an Everyman's Library edition; and the marvelous, brutal, and vivid *Saga of the Jomsvikings* (by an unknown writer) and *Heimskringla: History of the Kings of Norway* (attributed to Snorri Sturleson), both translated by Lee M. Hollander and published by the University of Texas Press.

I mention these works so that those who are interested can read about one small corner of that fascinating history of humankind which is our shared heritage. Writers don't work in a vacuum; it's a bit of a cliché to say that I could not have written what I have without those who came before, but nevertheless it's still true.

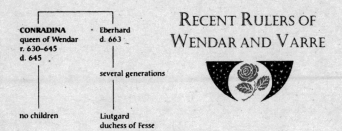

RECENT RULERS OF WENDAR AND VARRE

CONRADINA
queen of Wendar
r. 630–645
d. 645

Eberhard
d. 663

several generations

no children

Liutgard
duchess of Fesse

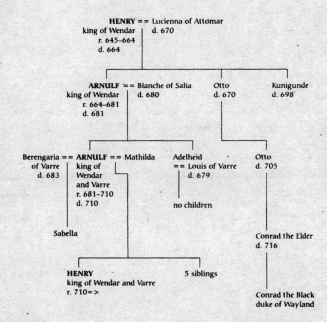

HENRY == Lucienna of Attomar
king of Wendar   d. 670
r. 645–664
d. 664

ARNULF == Blanche of Salia   Otto   Kunigunde
king of Wendar   d. 680   d. 670   d. 698
r. 664–681
d. 681

Berengaria == **ARNULF** == Mathilda   Adelheid   Otto
of Varre   king of   == Louis of Varre   d. 705
d. 683   Wendar   d. 679
           and Varre
           r. 681–710   no children
           d. 710

Sabella

                                                    Conrad the Elder
                                                    d. 716

HENRY   5 siblings
king of Wendar and Varre
r. 710=>

                                                    Conrad the Black
                                                    duke of Wayland

== married
r.   reigned
d.   died

CONTENTS

PROLOGUE

HE had run this far without being caught, but he knew his Quman master still followed him. Convulsive shudders shook him where he huddled in the brush that crowded a stream. His robes were still damp. Yesterday he had eluded them by swimming a river, but they hadn't given up. Prince Bulkezu would never allow a slave to taunt him publicly and then run free.

At last he calmed himself enough to listen to the lazy flow of water and to the wind rustling through leaves. Across the stream a pair of thrushes with spotted breasts stepped into view, plump and assertive. Ai, God he was starving.

The birds fluttered away as if they had gleaned his thoughts instead of insects. He dipped a hand in the water, sipped; then, seduced by its cold bite, he gulped down handfuls of it until his skin ached. By his knee a mat of dead leaves made a hummock. He turned it up and with the economy of long practice scooped up a mass of grubs and popped them in his mouth. Briefly he felt their writhing, but he had learned to swallow fast.

He coughed, hacking, wanting to vomit. He was a savage, to eat so. But what had the Quman left him? They had mocked him for his preaching, and therefore had taken his book and his freedom. They had mocked him for his robes, his clean-shaven chin, and his proud defense of Lady and Lord and the Circle of Unity between female and male, and therefore treated him as they did their own female slaves or any man they considered sheath instead of sword—with such indignity that he winced to recall it now. And they had done worse, far far worse, and laughed as they did it; it had been sport to them, to make a man into a woman in truth, an act they considered the second worst insult that could be given to a man. Ai, God! It had not been insult but pain and infection that had almost caused him to die.

But that was all over now. He had run before they took away his tongue, which truly mattered more to him than the other.

Water eddied along the bank. A hawk's piercing cry made him start. He had rested long enough. Cautiously he eased free of the brush, forded the stream, and fell into the steady lope that he used to cover ground. He was so tired. But west lay the land out of which he had walked in pride so many years ago that he had lost count: five or seven or nine. He meant to return there, or die. He would not remain a Quman slave any longer.

Dusk came. The waxing moon gave him enough light to see by as he walked on, a shadow among shadows on the colorless plain. Stars wheeled above, and he kept to a westerly course by keeping the pole star to his right.

Very late, a spark of light wavering on the gloomy landscape caught his attention. He cursed under his breath. Had the warband caught and passed him, and did they now wait as a spider waits for the fly to land? But that was not proud Bulkezu's way. Bulkezu was honorable in the way of his people—if that could be called honor—but he was also like a bull when it came to problems: he had no subtlety at all. Strength and prowess had always served him well enough.

No, this was someone—or something—else.

He circled in, creeping, until in the gray predawn light he saw the hulking shapes of standing stones at the height of a rise, alone out here on the plain as though a giant had once stridden by and placed them there carelessly, a trifle now forgotten. His own people called such stone circles "crowns," and this fire shone from within the crown. He knew then it was no Quman campsite—they were far too superstitious to venture into such a haunted place.

He crept closer on his hands and knees. Grass pricked his hands. The moon set as the first faint wash of light spread along the eastern horizon. The fire blazed higher and yet higher until his eyes stung from its glare. When he came to the nearest stone, he hid behind its bulk and peeked around.

That harsh glare was no campfire.

Within the ring of stones stood a smaller upright stone, no taller or thicker than a man. And it burned.

Stone could not burn.

Reflexively, he touched the wooden Circle of Unity he still wore. He would have prayed, but the Quman had taken his faith together with so much else.

A woman crouched beside the burning stone. She had the well-rounded curves of a creature that eats as much as it wants, and the sleek power of a predator, muscular and quick. Her hair had the same color as the height of flame that cast a net of fire into the empty air. Her skin, too, wore a golden-bronze gilding, a sheen of flame, and she wore necklaces that glittered and sparked under the light of that unearthly fire.

Witchfire.

She swayed, rocking from heel to heel as she chanted in a low voice.

The stone flared so brightly that his eyes teared, but he could not look away. He *saw* through the burning stone as through a gateway, saw another country, *heard* it, a place more shadow than real, as faint as the spirit world his ancient grandmother had told tales about but with the sudden gleam of color, bright feathers, white shells, a trail of dun-colored earth, a sharp whistle like that of a bird.

Then the vision vanished, and the stone snuffed out as though a blanket of earth thrown on the fire had smothered it.

Stone and fire both were utterly *gone*.

A moment later the lick and spit of everyday flame flowered into life. The woman fed a common campfire with dried dung and twigs. As soon as it burned briskly, she made a clucking sound with her tongue, stood, and turned to face *him*.

Ai, Lord! She wore leather sandals, bound by straps that wound up her calves, and a supple skirt sewn of pale leather that had been sliced off raggedly at knee length. And nothing else, unless one could count as clothing her wealth of necklaces. Made of gold and beads, they draped thickly enough that they almost covered her breasts—until she shifted. A witch, indeed.

She did not look human. In her right hand she held a spear tipped with an obsidian point.

"Come," she said in the Wendish tongue.

It had been so long since he had heard the language of his own people that at first he did not recognize what he heard.

"Come," she repeated. "Do you understand this tongue?" She tried again, speaking a word he did not know.

His knees ached as he straightened up. He shuffled forward

slowly, ready to bolt, but she only watched him. A double stripe of red paint like a savage's tattoo ran from the back of her left hand up around the curve of her elbow, all the way to her shoulder. She wore no curved felt hat on her head, as Quman women did, nor did she cover her hair with a shawl, as Wendish women were accustomed to do. Only leather strips decorated with beads bound her hair back from her face. A single bright feather trailed down behind, half hidden. The plume shone with such a pure, uncanny green that it seemed to be feathered with slivers from an emerald.

"Come forward," she repeated in Wendish. "What are you?"

"I am a man," he said hoarsely, then wondered bitterly if he could name himself such now.

"You are of the Wendish kin."

"I am of the Wendish kin." He was shocked to find how hard it was to speak out loud the language he had been forbidden to speak among the Quman. "I am called—" He broke off. *Dog, worm, slave-girl,* and *piece-of-dung* were the names given him among the Quman, and there had been little difference in meaning between the four. But he had escaped the Quman. "I—I was once called by the name Zacharias, son of Elseva and Volusianus."

"What are you to be called now?"

He blinked. "My name has not changed."

"All names change, as all things change. But I have seen among the human kin that you are blind to this truth."

To the east, the rim of sun pierced the horizon, and he had to shade his eyes. "What are you?" he whispered.

Wind had risen with the dawning of day.

But it was not wind. It sang in the air like the whirring of wings, and the sound of it tore the breath out of his chest. He tried to make a noise, to warn her, but the cry lodged in his throat. She watched him, unblinking. She was alone, as good as unarmed with only a spear to protect her; he knew with what disrespect the Quman treated women who were not their own kin.

"Run!" he croaked, to make her understand.

He spun, slammed up against stone, and swayed there, stunned. The towering stone block hid him from view. He could still flee, yet wasn't it too late once you could hear their wings spinning and humming in the air? Like the griffins who stalked

the deep grass, the Quman warriors took their prey with lightning swiftness and no warning but for that bodiless humming
vibrating in the air, the sound of their passage.

He had learned to mark their number by the sound: at least
a dozen, not more than twenty. Singing above the rest ran the
liquid iron thrum of true griffin wings.

He began, horribly, to weep with fear. The Quman had said,
"like a woman"; his own people would say, "like a coward and
unbeliever," one afflicted with weakness. But he was so tired,
and he *was* weak. If he had been strong, he would have embraced martyrdom for the greater glory of God, but he was too
afraid. He had chosen weakness and life. That was why They
had forsaken him.

She shifted to gaze east through the portal made by standing
stones and lintel. He was so shocked by her lack of fear that he
turned—and saw.

They rode with their wings scattering the light behind them
and the whir of their feathers drowning even the pounding of
their horses' hooves. Their wings streamed and spun and hummed
and vibrated. Once he had thought them real wings, but he knew
better now: They were feathers attached by wire to wooden
frames riveted to the body of their armored coats. That armor
had a scaly gleam, strips of metal sewn onto stiff leather coats.
On a standard fixed to a spear they bore the mark of the Pechanek
clan: the rake of a snow leopard's claw. The Quman had many
tribes. This one he knew well, to his sorrow.

At the fore rode a rider whose wings shone with the hard
iron fletching of griffin feathers. Like the others he wore a metal
visor shaped and forged into the likeness of a face, blank and
intimidating, but Zacharias did not need to see his face to know
who it was.

Bulkezu.

The name struck at his heart like a deathblow.

A band of fifteen riders approached the ring of stones, slowing now, the hum of their wings abating. From a prudent distance they examined the stone circle and split up to scout its
perimeter and assess the stone portals, the lay of the ground,
and the strength of its defenders. The horses shied at first, made
skittish by the great hulking stones or by the shadow of night
that still lingered inside the ring, but taking courage from their
masters, they settled and agreed to move in closer.

The woman braced herself at the eastern portal with her spear in one hand. She showed no fear as she waited. The riders called out to each other. Their words were torn away on a wind Zacharias could not feel on his skin—audible but so distant that he could make out no meaning to what they shouted to each other, as though the sound came to him through water.

At once the whirring began again as all the riders kicked into a gallop and charged, some from the left, some from the right, some from the other side of the circle. Wings hummed; hooves pounded; otherwise they came silently except for the creak and slap of their armored coats against the wooden saddles.

With the rising sun bright in his eyes, Zacharias saw Bulkezu as iron wings and iron face and gleaming strips of iron armor. The two feathers stuck on either side of his helmet flashed white and brown. The griffin feathers fletched in the curving wooden wings that were fastened to his back shone with a deadly iron gleam. Where the ground leveled off, just beyond the eastern portal, he galloped toward the waiting woman, lowering his spear.

Zacharias hissed out a breath, but he did not act. He already knew he was a coward and a weakling. He could not stand boldly against the man who had first mocked him, then violated him, and then wielded the knife.

He could not stand boldly—but he watched, at first numb and then with a surge of fierce longing for the woman who waited without flinching. With an imperceptible movement she opened her fingers. From within her uncurling hand mist swirled into being to engulf the world beyond. Only the air within the stone circle remained untouched, tinted with a vague blue haze. An unearthly fog swallowed the world beyond the stones.

All sound dissolved into that dampening fog, the whir and hum of spinning feathers, the approach of the horses, the distant skirl of wind through grass.

With a sudden sharp exclamation, the woman leaped to one side. A horse loomed, became solid as griffin feathers cut a burning path through the mist. In stillness the horse jumped out of the fog and galloped into the ring of stones, hooves clattering on pebbles. Bulkezu had to duck so that his wings did not strike the lintel stone above.

The other riders could be seen as fleeting figures searching for a portal to enter, yet they were no more substantial than fish swimming beneath the cloudy surface of a pond. They could not leave their fog-enshrouded world. They could not enter the circle.

The war leader quickly scanned the interior of the stone ring, but the woman had vanished. As he turned his horse in a tight circle the griffin feathers left sparks behind them in the blue haze. Of all things in this place, those feathers alone seemed immune to the witchcraft that had been brought to life.

"Dog!" he called, seeing Zacharias through the haze. "Crawling one! You have not escaped me!" He nudged his horse forward, tucked his spear between leg and horse's belly, and drew his sword. Zacharias shrank back, trapped against the stone. He had nowhere to run.

But the horse had taken no more than three steps when the earth began to shake and the huge stones groaned and creaked and seemed to swing wildly from side to side, although Zacharias felt nothing at his own back except solid, unmoving stone. Bulkezu's horse stumbled to its knees, neighing in terror, and Bulkezu himself was thrown. Stones swayed as if whatever spell had set them in place was at this moment unweaving itself, and Zacharias shrieked, flinging up his hands to protect himself, although mere flesh could not protect him against stone.

This was more than witchcraft.

The woman appeared again in the center of the circle, surefooted and unshaken by the earth's tremors except for the flashing shimmer and sway of beads dangling among her gold necklaces. Bulkezu struggled up from his hands and knees behind her. Zacharias tried to call a warning, but the breath sucked into his lungs congealed there and he could only gasp and choke and point.

With a grunt, the woman swung around to bring the flat of the obsidian blade down between the two arched spines of Bulkezu's wings, onto his head. The blow laid him flat on his stomach, and his helmet canted awkwardly to one side, almost torn off. Blood swelled from the base of his skull to mat his black hair. The shaking subsided, but the haze remained. Outside the circle the other riders flitted by this portal and that, still searching for an entrance.

The woman stepped closer to Bulkezu—that fast he rolled to one side and jerked himself up and back around in a half turn. The tips of his deadly wings hissed through the air to slice her across the abdomen and through her sheath of necklaces. Beads of jade and turquoise, pellets of gold, rained onto the ground around her. He leaped backward, up to his feet, sword held before him. His helmet he slapped down, and again when it would not settle right around his eyes, and then, with an angry grunt, he wrenched it off and flung it to one side so that, finally, his face was exposed—proud and handsome in the Quman way.

Ugly red welts bloomed on the woman's bronze-dark skin. Blood welled from the cuts and snaked down in vermilion beads to lodge in the waistband of her skirt.

They faced off, each wounded, each warrior now. In this way they measured each the other: the Quman warrior made fearsome by the glint of the griffin feathers bound into the wings at his back—only a man who had killed a griffin could wear such wings; and the foreign woman, not of human breed or birthing, with her bronze cast of skin and hair, her own blood seeping unheeded down her belly. Her gaze on her opponent was as unyielding as the stone behind Zacharias' back.

Bulkezu sprang forward, batting at the spear with his sword and closing the distance between them. Zacharias gasped aloud. But her spear circled around Bulkezu's blow, and as she stepped aside, she caught him with the haft, a strike behind his knee. She was neither frail nor slender; the force of her blow dropped him to his knees, but he sat down hard, locking the haft beneath him, and lashed out with his sword. She leaped back, abandoning the spear. But as he rose to pursue her, the spear *moved*. Like a serpent come to life, it twined around his legs. He fell, catching himself on his hands, but where his sword struck earth, it sank into the dirt as if hidden claws dragged it down into the depths. No matter how hard he scrabbled, he could not grab it.

She raised her arms again, chest naked now except for a single strand of gold that curved along the swell of a breast. The shaking resumed, more violent than before. The great lintel stones rocked and teetered and began to slide. Wind battered Zacharias to his knees. With his dagger Bulkezu hacked at the magicked spear wound around his legs, but to no avail. With each cut it merely grew spurs and flourishes, and these spurs sprouted roots that embedded themselves into the ground until its many-limbed net pinned his calves to the dirt and twined up his arms. In frustration he threw his dagger at her. With her arms outstretched and blood trickling down her breasts to pool in the folds of her skirt, she merely stared.

But the dagger slowed—or was that a trick of the haze and the trembling earth? As the shaking subsided, the dagger froze, suspended in the air.

Impossible. Zacharias staggered up to his feet, leaning on the stone for strength. *What was she?*

"Damn you, witch, what do you want?" cried Bulkezu, but she did not reply; she did not appear to understand him, and neither did she appear to care. In the seething fog beyond the stone circle, riders still quested back and forth and around the ring of stones for some way to get inside.

Bulkezu struggled on the ground but could not free himself from the rootlike tangle that bound him hand and foot. His sword had vanished into the earth. He looked furious. Brought down by a mere woman, and one armed with the most primitive of weapons! But Bulkezu's hatred could not be more tangible than Zacharias' exultation.

Zacharias actually crowed, the rooster's call. He had lived to see Bulkezu brought low.

"Sorcery is a weapon more powerful than a blade," Zacharias cried in the tongue of the Quman people. "What matter that she is a mere woman and you are a strong warrior? What matter that the tribes sing your praises because you slew a griffin, the first warrior in a generation to do so? You may be adept at war, mighty one, but she is armed with something more dangerous than brute strength. Her sorcery binds you. You can only kill her, never compel her to your will as she does to you now. And the truth is, you can't kill her either."

"Dogs can bark, but it is all noise," snapped Bulkezu without looking at him. He did not look away from his opponent. "As for you, you who are only a woman, you have made an enemy this day."

But the woman only smiled, as if she found his threats so insignificant as to be laughable. At that moment Zacharias fell in love with her—or with what she was, and what she had: She was no coward, and her gods walked with her. What matter that he no longer possessed that portion of a man that some considered to be all the measure of manhood? Hadn't the blessed Daisan himself said that the peace of true love lasts until the end of days, and has nothing to do with carnal desire? She was everything he was not.

"I beg you," he called hoarsely in the Wendish tongue, "let me serve you so that I may teach myself strength."

She looked at him, then turned away to catch the horse and hobble it. To one side of the fire lay a basket and a quiver. She unearthed bow and arrows, and with some care she approached the furious warrior and plucked a griffin's feather from the wooden frame which, like two shepherd's crooks, arched over his head. Her fingers bled at once, and profusely, but she only licked her fingers and murmured words, like a prayer, under her breath.

"Nay, I beg you, let me do it." Zacharias stumbled forward as Bulkezu cursed out loud. "Let me do it. For he has shamed me, and in this way I may return shame upon him threefold."

She stepped back to regard him with narrowed eyes. He had never seen eyes of such green before, fathomless, as luminous as polished jade. Measuring him, she came to a decision. Before he could flinch back, she nicked his left ear with her obsidian knife, and when he yelped in surprise, she licked welling blood from his skin—and then handed him the knife and turned her back on him as she would on a trusted servant.

"Strike now!" cried Bulkezu, "and I will give you an honorable position among my slaves!"

"There is no honor among slaves. You are no longer my master!"

"Do you not recognize what she is? *Ashioi*, the tribe of gold. The ones who vanished from the bones of earth."

A chill from the stones seeped into Zacharias' skin and soaked through to his bones. It all made sense now. She had come from the spirit world. She was one of the Aoi, the Lost Ones.

Bulkezu grunted, still struggling. Only a man who never ceased striving could stalk and slay a griffin. "I will lay a blood-price on her. My riders will track you, and kill her, and bring you back to grovel at my feet."

Zacharias laughed, and at once his fear sloughed off, a trifle compared to the prospect of victory over the man who had humiliated him. "You bargain and then threaten, Bulkezu, mightiest son of the Pechanek clan. But what you took from me is nothing to what I am about to take from you, because the flesh is given by the god to all men but your prowess and reputation can never be returned once they are taken from you. And by a

dog, a piece-of-dung who was used as you use slave women!"
He reached for a feather.

"I curse you! You will never be more than a slave, and always a worm! And I will kill you! I swear this on Tarkan's bones!"

Like an echo of the threat, the iron-hard feathers sliced Zacharias' skin with each least touch until his palms and fingers were a mass of seeping cuts. Blood smeared his hands and made them slick while Bulkezu struggled and cursed but could not free himself from his bindings as Zacharias denuded his wings.

He took everything, all but one, and when he was finished, his hands bled and his heart rejoiced. "Kill him now!" he cried.

"His blood will slow me down." She said it without emotion, and by that he understood there was no possible argument. "Nor will you touch him," she added. "If you will serve me, then you will serve my cause and not your own."

She grasped Zacharias' hands and licked them clean of blood, then let him go and indicated that he should stow most of the feathers in the quiver. She fletched several of her stone-tipped arrows with griffin feathers, afterward hefting them in her hand, testing their weight and balance. When she was satisfied, she went to the eastern portal and began to shoot, one by one, the riders who circled her sanctuary. At once they sprayed a killing rain of arrows back into the stones. She had downed four of them before they truly understood that although neither they nor their arrows could get into the circle, her arrows could come out. At last they retreated out of arrowshot with their wounded. As from a great distance Zacharias saw them examine the arrows and exclaim over them while one rider galloped away eastward.

"My tribe will come soon with more warriors," said Bulkezu, even though he knew by now that the woman did not understand his words. He had recovered himself and spoke without malice but with the certainty of a man who has won many battles and knows he will win more. "Then you will be helpless, even with my feathers."

"And you will be helpless without them!" cried Zacharias.

"I can kill another griffin. In your heart, crawling one, you will never be more than a worm."

"No," whispered Zacharias, but in his heart he knew it was true. Once he had been a man in the only way that truly counted:

He had held to his vows. But he had forsaken his vows when God had forsaken him.

Bulkezu glanced toward the woman. He could move his neck and shoulders, wiggle a bit to ease the weight on his knees and hands, but he was otherwise pinned to earth, no matter how he tried to force or twist his way free of her spell. "I will raise an army, and when I have, I will burn every village in my path until I stand with your throat under my heel and her head in my hands."

Zacharias shuddered. But he had come too far to let fear destroy him. Against all hope he was a free man again, bound by his own will into the service of another. He might be a worm in his heart, but hearts could change. *She* had said that all things change.

"Come, you who were once called Zacharias-son-of-Elseva-and-Volusianus." She had stepped back from the edge of the stone circle and hoisted two baskets woven of reeds and slung them from the ends of Bulkezu's spear, then balanced and bound the spear as a pole over the saddle. To the saddle she tied three pale skin pouches, odd looking things that each had five distended fingers probing out from the bottom as if they had been fashioned from a cow's misshapen udder or a bloated, boneless hand. She tossed dirt over the fire. She whistled tunelessly and wind rose, blowing the fog outside the sanctuary of the stone circle into tufts of a wicked, cutting gale. The distant riders retreated farther away.

Bulkezu strained against the spear with its many rootling arms that clasped him to the earth, but he still could not shift at all. The remaining griffin feather hissed and fluttered in the rising wind. While she tested the harness, ignoring him, he tested his shoulders to see how far he could slide his wings out, or if he could wedge himself down far enough to cut at the magicked staff with the iron edge of that last feather. "I will have my revenge!"

She took no notice of his threat. Instead, when everything was to her liking, she returned to the eastern portal to watch. Fog shrouded the land, and in this fog she—and Zacharias with her—could easily make their escape, concealed from the eyes and ears of the waiting riders. But how long would they have until the Quman riders tracked them down?

She turned to smile at him as if, like the spotted thrush, she had divined his thoughts. Carefully, she wiped drying blood from her abdomen, then clapped red-streaked hands together and spoke words. A flash of heat blasted Zacharias' face, and suddenly, as the burning stone winked back into existence in the center of the stone circle, he knew that the Aoi woman would not leave this sanctuary by any earthly road.

The woman regarded him unblinking, as if testing his courage. Bulkezu said nothing. Zacharias dropped the horse's reins and untied the bedroll behind the saddle, shook it out to reveal the fine knee-length leather jacket that Quman men wore when they did not wear armor. He offered this to her so that she could cover herself, because not even necklaces covered her upper body now, only the smears and drying tracks of her own blood.

The stone burned without sound. Wind swirled round them, whistling through the stones.

Bulkezu threw back his head and howled, the eerie ululation that according to the shamans was the cry of the he-griffin. Zacharias had heard that call once, from far away, when the Pechanek clan had wandered the borderwild of the deep grass— the land beyond human ken into which only heroes and shamans might venture. Ai, God! He had never forgotten it.

But he would not let it rip his hard-won courage from him now.

She stepped forward. Zacharias followed, leading the horse.

The heat of fire burned his face, but just before he could flinch back from the flame, they passed through the gateway. Bulkezu's call, the high-pitched song of wind through grass and stone, the moist heat of a midsummer day blanketed by fog— all of these vanished as completely as though they had been sliced away by a keen and merciless blade.

PART ONE

THE DEAD HAND

I
THAT WHICH BINDS

1

THE ruins stretched from the river's bank up along a grassy slope to where the last wall crumbled into the earth at the steep base of a hill. Here, on this broken wall under the light of a waning quarter moon, an owl came to rest. It folded its wings, and with that uncanny and direct gaze common to owls it regarded the ring of stones crowning the hilltop beyond.

Stars faded as light rose and with it, shrouded in a low-hanging mist, the sun. The moon vanished into the brightening sky. Still the owl waited. A mouse scurried by through the dew-laden grass, yet the owl did not stir to snatch it. Rabbits nosed out of their burrows, and yet it let them pass unregarded. Its gaze did not waver, although it blinked once. Twice. Thrice.

Perhaps the mist cleared enough for the rising sun to glint on the stones that made up the huge standing circle at the height of the hill. A light flashed, and the owl launched itself into the air, beating hard to gain height. From above the stones it swooped down into the circle, where certain other stones lay on the soil in a pattern unreadable to human eyes. Flame flickered along the ancient grain of a smallish standing stone in the center of the ring. Out of the flame came faint words overheard in the same way that whispers escape through a keyhole, two voices in conflict.

"*It seems to me that you have all been too gentle. A firmer hand would have solved the matter long ago and bent this one you seek to your will.*"

"*Nay, Sister. You do not fully understand the matter.*"

"*Yet do you not all admit that I have certain gifts none of the rest of you possess? Is that not why I was brought among your number? Is it not fitting that you let me try my hand in this in case your other plan fails? Then you will see what I am capable of.*"

"*I am against it.*"

"*Yours is not the final word. Let the others speak.*"

Wind sighed in the distant trees and hummed through the stones. A hare bounded into view, froze, its ears twitching, and then flinched and leaped away into the cover of mustard flower and sedge.

"*We risk nothing if she fails,*" said a third voice. "*If she succeeds, we benefit, for then our absent sister can return here quickly and we can return to our work that much sooner.*"

Hard upon these words came a fourth voice, "*I am curious. I would like a demonstration of these methods we have heard so much about.*"

"*I care not,*" said the fifth voice, so faint that the sound of it almost died on the wind. "*This is a trifle. Do as you wish.*"

Now the first spoke again. "*Then I will attempt it. What has eluded you for so long will not elude me!*"

The owl glided down in a spiral. With sudden grace it folded its wings and, heedless of the flames, came to rest on the smooth knob at the top of the burning stone. The sun's light pierced the last strings of mist and broke brightly across the grandeur of the stone circle.

Between one moment and the next, the burning stone vanished—and the owl with it.

2

IN any village, a stranger attracts notice—and distrust. But Eagles weren't strangers, precisely; they were interchangeable, an arm of the king—his wings, so to speak—and they might come flying through and, after a meal and a night's sleep, fly away again, never truly at rest.

Liath had discovered that as a King's Eagle her only solitude on any errand she rode for the king came while actually on the road itself, because the roads were lightly traveled. Wherever she stopped to break her fast or for a night's shelter, she had no rest as long as she stayed awake. Villagers, deacons, chatelaines, nuns, even simple day laborers: All of them wanted gossip of the world beyond because few of them had ever ventured more than a day's walk from their home—and even fewer had actually seen the king and his court.

"Did the foreign queen die?" they would ask, surprised, although Queen Sophia had died almost four years ago.

"Lady Sabella rebelled against King Henry's authority?" they would cry, aghast and amazed, although all this had taken place a full year before.

"We heard the Eika sacked the city of Gent and are laying the countryside waste all around," they would confide nervously, and then she would calm their fears by telling them of the second battle of Gent and how Count Lavastine and King Henry had routed the Eika army and restored the ruined city to human hands.

To them, she was an exotic bird, bright, fleeting, quickly come and quickly gone. No doubt they would remember her, and her words, long after she had forgotten them and theirs.

It was a sobering thought.

In the village of Laderne full twenty souls crowded the house of her host, turning her visit into a festive gathering. They entertained her with songs and local gossip while she ate, but as

soon as her host brought her a mug of beer after the meal, they
turned their questions on her.

"What's your errand, Eagle? Where did you come from?
Where are you going?"

She had learned to judge how much to say: when to keep
close counsel or when to be more forthcoming. Many people favored her with better food the more she told them, and this old
householder clearly thought her visitor important: She hadn't watered down the beer. "I'm riding to the palace at Weraushausen,
at the king's order. He left his schola there, many of his clerics
and most of the noble children who attend the progress. His own
young son, Prince Ekkehard, is among them. I'm to give them
word where they are to meet him."

"Weraushausen? Where's that?"

"Beyond the Bretwald," she said. They shook their heads,
hemmed and hawed, and advised her to ride carefully and on
no account to cut through the old forest itself.

"Young fools have tried it now and again," said Merla, the
old householder. She had about six teeth left and was proud of
them. "They always vanish. Killed by wolves and bears, no
doubt. Or worse things." She nodded with satisfaction, as if
pleased at their dreadful fate.

"Nay, I heard at market that foresters was cutting a road
through the heart of the Bretwald at the king's order," protested
one of the men. He had a face made bright red by many hours
working in the sun.

"As if any could do so," retorted the old woman. "But you've
said nothing of the king. Has he named an heir yet? This Prince
Ekkehard, perhaps?"

"He has an eldest daughter, Princess Sapientia. She's old
enough to be named as heir now that she's ridden to battle and
borne a child."

"Ach, yes, proven her fertility and led soldiers in war. God
have marked her as worthy to rule."

They nodded sagely all round, much struck by this sign of
God's favor, all except one thin man in the back. He sipped beer
and regarded Liath with pale eyes. He was almost as brown as
she was on his face and hands, but where his tunic lay unlaced
at his chest—for it was still warm—she could see how pale his
skin was where the sun didn't reach. "He'd another child, a son,
with a Salian name—*Sawnglawnt,* or something like that. He

was a grand fighter, captain of the King's Dragons. But I heard from a peddler that he and his Dragons died when the Eika took Gent."

She flushed, and was grateful that people who did not know her well could not see any change in her complexion, dark as it was. "Not dead," she said. How on God's earth did she manage to keep her voice from shaking? "He'd been held prisoner, but he was freed by troops under the command of Count Lavastine. He is now safe at the king's side."

They exclaimed over this miracle. She gulped down her beer. But the damage had already been done. That night she slept restlessly and in the morning blushed to recall her dreams.

Ai, Lady. What had he said to her six days ago as the dawn light rose over the king's camp, set up outside Gent?

"Marry me, Liath."

All day the sun shone as Liath rode northwest along the great northern loop of the Ringswaldweg. She passed only a few travelers during the day: two carters hauling coarse sailcloth weighted down by a dozen bars of pig iron; a quiet pack of day laborers seeking a harvest; a peddler pushing a handcart; and a trio of polite fraters walking south with bare feet, callused hands, and sun-chapped faces. The ancient forest known as the Bretwald loomed to her left, so thick that it was no wonder travelers did not bother to try to hack through it but rather suffered the long journey round its northern fringe. Land broken up by trees, pasture, and the occasional village surrounded by strips of fields marched along on her right. She was used to traveling. She liked the solitude, the changing landscape, the sense of being at one with the cosmos, a small moving particle in the great dance of light.

But now, as the late summer twilight overtook her, the wind began to blow, and for some reason she couldn't shake the feeling that something was following her. She glanced back along the road, but it lay empty.

Never trust the appearance of emptiness.

Clouds brought an early dusk, and she unrolled her cloak and threw it over her shoulders as rain spattered down. Because the summer had been dry, the road did not churn instantly to mud, but even so, the way bogged down and she soon despaired of reaching any kind of shelter for the night.

God knew she did not want to sleep outside on a night of storm and rain, far from any human habitation.

The rain slackened. From ahead, she heard a faint jingling of harness, and for an instant she breathed easier. She had no fear of lawful riders on the king's road.

For an instant.

Out of the darkening sky behind her, she heard a low reverberation, a tolling like that of a church bell. But she had passed no church since midday.

Was that sound the echo of a daimone's passing? Did such a creature pursue her again? She glanced back but saw no hollow-eyed daimone formed into the fair semblance of an angel gliding above the earth, saw no glass-feathered wings. Yet as the rising wind buffeted her, she felt a whisper:

"Liathano."

The air shuddered and rippled on the road far behind her, just where it hooked to the right around a bulge in the forest's girth. Columns of mist rose into the air like great tree trunks uprooted from the forest and spun into gauze.

Surely it was only a trick of the light. But claws seemed to sink into her, into her shoulders and deeper yet, right down to her heart, and those claws clutched at her, tugging her back toward the tolling bells. Why not just wait? Why not just slow down and wait?

"Come to me, Liathano. Do not run any longer. Only wait for us, and you will find peace."

Her horse snorted nervously and flattened its ears.

"Wait for us. Come to us."

She hesitated.

"Run," Da would answer. *"Run, Liath."*

The compulsion to wait slid from her like rainwater off a good roof. With fear and anger fueling her, she urged her mount forward. It eagerly broke into a canter. She glanced back, and her heart almost died within her. Creatures formed like columns of living oily smoke streamed along the road, chasing her. They had voices, a rustling murmur like countless leaves stirred in a gale, underscored by that terrible dull tolling bell-voice. That they were living creatures she did not doubt.

And they were gaining on her.

She freed her bow from its quiver, readied an arrow. On the wind she smelled a hot stench like that of the forge. Her horse bolted, and she let it run while she turned in the saddle and, drawing, measured the distance between her and her pursuers. She loosed, but the arrow fell harmlessly onto empty road.

The shout came as warning. "Hey, there! Look where you're going!"

Ahead, in the dimness, she saw a small party: two riders and an escort of four men-at-arms. A minor lord, perhaps, or a steward about the business of his lady: She did not recognize the sigil of a deer's head on white that marked the shields. They swung wide to make room for her headlong flight.

But as she drew breath to shout a warning to them in turn, light flashed to her right, and beyond the road where the ground swelled up to make a neat little tumulus, fire flashed and beckoned from a shadowy ring of standing stones.

An owl glided past, so close that her horse shied away rightward, breaking off the road. She needed no more urging than that. With her bow in one hand and the reins in the other, she let the horse have its head. It jumped a low ditch to reach the grassy slope that marked the tumulus. From the road, men shouted after her.

A moment later she heard screaming.

The horse took the slope with the speed of a creature fleeing fire, and yet it was fire that greeted them in the center of the tiny stone circle: seven small stones, two of them fallen, one listing. And in the center stood an eighth stone as tall as a man of middling height; it burned with a blue-white fire that gave off no heat.

The shrieking from the road turned into garbled noises that no human ought to be able to utter. She dared not look behind. Ahead, the owl settled with uncanny grace onto the top of the burning stone, and the horse leaped—

She shouted with surprise as blue-white flame flared all around her. Her horse landed, shied sideways, and stopped.

With reins held taut and the horse quiet under her, Liath stared around the clearing: beaten earth, a layer of yellowing scrub brush, and thin forest cover made up of small-leafed oak as well as trees she had never seen before. But her voice failed her when the man sitting on a rock rose to examine her with interest. Not a human man, by any measure: with his bronze-tinted skin and beardless face and his person decorated with all manner of beads and feathers and shells and polished stones, he was of another kinship entirely. Humans named his kind, Aoi, "the Lost Ones," the ancient elvish kin who had long since vanished from the cities and paths trodden by humanity.

But she knew him, and he knew her.

"You have come," he said. "Sooner than I expected. You must hide until the procession has passed, or I cannot speak for what judgment the council will pass on you and your presence here. Come now, dismount and give me the horse."

He looked no different than in the vision seen through fire, although he was smaller in stature than she expected. The feathers with which he decorated himself shone as boldly as if they had been painted. The flax rope at his thigh was perhaps a finger longer than when she had last seen him, weeks—or was it months?—ago. A tremulous moan sounded from the depths of the forest, and a moment later she recognized it as a horn call. She shaded her eyes, and there along a distant path seen dimly under shadows she saw a procession winding through the trees. At the head of the procession, a brilliant wheel of beaten gold and iridescent green plumes spun, although no wind blew.

"How did I come here?" she asked hoarsely. "The creatures were chasing me, and then I saw an owl ... and the burning stone." She turned in the saddle to see the stone still blazing, blue-white and cold. No owl flew.

"An owl," he mused, fingering a proud feather of mottled brown and white, one dull plume among the many bright ones that trimmed his forearm sheath. He smiled briefly, if not kindly. "My old enemy."

"Then the horse leaped, and I was here," she finished haltingly. She felt like a twig borne down a flooding stream. Too much was happening at once.

"Ah." He displayed the rope and the fiber he twined to create it. "Out of one thing, we make another, even if there is no change or addition of substance. Sometimes it is the pattern that matters most. These strands of flax, alone, cannot support me or aid me as this rope can, and yet are they not both the same thing?"

"I don't understand what you're saying."

"The burning stone is a gateway between the worlds. All of the stones are gateways, as we learned to our sorrow, but this one was not fashioned by means of mortal magics but rather is

part of the fabric of the universe. To use it, one must understand it."

"I don't know anything," she said bitterly. "So much was kept
hidden from me."

"Much is hidden," he agreed. "Yet nevertheless you have
come to me. If you are willing, I sense there is a great deal you
can learn."

"Ai, God. There's so much I need to know." Yet she hesitated. "But how long will it take? To learn everything I need to
know?"

He chuckled. "That depends on what you think you need to
know." But his expression became serious. "Once you have decided that, then it will take as long as it must." He glanced toward the procession in the forest, still mostly hidden from them
in their small clearing. "But if you mean to ask how long will
it take in the world of humankind, that I cannot answer. The
measure of days and years moves differently here than there."

"Ai, Lady!" She glanced at the stone. The fire had begun to
flicker down, dying.

"Why do you hesitate?" he pressed her. "Was this not the
wish of your heart?"

"The wish of my heart." Her voice died on the words as she
said them. Of course she must study. It was the only way to
protect herself. She wanted the knowledge so badly. She might
never have this chance again.

And yet—she could not help but look back.

"You are still bound to the other world," he said, not dismayed, not irritated, not cheerful. Simply stating what was true.
"Give me your hand."

He was not a person one disobeyed. She sheathed her bow
and held out a hand, then grunted with surprise and pain as he
cut her palm with an obsidian knife. But she held steady as blood
welled up, as he cut his hands in a similar fashion and clasped
one to hers so their blood flowed together. His free hand he
pressed against the stone. Fire flared, so bright she flinched away
from it, and her horse whickered nervously and shied. But the
old sorcerer's grip remained firm.

"Come with me," he said. "What has bound you to the world
of human kin?"

The fire opened, and together they saw within.

When he sprawls in the grass under the glorious heat of the sun, he can hear everything and nothing. He shuts his eyes, the better to listen.

A bee drones. A bird's repetitive whistle sounds from the trees. His horse grazes at the edge of the clearing, well out of reach of his other companions: three Eika dogs in iron collars and iron chains bound to an iron stake he has hammered into the ground. Bones crack under their jaws as they feed. These three are all that remain to him of the beasts who formed his war-band in Gent's cathedral. He hears their chains scraping each on the others as the dogs growl over the tastiest bits of marrow.

A stream gurgles and chuckles beyond them: he has washed there, although he will never truly wash the filth and the shame of Bloodheart's chains off himself no matter how often he spills water over his skin and cleanses himself with soap or sand or oil. Now he lies half-clothed in the sun to dry in merciful solitude.

Of human activity he hears nothing. He has fled the captivity of the king's court and found this clearing next to the track that leads northwest—in that direction she rode off on the king's errand eight days ago. Here, now, he relishes his freedom, bathing in sun and wind and the feel of good mellow earth and grass beneath his back.

A fly lands on his face and he brushes it away without opening his eyes. The heat melts pleasantly into his skin. Where his other hand lies splayed in the grass he has tossed down the square leather pouch, stiffened with metal plates and trimmed with ivory and gems, in which he shelters the book. He feels its weight just beyond his fingertips, although he does not need to touch it to know that it is still there, and what it means to him: a promise. He keeps it always with him or, when he hunts or bathes, ties it to the collar of one of the dogs. The dogs are the only ones among his new retinue he can trust.

Wind rustles in leaves, indifferent whispers so unlike the ones that follow his every movement among the courtiers—the one they think he can't hear.

Each day of the king's progress unfurls, flowers, and fades as in a haze. He waits.

Among the dogs, he has learned to be patient.

"That which binds you," said the sorcerer, but whether with surprise or recognition she could not tell.

"I made him a promise." As the vision faded, its passing throbbed in her like a new pain.

She knew better, she knew what she ought to do, what Da would tell her to do. But none of that mattered. For a year she had thought him dead.

"I have to go back." Then, hearing the words as if someone else had spoken them, she hurried on. "I'll come back to you. I swear it. I just have to go back—" She trailed off. She knew how foolish she sounded.

He merely let go of her hand and regarded her. He had no expression on his face except the quiescence of great age. "It is ever such with those who are young. But I do not believe your path will be a smooth one."

"Then I *can* come back?" Now that she had made the choice, she regretted having to go. But not so much that she could bring herself to stay.

"I cannot see into the future. Go, then."

"But there are creatures pursuing me—"

"So many mysteries. So much movement afoot. You must make your choice—there, or here. The gateway is closing."

The flames flickered lower until they rippled like a sheen of water trembling along the surface of the stone. If she waited too long, the choice would be made for her.

She reined the horse around and slapped its rump with the trailing end of her reins. It bolted forward, light surged, and her sight was still hazed with dancing spots and black dots and bright sparks when her shoulder brushed rough stone and they broke out of the ragged circle of stones with a flash of afternoon sun in her eyes.

Disoriented, she shaded her eyes with a hand until she could make out the road below. It was not yet twilight; an unseasonable chill stung the air. The Bretwald lay beyond the road, alive with birds come to feed at the verge. Crows flocked in the treetops. A vulture spiraled down and landed on a heap of rags that littered the roadside.

Of the fell creatures that had stalked her, there was no sign.

What had the old sorcerer said? *"The measure of days and years moves differently here than there."*

Had she arrived earlier than she had left? Was that even possible, to wait here beside the road when she was herself riding on that same road, not yet having reached this point? She shook herself and urged the horse forward, looking around cautiously. But nothing stirred. The crows flapped away with raucous cries. The vulture at last bestirred itself and flew, but only to a nearby branch, where it watched as she picked her way up to the road-side and dismounted to examine the litter: a jumble of bones scoured clean; damp tabards wilted on the turf or strewn with pebbles as though a wind had blown over them; and weapons left lying every which way. With her boot she turned over a shield: A white deer's head stared blankly at her.

She jumped back, found shelter in the bulk of her horse, who blew noisily into her ear, unimpressed by these remains.

The men-at-arms she had seen had borne shields marked with a white deer's head. And she had heard screaming. How long could it have been? It would take months for a body to rot to clean bone.

The light changed as a scrap of cloud scudded over the sun, and she shivered in the sudden cold. She mounted and rode on, northward, as she had before. As dusk lowered, she studied the heavens with apprehension throbbing in her chest. Stars came out one by one. Above her shone summer's evening sky. Had she lost an entire year?

Ahead, a torch flared, and then a second, and she urged her mount forward, smelling a village ahead. A low, square church steeple loomed, cutting off stars. They had not yet closed the palisade gates of the little town, which protected them against wild animals as well as the occasional depredations of what ban-dits still lurked in the Bretwald. The gatekeeper sent her on to the church, where the deacon kept mats for travelers and a sim-mering pot of leek stew for the hungry.

Liath was starving. Her hands shook so badly that she could barely gulp down stew and cider as the deacon watched with mild concern.

"What day is it?" Liath asked when at last her hands came back under her control, and the sting of hunger softened.

"Today we celebrated the nativity of St. Theodoret, and to-morrow we will sing the mass celebrating the martyrdom of St. Walaricus."

Today was the nineteenth of Quadrii, then; the day she had fled the creatures had been the eighteenth. For an instant she breathed more easily. Then she remembered the bones, and the party she had almost met on the road.

"What year?"

"An odd question," said the deacon, but she was a young woman and not inclined to question a King's Eagle. "It is the year 729 since the Proclamation of the Divine Logos by the blessed Daisan."

One day later. Only one day. The bones she had seen by the roadside had nothing to do with her, then. They must have lain there for months, picked clean by the crows and the vultures and the small vermin that feed on carrion.

Only later, rolled up in her blanket on a mat laid down in the dark entry hall of the church, did it occur to her that the clothing left behind with the bones on the roadside was damp but not rotted or torn. Had it lain there for months or years, it, too, would have begun to rot away.

3

THE hunting party burst out of the forest and then scattered aimlessly into small groups, having lost the scent. The king rode among a riot of his good companions, all laughing at a comment made by Count Lavastine. Alain had fallen back to the fringe, and now he reined in his horse to watch a trio of young men fishing in the river an arrow's shot upstream. Hip-deep in water, they flung nets wide over the glittering surface.

"Alain." Count Lavastine halted beside him. The black hounds snuffled in the grass that edged the cliff, which fell away about a man's height before hillside met river. A rock, dislodged by Fear, skittered down the slope, stirring up a shower of dust, and the other hounds all barked in a delighted frenzy as they scrambled back.

"Peace!" said Lavastine sternly, and at once they quieted, obedient to his wishes. He turned his gaze to Alain. "You must come ride closer to the king, Son."

"Their task seems easier than mine." Alain indicated the fishermen below. Stripped down to their breechclouts, the fishermen enjoyed the purl of the water around their bodies and the hot sun on their glistening backs without any thought except for the labor at hand. He heard their laughter ringing up from the distant shore.

"A drought, a late freeze, a rainy Aogoste. Any of these could ruin their crops."

"But at least the rivers always breed fish. I'm never quite sure what the noble parties are hunting."

"You do not like the form of this hunt. But it is one you must learn, and you must learn to judge which party will succeed and which will fail. In this way we make our alliances. The prince favors you."

"The princess does not."

"Only because you are favored by the prince."

"Because I am a bastard, as he is."

"*Were,*" said Lavastine with a sudden bite to his tone, like a hound's sharp nip, more warning than attack. "You are legitimately claimed and honored now."

"Yes, Father," said Alain obediently. "But when she sees me and then sees Lord Geoffrey, it reminds Princess Sapientia that the king may choose another claimant over her when it comes time to anoint his heir." The hounds sat, panting, in the sun: Rage, Sorrow, Ardent, Bliss, and Fear. Terror flopped down. Only Steadfast still sniffed along the verge of the bluff, intent on a scent that did not interest the others. A stone's toss back from the bluff, King Henry and his companions conferred, pointing toward the dense spur of woodland that thrust here into a scattering of orchard and fields of ripening oats cut into a neat patchwork by hedgerows.

"I have never much cared for the king's progress," said Lavastine finally. He, too, looked toward the forest. The bleat of a hunting horn floated on the air.

"You don't like the king?" asked Alain, daring much since they were alone, unheard except by the hounds.

Lavastine had a hard, compelling gaze; he turned it on Alain now. "The king stands beyond our likes or dislikes, Alain. I respect him, as he deserves. I hold no grievance against him as long as he leaves me and mine alone—and grants me that which I have won." The flash of approval in his eyes did not extend to his lips. "That which *we* won at Gent, you and I. There are many young men and some few women who would gladly join the ranks of your entourage, Alain, if you were to show them your favor. You have learned your manners perfectly, and you carry yourself as well—or better—than most of the young nobles whom we see here at court. You have done well to remain above their games and useless intrigues. But now it is time to build your own retinue."

Alain sighed. "My foster family brought me up to work and to be proud of that labor. Yet here, should I only gossip and hunt and drink? In truth, Father, I don't feel at ease in their company. But if I don't indulge in these amusements, then I fear they'll think me unworthy."

Lavastine smiled slightly. "You are not swayed by their levity, as you should not be. You have made a name for yourself in war. Others have noticed that you also apply yourself to the study of *scientia*. It's such practical knowledge that will allow you to administer Lavas lands as well as I have done in my time. Your serious manner proves in the eyes of the worthy that you are cast of noble metal."

The praise embarrassed Alain. He did not feel worthy. Below, the fishermen had hauled their nets out into the shallows and now shouted and whooped with the good cheer of young men who haven't a care in the world as they tossed fish into baskets that rested on the rocky shore. A few fish slipped from their hands in twisting leaps that spun them back into the river and freedom. But the baskets were by now almost full; their contents churned and slithered, scales flashing in the light like liquid silver.

The horn rang out again, closer. A large animal erupted from cover and scrambled into the orchard. The king's huntsmen began shouting all at once, bringing their hunting spears to bear. Lavastine's hounds sprang up and tore away, only to stop short when Lavastine whistled piercingly. They barked furiously as a huge boar appeared in the distance beneath the shelter of a cluster of apple trees.

At that moment, two parties of about equal numbers galloped free of the woods, one from the southern edge of the spur of woodland and the other from its center. Princess Sapientia led the first party. Her banner rippled blue and white from a lance carried by a servant, and her companions thundered along beside her so colorfully outfitted that they obliterated the serenity of cultivated land. Some few even jumped hedgerows and tram-

pled fields in their haste to reach the boar before the other party
did.

That other party had come clear of the woodland closer to
the hunted beast, but their leader made such a clear point of
avoiding any stands of oat and bypassing one stoutly growing
field of beans that they closed on the boar from the north just
as Princess Sapientia and her entourage circled in from the south.
For an instant the two parties faced each other, as do enemy
forces in a skirmish: the princess small and fierce on a skittish
gelding rather too large for her; her half brother so at his ease
with a hunting spear in one hand and the other light on the reins
of a magnificent gray that he seemed to shine under the glare
of the sun.

The king raised a hand, and his own companions paused,
holding back. Everyone watched. The boar bolted away toward
the river, the only stretch of open ground left to it.

At once, Prince Sanglant galloped after it, leaving his party
behind. He had so much natural grace that Sapientia, racing after
him, had somewhat the appearance of a mongrel chasing a sleek
greyhound. No one rode after them: to the victor, the spoils.

Sanglant broke wide to drive the boar back from the bluff
and cut in from behind. Then he deliberately reined up to let
Sapientia take the kill, as if it were her prerogative. As if he
did not want what he could easily take.

She saw only his hesitation, his turning aside. The boar
bunched, charged; she thrust at its ribs and lodged the point of
her spear behind its front shoulder, but the beast got under her
horse and the horse went crazy, bucking while she clung to the
saddle.

Huntsmen came running, their brindle boarhounds coursing
ahead. Sanglant vaulted off his horse and sprinted for the
wounded beast. It saw his movement, and in its blind fear and
fury charged him. Distantly, Alain heard King Henry cry out.
But the prince only braced himself, showing no fear. The boar
impaled itself on his spearpoint and drove itself into the lugs.
Sanglant plunged his dagger into its eye to kill it.

Sapientia had calmed her horse and now claimed first blood.
The boarhounds leaped yelping and biting in a mob around the
dead boar, but they slunk back, whimpering, ears pinned down,
as Prince Sanglant laid about him with his fist, battering them
back as if he were the beast being hunted.

Only when the other riders approached did he shake himself, like a dog newly come from water, and step away to become a man again, tall and handsome in his fine embroidered tunic and leggings with a gold brooch clasping a short half-cloak across his broad shoulders. Yet the iron collar he wore at his neck instead of a gold torque of royal kinship looked incongruous; that, and the odd habit he had of scenting like a hound for smells on the air and of starting 'round like a wild animal at unexpected movement behind him.

Princess Sapientia cut over to Prince Sanglant, but before she could swing down beside him, she was distracted by her chief adviser, Father Hugh. With elegant grace he lured her away to the heady congratulations of her entourage.

"There is one at least," said Lavastine softly, watching the scene through narrowed eyes, "who wishes for no reconciliation between brother and sister."

After twenty days riding with the king's progress, Alain could not bring himself to like, trust, or even respect the handsome, charming, and ingenious Father Hugh. But he felt obliged to be fair. "Father Hugh is well spoken of by everyone at court. Everyone says his influence has benefited the princess immeasurably."

"Certainly his manners are excellent, and his mother is a powerful prince. I would not like to make an enemy of him. Nevertheless, he has thrown his weight behind Sapientia, and all that influence comes to naught if she does not become regnant after her father."

"I don't like him because of what he did to Liath," muttered Alain.

Lavastine raised an eyebrow and regarded his son skeptically. "You have only her word—that of a kinless Eagle—that he behaved as she describes. In any case, if she was his legal slave, then he could do what he wished with her." That easily he dismissed Liath's fears and terrors. "Still, the Eagle has uncommon gifts. Keep an eye on her, if you will. We may yet use her again to our advantage."

Prince Sanglant had retreated to the river, away from the kill and the commotion. His new hangers-on, uncertain of his temper as always, kept a safe distance although they made an obvious effort to distinguish themselves from those who flocked around Sapientia. The prince stood on the verge where the bluff plunged away to the water. The fishermen had stopped to stare at the sight of a noble lord and his fine retinue.

"He'll go in," said Alain suddenly, and as if his words—surely too distant for the prince to hear—triggered the action, Sanglant abruptly began to strip at the bluff's edge.

Tittering came from Sapienta's entourage. They had seen this behavior before: Prince Sanglant had a mania for washing himself. But to be without clothing in such a public setting was to be without the dignity and honor granted one by noble birth. Only common folk making ready to wash themselves or to labor on a hot day would as unthinkingly strip before all and sundry as kneel before God to pray.

The prince left his clothing on the ground and scrambled down the slope into the water. He had an astonishing number of white scars on his body, but he had begun to fill out. Alain could no longer count his ribs.

As the wind turned and positions shifted, Alain heard Father Hugh's pleasant voice on the breeze. "Alas, and like some dogs, he'll leap into any body of water if not restrained. Come, Your Highness. This is not fitting."

Sapienta's party retreated to the woodland while the huntsmen dealt with the kill, although some few of the ladies with her could not resist a backward glance.

Lavastine sighed audibly. A flurry of movement came from within the king's party as certain riders—mostly women—made to leave with Princess Sapienta's party while others, including the king, began to dismount.

"Come," said Lavastine as he signaled to his attendants. "I return now to the king. Alain, you must choose your place as you think fit."

By this time half a dozen of Prince Sanglant's entourage had begun to strip, to follow him into the water, and Alain saw that the king meant to bathe as well, as if to lend royal sanction to his son's action.

Alain felt it prudent to stay near the king, so he followed Lavastine and in this way was able to jest with several young lords whom he had befriended. Steadfast forged ahead, still on a scent. She growled, and Fear padded forward to snuffle in the grass beside her.

Where the bluff gave way to a negotiable embankment, servants had come forward to hack through brush clinging to the slope to make a path for the king down to the water. The prince, waist-deep in the sluggish current, now plunged in over his head and struck out for the opposite shore. Upstream, the fishermen collected their baskets and made ready to leave. They lingered to stare as the king made his way down the embankment and left his rich clothing to the care of his servants while he took to the cool water. The splashing and shouting and laughter had long since drowned out any sound of Sapientia's party as it retreated into the forest.

"Do you mean to come in, Son?" Lavastine swung down off his horse. As soon as the count's feet touched the ground, Terror tried to herd the count away from a thicket of brambles while the other hounds set up such a racket of barking that the prince paused half out on the opposite shore to turn and see what the commotion was, and King Henry spoke a word to an attendant who scrambled back up the embankment.

"Peace!" Lavastine frowned at the hounds, who swarmed around him more like puppies frightened by thunder than loyal fighting hounds.

A creature rustled in the thicket. The hounds went wild. Terror closed his jaw over the count's hand and tugged him backward while Steadfast and Fear leaped into the brambles, teeth snapping on empty air. Hackles up, Sorrow and Rage circled the bramble bush and Ardent and Bliss tore up and down between Lavastine and the thicket.

But there was nothing there.

"Peace!" snapped Lavastine. He so disliked it when his orders were not obeyed instantly.

Steadfast yelped suddenly, a cry of pain. The other hounds went into such a wild frenzy around the thicket that servants and noblemen scattered in fear, and then the hounds spun and snapped and bolted away as if in hot pursuit, the entire pack running downstream along the embankment.

"Alain! Follow them!"

Alain quickly followed the hounds, with only a single servant in attendance. The hounds ran far ahead now, scrambling in a fluid, furious pack down to a rocky stretch of beach. He glanced back in time to see Lavastine strip and make his careful way—as had the other courtiers before him—down the slope to the river. While the younger men braved the crossing to follow after the prince, the king and his mature councillors took

their ease in the shallow water and talked no doubt of Gent and
the Eika and recent reports of Quman raids in the east and certain marriage alliances that must be accepted or declined.

The hounds had disappeared, so Alain broke into a trot and
found them clustered just around the river's bend on the last
strip of narrow beach. Stiff-legged, they barked at the water.
Alain thought he saw a flash of something tiny and white struggling in the current. Then, slowly, their barking subsided into
growls, growls to silence, and the hounds relaxed into a steady
vigilance as they regarded the flowing river.

Had he only imagined that flash of movement? The sun made
metal of the water as it streamed along. Its bright flash made
Alain's eyes tear, and he blinked rapidly, but that only made the
water shimmer and flow in uncanny forms like the shift of a
slick and scaly back seen beneath the waves or the swift passage of a ship along a canyon of water.

*Ahead lies the smoke of home, the cradle of his tribe. Who
has arrived before him? Will he and his soldiers have to fight
just to set foot on shore, or has he come first to make his claim
before OldMother so that she may prepare the knife of decision?*

*The fjord waters mirror the deep blush of the heavens, the
powerful blue of the afternoon sky. The waters are so still that
each tree along the shore lies mirrored in their depths. Off to
one side a merman's slick back parts the water and a ruddy eye
takes their measure; then, with a flick of its tail, the creature
vanishes into the seamless depths.*

Teeth closed on his hand and, coming to himself, he looked
down to see Sorrow pulling on him to get his attention. Only
three hounds remained; the others had vanished. He started
around to see his attendant sitting cross-legged, arms relaxed, as
if he'd been waiting a long time.

"My lord!" The man jumped up. "The other hounds ran back
to the count, and I didn't know how to stop them, but you was
so still for so long I didn't know how to interrupt you. . . ." Trailing off, he glanced nervously at the remaining hounds: Sorrow,
Rage, and poor Steadfast, who sat whimpering and licking her
right forepaw.

"No matter." Alain took Steadfast's paw into his hand to examine it. A bramble thorn had bitten deep into the flesh, and he

gentled her with his tone and then got hold of the thorn and pulled it out. She whimpered, then set to work licking again.

A flash of dead white out in the streaming flow of the river distracted him. Downstream, a fish appeared, belly up. Dead. Then a second, a third, and a fourth appeared farther downstream yet, dead white bellies turned up to sun and air, gleaming corpses drawn seaward by the current. Beyond that he could make out only light on the water.

Rage growled.

"My lord." The servant had brought his horse.

But he walked back instead, to keep an eye on Steadfast. The thorn had done no lasting damage. Soon she was loping along with the others in perfect good humor, biting and nipping at her cousins in play. Alain would have laughed to see them; it was, after all, a pleasant and carefree day.

But when, across the river, he saw the fishermen trudging home with their baskets full of plump fish, the image of the dead fish caught in the current flashed into his mind's eye and filled him with a troubling foreboding—only he did not know why.

4

THE quiet that pervaded the inner court of the palace of Weraushausen had such a soothing effect, combined with the heat of the sun, that Liath drowsed on the stone bench where she waited even though she wasn't tired. Fears and hopes mingled to become a tangled dream: Da's murder, Hugh, the curse of fire, Hanna's loyalty and love, Ivar's pledge, the shades of dead elves, Lord Alain and the friendship he had offered her, the death of Bloodheart, Sister Rosvita and *The Book of Secrets,* daimones hunting her and, more vivid than all the others, the tangible memory of Sanglant's hair caught in her fingers there by the stream where he had scoured away the filth of his captivity.

She started up heart pounding; she was hot, embarrassed, dismayed, and breathless with hope all at once.

She could not bear to think of him because she wanted only to think of him. A bee droned past. The gardener who weeded in the herb garden had moved to another row. No one had come to summon her. She did not know how much longer she would have to wait.

She walked to the well with its shingled roof and white-washed stone rim. The draft of air rising from the depths smelled of fresh water and damp stone. The deacon who cared for the chapel here had told her that a spring fed the wells; before the coming of the Daisanite fraters to these lands a hundred years ago its source had rested hidden in rocks and been worshiped as a goddess by the heathen tribes. Now a stone cistern contained it safely beneath the palace.

Was that the glint of water in the depths? if she looked hard enough with her salamander eyes, would she see in that mirror the face of the man she would marry, as old herbwomen claimed? Or was that only pagan superstition, as the church mothers wrote?

She drew back, suddenly afraid to see anything, and stepped out from the shadow of the little roof into the blast of the noon-day sun.

"I will never love any man but him." Was it that pledge which had bound her four days ago in the circle of stones where she'd crossed through an unseen gateway and ridden into unknown lands? Had she really been foolish enough to turn away from the learning offered to her by the old sorcerer?

She shaded her eyes from the sun and sat again on the bench. It had heavy feet fashioned in the likeness of a lion's paws, carved of a reddish-tinged marble. That same marble had been used for the pillars lining the inner court.

Because the king was not now in residence at Weraushausen, a mere Eagle like herself could sit in the court usually reserved for the king rather than stand attendance upon him. It was so quiet that she could believe for this while in the peace that God are said to grant to the tranquil soul—not that such peace was ever likely to be granted to *her.*

A sudden scream tore the silence, followed by laughter and the pounding of running feet.

"Nay, children. Walk with dignity. Slow down!"

The children of the king's schola had arrived to take their midday exercise, some more sedately than others. Liath watched as they tumbled out into the sunlight. She envied these children their freedom to study, their knowledge of their kin, and their future position in the king's court. One boy climbed a plinth and swung, dangling, from the legs of the old statue set there, an ancient Dariyan general.

"Lord Adelfred! Come down off there. I beg you!"

"There's the Eagle," said the boy, jumping down. "Why couldn't we hear her report about the battle at Gent?"

Next to the statue stood Ekkehard, the king's youngest child. He resembled his father although he had the slenderness of youth. At this moment, he wore a sullen expression as if it were as fine an adornment as his rich clothing and gem-studded rings, in sharp contrast to the austere expression of the stone soldier. "I asked if I could ride back with her, to my father," he said, "but it wasn't allowed."

"We must be going back to the king's court soon," retorted the other boy, looking alarmed. By the slight burr in the way he pronounced his Wendish, Liath guessed he was from Avaria, perhaps one of Duke Burchard's many nephews. "King Henry can't mean to leave us here forever! I'm to get my retinue next year and ride east to fight the Quman!"

"It won't matter, forever," muttered Prince Ekkehard. He had a sweet voice; Liath had heard him sing quite beautifully last night. In daylight, without a lute in his hand, he merely looked restless and ill-tempered. "Soon I'll be fifteen and have my own retinue, too, and then I won't be treated like a child. Then I can do what I want."

"Eagle."

Liath started to her feet and turned, expecting to see a cleric come to escort her to Cleric Monica. But she saw only the top of a black-haired head.

"Do you know who I am?" asked the child. For an instant it was like staring into a mirror and seeing a small shadow of herself, although they looked nothing alike except in complexion.

"You are Duke Conrad's daughter," said Liath.

The girl took hold of Liath's wrist and turned over the Eagle's hand to see the lighter skin of the palm. "I've never seen anyone but my father, my *avia*—my grandmother, that is—and my sister and myself with such skin. I did see a slave once, in the retinue of a presbyter. They said she had been born in the land of the Gyptos, but she was dark as pitch. Where do your kinfolk come from?"

"From Darre," said Liath, amused by her blithe arrogance.

The child regarded her with an imperious expression. "You just rode in from the king's progress. Has there been news? My mother, Lady Eadgifu, should have had her baby by now but no one will tell me anything."

"I have heard no news of your mother."

The girl glanced toward the other children. Ekkehard and his companion had moved off to toss dice in the shadow of the colonnade, and the others kept their distance. Only the old statue remained, like a trusted companion. He had once held a sword, but it was missing. Flecks of blue still colored his eyes, and in the sheltered curve of his elbow and the deeper folds of the cloak spun out in folds of stone from his left shoulder Liath could see the stain of gold paint not yet worn away by wind and weather. Lichen grew on his stone sandals and between his toes.

Was it not said that the Dariyan emperors and empresses and their noble court were the half-breed descendants of the Lost Ones? This stone general looked a little like Sanglant.

"I'm a prisoner here, you know," the girl added without heat. She had the rounded profile of youth, blurred still by baby-fat and the promise of later growth, but a distinctly self-aware expression for all that. No more than nine or ten, she already understood the intricate dance of court intrigue. With a sigh, the child released Liath's hand and turned half away. "I still miss Berthold," she murmured. "He was the only one who paid attention to me."

"Who is Berthold?" asked Liath, intrigued by the yearning in the girl's voice.

But the girl only glanced at her, as if surprised—as Hugh would say—to hear a dog speak.

A cleric hurried up the central colonnade and beckoned to Liath; she followed her into the palace. In a spacious wood-paneled chamber Cleric Monica sat at one end of a long table otherwise inhabited by clerics only half awake, writing with careful strokes or yawning while a scant breeze stirred the air. The shutters had been taken down. Through the windows Liath could see a corral for horses and beyond that the berm of earth that was part of the fortifications. Wildflowers bloomed along the berm, purple and pale yellow. Goats grazed on the steep slope.

"Come forward." Cleric Monica spoke in a low voice. The

clerics worked in silence, and only the distant bleat of a goat and an occasional shout from one of the children penetrated the room, and yet there lay between them all a companionable air as if this hush reflected labor done willingly together, with one heart and one striving. Two letters and several parchment documents lay at Monica's right hand. "Here is a letter for Sister Rosvita from Mother Rothgard at St. Valeria Convent. Here are four royal capitularies completed by the clerics at the king's order. To King Henry relate this message: the schola will leave Weraushausen in two days' time and travel south to meet him at Thersa, as His Majesty commands. Do you understand the whole?"

"Yes."

"Now." Cleric Monica beckoned to a tiny deacon almost as old as Monica herself. Liath towered over the old woman. "Deacon Ansfrida."

Deacon Ansfrida had a lisp which, combined with the hauteur of a noblewoman, gave her an air of slightly ridiculous abstraction. "There has been a new road built through the forest. If you follow it, it should save you four days of riding time toward Thersa."

"Is it safe to ride through the forest?"

Neither churchwoman appeared surprised by the question. The forests lay outside the grasp of the church; they were wild lands still. "I have heard no reports that the levy set to do the work met with any difficulty. Since the Eika came last year, we have been peculiarly untroubled by bandits."

"What of other creatures?"

Cleric Monica gave a little breath, a voiced "ah" that trailed away to blend with the shuffling of feet and the scratch of pens. But the deacon gave Liath a strange look. "Certainly one must watch out for wolves," replied Ansfrida. "Is that what you mean?"

Better, Liath realized, to have asked the forests that question and not good women of the church. "Yes, that's what I mean," she said quickly.

"You may wait outside," said Cleric Monica crisply. "A servant will bring you a horse."

Thus dismissed, Liath retreated, relieved to get out from under Monica's searching eye. Beyond the palace she found a log bench to sit on. Here she waited again. The palace lay enclosed by berms of more recent construction; in one place where ditch and

earth wall stood now, she could see the remains of an old building that had been torn up and dug through when the fortification was put in. The palace loomed before her. With windows
set high in its walls and six towers hugging the semicircular side
like sentries, it appeared from the outside more like a fort than
a palace. A jumble of outbuildings lay scattered within the protecting berms. A woman stood outside the cookhouse, searing a
side of beef over a smoking pit. A servant boy slept half hidden in the grass.

Without the king in residence, Weraushausen was a peaceful
place. From the chapel, she heard a single female voice raised
in prayer for the service of Sext, and in distant fields men sang
in robust chorus as they worked under the hot sun. Crickets
buzzed. Beyond the river lay the great green shoulder of the un-
tamed forest; a buzzard—scarcely more than a black speck—
soared along its outermost fringe.

What would it be like to live in such peace?

She flipped open her saddlebags. The letters were sealed with
wax and stamped with tiny figures. She recognized the seal from
St. Valeria Convent at once by the miniature orrery, symbol of
St. Valeria's victory in the city of Saïs when she confounded the
pagan astrologers. Liath dared not open the letter, of course. Did
it contain news of Princess Theophanu? Had she recovered from
her illness, or did this letter bring news of her death? Was Mother
Rothgard writing to warn Sister Rosvita that a sorcerer walked
veiled in the king's progress? Would Rosvita suspect Liath? Or
would she suspect Hugh?

Liath glanced through the capitularies: King Henry grants to
the nuns of Regensbach a certain estate named Felstatt for which
they owe the king and his heirs full accommodation and renders
of food and drink for the royal retinue as well as fodder for the
horses at such times as the king's progress may pass that way;
King Henry endows a monastery at Gent in the name of St. Perpetua in thanks for the victory at Gent and the return of his son;
King Henry grants immunity from all but royal service to the
foresters of the Bretwald in exchange for keeping the new road
through the Bret Forest clear; King Henry calls the elders of the
church to a council at Autun on the first day of the month of
Setentre, which in the calendar of the church is called Matthiasmass.

That day, according to the mathematici, was the autumn equinox.

Ai, God. If she held *The Book of Secrets*, could she open it freely here? Would she ever live in a place where there was leisure, and such safety as this palace offered? Was there any place she could study the secrets of the mathematici, wander in her city of memory, explore the curse of fire, and be left alone?

She laughed softly, a mixture of anger, regret, and giddy desire. Such a place had been offered her, when she had least expected it, and she had turned away in pursuit of a dream just as impossible.

A man emerged from the palace gateway leading a saddled horse, a sturdy bay mare with a white blaze and two white socks. She took the reins, thanked him politely, and went on her way.

5

AS the deacon had promised, the road ran straight east through the Bretwald. Birds trilled from the branches. A doe and half-grown twin fawns trotted into view and as quickly vanished into the foliage. She heard the grunt of a boar. She peered into the depths beyond the scar that was the road. Trees marched out on all sides into unknowable and impenetrable wilderness. The scent of growing lay over everything as heavily as spices at the king's feasting table. Like a rich mead, she could almost taste it simply by breathing it in.

But she could no longer ride through the deep forest without looking over her shoulder. She could not forget the diamone that had stalked her, or the creature of bells. She could not forget the elfshot that had killed her horse this past spring, although that pursuit had taken place in a different forest than this one. Yet surely all forests were only pieces of the same great and ancient forest. She had traveled enough to know that the wild places on earth were of far greater extent than those lands tamed by human hands.

There.

An aurochs bolted through the distant trees. Its curving horns caught a stray glance of sunlight, vivid, disturbing, and then it was gone. The noise of its passage faded into the heavier silence of the forest, which was not a true silence at all but rather woven of a hundred tiny sounds that blended so seamlessly as to make of themselves that kind of silence which has forgotten, or does not know of or care about, the chatter of human enterprise.

As the last rustle of the aurochs' passing faded, Liath heard, quite clearly, the clop of hooves behind her. She swung round in her saddle but could see nothing. What if it were Hugh?

Ai, Lady! That bastard Hugh had no reason to follow her. He would wait in the safety of the king's progress because he knew she had to return to the king. She had no freedom of her own to choose where she went and how she lived; she was a mere Eagle living on the sufferance of the king, and that was all and everything she had, her only safety, her only kin.

"Except Sanglant," she whispered. If she said his name too loudly, would she wake herself up from a long and almost painful dream and find the prince still dead at Gent and herself sobbing by a dying fire?

The sound of hooves faded as a wind came up, stirring the upper branches into movement punctuated by the eruption into flight of a dozen noisy wood pigeons. That suddenly, she saw a flash of red far back in the dim corridor of the road. At once she slipped her bow free of its quiver and drew an arrow to rest loosely along the curve of the bow.

A branch snapped to her left and she started 'round, but nothing showed itself in the thickets. What use was running, anyway? She and Da had scuttled from shadow to shadow, but in the end his enemies had caught them.

She reined up her horse and peered into every thicket and out along an unexpected vista of tree trunks marching away into shadow like so many pillars lining the aisles of a cathedral. Nothing. What approached came from the road. And she heard no tolling of bells.

Yet her face was flushed and she was sweating. She nocked her arrow and waited. A King's Eagle expected respect and safe passage. She had endured so much, she *had* escaped from Hugh twice.

She was strong enough to face down this enemy.

As the rider came clear of the shadow of the trees, she drew down on a figure dressed in ordinary clothing marked only by a gray cloak trimmed with scarlet. A familiar badge winked at his throat.

"Wolfhere!"

He laughed and, when he came close enough, called to her. "I'll thank you not to look quite so intimidating with that arrow aimed at my heart."

Startled, she lowered the bow. "Wolfhere!" she repeated, too dumbfounded to say anything else.

"I had hoped to catch you before nightfall." He reined in beside her. "No one likes to pass through the forest alone." He rode a surly-looking gelding. Her own mare, sensing trouble, gave a nip to the gelding's hindquarters to let it know at once which of them took precedence.

"You've ridden all the way from Darre," she said stupidly, still too amazed to think.

"That I have," he agreed mildly. He pressed his gelding forward into a walk and Liath rode beside him.

"It took Hanna months to track down the king, and it's only the twenty-fifth day of Quadrii."

"That it is, the feast day of St. Placidana, she who brought the Circle of Unities to the goblinkin of the Harenz Mountains." She saw immediately that he was trying not to smile.

"But you know perfectly well that no passes over the Alfar Mountains are clear until early summer. How did you get to Weraushausen so quickly?"

He slanted a glance at her, eyes serious, mouth quirking up. "I knew where the king was."

"You looked for him through fire."

"So I did. It was a mild winter, and I made my way across the Julier Pass earlier than I had hoped. I watched through fire when I could. I know Wendar well, Liath. I followed the king's progress with that vision and saw where they were bound. Once I saw that King Henry had left the children of the schola at Werauschausen, I knew he would have to return by that way or at the least send a message by one of his Eagles, who would know what route he planned to take. I had hoped it might be you."

How much had he seen of her? Did he know Hugh was tormenting her again? Had he seen her burn down the palace at Augensburg, or fight the lost shades in the forest east of Laar, or kill Bloodheart? Had he heard Sanglant's words to her? Had he seen her cross through the gateway of burning stone?

As if he read her thoughts in her expression, he spoke again. "Although I couldn't be sure you still rode with the king's progress and not with Princess Theophanu or on some other errand. You are difficult to vision through fire, Liath. It's as if there's a haze about you, concealing you. I suppose Bernard laid some kind of spell over you to hide you. I'm surprised the effect has survived so long after his death."

Like a challenge, the words seemed to hang in the air between them. They rode some paces in silence while in the branches above the purring coo of turtledoves serenaded them and was left behind.

"You strike straight to heart of the matter, and at once, do you not?"

"Alas, I'm not usually accused of such a weakness." His tone was dry and his smile brief. "To what do you refer, my child?"

She laughed, light-headed, a little dizzy. "I don't trust you, Wolfhere. Maybe I never will. But I'm grateful to you for saving me at Heart's Rest. And I'm not afraid of you anymore."

This time the smile sparked in his eyes, a pale flicker in gray.

She did not wait for his answer but went on, determined to bring it all to light immediately. "Why were you looking for me? Why did you save me at Heart's Rest?"

He blinked. She had surprised him. "When you were born, I promised Anne that I would look after you. I had been looking for you and your father for eight years, ever since you disappeared. I knew you were in danger." He looked away to the verge where road and forest met and intertwined. When he frowned, lines creased his forehead, and she could see how old he truly was; she had seen only a handful of people whom she supposed to be older than Wolfhere, and certainly none of them had been as hale and vigorous. What magic made him so strong although he was so old? Or was it magic at all but rather the kiss of Lady Fortune, who for her own fickle reasons blessed some with vigor while inflicting feebleness upon others? "Had I found you earlier," he continued, still not looking at her, "Bernard would not have died."

"You could have protected us?" He had not seen Da's body or the two arrows stuck uselessly in the wall.

"Only Our Lady and Lord see all that has happened and all

that will happen." A jay cried harshly and fluttered away from the path, its rump a flash of white among dense green. He turned his gaze away from his contemplation of a riot of flowering brambles that twined along the roadside, and with that pale keen gaze regarded her again. "What of you, Liath? Have you been well? You seem stronger."

Did he understand the fire she held within her, which Da had tried to protect her from? She didn't want him to see its existence, her knowledge of its existence, as if some change in her might betray it to his penetrating gaze; she was sure he watched her so keenly to see what she might unwittingly reveal. Da always said there were two ways to hide: to scuttle from shadow to shadow, or to talk in plain sight on a busy road at midday. *"Talk too much about nothing, or be silent about everything,"* he would say, but Wolfhere couldn't be misled by babble, and she no longer dared hide behind silence. Once she had thought silence would shield her. Now she knew that ignorance was more dangerous than knowledge.

"I was afraid to ask you questions before," she said finally, not without a catch in her voice. "Even though I wanted to know about Da and about my mother. I was afraid you would make me tell you things. That you were one of the ones hunting us. But I *know* you were one of the ones hunting us."

"I would not have phrased it so: 'hunting' you."

"Aren't you named for the wolf. Doesn't the wolf hunt?"

"The wolf does what it must. Unlike humankind, it only kills when it is threatened, or when it is hungry—and then only as much as it needs."

"How did you come to know my mother and father?"

"Our paths crossed." He smiled grimly, remembering as well as she did the conversation, more like a sparring contest, they had had last spring in the tower at Steleshame. "What do you know of magic, Liath?"

"Not enough!" She reconsidered these rash words, then added, "Enough to keep silent on that subject. I've only your word that you made a promise to my mother to protect me. But she's dead, and Da never once mentioned your name. Why should I trust you?"

He looked pained, as at a trust betrayed or a kindness spurned. "Because your mother—" Then he broke off.

She waited. There was more than one kind of silence: that

of the indifferent forest; that of a man hesitant to speak and a woman waiting to hear a truth; the silence that is choked by fear or that which wells up from a pure spring of joy. This silence spread from him into the forest; the sudden stillness of birds at an unexpected presence walking among them; the hush that descends when the sun's face is shrouded by cloud. His face had too much weight in it, as at a decision come to after a hard fight.

When he finally spoke, he said what she had never expected to hear. "Your mother isn't dead."

6

TEN steps, perhaps twelve, on a path through a dessicated forest whose branches rattled in a howling wind brought Zacharias and the woman to another hard bend in the path. Coming around it, coils of air whipped at his face as he followed the Aoi woman through a bubble of heat. The ground shifted under him, and suddenly he slipped down a pebbly slope and found himself slogging through calf-deep drifts of sand. The horse struggled behind him, and he had to haul on it to get it up a crumbling slope to where the Aoi woman stood on a pathway marked out in black stone. Barren land lay everywhere around them, nothing but sun and sand and the narrow path that cut sharply to the right.

Disorientation shook him, his vision hazed, and when he could see again, they walked through forest, although here the trees looked different, denser than that first glimpse of forest he had seen, like moving from the land where the short-grass grows to the borderwild beyond which the tall grass of the wilderness shrouds the earth and any who walk in its shadow.

The Aoi woman spoke in a sharp whisper, holding up a hand to stop them. Zacharias yanked the horse to a halt. In the distance, he heard a moaning horn call and saw a green-and-gold flash in the vegetation; someone was on the move out in the forest. They waited for what seemed an eternity, although Zacharias drew perhaps twenty breaths.

"Hei!" said the woman, waving him forward. She looked nervous, and her pace was brisk.

This time when the path veered left, Zacharias knew what to expect. The ground shifted, but he kept his balance, only to lose it as his boots sloshed in water and a salty wind stung his lips. Water lapped his ankles. He looked up in surprise to see waves surging all the way to the horizon. He staggered and barely caught himself on the horse's neck. Where had all this water come from? Where did it end?

On his other side, mercifully, lay a long strand of pebbles and beyond it hummocks of grass and scrub. A gleaming path shone under the water, cast in bronze.

"What is this place?" he whispered. The woman did not answer.

The ghost lands, his grandmother would have said. *The spirit world.* Was he dead?

The path veered right, and the Aoi woman disappeared into a dense bank of fog. Zacharias shook off his fear and followed her to where light streamed in the mist, a fire flaming blue-white and searing his face with its heat—and then it vanished.

He sucked in a breath of grass-laden air and collapsed to his knees next to a dead campfire. Water puddled from his robes and soaked onto the earth. An instant later he gulped, recognizing their surroundings. They had come back to the very stone circle where the witch had defeated Bulkezu. He groped for the knife, then saw the sky and hissed his surprise through his teeth.

It was night, and the waning gibbous moon laid bare the bones of the stone circle and the long horizon of grass, a pale silver expanse under moonlight.

Four turns on an unearthly path had brought them not to a different place but back to the same place at a different time.

He knelt beside the old campfire and stirred the cold ashes with a finger. Chaff had settled there together with a drying flower petal. "Six days, perhaps seven," he said aloud, touching ash to his tongue. He looked up, suddenly afraid that she would punish him for his fear . . . or for his knowledge. But if she had meant to kill him, surely she would have done so by now. "Did we walk through the ghost lands?" he asked.

She stood beneath a lintel, gazing west over the plain.

Bulkezu's jacket, laid over her shoulders, gave her the look of a Quman boy.

But she was no boy.

She lifted her spear toward the heavens and spoke incomprehensible words, calling, praying, commanding: Who could know? As she swayed, her leather skirt swayed, as supple as the finest calfskin.

Except it wasn't calfskin.

"Ah—Ah—Ah—! Lady!" Terror hung hitches into his words, forced out of him by shock.

The skirt she wore wasn't sewn of calfskin, nor of deerskin. It wasn't animal skin at all.

Under the lintel, the Aoi woman turned to look at him. Her leather skirt slipped gracefully around her, such a fine bronze sheen to it that it almost seemed to shimmer in the moonlight.

"Human skin," he breathed. The words died away onto the night breeze, then were answered by hers.

"You who were once called Zacharias-son-of-Elseva-and-Volusianus. I have taken your blood into my blood. You are bound to me now, and at last I have seen how you can be of service to me and my cause."

7

ALIVE.

At first Liath could only ride silent along the newly-cut road while the riot of forest tangled around her until she felt utterly confused. Why had Da lied to her? Had he even known? Ai, Lady. Why couldn't it be Da who still lived, instead of her mother?

At once she knew the thought for a sin. But her mother existed so distantly from her that she could grasp no feeling for that memory which came in the wake of Wolfhere's words more as dream than remembrance: a courtyard and herb garden, a stone bench carved with eagle claws, a slippery memory of silent servants half hidden in the shadows. Of her mother she recalled little except that her hair had been as pale as straw and her skin as light as if sun never touched it, although she remembered sitting sometimes for entire afternoons in the bright sun of an Aostan summer, a light more pure than beaten gold.

"You knew all the time."

"No," he said curtly. "I only discovered it now, on my journey to Aosta."

"Hanna didn't tell me."

"She had already left me to return to King Henry with news of Biscop Antonia's escape."

"Did you tell my mother you found me? Did you tell her Da was killed? What did she say?"

"She said I must bring you to her as soon as I can."

"But where is she now?"

Finally he shook his head. "I dare not say, Liath. I must take you to her myself. There are others looking for you—and for her."

"The ones who killed Da."

His silence was answer enough.

"Ai, Lady." She knew herself to be a young woman now, having left the last of her girl's innocence behind when Da had been killed and Hugh had taken her as his slave; she knew she must appear different to his eyes than she had on that day over a year ago when they had parted in Autun. She had grown, filled out, gotten stronger. But Wolfhere might have aged not a single day in the last year for all she could see any difference in him. White of hair, keen of eye, with the same imperturbable expression that all wise old souls wore in order to confound youthful rashness, he had weathered much in his life that she could only guess at. Surely it took some remarkable action for a common-born man to make an enemy of a king, for kings did not need to take notice of those so far beneath them in all but God's grace. Yet the grieving Henry, at Autun, had banished Wolfhere from court as punishment for his being the messenger who had brought him news of Sanglant's death at Gent.

Except Sanglant wasn't dead.

"If only I could have taken you with me to Darre instead of Hanna," Wolfhere murmured. Then he grinned wryly. "Not that I have any complaint of Hanna, mind you, but do not forget— as I have once or twice to my regret—that we Eagles do not

control our own movements. We must go as and where the king
sends us."

"If you dislike the king's command upon you, then why do
you remain an Eagle?"

"Ah, well." His smile gave little away. "I have been an Eagle
for many years."

They rode on for a time in silence as the afternoon sun drew
shadows across the road. A red kite glided into view along the
treetops and vanished as it swooped for prey. Vines trailed from
overhanging branches to brush the track.

"Is she well?" Liath asked finally.

"She is as she ever was."

"You might as well tell me nothing as tell me that. I hardly
remember her. Ai, Lady! Can you imagine what this means to
me?"

"It means," said Wolfhere with a somber expression, "that I
will lose you as an Eagle."

It struck her suddenly and profoundly. "I'm no longer kinless. I have a home." But she could make no picture in her mind
of what that home might look like.

"You will become what your birthright grants you, Liath. Although how much Bernard taught you I don't know, since you
will not tell me." Though there was a hint of accusation in his
voice, he did not let it show on his face.

"The art of the mathematici, which is forbidden by the
church."

"But which is studied in certain places nevertheless. Will you
go with me, Liath, when I leave the king?"

She could not answer. This, of all choices, was the one she
had never expected to have.

By late afternoon they heard a rhythmic chopping and soon
came to half-cleared land, undergrowth burned out between the
stumps of trees. A goshawk skimmed the clearing. Squirrels
bounded along branches, chittering at these intruders. Just past
a shallow stream they came to a natural clearing now inhabited
by three cottages built of logs and several turf outbuildings. A
garden fenced with stout sticks ran riot alongside the central
lane, which was also the road. Several young men labored to
build a palisade, but when they saw the Eagles, they set down
their tools to stare. One whistled to alert the rest, and soon Liath

and Wolfhere were surrounded by the entire community: some ten hardy adult souls and about a dozen children.

"Nay, you can't go this day," said the eldest woman there, Old Uta, whom the others deferred to. "You'll not come clear of the Bretwald before nightfall. Better you bide here with us than sleep where the beasts might make off with you. As it is, we've a wedding to celebrate tonight. It would be our shame not to show hospitality to guests at such a time!"

The young men put on deerskin tunics and then set up a long table and benches outdoors while the women and girls prepared a feast: baked eggs; rabbit; a haunch of venison roasted over the fire; a salad of greens; coarse brown bread baked into a pudding with milk and honey roasted mushrooms; and as many berries as Liath could eat without making herself sick, all washed down with fresh goat's milk and a pungent cider that went immediately to her head. She found it hard to concentrate as Wolfhere regaled the foresters with tales of the Alfar Mountains and a great avalanche and of the holy city of Darre and the palace of Her Holiness the skopos, our mother among the saints, Clementia, the second of that name.

The bride was easy to recognize: the youngest daughter of Old Uta, she wore flowers in her braided hair and she sat on the bench of honor next to her husband. The bridegroom was scarcely more than a boy, and all through the meal he stared at Liath. There was something familiar about him, but she could not pin it down and no doubt it was only the strength of the cider acting on the astounding news Wolfhere had burdened her with that made her so dizzy.

Her mother was alive.

"Eagle," said the young man, speaking up suddenly. "You were the one who led us out of Gent. Do you remember me? With no good humor, I'd wager. I'm the one as lost your horse, by the east gate." Ruddy-cheeked from working in the sun, he looked little like the thin-faced lad who had wept outside Gent over losing her horse and losing his home that awful day; he had filled out through the chest and gotten rounder in the face. But his eyes had that same quick gleam.

"Ach, lad, lost a horse!" The men groaned and the women clucked in displeasure. "A horse! If we only had a horse to haul those logs, or even a donkey—"

"We could have traded a horse for another iron ax!"

"Peace!" said Liath sharply. They quieted at once and turned to her respectfully. "Did he not tell you what occurred at Gent?"

"Gent's a long way from here," said Old Uta, "and is nothing to do with us. Indeed, I'd never heard tell of it before they came."

"What's Gent?" piped up one of the younger children.

"It's the place where Martin and Young Uta came from, child." The old woman indicated the bridegroom and then a stout girl with scars on her face and hands. "We took them in, for there were many young people left without family after the raiders came. We've always use for more hands to work. It took us and the other foresters ten years to cut that road." She nodded toward the track that led eastward out of the clearing into the dense forest. "Now we're done, we can cut a home out of this clearing and be free of our service to Lady Helmingard."

"Well, then," said Liath, looking at each in turn, "I'll thank you not to be thinking it's any fault of Martin's that he lost the horse. The king's own Dragons died saving what townsfolk they could from the Eika. There was nothing a boy could do against savages."

"Did all the Dragons die in the end?" Martin asked. She recalled now that he had been the kind of boy who yearned after the Dragons and followed them everywhere he could.

"Yes," said Wolfhere.

"No," said Liath, and she had the satisfaction of seeing Wolfhere astounded in his turn. "The prince survived."

"The prince survived," echoed Wolfhere, on an exhaled breath. Liath could not tell if he were ecstatic or dismayed.

"The prince," breathed the young man in tones more appropriate for a prayer to God. "But of course the prince must have lived. Not even the Eika could kill him. Are they still there in Gent? The Eika, I mean."

"Nay, for two great armies marched on Gent in order to avenge the attack last year." Her audience raptly awaited the tale, and even Wolfhere regarded her with that cool gray gaze, patient enough for obviously wanting to hear the story of how Prince Sanglant had survived the death both she and Wolfhere had visioned through fire.

So she told the tale of Count Lavastine's march and the terrible battle on the field before Gent, of Bloodheart's enchantments and the Eika horde. She told of how Lavastine himself had taken some few of his soldiers as a last gamble through the tunnel and how Bloodheart's death had shattered the Eika army, how King Henry's army arrived at the very end—just in time. She could not resist dwelling perhaps more than was seemly on Sanglant's great deeds that day, saving his sister's line from collapse, slaying more Eika than any other soldier on the field. To these isolated forest folk the tale no doubt could as well have been told about heroes who had lived a hundred years before; she might as well have sung the tale of Waltharia and Sigisfrid and the cursed gold of the Hevelli for all that her words truly meant no more to them than a good evening's tale.

But they proclaimed themselves well satisfied when she had done.

"A fitting tale for a wedding feast," said Old Uta. "Now we've somewhat for you to take to King Henry, as a token of our gratitude for his generosity in granting us freedom from Lady Helmingard's service, which she laid heavily on us."

Recalling the diploma she carried, Liath removed it from her saddlebags and read aloud to them King Henry's promise that the foresters would be free of service to any lady or lord as long as they kept the king's road passable for himself and his messengers and armies. The king had not yet put his seal on it, but the foresters nevertheless listened intently, touched the parchment with reverence, and examined the writing, which, of course, none of them could read.

"I've a wish to go back to Gent," said the scarred girl, Young Uta. "I don't like the forest."

"You've a few years to work off first," said Old Uta sternly, and the girl sighed.

But Martin was satisfied with his new life. He had a bride, a place of honor, and security among his new kin. The foresters had meat in abundance and wild plants and skins to trade to the farming folk for grain to supplement what vegetables they could grow in their garden. Even in years made lean by a scant harvest there was game to be caught in the deep forest. They showed off their iron tools: two axes and a shovel. The rest of the tools were made of wood, stone, or copper. They had a storehouse filled with baskets of nuts and pips, shriveled crab apples, leather vessels brimming with barley and unhulled wheat, herbs dried and hung in bundles, and several covered pots of lard. From the rafters they brought down four fine wolfskins and a bearskin

and these they rolled and tied and gave to Wolfhere to present
to the king as a token of their loyalty and in honor of his recent visit to Weraushausen and the pledge made between foresters
and king.

When twilight came, they all escorted bride and bridegroom
to the best bed in the hall and entertained them with songs and
lengthy toasts. Oaths were sworn—Martin would be given a
place in the family in exchange for his labor—and pledges of
consent exchanged. In a month or a year, a frater would probably walk out along the road into the forest, and then he could
sing a blessing over the couple. It was always good to get the
blessing of the church in such matters, when one could.

"Come now!" said Old Uta finally, taking pity on the new-
lyweds, who sat bolt upright in the bed enduring the jests and
singing. "It's time to leave these young folk alone to get on with
it!" With much laughter, the rest of them left the hall and went
to sleep outdoors.

But Liath was too restless to sleep. Wolfhere built a small
fire, and by this they sat as stars bloomed in the darkening sky.
Lying on her back, she pretended to sleep but instead studied
the heavens. Summer was known as "the Queen's sky." The
Queen, her Bow, her Staff, and her Sword all shone in splendor
above. The Queen's Cup stood at the zenith, the bright star known
as the Sapphire almost directly overhead. Her faithful Eagle rose
from the east behind her, flying eternally toward the River of
Heaven, which spanned the night sky much as the forest road
cut a swath through the dense woodland. The zodiac was obscured by trees and by a misty haze that had spread along the
southern horizon, but she caught a glimpse of the Dragon, sixth
House, between gaps among the tops of trees. Stately Mok
gleamed in the hindquarters of the Lion, a brilliant wink between leaves.

"I never thought to look for him," said Wolfhere suddenly
into the silence.

"For whom?" she asked, then knew the next instant whom
he meant. "Didn't you ever try looking for my mother through
fire?"

"We can only see the living, and then only ones we know
and have touched, have a link to."

"But I saw the Aoi through fire, after Gent fell." She rolled
to one side. He sat on the other side of the fire, his face in

shadow. "I'd never met any such creatures." She hesitated, then said nothing more about her encounter with the Aoi sorcerer.

"That is indeed a mystery. I have but small skill in these matters, though I am adept at seeing. Had I ever suspected Prince Sanglant was alive, I would have looked for him, but I did not. We both saw him take a killing blow—" Here he broke off.

"You are no more surprised than I was when I recognized him in the cathedral," she admitted. But she could not make herself describe to Wolfhere how like a wild beast Sanglant had looked—and acted. Instead she changed the subject. "Da said—"

Da's words on the last night of his life remained caught forever in her city of memory. "*If you touch anything their hands have touched, they have a further link to you. . . . They have the power of seeking and finding, but I have sealed you away from them.*" If Da had only known her mother wasn't dead, what then? Could she have saved him?

"How could Da have thought she was dead if she wasn't?"

"How could we have thought Prince Sanglant dead, when he wasn't?"

"But if she was alive, then why didn't she try to find us? She could see through fire. She knew we weren't dead!"

"She looked for you! But you are not alone in being hunted. Despite our small magics, distances are great and not easily traversed even for an Eagle who has a horse and the promise of lodging and food wherever she stops."

"But if she had to go into hiding, why couldn't she take us? How could Da have thought she was dead? I remember—" Like fire taking to pitch, the memory of that night ten years past flared into life.

"What do you remember?" he asked softly.

She could barely find her voice. "Everything burst into flame, the cottage, all the plants in the courtyard, the stables and the weaving house, all the other buildings . . ." She shut her eyes, and there in the forest clearing with the whispering of the night woodland pressing in on her she dredged into the depths of that old painful memory. "And the benches. The stone benches. *Even the stone burned.* That's when we ran. Da grabbed the book and we ran. And he said, " 'They've killed Anne and taken her gift to use as their own.' "

She had to stop because her throat was thick with grief, and with more questions than she knew how to ask. Opening her eyes, she stared up at a sky now so brilliant with stars that it seemed a thousand burning jewels had been casually strewn across the heavens. A streak of light blazed and vanished: a falling star. Was it an angel cast to earth by God's hand, sent to aid the prayers of the faithful, as the church mothers wrote? Or was it the track of one of those aetherical creatures born out of pure fire who, diving like a falcon, plunged from the Sun's sphere to those nesting below?

Wolfhere said nothing. The fire popped loudly and spit a red coal onto the end of her cloak. She shook it off and then sank forward to rest elbows on knees and stare into the fire. A long while passed in silence as the yellow flames flickered and died down into sullen coals. Wolfhere seemed to have fallen asleep.

He had looked for her, but he had not been able to see her through fire. Was Da's spell still hiding her? She had felt the presence of others looking for her, had felt the wind of their stalking, the blind grasp of their seeking hands. She had *seen* the glass-winged daimone. She had seen the creatures that stalked with a voice of bells and left flesh stripped to bone in their wake. Were they still out there? Could she, like a mouse, scuttle into places forbidden to her and spy them out?

She made of the coals a gateway and peered into its depths. If only she could recall her mother clearly enough in her mind's eye, then surely she could vision her through fire, actually *see* her again. But as the fire flared under the weight of her stare, she was suddenly seized by a foreboding of doom as real as a hand touching her shoulder—as Hugh's hand had imprisoned her, binding her to his will.

The fire leaped with sudden strength as if it were an unnatural being blooming into existence, wings unfurling into a sheet of fire, eyes like the strike of lightning, the breath of the fiery Sun coalesced into mind and will. Its voice rolled with the searing blaze of flame.

"Child."

She shrieked out loud and scrambled backward, so terrified that she couldn't gulp down the sobs that burst from her chest.

Wolfhere started up. The fire winked out, that fast, to become ashes and one last spark of heat, a dying cinder, gone. "Liath!"

She jumped up and ran out to the half-built palisade, logs felled and sharpened and driven into a ditch to make a barrier against the beasts of the forest. She leaned against one of the stout posts. With the bark peeled off, oak lay smooth against her shoulder and cheek; the foresters had done their work well, for the post did not shift beneath her weight.

She was still shaking.

An owl hooted and its shadow fluttered past, then vanished into the night.

"Ai, Lady," she whispered to the silent witness of stars and night breeze and the many busy animals about their nocturnal labors. "Sanglant."

II
A LILY AMONG THORNS

1

IVAR had never prayed so much in his life, not even in his first year as a novice at Quedlinhame. His knees ached constantly. But Baldwin had taken it into his head that if he prayed enough he could protect himself from his bride's attentions: He hoped that even a powerful margrave would be loath to disturb a young man at prayer, no matter how long she had been waiting to get her hands on him.

So it proved for the first five days after they left Quedlinhame. But Ivar had ears, and he had grown up with sisters. Margrave Judith wasn't so old that her holy courses had ceased. He even caught a glimpse of a stained cloth laid reverently on a blazing hearth fire.

Women were specially holy at their bleeding time, not to be corrupted by base desire. Even a noblewoman such as Judith followed the wisdom of the church mothers in such matters. Ivar suspected that all Baldwin's praying was a pretty show that counted for very little except to whet his bride's appetite; sometimes while praying, Ivar glanced sidelong at the margrave watching Baldwin, who did indeed pray beautifully.

"You oughtn't to pray unless you pray from your heart," said Ivar. "It's a sin."

It was late afternoon on yet another day of travel, west, toward the king. Ivar rode a donkey, as was fitting for a novice, but Baldwin had been given a proud black gelding to ride. No doubt Margrave Judith could not resist the chance to display two handsome creatures together.

Right now, however, Baldwin came as close to scowling as he ever could. "You scold like Master Pursed-Lips. I *am* praying from my heart! You don't imagine I want to marry her, do you?"

"As if you have a choice."

"If the marriage is not consummated, then it is no marriage."

Ivar sighed. "She's no worse than any other woman. You'll have fine clothes to wear, excellent armor, and a good iron sword. You'll have the Quman barbarians to fight in the march country. It won't be so bad."

"I don't like her," said Baldwin in the tone of a child who has never before had to accept anything he didn't like. "I don't *want* to be married to her." He cast a glance forward where Lady Tallia rode beside Margrave Judith. "I'd even rather marry—".

"She isn't to be married!" hissed Ivar in a low voice, suddenly angry. "Not by anyone! God has chosen her to be Her handmaiden, to be the uncorrupted bride of Her Son, the blessed Daisan, as all nuns ought to pledge themselves to be."

"Why can't I be chosen?" murmured Baldwin plaintively.

"Because you're a man. Women serve God by tending Her hearth, for they are made in God's image and it is their duty to administer to all that She creates."

"If you preach a heresy," whispered Baldwin, "then the church will punish you."

"Martyrdom isn't punishment! The heathen Dariyans rewarded the blessed Daisan by flaying him alive and cutting out his heart. But God gave him life again, just as martyrs live again in the Chamber of Light."

Baldwin flicked a fly away from his face as he considered the women riding at the front of the procession. "Do you suppose Margrave Judith will be lifted up to the Chamber of Light when she dies, or will she be flung into the Abyss?"

At the vanguard rode some twenty guardsmen, soldiers fitted out in tabards sewn with a leaping panther. After them came Margrave Judith herself. She had a proud carriage, silvering hair, and a handsome profile marked in particular by a strong nose; she wore a tunic of the richest purple, a hue Ivar had never seen before and marveled at now, embroidered so cunningly with falcons stooping upon fleeing hares and panthers springing upon unsuspecting deer that at odd moments he thought he had glimpsed a real scene, not one caught by silk thread on linen. Riding beside the margrave, Tallia looked frail with her head bowed humbly and her shoulders curved as though under a great weight; she still dressed as simply as a novice, in a coarse robe with a shawl draped modestly over her head. Other attendants surrounded them, laughing and joking. Judith preferred women as companions; of the nobles, clerics, stewards, servants, grooms, carters, and humble slaves who attended her, almost all were female, with the exception of most of her soldiers and two elderly fraters who had served her mother before her. She rode at the head of a magnificent procession. Of the entourages Ivar had seen, only the king's had been larger.

"Why would such a powerful noble be flung into the pit?" Ivar replied finally. "Except that she is in error about the Holy Word and the truth of the blessed Daisan's death and life. But that is the fault of the church, which denies the truth to those eager to hear the Holy Word. I suppose Margrave Judith will endow a convent at her death and the nuns there will pray for her soul every day. So why shouldn't she ascend to the Chamber of Light, with so many nuns praying so devoutly for the care of her soul once she is dead?"

Baldwin sighed expansively. "Then why should I bother to be good, if it only means that I'll endure for eternity next to her in the Chamber of Light after I'm dead?"

"Baldwin! Didn't you listen at all to the lessons?" Ivar realized at that moment that Baldwin's rapt attentive gaze, so often turned on Master Pursed-Lips, Brother Methodius, and their other teachers, might have all this time concealed his complete mental absence from their lessons. "In the Chamber of Light all of our earthly desires will be washed away in the glory of God's gaze."

At that instant the margrave chanced to look back toward them. The gleam in her eyes caused poor Baldwin to look startled and abruptly shy, but unfortunately Baldwin's modesty only highlighted the length of his eyelashes, the curve of his rosy cheeks, and the blush of his lips. The margrave smiled and returned her attention to her companions, who laughed uproariously at some comment she now made. Like a cat, she gained great pleasure in toying with the plump mouse she had snared.

Ivar shuddered. "But there's nothing you can do anyway," he said to Baldwin.

"That doesn't mean I have to like it." A half-gulped-down sob choked out of Baldwin's throat and was stifled. "At least you're with me, Ivar." He reached out and clasped Ivar's hand tightly, almost crushing Ivar's knuckles with the desperate strength of his grip.

"For now."

"I'll beg her to keep you by me," said Baldwin fiercely, releasing Ivar's hand. "You can be my attendant. Promise me you'll stay with me, Ivar." He turned the full force of those beautiful eyes on Ivar. Ivar flushed, felt the heat of it suffuse his face; that blush satisfied Baldwin, who first smiled softly at him and then glanced nervously toward the woman who now controlled his fate.

That evening Ivar was allowed to pour wine at the margrave's table. They had stopped for the night at a monastic estate, and Judith had commanded a fine feast. The margrave was in high spirits; the food was plentiful, the jesting so pointed that Baldwin could not take his gaze off the wooden trencher he shared with his bride. A poet who traveled with them performed "The Best of Songs," appropriate for a wedding night.

> "Bring me into your chamber, O queen.
> I have eaten my bread and honey.
> I have drunk my wine.
> Eat, friends, and drink, until you are drunk with love."

One of Judith's noble companions was questioning the elderly uncle, brother to Baldwin's mother, whose presence had been necessary to pry Baldwin loose from the monastery: The old man had explained to Mother Scholastica in a quavering voice that the betrothal between Judith and Baldwin had been formally confirmed by oaths when Baldwin was thirteen; thus the covenant superceded Baldwin's personal oath to the monastery.

Now drunk, the uncle confided in Lady Adelinde. "But the margrave was still married then, when she saw the lad. Ai, well, if her husband hadn't died fighting the Quman, no doubt she would have set him aside in Baldwin's favor. He was of a good family but nothing as well-favored as the boy."

Adelinde only smiled. "And when Judith sees a man she wants, she will have him despite what the church says about cleaving only to one spouse. No doubt it was a good match for the family."

"Yes, indeed," he agreed enthusiastically. "My sister saw how much she wanted the boy, so she drove a hard bargain and was able to expand her own holdings with several good estates."

Ai, God! Sold like a young bull at market. Ivar gulped the dregs of wine from the cup he was taking to refill. The wine burned his throat; his head was already swimming.

"She'll marry him tonight," said the old uncle, nodding toward the bridal pair. Judith kept a firm hand on the wine cup she and Baldwin shared, making sure he did not drink too much, but she did not fawn over him or pay him an unseemly amount of attention. "And a biscop will sing a blessing over the marriage when we reach the king."

> "Come, my beloved, let us go early to the vineyards.
> Let us see if the vine has budded or its blossom opened."

"You see, Adelinde," said the margrave, calling Lady Adelinde's attention away from Baldwin's aged relative. "No flower should be plucked before it blooms, or we will never see it in its full flowering." She indicated Baldwin who by this time was pink with embarrassment; yet like a flower under the hot gaze of the sun—and the abrupt attention of all the folk privileged to sit at the table with Margrave Judith—he did not wilt but rather flourished. But she had already turned her gaze elsewhere; she had a sudden and uncomfortable glint in her eyes. "Is that not so, Lady Tallia?"

The young woman did not look up. She had not even eaten the bread off her plate, and at once Ivar felt guilty for having eaten and drunk so lustily. Her face was as pale as a dusting of snow on spring fields, her voice so soft that he could scarcely hear her reply. " 'If a woman were to offer for love the whole wealth of her house, it would be utterly scorned.' "

This rebuke had no effect on Margrave Judith's good cheer. " 'But my vineyard is mine to give,' " she retorted to hearty laughter, and then signaled to her waiting attendants. "Come. Now we shall retire."

"What?" exclaimed her companion with drunken joviality. "So soon after fetching him from the monastery? You raise horses aplenty in the east. Surely you know you break them in a bit at a time. You don't just throw a saddle on them and ride them the first time you put a harness on them."

"I have been patient," said Judith with a pleasant smile, but there was iron in her tone. She gestured to Baldwin to rise, and Ivar hastily followed him, since poor Baldwin had now gone as white as a burial shroud.

In the bustle as they retreated from the hall Ivar found himself cornered by Judith's noble companion, who was so flushed with drink that her hands had no more discretion than her wine-loosened tongue. "Do you have those freckles everywhere?" she demanded, and with a hand on his thigh seemed likely to pull up his robe to find out.

"Nay, Adelinde." Judith put herself between the woman and Ivar. "This boy is sworn to the church. He's not even allowed to speak to women. I have pledged to see him safely to the monastery of St. Walaricus the Martyr. And that means safe in *all* parts." Her glance touched Ivar, but in her case it was her disinterest in him that was tangible. He could have been a chair she moved aside. "Go on, boy. Attend my bridegroom to his night's rest."

A chamber had been set aside for the margrave and her attendants. Several pallets had been set to one side on the floor; the bed, wide and soft, had a curtain hung about it like a shield. A breath of wind through open shutters stirred the curtain. Outside, twilight bled a buttery light into the room.

Baldwin was shaking as Ivar helped him out of his sandals and leggings and fine tunic, leaving him in his undertunic. He washed his face and hands and then went to kneel beside the bed in an attitude of devout prayer, as blank of expression as a handsome marble statue.

Judith arrived, flushed and full of energy. She was a good-sized woman, tall, stout, and strong. Baldwin was scarcely taller and, having all the slenderness of youth, seemed swallowed by her robust presence.

At a signal from one of the servants, Ivar left Baldwin and retreated to a corner. At the table, one of Judith's clerics chanted words over a strip of linen marked with letters—something in Dariyan that Ivar couldn't make out, although it had the cadence of one of those homely spells used by parish deacons to drive out pests or heal the sick. The cleric soaked the linen in vinegar and then wrapped it up around a pebble. Now Ivar turned away modestly while Judith's attendants flocked around her, undressing her. There was much giggling and whispering. A servingwoman drew the curtains shut. The other servants settled down on pallets or on the floor, but Ivar couldn't sleep. Facing the corner, he sank down to bruised knees, clenched his eyes shut, and clasped his hands tightly in prayer.

Even with his eyes squeezed shut, he couldn't help but hear. The good margrave seemed to take an unconscionably long time about her task.

His own body stirred in response to what he heard: a slip of cloth as bodies rolled, a grunt, a stifled chuckle, a sudden surprised gasp; a sigh. Ai, Lady protect him. He could imagine the man rousing, the woman opening, and whether his thoughts dwelt longest with bridegroom or bride he could not—must not—think on. His prayers fled from him like startled hares. He was sweating although it was not a particularly hot night.

A few short gasps which he recognized as Baldwin—and it was finally over.

He had held himself so tensely that to move made his muscles groan. Grimacing, he eased down onto the carpet that covered the wood floor, the only pallet granted him, and at last, wrung out by the ordeal, dozed off . . . only to be awakened much later in the night by the same thing.

When they had finished once again, he could finally sleep, but he was haunted by terrible dreams. Surely the Enemy had sent a hundred grasping, pinching, teasing minions to taunt him with visions of Liath warm, willing, and close against him.

In the morning only formalities remained. Judith presented her new husband with a traditional morning gift to celebrate the consummation of the marriage: a fine sword set in a jeweled scabbard; a silk tunic from Arethousa; a small ivory chest containing jeweled brooches and rings; and twelve *nomias,* gold coins minted in the Arethousan Empire. It was a handsome and impressive gift.

Baldwin's old uncle had brought a trifle for Baldwin to present to her in his turn, a gold bauble with bells hidden inside that tinkled when it was rolled along the floor.

The marriage-price paid by Judith to his parents was more substantial but none of it movable wealth: He now could lay claim to several rich estates in Austra and Olsatia. That had all been agreed upon five years before, and it was only a formality to read the charters now.

They left the estate late in the morning. Judith rode ahead with her attendants, leaving Ivar to keep pace beside Baldwin. The new bridegroom had a flush in his cheeks and a bit of pale fuzz along his jaw; he was a man now and was expected to grow a beard.

Ivar reached over to tap his leg, and Baldwin flinched as if any least touch startled him. "Are you well?" whispered Ivar. "You look as if you've taken a fever."

"I didn't know." His eyes had a feverish gleam and his gaze on Ivar had such intensity that all at once those thoughts which had tormented Ivar's waking prayers and restless sleep last night shuddered back into life and danced through his body. Both young men looked away, at once, and when Ivar looked up again it was to see Baldwin staring now at Lady Tallia with her pale face and frail profile. His lips were slightly swollen, and his eyes were wide.

"I didn't know," he repeated, as at a revelation, but of what he hadn't known then and did know now he spoke no further word. Ivar was left to ride in discomforting silence beside him.

2

WHEN Rosvita slept with the *Vita* of St. Radegundis tucked against her, the bequest given to her by the dying Brother Fidelis, she always had strange dreams. Voices whispered in her dreams in a language she could not quite understand. Creatures fluttered at the edge of her mind's vision as at the forest's verge, trying to catch her attention, then bolting as woodland animals did when they caught the scent of a predator.

A golden wheel flashed in harsh sunlight, turning. Young Berthold slept peacefully in a stone cavern, surrounded by six attendants. A blizzard tore at mountain peaks, and in the wings of a storm danced moon-pale daimones, formed out of the substance of the aetherical winds. A lion stalked a cold hillside of rock, and on the plain of dying grass below this escarpment black hounds coursed after their prey, an eight-pointed stag, while a great party of riders clothed in garments as brilliant as gems followed on their trail.

"Sister Rosvita!"

A hand descended on her shoulder and she woke, dragged out of the dream by the urgent summons of the waking world. She grunted and sat up, blinking.

"I beg you, Sister Rosvita." Nerves made young Constantine's voice squeak like a boy's. "The king wishes you to attend him. A steward is here to escort you."

"I beg you, Brother, recall your modesty."

He murmured apologies and turned his back as she slipped out from under the blanket and pulled on cleric's robes over her undertunic. Sister Amabilia snored pleasingly in the bed; Rosvita envied the young woman her ability to sleep through anything. She considered the *Vita* and on impulse picked it up.

The king was out behind the stables, fully dressed as if he had never lain down to sleep the night before. He stood with one foot braced on a stump and a hand braced on that leg as if to give him a place to grip patience as he watched his son pace back and forth, back and forth, along the ground in a curving line that would soon wear itself visibly into the grass. For an instant Rosvita thought the prince was on a leash, but it was only that the pattern of his restless pacing marked the same ground over and over: as if he still paced in a semicircle at the limit of chains. Yet he had been freed from the chains of his captivity to Bloodheart over twenty days ago.

Dogs growled as Rosvita approached, making her neck prickle. Horrible beasts, they had huge fangs coated with saliva, and eyes that sparked fire. Their iron-gray coats lay like a sheen of metal over thin flanks. They lunged, were brought up short by chains, and contented themselves with barking and slobbering.

Seeing Rosvita, Henry gestured toward his son. "He has taken a mad plan into his head to ride out after one of my Eagles, without even an escort. Your advice, good Sister, will surely make him see reason where Villam and I cannot."

Sanglant stopped pacing and stood alertly as if listening—to her, or to the birds singing their morning lauds. Was it true, as Brother Fidelis had said over a year ago, that the birds sang of this child born of the mingling of human and Aoi blood? Could the prince actually understand the language of the birds? Or was he listening for something else?

"Let me go, Your Majesty," said Sanglant harshly. "Call off your dogs."

The soldiers glanced toward the staked-down Eika dogs, who growled and yipped, sensing their disquiet. Henry looked toward Rosvita, expecting her to speak.

Quickly she collected her thoughts. "What troubles you, Your Highness? Where is it you wish to go?"

"She should have been back by now. I have been patient. But there are things stalking her." He cast his head back to scent. "I can smell them. There is something else, something I don't understand— What if she's met with disaster on the road? I must find her!"

That he did not bolt for freedom was due only to the presence of his father. Henry would not have been king had he not had a gaze as sharp as lightning and a force of will as strong as any ten men. That will set to bear on the prince was all that kept Sanglant from bolting.

"How will you find this Eagle you seek?" Rosvita continued. "There are many roads."

"But I smell death—! And the taint of the Enemy." He shook himself all over, barked out something more like a howl of frustration than a curse, and suddenly collapsed to his knees. "Ai, Lady, I feel a dead hand reaching out to poison her."

"As well chain him up like the dogs," muttered the king, "as get sense out of him. No one must see him like this."

"Your Highness." Rosvita knew how to soothe distraught men. As eldest daughter in her father's hall, that duty had fallen to her more than once as a child when rage overtook Count Harl. She had soothed Henry many times. She went forward now and cautiously but firmly laid a hand on the prince's shoulder. His whole body shook under her touch. "Would it not be better to remain with the king's progress than to risk missing her on the road? The Eagle you seek will return to the king. If you go hunting for her, how can you hope to find her when so much land lies between?"

He had a hand over his eyes and was, she now realized, weeping silently. But tears, at least, were a man's reaction, not a dog's. Emboldened by this small success, she went on. "We move again today, Your Highness. At Werlida they have stores enough to feed us all for a week or more. How many roads lead to Werlida? You could ride for months and miss her on the road. Only be patient."

"Child," said Villam gently, "all Eagles return to the king in time. If you wait with the king, then she will come to us eventually."

"She will come to *me* eventually," he whispered hoarsely.

Villam smiled. "There speaks a young man touched by the barb young men feel most keenly. You must be patient in your turn, Your Majesty. He has endured much."

The king frowned at his son but, as the clerics gathered in the manor hall behind them raised their voices in the opening verses of Prime, his expression lost some of its utter gloom.

"She's a handsome enough young woman," continued Villam, almost coaxingly. "It would do him good to recover his interest in women."

"What is it you mean, son," asked the king, "by the taint of the Enemy? By a 'dead hand'?"

Suddenly, as if alerted by a noise only he could hear, Sanglant bolted to his feet and yanked up the stake that held the dogs. With them yammering and dragging at the chains, he made for the horses watched over by a nervous groom. The horses shied away from the frenzied approach of the pack, and the prince had to beat the dogs back with his fists to make them stop lunging for the underbellies of the horses. With growls and whines they obeyed him, and he swung onto a horse and with the dogs' leashes still in his grip and a square pouch slung over his shoulder, he rode away toward the river.

The king looked toward Hathui. She nodded, as at a spoken command, and commandeered a horse to make haste after

Sanglant. With barely audible groans, the four soldiers followed her.

"I despair of him," muttered Henry.

"Let him recover," advised Villam. "Then give him the Dragons again. Battle will restore his wits."

But Henry only frowned. "Ungria's king has sent an envoy. He offers his younger brother as a bridegroom for Sapientia."

Rosvita regarded him with surprise. "I thought you favored the suit of the Salian, Prince Guillaime. Or the son of the Polenie king."

"Savages!" murmured Villam, who had fought against the Polenie before their conversation to the faith of the Unities. "You'd do better to marry her to young Rodulf of Varingia, and seal his sister the duke's loyalty in that way. Sapientia will need the loyalty of Duchess Yolande of Varingia when she comes to the throne."

"He's always been an obedient son," said Henry, still staring in the direction his son had ridden. "But I must set the foundation on stone, not sand."

Villam glanced at Rosvita and raised his eyebrows as if to question her. What on earth was the king speaking about? She could only shrug.

In the forecourt in front of the manor house where they had stayed the night, the servants were already loading wagons, beating feather beds, hauling the king's treasure chests out under guard. Rosvita watched as young Brother Constantine hurried out, bent over a loose bundle of pens and ink bottles; because he wasn't looking where he was going, he slammed into a servant, dropped a stoppered bottle and then, bending to retrieve it, several quills as well.

Rosvita smiled. "Your Majesty. If I may go to my clerics and make ready?"

Henry nodded absently. As she moved off, he called her name. "I thank you, good friend," he said with a sudden, brilliant smile, and she could only incline her head, staggered as always by the force of his approval.

Rosvita reached young Constantine in time to help him pick up the last goose quill. A moment later she heard a hail. Brother Fortunatus and Sister Amabilia had appeared on the steps, blinking sleepily, and now they swung around to look as a rider came into view.

"Where is the king?" the man called. Rosvita stepped forward to take his message. "Nay, I bring no message," the rider continued politely. "I ride as herald for Margrave Judith. She has returned to the king's progress with her bridegroom. She escorts Lady Tallia to the king."

"Her bridegroom!" said Fortunatus just as Amabilia exclaimed: "God Above! What has the girl done to get herself thrown out of Quedlinhame so quickly?"

A new set of riders clattered into view, and the clerics stared expectantly, but it was only an annoyed Prince Sanglant with his escort of Hathui and the four guardsmen made anxious by the Eika dogs. Servants scattered, running for safety. The dogs erupted into a frenzy of barking, and a moment later Count Lavastine and his hounds spilled into the courtyard. The noise became so deafening that Rosvita covered her ears.

Sanglant leaped down off his horse and yanked his dogs down, but they kept struggling up to bolt for the black hounds, who wisely kept their distance without stinting in threatening growls and ear-splitting barks even as the count called them to heel.

Then Lavastine's heir came out of the hall. Lord Alain knelt beside the hounds and spoke a few words to them, and at once they ceased barking and sat, tongues lolling, with patient vigilance.

Sanglant was still cursing his dogs, who barked and lunged and snapped at their rivals. His right hand dripped blood where the chain, dragged through his grip, had scraped the skin raw. Alain approached him cautiously, knelt with extended hand, and reached out to touch the nearest Eika dog.

Rosvita shut her eyes as Amabilia gasped and Fortunatus swore under his breath. Constantine whimpered in fright. Then Rosvita cursed herself for cowardice and opened her eyes just as an uncanny silence fell upon the scene.

Alain had laid a hand gently on the head of the biggest and ugliest of the Eika dogs. It sat meekly, trembling beneath his touch. The other two hunkered down. Gobs of saliva dribbled down their muzzles to stain the dirt at his feet.

"Peace," he said to them. "Poor troubled souls."

He stood up. Sanglant regarded the young man with astonishment. Count Lavastine's expression was so blank Rosvita could not read it.

A moment more they all stood so. Then raised voices drifted out to them from the hall behind. Sanglant grimaced and hastily dragged his dogs away just as Sapientia and Father Hugh emerged from the hall. An attendant carried infant Hippolyte, and the baby crowed and burbled as Hugh smiled at her and tickled her under her fat chin.

But Sapientia was staring around the courtyard, mouth pinched down. "Did we miss something?" she demanded as Sanglant vanished behind the stable. Hathui nodded curtly at Rosvita and left to find the king. Servants emerged cautiously from their bolt-holes and resumed their labors, and the messenger crept out from the safety of the stables and knelt before Father Hugh.

"My lord. Your mother rides not an hour behind me on the road."

Father Hugh turned his smile from baby to messenger. "Ah, you are the younger son of old Tortua, the crofter over by Lerchewald. You're much grown since I left Austra. You are wed now?"

"Nay, my lord. The farm has gone to my elder sisters and there was nothing left for me, so I came into your good mother's service."

"Indeed," said Hugh with a gentle smile but a glint like the spark of fire in his eye, "that is often the fate of sons. Here." He took a pouch from one of his attendants and gave a handful of silver coins to the young man. "For your dowry."

The messenger flushed scarlet. "My lord Hugh!" He kissed Hugh's hand. Hugh said a blessing over him and sent him off to find something to eat. As Count Lavastine came forward to pay his respects to Princess Sapientia, Hugh's gaze roved the courtyard and came to rest, briefly, on Rosvita.

She nodded at him, to acknowledge him, although they did not stand close enough to speak. His eyes had a fever in them, as of a man caught at the beginning of the onslaught of an all-encompassing illness. He frowned at her, recalled himself, and offered a pleasant smile instead, then turned away.

Did he suspect that she was the one who had stolen *The Book of Secrets* from him? And if he did, what action would he take against her?

3

IT was well past dawn, but the procession was not yet ready to leave. Loaded wagons jostled past crates of chickens; a file of soldiers stood at their ease beside the wagons which carried the king's treasure. As a mark of favor, the king had chosen to wait for Margrave Judith's party to arrive so that they could travel together to Werlida. Alain stood restlessly beside Lavastine, who himself waited on the king. The sun's glare made him wince as he squinted northeast, trying to make out the approaching party. It was so hard to wait.

Lord Geoffrey had caroused late the night before, and he finally emerged from the house rubbing his eyes, looking rather the worse for wear. "Cousin!" he said to Lavastine by way of greeting. He nodded at Alain, nothing more. "Is it true that Margrave Judith will arrive today?"

Lavastine's frown was comprehensive as he studied Geoffrey. "Had you risen earlier, you would know the whole."

"And missed the wrestling?" Geoffrey laughed heartily, and Alain flushed. A group of women who were no better than whores had come from the nearby town of Fuldas yesterday to entertain the king's court.

"I would not have called it wrestling," replied Lavastine. "Indeed, if you recall, their antics were so outrageous that in the end the king asked them to leave the hall."

"Yet he did not forbid any of us to follow after them. The king does not begrudge the young their diversions."

"The young will behave foolishly, as is their wont. But you are married, cousin."

"And glad of it! So could you be married again, cousin, if you took a wife."

Lavastine pressed his lips together so tightly that his skin went white at the corners of his mouth. He called Terror over to him, and Geoffrey fidgeted nervously, but the old hound merely snarled at him and then sat down to get his ears stroked. "I will not marry again. Alain will sire the next heir to Lavas county."

Geoffrey's smile in reply was as tight, and he did not look at Alain at all. But Alain knew he was thinking of his eldest and so far only child, Lavrentia, whom he had once believed would inherit the county of Lavas.

"Geoffrey!" cried one of the young lords from among a pack of them gathered by the stables. "You missed the best of it last night! Come, we'll tell you!"

Geoffrey excused himself and hurried over to them, stopping only to pay his respects to King Henry, who greeted him cheerfully enough.

Alain stared and stared "Look!" he cried, pointing to a haze of dust along the river.

"It was a terrible risk, Alain," said Lavastine suddenly. "What were you thinking to approach Prince Sanglant's dogs in that way?"

"Poor creatures. But I wasn't scared of them. That's why they didn't hurt me. If the prince would not treat them so brutally, they might have better natures." Then he flushed, aghast at his own harsh words.

"Eika dogs do not have 'better natures.' Prince Sanglant has shown great mercy toward them. I would have had them killed outright. That they didn't injure you is beyond my understanding, Son. You will not go near them again."

"Yes, Father," he said obediently. Then: "I see them!"

Margrave Judith's procession came into view on the road. Her banner, a panther leaping upon an antelope, flew beside a banner marked with the Arconian guivre set between three springing roes, two above and one below, the sigil of the old royal house of Varre. Lavastine hissed in breath between his teeth and with a smile of triumph turned to Alain.

"Make ready, my child. What we have worked for will come to pass at Werlida."

Suddenly, senses made sharp by anticipation, Alan could smell the harvest of summer's growth, hear chickens scratching on wood, the piping call of a bullfinch, and the purl of the distant river. Far away, clouds gathered on the horizon, a dull gray that promised rain. Ardent yawned, a gape-toothed swallowing of air, and flopped down beside Bliss. Alain smelled ripe cheese and the last faint perfume of frankincense used in the morning service.

"Tallia," he said softly, trying her name on his lips, but his throat clotted with emotion, and he could only stare as Margrave Judith's party approached in all their glory—a sight that two years ago would have left him speechless at the splendor of their passing but which now had become commonplace. Father Hugh walked forward to kiss his mother's hand; then Judith dismounted in her turn to greet King Henry.

Alain searched, but he could not see Tallia although he knew she must be among the group of women concealed by hoods and shawls.

Sister Rosvita and her clerics stood a few paces from him, and Alain heard their whispered comments.

"God Above! He has the face of an angel!"

"Sister Amabilia," replied Rosvita sternly. "Do not stare so. It is unseemly."

" 'A lily among thorns is my sweet flower among men,' " quoted the youngest of them, not without a quaver of awe in his voice.

"Brother Constantine and I are for once in agreement," muttered Amabilia.

"Where does she find these succulent young morsels?" asked the fourth.

"Brother Fortunatus!" Rosvita scolded. Then, on a gasp, she spoke again. "Ivar! What means this?"

"God help us," murmured Lavastine in a tone of astonishment. Alain tore his gaze away from his search for Tallia to see a blindingly handsome young man brought forward to be presented to the king. With him, like an attendant, walked another young man whose curling red-gold hair strayed out from the otherwise modest cowl of his novice's hood. Rosvita moved forward to intercept the young men, but before she could reach them through the crowd, King Henry signaled for the march to begin. At once the courtyard fell into such a clamor and with so much dust hazing the scene that Alain had everything he could do to keep the hounds and himself next to his father.

With Margrave Judith now in the procession, Count Lavastine and Alain were relegated to the second rank behind Henry, Helmut Villam, Judith, Hugh, and Princess Sapientia. But Alain did not mind; he kept craning his neck around to try to get a glimpse of Tallia, but her group was lost to his gaze in the crowd behind.

It took until the afternoon to reach Werlida, a magnificent palace set on a bluff overlooking a broad bend in the river. They wound up a road from the river bottom and past a berm and a palisade wall into the lower enclosure. Here most of the wagons rumbled to a halt, scattering out among a village made up of sunken pit-houses for quartering servants and craftsmen, four large weaving halls, and a half dozen timber-post graneries. Alain caught the dusty scent of old grain stored in sacks and pots, then they moved out of range, upward through gateways with no less than three ramparts with ditches cut away on their outer slopes. From the height of the upper enclosure, he saw the river at the steep base of the bluff below. It curved around on three sides. Fields lay scattered among copses of woodland, and beyond them spread forest.

Here, on the grounds of the palace, they waited in the large, open interior field—not quite a courtyard—for the king to make his way to his quarters, which lay on the other side of a stone chapel. A stately timber hall with its foundations set in stone graced the southern side of this complex of buildings. The king's stewards parceled out quarters according to rank and favor, but no sooner had Alain gotten the hounds settled in a makeshift kennel outside their assigned guesthouse than the count came looking for him.

"King Henry has asked that we attend him in a private council. Come, Son. Make yourself presentable." He glanced toward the kenneled hounds who, hoping for a caress, wagged their tails and whined. "Bring two of the hounds as well."

The king received them in a spacious room with all the shutters taken down to admit light and air. Only Helmut Villam, a half-dozen servingmen, and Sister Rosvita attended him. Henry sat on his traveling chair, carved cunningly with lions as the four legs, the back as the wings of an eagle, and the arms as the sinuous necks and heads of dragons. The king leaned forward as his favored Eagle spoke softly into his ear. Seeing Lavastine and Alain, he straightened.

"Let him come to me at once if you can coax him within the ramparts. Otherwise—" He glanced toward Villam, who gave a barely perceptible nod. "—let him range as widely as he wishes at this time. Better that the court not see him when he is in such a restless and wild humor."

She bowed and strode briskly out of the chamber. Henry gestured to a servingman, who left the chamber in the Eagle's wake. Then he nodded to Sister Rosvita and, with a troubled expression, she read aloud from a letter.

" 'To my brother, His Illustrious Majesty, Henry, regnant over Wendar and Varre. With a heavy heart and a disquieted mind I must relate to you these tidings, that our niece Tallia cannot remain at Quedlinhame. She has been spreading the taint of heresy among my novices and has polluted over twenty young innocents with her preaching. I advise caution even as I commend her into your hands. It seems to me that marriage would best distract her from these falsehoods.' "

Henry signed, and Rosvita stopped reading. "Do you still want the marriage to go forward?" he asked Lavastine bluntly. "The charge of heresy is a serious one. Mother Scholastica has taken Tallia's youth into account in judging her fit, at this time, for mercy. The girl claims to have had visions, but whether they have come to her through the agency of the Enemy or merely through her innocent trust in bad counselors we cannot say. If she does not repent of these views, the church may be forced to take more drastic action."

Lavastine raised an eyebrow, considering.

Heresy. Alain knew in his gut to whom Tallia had listened: Frater Agius. It was as if the heresy of the flaying knife and the sacrifice and redemption of the blessed Daisan was a plague, passing from one vulnerable soul on to the next. Agius had been granted the martyr's death he so desired. Wasn't that a mark of God's favor? But why should God favor a man who preached a heresy against God's own truth?

Yet the thought of losing Tallia because of Agius' preaching infuriated him. Anger welled up in his heart, and Rage growled beside him.

"Peace," murmured Lavastine, and the hound settled down to rest its head on its great paws. He turned to the king. "Lady Tallia is young yet, Your Majesty. And she has not, alas, been exposed to the wisest of counselors. A steadying influence—" He nodded toward Alain. "—will calm her young mind."

"So be it," said Henry, not without relief.

"The sooner this transaction takes place, the better," added

Lavastine. "I must return to my lands before autumn so that I and my son can oversee the autumn sowing. A hard winter awaits us because of the men who died at Gent ... those same men who gave up their lives to return Gent—and your son Sanglant—into your hands."

The door opened and the servingman returned with two young women in tow. One, with a plump and eager face, stared at the king with mouth agape and then recalled herself and knelt obediently. The other, shawl askew to reveal wheat-pale hair, was Tallia.

Alain had to shut his eyes. He was overtaken by such a surge of anticipation and relief and simple, terrible desire that he swayed, trembling all over, until Sorrow nudged up under a hand to give him a foundation to steady himself on.

"Uncle," said Tallia so softly that the commonplace noises from outside almost drowned out her words "I beg you, Uncle, let me retire in peace to a nun's cell. I will take vows of silence, if that must be, but do not—"

"Silence! You are not meant for the church, Tallia. In two days' time you will be wed to Lord Alain. Do not seek to argue with me. My mind is made up."

Alain looked up to see Tallia kneeling before the king. Her cheeks were scoured to a dreadful pallor, and she was as thin as a beggar in a year of bad harvests, but she was still beautiful to his eyes. It was more than her beauty that affected him; another inexplicable, unnamable force had taken hold of him and he could only stare, stricken dumb with shame for the desire he felt even as she turned a pleading gaze on him and with tears rolling down her cheeks bent her head as in submission to the terrible fate that had overtaken her.

4

FATHER Hugh never argued. He merely smiled when another disagreed with him, then spoke with such gentle persuasion that his disputants rarely recognized that he almost always got his way. But Hanna had learned to read signs of his agitation. Right now he was wringing the finger of one of his gloves, held lightly in his left hand, twisting it round and round as he listened to his mother's advice to Princess Sapientia.

"Prince Sanglant is a threat to your position only if you let him become one, Your Highness," Margrave Judith was saying. Hanna stood behind Sapientia's chair; the margrave sat like an equal beside the princess in a chair almost as elaborate as the regnant's throne. All of her other attendants—including her new husband and her bastard son—stood while the two noblewomen conversed. "It is true that your father the king has neglected you because of his affection for the prince. I speak bluntly because it is only the common truth."

She spoke bluntly because she was powerful enough to do so. A sidewise glance brought Hanna a glimpse of Ivar's bowed head. He had a flush in his cheeks that bothered Hanna, as if a disease had come to roost within him that he was not yet aware of. Yet in such a situation, she could not hope to speak to him.

"What do you advise?" Too restless to sit still for long, Sapientia jumped up and began to pace. "I do not dislike my brother, although I admit since we rescued him from Gent he behaves strangely, more like a dog than a man."

"His mother was not even human, which no doubt accounts for it." Judith lifted a hand and Hugh, obedient son, brought her a cup of wine. He moved so gracefully. Hanna could scarcely believe she had seen this elegant courtier strike Liath with cold fury. He was so different, here at court. Indeed, he was so very different in all ways from the men in Heart's Rest, the village where she had grown up: his elegant manners; his fine clothes; his beautiful voice; his clean hands. "But women were made by God to administer and create and men to fight and toil," continued Judith. "Cultivate your brother as a wise farming-woman cultivates her fields, and you will gain a rich harvest for your efforts. He is a notable fighter, and he carries the luck of your family with him on the battlefield. Use his good qualities to support your own position as heir to the regnant. Do not be so foolish as to believe the whispers that Henry wishes to make him Heir. The princes of Wendar and Varre will not let themselves be ruled by a bastard, certainly not a male bastard, and one as well who has only half the blood of humankind in him."

Sapientia paused by the window. Something she saw outside

caused her to turn back and regard Margrave Judith with a half smile. "Count Lavastine's heir was once named a bastard. And now he is legitimate—and marrying my cousin this very night!"

"Tallia is an embarrassment. Henry did well to give her as a gift to Count Lavastine as reward for Lavastine's service to him at Gent. It rids Henry of Tallia."

"And gives Lavastine a bride with royal connections for his heir," said Sapientia thoughtfully. "I think you did not meet Lord Geoffrey, who is Lavastine's cousin and was his heir before Lord Alain appeared. He is a nobleman in every respect, certainly worthy of the county and title."

"Lavastine is cunning. Once Lord Alain and Lady Tallia produce an heir, Henry will be forced to support Alain if Lord Geoffrey contests the succession."

Hugh spoke suddenly. "What if King Henry decides to marry Prince Sanglant in like manner, to give him legitimacy?"

Startled, Judith glanced at him as if she had forgotten he was there. "Do you actually think Henry so far gone in his affection for Sanglant that he would consider such a thing?"

"Yes," he said curtly.

"No," retorted Sapientia. "I am Heir. I have Hippolyte to prove my worthiness. It's just that you hate Sanglant, Hugh. I see how you detest him. You can't bear that I might like him, even though we grew up together and he always treated me kindly when we were children. But your mother is right." Judith nodded in acknowledgment, but Hanna noted how hard her gaze was upon her son, as if she sought to plumb his depths and thereby know his mind. "Sanglant is no threat to my position—unless I let him become one. And by seeming to fear him because my father favors him and shows an old fondness for him, it weakens me—not him." She spun around to look at Hanna. "Is that not so, Eagle? Is that not exactly what you said to me yesterday?"

Ai, Lady! They all looked at her. She wished abruptly that she had never spoken such rash words to Sapientia. But Sapientia, if young and foolish, had promise if only someone bothered to give her practical advice, and Hanna had a store of practical advice harvested from her own mother.

"Wise counsel," said Margrave Judith with a gleam in her eyes that made Hanna exceedingly nervous. "What do *you* say, Hugh?"

Hugh had a certain quirk to his lips that betrayed irritation. He smiled to cover it now. His voice remained as smooth as honey, and as sweet. "It is God's will that sister love brother. For the rest of us, we must treat weak and strong alike with equal compassion."

"Still," mused Judith, "I had not considered the possibility of a marriage for Prince Sanglant. I will propose to Henry that he marry Sanglant to my Theucinda."

"You would marry your own legitimate daughter to my bastard brother?" asked Sapientia, astonished.

In her mind's ear, Hanna could hear her mother's voice commenting. She knew exactly what Mistress Birta would say: that Margrave Judith, a wise administrator, was merely gathering the entire flock of chickens into her own henhouse.

"Theucinda is my third daughter, just now of age. Gerberga and Bertha have their duties, their estates, and their husbands and heirs in Austra and Olsatia. Theucinda can serve me in this way, if I think it advantageous." She drained her cup, still watching her son. "But I do not concern myself as much with Sanglant's marriage. Do not forget that Henry may marry again."

"As you did," said Hugh stiffly, glancing toward Baldwin and as quickly away as if embarrassed to be caught looking.

Judith chuckled. "What is this frown, my pet? I must have my amusements." By *not* glancing toward Baldwin she called attention to his presence because everyone else then looked at him. The poor boy was, truthfully, the prettiest creature Hanna had ever seen; as was now commonly said among the serving-folk, he had the face of an angel.

Hugh seemed about to speak. Abruptly he moved forward to take his mother's empty wine cup and have it refilled. When he returned it to her, she touched his wrist as lightly as a butterfly lights on a flower to sip its nectar, and for a moment Hanna thought that something passed between them, mother and son, an unspoken message understood by what could be read in the gaze and in the language of the body. But she did not hold the key to interpret it.

When Judith left, Ivar was hustled away together with Baldwin, and Hanna could only catch his eye as he crossed the threshold. He lifted a hand as if in reply, and then was gone. For the rest of the day, preparations for the wedding feast consumed her attention. Mercifully, Hathui pressed her into service to escort two wagons to an outlying farmstead where stores of honey and beeswax candles had been set aside for the regnant's use as their yearly rent.

She loitered at the farmstead, talking to the old beekeeper while his adult children and two laborers loaded the two wagons with casks of honey and carefully wrapped bundles of delicate wax. His youngest son eyed her with interest.

"Ach, the king himself!" said the old man, whom Hanna quite liked. "I've never seen King Henry. It's said he's a handsome man, strong and tall and a fine general."

"So he is."

"But I have seen Arnulf the Younger with these own eyes, and that sight I'll never forget. He came here by this very farm when I was a young man, with his escort all in rich clothes and with such fine horses that it nearly blinded a man to see them. I remember that he had a scar under his left ear, somewhat fresh. He rode with an Eagle at his right side, just like you, a common Eagle! Only it were a man. Strange it were, to see a common man riding next to the king like his best companion. But he died."

"The Eagle?" asked Hanna, curious now.

"Nay, King Arnulf. Died many a year ago and the son come onto the throne for the elder girl couldn't bear children and it isn't any use to have an heir if she can't bear children in her turn, is it now?" He glanced toward one of the adults, a tired-looking woman who had an angry lift to her mouth. A number of small children helped—or hindered—the labor, but none of them ran to her. "Ach, well, they say Henry has children of his own and a fine son who got him the throne, who's captain of the Dragons, they say."

"That would be Prince Sanglant." They all looked at her so expectantly that she felt obliged to give them a quick tale of the fall of Gent and its retaking.

"Ach, now!" exclaimed the old man when she had finished. "That's a story!" He gestured to his youngest son, and the lad brought a mug of sweetened vinegar so tart despite the honeyed flavor that Hanna could not keep from puckering her mouth while her hosts laughed good-naturedly.

"Now, then," said the old beekeeper, gesturing toward the son. "Can you do me a favor, Eagle? If you'd take the lad with you, he could see the king and walk back home after. He's got a yearning to see the king, and how can I say 'nay' to him, who was the last gift my poor dead wife gave me?"

The lad's name was Arnulf, no doubt in memory of the dead king; he had light hair and a pleasant if undistinguished face except for a pair of stark blue eyes that held such a wealth of wordless pleading in them that Hanna did not have the heart to say no. Arnulf proved to be no trouble, although he asked a hundred questions as he walked alongside the wagons, driven by two skeptical wagoneers in the service of the king's stewards who had grown so accustomed to the presence of the king on their daily travels that they were amused by the lad's excitement.

As they passed a stand of woods, a pack of riders swept by to the right. Hanna recognized them because of the dogs. She called out: "Look there. That is Prince Sanglant." The lad gaped.

"They say he's run mad," said the first wagoneer, to which the second retorted, "He's never harmed any but the king's enemies. You won't find a better captain than Prince Sanglant. I hear such stories. . . ."

Hanna caught sight of Hathui riding down the track, and hailed her.

"I see you have what you came for," said Hathui, reining in beside Hanna. "Wish me good fortune in my own hunt. I'm to bring him back in time for the feasting tonight." She lifted a chin to indicate the riders who had just vanished into the copse.

"What's wrong with him? Many things are whispered, that he's more dog than man now."

Hathui shaded a hand to get a better look at the trees. "Chained among the Eika for a year?" She shrugged. "At least those prisoners the Quman take are made slaves and given work to do. It's a miracle he's alive at all." Her gaze had a sharp sympathy. "Don't forget how he fought outside Gent when he was finally released."

Hanna smiled. "Nay, I've not become Sapientia's advocate against him. But do you think it's true, what's rumored, that Henry has it in mind to name Sanglant as his heir instead of his legitimate daughter?"

Hathui's frown was all the answer she would give as she nodded at Hanna and rode away.

Hanna left the wagons and wagoneers by the pit-houses that

served the kitchens and let Arnulf follow her to the great open yard that fronted chapel, hall, and the royal residence. There, as luck would have it, king and court had gathered outside to cheer on bouts of wrestling. Hanna made her way through the crowd to the side of Princess Sapientia. Catching the princess' eye, Hanna knelt before her. With a graceless exhalation of surprise, the lad plopped down beside her.

"Your Highness." Sapientia was in a good mood, all light and charm made bright by that very energy that so often made her look foolish. "Here is Arnulf, the beekeeper's son. He has escorted us from his father's farmstead with honey and candlewax.

Sapientia smiled on the young man, called over the steward who oversaw her treasury, and handed young Arnulf two silver sceattas. "For your dowry," she said. She hailed her father.

Henry came attended by Villam and Judith. He was laughing, not immoderately but with pure good humor, infectious and yet dignified. But when Sapientia indicated the young man who stared in awe at this apparition, the king's posture changed.

He sobered; he turned the full force of his gaze on the young man and, with a firm hand, touched him on the head. "My blessing on you and your kin," he said, then removed his hand. That quickly, he returned to his jest with his companions, and they strolled away while Margrave Judith pointed out the young man-at-arms who was next to challenge the champion.

Hanna led the quaking Arnulf away. "What are these?" he whispered, holding out the sceattas.

"They're coins. You can exchange them for goods in the marketplace down in the lower enclosure, although you'd best not do so today, for they'll know you're not used to bargaining and they'll cheat you."

"My dowry," he murmured. He blinked so many times she thought for a moment he was about to faint. He turned to her. "Will *you* marry me?" he demanded.

Hanna choked down a laugh and instead smiled kindly. "Go on, lad," she said, feeling immeasurably older although she guessed they were of an age. "Take the coins and your blessing home to your kinfolk." She led him to the gate and watched him walk away, still unsteady on his feet.

On her way back to Sapientia, she saw Ivar standing in the doorway to the residence where Margrave Judith had taken up quarters. He saw her, beckoned, and ducked inside. She followed him over the threshold. "Ivar?"

"Hush!" He drew her into a small storeroom where servants' pallets lined one wall. The closed shutters made the room dim and stuffy. He embraced her. "Oh, Hanna! I thought I would never see you again! I'm not allowed to speak to women."

She kissed him on either cheek, the kinswoman's greeting. "I'm not just any woman!" she said unsteadily. "I nursed at the same breast. Surely we can speak together without fear of punishment."

"Nay," he whispered, opening the door a crack to see out into the corridor, then returning to her. "Rosvita wanted to see me, but it was forbidden, though she's a cleric, and my sister. But she would only have scolded me anyway, so I'm glad I didn't see her!"

Hanna sighed. He was as passionately thoughtless as ever. "Well, you've certainly filled out through the shoulders, Ivar. You look more like your father than ever. But are you well? Why aren't you at Quedlinhame?"

He still shook his head the same way, red curls all unruly, face gone stubborn. He always jumped before he measured the ground. "Is it true? That the king means Lady Tallia to marry? They mustn't despoil her! She must remain the pure vessel of God's truth." He wrenched away from her again, clapping his hands to his forehead in an attitude of despair and frustration. "They'll do to her what they did to Baldwin! They care nothing for vows sworn honestly to the church!"

"Hush, Ivar. Hush, now." She drew his hands down from his head and pressed a palm against his forehead, but he wasn't hot. His voice had the fever in it, not his skin. "Why aren't you at Quedlinhame? Did your father send for you?"

He made a strange gesture, left index finger drawn down his chest over his breastbone. "If you'd seen—"

"Seen *what?*"

"The miracle of the rose. The marks of flaying on her palms. You'd believe in the sacrifice and redemption. You'd know the truth which has been concealed."

Nervous, she pulled away from him and bumped up against the wall. "I don't know what you're talking about, Ivar. Is this some madness that's gotten into you?"

"No madness." He groped for her hand, found it, and tugged

her against the wall. Her boot wrinkled the edge of a neatly-folded wool blanket, uncovering a posy of pressed flowers beneath, a love token. "The Translatus is a lie, Hanna. The blessed Daisan didn't pray for seven days, as they wrote in the Holy Verses. He wasn't lifted bodily into the Chamber of Light. It's all a lie."

"You're scaring me. Isn't that a heresy?" Surely the minions of the Enemy had burrowed inside him and now spoke through his lips. She tried to edge away, but his grip was strong.

"So has the church taught falsely for years. The blessed Daisan was flayed alive by the order of the Empress Thaisannia. His heart was cut out of him, but his heart's blood bloomed on the Earth as a red rose. He suffered, and he died. But he lived again and ascended to the Chamber of Light and through his suffering cleansed us of our sin."

"Ivar!" Perhaps the curtness of her voice shocked him into silence. "Let me go!"

He dropped her hand. "You'll do as Liath did. Abandon me. Only Lady Tallia wasn't afraid to walk where the rest of us were imprisoned. Only *she* brought us hope."

"Lady Tallia is spreading these lies?"

"It's the truth! Hanna—"

"Nay, Ivar. I won't speak of such things with you. Now hush and listen to me, and please answer me this time, I beg you. Why aren't you at Quedlinhame?"

"I'm being taken to the monastery founded in the memory of St. Walaricus the Martyr. In Eastfall."

"That's a fair long way. Did you ask to be sent there?"

"Nay. They separated the four of us—that is, me, and Baldwin, and Ermanrich, and Sigrid—because we listened to Lady Tallia's preaching. Because we saw the miracle of the rose, and they don't want anyone to know. That's why they cast Lady Tallia out of the convent."

"Oh, Ivar." Despite the fever that had overtaken him, she could only see him as the overeager boy she had grown up with. "You must pray to God to bring peace to your spirit."

"How can I have peace?" Suddenly he began to cry. His voice got hoarse. "Have you seen Liath? Is she here? Why haven't I seen her?"

"Ivar!" She felt obliged to scold him despite what he'd said about Rosvita. "Listen to the words of a sister, for I can call myself that. Liath isn't meant for you. She rides as an Eagle now."

"She abandoned me at Quedlinhame! I said I would marry her, I said we would ride away together—"

"After you'd sworn vows as a novice?"

"Against my will! She said she'd marry me, but then she just rode away when the king left!"

"That isn't fair! She told me of your meeting. God Above! What was she to do? You'd already sworn vows. You had no prospects, no support—and she has no kinfolk—"

"She said she loved someone else, another man," said Ivar stubbornly. "I think she abandoned me to be with *him*. I think she still loves Hugh."

"She never loved Hugh! You know what he did to her!"

"Then what man did she mean?"

She knew then, at once, whom Liath had meant, and a sick foreboding filled her heart. "That doesn't matter," she said hastily. "She's an Eagle. And you're traveling east. Ai, God, Ivar! I might never see you again."

He gripped her elbows. "Can't you help me escape?" Letting her go, he answered himself. "But I can't abandoned Baldwin. He needs me. Ai, Lady. If only Liath had married me, if only we had run away, then none of this would have happened."

They heard voices at the door, and she hid under a cot as several of Judith's stewards came in. "Ah, there he is! Lord Baldwin is asking for you, boy. Go attend him now."

Ivar had no choice but to leave. They rummaged around on other errands that at length took them into other chambers, and she slipped out, unseen. But Ivar's words troubled her into the evening, when at last king and court gathered for the wedding feast. The bridal couple were led forward wearing their best clothes. A cleric read out loud the details of the dower, what each party would bring to the marriage. Lord Alain spoke his consent in a clear, if unsteady, voice, but when it came Tallia's turn, King Henry spoke for her. *Was* she being forced into the marriage against her will, as Ivar claimed? Yet who would quarrel with the regnant's decision? The children of the nobility married to give advantage to their families; they had no say in the matter. Tallia was Henry's to dispose of, now that he had defeated her parents in battle.

The local biscop had been brought in from the nearby town

of Fuldas to speak a blessing over the young couple, who knelt before her to receive it. Lord Alain looked nervous and flushed and agitated. Lady Tallia looked so pale and thin that Hanna wondered if she would faint. But she did not. With hands clasped tightly before her, she merely kept her head bowed and looked at no one or no thing, not even her bridegroom.

The long summer twilight stretched before them as they crowded into the hall. Fresh rushes had been strewn over the floor. Servants scurried in and out with trays of steaming meat or pitchers of wine and mead. Slender greyhounds slunk away under tables, waiting for scraps. Sapientia allowed Hanna to stand behind her chair and occasionally offered her morsels from her platter, a marked sign of favor which Father Hugh noted with a surprised glance and then ignored as he directed Sapientia's attention to the poet who came forward to sing.

The poem was delivered in Dariyan, but Hugh murmured a translation to Sapientia.

"She said: Come now, you who are my own love. Come forward.
You are the light which flames in my heart.
Where once were only thorns there now blooms a lily.
He replied: I walked alone in the wood.
The solitude eased my heart.
But now the ice melts. The flowers bloom.
She bids him: Come! I cannot live without you.
Roses and lilies I will strew before you.
Let there be no delay."

Hanna flushed although she knew well enough that the words were not directed at her, but surely no man had a more beautiful voice than Hugh, and when he spoke such phrases so sweetly and with so much music in the words, even a practical young woman might feel faint with desire.

Quickly enough she steadied herself. Lady Above! No need to be foolish. No need to let Ivar's madness infect her. There was plenty else to distract her, here at the feast. At the heart of the king's progress, she could never be bored.

Her faithful companions from the long journey out of the Alfar Mountains, the Lions Ingo, Folquin, Leo and young Stephen, stood guard at the door. Catching her eye, Ingo nodded at her. Perhaps he winked.

At the king's table, Margrave Judith shared a platter with Helmut Villam. Heads together, they talked with great seriousness. Baldwin sat a table down from them; despite his status as Judith's new consort and his breathtaking beauty, he did not warrant a seat at the king's table. And there sat Ivar, beside Baldwin, but he ate nothing except a few crusts of bread and a sip of wine.

The royal clerics ate and talked with gusto, but now and again Sister Rosvita would pause and stare at her young brother with a troubled gaze.

The bridal pair sat on the other side of the king, so Hanna couldn't get a good look at them. But in any case the tableau that interested Hanna most was that of Hathui and Prince Sanglant. Hathui hovered behind Sanglant's chair and certain small communications seemed to pass between the Eagle and the king at intervals, unspoken but understood. The prince sat with the awkward stillness of an active man forced to stay in one place when he would rather be moving. With fists on the table, he stared at the opposite wall—that is, at nothing. On occasion Hathui would jostle him and he would recall himself and bolt down a scrap of cut meat, then hesitate, shake himself, and eat like a man—only to sink again into a stupor. Of the feasting and merriment around him he seemed unaware.

After a suitable interval of singing, King Henry called Sister Rosvita forward. Candles were set out but not yet lit since, with all the doors flung open and the shutters taken down, the evening still bled light into the hall. The gathered folk quieted expectantly as Sister Rosvita opened a book and began to read out loud in a clear voice.

" 'Many tales of the young Radegundis' holy deeds came to the ears of His Gracious Majesty, the illustrious Taillefer, and he had her brought to his court at Autun. The emperor could not but be swayed by her great holiness, and he determined at once to make her his queen. He entreated her to pray with him and by diverse almsgiving and acts of mercy to beggars brought her into charity with him. As her morning gift he gave her not just lands but every manner of fine gifts that she could distribute to the poor, and he pledged to feed the paupers at Baralcha every Hefensday.'

" 'In this way the saintly young woman, so determined in her vow to remain a chaste vessel so that she could embrace God with a pure heart, was overcome by the nobility of the emperor Taillefer. Wooing her in this fashion, he overcame her reluctance. Her love for his great virtues and imperial honor softened her heart, and they were married.'

" 'It is only possible to write here of a few of the many good works she accomplished in this period of her life. Early glory did not dim her ardor for God, nor did she take upon herself the trappings of royalty only to forget that the garments of the poor conceal the limbs of God.'

" 'Whenever she received part of the tribute brought before the emperor, she gave away fully half of it as her tithe to God before any was put in her own treasury. To the needy she gave clothes, and to the hungry, feasts. She built a house for poor women at Athies, and bathed the hair and sores of paupers with her own hands. To convents and monasteries she gave princely gifts. No hermit was safe from her generosity.'

" 'When his last illness laid low the emperor, she could not be torn from his side although she was great with child. She knelt beside him with such devotion that her attendants feared for her health, but she could not be shaken from her prayers and at last his passing, made gentle by her efforts, came about, and his soul was lifted to the Chamber of Light.'

" 'At that time many powerful princes flocked like carrion crows to the side of the illustrious emperor, desirous of obtaining by guile or force what he would leave behind him. Not least among these treasures stood the blessed Radegundis, a jewel among women. But she had no kin to protect her from their greed.'

" 'Still heavy with child, Radegundis clothed herself and her closest companion, a woman named Clothilde, in the garb of poor women. She chose exile over the torments of power, and she swore to marry no earthly prince but from this time on to bind herself over into God's service alone. In this way, they escaped in the night and fled to the convent of Poiterri, where they took refuge—' "

A crash and a startled scream shuddered through the hall. Sanglant had leaped to his feet in such a state of wild excitement that he had overturned the table at which he and several others sat. A stunned silence held the feasting crowd, like a deeply indrawn breath before a shout, while he stood with head thrown back, like a beast listening for the snap of a twig in the forest.

Then he sprang over the overturned table and bolted toward the doors, heedless of food and platters scattered under his feet, of wine splashed everywhere and now soaking into the rushes. Whippets scurried forward to snap at the spilled trays while servants scrambled to save what they could.

"Sanglant!" cried the king, coming to his feet, and the young man jerked to a halt as if brought up short by a chain. Perhaps only that voice could have stopped him. He did not turn to face his father. His hands shook noticeably, and he stared at the main doors so fixedly that Hanna expected a brace of Eika to come clamoring in, axes raised for a fight.

But no one entered. All was still except for the scuff and tap of servants cleaning up and the groan and heavy thunk of the table being tipped back onto its feet by the combined efforts of three men.

"As I was telling you, Your Highness," remarked Hugh to Sapientia in a pleasant voice that carried easily in the hush that now pervaded the hall, "when Queen Athelthyri of Alba was angry with certain of her subjects for fomenting rebellion against her, she set her dog Contumelus over them as their count. And quite a fine count he was, this dog, for it is said that besides wearing a neckband and a gold chain as a mark of his rank, he had a certain gift, that after he barked twice he could speak every third word."

Half the assembly tittered. Henry did not laugh, and an instant later a rash of barking came from out of doors, hounds singing a warning.

"Make way!" a man shouted outside. Hanna heard horses, the buzz of voices, and caught a glimpse of movement in the twilight beyond the threshold.

Two Eagles came into the hall.

"Liath!" Hugh stood up so quickly that his chair tipped over behind him.

On the other side of the hall, Ivar had to be restrained from bolting forward by Baldwin.

Sanglant took a step forward and then froze. A thin flush of red stained his cheeks. Liath marked him; Hanna saw it by the way her step faltered, and she supposed everyone else saw it, too. He stared at her, his body turned as a flower turns with the sun so he could follow her with his gaze as she strode forward with Wolfhere to the king.

Hugh muttered words under his breath, Hanna could not make them out.

The two Eagles knelt before the king's table.

"Wolfhere," said Henry with such dislike that the old Eagle actually winced. The king gestured. A servingman hastened around the table to give a cup of wine to Liath; she took a draught, then gave the cup to Wolfhere, who drained it.

"Your Majesty," he began with cup still in hand.

The king indicated that Liath should relay her messages first, but he caught her in the act of glancing over her shoulder toward Sanglant, and she stuttered out something meaningless as many among the assembly giggled, or coughed.

"I come from Weraushausen, Your Majesty," she said, recovering quickly. "I bring this message from Cleric Monica: She will join you with the schola. I bring also capitularies needing your seal, and a letter for Sister Rosvita from Mother Rothgard of St. Valeria Convent."

"I pray it brings news of Theophanu." At last Henry deigned to look upon Wolfhere, who had waited patiently under the king's censure.

"Your Majesty," Wolfhere said briskly. "I bring news from the south. Duke Conrad sends this message: That he will wait upon Your Majesty before Matthiasmass."

"Why has it taken him so long to come before me after the insult he gave my Eagle?"

"His wife, Lady Eadgifu, died in childbed, Your Majesty."

A murmur rolled through the hall, and several women wailed out loud. The king drew the Circle at his breast. "May God have mercy upon her." He leaned forward to rest a fist on the table. "What of the message you took to the skopos? Is it true that you believe Biscop Antonia did not die in this avalanche we have been told of?"

"She did not die, Your Majesty."

"You have seen her alive?"

"I do not need to see her to know she still lives—although I do not know how she escaped or where she is now."

"I see. Go on."

"Her Holiness Clementia, skopos and Mother to us all, has passed this judgment on Antonia of Karrone, once biscop of Mainni: that she be excommunicated for indulging in the arts of the malefici. 'Let neither woman nor man who stand within the Light of the Circle of Unity give her shelter. Let no deacon or frater take her confession or give her blessing until she bring herself before the throne of the skopos and repent of her deeds. She may no longer enter into a church and take mass. Any who consort with her or give her shelter will also be excommunicate.' These were the words of the skopos."

"A harsh judgment," said Henry, musing, then smiled grimly. "But a just one."

"That is not all the news I bring," continued Wolfhere, and the king looked at him expectantly, inclined, perhaps, to look kindly on him for bringing news so favorable to Henry's interests. He gestured for Wolfhere to go on. "Queen Gertrudis of Aosta is dead, Your Majesty, and in Ventuno King Demetrius lies on his deathbed and has received last rites."

A profound stillness, coming over the face of the king, spread quickly until the hush that pervaded the hall caused even the greyhounds to sink down and lay their heads on their paws.

"King Demetrius is without heirs, as you yourself know, my lord king. His heirs and those who contested for his share of the Aostan throne long since wasted themselves in wars in the south or else they were carried off by the pestilence brought by Jinna raiders into the southern ports. But Queen Gertrudis left one child, her daughter Adelheid, who is recently widowed."

"Widowed," said Henry. He looked—and everyone turned to look at him—at his son. Sangant stood as quiescent, or as stupefied, as the greyhounds, staring at Liath. "She is the legitimate claimant to the throne of Aosta."

"So she is, Your Majesty," said Wolfhere, who alone in the hall did not look at Prince Sanglant. "And but twenty years of age. Rumor has it that her kinfolk are now so denuded by plague and war that she has no male relatives to fight with her for her claim."

Henry shut his eyes briefly. Opening them, he gestured to the two Eagles to rise. "The Lord and Lady have heard me," he said in a voice made thick with emotion, "and listened to my prayers." He spoke softly into the ear of a steward, and as Liath and

Wolfhere retreated and were escorted outside, a party of tumblers hurried forward to entertain the court.

So the merriment and feasting resumed.

But Sanglant, moving aside to make room for the tumblers, pressed himself against the wall and instead of returning to his seat made his way to the door and slipped outside. A moment later, Hugh excused himself and left. Ivar made to get up, but Judith's young husband pulled him back into his chair and whispered urgently into his ear.

When Hanna moved to follow him, Sapientia called to her. "Eagle! Look there! How do you think that girl balances on that rope?"

Given no choice, she had to stay where she was.

III
THE LOCKED CHEST

1

"WHAT means this?" asked Wolfhere harshly as they left the hall.

A servingwoman brought them food and ale and left them to sit on a bench to take their supper in peace. Liath smiled wryly as Wolfhere glared at her. *Peace*, indeed. The first stars had bloomed in the heavens above—the three jewels of the Queen's sky promising momentary splendor—but in the west the sky still wore the blush of sunset.

"You are silent," Wolfhere observed. They hadn't eaten since taking bread and cider at midday at an isolated farm, but he ignored the platter set on the bench beside him, although a fresh cut of roast pig steamed up most invitingly.

Liath concentrated on the food because she was starving. Wolfhere would get his answer soon enough. She had gulped down most of the food on her half of the platter when she saw him make his way through the crowd of retainers who had flocked around the entrance to watch the entertainment within. Embarrassed to be caught bolting her food, she wiped her mouth with the back of a hand and stood. Wolfhere jumped up as Sanglant eased free of the crowd and walked toward them.

"What means this?" Wolfhere demanded again.

"What matters it to you? What right do you have to interfere?" But she was only angry at him because of the fearful pounding of her own heart as the prince stopped before her. He had filled out in the past twenty days and had his hair trimmed neatly, but the haunted look in his eyes hadn't dissipated. He wore a rich linen tunic trimmed with silver-and-gold-threaded embroidery, cut to fit his height; with a sword swinging in a magnificent red-leather sheath at his belt and several fine rings on his fingers, he looked very much the royal prince and courtier. Only the rough iron collar bound at his neck spoiled the picture. Perhaps it choked him: He seemed unable to speak, and now that he stood so close she could not think of one single word.

"Do not forget the oath you took as an Eagle," said Wolfhere suddenly. "Do not forget the news I brought you, Liath!"

"Leave us," said Sanglant without taking his gaze off Liath.

Not even Wolfhere dared disobey a direct command. He grunted with irritation, spun, and stalked off without taking supper or ale with him.

"I kept the book safe for you, as I promised." His hoarse voice made the words seem even more fraught with meaning; but his voice always sounded like that. "The question I asked you . . . have you an answer for me?" Shouts and laughter swelled out from the hall, and he glanced back toward the doors and muttered something under his voice more growl than words.

"You were half mad. How can I be sure you meant what you asked?"

He laughed—the old laugh she recalled from Gent when, under siege, he had lived each day as if he cared not whether another came for him. "Ai, Lady! Say you will marry me, and let us have done with this!"

Impulsively, she raised a hand to touch his face. No trace of beard chafed her fingers. This close, she could smell him: sweat, dust, the fading scent of recently-dyed cloth, all of it sharp and overwhelming. Nothing of his Eika prison remained. In the wild lands beyond the city of memory, frozen under ice, the summer sun flooded the wilderness smothered in ice with a heat so intense that it ripped through her with the power of liquid fire: A torch flared across the yard, surprised murmurs rose from inside the hall, and she staggered under the hideous memory of the palace at Augensburg going up in flames.

He drew her hand down to his chest. His touch was like the wash of cool water, soothing, quieting, healing. Where he held her hand pressed against his tunic, she felt the beat of his heart. He was not less unsteady than she was.

Lady Above! This was madness. But she couldn't bring herself to move away.

Suddenly, Sanglant threw back his head and half-growled, pushed her brusquely aside as he stepped forward. Surprised, turning, she saw Hugh behind her with an arm outstretched to grab her. She yelped and began to bolt, but Sanglant had already put himself between her and the enemy. She began to shake, could do nothing more than press a hand weakly against Sanglant's back.

"Hugh," said Sanglant in the way that a devout man utters one of the thousand names of the Enemy.

"She is mine." Hugh looked so consumed by rage that for an instant she scarcely recognized the elegant courtier who graced the king's progress. Then he controlled himself. "And I will have her back."

Sanglant snorted. "She belongs to no man, nor woman either. Her service as a King's Eagle is pledged to the regnant."

Hugh did not back down. Sanglant was taller, and broader across the shoulders; certainly Sanglant had the posture of a man well-trained at war. But Hugh had that indefinable aura of confidence of a man who always gets what he wants. "We may as well set this straight now so that there are no further misunderstandings between us, my lord prince. She is my slave and has been in the past my concubine. Do not believe otherwise, no matter what she tells you."

The words fell like ice, but Sanglant did not move to expose her. "At least I do not number among my faults having to compel women to lie with me."

The difference between them was that Hugh made no unstudied movement, allowed no unthought expression to mar either his beauty or his poise, while Sanglant made no such pretense—or perhaps he had simply forgotten what it meant to be a man, a creature halfway between the beasts and the angels.

The smile that touched Hugh's lips fell short of a sneer; rather, he looked saddened and amused as he slid his gaze past Sanglant to fix on Liath. She could not look away from him. " 'Whoever

has unnatural connection with a beast shall be put to death,' "
he said softly.

She grabbed the cup of ale and dashed the liquid into his
face. Shaking, she lost hold of the cup. It thudded onto the
bench, rolled, and struck her foot. But the pain only brought her
fully awake, out of the blinding haze of desire that had surged
over her when she first walked into the hall and saw Sanglant
waiting for her.

Someone laughed; not Sanglant. The prince's fingers touched
her sleeve, to rein her back.

Hugh laughed, delighted, even as he licked ale from his lips.
He did not wipe the ale from his face or blot it from the damp
front of his handsomely-embroidered tunic, grape leaves en-
twined with purple flowers. She was so painfully alive to the
currents running between them that Hugh's laughter came this
time with revelation: Her defiance excited him physically. He
laughed to cover it, to release an energy fueled of fury and lust.

"I am an Eagle." The hate she felt for what he'd done to her
spilled into the words. "I pledged my service to King Henry."
But with each of her defiant words, *his* fury built; she could
feel it like an actual hand gripping her throat. He would hit her
again. And again. No matter how much anger she spat at him
he was still stronger. If Sanglant's fingers had not steadied her,
she would have fled.

But Hugh liked the chase.

"I'm not your slave!"

"We shall see," said Hugh, all elegance and hauteur even with
the last traces of ale trickling along the curve of his jaw. "We
shall see, my rose, whether King Henry judges the matter in my
favor—or in Wolfhere's." With a thin smile, confident of victory, he left them.

It took five heartbeats for the words to register, and when
they did, she went weak at the knees and collapsed onto the
bench. "He'll take it before the king. He'll protest he didn't consent to give me up, that Wolfhere bought off the debt price un-
lawfully. You know how the king hates Wolfhere!" Her chest
felt caught in a vise. "I'm lost!"

"Liath!" His hand cupped her elbow and he lifted her up. "I
beg you, Liath, look at me."

She looked up. She had forgotten how green his eyes were.
The wildish underglaze in them had not vanished entirely, but

it had fled back as if to hide, leaving him with a clear gaze, determined and dead stubborn.

"Liath, if you consent to marry me, then I can protect you from him."

"You're half mad, Sanglant," she murmured.

"So I am. God Above! I'd be nothing but a beast in truth if you hadn't saved me! No better than those dogs that bite at my heels. But you waited for me all that time. Knowing that, I kept hold of what it means to be a man instead of becoming only a chained beast for him to torment."

"I don't understand you. Ai, Lady! It's true what Hugh said of me, made his slave and his—" The shame was too deep. She could not get the word out.

He shrugged it away as if it meant nothing to him, then drew her aside. "Let us move away from here. Half the crowd is watching us instead of the entertainers." But he paused abruptly, glanced back. A not inconsiderable number of the folk gathered outside the hall, having no good view in to where the tumbling troupe entertained king and company, had turned to watch a scene no doubt as entertaining, as well as one sure to make them the center of attention at every table and fire for the next few days when it came time to gossip about court. Some pointed; other simply stared, servants beside wagoneers, grooms and doghandlers, laundresses with their chapped hands and serving-women with trays wedged against their hips, giggling or whispering although they stood too far away to hear words. Had they all seen her throw the ale into Hugh's face? Could they possibly wonder what Sanglant's interest in her betokened? Hadn't he been famous for his love of women?

That had all been before Bloodheart.

"Nay, let them see," he muttered. "Let them know, and carry the tale as they will in any case." He took her hands in his, fingers curling over hers, enveloping them. "Liath, marry me. But if you will not, I will still protect you. I so swear. I know I am—am—" He winced, slapping at his ear as if to drive off an annoying bug. "—I am not what I was. Lord in Heaven! They whisper of me. They say things. They ridicule me. If I only— Ai!" He could not get words out. He seemed helpless, and furious at his helplessness like a captured wolf beating itself into a stupor against the bars of its cage. "If only my father would give me lands, then there I could find peace. Ai, God, and the quiet I pray for, with you at my side. I only want healing." His voice was ragged with heart's pain; but then, his voice always sounded like that.

But to whom else would he have made such a confession? To no one but her.

Hadn't she turned away from the Aoi sorcerer for this? She kissed him.

It didn't last long, her lips touching his, although it was utterly intoxicating. He jerked back, stumbling.

"Not out here!" A flush suffused him.

"Wise counsel, Your Highness," said a new voice, flatly calm and wry along with it. "Liath!" Hathui walked toward them out of the gloom. She stopped neatly between them, fittingly so: taller than Liath, she was not of course nearly as tall as Sanglant but substantial nevertheless. "Your Highness." The bow she gave him was curt but not disrespectful. "The king your father is concerned that you have been absent for so long. He asks that you attend him."

"No," said Sanglant.

"I beg you, Your Highness." She faced him squarely. "My comrade is safe with me. I will keep an eye on her."

"Liath, you haven't yet—"

"Nay, she's right." It was like struggling to keep your head above water in a strong current. She had to stroke on her own. "Just—now—it would be better." It had all happened so quickly.

He stilled, took in a shuddering breath. "I have the book." He strode off.

"He looks like he's headed down to the river for a long cold swim," observed Hathui. She made a sign, and half a dozen Lions took off after him, keeping their distance.

Liath nudged the empty cup with her toe and bent to pick it up.

"Rumor flies fast," added Hathui, taking the cup out of Liath's hand and spinning it around. It had a coarse wood surface, nothing fine—but sturdy and serviceable. She snorted. "Did you really toss ale in his face?"

"What am I to do?" she wailed.

"Courageously spoken. You, my friend, stick next to me or to Wolfhere. Else I fear you'll do something very foolish indeed."

"But Hugh means to protest the debt price. He'll take the

case before the king, and you know how the king hates Wolfhere. What if he gives me back to Hugh?"

"You don't understand King Henry very well, do you?" said Hathui coolly. "Now come. There's a place above the stables set aside for Eagles—and well protected by Lions. You'll be safe to sleep there. Perhaps your head will be clearer in the morning."

She followed Hathui meekly. "Prince Sanglant has nothing, you know," said Hathui suddenly. "Nothing but what the king gives him, no arms, no horse, no retinue, no lands, no inheritance from his mother except his blood—and that is distrusted by most of the court."

"Nothing!" Liath retorted, furious on his behalf that he could be judged and found wanting in such a crass material manner, then faltered. Hathui spoke truth in the only way that mattered outside the spiritual walls of the church. "But I don't care," she murmured stubbornly, and in response heard only Hathui's gusting sigh.

In a way, it was a relief to find the stables tenanted by dozing Lions, a few Eagles, and by Wolfhere sitting outside on a log with a lantern burning at his feet while he ate supper. He looked mightily irritated but mercifully said nothing, only touched Hathui's shoulder by way of greeting and whispered something into her ear which Liath could not hear. But she didn't have Sanglant's unnaturally acute hearing.

"Go to sleep, Liath," he said stiffly once he deigned to acknowledge her. He was still angry. "We'll speak in the morning."

Shouts rang out from the distant hall, followed by laughter and a burst of song.

"They're carrying bride and groom to their wedding bed," said Hathui.

"Bride and groom?" asked Liath, startled. "Who is wed this night?" *She* could have been wed this night, by the law of consent. But it *had* happened too fast. She had to catch her breath before she took the irrevocable step.

Hathui laughed but Wolfhere only grunted, still annoyed. "I like this not," he muttered.

"That there's a wedding?" she asked, still confused.

"That you were blind to it and everything else going on here—

abouts," he retorted. "Go on, Hathui. The king will be looking for you."

She nodded and left, her proud figure fading into the gloom.

Liath did not like to be alone with Wolfhere. He had a way of looking at her, mild but with a grim glint deep in his eyes, that made her horribly uncomfortable.

"I beg you, Liath," he said, his voice made harsh by an emotion she could not identify, "don't be tempted by him."

Torches flared distantly and pipes skirled as drums took up a brisk four-square rhythm. Dancing had begun out in the yard. No doubt the celebration would last all night. Wolfhere scuffed at the dirt and took a sip of ale, then held out the cup as a peace offering.

"Hugh will ask the king to give me back to him," she said abruptly.

Wolfhere raised an eyebrow, surprised. "So he will, I suppose. He threatened as much in Heart's Rest the day I freed you from him."

"The king hates you, Wolfhere. Why?"

The smile that quirked up his mouth was touched with an irony that made his expression look strangely comforting and, even, trustworthy: A man who faces his own faults so openly surely cannot mean to harm others for the sake of his own vanity or greed.

"Why?" he echoed her. "Why, indeed. It's an old story and one I thought had been put to rest. But so it has not proved."

Still she did not take the cup from him. "It has to do with Sanglant."

"Everything has to do with Sanglant," said Wolfhere cryptically, and would say no more.

2

THE day passed in quiet solitude. A heavy mist bound the circle of stones, cutting them off from the world beyond. The Aoi woman meditated, seated cross-legged on the ground, her eyes closed, her body as still as if no soul inhabited it. Once, Zacharias would have prayed, but he no longer had anyone to pray to. For part of the day he dozed; later, he plucked and gutted the two grouse the Aoi woman had shot at dawn.

It had been a great honor for his kinfolk when he, a free-holder's son, had been ordained as a frater in the church by reason of his true singing voice, his clever tongue, and his excellent memory for scripture. But none of these were qualities the Quman respected in a man. They had cut so much from him that he could scarcely recall the man he had once been, proud and determined and eager to walk alone into the land of the savages to bring them into the Light of the Unities. It had all seemed so clear, then. He had had many names: son, nephew, brother. *Brother Zacharias,* a title his mother had repeated with pride. His younger sister had admired him. Would she admire him now?

At twilight the mist cleared off, and he walked nervously to the edge of the stone circle, but saw nothing, no one, no sign of Bulkezu or his riders on the grass or along the horizon.

"We need a fire."

He started, surprised and startled by her voice, but she had already turned away to rummage in one of her strange five-fingered pouches. He checked the horse's hobble, then descended the hill to the stream that ran along the low ground. With the moon to light him, he found it easy enough to pick up sticks. The night was alive with animals, and each least rustle in the undergrowth made him snap around in fear that one of Bulkezu's warriors waited to capture him and drag him back to slavery.

It seemed mere breaths ago that he had heard Bulkezu's howl. The sound of it still echoed in his ears, but slowly the gurgle of the stream and the sighing of wind through reeds and undergrowth smeared the memory into silence.

He sloshed in the stream, testing reed grass with his fingers until he found stalks to twist together into rope as his grandmother had taught him. But he was still skittish, and he made such a hasty job of it that no sooner had he returned to the stone circle than the reed rope splayed and unraveled, spilling sticks everywhere.

The Aoi woman merely glanced at him, then indicated where to pile the wood.

"I will be worthy of you," he whispered. If she heard him, she made no answer.

She crouched on her haunches to build the fire, sparked flint until wood lit. As she spoke lilting words, odd swirls of light fled through the leaping fire, twining and unraveling to make patterns within. Reflexively, Zacharias began to trace the Circle at his chest, the sign to avert witchcraft. But he stopped himself. If the old gods had been good enough for his grandmother, they would be good enough for him. The old gods had protected his grandmother; she had lived to an incredible age, and she had outlived all but two of her twelve children. Her luck had always held.

And anyway, if the Aoi woman meant to harm him with witchcraft, then there was nothing he could do about it now.

"Blessed Mother!" he whispered, staring as the fire shifted and changed.

He crept forward and stared into the whip of flames. It was like looking through an insubstantial archway of fire into another world.

A figure, tall, broad-shouldered but thin at the ribs, shed its clothing and dove into the streaming currents of a river. He was, manifestly, male. That he would willingly enter water meant he was no kin of the Quman tribe, and although the flicker of fire gave Zacharias no clear picture of the figure's features, the man somewhat resembled his Aoi mistress. But his clothing, lying in a careless heap on the shore, betrayed his origins: It was what civilized men wore, the rich clothing of a lord. A moment later six men scurried down to the river's bank as if on his trail. Bearded and armed, they wore tabards marked with a black lion: Wendish soldiers, serving the regnant. And if that was so, then who was the man who had gone into the water, and why were they following him?

The Aoi woman whispered a word, "Sawn-glawnt." The fire whuffed out. She rose and lifted her staff, a stout ebony length of wood scored with white marks along its length, and measured the staff against the stars above.

Then she grunted, satisfied, gestured to him, and Zacharias had to unhobble the horse and mount quickly. She strode out of the stone circle, heading north, and as soon as they were clear of the stones, she broke into a steady lope which he had perforce to follow along at a jarring trot.

In this way they ran through half the night. She never let up. He wanted finally to tell her that his rump was sore, or that the

horse needed a rest, but in truth woman and horse seemed equally
hardy creatures. He was the weak one, so he refused to complain. The moon crested above and began to sink westward. Light
spilled along the landscape, a low rise and fall of grassland broken here and there by a stream or a copse of trees, roots sunk
into a swale. Grass sighed in the middle night wind, a breath of
summer's heat from the east. He could almost smell the campfires of the Pechanek tribe on that wind, the sting of fermented
mare's milk, the damp weight of felt being prepared, the rich
flavor of a greasy stew made of fat and sheep guts, the spice
of *kilkim* tea that had been traded across the deep grass where
griffins and Bwrmen roamed, all the way from the empire of
the Katai peoples whose impenetrable borders it was said were
guarded by rank upon rank of golden dragons.

Suddenly, the woman slowed to a walk and approached a hollow of ragged trees, stopping just beyond their edge. "We need
a fire," she said, then crouched to dig a fire circle.

Zacharias groaned as he dismounted. His rump ached miser-
ably. Just inside the ring of trees he paused to urinate. Ai, God,
it still hurt to do so; perhaps it would always hurt. But he still
had his tongue, and he meant to keep it. So much tree litter covered the ground that it took him little time to gather enough for
a fire. He dumped it beside the pit she had dug into the earth,
then turned to the horse. "Can we bide here long enough to cook
these grouse?" he asked.

"Sawn-glawnt." Her voice rang clear in the silence.

He spun in time to see in the archway of fire the same man,
now fully clothed and cast out on the ground in an attitude of
sleep while the six Lions stood back in the gloom, standing
watch around him. Then the archway unfolded and vanished into
the ordinary lick of flames.

His mistress stood, lifted her staff again, and again measured
it against the stars. Her smile came brief, fierce, and sharp. *"Co-
yoi-tohn,"* she said, pointing northwest.

"You're looking for him," said Zacharias suddenly.

From behind, a panther coughed and then, more distantly,
wings whirred.

Zacharias yelped, drew his knife and peered eastward, but
saw nothing—no winged riders among the silver-painted grass.
The woman cast a glance over her shoulder. She scented the
wind, then shrugged her pack down from her shoulders, pulled

out a hard, round cake, and sat to eat. She offered none to him. Zacharias sharpened a stick and spitted the grouse, careful to make sure the viscera he had cleaned out and stuffed back in did not fall out of the cavity. He was too hungry to wait long. He offered the first grouse to her; she sniffed, made a face that actually made him laugh out loud.

Then he caught himself, cringing, but she took no offense. She tore off a strip of meat, fingered it, touched it to her lips, licked it, chewed a corner, grunted with surprise, and finished it off, then extended a hand imperiously for more. He was starving, and he ate every bit of his own grouse even though it made his belly ache. She went so far as to crack the bones and suck the marrow out.

But when they were done, they did not rest. She rose, licked her fingers a final time, kicked dirt over the fire, and indicated the direction she had earlier pointed out.

"*Co-yoi-tohn,*" she repeated. "What you would call, west of northwest."

"But where are we going?" he asked. "Who was the man we saw in the fire?"

She only shrugged. Light tinged the east, the first herald of dawn. "Now we begin the hunt."

3

SURELY, wicked souls consigned to the pit could not have spent an evening's span of hours in more torment than did Alain at his wedding feast.

The merriment he could stomach, barely, but the constant laughing toasts and crude jokes made him want to curl up and shrink away, and he was acutely conscious of Tallia beside him so still and withdrawn that he felt like a monster for wanting so badly what she clearly feared.

But surely, when all was quiet and they were alone, he could persuade her to trust him. Surely, if he could gentle the fero-

cious Lavas hounds and win the trust of Liath, he could coax
love from Tallia.

She had on a blue linen gown fantastically embroidered with
gems and the springing roes that signified her Varren ancestry.
A slim silver coronet topped her brow, Henry's only concession
to her royal kinship except of course for the delicate twist of
gold braid that circled her neck. She wore her wheat-colored
hair braided and pinned up at the back of her head; the style
made her slim neck seem both more frail and more graceful.
Wanting simply to touch it, to feel the pulse beating at her throat,
made him ache in a peculiarly uncomfortable spot and even when
he had to go pee he dared not stand to leave the table for fear
of calling attention to himself in a most embarrassing way.

He and Tallia shared a platter. He tried hard not to dip the
elaborate sleeves of his tunic into the sauces that accompanied
each course of the meal. Tallia did not eat more than a crust of
bread and drink two sips of wine, but he was ravenous and
though he feared it made him look gross and slovenly in her
eyes, he could not help but eat heartily until a new toast would
remind him—like a kick in the head from a panicked cow—that
later this night he would at long last meet his heart's desire on
the wedding bed, where nothing more could come between them.
Then he would be so stricken with nausea that he was sorry he
had eaten anything.

Likewise, he gulped down wine one moment out of sheer
nerves only to refuse the cup the next when with sick fear he
recalled jokes he had heard at his Aunt Bel's table about bride-
grooms who had drunk themselves into such a sodden fog that
they could not perform their husbandly duty.

Lavastine spoke little and then only to respond laconically to
congratulations thrown his way. He needed to say nothing; this
triumph had cost him plenty in the lives of his men, but he had
gained a nobly-connected bride for his heir together with a seat,
by virtue of her lineage, among the great princes of the realm.

Certain distractions gnawed at the edges of the feast: Liath
returned, and Prince Sanglant made such a spectacle of himself
that Alain was briefly diverted from his fear that Tallia would
faint dead away at the high table; the tumblers caught Tallia's
attention with their tricks, and for a happy if short span of time
he got her to smile at him as he admired—not her, never her,
let him show no interest in her or she would retreat as totally

in spirit as a turtle pulls into its shell—but rather the lively cart-wheelers and rope-balancers, thin girls of about Tallia's age who had a kind of hard beauty to their faces composed of equal parts skill and coarse living.

The tumblers retreated. Wine flowed. Toasts came fast and furious and then—Ai, God!—it was time.

Servingwomen cleared off their table, he hoisted Tallia up and climbed on after, and eight young lords actually carried the table with the pair of them on it to the guesthouse set aside for their bridal night; crude, certainly, and boisterous as every person there laughed and called out suggestions, but Alain didn't mind the old tradition if only because Tallia had to hold on to him to keep from sliding off. She looked terrified, and actually shrank against him when he put an arm around her to pull her firmly to his side. She was as delicate as a sparrow.

"Here, now," he whispered. "I'll hold you safe." She trustingly pressed her face against his shoulder.

The crowd roared approvingly.

Ai, Lady, Perhaps it was he who would faint. He was deliriously happy.

They let the table down unsteadily by the threshold, and he helped Tallia down. She still clung to him, more afraid of the crowd than of him.

"Who witnesses?" cried out someone in the crowd.

A hundred voices answered.

The king himself came forward to speak the traditional words. "Your consent having been obtained, let this marriage be fittingly consummated so that it can be legal and binding. Let there be an exchange of morning gifts at this door after dawn to signify that consummation." He laughed, in a fine good humor after enough wine to soak a pig, a good meal, and the company of thrilling entertainers and all his good companions. "May you have God's blessing this night," he added, and as a mark of his extreme favor offered Alain his hand to kiss. Alain bent to one knee, took the king's callused hand, and kissed the knuckles. Tallia, sinking to both knees beside him, pressed her uncle's hand to her lips with a faint sigh. The lantern light made their shadows huge along the wall, like elongated giants.

Lavastine stepped forward to open the door for them, an unexpected gesture more like that of servant than lord and father. Alain caught his hands as well and pressed them to his lips.

Everything seemed so much larger and fuller this night: the noise
of the crowd, the brush of wind on his face, his love for his
father which suddenly seemed to swell until it encompassed the
heavens, the joyous barking of the hounds, who had not been
allowed to escort them for fear that they would frighten Tallia
and become too unruly among such a large and boisterous crowd.

Lavastine took him under the elbow and raised him up. This
close, Alain saw a single tear snaking a path down the count's
face. Lavastine paused, then took Alain's head gently between
his hands and kissed him on the forehead.

"I beg you, Daughter," he said, turning to Tallia. "Make him
happy."

Tallia seemed ready to swoon. Alain put an arm around her
to support her and, with cheers and lewd suggestions ringing out
behind them, helped her in over the threshold.

Servants waited within. A good broad bed stood with its head
against one wall of the simple chamber, made comfortable with
a feather bed and quilt and a huge bedspread embroidered with
the roes of Varre and the black hounds of Lavas. Obviously the
bedspread had been in the making for some months. At the other
wall stood a table and two handsome chairs. On the table sat a
finely-glazed pitcher and a basin, for washing hands and face,
and next to them a wooden bowl carved with turtledoves that
held ripe berries, and also two gilded cups filled with a heady-
scented wine. A wedding loaf, half-wrapped in a linen cloth,
steamed in the close air of the little chamber, making his stomach growl. The shutters had been put up to afford privacy for
this one night.

The servants unlaced his sandals, untangled him from the
complicated knotwork that belted his tunic, removed her blue
linen gown, and quickly enough they both stood silent, she in a
thin calf-length linen shift and he in knee-length shift and bare
legs.

"Go on," he said, giving each of the servants a few silver
sceattas as they slipped out. "May God bless you this night."

At last he was alone with Tallia.

She sank down beside the bed in an attitude of prayer, lips
pressed to her hands. He could not hear her words. She shivered as at a cold wind, and he saw briefly the shape of her body
beneath her shift, the curve of a hip, the ridge of her collarbone, the slight fleeting swell of a breast.

Ai, Lord! He spun to the table, poured out some cold water, and splashed it in his face. He had to lean his weight on the table while he fought to recover himself. Distantly he heard the hounds barking wildly. From the great yard he heard music, the nasal squeal of pipes and the thump of drums. No doubt the celebration would go on all night.

At last he turned. She had not moved. On a whim, he poured more water into the basin and carried it and a soft cloth over to the bed. Setting it on the floor, he knelt beside her.

"I beg you, my lady," he said as softly as if he were coaxing a mouse out from its hiding place beneath St. Lavrentius' altar in the old church at Lavas Holding, "give me leave to wash your face and hands."

She did not respond at first. She still seemed to be praying. But at last she turned those pale eyes on him as a prisoner pleads wordlessly for a stay of execution. Slowly, she uncurled her hands and held them out to him.

He gasped. Down the center of each palm an ugly scar, still suppurating on her left hand, scored the flesh. Her skin was like a delicate parchment, thin and almost translucent but for those horrible gashes.

He touched them gently with the damp cloth, letting the water soak in to soften the scabbing and the hard runnels of pus. "These must be tended, Tallia! How did you come by these?"

He looked up to see a faint blush stir on her pallid cheeks. Her lips parted; her eyes were very wide. He shut his eyes and swayed into her, caught the scent of her, the dry powder of wheat just before harvest and a trace of incense so fleeting that it was as if it retreated before him. Their lips did not touch.

She whimpered, and he opened his eyes to discover that she had recoiled from him and now, with a hand caught in his grasp, had begun to cry.

"God's mercy! I beg you! Forgive me!" He was a monster to force himself on her in this way. But he could not bear simply to let go of her. Without looking her again in the face, he tended her hands, patiently wetting the scars and gently swabbing the pus from them. When he finished, he dropped the now-dirty cloth into the basin.

She was still crying.

"It hurts you. I'm sorry." He could only stammer it. He could not bear to see her in pain.

"Nay, nay,". she whispered as he imagined a woman might who, having been violated, is compelled to grant forgiveness to the one who assaulted her. "The pain is nothing. It is not for us to tend the wounds given to us by God's mercy."

"What do you mean?"

The blush still bled color.into her cheeks. "I cannot speak of it. It would be prideful if people were to think that God had favored me, for I am no more worthy than any other vessel."

"Do you think this a sign from God—?" He broke off as understanding flooded him. "This is the mark of flaying, is it not?"

"Do you know of the blessed Daisan's sacrifice and redemption?" she asked eagerly, leaning toward him. "But of course you must! You were privileged to walk beside Frater Agius, he who revealed the truth to me!" She was very close to him, her breath a sweet mist on his cheek. "Do you believe in the Redemption?"

He scarcely trusted himself to breathe. Her gaze on him was impassioned, her pulse under his fingers drumming like a racing stag, and he knew in his gut that she had unknowingly revealed to him the means to soften her heart.

But it would be a lie.

"Nay," he said softly. "Frater Agius was a good man, but misguided. I don't believe in the sacrifice and redemption. I can't lie to you, Tallia." Not even if it meant the chance she would open fully to him.

She pulled her hands away from him and clasped them before her, resuming an attitude of prayer. "I beg you, Lord Alain," she said into her hands, her voice falling away until the mice scrabbling in the walls made a greater sound. "I beg you, I have sworn myself to God's service as a pure vessel, a bride to the blessed Daisan, the Redeemer, who sits enthroned in Heaven beside his mother, She who is God and Mercy and Judgment, She who gave breath to the Holy Word. I beg you, do not pollute me here on earth for mere earthly gain."

"But I love you, Tallia!" To have her so close! Her hands pressed against an embroidered golden stag, covering its antlers and head. A pair of slender hind legs, a gold rump and little tuft of a tail peeked out from under her right wrist. "God made us to be husband and wife together, and to bring children into the world!"

The sigh shuddered her whole body. She climbed onto the

bed and lay on her back, utterly still, arms limp at her side.
"Then do what you must," she murmured in the tone of a woman
who has reached the station of her martyrdom.

It was too much. He buried his face in his hands.

After a long time, still hearing her ragged breathing in anticipation of the brute act she expected, he lifted his head. "I
won't touch you." He was barely able to force the words out.
"Not until you get used to the idea of— But I beg you, Tallia,
try to think of me as your husband. For—we must in time—the
county needs its heir, and it is our duty—Ai, God, I—I—" His
voice failed. He wanted her so badly.

She heaved herself up and knelt on the bed, offering him her
hands. "I knew Frater Agius could not be wrong, to speak so
well of you."

He dared not clasp her hands in his. It would only waken the
feelings he struggled to control. "Agius spoke well of me?" That
Agius had thought of him at all astonished him.

"He praised you. So I always held his praise for you in my
heart, he whom God allowed a martyr's death. Here." She patted the bed beside her. "Though I am the vessel through which
God has sent a holy vision, do not be afraid to lie next to me.
I know your heart is pure."

She arranged herself so modestly on her side of the bed that
he knew what she meant him to endure, although perhaps it did
not seem like endurance to her. But he must do what would
please her if he meant to teach her to trust him—and to love
him. Wincing, he lay down stiffly on his back and closed his
eyes.

Her breathing slowed, gentled, and she slept. He ached too
much to sleep, yet he dared not toss and turn. He dared not rise
from the bed to pace, for fear of waking her. If he woke her,
so close beside him, and she opened her eyes to see him there,
limbs brushing, fingers caught in unwitting embrace, lips touching—

Madness lay that way, thinking on in this fashion. He did not
know what to do, could not do anything but breathe, in and out,
in and out. A plank creaked in the next chamber. Mice skittered
in the walls, and he could almost taste the patience of a spider
which, having spun out its final filament in one upper corner of
the chamber, settled down to wait for its first victim. He had
forgotten about the bread. Now, cooling, its mellow scent per-

meated the room and tickled his nose. Tallia shifted on the bed, murmuring in her sleep. Her fingers brushed his.

He could not bear it.

He slid off the bed and lay down on the floor. The hard wood gave him more welcome than the luxurious softness of the feather bed, and here, with his head pillowed on his arms, he finally fell into an exhausted sleep.

He arrived back at Rikin Fjord first of all the sons of Blood-heart—those who survived Gent—and Rikin's OldMother welcomed him without surprise.

"Fifth Son of the Fifth Litter." An OldMother never forgets the smell of each individual blind, seeking pupa that bursts from her nests. But she will stand aside once the battle is joined, as all OldMothers do. She does not care which of her sons leads Rikin's warband now that Bloodheart is dead, only that the strongest among them succeeds. Yet the WiseMothers know that the greatest strength lies in wisdom.

Now he waits in the shield of the Lightfell Waterfall whose ice-cold water pours down the jagged cliff face into the deep blue waters of the fjord, where stillness triumphs over movement. He waits, watching six ships round the far point and close in on the beach. Beyond them in the deepest central waters a tail flips, slaps, vanishes. The merfolk are out; they have the magic to smell blood not yet spilled, and now they gather, waiting to feed. Eighteen ships have so far returned from Gent and the southlands. Tonight when the midnight sun sinks to her low ebb, OldMother will begin the dance.

Has he built enough traps? Are his preparations adequate?

That is the weakness of his brothers: They think strength and ferocity are everything. He knows better.

He tucks the little wooden chest that he dug out from the base of the fall tight under his elbow and slips out from the ledge. Water sprays him and slides off his skin to fall onto moss and moist rock as he picks his way up the ladder rocks to the top of the cliff. There the priest waits, anxious. He wails out loud when he sees the box.

"I would have found it eventually," Fifth Son says, but not because he wishes to gloat. He merely states the truth. Gloating is a waste of time. He does not open the little casket. He doesn't need to. They both know what lies inside, nestled in spells

and downy feathers. "You have grown lazy, old one. Your magic cannot triumph over cunning."

"What do you want?" wails the priest. "Do you want the power of illusion, that Bloodheart stole from me? Your heart hidden in the fjall to protect you from death in battle?"

"My heart will stay where it is. Nor do I want your illusions. I want immunity."

"From death?" squeaks the priest.

"From your magic. And from the magic of the Soft Ones. For myself and the army I mean to build. Once I have that, I can do the rest."

"Impossible!" says the priest emphatically.

"For you working alone, perhaps." The priests keep their arcane studies a mystery even from the OldMothers, such as they can. "But there are others like you. In concert, you can surely work a magic that has a practical use. And once I triumph, you can share in the booty."

The priest laughs, a reedy sound like wind caught in stones. "Why would you think I and those like me want booty? What good does it do us?"

"Then what do you and those like you want?"

The old priest leans forward. Hands trembling, he reaches for the casket, but Fifth Son merely draws it away. He does not fear the priest; his magics seem mostly show, but he knows that a keener mind could wreak havoc with them.

He does not trust magic.

"Freedom from the OldMothers," whispers the priest hoarsely.

Fifth Son lets out a breath, satisfied and surprised by this confession. The jewels drilled into his teeth glint in the sun as he bares his teeth. "I can give you that. After you and those like you have given me what I need."

"But how am I to convince them?"

"That problem is yours to solve."

He leaves the old priest behind then, and runs ahead. The priest will search, of course, and use his magic to call to his hidden heart. But there are other magics that know the power of concealment. Before he goes to the OldMother's hall to assemble with the others, he takes the chest to the homesteads of his human slaves and there he gives it into the care of Ursuline, she who has made herself OldMother among the Soft Ones.

She has assured him that the circle-god has magic fully as strong as that of the RockChildren's priests—this will prove the test of her god's magic. And in any case, no RockChild will imagine that he might entrust a mere weak slave with something so powerful and precious.

She is curious but not foolhardy. She takes the casket from him and without attempting to look inside—for he has told her what it contains—confines it within the blanket-covered box that she calls the holy Hearth of their god. Then she places withered herbs, a cracked jug, and a crude carved circle on the altar and sings a spell over it, what she calls a psalm.

"Our bargain?" she asks boldly. She is no longer afraid of him, because she has seen that when he kills, he kills quickly, and she does not fear death. He admires that in her. Like the WiseMothers, she understands inexorable fate.

"Our bargain," he replies. She wants a token. The Soft Ones are ever like that, needing things to carry with them, objects to touch, in order to keep their word. He traces the wooden circle that hangs at his chest, his gift from Alain Henrisson. "I swear on my bond with the one who gifted me with my freedom that I will give you what you ask for if you keep this chest safe until I need it. Do that, and I will keep my bargain—as long as I become chieftain. Otherwise I will be dead, and you will be as well."

She chuckles, but he knows enough about the Soft Ones to see this laughter does not insult him but is instead a compliment. "You are different than the others. God give Their blessing to the merciful and the just. They will guide you to success."

"So you hope," he agrees.

He leaves her hovel, whistles in his dogs, and heads down the long valley to OldMother's compound. The path runs silent before and behind him; only a few slaves mewl and whine in their pens, dumb beasts shut away until the great events of the next hand of days have played out their course. His slaves, unconfined, are at their work—or hidden in certain places according to his plan. He has entrusted them with a great deal, but they know that if he does not succeed, they will die at the hands of the victor.

OldMother's drone rises up, a low rumble that lies as close along the steep valleys of Rikin as the blanket of spruce and pine and the mixed thickets of heather and fern; her song makes the lichen quicken and grow on rock faces, a pattern readable only by the SwiftDaughters. He strolls out onto the dancing ground of beaten earth alone but for his dogs.

His brothers howl with derision when they see him.

"WeakBrother, do you mean to be the first one to bare your throat?"

"Coward! Where were you when the fighting came to Gent?"

"What treasures did you give to Bloodheart, tongueless one?"

So they howl, taunting him. Their warbands cluster in packs, each pack striving to be the loudest—as if loudness denotes strength. He has ordered his soldiers to remain silent, and they do so. He, too, remains silent as OldMother slides the knife of decision out of the pouch in her thigh and raises it to point at the fiery heart of the sun, now riding low along the southern range. With a slashing motion, she brings their noise, and her drone, to a sudden end.

Six of Bloodheart's sons come forward into the center of the dancing ground, and when he steps forward last of all, there are seven. All the other RockChildren have chosen not to contend but instead to bare their throats to the victor. No doubt those who choose submission are showing wisdom in knowing just how weak they are.

The seven who will contend turn their backs to each other, and kneel. SwiftDaughters glide forward over the dirt and form the net of story, hands linked, gold and silver and copper and tin and iron hair gleaming as they begin to sway, humming.

Silence except for that low humming permeates the clearing. Even the dogs do not bark. Distantly, he can almost hear the WiseMothers hearing that silence as speech, turning their attention to this mortal instant.

Do they know how momentous this day will be? That one day the SwiftDaughters will weave it into their song of history? Or do they laugh at his ambition?

Soon he will find out.

The heavy tread of OldMother shudders the ground beneath his knees. She alone judges the worthiness of the contestants. The SwiftDaughters part to let her bulk through. He, with his brothers, bows his head.

She makes a slow circle. Suddenly, there comes a grunt, the sharp copper taint of blood, and a thud as one of Bloodheart's *sons topples over. His blood soaks into the soil of the dancing ground. Dogs growl, and a few bark and are hushed, or killed.*

He feels the knife of decision brush his head, his throat, and linger at the girdle of shimmering gold he wears at his hips: the girdle woven of the hair of a Hakonin SwiftDaughter.

Then it moves away. Six sons remain.

The SwiftDaughters rock back and forth, foot to foot, and begin the long chant, the history of Rikin's tribe. It will take three days to tell, and when they are done, only one of Blood-heart's sons will stand on the blood-soaked ground and claim victory.

The circle parts. He leaps up, knowing better than to be caught by one of the other five and forced into a brute fight: they all outweigh him, they are bigger, brawnier, and stronger.

But he has strength of a different kind.

With the dogs and the warriors yammering and howling and barking behind, he races up toward the fjall where the first of his traps lies waiting.

Alain woke to frenzied barking, the Eika dogs going crazy—

Only it wasn't the Eika dogs. Rage barked at his door, scratching insistently, and he heard the others howling and barking from Lavastine's chambers as if they had gone mad.

He scrambled to throw his tunic on over his shift. Without bothering with hose he flung open the door. Tallia called out behind him, but he ran on, to Lavastine's chambers.

The servants parted before him. They had not dared come too close. One had been bitten, and his arm wept blood. Alain waded into a seething whirlpool of hounds, all of them tearing around the chamber like a dog chasing its tail; only old Terror stood, legs up on the embrasure of the window, growling menacingly. Alain stuck his head out the window, but he saw only worried servingmen and a few curious onlookers who had paused to stare at the commotion. Wind stirred the flowering bushes just outside. A rodent—or an unseen bird—rustled in the leaves, and Fear, Sorrow, and Rage bolted out of the chamber and raced around the long building. People scattered from their path.

"Peace!" Alain cried, leaning out of the window, as they skittered to a halt on the other side. "Sit." They sat, but they still growled softly at wind and leaves. They sniffed in the bushes. Behind him, in the chamber, the barking settled and ceased, and the silence that weighed down made his ears ring. He turned to see Lavastine sitting on the bed, half clothed, examining Ardent's paw. She whimpered as he spread the pads and examined the flesh with a frown.

Alain crossed to him at once and knelt beside him, then set a hand on Ardent's flank. Her nose was dry and her breathing came in a labored pant.

"Bitten," said Lavastine, "but I know not by what."

Alain sat on the bed to examine her paw. She nipped at him weakly when he probed at the flesh, but she trusted him too well to bite him. At first he felt only how hot her paw was; a swelling bubble grew between the pad of two toes. Finally he found the wound, two tiny red punctures.

"Was she bitten by a snake?"

Lavastine rose and went to speak to a servant, who quickly left. "We'll speak with the stablemaster." The count paced over to the window and stood there, silent, with a hand resting on Terror's great head.

Alain swung a leg over Ardent to pin her down, cut the pad of her paw with his knife, and sucked out what of the poison he could, if indeed she had been bitten by something poisonous, then spat it out onto the floor. Her blood had a sour, metallic taste, and it clotted at once, did not even bleed—only seeped from the cut. He offered her water in a basin, but she would not drink.

Lavastine returned from the window and signed to a servant to help him dress. Another left to get Alain's clothing. Then Lavastine sat down beside Alain on the bed. He considered Ardent, stroked her head while she lay shuddering and panting hoarsely, not moving otherwise.

"it is time we returned to Lavas," he said, "since we have what we came for. I will ask my cleric to name a day propitious for a long journey, and on that day we will take our leave of the king and ride west."

"Father." Alain stuttered to a halt. His blush certainly had as much heat as the infection on poor Ardent's paw. He glanced up to see the servants busy at their tasks, pouring water to wash in, sweeping the steps outside. "I didn't—we didn't—" He could not continue, and yet he could not lie to his father.

Lavastine raised a pale eyebrow. "She has just come from the convent. She might still feel some hesitation." Terror padded over from the window and sat stiffly beside the count, on guard. "Still," he continued, "the practical thing for a woman is to get herself with child as quickly as possible so that she has an heir."

Even thinking of Tallia lying pale and fragile on the bed beside him made Alain flush, and he felt all over again the ache of last night. "But it would be—" He dropped his voice to a whisper because he could not bear for anyone else, even the servants, to hear. "—a lie to exchange morning gifts."

Lavastine massaged Ardent's foot. He wore his most intent look as he focused on the hound's paw. "Perhaps. But I lied to you about my intentions, at the battle at Gent. I had to, knowing you could see the Eika prince in your dreams and that he could, perhaps, see yours. Others envy us what we have gained here. If they believe that the marriage has gone unconsummated, some may even begin to whisper that it is invalid, even though a biscop blessed your union and the king himself gave his consent. We cannot afford to give them a weapon to strike against us." All but one of the servingmen had retreated from the chamber, responsive as always to Lavastine's moods. He glanced at the one man remaining, gave a brief nod as at a job well done, and turned to look directly at Alain. "Therefore, exchange morning gifts. She is a woman, and even if she is timid now, women above all things want heirs for their lands and titles."

Alain wasn't so sure, but he nodded obediently, and as if his nod had summoned her, there came a swell of voices outside the door, and then Tallia entered the chamber, stopped short, and cowered back against the wall away from the hounds.

Lavastine stood but not before glancing at Alain as if to say: "And so here she is."

Alain's servingman came in behind her, and Tallia covered her eyes with a corner of her shawl as Alain, settling Ardent comfortably on the bed, stood to dress. When he was decently clothed, he coaxed her over to sit on the bed beside Ardent. Once she saw that the huge hound was too weak to snap at her, she gingerly sat down, clinging to Alain's hand.

She trusted him. That much he had won from her.

Lavastine smiled slightly and, with hands clasped behind his back, nodded to his servants to fetch the morning gift which Alain would present to his bride. Alain waited nervously, half on fire from the innocent clasp of Tallia's hand in his, half terrified that she would find inappropriate the gift he had himself

commissioned. It was not his place as the one of lesser rank to
attempt to outdo her gift to him. He could not in any case, since
Henry had already settled rich estates on Lavas as part of the
dower. But neither could the heir to the count of Lavas permit
himself to appear like a pauper before the assembled nobles of
the king's progress.

Many people had gathered outside to witness the morning
gifts. When the king arrived, Alain coaxed Tallia to her feet, and
they went outside to greet him.

What raucous and lewd comments greeted their appearance
Alain tried not to hear. Tallia had pulled her shawl almost over
her face, and she huddled against him, which only made people
laugh and call out the louder, seeing it as a sign of the very
transaction that had not taken place last night.

Henry was generous with his disgraced sister Sabella's lands:
together with the estates marked as part of Tallia's dowry yesterday, the full extent of the gift in lands made as the marriage
settlement doubled the size of the Lavas Holdings. Lavastine
had a thin smile on his face, the closest he came to outright
glee. Henry gestured, and his stewards brought two chests forward: silks, a magnificent fur-lined cape, silver plate and gold
cups, handsome vestments for the Lavas clergy, rich clothing for
Tallia and Alain, and brass dog collars embossed with springing
roes and sportive hounds.

The crowd murmured in appreciation for Henry's generosity.
Lavastine had known better than to attempt to outdo a king.
His own servants brought forward chests filled with good cloth
suitable for a noblewoman of royal lineage to clothe her servants in, silver-and-gold vessels for her to present to her clerics, and handsomely carved small chests that contained enough
coins to grace an army of beggars. Last, Alain himself gave her
the tiny ivory reliquary inlaid with jewels that he had commissioned. Unlocked by a delicate silver key, it contained dust from
the shawl worn by the holy discipla, St. Johanna the Doubter,
together with a perfect jeweled replica of a rose.

Tallia wept over the holy relic and kissed the petals of the
jeweled rose. She gave the reliquary into the keeping of Hathumod, the young woman who had come with her from Quedlinhame. Lavastine gave Alain an approving nod, but her reaction
troubled Alain. He had meant the jeweled rose to represent the
Rose of Healing—the healing grace granted every soul by God's

mercy—but now he feared she saw it only as the symbol of her heretical belief, the rose that bloomed out of the blood of the blessed Daisan.

But when she thanked him so earnestly and with her eyes so untroubled by any memory of their awkward night together, hope surged again in his heart—and not least an uncomfortable tingling elsewhere. He need only be patient.

The crowd began to disperse. The king's steward announced that Henry would hold audience in the great open yard after the service of Terce. Lavastine ducked inside his chamber, and quickly Alain followed him with Tallia drawn along behind as if she wanted only to stay beside him—or did not know where else to go.

Ardent still lay on the bed, whimpering softly. Alain went over to soothe her. Under his hands, she quieted. Lavastine had drawn Tallia over to the window and was laboriously attempting to converse with her. Alain caught the eye of a steward.

"Christof, an Eagle arrived at the palace last night, one called Liathano. Send for her to attend me."

The steward concealed his astonishment poorly. He was a jovial fellow, and too late Alain recalled that he was also a terrible gossip. "I know the one you speak of, my lord," he replied obediently, but not without a glance at Count Lavastine. He went out.

When he returned, he brought Liath with him. As soon as she crossed the threshold, the hounds began to whimper and growl, scrambling back to cluster around Lavastine like terrified pups. Ardent tried to shove her head under Alain's thigh.

"Peace!" said Lavastine sternly. They hunkered down nervously at his feet. "Alain?"

"Your Highness," said Liath, seeing Tallia. Although she was obviously surprised, she did not stumble over the formalities. "My lord count. Lord Alain, I have come as you requested."

"Alain?" repeated Lavastine. He stood with one hand on Terror's head, but his intent gaze never left Liath. "What means this?"

Alain could not rise because of Ardent, and in any case he was lord and she a mere Eagle, not a person he could meet publicly on an equal standing whatever private confidences they had once shared. For an instant he didn't know how to answer because he saw Tallia's expression: Was Tallia jealous? Or did he only hope she would be?

"I am reminded of this Eagle's service to us at Gent," he said finally, and firmly, because everyone was watching him expectantly, "and I am minded to gift her with some token as a reward for her efforts there."

Lavastine took a step forward and stopped short as Terror nipped at him, took his master's hand in that great jaw, and growled softly while trying to tug Lavastine back. The count shook his hand free impatiently. "Resolve," he muttered under his breath, so softly that maybe only Alain heard him, and he continued to stare at Liath as a man stares at that woman with whom he discovers some deep kinship of blood, or spirit.

"Resuelto," he repeated, looking now at his servants.

"The gray gelding?" they repeated, dumbfounded that a lord would blithely give away his second best warhorse to a common Eagle.

"And the saddle and bridle from Asselda," he added. "Rope. And saddlebags. And the good leather belt crafted by Master Hosel, the one inscribed with salamanders so that as the Holy Verses say, 'if you walk through fire, the flame shall not consume you.'"

"I would give her a token as well," said Alain hastily to divert attention from the count, who seemed inclined to arm her as he would a relative. "A quiver of arrows and—" What he wanted to say to her, to ask, he could not communicate in front of such an audience. His gaze lit on one of his rings, a gold band set with a brilliantly blue stone. He pulled it off. "Let this ring of lapis lazuli protect you from evil," he said, giving it to her. "Know that you can find refuge here if you need it."

"I thank you, my lord count. Lord Alain." But her gaze was more eloquent. He read gratitude in her expression, and yet he saw that she was still frightened, apprehensive of some event she feared would come to pass. Was Lord Hugh still stalking her? He had no way of asking, and even as he paused, a steward came in from outside.

"I beg your pardon, my lord count," the man said to Lavastine. "An Eagle stands outside with an urgent summons for her comrade—from the king."

One look she gave to Alain, nothing more. Then she was

gone. As she left the chamber, the hounds rose unsteadily and shook themselves.

"My lord count, I have come as you requested." The king's stablemaster appeared at the threshold and Lavastine gave him permission to enter, although the man glanced nervously at the hounds. Still subdued, they growled softly and let him be.

The stablemaster examined Ardent, stroked his beard and looked puzzled. Neither adders nor any poisonous snakes were commonly found in this district, he explained, but he sent men at once to beat the bushes around the complex and to warn the king.

"Come, Son." Lavastine gave Ardent a pat on the head and rose to collect gloves and spear. "We must attend the king." Alain hesitated. "I will do what I can to help the girl," added Lavastine softly.

"Then I pray you, Father, let me stay with Ardent."

Lavastine glanced at Tallia, who still stood by the window, nodded curtly, and left.

"She's a strange-looking woman," said Tallia. "I remember seeing her before, when we rode to Quedlinhame."

"She fought with us at Gent."

"Then she was given a handsome reward by you and your father. People will speak of your generosity, and you will be known as a Godly man."

So was he reproved however gently for that brief desire that envy would prick her until she bled and, bleeding from jealousy, fell into his arms. He would have to win her over in a nobler manner than this. Ardent burrowed her head more deeply into Alain's lap and whimpered, and he stroked her ears and scratched her head, giving her such comfort as he could, knowing that his presence itself was comfort to her.

"Poor suffering soul," murmured Tallia. "I will pray to God for healing." She knelt, bent her head, and lapsed at once into a melisma of prayer.

Several young nobles stuck their heads inside the chamber to check on the progress of the hound. They all had their own dearly-loved hounds, and Alain could not help but be touched by their concern. But though they urged Alain to join them in their hunt for snakes, he would not. He could not bear to leave Ardent's side all through that long, hazy morning as she struggled to breathe and by degrees her leg turned, seemingly, into stone.

4

SANGLANT woke stiff and sore somewhat after dawn. After twenty-nine days sleeping in the second finest bed on the king's progress, his limbs had grown used to comfort. Now, rising from the ground, he ached everywhere, but he didn't mind it. The pain of freedom is never as harsh as that of slavery.

"My lord prince!" said one of the Lions in an urgent whisper.

He heard them coming down the narrow footpath that led from the bluff's height far above to the river's shore below: the king and a small entourage.

"Prince Sanglant." The Lion had a shock of red hair and part of one ear missing, the lobe sliced cleanly off and healed into a white dimple. "If we may—your clothing—"

Only now did he glance at himself to see in what disarray he stood; tunic skewed around his body and stained with dirt; sandals scuffed; leggings half unwound on his right calf; his belt lying like a sleeping snake, all curves and loops, on the ground by his feet. Two of the Lions ventured forward—he smelled their caution—and tidied him up so that by the time his father appeared, skirting an old fall of rocks that had half obliterated the last bend in the footpath, he looked presentable.

Henry shaded his eyes against the rising sun. "Sanglant." Sanglant knelt obediently. Henry's hand, coming to rest on his hair, had uncomfortable weight. "You did not come in last night."

"I slept outside."

Henry removed his hand. Sanglant looked up in time to see the king gesture to the others and, together, entourage and Lions moved away until they waited out of earshot. "We must talk, Son, before I hold my morning's audience. Walk with me."

Sanglant rose. Though he was half a head taller than the king, he never felt he dwarfed him; Henry used his power too well.

"You are restless," observed Henry as they strolled down along the river, away from his entourage, which consisted of the

six Lions who had guarded Sanglant through the night, four servingmen, Margrave Villam, and Sister Rosvita. "You heard the
news brought last night, that both regnants in Aosta are dead.
There is a single heir, the Princess Adelheid."

Sanglant shrugged. He had not heard the news; once Liath
had entered the hall, everything else had become a roar of meaningless chatter. She had a distinct way of walking, that of a person who has covered many leagues on her feet and found no
weariness from walking as would a man or woman used to riding. The quiver rode easily on her back; she was used to its
weight, and confident with it. Her braid had a distracting habit
of swaying as she walked, drawing the eye down her back to
the swell of her hips. She had looked at him over her shoulder.
And then, when he had followed her outside, she had kissed him
despite his confused confession that would have made another
woman scorn him. Surely that kiss—however greatly it had disturbed him bodily—revealed the wish of her heart.

"Sanglant! You are not listening."

It took him a moment to remember where he was. He bent,
scooped up a long branch, and commenced snapping it in half,
and the halves in half again. It was the only way he could keep
his attention from wandering back to her.

"You will lead an army to Aosta. There, you will place Lady
Adelheid on the queen regnant's throne, and you will marry her.
Once that is accomplished, and with my power behind you, the
Aostan princes will not contest your election as king regnant.
You will reign beside Adelheid, as her equal. No one can doubt
your worthiness for the Aostan throne, since it is as often claimed
by force as by inheritance. That is what the Aostan princes prefer, to keep their regnants weak and dependent on their power
as queenmakers. Once you have established yourself in Aosta,
with a royal wife and a child to prove your fertility, then it is
only a small step for me to name you as my heir here in Wendar and Varre as well. Who will contest us then, if the prize is
the restoration of the Holy Dariyan Empire? The Empire lies
within our grasp at last. With you on the Aostan throne, I can
march south and have myself crowned as emperor and you as
my successor and heir."

The branch lay in pieces at his feet. An osprey soared above,
heading upriver. The river flowed steadily along behind him; he
could almost hear each least grain of dirt being spun off from

the shoreline and washed away downstream, caught up in an irresistible current that would drag it all the way to the sea. He
was suddenly tired. Henry, like the river, was an unstoppable
force.

"Liath," he whispered. It was the only word he knew how to
say.

Henry grunted in the way of a man prepared for the blow
that strikes him. "As Villam warned me," he muttered. "I swear
that Wolfhere sent her to plague me and ruin you."

Henry regarded the river with a frown, and Sanglant watched
him, caught up without meaning to be in that strong attraction
that a regnant must necessarily wind around himself, like a cloak.
A regnant is no regnant without it. Henry had a strong profile,
most often stern, with the dignity appropriate to the responsibility God had given him. He had as much silver as brown in
his hair now, and a neat beard laced with white. Sanglant touched
his own—beardless—chin, but the movement brought Henry's
attention back to him.

"Very well." Henry could not conceal his annoyance, but he
attempted to. "Take her as a concubine, if you must. You won't
be the first man—or woman—to keep a concubine. The Emperor Taillefer was known to keep concubines while between
wives. But—"

"I don't want to marry Princess Adelheid. I intend to marry
Liath."

Henry laughed as if Sanglant had made a jest. "A common-
born woman?"

"Her father's kin have estates at Bodfeld."

"Bodfeld?" Henry had a capacious memory; he exercised it
now. "The lady of Bodfeld sends only twenty milites when called
to service. Such a family can scarcely expect a match with a
man of your position, and it isn't clear if the girl is of legitimate birth."

"All the better," said Sanglant sarcastically, "for one such as
me. Why do you refuse to understand? I don't want to be king
with princes all biting at my heels and waiting for me to go
down so they can rip out my throat. I endured that for a year.
I want a grant of land, Liath as my wife, and peace."

"*Peace*! What man or woman of royal blood can expect peace
with the Eika plaguing our northern shores and Quman raids in
the east? Since when have the princes of the realm allowed us

to luxuriate in peace? Even the lowliest lady with her small estate and dozen servants must contend against bandits and the depredations of her ambitious neighbors. If we live our lives according to the teaching of the blessed Daisan, then we can expect peace when our souls ascend to the Chamber of Light. Not before."

Henry paced to the river's edge, where water swirled over a nest of rocks the size of eggs. Picking one up, he flung it with some impatience into the center of the current. It vanished into the slate-gray waters with a plop. He heaved a sigh; from this angle Sanglant could not see his face, only the tense set of his shoulders. He wore this morning a linen tunic of intense blue, its neck and sleeves and hem embroidered with gold lions curling around eight-pointed purple starbursts, the sigil in needlework of his wedding to quiet, cunning, luxury-loving Sophia, dead these three years.

"You have not yet recovered from your captivity," the king said finally, addressing the streaming waters. "When you do, you will regret these rash words and see the wisdom of my plan. Sapientia is brave and willing, but she was not gifted by God with the mantle of queenship. Theophanu—perhaps—if she lives—" Here he faltered, one hand clenching. "She has a cool nature, not one to inspire soldiers to follow her into the thick of battle. And Ekkehard—" The shake of his shoulders was dismissive. "Too young, untried, and foolish. He belongs in the church so that he can sing praises to God with that beautiful voice. That leaves you." Now he turned. "You wear the mantle, Sanglant. You have always worn it. They follow you into battle. They trust and admire you. You must be king after me."

"I don't want to be king. Or heir. Or emperor. Is there some other way to state it so you understand?"

The red tinge to Henry's cheeks betrayed that one of his famous rages was descending, but Sanglant surveyed the king dispassionately. Rage never frightened him in others, only in himself. Ai, Lady, but the revelation hit hard enough: Henry could do nothing to harm him, nothing worse than what Bloodheart had already done. By making Sanglant his prisoner, Bloodheart had freed him from the chains that bound him to his father's will.

"You will do as I tell you!"

"No."

Now, at last, Henry looked surprised—so surprised, indeed, that for an instant he forgot to be furious. For an instant. A moment later the mask of stone crashed down, freezing his face, and the father intent on his son's rising fortune vanished to be replaced by the visage of the king whose subjects have unexpectedly cried rebellion. "If I disinherit you, you will have nothing, not even the sword you wear. Not even a horse to ride. Not even the clothes on your back."

"Did I have any of those things before? The only thing a man can truly claim as his own is the inheritance he receives from his mother."

"She abandoned you." Henry touched his own chest at the heart. Sanglant knew what lay there, tucked away between tunic and breast: a yellowing scrap of bloodied cloth, the only earthly remains of his mother, who had left him, and Henry, and human lands long ago. "She abandoned you with nothing."

"Except her curse upon me," hissed Sanglant.

"She was not meant to live upon this earth," said Henry, voice ragged with old grief.

They looked at each other, then: the two who had been left behind. Sanglant sank down abruptly to his knees before his father, and Henry came forward to rest a hand—that careless, most affectionate gesture—on his son's black hair.

"Ai, Lady," Sanglant whispered, "I'm tired of fighting. I just want to rest."

Henry said nothing for a while, but his hand stroked Sanglant's hair gently. Wind made ripples in the water, tiny scalloped waves that shivered in the sunlight and vanished. Henry's entourage stood out of human earshot, but in the eddy of silence that lapped around the king's affection and forgiveness, Sanglant could hear them speaking to each other as they watched the scene.

"I still think it unwise." That was Sister Rosvita.

"Perhaps." That was Villam. "But I think it wise to strike for Aosta when they are weakest, and there is no question but that the prince can lead such a campaign. What comes of it in the end once Aosta is in our hands and Henry crowned emperor . . . well, we cannot see into the future, so we must struggle forward blindly. We must not undercut the support the other princes and nobles will give Sanglant while they do not yet know Henry's full intentions."

"Did you hear about the adder?" This voice belonged to one

of Henry's stewards who stood somewhat away from Villam and Rosvita; Sanglant recognized the voice but not the name.

"Nay. An adder? Here?" That was a Lion, the red-haired one.

"Ach, yes. Bit one of Count Lavastine's hounds and then vanished. Stablemaster sent men to beat the bushes all round and smoke out any snake holes, but the local folk say they've not seen vipers 'round here for years and years. Still. It weren't no rat that bit that hound."

A thrill of alarm stung him. He staggered up to his feet, surprising his father. "What is this talk of an adder and Lavastine's hounds?"

Henry recovered his composure quickly, mingled affection, grief, and surprise smoothing back into the mask of stone, an expression that gave away nothing of his inner thoughts: Henry at his most cunning. "Indeed." He related the story, what he knew of it. "It happened at dawn. Men have beaten through the palace grounds. But none have scoured these slopes or this land here along the river." He sighed expansively. "Nay, what use? The creature has long since escaped into earth or brush."

"Not if I hunt it." Sanglant flung back his head and took a draught of air, but he smelled nothing out of the ordinary: sweat-tinged men; an aftertaste of frankincense from the dawn service, a dead fish, the evanescent perfume of lavender and comfrey growing along the far bank, manure and urine from the distant stables, the dense, faint underlay of women's holy bleeding, cook fires from the palace and the searing flesh of pork.

"Go, then," said the king quickly. "Send those Lions back, for they've been at their watch all night, and they'll send others to take their place. Where will you start?"

"Here at the base of the bluff. It may have come down through the brush."

"Take care you're not bitten, Son."

"And if I am?" he retorted bitterly. "Female and male God created them. It can't kill me."

"Search with my blessing, then."

But Sanglant had already begun the hunt, and gave no further thought to his father's swift retreat.

5

HANNA waited for Liath outside Count Lavastine's chamber. Liath was still stunned from the rain of gifts that had been showered on her inside. Ai, God, had Count Lavastine really given her a *horse*? She clutched Alain's ring in her hand and stared at Hanna, speechless.

"You've been called before the king." Hanna kissed her, they embraced, and then Hanna pushed back to survey Liath critically. "Everything looks in place."

"Called before the king?"

"Liath!" Hanna's tone made her jump. "Run if you want, or face it with courage. How you present yourself to the king will make a difference in whether he rules in your favor—or in Father Hugh's."

It was good advice, of course, but Liath had a claw stuck in her throat and could not get any words out.

As they walked to the great yard, they passed several Lions loitering as if waiting for her, among them her acquaintance Thiadbold. He winked at her and said, "You know where we are if you've need of aught, friend."

Did everyone know or suspect? But it took far more caution than she and Sanglant had shown to keep something secret on the king's progress. That Hugh had hidden his interest in her, until now, only betrayed how cunning he was.

"You've gained their regard," observed Hanna. "But then, you saved the lives of Lions at Augensburg."

Yet killed more than she had saved.

It was midmorning, just after Terce. The king held court out in the yard, his throne set up in the shadow of the great hall. From the kennels she heard barking as huntsmen readied hounds. Hugh and Wolfhere knelt in front of the king, Hugh somewhat closer to Henry than was Wolfhere, as befit his higher rank. Wolfhere marked her briefly; his composure irritated her. Hugh did not look toward her as Hanna walked forward beside her

and then peeled away to go stand in attendance on Princess Sapientia, but Henry examined her keenly as she knelt. She was careful to keep Wolfhere between her and Hugh. Nobles surrounded
Henry's seat, spread out like wings arching away from his chair:
Sapientia, Villam, Judith, Sister Rosvita, and others, faceless to
her dizzied sight. The eager crowd stirred like a nest of hornets
swept by a gust of smoke.

She did not see Sanglant.

Trembling, she slipped Alain's ring onto a finger.

"So this is the Eagle who has caused so much agitation in
my court. You are called Liathano. An Arethousan name." Henry
had a leash in one hand, studded with brass fittings, and he
played with it as he studied her. "What am I to do with you?"

"I beg you, Your Majesty," said Hugh. "This woman is my
slave. She came to me because her father died leaving a debt,
which I purchased. As his sole heir, she inherited the debt and
could not pay it—"

"I could have paid it if you'd not stolen Da's books—!"

"Quiet," said the king without raising his voice. "Go on,
Father Hugh."

She clenched her hands but could do nothing.

Hugh inclined his head graciously. "As his sole heir, she inherited the debt, which she could not pay, and because I paid
the debt, she came legally into my keeping. I knew very well
that a young woman left alone without kin to watch over her
would be in danger, especially in the north. I did what I could
to make her safe."

"What are these books she speaks of?" asked Henry.

Hugh shrugged. "All acknowledge the right of the church to
confiscate books that may prove dangerous." Unexpectedly, he
sought approval from a new quarter. "Is that not so, Sister
Rosvita? It was first stated at the Council of Orialle, was it not?"

The cleric nodded, but she was frowning. "This right the
church has kept in its own hands."

"And in my capacity as an ordained frater, a servant of God,
I judged these works dangerous to any not educated in their use.
I acted as I thought proper. In any case, it is not yet clear to me
that the books rightfully belonged to her father at all."

"That's not true—!"

"I have not given you leave to speak," said Henry without

looking at her. "But her charge of theft is a serious one, Father Hugh."

He sighed, with a tiny, sad frown. "It is indeed a serious charge, Your Majesty. But there remains another charge as serious: that I purchased her father's debt price, and thus her bond of slavery, illegally. I am sworn to the church. It is slander to suggest that I dealt dishonestly or unfairly in such a transaction." For an instant, she heard real anger in his voice, honor stung by false accusation. He did not look at her. She looked away from him quickly and became aware all at once that many people in the crowd were watching her watching him. What had her face revealed? More than his did, surely. He went on. "As for the books, to whom could she have expected to sell books? And for what price? To a freeholder to burn in the hearth for heat over the winter? I must point out that after the sale of his remaining belongings, her father *still* left debts totaling fully two nomias—"

Murmurs arose in the crowd. People pointed. Whispers buzzed.

"Two nomias! For a slave! That's as much as for a fine stallion!"

To one side, she glimpsed Count Lavastine slipping into place among the crowd of nobles.

"In truth, Your Majesty," Hugh went on smoothly, "she could not have met the debt price, books or no books, no matter what she believes—or wishes to believe. I kept her safe, clothed, fed, and housed. And I was repaid in this manner: Your Eagle, Wolfhere, stole her from me without my consent—and, evidently, without yours."

"I pray you, Your Majesty!" The words burst out of Wolfhere. "May I speak?"

The king considered for a long time. Finally, he lifted a hand in consent.

Wolfhere spoke crisply. "Liath came with me freely. I paid the full debt price that Father Hugh had taken on himself: two nomias. The transaction was witnessed by Marshal Liudolf of Heart's Rest, and sealed with your own mark—the mark of the Eagles which you grant to each of us who serves the crown of Wendar and Varre. It is well known that your servants hold the right to take what they need when they need it. I had need of more Eagles, in such troubled times. Liath and Hanna served

me well, and indeed I lost two Eagles at Gent, one of them my
own discipla. I did not purchase Liath's freedom trivially, but
out of necessity. She has served you well, Your Majesty. I beg
you to take her service into account."

"But she was still taken without my consent," said Hugh quietly. "I did not take the nomias that were offered me. I did not
agree to the transaction."

Henry shifted in his chair. "Do you begrudge me a gift as insignificant as this girl?"

"Not at all, Your Majesty," he replied without missing a beat.
His golden-blond hair gleamed in the sun, as did he. "But I dislike seeing such disgrace brought onto your Eagles, for isn't it
true that Eagles must be free men and women to ride in your
service?"

"Free*born* men and women," said Wolfhere quickly. "It was
no fault of Liath's that her father died in debt. But she is free-
born."

"How do we know that?" asked Hugh.

"I will swear it on the Holy Verses!" cried Liath fiercely.
"Both my mother and father were freeborn—"

"Peace," said the king softly, and she winced, cursed herself.
Could she never just keep quiet? This was not the way to win
the king's favor. He regarded Hugh and Wolfhere with a frown,
but she could not guess at his thoughts. Finally, he gestured toward Sister Rosvita. "You wish to speak, Sister?"

"Only in this way, Your Majesty. I advise you to send this
young woman to the convent of St. Valeria."

That surprised him. "I begin to think there is more here than
meets the eye. St. Valeria! Why should I send her to St. Valeria? To see why Theophanu is delayed for so long there?"

"A good enough reason, Your Majesty. One that will serve
the purpose."

"You speak in riddles, my good counselor. Is there more you
would say?"

Rosvita hesitated. Liath's heart beat so hard she thought everyone around her could hear its hammering. Rosvita knew what
was written in *The Book of Secrets;* her testimony alone could
condemn Liath.

"Nay, Your Majesty," she said at last, and reluctantly. "There
is nothing more I would say in such an assembly."

Whispers threaded through the crowd like a weaving gone

awry. Hugh's eyes narrowed as he gazed at the cleric; then he recalled himself and bowed his head modestly. He did it so well. Never a hair out of place, never a smile too many or a frown at the wrong time.

Henry chuckled, but more in exasperation than good cheer. He gestured expansively. "Are there others who wish to speak?" he demanded.

That brought silence. No one was foolish—or brave—enough to speak into such silence.

Until Count Lavastine stepped forward, unruffled although he immediately became the center of attention. "I see that this Eagle has caused a great deal of disturbance on your progress, Your Majesty. But she served me well at Gent. If you wish to be rid of her, I will take her into my retinue."

"Would you, indeed?" The king quirked an eyebrow, curious, not entirely pleased. "So many show such an interest in a simple Eagle," he mused. His tone made her nervous, and as if her fear attracted him, he looked right at her, the gaze of lightning, blazing, bright, and overwhelming. "Have you anything to say to this, Eagle?"

She blurted it out without thinking. "Where is Sanglant?"

"Sanglant is not *here*, because I have ordered it so." There was nothing more to be said, no petition, no recourse. She bent her head in submission. What else could she do? "Wolfhere leaves today to ride south to Aosta. You have served me well, Liathano."

To hear her name pronounced so firmly in his resonant baritone made her shiver; Da would have said: *"Beware the notice of those who can seal your death warrant; if they don't know you exist, then they'll likely ignore you."* But the king knew she existed. He knew her name, and names are power. She waited, toying with Alain's ring, praying that it might miraculously protect her. What else could she do?

"You have served me well," he repeated, "so I offer you a choice. Remain an Eagle and continue to serve me faithfully, as you have done up to now. If you so choose, you will leave with your comrade Wolfhere this morning. Renounce your oaths as an Eagle, if you will, and I will return you to Father Hugh, as he has asked. This is the king's will. Let none contest my judgment."

He spoke the words harshly, and the instant he uttered them

she could have sworn the words were meant for his absent son.
A kick of rebellion started alive in her gut. What had the king
threatened Sanglant with to make him stay away?

But· as the silence spread, waiting on her choice, she heard
Hugh's ragged breathing; she heard murmurs and the distant
sound of dogs yipping. A horse neighed. A drover shouted in
the lower enclosure, so faint that even the scuff of her knee on
the dirt made a louder sound.

"I will ride with Wolfhere, Your Majesty." Each word stabbed
like a knife in the heart.

Hugh stirred. She knew he was spitting furious, but nothing
of his rage showed on his fine, handsome face. Ai, Lady! She
was free of him at last. But all she felt was a cold emptiness in
her chest.

"Take what you will in recompense from my treasury, Father
Hugh," continued Henry. "You have served my daughter and my
kingdom well, and I am pleased with your counsel."

"Your Majesty." Hugh rose gracefully and, as he stepped back,
he bowed in submission to the king's decree. " 'In his days righteousness shall flourish, and prosperity abound until the moon is
no more.' "

"You may go," said the king to the two Eagles in the tone
of one who has been tried beyond his patience.

"Come, Liath," murmured Wolfhere. "We have outstayed our
welcome." But he did not look unhappy.

She was nothing, an empty vessel drained dry, all her hopes
gone for nothing, but Da hadn't raised a fool. She insisted they
stop at the count's stables, and here she took possession of her
fine horse, her saddle and bridle, rope and saddlebags, a quiver's
worth of arrows, and the beautifully worked leather belt by the
renowned Master Hosel, whoever he was. Wolfhere was astounded by this largesse, but he raised no objections. He was
too eager to leave.

She cried soundlessly when they rode down through the ramparts of Werlida and set their horses' heads to follow the southern road, but she dared not look back.

IV
THE SCENT
OF BLOOD

1

THROUGH birch and spruce he runs, aware that another runs behind him: Second Son of the Sixth Litter, the least of his enemies because of all the brothers he is the first to stalk him. The others deem him so worthless that they will leave him until the end. But he has planned it out all carefully: the first, and least, of the traps will be good enough to dispose of the least of his opponents.

Along the ground a wealth of ferns shatters under him; sedge and bramble give way as he leaps up a slope. He hears the roar of his pursuer, who is tired of running and wishes simply to bring his quarry to bay and fight to the death. May the strongest win.

Ahead, a boulder painted with lichen shoulders up out of the undergrowth: his marker. Beyond it a thick stand of trees awaits. He can almost feel the breath of Second Son on his back, feel the swipe of a clawed hand stirring the delicate links of his golden girdle as Second Son lunges—and misses.

Too late. He cuts in among the trees to a clearing hollowed out by dense growth shading away bracken. Old needles give

*him spring as he jumps, tucks, rolls in the air and out onto safe
ground just as Second Son blunders into the clearing and roars
triumph . . .*

*. . . and the ground shudders beneath him as ropes slither up
on all sides, tugged into the trees by ten slaves hidden in the
branches. The trap closes, a net sewn with fishhooks, and Second Son is tumbled into it. He writhes, howling in fury.*

*As he fights to free himself from the net, fishhooks bound
along the rope catch against his skin with each twist and turn.
Each barb finds purchase under the finely-layered scales that
protect his hide. As he fights, more catch and tug and tear, yet
it is not the pain that makes Second Son howl but the knowledge of defeat. He thrashes helplessly, gets a claw loose, and
begins to rip at the rope, woven of kelp and flax and strips of
bark and hair blessed by the Soft Ones' deacon. But his arm
catches on more fishhooks; as each one sinks in, it sticks stubbornly, and he must rip his skin free in order to begin again.*

*For one moment Fifth Son allows himself to watch the shud-
dering of the net in the air. Through the branches he sees his
slaves straining to hold it taut while the net convulses around
Second Son. Struggling in a net woven of ropes sewn with fishhooks is like struggling against fate: Resistance only sinks the
barbs in more deeply.*

*He steps forward onto ground churned and disordered by the
sudden hoisting of the net. Second Son spits curses at him but
has no power to make those curses stick. He is helpless, and in
moments he will be dead. Fifth Son steps close and unsheathes
his claws.*

Alain blinked, dizzy, and came abruptly awake out of an uncomfortable doze. He heard clerics singing the service of Nones,
but the music rang in his ears like a dirge for the forgotten dead
and he was pierced with such a vivid memory of Lackling joy-
fully feeding the sparrows that he thought his heart would rend
in two from sorrow. Afternoon light splashed across the chamber. Ardent lay still beneath his hands, and he moved to shift
her gently off his legs—only to bruise himself, crushed beneath
her weight. She might have been stone.

"Son." Lavastine stood at the window and now hurried over
to brush a finger against Alain's cheek. "Don't fight her weight.

I didn't want to disturb you before. She's rested so peacefully because she lay with you. There, you see. She's almost gone."

Ardent whimpered softly, but as he stroked her head, he could see the suck of her lungs grow shallow.

"Where is Tallia?" he whispered.

"When you slept, she took her attendants and went to pray in the chapel. It is better so. God have mercy." Only the scrape in his voice revealed his grief; his expression was as smooth as Ardent's coat. He sat on the bed, rested fingers lightly on her muzzle as she stiffened entirely and, at last, ceased to breathe.

The other hounds, who had remained silent at their vigil throughout the day, began to howl. A musky odor seemed to steam up from their bodies, like the heavy scent of mourning. From across the palace grounds, all the other dogs and hounds joined in until their mourning became cacophony.

Lavastine sat on the bed with head bowed and chin resting on his folded hands. With some difficulty, Alain got out from under Ardent's weight and, with his legs tingling, grimaced as he knelt beside her. Tears came. He could not bear to take his hand off her cold head. Her ears had the same stiff curl as would a sheet of metal molded to form such a shape. The servants stayed back, well aware of the uncertain temper of the other hounds, who might lunge without warning.

Finally Lavastine stirred, and rested a hand on Alain's hair. "Hush, Son. There is nothing you can do for her now."

Sorrow barked and the other hounds growled as the servants moved aside to make way for a tall figure.

"Your Highness." Lavastine stood.

Terror took two stiff steps forward to growl at the prince as he entered the chamber, and immediately all the hounds coursed forward protectively. The servants bolted back out of range. The prince lifted a gloved hand like a weapon and, seemingly without thinking, growled back at the hounds from deep in his throat, a hoarse sound as threatening as the one made by the hounds.

Prince and hounds faced off, not retreating, not attacking. Then, hackles still raised, Terror took a wary sidestep as if to signal to the rest that this foe was worthy of respect—if not friendship. The prince glanced once around to check their positions, then knelt beside Ardent. By every twitch of Prince Sanglant's body, by his very stance, Alain could see he would strike at any aggressive movement, but the hounds behaved themselves except for a low growl that escaped Rage at intervals.

Alain wiped his nose and tried to speak in greeting, but he could not get words past the grief lodged in his throat.

"I heard the tale," said the prince, "and I helped the huntsmen beat the bushes on the cliffs and down by the river, but we found nothing. The adder must have gone back into its den." He glanced again toward the hounds, aware of their least shifting movements. Rage growled again, all stiff-legged, but did not rush in: She knew a worthy opponent when she saw one. "May I look at the wound?"

"I thank you," said Lavastine.

Alain made to shift Ardent's right foreleg to turn over her paw . . . and for a moment could not, until he braced himself and heaved. She was almost too heavy to be moved.

"Strange," said Sanglant as he examined the paw. "It's as if she's turned to stone." He bent to sniff along her body exactly as a dog would.

Behind, the servants whispered as they watched him, and abruptly Sanglant jerked up, hands clenching at his side, as if he'd heard them. Bliss barked a warning. Outside, the baying and howling had subsided.

"She smells like the Eika." He shook his head as a hound flings off water. He traced the curve of her ear and the grain of her nose, dry and as cold as stone. "Are you sure it was an adder that bit her?"

"What else could it have been?" asked Lavastine. "She was at the threshold, there—" He pointed to the door of the chamber.

"You saw nothing?" The prince looked at Alain. He had startlingly green eyes and an expression as guarded as that of a caged panther which, given room to bolt free, suspects a hidden weapon is poised to strike it down as it runs.

"I wasn't here—" Alain felt himself blush.

"Of course not," said the prince curtly. "I beg your pardon." He paced to the window, stared out as if searching for someone, then abruptly turned back. "I saw a creature among the Eika that was dead and yet was animated by Bloodheart's magic." When he spoke the name of his captor, his gaze flinched inward. He touched the iron collar that ringed his neck, noticed that he had touched it, and jerked his hand down to his belt. A flush spread across his fine, high cheekbones, a dull stain over his golden-bronze complexion.

Lavastine waited, toying with Ardent's leash, tying it into knots and untying it again without once glancing at his hands.

At last Sanglant shook his head impatiently. "Nay, it is impossible that such a thing could live past Bloodheart's death. Or that it could follow us so far, when only sunlight animates it and we travel swiftly by horse and it is no bigger than a rat."

"What you speak of is not at all clear to me, Your Highness." Lavastine gestured to the servants and, as one, they retreated out the door to leave the count, his heir, and the half-wild prince alone with the living hounds and their dead companion.

Sanglant hissed between his teeth. "Lady preserve me," he whispered as if struggling against some inner demon. "It was a curse, that's all I know." He measured his words slowly, as if he did not quite have control of them—like a nervous horseman given an untried mount to ride. "A curse Bloodheart wove to protect himself from any man or Eika who wished to kill him. Let you and your people accompany me, Count Lavastine. I have certain . . . skills. Together with your hounds, if there is aught that stalks this place, we can catch it." He paused, set a hand on Ardent's cold paw, and shut his eyes as he considered.

Suddenly he started up with such violence that the hounds began barking madly.

"Peace!" said Lavastine over their noise, and they subsided.

"It isn't you at all," said the prince. "It's seeking *her*. She's the one who killed him."

That quickly, and without warning or any least polite words of parting, he was out the door and vanished from their sight. They heard the servants scattering out of his way as he strode down the corridor, and then much murmuring, leaves settling to earth after a gale blows through.

Lavastine sat for a long while in silence, so stern of face that the servants, glancing in, retreated at once. "A curse," he muttered finally. He lowered his eyes to the tangled leash, and sighed as Alain wiped a tear from his own eye. Poor, good-natured Ardent. It seemed impossible that she wasn't barking cheerfully, begging to be let out for a run.

Then he lifted a hand and touched a finger to his lips as he did when he meant Alain to listen closely. "Prince Sanglant is beholden to me for rescuing him. He favors you, and Henry favors him—which is not surprising. Princess Sapientia is brave but impulsive and unsteady. I have not seen Princess Theophanu, but she is said to be coldhearted. Alas for Henry that the prince is only half of human kin, and a bastard besides. Watch and listen carefully as we ride with the king's progress. I believe the king wishes to make Sanglant his heir—"

"But Prince Sanglant was conceived and borne to give King Henry the right by fertility to reign. Not to rule after him!"

"Henry must give him legitimacy, but he cannot simply confer it upon him as he—and I—conferred legitimacy upon you. The princes of the realm will not stand aside and watch a half-human bastard become regnant, no matter how respected a war leader he is. Nay, he's scarcely better than a dog at times now." He nudged Ardent's corpse with his shoe, then looked surprised and rubbed his toe. With a frown, he touched the hound's ears and with that same hand wiped away tears before turning back to his son. "Which is why the prince seeks to bring me into his circle by showing me such marked favor. He must cultivate powerful allies, and he must marry well."

"Someone like Tallia." Heat flushed Alain's skin and scalded his tears away.

"Yes. Now that you are married to Tallia, no one will remember that you were once a bastard. I believe that Henry will send Prince Sanglant to Aosta. It is what I would do in his place, and Henry is a strong and cunning king." He whistled the dogs to heel. "Come. Let us lay poor Ardent to rest."

They made a solemn procession: the count, his heir, their servants, and the six black hounds. It took six men to carry the corpse on a litter, whose woven branches had to be reinforced twice over before it could take the weight of the dead hound.

Servants had gone ahead to dig a grave outside the lower ramparts. Robins hunting for worms along the banks of newly-turned earth fluttered away as the funeral procession came up beside the open pit. The men carrying the litter set it at the lip of the grave and heaved up one side to roll the body out. The corpse did not budge until they hoisted the litter almost perpendicular, faces strained and backs sweating, and then the body tumbled down. It hit dirt with an audible thud.

Alain winced. Ai, Lady, what a strange death had overtaken her! The hounds snuffled around the upturned earth, but they seemed not to recognize the remains which lay in the grave as those of their sister and cousin. She no longer smelled of the pack.

A space chipped into the bank of soil as the servingmen began to fill in the grave. Clumps of dirt rained down, drowning her, as if sorrow could be buried together with the corpse of a loved one. The patter fell like hailstones. Somewhere, in the distance, he heard a horse galloping off down the southward road. He smelled the perfume of soil, roots and earth and crawling things intertwined. A worm wiggled out of the unforgiving stare of the sun where it had been upended by the grave-digging and slid away into a heap of moist earth.

The fragrance engulfed him, made his head spin. . . .

He smells blood and cautiously approaches the tumble of boulders. Tenth Son of the Fourth Litter lies splayed in death, limbs bent at awkward angles, throat ripped clean and one arm torn off. The pebbles sprayed everywhere, scuffed ground, moss torn into scraps all around the bloody soil might as well be signs recording in their ephemeral writing the course and outcome of the duel. By next summer, after winter scours the earth clean, no one will be able to trace in this arena that one fought and the other died.

He grips one copper-skinned shoulder of the corpse and rolls it over to reveal the back of the neck: The braid is shorn free. He touches the braid now coiled around his right arm. After he cut it off Second Son, he bound it to his own arm as both trophy and proof, just as one of the other brothers now carries the cut braid of Tenth Son in like manner. Where is that brother now?

He hears a scuff, and the wind shifts to bring him the whisper of a girdle shifting along thick flanks as someone steps stealthily toward him behind the cover of rocks. That quickly, he bolts.

That he is slender makes him swift. Fourth Son of the Ninth Litter thunders after him, but his vast girth makes him as slow as he is brutishly strong. This brother could rend him limb from body with a casual yank—as he did to Tenth Son.

Fifth Son gauges distance and speed and, like lightning forking, veers right to sprint for Lightwoven River, where his second trap waits.

"Hai! Hai! Hai! Coward and weakling!" howls Fourth Son. He minds it not but keeps running, although he slows to a

lope, knowing that Fourth Son cannot catch him even with a burst of speed. He need only stay far enough ahead to be free of that overpowering grip and yet close enough that Fourth Son will keep after him rather than give up to go hunt one of the others.

River gravel spins under his feet. He leaps for the narrow footbridge that spans the rushing waters here where they funnel toward the cliff and the great spill of Lightfell Waterfall. The planks sway dangerously under him; he feels the weakened ropes creak and can almost smell the strands fray further.

Then he is across, and he spins back just as Fourth Son hits the planks with his heavy pounding run. With the merest snick of his claws, he finishes off the rope struts that are already cut through and frayed to the breaking point.

The bridge collapses under Fourth Son's considerable weight. Planks skitter and tumble and rope handholds drop away. He falls into the icy water—not that the water will drown him, but here the current runs narrow and strong as it pours itself over the cliff and spills and spins and sprays down.

Down he falls over the Lightfell Waterfall. His body strikes rocks, spins, bumps, tumbles down the ragged cliff face and finally is doused in the pounding roar at the base where the rush of water hammers into the fjordwaters and erupts as mist.

He goes under.

Fifth Son waits atop the ridge, scanning the waters.

There! A head bobs up, ice-white braid a snake upon the water. Arms stroke with stubborn resolve. Beaten, bloodied, and battered by the fall, Fourth Son is yet alive.

He expected this.

But he does not have to wait long for what he knows will come next.

Farther out, where the fjordwaters lie still, movement eddies. A slick back surfaces and vanishes, swift and silent as it circles in. There, to its left, another ripple stirs the surface of the water. And another.

Fourth Son strokes toward shore. He is not dead, of course, but he does not need to be dead. He only needs to be bleeding.

Waters part as a tail skims, flicks up, and slaps down. Too late Fourth Son realizes his danger. The waters swirl with sudden violence around him. He thrashes, goes under. Wet scales gleam, curving backs swirl, a ghastly head rears up, water streaming from the netlike hair which itself winds and coils like a living thing. Fourth Son emerges from the roiling waters clawing at his attackers. From his station at the height of the cliff, Fifth Son hears a howl of triumph as one of the merfolk shudders and sinks, while an inky black trail bubbles in its wake. The merfolk close in. Water boils. Fourth Son vanishes beneath the cold gleam of the fjordwaters. Like a churning mill, the eddies run round, slow into ripples, smooth over.

All is still again—except for the shattering roar of the falls. Blood stains the water and mingles with inky fluid torn out of the merman.

A back breaks the surface, slides in a graceful curve back into the depths, and turns toward shore. He waits. A rock shelf juts out along one side of the base of the waterfall. Suddenly, the waters part and the creature rears up to reveal its face: flat red eyes gleaming like banked fires, noseless but for dark slits over a nodelike swelling, and a mouth grinning with rows of glittering sharp teeth. As it rises, its hair and mane begin to writhe wildly, each strand with its own snapping mouth as if eels had affixed themselves to its head and neck. It has shoulder and arms, hands tipped with razor-sharp nails, and a ridged back that the light gilds to a silvery shine. The huge tail, longer than legs and far more powerful, heaves out of the water and slaps once, hard, echoing, on the rock. It makes no other sound.

It tosses two braids—one neatly shorn, one slightly bloody— onto the rocky shelf. The merfolk are as much beast as intelligent being—or so he has always believed. But they know the contest, and they know the rules. It would not do to underestimate them. An ambitious general can never have enough allies.

With an awkward roll, arching backward, the merman spills off the shelf and hits the water hard. The huge splash melds with the waterfall's mist. The tail flicks up, as if in salute, slaps down again, and it is gone.

All lies still.

He climbs down the steps carved into the rock beside the falls. Down here, in the cavern hidden behind the spray, the priest hid his heart in a chest. He discovered it because he was patient; he waited and watched, and he listened to the priest murmur and sing about his hidden heart. And when at last one night the priest scurried from his nest cloaked with such shad-

ows as he could grasp in the midsummer twilight, Fifth Son followed him.

Now he controls the priest's heart—and the priest's obedience.

He wonders, briefly, about Bloodheart's curse. By his own testimony the priest turned the curse away from himself. But where did it fall? Who will be cursed by the poison of Bloodheart's hatred and thwarted greed?

Hate is the worst poison of all because it blinds.

He reaches the shelf, pauses to scan the waters, but they lie unsullied by any evidence of the gruesome fight conducted a short while before. Water speaks in a short-lived voice, ever-changing, mortal by reason of its endless fluidity.

Yet even water wears away rock in time, so the WiseMothers say.

Out beyond the thrumming roar of the waterfall, the sun makes the water gleam until it shines like a painted surface. Is that a ripple of movement, or only a trick of the light?

He kneels to pick up the two braids. Deftly he binds them around his upper arms like armbands. Three brothers dead. He touches his own braid, making of it a talisman.

Only two left to kill . . .

. . . but they will be the wiliest and smartest and strongest of Bloodheart's sons—besides himself, of course. For them, he has laid the most dangerous trap of all—the one not even he may survive.

Rage snapped at a butterfly and the bright creature skimmed away, lost in the spinning air.

Alain stood alone by the filled-in grave. Only Rage and Sorrow and a single servant, standing at a safe distance, attended him. Everyone else had gone. His knees almost gave out and his head swam as he staggered to kneel beside the fresh grave. But when he touched the soil, he felt nothing but dirt. Ardent's spirit, with her body, had vanished. A bold robin had returned to hunt these rich fields and now looked him over from a safe distance, head cocked to one side.

"My lord?" The servant came forward tentatively.

He sighed and rose. Now the rest of them would go on, and leave her behind. "Where are the others?"

"My lord count has gone to begin preparations for leave-taking. The clerics have told him that tomorrow is a propitious day to undertake a long journey."

"The curse," Alain whispered, recalling his dream. "I must find out what he knows."

"I beg your pardon, my lord?"

"I must speak to Prince Sanglant." He whistled the hounds to him and went to seek out Prince Sanglant.

There was a commotion in the great yard that fronted the king's residence: two riders spoke urgently with the king's favored Eagle while a cleric stood to one side, listening intently. Princess Sapientia and a party of riders attired for a pleasure ride waited impatiently, but because Father Hugh lingered to hear the news, none of them dared ride out yet. The folk gathered to hear the news parted quickly to let Alain and the hounds through. But he had no sooner come up beside the Eagle when the doors into the king's residence swung open and King Henry strode out into the glare of the afternoon sun. Dressed for riding in a handsomely trimmed tunic, a light knee-length cloak clasped with an elaborate brooch at his right shoulder, and soft leather boots, he waved away the horse brought up for him and turned on the steward who stood white-faced and nervous behind him.

"What do you mean, with *no* attendants?"

"He was in a foul temper, Your Majesty, after he went to the stables, and he was not inclined to answer our questions. And he took the ... dogs ... with him, and a spare mount."

"No one thought to ride after him?"

"I pray you, Eagle," said Alain, cutting in now that all others had fallen silent. "Do you know where I might find Prince Sanglant?"

The Eagle looked at him strangely, but she inclined her head. "He rode out alone, my lord, in great haste, as if a madness convulsed him." She seemed about to say more, then did not.

"Two men rode after him, at a discreet distance," replied the steward who had by now gone red in the face from the heat of the king's anger.

The king grunted. "The southern road," he said furiously. "That is where you'll find him. It takes no scouts to tell me that." His gaze swept the forecourt, dismissing daughter and noble attendants until it came to rest on his favored Eagle. Her, he beckoned to. "Send a dozen riders to track him down. But discreetly, as you say. That would be best."

The Eagle retired graciously, but with haste, toward the stables. The cleric led the two dust-covered riders away as they questioned her about the accommodations that would be available—and Alain suddenly realized that they were not the king's riders but one man and one woman, each wearing the badge of a hawk. Father Hugh had a pleasant smile on his face, and he swung back beside Princess Sapientia and spoke to her in a low voice as they rode away.

Helmut Villam came out to stand beside the king, who lingered, slapping a dog leash trimmed with brass against his palm. Henry beckoned to Alain. "So, young Alain, you seek my son as well."

"So I do, Your Majesty. I saw him earlier this morning. He was agitated, and he spoke of some kind of curse, a trap laid by Bloodheart against any person who sought to kill him."

"Bloodheart! Yet he's dead and safely gone." But abruptly he looked hopeful. "Do you think Sanglant might have ridden north toward Gent?"

Any man would have been tempted to coax the king into a better humor, but Alain saw no point in lying. "Nay, Your Majesty. I think he rode after the Eagle, as you said before."

Henry's expression clouded.

"You should have offered her as a concubine to him," said Villam in the tone of a man who has seen the storm coming for hours and is disgusted because his companion refused to take shelter before the rains hit.

"I did! But I don't trust Wolfhere. She's his discipla. I'm sure it's a plot."

Villam grunted. "Perhaps. But Wolfhere seemed eager enough to remove her from court. On this matter I do not think that your wish and his are far apart."

"That may be," admitted the king in a grudging tone. "What am I to do? If I make Sapientia margrave of Eastfall, then she'll be out of the way, but if I cannot make Sanglant cooperate, see the wisdom of marrying onto the Aostan throne, then what do I do with him?"

"Do not despair yet. I have said before and I say it again: Encourage him in his suit. No lord or lady will follow him if he does not . . ." He hesitated.

"Speak your mind, Villam! If you do not, then who will?"

Villam's sigh had as much meaning as any hundred words.

"He is half a dog. That everyone whispers it doesn't make it less true. He must become a man again and, as the philosopher says, young people are at first likely to fall in love with one particular beautiful person and only later observe that the beauty exhibited in one body is one and the same as in any other."

Henry laughed. "How long did it take you to come to this conclusion, my good friend?"

Villam chuckled. "I am not given up on my study yet. Let the young man make his. He will become more tractable after. Right now he is like to a dog who has sniffed a bitch in heat— he is all madness for her and can't control himself."

Alain blushed furiously, and suddenly the king smiled, looking right at him. "Go on, son," he said genially. "I saw Tallia enter the chapel earlier. That's where you'll find her."

Alain said the correct polite leave-takings, and retreated. The chapel doors yawned invitingly. Inside, he would find Tallia. But the thought of her only made him blush the harder.

She reached the threshold before him, escorted by Lavastine, who smiled to see him coming. Tallia shrank away from Rage and Sorrow, and Alain took her aside, away from the hounds.

"Will you ride out?" he asked, eager to make her happy.

"Nay," she said faintly. She looked unwell, quite tired and drawn.

"Then we will sit quietly together."

"Alain." Lavastine nodded toward the king. "I have already made known my intention to leave tomorrow. It is long past time we return to Lavas."

Tallia had the look of a cornered deer.

"We'll rest this evening," said Alain. "You needn't attend the feast if you're unwell."

"Yes," she murmured so quietly that he could barely hear her.

He glanced at Lavastine, who gave a bare nod of approval and then went to instruct his servants about the packing. They retired to their chamber, where she prayed for such a long time that Alain, kneeling beside her bodily but not truly in spirit, had finally to stand up because his knees hurt. He ordered a platter of food brought in, but although it was now twilight and she had fasted all day, she ate only some gruel and two crusts of bread. He felt like a glutton beside her.

"What is it like in Lavas?" she asked fearfully. "I'll be at your mercy."

"Of course you won't be at my mercy!" How could she think of him in such an unflattering light? "You are the daughter of Duke Berengar and Duchess Sabella. How can you imagine that I or anyone could take advantage of you when you are born into the royal kin?"

"I am merely a Lion in the king's chess game, a pawn, nothing more than that," she said bitterly. "As are you, only you do not see it."

"We aren't pawns! God have given us free will."

"That is not what I meant," she said with such a sigh that he thought her in pain. "It is the world I wish to be free of. I want only to devote my life to our Holy Mother, who is God, and to pledge myself as a bridge to the blessed Daisan and in this way live a pure life of holy good deeds as did St. Radegundis."

"She married and bore a child," he said with sudden anger, stung by her words.

"She was pregnant when Emperor Taillefer died. No one knows what happened to the child. I asked Sister Rosvita, and she says the matter is not mentioned again in the *Vita*. If our Holy Mother had intended St. Radegundis for earthly glory and a wealth of children, She would have showered her with these riches, since it is easily within Her power to grant something so trivial. She had greater plans for Radegundis, who made of herself a holy vessel for this purpose."

"A child doesn't just vanish!" retorted Alain, who could just imagine what his Aunt Bel—not his aunt any longer—would say to the notion of children and prosperity being trivial things in the eyes of the Lord and Lady, through Whose agency all that is bountiful arises.

Tallia laughed, sounding for a moment so heartless that he wondered if he knew her at all. "What do you think would happen to a newborn child of a dead emperor whose last wife has no kin to protect her from the vultures who have flocked to feed on the corpse? I believe Our Lady was merciful, and that the child was born dead."

"That isn't mercy!"

But she only bowed her head and turned away from him to kneel again by the bed, hands clasped atop the beautifully-embroidered bedspread, forehead resting on her hands as she murmured a prayer. He signed for the servants to leave.

"Tallia—" he began, when they were alone.

She raised her eyes to him reproachfully.

"Tallia." But her fawnlike eyes, the slender tower of her neck, the beat of her pulse at her throat—all this enflamed him. He had to pace to the window, leaning out to get any least draft of cooling air on his face. He had only to be patient, to coax her.

When at last he turned back, she had fallen asleep, slumped over the bed. She looked so frail that he couldn't bring himself to disturb her but instead gently lifted her onto the bed. Her eyelids fluttered, but she did not wake. He wanted to lie beside her, to keep that contact between them, but it felt somehow obscene because she was so limp, so resistless—as if he had unnatural feelings toward a corpse. He shuddered and eased off the bed.

Restless, he paced a while longer. He sent a servant to inquire after Prince Sanglant, but the prince had not returned to the palace, nor had those sent out to look for him.

Much later he heard the six hounds, confined to Lavastine's chamber, welcome the count with whines and whimpers as he came in from the night's feasting. He kept listening, expecting to hear a seventh familiar voice, but it never came: Ardent was truly gone.

2

WITH two horses, changing off, he made good time, and the dogs never seemed to tire. There was only one road to follow until the village of Ferse, nestled in the heel of a portion of land protected by the confluence of two rivers. There he questioned the ferryman about two Eagles who had passed earlier in the day: They had continued south into the forest rather than splitting off on the east-west path. Several startled farmers walking home from their fields along the roadside confirmed that they had seen Eagles riding past.

Neat strips of cultivated fields became scattered woods and pastureland, then forest swallowed everything but the cut of the road. Beneath the trees, summer's evening light filtered into a haze of fading color. The wind blew in his favor: He heard them before he saw them, two riders and two spare horses.

Wolfhere turned first to see who approached from behind. Sanglant heard the old Eagle swear under his breath, and he smiled with grim satisfaction. Then Liath turned to look over her shoulder. She reined in her horse at once, forcing Wolfhere to pull up as well.

"We have farther to go this night if we mean to sleep in the way station that lies ahead," warned Wolfhere.

Liath did not reply, did not need to; Sanglant knew how a woman's body spoke, how her expression betrayed her desire. She tried to master her expression, to give nothing away, but her entire face had lit and a grin kept tugging at her mouth. He knew then that he could succeed if only he behaved as a man, not a dog.

Wolfhere minced no words. "This is madness. Liath, we must ride on."

"No. I will hear what Sanglant has to say."

"You know what I have to say." Sanglant dismounted, staked down the dogs, then crossed to her and offered to take her reins as would a groom. She gave them to him, but did not dismount.

"You are not thinking this through, Liath," continued Wolfhere furiously. "You will lose the protection of the Eagles, which is all that saved you from Hugh first at Heart's Rest and this very morning at the king's court. All this to go to a man who has nothing, not land, not arms, no retinue, no control over his own destiny because he has no inheritance from his mother—"

"Save my blood," said Sanglant softly, and was happy to see Wolfhere glance angrily at him and then away.

"—and you will live at his mercy. Without the protection of the Eagles or any other kin he is the only protection you will have against those like Hugh who seek to enslave you. And that protection will be offered to you only for as long as he desires you."

"Marriage is a holy sacrament," observed Sanglant, "and not to be split asunder on a whim."

"Marriage?" exclaimed Wolfhere, and for the breath of an instant, Sanglant had the satisfaction of seeing him look panicked. But Wolfhere was too old and wily to remain so for long. He recovered as quickly as an experienced soldier who has lost his footing in the midst of battle: with an aggressive stab. "Mind

you, Liath, King Henry's displeasure is not a thing to be undertaken lightly. He will refuse to recognize the marriage. He has passed judgment: that you serve in his Eagles or return to Hugh. Will he rule differently if you return claiming marriage to his favored son? Or will he wish to be rid of you? And if so, where can you flee, neither of you with kin to support you? *Your mother is waiting for you, Liath.*"

Sanglant recognized danger instantly. "Your mother?"

"I've given up more than you know, Wolfhere," retorted Liath. "If I go to my mother, then I must leave the Eagles in any case. Why would Henry not object then? Only because he would not know and thus could not return me to Hugh? Is my reunion with my mother to be based on deceit? Why should I trust you?"

"Why should you trust Sanglant?" Wolfhere demanded.

But she only laughed, and her laughter made his heart sing with joy, although the words that came next were bitter and angry. "Because he's no more capable of lying than are those dogs. Even Da lied to me. You lied to me, Wolfhere, and I wonder if my mother lied as well. If she had made any kind of effort to find us, wouldn't he still be alive?"

A whiff of smoke rose on the breeze, some distant sparking fire that faded as Liath stared Wolfhere down, her expression as fierce as the king's when he allowed himself to succumb to one of his famous wraths. But a kind of unearthly fire shone from her, something he could almost smell more than see, an uncanny, pure scent. Sanglant took hold of one of her wrists, and she, startled, glanced at him, then sighed. That scent burned in her, almost a living creature in its own right. Her skin seemed to steam with her anger.

Made humble before it, Wolfhere said only: "She must teach you, Liath. You know by now that you desperately need teaching."

There was the danger. He saw the shadow of it flicker over her expression: she needed something he could not give her, and Wolfhere would use that need to sway her. But Sanglant had no intention of losing her again. "Wherever you need to go," he said, "I will take you there."

"What if your father objects?" Liath asked. "What if he won't give you horses, or arms, or an escort?"

He laughed recklessly. "I don't know. What does it matter what *might* happen—only what can, now, this night."

"Bred and trained for war," muttered Wolfhere, "with no thought beyond the current battle."

She had a sharp flush on her cheeks and looked away from both of them, but he knew what she was thinking of. He found it hard not to think of it himself. He released her wrist abruptly. Suddenly his grasp on her seemed too much like Bloodheart's iron collar, a means to force her to do what he wanted her to do rather than to let her make the choice. "It is true I have nothing to offer you by way of estates or income as part of the marriage agreement. It is true that my father will object. But he may also see reason when presented with a vow witnessed, legal, and binding. I am not the only man available to marry Princess Adelheid. Let my father object first, then we will see. We may both be set upon by bandits and killed before we can get back to Werlida to receive the king's judgment! And I have other resources."

"Such as?" asked Wolfhere, not without sarcasm.

"Where is my mother now, Wolfhere?" asked Liath, cutting him off.

But he remained stubbornly silent.

"You won't tell me," she said harshly.

"I can't speak freely now."

"Because of Sanglant?" She looked astounded.

"We are not always alone," said Wolfhere cryptically, and as if in answer an owl suddenly glided into view. It came to rest quite boldly on an outstretched branch that jutted out over the road a few paces beyond Wolfhere's horse. Could it be the same owl that had led her to the burning stone? It was certainly as large. Its sudden arrival set the dogs to yammering until the creature noiselessly launched itself into the air and vanished into the darkening forest. The trees and undergrowth turned to blue-gray as the late summer evening faded toward night.

When Wolfhere spoke again, it was with suppressed anger and a fierce intensity. "You must accept, Liath, that we are caught in greater currents than you understand—and until you do understand more fully, I must be circumspect."

"Why does King Henry hate you?" she asked. He betrayed himself by glancing at Sanglant, and that caused her to look at him as well. "Do *you* know?" she asked, amazed.

"Of course I know." The old story had long since ceased to

stir in him anything more than a faint amusement. "He tried to drown me when I was an infant."

"Is that true?" she demanded of Wolfhere.

He merely nodded. He could no longer disguise his anger— the annoyance of a man whose quiet plans are rarely thwarted.

"Alas that he didn't succeed," added Sanglant, now beginning to be truly amused at Wolfhere's sullen silence. "Then I wouldn't have had to suffer through so many of his later attempts to convince me that I was part of a terrible plot contrived by my mother and her kin. 'Who knows what will happen when the crown of stars crowns the heavens?' If only I had known, perhaps I might not have been abandoned by my mother, her unwanted child. At least my father cared for me."

"And will he care for you still, my lord prince," asked Wolfhere in a harsh voice, "when you return with a bride not of his choosing?"

Sanglant's smile now was grim and sure, his voice steady. "I have other resources because I have made my reputation as a warrior. There are many princes in this world who would be happy to have me fight at their side, even at the risk of King Henry's displeasure. I am no longer dragon—or pawn—to be used in your chess games, Wolfhere, nor in my father's. I have left the board, and I will make my way with his blessing . . . or without it. So do I swear."

Wolfhere did not reply. Nor did Liath—or at least, not in words. Instead, she unpinned her Eagle's cloak and rolled it up, then unclasped her Eagle's badge and fastened it to the cloak.

"I'm sorry," she said, holding them out. "But I made this choice days ago, and in far stranger circumstances than these. My mother now knows where to find me."

"This was not to be! It is not possible that you should cleave unto him!"

"Because you will it otherwise?" she demanded. "I refuse to be bound by the fate others have determined for me!"

"Liath!" Still he did not lean forward to take cloak and badge. "If you go with him, you will be without any support—"

"What other life do you think I have known? Da and I managed."

"For a time." Was his reply meant to be ominous, or was that only his frustration surfacing? He genuinely seemed to care about Liath's fate. "Reflect on this, then. It is not only the cloak and badge I must take, but the horse. Provision was made for an Eagle, not for Sanglant's concubine."

She smiled triumphantly. "Then it's as well I have my own horse, isn't it?" She dismounted, tied the cloak neatly onto the abandoned saddle, and removed the blanket roll. "This, too, is mine. It came to me as a gift from Mistress Birta." She took the reins from Sanglant and offered them to Wolfhere, who did not yet move.

"What of the sword and bow?" he demanded instead.

Her expression did not change. The speed with which she had made her decision and the ruthlessness with which she now executed it impressed Sanglant—and made him a bit apprehensive. She began to unbuckle her belt to loose the sheath and thereby the sword.

"Nay," said Wolfhere quickly. "I cannot leave you defenseless. If I have not persuaded you to come with me, then let that fault lie with me. You may change your mind." Now he did take the reins, but he fixed his gaze on Liath's face as if to peer into her heart. "You can still change your mind—" Here he winced slightly, as at a thorn in his foot. "—until and unless you get pregnant by him. Ai, God, why won't you trust me? There are greater things than you know—"

"Then tell me what they are!"

But he only glanced toward the tree where the owl had alighted.

"Here," said Sanglant, trying very hard to speak steadily, although he wanted to shout with triumph, "I have two horses. The bay is more tractable."

"Nay, let me only tighten the girth on Resuelto. I'll ride him now."

They left Wolfhere on the road, still caught as if by an invisible hand in that pose with one hand on his own reins and one holding that of the horse Liath had ridden. Liath looked back once as they rounded a bend, heading north, to catch a last sight of him. Sanglant did not bother.

At first they had nothing to say, simply rode with eyes intent on the darkening road as they followed the track back toward Ferse. Her breathing, the thud of horses' hooves, and the scrabbling of the dogs as they padded alongside with occasional forays toward the roadside or nipping at each other all melded together with the shush of wind in the branches and the night sounds of animals coming awake.

"Where did you come by the horse?" he asked finally. "He's very fine. It seems to me I've seen him before."

"Count Lavastine gave Resuelto to me as a reward for my service to him at Gent. And all the gear, too."

It stirred, then, a spark of jealousy—quickly extinguished. She wasn't riding with Count Lavastine. She was riding with *him*.

"Will King Henry be very angry?" she asked in a tremulous voice.

"Yes. He wants me to ride south to Aosta to place Princess Adelheid on the Aostan throne, marry her, and name myself as king regnant. Then he can march south, have the skopos crown him emperor, and name me as his heir and successor because of the legitimacy conferred upon me by my title as king."

Her reply came more as a kind of stifled grunt than anything. They rode out into a clearing, vanguard of the open land that lay before them, and here he could see her expression clearly in the muted light of late evening. "But then, if you marry *me*—"

He reined in and she had to halt. "Let us speak of this once and not again," he said, impatient not truly with her but with the arguments he knew would come once they returned to the king's progress. "As Bloodheart's prisoner I saw what it meant to be a king. This, my retinue—" He gestured toward the dogs who were by now well trained enough that they didn't try to rip out the horses' underbellies. "—would have torn out my throat any time I showed weakness. So would the great princes do to my father, were he to show weakness. Imagine how they would lie in wait for me, because I am a bastard and only half of human kin. For one year I lived that way trapped in the cathedral in Gent. I will not live so again. I do not want to be king or emperor. But if you cannot believe me, Liath, then return to Wolfhere. Or break with the king and offer your service to Count Lavastine, who obviously values you. I will not have this conversation over and over if you in your heart doubt my intention."

She said nothing at first. Finally, she nudged her horse forward and commenced riding north along the road. He followed her. His heart pounded fiercely and a wave of dizziness swept

through him so powerfully that he clutched the saddle to keep
his seat. The pounding in his ears swelled until he started up,
realizing he heard hoofbeats ahead.

"Pull up," he said curtly, and she did so.

"What is it?" But then she, too, heard. A moment later they
saw riders.

Two men reined in, looking relieved. "My lord prince!" Their
horses were in a bad state; they had not thought to take re-
mounts.

"We'll return to the village," said Sanglant to them, "where
we'll rest for the night. Then we'll rejoin the king."

They nodded, not asking questions.

The sun had finally set, and they pressed forward through the
moon-fed twilight, walking the horses in part to spare the blown
mounts of their escort and in part because of the dim light. He
had nothing to say to Liath, not with the two servingmen so
close behind them. He did not really know what to say in any
case. What point was there in saying anything? The decision had
been made. There was, thank God, nothing left to discuss.

She rode with a straight back and a proud, confident carriage.
Did she have second thoughts as she rode beside him? He could
not tell by her expression, half hidden by the deepening twilight. She seemed resolute, with her chin tilted back.

A single lantern burned at the gate to Ferse, like a star fallen
to earth—the only light besides that glistening down upon them
from the heavens. Clouds had smothered the southern sky, blowing a brisk wind before it: a coming storm.

He let one of the servingmen pound at the closed gate while
he tried not to think of what lay ahead: a cold supper, and a
bed. Certainly a few women had approached him in the last
month—some, he suspected, at the instigation of Helmut Villam, who seemed to believe that every ill that assailed the male
body could be cured by the vigorous application of sex—but he
had not touched even one. He was afraid that he would make a
fool of himself.

Now, as the gate creaked open and they were admitted within
the palisade by a suitably overawed young man acting as watchman, he was sorry he had not. Then at least he would have taken
the edge off that terrible appetite which is desire unfulfilled.
Even the mothers and fathers of the church understood that it

is easier to cure the body of its lust for eat and drink than of the inclination toward concupiscence.

In Ferse, a dozen riders waited, men-at-arms sent by the king who had stopped for that selfsame cold supper before riding on. They stared at Liath when the young watchman led her and Sanglant into the longhouse of his mother, a woman called Hilda. The householder was eager to serve a royal prince. She fed them with roasted chicken, greens, baked turnips, and a piece of honey cake.

"There are two other things we need from you this night," said Sanglant when he had finished his cup of ale. "A bed." Some of the men-at-arms gulped down laughter—but he heard no ridicule, only sympathetic amusement. He recognized all of these men as soldiers who had followed his command at the battle outside Gent. "And your witness, Mistress Hilda, together with that of these men."

They waited expectantly. Mistress Hilda made a gesture for her son to fill the cups again, and the rest of her household huddled among the shadows under the interior eaves to listen.

Liath had spoken no word since the first riders had caught up with them, but she stood now, hand trembling slightly as she took hold of the wooden cup. He stood hastily beside her, taut, like a hound held to a tight leash. "With these folk as my witness, I thee pledge—" She stumbled, tried again, this time looking at him, holding his gaze. "I freely state my intention before God and these witnesses to bind myself in marriage with this man, given by his mother the name of Sanglant."

He did not stumble, but only because he simply repeated her words. "I freely state my intention before God and these witnesses to bind myself in marriage with this woman, given by her father the name of Liathano."

"I so witness," said Mistress Hilda in a carrying voice.

"I so witness," mumbled the poor soldiers, who well knew they would be called to explain the whole thing once they had returned to court.

Then everyone drained their cups and there came one of those awkward pauses while everyone waited for someone else to make the first move.

Mistress Hilda acted first. She made such a great fuss about surrendering the use of her best bed that Sanglant would have laughed if he hadn't been so damned nervous. No doubt once word spread that a king's son had spent his wedding night there many a villager would offer a basket of their best fruit, a prize chicken, or several plump partridges for the privilege of letting their own sons or daughters spend their wedding night in that same bed in the hope that some portion of the king's luck and fertility would rub off.

The bed, built under the low slanting roof, boasted a luxurious feather mattress and a good stout curtain that could be drawn closed around it. Mistress Hilda herself chased off the two whippets curled up at the foot of the mattress. While a daughter shook out the blankets outside, the householder made a valiant attempt to brush out fleas and bugs. Then she herded the soldiers down to the empty half of the longhouse where, during the winter, the family stabled their livestock.

One lantern still burned, and the longhouse doors, thrown open to admit the breeze, allowed a pearlescent gleam of moonlight to gild the darkest confines of the longhouse. Mistress Hilda made much of escorting them to the bed and drew the curtains shut behind them. With curtains drawn it was astoundingly black; he could not see at all. The air within was stuffy. Liath sat next to him. She did not move, nor did he. He was inordinately pleased with his self-control. He sat there, thinking that he ought to unwrap his sandals and leggings. Sweat prickled on his neck and a few beads of sweat trickled down his back. The bed still smelled of dog, and of the wool stored under the bed. Outside, where he had staked them, the Eika dogs barked, then settled down.

"Sanglant," she whispered. She let out a sigh, and he almost lost himself. But he did not move. He was afraid to move.

But she moved. Her fingers touched his cheek, the old remembered gesture from the crypt in the cathedral of Gent, then wandered to his ear and finally down to his neck, where she traced the rough surface of the slave collar around to its clasp.

"I swore that I would never love any man but you." Her voice was tense with amazement. Without asking permission, she found the cunning mechanism that clasped the collar closed. Without chains locking it closed, it was easy for her to undo it. That quickly, she eased it off, then hissed between her teeth as she gently touched the skin beneath. He hissed, too, in pain; it was very tender. She leaned forward to kiss him at the base of his throat, over the scar from the wound that had ruined his voice, taken four years ago—or was it five? Her lips burned as if with fire, but it was very hot within the curtains. Indeed, the only way to be at all comfortable was to take off his clothes—although in such a confined space, and with her fumbling at her own next to him in such a distracting manner, it was not an easy task.

She brushed him, naked now, her skin hot to the touch, and he most willingly lay down beside her although it took incredible strength of will not simply to have the matter done with in an instant—all the time it would no doubt take him—and be relieved however briefly of this horrible pressure of arousal.

She had no such strength of will, or considered it unnecessary. What passed next went rather faster than he would have wished, but he did not disgrace himself; his prayers did not go in vain, for the Lord watched over him and he managed to get through it as a man would, not losing control like a dog.

"Ai, Lady," she whispered urgently, as if the strength of her passion scared her. "I'll burn everything down." He closed his arms around her, to be a shield against that fear. With her face pressed sideways against his neck she spoke in a slow murmur. "I'm not—I'm not what I seem. You felt it before. Da hid it from me, locked it away—"

This close, with her pressed bodily against him and nothing between them, *nothing,* he finally understood what it was that stirred there, inchoate, restless, almost like a second being trapped within her skin.

Fire.

"You're like me," he said, and heard how the hoarseness in his voice made him sound astonished. As indeed he was.

"What do you mean?" She pushed up, weight shifting, and looked down at him, although she couldn't possibly see him in this darkness.

He chose his words slowly, to be precise. "There's more than human blood in you."

"Aoi blood?" She sounded stunned.

"Nay, I know the scent of Aoi blood, and it isn't that. It's nothing I recognize."

"Lady have mercy." She collapsed so hard on top of him that he grunted, all the breath forced out of his chest.

For a long while he spun in an oblivion of contentment, simply lost track of anything except the actual physical contact between them, her breath on his cheek, her unbound hair spilling

over his shoulders, her weight on his hip and chest, the sticky
contact of their skin. He might have lain there for the space of
ten breaths or a thousand. He simply existed together with her,
nothing more, nothing less, they alone in the whole wide world
all that mattered.

She said into the silence: "You still have the book."

"I do. Did you intend to leave it with me all along?"

"It all happened so fast. I didn't know what to do." She wiggled to blow on his neck, as if her breath would heal the ring
of chafed skin that was now all that remained to remind him of
his slavery. "Do you know what is in that book?"

"No."

"My father was a mathematicus, a sorcerer. I suspect he was
thrown out of the church before of it, before he married my
mother—who was also a sorcerer—and they had me. That book
contains his compilation of all learning on the art of the mathematici that he could find—" She hesitated, again touched the
scar at his throat.

He waited. She seemed to expect something from him.

"That doesn't trouble you?" she demanded finally.

"Ought it to?"

"That isn't all." He heard a hint of annoyance in her voice—
that he hadn't responded as she expected him to—and he grinned.
Her eyes sparked in the blackness with a flicker of blue fire.
From beyond the curtains he heard snoring, a child's cough, the
restless whining of a dog, and the faint pop of a log shifting on
the outdoor hearth fire, banked down for the night. "What Hugh
said about me is true. It's true he wanted me for the knowledge
he thought I had, but that wasn't all. He knew all along. He still
knows there's something more. When we return to court, he
won't give up trying to get me back." Her voice caught. "Do
you despise me for what I was to him?"

"Can you possibly believe that after Gent I would judge you?
Easier for you to despise me for becoming no better than a
dog." He could not help himself. The growl that emerged from
his throat came unbidden and unwanted; he could not control
this vestige of his time among the dogs, and he hated himself
for it.

"Hush," she said matter-of-factly, pressing her finger to his
throat again. "You no longer wear Bloodheart's slave collar."

"And you no longer wear Hugh's," he retorted. "I tire of

Hugh. Whatever power he may still have over you, he has none over me."

"Do you think not? He tried to murder Theophanu!"

He sat up abruptly. "Not so loud," he whispered. "What do you mean?" Her education had given her the ability to recount a tale succinctly and with all necessary details intact. She told him now of the incident in the forest where Theophanu had been mistaken for a deer; then, haltingly at first but when he made no horrified reaction more confidently, told him of the vision seen through fire of Theophanu burning with fever and of the panther brooch that Mother Rothgard had proclaimed a ligatura wrought by a maleficus—that of a sorcerer determined only to advance his own selfish desires.

She had slid a little away from him during the telling, although the bed sagged heavily between them. It was easy enough to take hold of her shoulder and gently pull her into him. He could not get enough of the simple touch of her—but he must pursue this other line of thought, not allow himself to be distracted by her body.

"If Hugh has practiced sorcery, then what other weapon do I need against him as long as he knows I can make such an accusation? But you must tell me what else you have done, if there is more to tell."

At once, he felt her pull away from him—not bodily, but in an intangible way, a sudden retraction of the bond between them. "W-why?"

"So that we can be prepared. So that we can plan our tactics. It isn't just Hugh's interest you've attracted. Ai, Lord! I have never trusted Wolfhere, though I don't dislike him."

"Even after—?"

He smiled. "It is hard to hate a man for a deed you don't remember and were only told about. He has never attempted to harm me that I recall, only plagued me with his endless accusations about a 'crown of stars' and some kind of unfathomable plot fashioned by my mother and her kin. But now it seems clear why he is interested in you, if it's true you're the child of sorcerers. Does he know everything about you?"

"Not everything," she admitted. "I can't trust him, even though he freed me from Hugh. But I don't dislike him. Yet whom can I trust? Who will not condemn me for what I am? Who will not call me a maleficus?"

"I will not condemn you."

"Will you not?" she asked bitterly, and she told him about the burning of the palace at Augensburg. "That isn't all. While riding to Lavas, I burned down a bridge in the same way. I saw the shades of dead elves hunting in the deep forest. I've spoken with an Aoi sorcerer, who offered to teach me. I've been stalked by daimones. One of them was as beautiful as an angel but a monster nevertheless for having no soul. You could see that in its eyes. It called for me in a terrible voice, but it passed right by and couldn't see me though I sat in plain sight. I was too terrified to move. Ai, Lady! I don't know what I am. I don't know what Da hid from me!"

"Hush." He pressed a finger to her lips to silence her helpless fury. "But Wolfhere is right: You need teaching."

"Who on this earth will teach such as me without condemning me? Without sending me to the skopos to stand trial as a maleficus?"

"Your mother?"

"Wolfhere wouldn't tell me where she is. I don't trust his secrecy."

"Nor should you."

"And I don't know—I just don't know— It seems so odd for this news to come now, after Da and I struggled so many years alone."

"Then we must find out who can teach you without condemning you. You're like a boy who is quick and strong and gifted, who's taken up a sword but has had no training. He is as likely to hurt himself and his comrades as fell his enemies."

"Sanglant," she said softly, "why aren't you afraid of me? Everyone else seems to be!" Her hand wandered to splay itself across his left shoulder blade. He became overpoweringly aware of every part of her, all that was soft, all that was hard, pressed against him.

The absurdity of it made him laugh. "What more can you do to me that you haven't already done? I am at your mercy. Thank God!"

He literally felt indignation shudder through her. He understood at once that she did not know how to be laughed at. But even after that year among the dogs, he remembered something of the intricate dance eternally played out between female and male. There are places a woman's indignation can be taken, and he knew how to get there.

3

LIATH woke with a strange sensation suffusing her chest and limbs. Sanglant slept beside her, touching her only where an ankle crossed hers, weighting it down. In fact it was too stifling within the curtained bed to press together. She had no cover drawn over her, yet even so, something lay on her so calming that the sweat and stuffy heat did not bother her. It took her a long while, lying completely still so as not to scare it away, to identify what it was.

Peace.

Thunder rumbled in the distance. A rooster crowed outside. A flea crawled up her arm and she pinched it between two fingers.

Sanglant bolted upright, arms raised defensively, and almost hit her as he growled. "I can't see!" he hissed desperately.

"You aren't in Gent."

"Liath?" He sounded more astonished than pleased. He groped, caught her, and hugged her against him so tightly that she choked out a breath. "Ai, God! You're real."

"What did you think I was?"

He was weeping. "I dreamed of you so often in Gent, I forgot what was dream and what was real, and then I would wake up. Ai, Lady. That was when it was worst, when I would wake up to discover I was still Bloodheart's prisoner."

"Hush," she said, kissing him. "You're free."

He only shook his head. He rocked back and forth, unable to keep still, but with her still clasped in his arms. Then, as suddenly as he had begun, he ceased and lifted his face to look at her. Light seeped in where wooden rings fastened the curtain to rods attached to the ceiling; she saw his expression as a gray mask, bewildered, joyous, determined.

"Make no marriage, Liath," he whispered, echoing words he

had said to her a long time ago, before the fall of Gent. Then
he smiled. "Unless it be with me."

"Foolhardy," she murmured.

"What is?"

"This. Marrying."

His voice sharpened. "Do you regret it already?"

She laughed. It was spectacularly disconcerting to have this
need consume her. She just could not keep her hands off him.
"Oh, no. No. Never." It was a different kind of fire, just as intense but more satisfying. He did not try to resist her even knowing that the village woke beyond the curtains as a new day began,
but he was far more restrained than she was—although now and
again he would forget himself and nip.

They did, finally, have to dress. They could hear Mistress
Hilda and her household moving around, hear the soldiers moving restlessly outside the longhouse, talking and joking, although
no one dared disturb the two hidden behind the curtains. She
was embarrassed when they at last drew the curtains aside.
Sanglant did not seem aware of the stares, the whispers, the giggles, the jocular congratulations. He wound up his leggings and
laced up his sandals with intense concentration, obviously making plans. He took in a deep draught of air and held it, then
shook his head as a dog shakes off water.

"Nothing," he murmured. "I do not smell his scent here."

"Whose scent?"

"Bloodheart's." He belted on his sword. "Bloodheart laid a
curse as a protection against any person who sought to kill him.
Your hand drew the bow whose arrow struck him down."

Mistress Hilda bustled over with two cups of cider. As they
drained the cups, she surveyed the tangled bedcovers with satisfaction.

The bite of the cider cleared Liath's head. "A curse is woven
of magic," she said in a low voice, "and Da protected me against
magic. It can't harm me."

He swore. "Rash words!"

"I don't mean them to be! You didn't see the daimone stalk
past me, calling my name and yet not seeing me. That's not the
only time it happened."

"That you were protected from magic? What do you mean?"

"I suppose the way armor protects you from a sword blow.
It's as if I'm invisible to magic."

He considered this seriously. "Do you remember when Blood-heart died?"

She touched her quiver, propped up against the bed. "How could I forget it? When I first saw you—" She broke off, aware that her voice had risen. Everyone had turned to watch them: children, adults, slaves, even the soldiers who had crowded to the door as soon as they heard Sanglant's voice. It wasn't every day that such folk got to witness a royal marriage.

"Ah," said Sanglant, looking embarrassed—but she had a sudden feeling that it wasn't their audience that bothered him but the memory of Gent and the bestial condition in which she and Lavastine had found him. He headed for the door, and Liath hurried in his wake, not at all sure where he was going. But he was headed for the three Eika dogs, who barked and scrabbled to reach them as he approached. He cuffed them down, then retrieved the handsome reinforced pouch. Inside she saw *The Book of Secrets,* but he did not remove it; instead, he pulled out his gold torque, the sign of his royal kinship. He turned.

"This is all I have to give you. My morning gift to you."

The assembled audience gasped at the magnificence of the gift, although Liath knew that among the nobility such a piece of jewelry, while very fine in its own right, would be but one among many such gifts—except that only women and men born into the royal lineage had the right to wear a torque braided of solid gold.

"I can't—" she choked.

"I beg you," he whispered.

It was all he had.

She received it from him, then flushed, humiliated. "I have nothing to give you—" Nothing but the gifts given to her by Lavastine and Alain the day before, and to hand them over now seemed demeaning, to him, to her, and to the lords who had rewarded her. She glanced toward the waiting soldiers, and inspiration seized her. "But I will have, if you are willing to wait."

His laughter came sharp and bright on the morning air. "I have learned to be patient." He sobered, seeing the soldiers waiting, horses saddled, everyone ready to go, and the villagers waiting expectantly. Thunder rumbled again as rain spattered down on the dirt.

"What do I do, Liath?" he muttered. "I've nothing to gift them with for their night's hospitality. I can't just leave without giving them something. It would be a disgrace to my reputation—and my father's. Ai, God!" He winced, hid the expression, then abruptly unsheathed his knife and pried the jewels off the fine leather case in which he carried the book, muttering under his breath as he did so. "Wolfhere was right. I've nothing of my own. Everything comes at my father's sufferance."

She didn't know what to reply. She, too, had nothing—except the book, the horse, and her weapons. Yet in truth few people possessed so much. Still, would it have been wiser to go to her mother, who presumably had the means to feed and house and teach her?

Perhaps.

But as she watched Sanglant distribute this largesse—and jewels certainly impressed the villagers—she could not imagine any decision other than the one she had made last night.

They rode out of Ferse with the wind at their backs only to find that the ferryman wouldn't take them across the water. So they huddled under the trees while the storm moved through, brief but strong. Rain lashed the ground, pounding dirt into mud. Wind whipped the river into a surface of choppy waves. She used her blanket like a cloak to cover herself while Sanglant walked out in the full force of the rainstorm, heedless of the rain pouring over him. It drenched him until his hair lay slick along his head and his clothes stuck to him in a most inviting fashion. The fresh scar left by his slave collar stood out starkly against his dark skin.

"You left behind Bloodheart's collar," she said suddenly.

He mopped rain from his forehead and flicked a slick mat of hair out of his eyes. "The villagers will make use of it." Then he grinned, the familiar charming smile she had first seen at Gent. At once he began bantering with the soldiers who, like Liath, huddled under the tree in the vain hope of staying dry. He soon had them laughing—*eating out of his hand,* as Da had once said years ago when they had watched an Andallan captain-at-arms ready his men to march into battle—and the delay passed remarkably swiftly.

With all the horses, it took six trips to get them over on the ferry, and even then seven of the horses balked at getting on board the rocking ferry and had to be let swim across. Sanglant and two of the soldiers stripped to go in with the horses, and Liath had to look away with her face burning while she listened to their companions, now unable to restrain themselves, making jests about wedding nights and "riding" and other coarse jokes.

"I pray you," said Sanglant sternly when he rejoined them, "do not make light of the marriage bed, or my bride, who will have a difficult enough time at the king's court as it is." They looked a little shamefaced, but he soon pried them out of it by asking each man about his home and family and what battles he had fought in.

Mud and a second squall made for slow going, and Sanglant seemed in no hurry to return. Nor was she. The farther they rode the more nervous she got. But nevertheless they came within sight of Werlida by midafternoon. Even from the road beneath the ramparts it seemed a veritable hive of activity—more so than when she had left.

At the gates, guards greeted them. "Prince Sanglant, you have returned!" They looked relieved.

"What's all this?" Sanglant gestured toward the lower enclosure, which was bustling with movement. Just ahead a herd of squealing pigs had been confined in a fenced enclosure from which they were now being removed one by one to be slaughtered.

"They rode in not one hour before you, my lord prince!" exclaimed the guards.

"Who did?"

A horn blasted from the road behind, and two dozen riders wearing the sigil of a hawk galloped up behind them, looking irritated to be kept waiting—until they recognized the prince.

Sanglant began to laugh. "Lady Fortune is with us this day. My father will be far too busy to remember me!"

The hawk: symbol of the duchy of Wayland.

Duke Conrad had arrived at last.

4

DUKE Conrad had arrived at last.

King Henry was in a foul mood, furious about Sanglant's disappearance. Rosvita feared it would bode ill for Conrad when

Henry, upon being told the news that the duke of Wayland would arrive soon after Nones, smiled grimly. He went at once to pray and refused to break his fast at midday, since it was his habit to honor God in this way before wearing the crown.

"Will there be some kind of ceremony?" asked young Brother Constantine, who had only seen the king crowned and robed in splendor once, at Quedlinhame.

Brother Fortunatus shook his head. "He means to show his displeasure by meeting Conrad in full royal dignity." He clicked his tongue softly. "Poor Conrad."

"Poor Conrad!" objected Sister Amabilia. "Do you suppose Duke Conrad is a fool? I don't think he is."

And indeed, Conrad the Black was no fool. He rode in at the head of a magnificent procession, befitting his dignity and his rank, and beside him in the place of honor—and on a very fine white mare—rode Princess Theophanu fitted out in equally fine clothing, obviously a gift from him. She looked at her ease, handsome, vigorous, and elegant in her composure—thank God!

Only now, seeing her, did Rosvita realize how deeply she had missed her composed and sometimes ironic presence over the past months.

Because of the uproar surrounding Sanglant, Rosvita had only that morning discovered among the capitularies sent from the schola the letter from Mother Rothgard and its terrifying contents: malefici—malevolent sorcerers—lurking in the court! Mother Rothgard named no names, and perhaps knew none since she had written the letter while Theophanu was still gravely ill, but Rosvita had recognized the panther brooch sketched onto the parchment. Only the margraviate of Austra and Olsatia displayed a panther as part of its sigil.

"*This is a matter for the church,*" Mother Rothgard had written after detailing her suspicions and what manner of instruments and bindings a maleficus would have hidden about her person. "*Speak to no one until my representative, a certain Sister Anne whose integrity and knowledge are irreproachable, reaches you. Without her aid, and with no experience in these matters, you will not be able to defeat the maleficus, and will indeed be at her mercy. Once you have the support of Sister Anne, then together you must decide what action to take, if indeed you can flush the maleficus from its lair. This is not a matter for the king's justice.*"

She dared not show the letter even to Amabilia or Fortunatus. Now she had to wait until the audience had finished, when
she could hope to speak privately with Theophanu.

The king received Duke Conrad in kingly state, crowned, with
scepter in hand and his entire court in attendance. The yard in
front of the great hall was mobbed with people; the king had
had his throne brought outside and raised up on a hastily-built
platform. To his right sat Princess Sapientia, the only person so
honored among the company.

Into this assembly Duke Conrad rode with all the pride of a
prince born into the royal kinship. He had a nobleman's seat on
a horse, easy and natural, and a soldier's broad shoulders and
tough hands. He was a good-looking man, striking in appearance, with all the vitality of a man in his prime—he was not
over thirty years of age. Conrad's dark complexion and black
hair were indeed startling, but he had keen blue eyes and a
wicked grin, which he used now to swift effect on Princess Theophanu as they halted before the king. Rosvita found him rather
more to her taste than young Baldwin, who was all beauty and
no stature. A servant supported his foot as he dismounted. He
himself assisted Theophanu to dismount.

"Your Majesty." He did not kneel. After all, he wore the gold
torque—in handsome contrast to his smoky-brown complexion—
around his neck to mark his royal kinship. "I give you greetings, cousin, and I bring these gifts to honor you, and I bring
as well your daughter, who has ridden beside me from St. Valeria Convent."

Henry gestured to a servant, and a chair was squeezed in to
the left of his throne. Theophanu climbed the two steps to the
platform and knelt before her father to receive his blessing and
his kiss. Then, coolly, she kissed Sapientia on either cheek, and
sat down. She had not changed in outward appearance, except
perhaps for a flush in her cheeks when she glanced at Conrad;
after that, she kept her gaze fixed on the horizon where forest
met sky in a haze. Seeing her so healthy, it was hard to believe
that she had almost died at St. Valeria Convent of a fever brought
upon her by magic most foul. Yet Mother Rothgard had no reason to lie.

Conrad waited until she was seated, then made a sign to his
retinue. Servants came forward with boxes and chests. The display took some time, all of it artfully handled with clasps un-

done, cloth unwrapped and wafted aside, fine tapestries unrolled to reveal more precious treasures inside. Conrad had not stinted in his offerings: carved ivory plaques; gold vessels; a dozen finely-crafted saddles; glass pitchers packed in wood shavings; tiny cloisonne pots filled with spices; silver basins so cunningly worked that entire scenes from old tales could be read on their sides; and two delightful creatures he called *monkeys* that chittered excitedly and gamboled in a large cage.

Henry regarded this munificence without expression. When Conrad had finished, Henry merely raised a hand for silence. The assembly, whispering and jostling the better to see, quieted expectantly.

"Is this how you hope to expiate your treachery?"

Conrad's nostrils flared, and his shoulders stiffened. "I didn't join Sabella!"

"You didn't join *me*!"

He regained his composure. "Yet I am here now, cousin."

"So you are. What am I to make of your appearance? Why did you turn my Eagle back at your border, in the Alfar Mountains? Why have you troubled my brother Benedict and Queen Marozia of Karrone with your disputes? Why did you not support me against the Eika, and against Sabella's unlawful rebellion against my authority?"

For an instant Rosvita thought Conrad would turn around right then, mount, and ride off in a rage. Unexpectedly, Father Hugh stepped forward from his place in the front ranks, near Sapientia's chair, and placed himself between the two men.

"Your Majesty," he began, "let me with these poor words humbly beg you and your noble cousin to feast together, for as the blessed Daisan once said, 'The measure you give is the measure you will receive.' Greet your kin with wine and food. It is better to enter into a dispute on a full stomach than an empty one, for a hungry woman will feed on angry words while she who has eaten of the feast provided by God will know how to set aside anger for conciliation."

He was right, of course. She took a step forward to add her voice to his.

"What better conciliation," said Conrad suddenly, "than a betrothal feast? Give us only your blessing, cousin, and your daughter Theophanu and I will speak our consent to be wed."

Henry rose slowly. Rosvita caught in her breath and waited.

Rashly suggested! What did Conrad hope to gain from such bluntness?

But Henry said nothing of marriage. He descended the steps with kingly dignity and raised an arm to clasp Conrad's in cousinly affection. "The news came to us only two days ago, and it was received with many tears. Let us have peace between us, cousin, while we mourn the passing of Lady Eadgifu."

Conrad wept manfully, and with evident sincerity. "We must put our trust in God, They who rule over all things. She was the best of women."

Now many sighs and groans arose from the assembly, both from those who had known the Lady Eadgifu and those whose hearts were touched by the sorrow shown by duke and king. Rosvita could not help but shed a few tears, although she had met the Alban princess on only three occasions, and mostly remembered her because her fair hair and ivory-light skin had contrasted handsomely with the black hair and dusky complexion of her husband; on first arriving from Alba, Eadgifu had spoken Wendish poorly and therefore refrained from speaking much except to her Alban retinue.

One woman among the assembly was not weeping: Theophanu. She had lowered her gaze but under those heavy, dark lids—so like Queen Sophia's—she examined Father Hugh. Her expression had the placid innocence of a holy mosaic, pieced together out of colored stone, and not even Rosvita, who knew her as well as anyone, could tell what she was thinking. Did she want to marry Conrad? Did she still hoard her infatuation for Father Hugh? Did she know the name of the maleficus who had tried to kill her?

Hugh had taken a book of forbidden magic from the young Eagle, Liath. Was it only coincidence that the unnamed magus had attempted to sicken Theophanu through the agency of a ligatura woven into a brooch shaped as a panther?

"Make way! Make way!"

Henry dropped Conrad's arm as a small procession appeared. Everyone began to talk at once, pointing and whispering. The king stepped back up onto the first of the two steps that mounted the platform, but there he paused, waiting, and Duke Conrad turned and with a surprised expression moved aside to make room.

"Your Majesty." Prince Sanglant pulled up his horse at a re-

spectful distance from the throne. He looked travel-worn and unkempt with his rich tunic damp from rain and his hair uncombed,
but by some indefinable air he wore as always the mantle of authority. But the Eika dogs that trailed at his heels reminded everyone of what he had been—and what he still harbored within
himself. He made a sign, and his escort of a dozen soldiers and
two servingmen turned aside and dismounted.

There was one other person with them: a dark young woman
with a regal air and a look of tense hauteur, held distant from
the crowd that surrounded her. It took Rosvita a moment to recognize her, although it should not have. What on God's earth
was the Eagle—as good as banished yesterday together with
Wolfhere—doing with him? Or was she still an Eagle? She no
longer wore badge or cloak, although she rode a very fine gray
gelding.

Prince Sanglant was not a subtle man. Liath glanced toward
him, and he reached to touch her on the elbow. The glance, the
movement, the touch: these spoke as eloquently as words.

"What means this?" demanded Henry.

But every soul there knew what it meant: Sanglant, the obedient son, had defied his father.

Rosvita knew well the signs of Henry's wrath; he wore them
now: the tic in his upper lip, the stark lightning glare in his eyes,
the threatening way he rested his royal staff on his forearm as
if in preparation for a sharp blow. She stepped forward in the
hope of turning his anger aside, but Hugh had already moved
to place himself before the king.

"I beg you, Your Majesty." His expression was smooth but
his hands were trembling. "She no longer wears the Eagle's
badge that marks her as in your service. Therefore, she is now
by right—*and your judgment*—my slave."

"She is my wife," said Sanglant suddenly. His hoarse tenor,
accustomed to the battlefield, carried easily over the noise of
the throng. Everyone burst into exclamations at once, and after
a furious but short-lived uproar, the assembly like a huge beast
quieted, the better to hear. Even the king's favorite poet or a
juggling troupe from Aosta did not provide as thrilling an entertainment as this.

The prince dismounted and everyone stared as he hammered
an iron stake into the ground and staked down the dogs. From
their savage presence all shrank back as the prince walked for-

ward to stand before his father. Clouds covered the sun, and rain
spattered the crowd, enough to keep the dust down and to wet
tongues made dry by anticipation.

"She is my wife," Sanglant repeated, "by mutual consent, witnessed by these soldiers and a freewoman of Ferse village, and
made legal and binding by the act of consummation and by the
exchange of morning gifts."

" 'Let the children be satisfied first,' " said Hugh in a low,
furious voice. She had never before seen him lose his composure, but he was shaking visibly now, flushed and agitated. " 'It
is not fair to take the children's bread and throw it to the dogs.' "

"Hugh," warned his mother from her place near the king.

Abruptly, Liath replied in a bold and angry voice. " 'Even
the dogs under the table eat the children's scraps.' "

Hugh looked as if he had been slapped. He bolted toward
her. That fast, and more smoothly than Rosvita believed possible, Sanglant stepped between them, and Hugh actually bumped
up against him. But to go around the prince would be to make
a fool of himself. Even so he hesitated, as if actually contemplating fighting it out hand to hand, the gracious cleric and the
half-wild prince.

"I did not give my permission for you to marry," said Henry.

"I did not ask permission to marry, nor need I do so, since
I am of age, and of free birth."

"*She* is not free," retorted Hugh, recovering his composure
so completely that she might have dreamed that flash of rage.
"She is either in the king's service, and thus needs his permission to marry, or she is my slave. As a slave, she has no right
to marry a man of free birth—much less, my lord prince," he
added, with a humble bow, "a man of your exalted rank and
birth." He turned back to the king. "Yet I would not dare to pass
judgment when we must bow before your wisdom, Your
Majesty."

"I gave her a choice." Henry gestured toward the young
woman. "Did I not give that choice, Eagle? Have you forsaken
my service and thus rebelled against my rightful authority?"

She blanched.

"Let me speak," said Sanglant.

"Sanglant," she murmured, as softly as a person caught in
the whirlpool whispers with her last breath before she goes under.
"Do not—"

"Sanglant." The king uttered his name with that same tone of warning with which Margrave Judith had moments before spoken her own son's name.

"I will speak! The blessed Daisan said that it is not the things that go into a man from outside that defile him but the things that come out of him that defile him. Look upon him, whom you all admire and love, who is charming and elegant and handsome. Yet out of this man's heart come evil thoughts, acts of fornication forced upon a helpless woman, theft, murder, ruthless greed and malice, fraud, indecency for a man sworn to the church to cohabit with a woman, envy, slander, arrogance—and with his hands and his fine manners he has blinded you all with *sorcery*—"

Theophanu started up out of her chair.

Margrave Judith strode forward, flushed with anger. "I will not stand by quietly while my son is insulted and abused—"

"Silence!" roared the king. "How dare you question my judgment in this way, Sanglant!"

"Nay, Your Majesty," said Hugh with humble amiability, grave and patient. "Let him speak. Everything Prince Sanglant says is true, for I am sure that he hates lying and loves me. Who among us is worthy? I know only too well that I am a sinner. None censures me more than I do myself, for I have often failed in my service toward my king, and toward God."

Did Hugh say one thing more to Sanglant? His lips moved, but Rosvita could not hear—

Sanglant growled in rage and struck in fury: He hit the unresisting Hugh so hard backhanded that Hugh crumpled to the ground, teeth cracking, and before anyone else could move Sanglant dove for him like a dog leaping for the kill. The Eika dogs went wild, yammering and tugging on their chains as they dragged the stake out of the dirt and bolted forward.

People screamed and stumbled back. Liath flung herself off her horse and grabbed for the chains, getting brief hold of the stake before it was yanked out of her hands. Rosvita was too shocked to move while all around her the court scattered—all but Judith, who unsheathed her knife to defend her son. All but the king himself, who bellowed Sanglant's name and jumped forward to grab him by the back of the tunic to haul him off Hugh.

The dogs hit Henry with the full force of their charge.

Rosvita shrieked. She heard it as from a distance, unaware

she could utter such a terrible sound. Someone tugged frantically at her robe. Sanglant beat back the dogs in a frenzy, away
from his father, and behind him Liath shouted a warning to Villam—who had dashed forward to the king—while she scrabbled
in the dirt for the hammer and grasped the stake, trying to drag
back on the chains. Lions charged in. They clubbed down the
dogs, braved their fierce jaws to grab their legs and drag them
off the king, and hacked at them mercilessly until blood spattered the ground like rain.

Pity stabbed briefly, vanished as Sanglant emerged from the
maelstrom with Henry supported in his arms. Ai, God! The king
was injured! She hurried to his side, vaguely aware of three attendants pressed close behind her: her clerics, who had not deserted her.

Sanglant thrust Henry into the arms of the princesses and
plunged back in the fray.

"Down!" His voice rang out above everything else. "Hold!
Withdraw!"

The Lions obeyed. How could they not? The prince knew
how to command in battle. They withdrew cautiously, and he
knelt beside the dogs.

Rosvita knelt beside the king, who had a weeping tear in his
left arm, cloth mangled and stained with saliva and blood, threads
shredded into skin. Claws had ripped the tunic along his back,
too, but mercifully the thick royal robe had protected him from
all but a shallow scratch. He shook off the shock of the impact
and pushed himself upright. "Your Majesty!" she protested.

"Nay!" He shook off all who ran to assist him, even his
daughters, as he limped forward.

"Your Majesty!" cried Villam, and a dozen others, as he approached Sanglant and the dogs, but he did not heed them.

One of the dogs was dead. As Henry halted beside him, Sanglant
took out his knife and cut the throat of the second, so badly hacked
that it could not possibly survive. The third whimpered softly and
rolled to bare its throat to the prince. He stared into its yellow
eyes. Blood dripped from its fangs; dust and the vile greenish blood
born of its own foul body smeared its iron-gray coat.

"Kill it," said Henry in a voice made dull by rage.

Sanglant looked up at him, glanced at Liath, who stood holding the iron stake in a bloodied hand . . . then sheathed the knife.

The shock of Sanglant's defiance hit Henry harder than the

dogs had. He staggered, caught himself on Villam, who got under
his arm just in time to steady him. Rosvita's mind seemed to be
working at a pace so sluggish that not until this moment did she
register Father Hugh, who had somehow gotten out of range and
now, supported by his mother, spit bits of tooth onto the ground.
Blood stained his lips, and his right cheek had the red bloom of
a terrible bruise making ready to flower.

"I will retire to my chamber," said Henry, so far gone in
wrath that all the heat had boiled off to make a fearsomely cold
rage beneath. "There, he will be brought to meet my judgment."

Villam helped him away. Servingmen swarmed around them.

Rosvita knew she ought to follow, but she could not make her
legs work. She stared at the assembly as they parted to make way
for the king, dissolved into their constituent groups to slip away
and plot in private over the upheaval sure to follow. Images caught
and burned into her mind: Duke Conrad staying Princess Theophanu with a hand lightly touching her elbow, a comment exchanged, the shake of her head in negation, his eyes narrowing
as he frowned and stepped back from her to let her by when she
walked after her father; Sapientia flushed red with anger and humiliation, taking the arm of her young Eagle and turning deliberately away from Hugh as if to make clear that he had fallen
into disfavor; Judith with her lips pressed tight in a foreboding
glower; Ivar trying to break through the crowd to get to Liath but
being hopelessly caught up in the tide that washed him away from
her and then held back bodily by young Baldwin.

"Sister!" whispered Amabilia. Fortunatus had hold of her right
arm, whether to support her or himself she could not tell. Constantine wept quietly. "Come, Sister, let us withdraw."

Everyone, eddying, swirled away to leave at last several dozen
soldiers, two dead dogs and an injured one, the bride, and the
prince amid a spray of blood. Left alone, abandoned even by
those who had championed him before.

This was the price of the king's displeasure.

V
THE GENTLE BREATH
OF GOD

1

IN an odd way, the disaster only made her more stubbornly resolute. She stood beside one of the dead dogs, and as its copperish blood leached away into the dirt, she felt a desperate obstinance swell in her heart as if the creature's heart's blood, soaking into the earth, made a transference of substance up through her feet to harden her own.

She was not going to let the king take Sanglant away from her.

Sanglant looked to see if anyone remained. It was worse even than she expected: everyone had abandoned them except for a dozen Lions and the soldiers who had escorted them from Ferse.

Now the captain of these men stepped forward. "My lord prince. We will gladly help you with the dogs. Then we must take you before the king, at his order."

"Bury them," said Sanglant. "I doubt if they'll burn." He got his arms under the injured dog, hoisted it, and lugged it to the chamber set aside for his use. Lions fanned out to give him room to walk. The courtyard had emptied except for servants, who whispered, staring, and fluttered away. Dust spun around the corners of buildings. She smelled pork roasting over fires. A sheep bleated. Distant thunder growled and faded.

"Eagle!" whispered one of the Lions as they halted before the door while Sanglant carried the limp dog over the threshold. She recognized her old comrade, Thiadbold; his scar stood stark white against tanned skin. "I beg your pardon!"

"Call me Liath, I beg you, friend." She was desperate for friends. That Sanglant's own loyal dogs had set upon the king . . .

"Liath," Thiadbold glanced toward the door, which still yawned open. From within she heard Sanglant grunt as he got the dog down to the floor. "We Lions have not forgotten. If there is aught we can do to aid you, we will, as long as it does not go against our oath to the king."

Tears stung at his unexpected kindness. "I thank you," she said stiffly. "Please see that my horse is stabled, if you will." Then she remembered Ferse and the morning gift. "There is one thing. . . ." She had only finished explaining it when Sanglant called to her.

The Lion nodded gravely. "It is little enough to do for him." She went inside.

"Have we no servants available to us?" Sanglant asked her.

"Only the soldiers set on guard."

He knelt beside the dog, which lay silent at the foot of the bed as at the approach of an expected kindness—or of death. It did not move as he ran his hands along its body to probe its injuries: a smashed paw, a slashed foreleg, a deep wound to the ribs and another to the head that had shorn off one ear. Its shallow panting, the grotesque tongue lolling out, was as quiet as a baby's breath. She had never been this close to an Eika dog before. She shuddered.

He smiled grimly. "Best that we save this one, since it's all that remains of my retinue." He drew from the collar the short chain affixed to the leather pouch, now scarred where gems had been pried off. "It guarded your book most faithfully."

Despite his disgrace, the soldiers had not deserted Sanglant. Their captain, Fulk, brought him water in a basin together with an old cloth which he tore into strips to bind up the dog's wounds. She tidied her clothing, unbelted sword and quiver and bow and laid them beside the bed with rest of her gear. She dared not approach the king wearing arms. When Sanglant finished with the dog, and she had taken a draught of wine for her parched throat and reminded him to straighten up his own tunic so he should not appear completely disreputable, the soldiers escorted them to the king's audience chamber. It was not far, because the king had given Sanglant a chamber in one wing of his own residence.

They found the king seated on a couch with his arm bandaged and his expression severe. Sapientia sat at his right hand, Theophanu at his left. He dismissed all of his attendants except for Helmut Villam, Sister Rosvita, and Hathui. Liath caught a glimpse of Hanna, face drawn tight with fear, before she vanished with the others. A half-dozen stewards remained.

Liath knelt. But her hands were steady. Sanglant hesitated, but then, slowly, he knelt also: supplicant before the king's displeasure.

"What did Hugh say to you?" Henry asked Sanglant in a perfectly collected voice.

The question surprised her, but Sanglant got a stubborn look on his face and set his mouth mulishly.

"What did he say to make you attack him in that way?" repeated the king, each word uttered so distinctly that they fell like stones.

Sanglant shut his eyes. " 'Do you cover her as a dog covers a bitch?' " He croaked out the words, his voice so harsh she could barely understand him. Then he buried his face in his hands in shame. And she burned.

An unlit candle set on the side table snapped into flame.

Henry started up in surprise, and Sapientia leaped up beside him and took hold of his elbow, to steady him. Villam murmured a prayer and drew the sign of the Circle at his breast. But Theophanu only glanced at the candle and then nodded to Rosvita, as if to answer a question. Hathui sighed softly from her station behind the king's couch.

"What is this, Sanglant?" demanded Henry. "A sign of your mother's blood at last?"

"Merely a trick, learned as a child and then forgotten," said Sanglant without looking at Liath.

"Nay," Liath said, although her voice shook. "I cannot let you shoulder the burden which is properly mine."

"Sorcery!" hissed Sapientia. "She's bewitched Hugh. That's why he's gone mad for her. Just like she's bewitched Sanglant."

"You're a fool, sister!" retorted Theophanu. "She saved my life. It's your beloved Hugh who is the maleficus!"

"Hush," said the king. He touched Sapientia on the arm and she let him go at once so that he could walk forward. The injury to his shoulder had not wounded the dignity of his gait. Frozen, Liath dared not move as he stopped in front of her and then circled her as a man does a caged leopard he means to slay. "Have you bewitched my son?"

"Nay, Your Majesty," she stammered, dry-eyed with terror.

"How can I believe you?"

"She has not—!" Sanglant began, head flung back.

"Silence! Or I will have you thrown out while I conduct this interview in your absence. Now. Speak."

The king could crush her flat in an instant, with the merest flick of his hand command his soldiers to kill her. "It's true I know some few of the arts of sorcery, as part of the education my father gave me," she began hesitantly, "but I'm untrained."

"Hah!" said Sapientia as she paced behind Henry's couch. Sanglant shifted where he knelt, as if he, too, wanted to pace.

"Go on," said the king without looking toward his daughter. His gaze, fixed so unerringly on Liath, made her wonder if perhaps it wasn't better just to get that spear through the guts and have done with it.

"My Da protected me against magic, that's all. He told me I'd never be a sorcerer." It all sounded very foolish. And dangerous.

"Her father was a mathematicus," said Rosvita suddenly. Ai, Lady: the voice of doom.

Henry snorted. "She arrived at my progress an avowed discipla of Wolfhere. It *is* a plot."

"Wolfhere didn't want her to leave," said Sanglant. "He argued against her leaving him, most furiously. He wanted her to stay with him."

"The better to fool you into taking her with you. And *marrying* her! A royal prince!"

"Nay, Father. Hear me out." Sanglant did rise now. Sapientia stopped pacing and with flushed cheeks studied her half brother. Theophanu, as cool as ever, had clasped her hands at her belt. Villam looked anxious, and Rosvita, who might be her best ally or her worst enemy, wore a grave expression indeed. "Hear me out, I beg you."

Henry hesitated, fingered the bandage that wrapped his arm. Oddly, he glanced back toward Hathui.

"I cannot know everything that is in Wolfhere's mind," Hathui said, as if in response to a spoken question. "I have no doubt he has seen and done much that I have never—and will never—hear about. But I do not think he ever intended Liath for any path but following him—and—" She glanced toward Sapientia, who had paused beside the window to run her fingers down the ridges of the closed shutters. "—to free her from Father Hugh."

Amazingly, Sapientia said nothing, appeared not even to hear the remark except that her tracing faltered, stopped, and began again.

At last, Henry nodded to Sanglant. "You may speak."

"You wouldn't have taken Gent without her aid. She killed Bloodheart."

"She? This one?"

"You did not hear the story from Lavastine?"

"She was under his command. What story is there to tell?"

"If you cannot believe me, then let Lavastine come before you and tell the tale."

"Lavastine was ensorcelled before," began Sapientia. "Why not again—?"

"He and his retinue left this morning," said Henry, cutting her off, "So his tale must be left untold."

"Count Lavastine has gone?" Now Sanglant paced to the door, and back, like a dog caught on a chain. Liath hissed his name softly, but he worried at his knuckles until Henry brought him up short by placing an open hand on his chest and stopping him. "I must ride after him—to warn him— If the curse does not follow her—" He faltered, came back to himself, and glanced around the room. "A messenger must be sent. You cannot begin to imagine Bloodheart's power."

"It was rumored that he was an enchanter," said Villam.

Sanglant laughed sourly. "No rumor. I myself witnessed—" He swiped at his face as if brushing away a swarm of gnats that no one else could see. "No use telling it. No use recalling it now, what he did to me."

That quickly, she saw Henry's face soften. But it was brief. He touched the bandage again, and his mouth set in a grim line. "There is much to explain."

Sanglant spun, took Liath by the elbow, and pulled her up.

She did not want to fight against that pull, but she also did not want to stand rather than kneel before the king. "Only someone with magic could have killed an enchanter as powerful as Bloodheart."

"Explain yourself."

"You know yourself he had powers of illusion, that he could make things appear in the air that had no true existence. Or perhaps you didn't see that. We saw it." He grimaced and turned to look at Liath. "She alone—Ai, Lord! Had I only listened to her at Gent, my Dragons would still be alive. But we let them in, we opened the gates, thinking they were our allies."

"Young Alain spoke of a curse," said Henry, "but I don't understand what you're trying to say."

"He had protected himself against death," Sanglant went on, not hearing the comment. "He had taken his heart out of his own body so that he could not be killed. He protected himself with some kind of grotesque creature that he kept in a chest. He spoke a curse at the end, but whether he released the creature I can't know. I didn't see it again. By all these means did Bloodheart protect himself." He turned to gesture toward her, and with that gesture everyone looked at her. "No man or woman acting alone could have killed Bloodheart. But *she* did."

The silence made Liath nervous. She stared at the couch, finest linen dyed a blood red and embroidered with a magnificent hunting scene in gold-and-silver thread: Henry, standing in front of her, obscured part of it, but she could see lions grappling with deer, and a stag bounding away in front of three riders while partridges flushed from cover.

"That is why a messenger must be sent to Count Lavastine," finished Sanglant. "If Bloodheart's vengeance doesn't stalk Liath, if she is somehow protected against magic by her father's spells, then it must be stalking Count Lavastine. Bloodheart's magic was powerful—"

"Bloodheart is dead," said Henry.

"Yet no harm can come," said Hathui suddenly, "in sending an Eagle to warn him, even if naught comes of it."

"It was the hound," said Sanglant. "The hound that died. It smelled of Bloodheart."

"What must we tell him?" asked Hathui. "How does one overcome such a curse?"

Sanglant looked helplessly at Liath, but she could only shrug.

In truth, like Henry, she didn't truly understand what he was talking about: Was this a madness brought on by his captivity, the months in chains he had spent at Bloodheart's feet? Or was he right? Did some terrible curse stalk her or, thwarted by Da's magic, stalk Lavastine instead?

"Send an Eagle," said Henry to Hathui, "telling everything you have learned here. Then return." She nodded and left quickly.

Henry touched his injured arm, winced—and caught Sanglant wincing at the same time, as if in sympathy, or guilt. Villam helped the king seat himself on the couch. Henry looked tired, but thoughtful.

"Others have noticed her," Henry said, studying Liath.

"Never be noticed." Da had been right all along: That way lay ruin. But it was too late now. She could have stayed with the Aoi sorcerer, but she had not. She could have ridden on with Wolfhere, but she had not. She could not undo what had been done.

And she did not want to, not even now.

"Count Lavastine would have taken her into his retinue, and he is no fool. Even my trusted cleric, Sister Rosvita, has taken an interest in her. No doubt others have as well." Villam coughed, then cleared his throat. "The church is right to control such powers," Henry mused, "yet they exist nevertheless. Given what you have seen, Sanglant . . ." He gestured, and the steward hurried forward with a cup of wine, which the king drank from and then offered, in turn, to his daughters, to Rosvita, and to Villam. "It may have seemed more advantageous to marry a woman connected with sorcery than one who shares a claim to the Aostan throne."

"Why should I care what advantage she brings me? She saved my life."

"By killing Bloodheart. You saw the worth of such power as she has."

"Nay." He flushed, a darker tone in his bronze complexion. In a low voice, he spoke quickly, as if he feared the words would condemn him. "I would have gone mad there in my chains if I hadn't had my memory of her to sustain me."

"Ah," said Villam in the tone of a man who has just seen and understood a miracle. He glanced at Liath, and she flushed, recalling the proposition he had made to her many months ago.

Henry looked pained, then rested head on hands, as if his

head ached. When he looked up, he frowned, brow furrowed. "Sanglant, folk of our station do not marry for pleasure or sentiment. That is what concubines are for. We marry for advantage. For alliance."

"How many times was it made clear to me that I was never to marry? That I could not be allowed to? Why should I have taken such a lesson to heart? *She* is the one I have married, and I have given my consent and sworn an oath before God. *You* cannot dissolve that oath."

"But I can judge whether she is free to marry at all. Father Hugh was right: As my servant, she must have my permission to marry. If she is not my servant, then she is his slave, and thus his to dispose of."

Sapientia groaned under her breath, like a woman mourning. Theophanu made a movement toward her, as though to comfort her, but Sapientia thrust her away and hid her face with a hand. Quickly, Sister Rosvita hurried over to her.

"We have not yet spoken of Father Hugh," sad Theophanu in a low voice, "and the accusations I have laid before you, Father. I have also brought with me—in writing—Mother Rothgard's testimony."

"I, too, have a letter from Mother Rothgard," said Rosvita. Sapientia was weeping softly on her shoulder. "Is there not a holy nun in your party, Your Highness?" she asked Theophanu. "One Sister Anne, by name, who has come to investigate these matters?"

Theophanu blinked, looking confused. "Sister Anne? She came with us from St. Valeria. A very wise and ancient woman, devout, and knowledgeable. Incorruptible. But she fell ill on the journey and had to be nursed in a cottage for several days. When she emerged, she always wore a veil because the sun hurt her eyes so. I will send for her."

"How do we know," sobbed Sapientia, "that it is not this Eagle who is the maleficus? If she has bound a spell onto Hugh—?" But her heart wasn't in it. Even she did not believe her own words. "God have mercy! That he should betray a preference for her, a common-born woman, and in front of everyone, and humiliate me by so doing!"

"Hush, Your Highness," said Rosvita softly. "All will be set right."

"I am not yet done with these two," said Henry. "But be assured that any accusation of malevolent sorcery in *my* court will be dealt with harshly should it prove unfounded, and more harshly yet should it prove true. Sanglant." He gestured, and Sanglant knelt beside Liath.

"Eagle." Liath flinched. The king had so completely recovered his composure that she felt more keenly the power he held over her. What soul, struggling to free itself from the eddy surrounding the dreaded Abyss, does not fear the gentle breath of God? With one puff of air They sweep damned souls irrevocably into the pit. "Liathano, so they call you. What do you have to say for yourself?"

She choked out the words. "I am at your mercy, Your Majesty."

"So you are. Why did you marry my son?"

She flushed, could look at no one, not even Sanglant, especially not Sanglant, because that would only recall too vividly the night they had passed so sweetly together. Instead, she fixed her gaze on the flagstone floor partly covered with a rug elaborately woven in imperial purple and pale ivory: the eight-pointed Arethousan star. "I—I swear to you, Your Majesty. I gave no thought to advantage. I just—" She faltered. "I—"

"Well," said Villam with a snort of laughter, "I fear me, my good friend Henry, that I see nothing here I have not seen a hundred times before. They are young and they are handsome and they are hungry for that with which the body feeds them."

"Is it only the young who think in this way, my good friend Helmut?" asked Henry with a laugh. "So be it. If there is threat in her beyond the sorcery her father evidently taught her and that others seek to exploit by gaining control of her, I do not see it. But."

But.

The word cut like a blade.

"I will not tolerate my son's disobedience. Naked he came into the world, and I clothed him. He walked, until I gave him a horse to ride. My captains trained him, and he bore the arms I gifted him with. All that he has came from me, and in his arrogance he has forgotten that."

"I have not forgotten it." Sanglant said it hoarsely, as if the knowledge pained him—but his voice always sounded like that.

"You no longer wear the iron collar set upon you by Bloodheart. Where is the gold torque that marks you as blood of my blood, descendant of the royal line of Wendar and Varre?"

"I will not wear it." At his most stubborn, with high cheekbones in relief, the un-Wendish slant of his nose, the way he
held his jaw taut, he was very much the arrogant prince, one
born out of an exotic line.

"You defy me." Henry's tone made the statement into a question. She heard it as a warning.

Surely Sanglant understood that it was pointless to set himself against the king? They could not win against the king, who
had all the power where they had none.

"I am no longer a King's Dragon."

"Then give me the belt of honor which I myself fastened on
you when you were fifteen. Give me the sword that I myself
gave into your hands after Gent."

Villam gasped. Even Sapientia looked up, tears streaking her
face. Liath's throat burned with the bile of defeat. But Sanglant
looked grimly satisfied as he lay belt, sheath, and sword at the
king's feet.

"You are what I make you." Henry's words rang like a hammer on iron. "You will do as I tell you. I am not unsympathetic
to the needs of the flesh, which are manifold. Therefore, keep
this woman as your concubine, if you will, but since she, my
servant, has not received my permission to wed, then her consent even before witnesses is not valid. I will equip an army,
and arm you for this duty, and you will lead this army south to
Aosta. When you have restored Princess Adelheid to her throne,
you will marry her. I think you will find a queen's bed more
satisfying than that of a magus' get—no matter how handsome
she may be."

"But what about me, Father?" demanded Sapientia, whose
tears had dried suddenly.

"You I will invest as Margrave of Eastfall, so that you may
learn to rule yourself."

She flushed, stung as by a slap in the face, but she did not
protest.

"And what of me, Father?" asked Theophanu more quietly.
"What of Duke Conrad's suit?"

Henry snorted. "I do not trust Conrad, and I will not send
one of my most valuable treasures into the treasure house of a
man who may harbor his own ambitions."

"But, Father—"

"No." He cut her off, and she was far too cool to show any

emotion, whether relief or anger or despair. "In any case, the church will rule that you are too closely related, with a common ancestor in the—" He gestured toward Rosvita.

"In the seventh degree, if we calculate by the old imperial method. In the fourth degree, if we calculate by the method outlined in an encyclical circulated under the holy rule of our Holy Mother Honoria, who reigned at the Hearth before Clementia, she who is now skopos in Darre."

"No marriage may be consummated within the fifth degree of relation," said Henry, with satisfaction. "Conrad will not get a bride from my house." The door opened, and Hathui returned, making her bow, but she had hardly gotten inside the door when Henry addressed her: "Eagle, tell Duke Conrad that I will hold audience with him. Now. As for Father Hugh—well—"

"Send him to the skopos," hissed Sapienta. "I will see him condemned!" Then she burst into noisy sobs.

"Well," continued Henry, "I will have the letters read to me, and I wish to speak with this Sister Anne." He caught sight of Sanglant, still kneeling with mute obstinacy, and frowned. "You will return to your chamber, and you may come before me again when you are ready to beg my forgiveness."

It was a dismissal. Liath rose. She desperately wanted to rub her aching knees, but dared not. Sanglant hesitated. Was it rebellion? Had he not heard? Henry grunted with annoyance, and then the prince rose, glanced once at Liath, once toward his sisters—

"Come," said Villam, not without sympathy. "It is time for you to go."

When they returned to the chamber set aside for Sanglant's use and the door shut behind them, she simply walked into his arms and stood there for a long while, not wanting to move. He was solid and strong, and she felt as if she could pour all her anger and fire and fear into the cool endless depths of him without ever filling him up. He seemed content simply to stand there, rocking slightly side to side: he was never completely at rest. But she was at rest here, with him—even in such disgrace. She had lived on the fringe of society for so long, she and Da, that she could scarcely feel she had lost something precious to her.

Yet what if he decided that a queen's bed was more satisfying than the one he shared with her?

The Eika dog whined weakly, then collapsed back to lick a paw with its dry tongue. Sanglant released her, took water from the basin, and knelt so the poor beast could lap from his palms. Someone had put up the shutters, and the corners of the room lay dim with shadows. Light shone in lines through the shutters, striping the floor and the dog and the prince and a strange creature concocted of metal that lay slumped over the back of the only chair. Standing, he wiped his hands on his leggings and said, suddenly:

"What's this? It's a coat of mail!" He ran his fingers over coarse iron links. "A quilted coat. A helm. Lord Above! A good stout spear. A sword. A sheath." And a teardrop shield, without marking or color: suitable for a cavalryman. He hoisted it up and slipped his left arm through the straps, testing weight and balance. He unsheathed the sword.

"Ai, Lady!" she murmured, staring at these riches. It was far more than what she had asked Thiadbold for: she had asked only for a sword and helmet.

"But what is it?" he asked.

She found Master Hosel's belt among her gear and slid the sheath onto it, then with her own hands fastened the belt about Sanglant's hips as she swallowed tears brought on by the generosity of the Lions. "It's your morning gift." She tied off the belt and stood back, remembering what Lavastine had said. " 'If you walk through fire, the flame shall not consume you.' "

He gave a curt laugh. "Let *them* declare we are not wed, if they will, but God have witnessed our oath, and God will honor our pledge." Taking her face between his hands, he kissed her on the forehead.

There were two unlit candles in this chamber; both of them flared abruptly to life, and he laughed, swung her up and around, and they landed on the bed in a breathless heap. It was a measure of his disgrace that, even in the late afternoon with preparations for a feast underway and the palace swarming with servants and nobles and hangers-on, no one disturbed them.

Afterward, he lay beside her with a leg flung over her buttocks, head turned away as he examined the sword, good, strong iron meant for war, not show. "Where did it all come from?"

"The Lions felt they owed me a favor, but they respect you even more than they felt grateful to me. This is a tribute to you—and to your reputation."

He rolled up to sit, rubbing his forehead with one hand. "If I have not destroyed it entirely now." He drew his knees up and pounded his head against them, too restless to sit still. "Why didn't I see it before? There's no trace of Bloodheart's scent around you. There never has been. Yet it attacked Lavastine's hounds. It can't have been an adder—yet if it were only an adder, if I mistook the scent . . ." From the floor, the dog whimpered restlessly and tried to stand, but had not the strength. Sanglant tugged at his own hair, twining it into a single thick strand so tightly that it strained at his scalp, and then shaking it out. "No Eagle can do my message justice. No Eagle knows Bloodheart's scent, or can listen for it in the bushes. I must go after him myself."

"Hush. Of course you must. But I'll ride with you."

"I wouldn't leave you here alone!" he said indignantly. Then he groaned and shut his eyes in despair. "But I have no horse except on my father's sufferance. I wish he had invested me as margrave of Eastfall and let Sapientia march to Aosta! Then we could have been left in peace!"

"If there can be peace in the marchlands, with bandits and Quman raiders."

"If there is peace in my heart, then I will be at peace no matter what troubles come my way." He buried his face against her neck.

The dog whined. She heard voices. Sanglant grabbed for her tunic, and the door slammed open to admit—

"Conrad!" exclaimed Sanglant. He jumped out of bed and stood there stark naked in the middle of the floor. "Well met, cousin. I could not greet you earlier as you deserved." She could not help but admire his insouciance—and his backside—even as she scrambled to get her clothes on under the covers.

The man who had just entered dismissed his servants. He had a deep, resonant laugh, and a voice to go with it. "Is this the greeting I deserve? I beg your pardon, cousin." But he did not seem inclined to leave. Liath was furiously embarrassed; after eight years alone with Da, she was not used to a constant audience—although Sanglant clearly was. "You have a bride hidden in here somewhere, I hear. I caught a glimpse of her when you rode in, and I confess myself eager to be introduced to her now."

Sanglant took his time getting dressed and did not move out

of the other man's way. "Let there be no confusion. She *is* my
wife."

"Did I say otherwise? Surely, cousin, you do not think I intend to steal her from you as I might if she were only your concubine. Ah, but what's this?"

She slipped out of bed, straightened her tunic, and stood.
Duke Conrad, in the flesh, was rather like Sanglant made shorter
and broader. He had the same kind of leashed vigor as Henry,
and the powerful hands of a man who is used to gripping spear
and shield. He stepped forward, took her hand, and turned it
over to show the lighter palm, then held it against his own. His
skin had a different tone; where hers was more golden-brown
like sun burned into skin, his had a more olive-yellow tint. "Who
are your kin?"

She extricated her hand from his grip. He was barely taller
than she was, but she felt slight beside him. "My father's cousin
is the lady of Bodfeld. I don't know my mother's kin."

He misunderstood her. "A Gyptos whore, no doubt. That
would explain it. How comes she to you, cousin?" He had an
open face, quick to laughter.

"God have brought her to me," retorted Sanglant, looking annoyed.

"They whom God have joined, let no man or woman—even
the regnant—tear asunder." Quick to anger as well, that face.
He boiled with it, a flush staining his neck and the tendons standing out. "Ride out with me, Sanglant. I offer you a place in Wayland."

"Ride out with you?"

Conrad spat in anger. "Henry refused my suit. He will not
let me marry Theophanu." He swore colorfully, describing what
Henry could in his opinion do with his horses and his hounds
and whatever sheep he might come across in the course of his
travels. Liath blushed. "I see no reason to stay feasting and drinking with a man who does not trust me to marry his own daughter! What do you say?"

"What kind of place? As a captain in your retinue?"

Conrad grinned, but with a subtle coating to it, cunning and
sweet. "Nay, cousin. You have too fierce a reputation and I am
far too respectful of your rank. I have certain lands that came
to me in a recent dispute that I can settle on someone willing
to support me, even against the king's displeasure."

"I will not make war upon my father," said Sanglant stubbornly.

The door was still open. Conrad signed to his servants to shut it. "I do not speak of war, not with Henry. Even were I tempted, I don't have enough support."

The "yet" might as well have been spoken out loud, it hung so heavily in the air.

"I will not make war upon my father," repeated Sanglant.

"Nor do I ask you to." Conrad grunted impatiently. "I ride out in the morning. You and your bride may ride with me, or not. As you wish." He looked Liath over once, in the way of a powerful man who has bedded many women and intends to bed many more, and when Sanglant growled low in his throat, he laughed. "So I heard, but I didn't believe it. Is it true that you lived for a year among dogs, my lord prince?" He raised an eyebrow, seeing Sanglant's anger. "Yet the dogs are scarcely different than the nobles who flock 'round the throne, are they not?"

With that, he signed to his servant to open the door, and swept out. The hard glare of the afternoon sun lanced into Liath's eyes, and she had to shade herself with an arm until a Lion latched the door shut from outside.

Sanglant began to pace, then unfastened one of the shutters and took it down so they could get air into the room.

"He offered you land," said Liath as she watched him. She dared not think of it: land, an estate, a place to live in peace.

He turned away from the window to sort impatiently through the contents of his belt pouch, which had fallen to the floor in his haste to undress earlier. He found a comb and with it in his hand steered her to the chair, sat her down, and undid her braid. With a sigh of satisfaction, he began to comb out her hair, which fell to her waist. The strokes soothed her.

"I don't trust him," he said as he worked through a knot. "But you are right. He offered me land. He will not contest my marriage to you. And unlike any other soul in this land, he will not care if my father contests it."

"Will we ride out with him in the morning?"

"Do we have another choice?" But for that question, she had no answer.

2

"YOU'VE made a fool of yourself, Hugh."

Margrave Judith did not mince words when she was angry, and she was very angry now. Ivar huddled in a corner of the spacious chamber reserved for her use, clinging to an equally frightened Baldwin. She had already hit Baldwin once for not getting out of her way quickly enough; his cheek was still pink from the slap. She was so angry that Ivar could not even get any pleasure out of her castigation of Hugh, which she conducted in front of her entire household.

Not that any of them appeared to be enjoying it either. Her servants and courtiers admired and loved Hugh, who treated high and low alike with graciousness and perfect amiability.

Now he stood with hands clasped behind him, a bruise purpling on one cheek, and his gaze fixed not on his mother but on a gaudy spray of white-and-pink flowers outside that shielded the open window from the glare of the late afternoon sun.

"Your conduct has embarrassed *me*," she continued mercilessly, "and, God help me, may have lost you your influence with Princess Sapientia. Fool! And more fool I for thinking I could raise a son who would not fall prey to his male weakness! What hope does a man have if he betrays a consuming lust for a woman of unknown birth who brings no advantage to his kin and kind? By the amount you desire her, you give her that much power over you."

"But she has power," he said in a low voice, still flushed. "More power than anyone here knows or suspects. Except Wolfhere."

"Power! A handsome face is not power. Even grant you that her father was a magus, as they're all saying now, even grant that magus' blood has lent her power, then what use is it to you since you have become her prisoner by reason of this unseemly obsession?"

"She is mine," he said with such zeal that cold ran down

Ivar's spine like the fingers of the Enemy, probing toward the heart for weakness.

"She is Prince Sanglant's, as is apparent to anyone with eyes not blinded by lust."

"Never his!" He reached out suddenly, broke off a spray of glorious flowers, and began shredding them into bits. Petals spun down around him.

"Has she bewitched you? Bound some kind of spell onto you? They're saying that her father was a fallen monastic who dabbled in the black arts as well as in some Jinna whore's belly, and who paid for his sins by being eaten alive by the minions of the Enemy. It would make sense that she had learned a few tricks from him before he died."

"Yes," he said hoarsely, "she has bewitched me." He clenched both hands. Astonishingly, he began to weep with thwarted fury—just utterly lost control of himself.

Liath had done this to him.

Ivar could not help but exult at Hugh's humiliation and rage. The Holy Mother had visited this punishment upon him for his arrogance. But when he thought of Liath, a stuttering sickness gripped his heart.

She had not even noticed him! Not two days ago when she first arrived at the king's progress, not yesterday when the king had passed judgment by letting her remain his servant, and not today, when she had returned in defiance of the king's command. By what right did she ignore him, who had done everything he could to help her? Did the love they had pledged each other mean nothing to her? What on God's earth did Prince Sanglant have that he didn't—?

"Hush," said Baldwin, caressing his arm to distract him, though he hadn't realized that he was grunting and muttering out loud. "Don't draw attention to us, or she'll hit me again."

"How can she love him?" Ivar choked out.

"Of course a mother loves her son."

"I didn't mean—"

Margrave Judith stood up, and both boys instinctively flinched back, but she did not even glance their way. She picked up a fine silver basin filled with water and dashed it full in Hugh's face.

"Control yourself!" She replaced the basin with perfect composure and sat back down. "I see I am almost too late."

The shock of it brought him back. Trembling, he wiped his face dry with a sleeve.

"Kneel before me." Slowly, he did so. "Am I not first in your heart?" she asked grimly.

"You are my mother," he replied in a dull voice.

"I nurtured you within my body, bore you with great effort, and raised you with care. Is this how you repay my efforts?" He began to speak, but she cut him off. "Now you will listen to me. Three years ago I had to agree to have you sent to the North Mark after the incident in Zeitsenburg. You swore to me then there would be no more such incidents, yet I now find you entangled with a girl born of a magus' breeding. Have you gone against my wishes in this matter? Have you, Hugh?"

Stubbornly, he did not reply.

Her hiss, between gritted teeth, gave Ivar a shiver of fear.

"The court is a bad influence on you! You still bear a personal grudge against the prince, do you not? That he, a bastard, was given power in the secular world and you were not, is that not so, Hugh?"

With one hand he gripped the cloth of his tunic, folded around one knee; the other lay open, pressed against the floorboards palm down to hold himself up. His breath came ragged, and his gaze seemed fixed on something invisible to everyone else in the room. "That she should go willingly to *him* when she has spurned me—!"

She extended a leg, caught him under the chin with the toe of her sandal, and tipped his head back so that he had to look at her. "You have gone mad with jealousy." She stated it in the same way any noble lady might examine her cattle and see that some were afflicted with hoof-rot: calmly, but with a little disgust at her own bad luck. "Your mind has been afflicted by her spells."

She lowered her foot and stood. "Go," she said to her courtiers. "Speak of this to the folk hereabouts, what you have heard here— that the girl has bound him with her evil spells. See how she has reduced him. We all know Father Hugh's elegant manners. This is no natural state." They scurried away obediently.

"Go heat a bath for him so that we may wash some of the poison out," she said, and a half dozen servants hurried into the adjoining room. Then she turned to her entourage. "Lord Atto, I haven't forgotten the matter of the king's stallion, Potentis. I have spoken with the king myself, and if that bay mare of yours comes into season while we are on progress with the king, you may try for a foal out of Potentis. Go speak with the king's stablemaster, if you will, to arrange it."

Lord Atto was all effusive thanks as he retreated, but Judith had already beckoned forward one of her servingwomen. "Hemma, I have considered this matter of your daughter's betrothal, and I think it a good match for her to wed Minister Oda's son. But I have it in mind to gift her with that length of fine linen cloth we picked up in Quedlinhame. If you will see to it that it is packed and made ready, I will have it sent with the messengers who are returning east. Then your daughter will have time to sew some clothing out of it for the wedding feast."

With one pretext or another, she sent them away until only she, Hugh, her two eldest servingwomen, and Baldwin and Ivar remained. Her pleasant manner vanished, and she spoke in a hard voice. "Now you will tell me truly what this means." She took Hugh's chin in a hand and turned his head up to look at her. "I can scarcely believe the rumors I hear. Did you try to murder Princess Theophanu? After it was forbidden you at Zeitsenburg, have you soiled your hands again with bindings and workings, this pollution that you call sorcery?"

The light from the open window dappled Hugh's face, mottling it with shadow and light and the discoloring bruise. His expression, nakedly anguished, underwent some cataclysmic change as he stared up at his mother, who had bent the full force of her will upon him. A shudder shook through his body and he collapsed at her feet.

"I beg you, Mother," he whispered. "Forgive me. I have sinned."

She grunted, but that was all the reply she made, and she seemed to be expecting more.

"Ai, God," he prayed, "protect me from temptation." His hands hid his face. "I know now what came over me. It was a trap her father laid. As soon as I saw her, I burned for her despite my prayers day upon night offered up to Our Lady and Lord, Whom I begged to protect me. But he bound me and trapped me, and even after he died, I could not escape from her."

She appeared unmoved by this recital. Ivar could not tell whether she believed it, but it seemed to satisfy her. "You are bored as abbot," she said finally, "and when a man of your intelligence becomes bored, then the Enemy sends his minions to tempt him. And indeed a mere abbacy is not the position due your consequence."

He looked up, strangely dry-eyed after his weeping confession. "What do you mean?"

"Be obedient to my wishes, Hugh, and you shall have more." She took hold of his ear, twisted it so that one more tweak would cause pain, and with the other hand brushed a finger affectionately over his moist lips and with that same finger touched her own lips, as if sipping off his sweetness. "I have never failed you, Hugh. I have given you everything you have asked me for."

"You have," he said softly. Hesitated, then fell silent.

She let go, stepped back, and let him stand. "You will not fail me. Do not see her again, and we can salvage your reputation."

He bowed his head humbly. "I am your obedient servant, my lady mother."

She looked at Baldwin, and Ivar knew with a nauseating wrench in his gut that this was also a message meant for her young husband: Those who lived within the circle of her power were not allowed to be disobedient.

Baldwin bent his head and abruptly launched into an impassioned prayer. Halfway through, he nudged Ivar with a foot, and Ivar, startled and now seeing Hugh kiss his mother on either cheek and retreat to the room where his bath awaited him, clasped his hands as well and joined the whispered prayer. "Our Mother, Who art in Heaven—"

Seeing them so occupied, Judith left the chamber with her two servants at her heels and a slender whippet slinking behind. No doubt she had decided it was time to venture out onto the field of battle to save her son's reputation. And what of Liath?

Ai, Lord. *Liath.*

"You're not concentrating," murmured Baldwin, who sounded insulted.

"What will become of her?" Ivar muttered.

This time, Baldwin understood him. "Do you desire her body, Ivar?" He rested a hand on Ivar's thigh. His sweet breath, like the breath of angels, brushed softly along his neck.

Ivar shivered convulsively. "God help me!" he prayed. It hurt too much to think of her. It was easier to drown himself in thoughts of God. He set to praying with a vengeance and, after a pause, Baldwin joined him.

3

THE king did not summon them to the feast celebrating the return of Theophanu and the arrival of Duke Conrad. No royal steward saw fit to bring them platters of choice tidbits from the feast table. But soldiers brought offerings: bread, baked turnips, roast pork, and greens, such fare as milites could expect and would generously share with a captain they admired and respected and a disgraced Eagle toward whom they had cause to be grateful.

The twilight hours in summer ran long and leisurely and, as Sanglant braided her hair, Liath listened to the sweet singing of the clerics from the hall as they entertained the king with the hymn celebrating St. Casceil's Ascension, whose feast day they observed.

> "The holy St. Casceil made a pilgrimage from her home in rain-drenched Alba to the dry desert shores of Saïs the Younger. There she dwelt in blessed solitude in the east with only a tame lion as companion, and there she knelt to pray day after day under the constant hammer blow of the desert sun while angels fanned her with their wings to cool her brow and body. Yet the heat so burned away her mortal substance, and her holy prayers so inflamed her soul with purity and truth that the wind made by the angels' wings, which is also the gentle breath of God, lifted her into the heavens. There she found her place among the righteous."

Braiding the hair he had earlier combed out gave Sanglant something to do with his hands, but he shifted restlessly from one foot to the other, seeming about to start talking but grunting softly instead. She had said everything she knew to say to

him. No decision had been reached: Would they ride out with
Conrad, or not?

"My lord prince." Hathui stood at the door. Liath could smell
the feast on her. The pungent scent of spices and sauces made
Liath's mouth water.

He nodded, giving her permission to enter. "Do you bring a
message from my father?"

"I come on my own, to speak with my old comrade, Liath,
if you will."

"That is for her to choose, not me to choose for her!" he said
as he tied off the braid and stepped away from Liath.

Liath started up when Hanna stepped into the room behind
Hathui. The badge winking at the throat of her short summer cloak
seemed like accusation. Hanna had given up Kinfolk, home, and
all that was familiar to her to follow Liath, and yet Liath had
turned aside from that jointly-sworn oath to bind her life with
Sanglant's. Hanna had been crying, and Hathui looked solemn.

"This is—this is—my comrade—" Liath stuttered, not wanting to ignore Hanna as one would a simple servant, yet not
knowing if a prince and a common Eagle could have any ground
on which to meet as equals. Ai, Lady! Had she never truly
thought of herself as a "common Eagle" but rather as an equal
to the great princes in some intangible way she had inherited
from Da's manner and education? Had she never truly treated
Hanna as an equal, through those years when Hanna had generously offered friendship to a friendless, foreign-born girl?

She was ashamed.

"This is the Eagle who serves Sapientia," said Sanglant into
the silence made by her stumbling. "She is called Hanna. Did
you not know her in Heart's Rest?" He turned his gaze on Hanna.
"You called my wife 'friend' there, I believe."

"My lord prince," said Hanna, kneeling abruptly. Hathui, with
a tight smile, remained standing, but she inclined her head respectfully. Then Hanna saw the Eika dog, and she recoiled, jumping back to stand beside the table.

"Fear not," said Sanglant. "It doesn't have enough strength
to harm you."

"Will it live?" asked Hathui softly.

"You may tell my father that I will nurse it as I am able,
since it alone of all my possessions did not come to me through
his power."

Her eyes glinted. "Shall I tell him so in those exact words, my lord prince? I would humbly advise against it, while the king remains in such a humor toward you as he is this day."

"Plainly spoken, Eagle. Say what you came to say to my wife. I will not interfere."

Hathui nodded and began. "You ought to have ridden on with Wolfhere, Liath. How can you have traveled with the king's progress for so many months and not seen what a pit of intrigue it is? How will you fare, here, with the king turned against you and the prince without support? What will you say when princes and nobles come to seek your favor, to gain the attention of the prince? There will always be supplicants at your door, and beggars and lepers and every kind of pauper and sick person, seeking healing, and noble ladies and lords who hope that your influence can give them audience with the king or his children—or who wish to sway the prince to their cause, whether it be just or no."

Like Conrad. Liath picked up the comb that lay on the table. Such a simple thing to be so finely made. With its bone surface incised with a pair of twined dragons and trimmed with ivory and pearls set into the handle at either end, it marked Sanglant as a great prince who need not untangle his hair with sticks or a plain wood comb but only with something fashioned by a master craftsman.

Hathui went on. "Father Hugh stands accused of sorcery by Princess Theophanu, but if you are called upon to testify before the king against him, how will it fare with you when Margrave Judith's anger is turned upon you? What if you are accused in your turn of sorcery? The king will never allow you to be recognized as Prince Sanglant's wife. All that I have named above you will suffer without even the legal standing of wife but only that of concubine. Do you think an Eagle's oath and freedom—beholden to no one but the king—a fair exchange for the bed of a prince?"

"Liath," whispered Hanna, "are you sure this is wise?"

"Of course it isn't wise!" she retorted.

Sanglant stood by the window staring outside. The wind stirred his hair, and the graying light made of his profile—the arch of the nose, the high cheekbones, the set of his beardless jaw—a proud mask. He made no move to interfere.

"Of course it isn't wise," Liath repeated bitterly. "It just *is*.

I won't leave him. Oh, Hanna. You followed me from Heart's Rest, and now I've deserted you—" She grabbed Hanna's hands and Hanna snorted, still pale, and hugged her suddenly.

"As if I only took an Eagle's oaths to follow you! Maybe I wanted to see something more of the world. Maybe I wanted to escape young Johan."

Liath laughed unsteadily, more like a sob. Hanna's body felt familiar, and safe, caught against her. "Maybe you did. I'm sorry."

"I still think you're being a fool," whispered Hanna. "My mother would never have let any of her children marry because of . . . well . . ."

"What?"

Hanna spoke so softly that Liath, pressed against her, could barely hear her. "Lust alone. It might be said that you've gained advantage by attracting his interest, but you don't bring anything to him, that would be useful to him—"

Sanglant laughed without turning away from the window, and Hanna blushed furiously. "More use than anyone here can know," he said as if addressing the bushes, "although I confess freely that I am not immune to the weaknesses of the flesh."

"But no one makes a marriage only for . . ." Hanna stuttered to a halt. "My good mother always said that God made marriage as a useful tool, not as a pleasure bed."

"Ought we to be good, or useful?" asked Hathui sardonically.

"Ought we to be chattering on like the clerics?" retorted Sanglant. "We ought to be seeing that the crops are brought in, and that our borders are safe from bandits and raiders, and that our retainers are fed and their children healthy. And that we pray to God to spare us from the howling dogs who nip at our heels!"

Hanna started back from Liath as if she had been slapped. Hathui nodded curtly. "If you wish us to leave, my lord prince."

"Nay." He tossed his head impatiently and finally slewed round to look at them. "I did not mean it of you, but of the ladies and lords who flock round the court. I beg you, take no offense from my coarse way of speaking."

"You are not coarse, my lord, but blunt." Hathui grinned charmingly.

"Not as eloquent as my wife," he said, with a pride that startled Liath.

At this moment Liath had more pressing concerns. She tugged

on Hanna's sleeve. "Come with me outside, Hanna, I beg you. I'm not accustomed to—with so many people about—"

She was in disgrace, not in prison, and while she preferred to use the privies built up over the edge of the ramparts rather than the chamber pot, she dared not venture out alone for fear of meeting Hugh. Hanna seemed more cheerful out of the close chamber, or away from Sanglant. Servants wandering the grounds pointed and whispered.

"Do you think I'm a fool, Hanna?" The constant scrutiny made her uneasy. Her entrance onto the stage as Sanglant's declared wife had made her a beacon, visible to everyone.

"Yes. Better to serve him as an Eagle than as his mistress. As an Eagle you are bound to the king by oaths. As his mistress, he can put you aside whenever he tires of you, and then where will you go?"

"Spoken like Wolfhere!"

"Like Wolfhere, indeed!" Hanna waited to one side while Liath used the privies, but she started up again as soon as Liath rejoined her. "Wolfhere became an Eagle during King Arnulf's reign. Everyone knows he was one of Arnulf's favorites. Then Henry took the throne, and dismissed Wolfhere from court—but he could not dismiss him from the Eagles! That is the measure of an Eagle's security."

"Such as any of us have security," murmured Liath, remembering bones scoured clean on a roadside. She scrambled up the rampart to view the surrounding countryside. Up here the evening wind blew fresh into her face. Below the bluff, the river wound away into darkening forest. Fields patched the nearer ground in narrow strips of lush growth: beans, vetch, and barley. Small figures walked in a village that seemed only a stone's throw from her position, although she knew it lay much farther away. The morning thunderclouds had long since vanished into the northeast, and the sky was clear with the moon already risen halfway to the zenith. The sun had set, but its glow colored the western sky. Brilliant Somorhas rode low on the horizon; the sky was still too bright to see any but the brightest stars in summer's sky: the Queen's sky.

"Would I be a queen?" she murmured, and was then so appalled at the thought of presiding over a court—a pit of intrigue, indeed!—that she shuddered.

"Are you cold?" Hanna draped a companionable arm over

her shoulders. A roar of laughter erupted from the great hall, which lay hidden behind them by chapel tower and stables.

"It's only because he can't rule," said Liath suddenly. "If he'd had any ambition to be king after his father, I couldn't have endured that!"

Hanna laughed sharply. "If he'd had any ambition to be king, he'd never have married *you!* He'd have married a noblewoman whose kin will support him."

"I deserved that, I suppose!"

"Maybe he's right." Hanna's expression drew taut in an expression of wonder and worry. "You aren't what you seem, Liath. Maybe he's wiser than the rest of us. They say Aoi blood tunes you to magic just as a poet tunes his lyre before he sings, knowing what sounds sweetest."

"Is that what they say?"

"Some at court say that Prince Sanglant grew so strange under Eika captivity because the enchantments polluted his mind. That's why—" She broke off, then smiled apologetically. "That's why he acts like a dog. The dogs became part of him, or he of the dogs, like a spell bound into his body by the Eika chieftain."

It arrived noiselessly and settled down on a ragged outcropping of rock. At first, Hanna didn't notice it, but Liath saw the owl immediately.

She gently shook off Hanna's arm and took a cautious step forward, then knelt. "Who are you?" she asked of the owl. It blinked huge golden eyes but did not move.

"Liath," whispered Hanna. "Why are you talking to an owl?"

"It isn't an ordinary owl." She kept her gaze fixed on the bird. It had ear tufts and a coat of mottled feathers, streaked with white at the breast. It was the largest owl she had ever seen—she who had spent many a night in silent contemplation of the stars and thus with her keen night vision seen the animals that woke and fed in the night. "Who are you?"

Its hoot echoed like a warning, "Who? Who?" and then it launched itself up from the rock and glided away.

"Eagle! I did not expect you to be gone for so long." Princess Sapientia appeared with a handful of servingwomen, having just come from the privies.

"Your Highness!" Hanna's expression betrayed her surprise no less than did her voice.

"Has she bewitched you, too?" demanded Sapientia as Hanna

knelt before her. Liath hesitated, then felt it prudent to kneel in her turn. "Made proud by my brother's attention!"

"I beg your pardon, Your Highness, for being so long away from you," replied Hanna in a calm voice. "We knew each other before we became Eagles. We are almost like kin—"

"But you are not kin."

"No—"

"You are a good, honest freewoman, Hanna. What she is no one here yet knows." She beckoned to a pair of guards who had remained respectfully behind. "Bring her."

"I must return—!" Liath began.

"You must come with me." Sapientia's eyes gleamed with triumph. "You will not have your way so easily with the rest of us, Eagle!"

"Sanglant." But the wind blew her voice out into the gulf of air beyond the ramparts, where the bluff tumbled down and down to the land below. To fight would only cause more of a scene, as well as make her life immeasurably harder, so she went, and then was sorry she had done so when Sapientia returned directly to the hall. It was swarming with as many of the court who could crowd in, and the rest of their retainers and servants sat at trestle tables outside. With Duke Conrad and Margrave Judith and various local ladies who had ridden in to offer gifts before the king and share in his generosity in return, the king's progress had blossomed into a field crowded with life, hundreds of folk crammed together all eager to enjoy the night no matter what form their entertainment took. And when Sapientia led her into the great hall, so stuffed with people that it seemed to bulge at the seams, she would have sworn that every gaze turned to scrutinize her. Nausea swept her, washed down by the brush of Hanna's arm or her elbow, her last—and briefest—reassurance.

They had all been drinking, of course; it was a feast, and wine flowed freely. But the king rose, seeing her, and she knew at once—because she had known the signs intimately in Da's face—that he had been drinking hard to drown anger in his heart.

But he was still the king in dignity and voice.

"Has my son's mistress come to pay her respects?" he asked, gesturing toward her to make sure any soul in court who had not yet noticed her would notice her now.

"Or has she simply tired of her new conquest?" drawled Margrave Judith, "and thrown him aside as she did my son once she had polluted him with her magics?" Her glare was as frightening as that of a guivre, turning Liath to stone. Hugh did not appear to her among the sea of faces, all of them staring, but she was sure *he* was behind this humiliation.

"That is not for us to judge, but rather a matter for the church." Yes, Henry was drunk, but coldly angry beneath and able to control himself in his cups far better than Da had ever been able to. But Da had been nothing but a disgraced frater. Henry was king. "Seat her beside me," he continued with that iron gaze, edged like a sword. "Let the royal mistress be given honor as she deserves, who graces my son's bed." He knew what he was doing. "But not dressed like that! Not dressed like a common Eagle! Has my son not gifted you with clothing fit for your rank?"

He did not mean her to reply; he only meant to remind her of his power, as if she had ever forgotten it.

Theophanu rose from her seat to the left of her father. A servingwoman hurried forward, and the princess whispered in her ear before turning back to the king. "Your Majesty, I have reason to be beholden to this woman. Let me clothe her in a fitting manner."

The blow came from an unexpected source. Henry hesitated, but that hesitation gave Theophanu time to gesture peremptorily. Liath slipped out from the circle of Sapientia's retainers and into the cool but not unfriendly clime of Theophanu's followers.

They led her away to a room tucked under the eaves in the hall, and here the first servingwoman arrived out of breath with her arms draped with cloth. She shook out the bundle to display a fine linen undertunic and an indigo silk overdress embroidered with tiny gold eight-pointed stars. The cloth rippled like a glimpse of the night sky, pure and mysterious.

"I've never worn anything so fine!" Liath whispered in awe, but they dressed her ruthlessly, measured her frame—as tall as the princess but more slender—and belted the overdress with a simple chain of gold links. They announced themselves satisfied with the condition of her hair but wove a golden net of delicate knotwork studded with pearls around the crown of her head as ornament.

"Lord have mercy," they murmured, surveying her. "It's no wonder the prince took a fancy to this one."

They led her back out into the hall. If she had thought herself fallen into the pit of misery before, it was nothing to what happened now: Even Henry, caught in mid-sentence as he addressed Sapientia, fell silent when he saw her. They all fell silent, every soul in the hall. A moment later when Theophanu rose to relinquish her own seat beside the king, they all broke into voice at once.

"No dogs set over her to guard her?" Conrad's battle-trained voice carried easily over the throng. "I'd not leave such a precious treasure unattended."

She felt a blush flow like fire through her cheeks and down all her limbs, then furiously wished it cool for fear of causing an untimely and horrible conflagration. The king had a very odd look in his eye, and he offered her his own cup to drink from. She dared not refuse. The wine hit her throat with a rich bouquet and glowed in her stomach. She had to share the king's platter—an honor of such distinction that it branded her forever among the folk present here tonight. She would never be anonymous again, not on the king's progress. And the worst of it was that his fingers kept touching and tangling with hers in the dish so that despite the wonderful aroma and flavor of the food, she could scarcely get it down her throat which stayed parched no matter how much wine she drank.

Hathui slipped into the hall and stood in disapproving attendance behind the king's chair. Hanna, trapped in Sapientia's service, could only throw her despairing glances, helpless to help her. All other faces blurred together.

Young men wrestled before the king and threw her tokens in competition for her favor, and she had to give a kiss to the winner—a brawny lad whose breath smelled of onions. Jugglers and tumblers entertained, and she had to shower them with silver sceattas brought to her by the stewards. She had to pass judgment on the poets who came forward in the hope of gaining the fancy—and the favor—of the king, and the king demurred on all counts to her judgment. He sat with heavy-lidded eyes and watched her when he was not watching his court. His limbs brushed hers at intervals, but surely that was accident because they sat so close together. The sick feeling that afflicted her heart would not go away.

"How can you honor her, Your Majesty," said Judith finally, pushed to the edge of her patience, "when my son lies in a fever

in his chamber, sweating away the pollution she brought onto
him?"

Henry turned in his chair to regard the margrave. "I will act
as is fitting, considering the accusations brought before me this
day. I have already convened a council of biscops, to be held
at Matthias-mass in Autun. There your son and this woman will
be brought before those most fit to judge in such matters." His
gaze lit on Liath again, and he toasted her with wine. "Yet as
my dear cousin Conrad has so wisely warned me, I dare not let
such a treasure go unguarded. She will remain by my side until
then—"

"By *your* side, cousin?" shouted Conrad, then roared with
laughter. "Will that be after the prince tires of her, or before?
But I am much struck by her beauty, too. I am not ashamed to
state here in front of witnesses that no matter how many royal
beds she graces, I will gladly take her off your hands when you
are through."

When Henry laughed, other noblemen took up the jest, took
up wagers: How many months until Sanglant tired of her—or
the king—or then Conrad? Who would have her next?

Ai, God. She was desperately ashamed to be made mock of
in this fashion. Better to be spinning above the Abyss waiting
for God to blow her into the pit then suffer this any longer!

To her left, Princess Theophanu sat as still as stone. Beyond
Theophanu, Helmut Villam frowned at the assembly and did not
join in the jesting. But Henry had a grim smile of perverse satisfaction on his face even as he watched her with that terrible
glint of wine-inflamed desire on his face. She recognized it now.
Hugh had looked at her so on certain winter nights in Heart's
Rest; what always followed was never pleasant, at least not for
her.

"You see by this spectacle, my friends," said Judith in a voice
that carried to the four corners of the hall, "that she has now
bewitched even our good king. What more proof do you need
that she has stained her hands with malevolent sorcery?"

Ai, Lady! At long last he appeared at the door with twilight
at his back, alone, without retinue, although thank God he had
taken pains to make his clothing look neat. Perhaps the soldiers
had done it for him. Master Hosel's belt looked perfectly in place
with his rich tunic and hose. The salamanders worked into the
leather almost seemed to slide and shine in the torchlight.

He strode forward down the ranks of tables and without a word or any least gesture of acknowledgment halted with arrogant grace before the king's table. There, he held out his hand. She staggered to her feet, but the king caught her by the wrist.

"My bed, or his," the king murmured.

Sanglant's nostrils flared in anger. But he did not move.

Henry's hand tightened on her arm. A whippet growled softly and was hushed. Even the jugglers and tumblers peeked out from where they sat tucked under the king's table. Everyone watched.

The king's bed.

She stood stunned for a good long time. Henry was about the age Da would have been, had he survived, but Henry wore his years with vigor and he had the fine, handsome, noble appearance that God of necessity grant to a regnant.

The king's protection.

Hugh would never dare touch her. Even the biscops, called to council, would surely be lenient with the king's mistress.

Sanglant waited with the dead calm of a man who knows the death blow is moments away.

"I beg your pardon, Your Majesty," she said. "But I swore an oath before God long ago."

He let her go. She cared for nothing now except getting out fast; ducking under the table, she crawled over fresh rushes, chicken bones, and the dregs of wine cups, and when she emerged on the other side Sanglant was there to hoist her up, assisted, unexpectedly, by one of the jugglers giving a hearty shove to her backside.

Everyone began talking at once.

She saw the door so far in the distance that she was sure they would never make it there, and then it gaped open before her and they stepped out under the night sky. She would have run, but he made her walk so that they would not look undignified.

He said nothing. When they got back to his chamber, he dug into her saddlebag without asking her leave and pulled out the gold torque. She began to shake. He caught her hands and still without a word twisted the torque around her neck—and *stared* at her, in her fine gown ornamented with the night sky.

The torque weighed heavily, a slave collar indeed.

"Take it off, I beg you." The words choked her. "It's wrong for me to wear it."

"Nay, it's meant for you." He passed a hand over his eyes as at a vision he dared not dream of seeing. "Had it been Taille-fer's court, you still would have outshone them all."

She slid her fingers under the curve of gold braid, twisted it off, and set it down hard on the table as if the touch of it burned her skin to ice. "There must have been three hundred people in there, and all of them staring at me!"

"You'll get used to it."

"I'll never get used to it! I don't want to get used to it!"

"Hush, Liath." He tried to kiss her, to calm her, but she was too agitated to be calmed. She went to the window and leaned out. Many figures moved beyond the corner of the residence: and by their voices, and coarse jesting, and the tidal flow of the crowd, she knew the feast had ended with her departure. "He meant to shame you," said Sanglant as he came up beside her. He was careful not to touch her.

"Ai, God."

"Did you bewitch him?" he asked casually, flicking a finger along her cheek.

"I did nothing!"

"You did nothing, and yet he offered you his bed and his pro-tection. My father is well known for his piety and his conti-nence. In all my years at his side, I have never seen a display such as he gave us this night."

"I did nothing!" she repeated, furious now because the hu-miliation was still so raw. She remembered his own words of yesterday. "I will not have this conversation over and over if you in your heart doubt my intention!"

He laughed, relaxing suddenly. "No, I think you are the one who is witched somehow. Any man in that hall tonight would have taken you to his bed and given you half his estates and a third of his mother's treasure in return for your favor. The Lord and Lady know that you are beautiful, Liath." He leaned so close that his breath stirred her hair. "But not even the fair Baldwin makes all the ladies of the court go mad with desire for him. And I think God have molded him more like to the angels even than you."

"Who is the fair Baldwin?" she asked indignantly.

He bent away from her, shut his eyes as he stood silent, lis-tening to the distant chatter of the assembly as it broke into groups and eddied away. She heard only a meaningless murmur, but she knew he could hear far more. "Nay," he said finally, "there is something else at work here, some spell laid on you."

"Is that the only reason you asked me to marry you, then," she asked harshly, "because of a spell? And if the biscops so choose, can they can condemn me for something I had no part in?"

He shook his head, having come to a decision. "You will not appear before the biscops. We will ride out with Conrad."

"Conrad was the worst of them!"

"We can't stay at court! Not after the king—my own holy father—tried to take you away from me!" Then he paused, made certain hesitant gestures as a prelude to speaking so that she knew what was coming next. "Were you tempted?"

Because he asked so timidly, the question made her laugh. "Of course I was tempted. The king's bed. The king's protection! I'd be a fool to cast that aside, wouldn't I? But I swore before God that I would never love any man but you."

"Ai, Lady, Liath." He embraced her, although he was unsteady. "We will make many strong children together, each one a blessing on our house." He pulled her gently toward the bed, but she slid out of his arms.

"Let me just stand here for a while," she said, going back to the window. "I'm dizzy." She had drunk so much wine that her head still spun with it. He only smiled and went to sit on the bed, content to watch her.

She leaned out for a draught of air. She could see stars now in the vault of heaven: the Queen's Sword stood at zenith, but from this angle she could not see it. The River of Heaven poured westward, and the Guivre rose from its waters with stars streaming off its back. Like Judith's eye, turned on her with malice. So many stars, a thousand at least, as numerous as the courtiers and servants and hangers-on who followed the king.

"Da and I were always alone. Even at the court in Qurtubah where everything was rich and crowded, we stayed hidden on the fringe, mostly. We were always alone."

"Qurtubah," murmured Sanglant from the bed, a soft echo. "I saw a sword from Qurtubah once, light but strong. It had a curve to it."

Directly north she saw Kokab, the north star, and below it the Ladle, forever poised to catch the heavenly waters and bring them to the mouths of the gods should the gods thirst for such nectar. That was the story the old Dariyans told, but it was not the explanation which the Jinna astronomers, beholden to the great Gyptian philosopher Ptolomaia, set down in their books.

" 'The highest sphere encompasses all existing things,' " she said softly. *The Book of Secrets* lay so close behind her that she could feel its quiescent presence; she did not need to open its pages to quote from the text of the Jinna scholar al-Haytham whom she and Da had once met. " 'It surrounds the sphere of the fixed stars and touches it. It moves with a swift motion from east to west on two fixed poles and makes one revolution in every day and night. All the orbs which it surrounds move with its motion.' "

"Does this mean something I ought to understand?" Lounging on the bed, he yawned.

"We call Kokab the north star because it marks the north pole. There must be a south pole, too, which I haven't seen."

"Has someone seen it?"

"I don't know if any of the Jinna astronomers traveled so far. I don't know if there's any land in the south. They say it's all a desert, baked to sand under the sun's heat." Out among the palace buildings, people filtered away in ripples made of laughter and song and movement as hall and courtyard emptied. "Al-Haytham says that day and night increase the closer you are to the place where you would stand under the pole. It would be at zenith—"

He yawned the question more than spoke it.

She pointed, realized it had grown too dark for him to see her. "Zenith is straight above us. At that place, where you would stand right under the pole, the axis of the world is perpendicular. And the horizon then must coincide exactly with the circle of the celestial equator." The misery of the evening slid off of her as she stared at the stars. Their mysteries never failed to catch hold in her spirit and set her free to wonder. "But then daylight would be almost six months long. Well, as long as the sun remains in the northern signs. Because the sun would always be above the horizon. And night would be almost six months long when the sun was in the southern signs, because the sun would always be below the horizon. So it must also be true at the southern pole, only day and night would be the opposite of that which held at the northern pole. Isn't that elegant?" Now she yawned, the spell of the night wearing even on her. "Sanglant?"

He had fallen asleep.

All at once she realized how an unnatural quiet had spread like a cloud creeping out from the horizon to blanket the sky. She yawned again, shook it off.

"Sanglant?"

He grunted softly, but only to turn over. He was still fully clothed.

She leaned farther out the window, but only wind crackled in the branches. No sign of life stirred, not hounds sniffing after scraps, not an owl spying for mice, not even servants or rats picking clean platters left half full by drunken nobles. It was as if everyone had fallen abruptly into a profound sleep. The stars shimmered under a veil of haze, sundered from her who was trapped here in the mortal plane.

"Da?" If his soul streamed above her in the River of Heaven, pouring toward the Chamber of Light with the thousands of others released from the flesh, she could not see it.

Nervous, she crossed to the door and peeked out. Four Lions lay slumped, asleep, by the threshold. In the great courtyard, no living thing moved; dust swirled around abandoned tables.

The terror hit so hard that she could barely get the door closed, she began to shake so violently; she could barely hoist the bar and wedge it down in its place, barring them in. She turned to go to the window, but it was too late.

A shadow moved at the open window. A leg thrown over. The glint of gold hair by candlelight. His face, bruised but still beautiful. He set the candle down on the table. The Eika dog whined a warning and he kicked it as he strode past, crossing the chamber to her. He slapped her, hard, before she could even think to defend herself, then shoved her up against the door. With his body pressed against her she could feel his arousal, and, God help her, for an instant a spike of lust coursed through her only because her body was so alive to desire, made so by Sanglant's presence.

Then he hit her again.

She fought back, but he was in a frenzy; he was too far gone even to speak in that eloquent, beautiful voice. He grabbed her by the shoulders and wrestled her to the bed, flung her down beside Sanglant. Who did not wake. Who breathed most gently, eyes closed, face peaceful and yet, even in repose, proud and strong.

"Now you will give me what you give him!"

"Won't!" The word was forced out of her by his weight as

he dropped down on top of her, knee pressed against her chest and a hand on either shoulder. His face was bruised and his front teeth chipped; his beauty spoiled.

He let go of one shoulder to grope for his knife. "Or I'll kill him. I'll slit his throat while he sleeps here helplessly, and if you burn down this room around us he'll be the first to die!"

It was only a bad dream, wasn't it? She would wake up in an instant and everything would be fine.

The Eika dog whined, claws scrabbling weakly at the floor. Ai, God! Let her keep her wits about her even while terror drowned her. It was so hard not simply to slide away into the frozen tower where she had hidden all those months in Heart's Rest. But she could not. She must not.

"How can I know you won't kill him anyway, after you're done?" she asked hoarsely.

"You can't know! They're all asleep, Liath." His voice gentled. "No one can help you now, and do you dare risk burning down this place knowing the king rests next door, asleep? He'll not escape in time; he'll be the second to die. Will his death be on your head, too?" His face twisted again, and the bruise mottled in the inconstant light to become like the mark of the Enemy. "I will have what he has enjoyed! He's no better than a dog. How could you possibly prefer him to me!"

"I hate you."

He smiled with the old familiar beauty—not lost after all but merely poisoned. "Hate is only the other face of love, my beauty. You cannot hate what you cannot also love. You cannot possibly imagine how beautiful you looked seated beside the king. You looked truly to be a queen, set higher than the rest. I can't believe you were foolish enough to turn away from the king's favor for—this—this *dog!*"

"Jealousy is a sin." Just yesterday she had been able to hate him with all her passion, but, trapped by him against the bed, all that anger drained away. Numbness oozed from his hand like poison down her arm, invaded her chest, spread with the inevitable doom of a plague brought down by angels upon those who have turned their back on God's Holy Word.

"Then I will fall forever into the Abyss—but you will be at my side! Forever. We will ride out in the morning, back to Firsebarg. You and I—"

"Princess Sapientia—"

"What do I care for Sapientia? Ah, my beauty, how long I have waited for this. Perhaps the wait truly only makes it sweeter."

He pressed the knife against Sanglant's vulnerable throat. A line of red started up, not quite seeping.

"Ai, God," she breathed. She had nothing but fire, and fire would destroy what she loved.

"Take off your clothes, so I can see you who are dark and lovely."

Why hadn't Da's spell that protected her against all other magics protected her against Hugh's? Unless what Hugh had woven onto her during that long winter in Heart's Rest had not been any kind of spell at all but only cruelty and abuse.

Was it better to die with Sanglant?

"I told you what I wanted." He pressed the knife harder, and Sanglant actually murmured and shifted—but he did not wake. He could not wake. Hugh pressed the knife harder until blood trickled down the prince's neck.

The dog lunged, dragged itself forward, and gripped Hugh's trailing foot in its mouth; even weakened the dog had a sharp bite. Hugh jerked back and swore in pain, kicked free of the dog, and then kicked it back into the corner.

Which gave her time and chance.

She dove for her short sword.

He wrenched her back just as she got a grip on the handle. Slammed her against the wall. "I'll kill him! I promise you, I'll kill him. You're mine, damn you."

She fought him, trying to catch his hands so the blows wouldn't land; trying not to explode into a fire made manifest by terror. There Sanglant breathed, so peaceful, but so far away now that Hugh loomed everywhere. She would never be free of him. But at least if she fought, she would be dead.

"God damn you!" He took her throat in his hands. *"You are mine!* Or no one's."

"Hush, Brother. Calm yourself. I fear you are overwrought."

Hugh did not register the voice. Over his shoulder, Liath saw the door standing open. *She had barred that door.* Stunned into immobility, she felt the back of her head hit the wall as Hugh shook her by the throat, but she could only stare, limp and passive, as a veiled figure crossed the threshold and glided into the room.

"Brother," it said in a woman's sorrowful yet commanding alto, "this is unseemly behavior for any soul indeed and yet how much worse in a man sworn to the church and educated in its ways. Alas, how God's children have fallen!"

Now his grip slackened. His eyes widened, and his lips parted with astonishment. He let Liath go and she slid down the wall as though she hadn't any bones left and sat hard, jolting her spine, on the floor. Beside her, the Eika dog lay under the window like a dead thing.

He raised a hand, pointed it at the hooded figure as a threat— or as prelude to a spell.

But her hand, pale and smooth, rose in response, and abruptly Hugh clapped a hand to his throat. His mouth worked, but no sound came out.

"Such a lovely countenance, such an elegant voice, to be poisoned by such trivial weaknesses as lust and envy. I pity you, Brother." She stepped aside from the door. The opening yawned wide and as dark as the pit beyond, where nothing stirred. She might have walked into the chamber from out of thin air, and yet she had weight and substance and her footfalls made a faint noise as she moved. "You are not as powerful as you think you are, although I admit you have strength of will and a promising intelligence. Such a great talent to be wasted tormenting a helpless girl. You must scour all such base feelings from your soul and be purified by God's love. Then you will understand that the power we have on earth, the lusts that hunger in our flesh, are as nothing compared to the promise of the Chamber of Light. All is darkness, below. Above—" She gestured eloquently toward the ceiling, but by the sweep of her arm she included the high heavens in that gesture. "—there is only that light which is God's gentle breath."

Hugh could not speak, although he tried to. He tried to grasp his knife, but it kept slipping out of his fingers. He was helpless. And Liath exulted in her heart to see him so.

"Go, Brother. 'Heal thyself.' But do not trouble me or this child any longer."

He coughed out something, not words—perhaps a curse that had gotten stuck in his throat. He stumbled over to the table and fumbled for the candle and at last got the bronze handle squeezed between thumb and forefinger. Even so, he could barely stay upright; he grunted like a pig as he groped along the table. Then, suddenly, he dropped to his knees and got his arm under the strap to the leather pouch which before the struggle had been hooked to the dog.

"The book!" Liath tried to get up, but her bones had all melted and she could not move.

He staggered out, and the veiled figure just let him go.

With the candle gone, night shuttered the chamber in layers of shadow. Silence settled like so many owls coming to roost in the eaves.

Liath began to cry, and then to hiccup as she cried. Pain cut into her throat like a rope burn, winching tighter. Her shoulder hurt; her ribs ached; on her left hip a bruise throbbed painfully. Sanglant gave a soft sleeping snort and shifted on the bed.

"The book!" she said again, her voice made harsh by Hugh's grip.

The figure moved to the bed. "He will not find a mathematicus to train him in its use, unless he comes to us."

A light appeared suddenly from her upraised palm, a gently glowing globe lined with silver. She held it over the bed and its sheen of light illuminated the sleeping Sanglant—and the line of blood that traced the curve of his throat. With a casual gesture, she tipped back her cowl and veil so that the fabric draped along her shoulders rather like a small creature curled there.

She had pale hair drawn back into a braid that, curled into a bun, nestled at the back of her head. She wore no other head covering, and the shapeless robes concealed all else. From this angle, Liath could not see her face, only an ear and the suggestion of a strong profile, neither young nor old.

The woman bent forward and with the light held before her examined Sanglant with great interest. She touched his knees. She lifted each hand in turn to scrutinize palm and fingers before letting it fall limply back on the bed. She traced the swell of bone in his cheeks, parted his lips to study his teeth, and clasped his shoulders as if to gauge their strength. She pressed a hand on the old scar at the base of his throat, the visible mark of the wound that had ruined his voice, rubbed softly at the fresh raw wound only now beginning to heal, the mark of Bloodheart's iron collar, and then ran a finger along the shallow cut made by Hugh's knife to collect and taste his blood. Indeed, she behaved very like a noble lady who prefers to personally ex-

amine the fine stallion in question before she buys it to breed
into her herd.

"So this is Sanglant," she said in a tone of detached curiosity.

The name, uttered so dispassionately and yet with such a
sense of ancient and hoarded knowledge, startled Liath into
speaking. "Do you know him?"

"No mathematicus who studies the geometry of the heavens,
who is aware of that which exists beyond human ken, is unaware of him. Even the diomenes of the upper air whisper of
his progress from child to youth to man."

"Who are you?" Liath whispered. Her hands tingled sharply
as blood flooded back into them. She tried to stand, but her
knees gave out. She ached everywhere.

"Those in Duke Conrad's party know me as Sister Anne from
St. Valeria Convent." She displayed a pleasant smile that by no
means touched her eyes. She had an ageless face, hair made
paler by the silvery light of the globe that hovered at her fingertips, and, most astonishingly, a torque nestled around her neck,
braided gold that glittered in the magelight with each end twisted
off into a nub that an unknown master craftsman had formed
into a face resembling nothing as much as an angel resting in
beatific ecstasy.

"You aren't Sister Anne," Liath blurted out. "I saw her. She
was small, and old, and had wrinkled hands covered with age
spots, and different eyes, brown eyes."

"How can you have seen Sister Anne? Did you bide at St.
Valeria Convent for a time?"

Liath hesitated, then realized how foolish it was to fear her.
If this woman could turn aside Hugh's spells so easily, then
whatever she meant to do to Liath would be done whether or
not Liath fought against it. "I saw her in a vision through fire."

She smiled at this, looking truly pleased this time—no longer
a mask. She lifted her arm slightly to let the globe better illuminate her face. "Don't you know who I am, Liath?"

The globe pulsed with light. Liath struggled to her feet. She
had a terrible bruise forming in her right thigh where Hugh had
jammed his knee into it, and her shins throbbed where he had
kicked her. The silvery gleam grew stronger, the globe spit white
sparks, and suddenly the sparks blossomed into butterflies, flit-
ting everywhere, winged light like glass flying off all around
the room so that every corner became a field of splintering,

swooping light. As with a breath breathed onto them from an unseen source, each white spark bloomed into color: ruby, carnelian, amber, citrine, emerald, lapis lazuli, and amethyst, stars fallen to earth and caught within this chamber, and each one engaged in a dance of such peculiar beauty that she could only stare in awe.

Then she knew, of course. But she could not at first speak, not because of magic but simply because she could not remember how to speak.

Ai, God. Memory flooded, surfacing, as she turned back to face the one who held the globe of light. "Muh—Mother?"

She had a headache from the pounding her head had taken against the wall. Sparks swirled around her eyes, and then everything vanished, leaving her with a steady gleam of magelight and a cool, pale woman of vast power and middling height who regarded her with a thoughtful gaze unsullied by emotion.

"You have grown up, of course. Your beauty is unexpected and has caused you trouble, I see."

"Why have you come?" Liath asked stupidly.

She released the globe and it bobbed to the ceiling, sank, and drifted to a balance just below the eaves. "I have come for you, of course. I have been looking for you and Bernard for a long time. And now, at last, I have found you."

4

DURING her reign as Queen of Wendar and Varre, Sophia of Arethousa had been accused by certain clerics of the sin of living in luxury beyond what was seemly for humankind, and some had muttered that God had punished her for the excessive luxury of her habits by striking her down with a festering sore: as inside, so outside.

But Sanglant recalled her fondly. She had always in her cool way suffered Sanglant to roam in chambers made opulent by the extravagant display of the many fine possessions she had brought with her from Arethousa. As a child he had loved to

explore those chambers: the bold tapestries, the rich fragrance
of incense smothering the air, the bright reliquaries and crosses
set on elaborately-carved Hearths inlaid with ivory and gems,
the plush carpets on which a young boy could lie for hours
while tracing their intricacies with a finger, the sumptuous silks
that he would run his hands through just to feel their softness.
Once he had accidentally broken a crystal chessman, one of the
handsome horsemen he loved to play with as he imagined himself among their number, and although the piece was irre-
placeable, she had merely ordered a matching piece carved out
of wood and had said no more about the incident. His freedom
in her chambers had ended when he turned nine and was sent
off to learn to fight—to his fate, as he thought of it then.

But he had never forgotten the feel of that cloth. Around
Queen Sophia's bed had hung a gauzy veil that seemed to dissolve like mist when he clenched it in his small fist.

Now he clawed at a substance as filmy, struggling to free
himself from a tangle of gauzelike sleep that had wrapped around
him: The dogs would kill him if he couldn't wake up.

Never let it be said that he did not fight until his last breath.

Dreams fluttered at the edge of his vision: Hugh of Austra,
his handsome face poisoned by jealousy, setting a knife to his
throat; people and animals dead asleep throughout the palace
grounds like so many corpses left strewn on the field after a battle; an owl skimming east; depthless waters roiled suddenly by
the movement of creatures more man than fish; the Aoi woman
whose blood had healed him loping at a steady pace over interminable grasslands with a filthy servant riding at her heels on
a pony decked out in Quman style.

*She stops to scent the air, brushes her hand through the wind
as if reading a message. The servant watches her almost wor-
shipfully; he has no beard, and wears a torn and dirty robe that
might once have belonged to a frater as well as a Circle of Unity
at his neck. He waits as she lifts her stone-tipped spear and rattles it in the wind. The bells attached to its base tinkle, shattering the silence around him—*

"And now, at last, I have found you."

He bolted up, growling, and was on his feet with arms raised
to strike before he came entirely awake. In Bloodheart's hall,
speed had been his only defense. Speed—and a stubborn refusal

to die. From under the window the Eika dog growled weakly but did not otherwise stir.

"Sanglant!" Liath crossed to him and pulled his arms down, then stood there with one hand on his wrist. An uncanny light gleamed in the chamber, sorcerer's fire: heatless and fuelless. He steadied himself on her shoulder, and she winced—not from his touch, but from pain.

"What has happened?" He moved to stand in front of Liath, to protect her from the intruder, but she stopped him.

"This is my mother."

The gauze still entangled his mind. *Her mother.* He could see no trace of Liath in this woman's face, except that the unconscious pride with which Liath carried herself was made manifest in this noblewoman's carriage and expression: That she wore a gold torque did not astonish him, although it surprised him. Was she of Salian descent? She watched him without speaking and indeed without any apparent emotion except a touch of curiosity.

"What do you want?" he asked bluntly. "We are wed, she and I."

"So I have heard, as well as a great deal else. It is time Liath left this place."

"For where?" asked Liath.

"And with whom?" added Sanglant.

"It is time for Liath to fulfill that charge which is rightfully hers by birth. She will come with me to my villa at Verna where she will study the arts of the mathematici."

Sanglant smiled softly. Liath tensed, but whether with worry—or excitement—at the prospect he could not tell. And in truth, how well did he know her? The image he had made of her in his mind had little to do with her: In the brief days since she had returned, he had seen her to be both more—and less—than the imagined woman he had built his life around during those months of captivity. But he was willing to be patient.

"You speak of forbidden sorcery," he observed. "One that the church has condemned."

"The church does not condemn what is needful," Anne replied. "Thus I am assured that God approve our work."

"*Our* work?" he murmured.

Liath dropped his wrist and stepped forward. "Why did you

abandon Da and me? Why did you let us think you were dead for all those years?"

"I did not abandon you, child. You had already fled, and *we* could not find you."

"You must have known Da couldn't take care of us!"

She had a puzzling face, one that didn't show her years, yet neither did she appear young. "Bernard loved the world too much," she said sadly, although her expression never varied from that face that reminded him most of Sister Rosvita when she was soothing Henry: the mask of affability that all successful courtiers wear. "It was his great weakness. He could not turn away from the things of the flesh—all that is transient and mortal. He delighted in the spring plants, in the little fawns running among the trees, in your first steps and first words, but these delights are also a trap for the unwary, for by these means the Enemy wraps his tendrils around those of good heart who are seduced by the beauty of the world." She sighed in the way of a teacher who regards a well-loved if exasperating pupil. "I see his mark on you, Daughter. But his alone. No other hand has worked in your soul to corrupt you. To change you."

"To change me?"

"From what you are meant to be."

"Which is?" asked Sanglant.

"A mathematicus," said Anne firmly. "Gather your things, Liath. We will leave now and be gone long before day breaks."

"With what retinue do we travel?" asked Sanglant.

She regarded him with that unfathomable gaze, and for an instant the chamber dimmed, and his skin trembled as if snakes crawled up his arms and legs, and he was shaken by a fear like nothing he had ever felt before: what an ant might feel in that shadowed moment before a hand reaches down to crush it.

Then the moment passed, and he merely stood in an ordinary chamber fitted out with the usual luxuries due to a fighting man of noble birth: two carpets thrown over the plank floor; a chest filled with clothing and linens; a table and, with it, a chair rather than a common bench; an engraved copper basin and pitcher for washing his face and hands as well an enamel tray, several wooden platters, two bone spoons, two silver goblets and one bowl fashioned out of gold; a plush feather bed covered by a spread magnificently embroidered with the figure of a black dragon, sigil of his triumphs as a soldier. The globe of magelight illuminated every corner of the room and all that it held: every piece of it come to him out of his father's treasury and his father's favor, which was itself a kind of prison. His armor and weapons—his morning gift—gleamed under the light as if they had been enchanted with unknown powers. And perhaps they were: They had come to him through his own efforts.

"You propose to travel with us?" Anne asked finally.

"I am a king's son, and whatever your lineage, my lady, you cannot look down upon my kin and my noble birth."

"It is the sins of the world and the weaknesses of the flesh that I look down upon. Shall I subject my daughter to them further? Or save her from them by taking her away from all that tempts her?"

"The blessed Daisan said that within marriage we may find purification. Salvation arises out of creation."

She folded her hands before her like a saint readying for prayer. "You are a learned man, Prince Sanglant."

"Not at all. But I listen when the clerics read from the Holy Verses." He allowed himself a smile, half lost on his lips and quickly passing away. He knew a battle joined when he met one; and, as always, he intended to win.

"What have you to offer me?" she asked.

"The protection I can bring you as we travel, in exchange for which you will agree to feed and clothe me, and supply me with a suitable mount."

"I do not need that kind of brute protection. In addition, I have only two mounts suitable for riding. You have nothing but service to offer me, Prince Sanglant. Will you bind yourself to me as a servant, one who *walks* at my side?"

The first blow that lands always comes as a surprise. But he knew better than to flail.

Liath did not. Her anger fairly sparked off her. "I have something you want," she cried furiously.

Her anger had no effect on the depthless calm worn by her mother. "What is that?"

"Myself!"

"Earthly ties can only interfere with the concentration and detachment required of any person who wishes to learn the arts of the mind."

"I have a horse, and I will only go with you if Sanglant

comes with us. He will ride beside us on my horse not as a servant but as a soldier. As a captain."

"As he was once captain of the King's Dragons." Anne studied him. He recognized the measuring gaze of one whose course
of action is not yet fixed. But he chose to wait. Perhaps Liath's
flanking action would serve the purpose, and the truth was that
he did not care how the victory was won. He simply would not
leave her.

"His name is famous among the people of Wendar and Varre,
and among their enemies," Liath continued. "He is worth more
than you know."

Anne lifted a hand to capture the magelit globe and turn its
light directly upon him. He had to blink at first because the light
was so strong, but he did not shrink from her scrutiny. "Nay,
Liathano, I am not unaware of his worth, the child of human
and Aoi blood. Not at all."

Like a warning finger run up his back, his spine tingled.

"It is not what I expected," she said, still studying him in the
way an eagle gliding above the earth surveys the landscape below
and all that runs there. "But still . . . We can learn more than we
have known up until now."

"Then it's agreed?" Liath stuck stubbornly to the issue at
hand.

"It is agreed."

"Ai, Lady!" Liath embraced him, shedding a few tears. "I
pray God that we find the peace you long for when we reach
Verna."

He kept his arms around her but his gaze on her mother, who
watched them without approval and yet without any obvious cen-
sorious *dis*approval. Her gaze had its own disconcerting backwash. He did not trust her. Yet neither did he feel in his gut that
Liath's choice to go with her was the wrong one. This contra-
diction he could not explain to himself.

Liath sighed with satisfaction and raised her head to get a
kiss, and of course he complied.

But that did not mean he stopped listening.

"This, too, is unexpected," Anne murmured, too softly for
Liath to hear, but he heard very well, as well as a dog. "But not
without advantage for our cause."

*   *   *

The palace slept as they made their way through the upper enclosure, but it was a natural sleep; he recognized its rustlings and murmurings. As they packed their few possessions, Liath had haltingly told him the entire story of Hugh's attack, and while at first he had certainly wanted nothing more than to get his hands around Hugh's throat and throttle him, he knew enough to let the feeling swell and then burst. They were in enough trouble. Henry would refuse to let them leave; all three of them knew that unsavory fact, and they worked more quickly, and in such silence as they could, because of it, although it was a tricky business getting the gelding out of the stable.

When at last they arrived at the gate where three mules and one horse waited, he began to doubt Anne's princely appearance because she had no retinue. An instant later, he knew himself mistaken when he heard whispering on the air. They spoke in a language he did not recognize, more wind than voice, and he could not see them, but he heard the breath of their movement and the rustling of that portion of their invisible bodies which gave them substance.

"Who is there?" murmured Liath, as if afraid her whisper would wake the palace. The magelight seemed now to Sanglant merely a particularly bright lantern—although its glow had too steady a flame to be natural.

"My servants," said Anne softly.

He shuddered as fingers trailed over his back, searching, then vanished. Breath tickled an ear, and his hair stirred, blown into his eyes. By the time he brushed it away, he was alone again. He threw his armor—muffled in the dragon-sigil-bedspread—over the back of one of the pack mules and tied it on securely, then handed the spear to Liath. "I must get the dog."

"The dog!" He had surprised Anne.

"My retinue," he said sardonically. "If I leave it here, they will kill it. It saved my life more than once."

"Ghastly creature!" she muttered, but then that flicker of emotion fled and she merely nodded, as if the exchange—and the presence of the dog—were too trivial for her to notice.

He had to go quietly. In the chapel, clerics sang Vigils. Their voices rose and fell so sinuously that he almost lost step and forgot to walk, caught in their melodious prayer. Lions snored lustily at his door; none had woken from their magicked sleep. He crossed the threshold, hoisted the dog, and hauled it back to the gates. He threw it like a sack of grain over the back of one of the pack mules and fastened it there with rope, then calmed the mule, who did not take well to the smell of Eika on its back. But even working quickly, he did not finish in time.

Soldiers came out of the gloom, twenty or thirty of them, all of them leading horses burdened with a soldier's kit.

"My lord prince!"

Yet they spoke in whispers, not in a shout that would wake the palace and the gate guards who still slept at their posts.

"Who are these?" asked Anne mildly.

"My lady Sister!" Well trained to a man, they knelt respectfully as such milites would before any noble cleric. Surprised, Sanglant glanced at her. She had pulled a golden strip of cloth over her hair to cover it; no gold gleamed at her throat to betray her exalted rank. "I beg your pardon, my lord prince," continued their spokesman, the same Captain Fulk, "but when your recent trouble came upon you, we met together and pledged an oath all as one: That we would follow you if you left the king. We beg you, Prince Sanglant. Let us ride with you. We will follow you even into death if only you will give us your pledge to lead us faithfully."

"Ai, God." How could he answer them? Yet such a thrill of joy throbbed through him at the thought of men he could lead, comrades to live and fight beside, that he was at once stricken to tears at the memory of his brave Dragons.

Anne answered before he could find his voice. "Nobly offered. But where we go, they cannot follow. We cannot support so many in idleness, and in idleness they would grow bored and difficult. Nay, the contemplative life is not for such as these."

The men muttered at her words, but they waited for *his* answer. So many faces turned up to him: all of them young and newly come to soldiering except for two weathered-looking men, one of whom was Captain Fulk. Sanglant met each man's gaze and nodded at him, and each in turn responded in his own way: with an answering nod, a cocky grin, a serious frown, a bob of excitement, a tightening of the jaw as resolve set in.

"Sister Anne's words ring true enough," he said finally. His heart ached for what had been offered but was not his to take. Not now. Not yet. "I mean to go into seclusion . . . until my father's anger toward me cools. I would gladly lead you, my comrades, but it would be no fit life for you, and it is true you would only grow bored and contentious, and you would fight among yourselves."

"Then what are we to do, my lord prince?" asked Captain Fulk, almost pleading.

He owed them consideration. They had offered him everything that mattered to a soldier: to stand beside him. He could not simply dismiss them. "Go to Princess Theophanu. I tender you into her care. She keeps her own counsel, and she will watch over you. She rides south to Aosta soon enough, where you will see plenty of fighting. When I have need of you, then I will know where to find you. I will fight no battle without you at my side."

"We will do as you wish, my lord prince. But we will be waiting for your call."

He walked in among them, then, took each man's hand between his own as a sign of their fidelity. He recalled the names of those who had been at Ferse, and asked the names of the others. All twenty-seven had strong shoulders and an iron glint in their eyes: Men who dared defy the king to ride with him. He admired them, and he knew their worth.

Anne and Liath had already mounted, Anne upon one of the mules like a good churchwoman and Liath on the smaller horse, leaving Resuelto for his greater weight. They waited for him, and in the end he had already made his choice. It was time to go.

But God knew how hard it was to leave behind his life as prince, lord, and captain, made doubly hard by the oaths just freely offered to him.

"We will wait for you, Prince Sanglant," repeated Captain Fulk, and the men murmured those same words and by speaking them made them binding. Then, as if Fulk understood that their presence was a chain binding the prince, he directed the soldiers to disperse, which they did with dispatch and admirable efficiency. They had even muffled their horses' hooves in cloth to cover the sound of so many riding out.

Sanglant mounted Resuelto and hurried to catch Anne and Liath, who had already vanished through the gate and now rode down the road through the lower enclosure. The pack mules plodded behind them, burdens swaying in a steady rhythm. Of Anne's servants he saw no sign. An owl hooted but remained hidden in the darkness. The waning gibbous moon rode low in the west, and its light made the road gleam as though an enchanter's hand had laid that light down before them to make their way easy—and safe from anything that might harm them.

Anne did not even look back as they crossed out of the lower enclosure and picked their way down through the ramparts. Liath glanced back once at the palace grounds now high above them, walls washed a pale gray under the moon, and she looked relieved more than anything. But he wept softly, in grief for the estrangement from his father and in regret for the brave men he had left behind.

VI
ONE STONE AT
A TIME

1

HE *gathers stones, none larger than his fist, none smaller than a hen's egg, and collects them in a leather pouch. The stones must not be too large, all together, for him to carry, but they must not be too small to serve his purpose—and there must not be too few of them. Here in the northlands, stone offers a rich harvest, and although his specifications are strict, he has no trouble finding what he seeks.*

He hears footsteps, but it is only one of his slaves, come to report. He sends the slave on her way. Armed with this intelligence, for he has made of his slaves a net of listening posts to seek out his rivals, he makes his way up along the vale to the spot where his last two rivals face off.

He finds a vantage point between two boulders. With interest he watches the duel: First Son of the First Litter, calm, canny, and strong, waits as Seventh Son of the Second Litter circles in aggressively. Too aggressively. He watches dispassionately as the two brothers meet, clash, rip, and leap back. Seventh Son is quick and ruthless. First Son has greater strength, but he wastes it not, for the duel is still young. He lets Seventh Son feint and circle, lunge, parry, and retreat, and hoards his own strength meanwhile.

Another lunge, another blow. Blood flows, eases. First Son wears a gash in his left shoulder. Seventh Son limps. They begin again.

In the end it is simply a matter of time. Seventh Son is fierce, but fierceness does not count for everything. First Son did not escape from the ruin of Gent with a large portion of his warband intact by being foolish. Nor is he foolish here.

In the end, it is Seventh Son who lies bloody and torn upon the earth. Fifth Son does not wait for First Son to cut the braid that will mark his victory, but retreats from his hiding place and cuts through trees to the path that leads up to the fjall, to the nest of the WiseMothers. He passes the newest WiseMother, still on her slow journey to the fjall, but he does not stop to speak to her. He must have time if he is to defeat First Son.

At this elevation all vegetation has been scoured away by the unceasing wind and the unforgiving chill, all but moss, moss everywhere except on those slopes where there is a recent fall of scree. Snowmelt streams flow downslope, as clear as air and bitterly cold. Everywhere rock lies, tumbled in the streambeds, smothered in moss, blanketing the slopes; rock is the mantle that shrouds the deep earth and the hidden fire.

Here an arm of the fjord has sliced into the high fjall, and a stream spills over a cliff that plunges straight down like a knife cut. The falling water booms down to the tongue of fjord. The cliff he stands on is mirrored in the still water far below. For a moment, he sees his own shape, indistinct and tiny, a transitory blot upon the ancient land, and then the wind moving over the water obliterates him—as will his own mortality, in time. But not this day.

A dog howls in the distance. A hawk soars above the opposite cliff face, joined by a second hawk, then a third.

Wind stirs on his shoulders, and he turns away from the edge and makes his way to the ring of WiseMothers. He watches the ground with care, because here on the fjall the silvery nets of the ice wyrms change from season to season as their paths change, snaking lines of glimmering sand, each grain a crystal shard of venom: Their trail.

It is a peculiarly still day, wearing away to what passes for night at this season. Here on the fjall the wind usually cuts un-

ceasingly, sawing and grinding away at the rock. Today it rests quiescent, stirring only occasionally as if it, too, awaits the decision soon to be reached on the nesting ground of the Wise-Mothers.

The land dips to make a hollow, where the Rikin WiseMothers congregate and whisper. Their thoughts reverberate into the heavens, and touch OldMan, the moon, the priest who in ancient days was banished to the fjall of the heavens as punishment for his transgressions. That is why the moon alone among all the heavenly creatures fades and dies, and is born again out of darkness. Such is the fate of all sons of the RockChildren.

The WiseMothers stand hunched in a rough circle, huge bodies ossifying, too heavy now to move. Each one stands with her toes just grazing on the expanse of silver sand. The sand lies smooth; no trace of the ever-present wind touches it; no debris lies scattered from recent storms; no scallops ripple its surface, for the nest of the WiseMothers is impervious to wind and guarded by the ice-wyrms.

Only the WiseMothers know what they are incubating here.

For a long while he watches the glimmering hollow. Nothing stirs. Nothing.

But that is illusion.

Even the small creatures that haunt the fjall know to avoid the nesting grounds.

He takes a rock from the pouch and tosses it. Where it hits the sand with a thunk, a shudder ripples out from it actually visible in the surface just as a tossed stone ripples still water. As the vibrations stir the sand away on the other side, where the rock fell, he slides one foot onto the hard surface and follows with the second.

The stone tilts, rocks. A gleaming claw, translucent like ice, surfaces to hook the stone. That fast, stone and claw vanish. He stops dead still. The sand where the stone hit eddies, smooths over, and lies still again.

He waits.

He dares not move.

He does not fear the claws of the ice-wyrms. They are fragile creatures, sightless, as thin as rope, at home only when they burrow deep in their nests of crystallized venom. Even starlight burns them.

But there is no creature the RockChildren fear as much as

the ice-wyrms. *No death compares to the wretched fate that awaits one who is stung. The venom of the ice-wyrms nourishes the WiseMothers, who nurse the roots of the earth. They alone are strong enough to take succor from it.*

To all other creatures, it brings that which is worse than death. In this way Bloodheart protected himself, with a dead nestbrother animated by magic and fueled with venom. That is the mark of an enchanter: Even after death his hand can strike down the one who killed him.

He reaches into the pouch, draws out another stone, and tosses it. One stone at a time, he slides out across the nesting ground toward a small hummock that emerges from the silver sands in the center. As hard as iron, the surface of the hummock is polished to a pearlescent gleam.

It takes him half the short summer's night to get there, but when he reaches the hummock and takes that last step onto its slick surface, he can shake out his tense limbs. The rounded dome warms his feet, and it smells faintly of sulfur. He is safe.

Safe, that is, until he has to cross back.

He has made this journey before. Only here, in the center of the nesting ground, can mortal ears hear the whispering of the WiseMothers. No creature enslaved to the earth lives long enough to hear even one of their thoughts in its entirety. But the youngest of the WiseMothers can still speak, if only one has the patience to listen. He has listened to them before. He has brashly asked their advice.

Yet it is not their advice he seeks this day.

Night fades to morning. He waits. First Son does not come. He waits, and listens.

"They. Will. Pass. The. Bridge. And. The. Cataract."

"They. Will. Part. The. Waters. The. Fire. Rivers. Will. Change. In. Their. Course."

"Make. Room. Make. Room."

A sigh passes through them, wind groaning down from the northern fjalls, murmuring out of the eastern fjalls, and whispering in the faint voices of those few scattered to the south where the land has been worn away one stone at a time by tide and current, where sea and ocean meld and mingle to breathe the vapor of their disparate perfumes into the salt-strewn air.

What the WiseMothers speak of is mystery to him. The sun passes its noonday height and begins to sink before he hears a *stealthy footfall, followed by the frustrated roar of First Son of the First Litter as he springs out from the rocks and stands on the brink of the nesting ground.*

"Coward!" he cries. "Do you think to hide from me there? Weakling! You must have water and food in time, or you will wither away and return to dust. Come and fight."

"Come and get my braids," says Fifth Son. He displays the three braids he has tied around his arm. "If I die out here, you will still have to come and get these to prove your worthiness before OldMother."

For a moment only First Son gapes, taken by surprise. He, strongest and canniest among them all, wears only a single braid wound round one arm. But he will not ask how his rival gained so much while he was gaining so little; he controls his surprise quickly. He is not foolish.

He gathers stones from the verge of the nesting ground, and when he has gathered enough, he tosses the first one to the opposite side of the sandy surface. The surface ripples as he slides a foot out onto the sand, then freezes. A claw spikes into the air and curls around the distant stone. Stone and claw vanish. First Son tosses another.

Fifth Son waits as the sun sinks and First Son slowly crosses the glimmering sand. He waits until First Son has come about half the distance between him and the rock. Then, casually, as soon as First Son has gone still and the last stone thrown by him has vanished under the surface, he takes a stone from his pouch, measures the distance, and tosses it to land at First Son's feet.

There is a moment of stillness. Wind whispers at his back. The long afternoon shadows of the WiseMothers stripe the nesting ground, cloudy, bright, cloudy, bright.

First Son springs, dashing for the safety of the central hummock. But no creature can run faster than the ice wyrms.

Three claws pierce the sand, engulfing the stone, and then the thick shaft of a tail thrusts through, whipping back and forth, seeking. The creature's skin is so clear, like ice, that Fifth Son sees the venom curdling beneath. It strikes. The spiked tail recoils faster than the eye can see. Three times it strikes, for First Son is nimble and desperate enough that his luck holds twice as he dodges; but on the third it stings. And vanishes beneath the sand.

First Son howls in pain, in fury. In fear.

In his convulsions, he drops all the stones he has gathered for the return trip. They rain down around him like so much fist-sized hail. Tiny claws seek, find, and gather them into their grave, where they will lie for aeons in the clutches of the ice-wyrms. What use do the ice wyrms have for stones?

Who can know?

As First Son shakes and jerks, as spittle and frothy copperish blood foam from his mouth and nostrils and ears and eyes, Fifth Son cautiously slides off the hummock and circles it. First Son's thrashing and spasms certainly will disorder the filaments that carry sound and motion to the burrowing ice-wyrms. But he still has to get the braids off First Son before he vanishes beneath the sands and thus those two trophies become lost to him. This is the most dangerous part, because it must be timed just right so that he reaches First Son after he can no longer struggle but before the ice wyrms drag him beneath.

Slowly Fifth Son circles. Slowly his rival stiffens or really, more precisely, solidifies.

His convulsions slow, stall, and the tiny claw stalks, the tendrils of the ice-wyrms, twine like vines up his legs and begin to haul him down, an ungainly process with something this large. First Son's eyes are frantic with fear, the only fear one of the RockChildren is ever allowed to express without losing all honor and position. Fifth Son tosses a stone to the opposite side of the nesting ground and as the movement ripples out, attracting attention over there, he slides in toward his rival, who can see him but no longer resist.

He cuts off his brother's braid. He takes for himself the braid of Seventh Son, gained only yesterday. The day grows dim, as dim as it will get at this time of year. Only the brightest stars in the fjall of the heavens can pierce midsummer's cloak.

He tosses a stone and slide-steps away, far enough to watch safely, and then he waits, still and silent with his feet on the venomous sands.

He watches as First Son is swallowed under the sands. He is helpless, and will remain so for a very, very long time. The priests say that the ice-wyrms digest that which they drag down into their nest, or that the thing which incubates there and which they protect digests it.

Who can know? Who has ever returned to speak of such a thing?

The WiseMothers do not answer that particular question.

According to the priest, who may or may not know the truth of these matters, for it is in their interest to claim knowledge that they might not actually possess, it can take up to a thousand years for the living rock—that which First Son has now become—to be digested in the belly of the nesting ground. A thousand years is the life span of twenty-five RockChildren, each one measured from the ending of the last. That is a long time to take to die, and every moment of it—so the priests say— awake, aware, and in agony.

But a thousand years is nothing to the sea. A thousand years is nothing to the wind. And to the bones of the earth laid bare at the surface as rock, a thousand years might encompass the merest shifting of one finger of a WiseMother's hand. To the stars that lie above in the fjall of the heavens, a thousand years does not even encompass a thought.

One stone at a time he moves out of the hollow, and he reaches safe ground as dawn brightens the short summer's gloom that passes as night.

From far below he dreams he hears the singing of Swift-Daughters and the stamp and scrape of their feet on the dancing ground. He counts his braids: one, two, three, four, five. And the sixth his own, still attached to his head.

Triumphant, he descends from the fjall to proclaim his victory.

When Alain woke, finding himself tangled in the bedclothes and alone in the bed, he heard Tallia praying. She spoke the words in a rush, as if she feared she would not have time to say them all. It was near dawn. She knelt by the unshuttered window, modestly clothed in a shift, with her head bent and her slight shoulders curled as under a great weight.

Even this sight stirred him. He flushed and rolled onto his stomach, but it was no good. Sorrow stirred and rose to follow him as he heaved himself off the bed, stumbled against the sleeping Rage, and hurried outside. Tallia paid him no mind, or perhaps she truly did not notice him because she was too caught up in her prayers. Because she insisted on such modesty, he, too, slept in a shift. Now, in the gray dawn rising, he was glad of the covering. A stream ran by the monastery guesthouse where they had sheltered for the night. The shock of it on his legs calmed him. He splashed his face, shuddering, and then climbed out to the opposite side to relieve himself in the bushes. Sorrow growled softly, sniffing through the bracken, nosing up forest litter. The hound had a fondness for beetles, and he snapped one up now. Wind sighed through leaves. A drizzle began to fall. With his feet muddy and his hands chilled, Alain staggered back inside. He had recovered his equanimity enough to sit on the bed, although he dared not kneel beside her. She could go on for hours like this.

As soon as it was light, the servants came, washed his feet, took away the chamber pot and brought out his clothing. Tallia had to cease praying so that they could make ready to leave. Count Lavastine, riding home triumphant, did not intend to waste time on a leisurely journey.

Outside, Lavastine greeted him with that brief smile which in him signaled his deepest. approval. He greeted Alain in this fashion every morning, and occasionally in a most uncharacteristic manner made labored and mercifully brief jests about becoming a grandfather. It made Alain sick at heart to hear him speak so. Surely the servants, who slept on pallets or on the floor beside the bed of their master and mistress, suspected that the marriage went unconsummated. Yet Tallia had twice now rebuked him for tossing and turning so on the bed when he was deep in sleep, dreaming, no doubt, of Fifth Son. Servants might assume anything from such small noises. Why should they believe anything else? God in Unity had made female and male in Their image, to live in harmony together, and had conferred immortality upon them in this way: that through their congress they could make children, and their children make children in their turn. In this way humankind had prospered, as had all the creatures of earth, air, and water.

In this way the county of Lavas would prosper.

He tried not to think about it too much. When he was near Tallia, his body had an unfortunate tendency to react in ways that embarrassed him. Was she so much holier than he was? Was it a sign of her worthiness in God's eyes that she could pray half the night to God's glory while he slept soundly? That she cleansed herself with fasting while he wolfed down his meals as eagerly as his hounds? That she begged him for a marriage of two pure souls unsullied by earthly lust while he knew in his heart—and elsewhere—that his soul was already stained by desiring her so fiercely?

"You are quiet, Son," said Lavastine. "This is a fine morning. The rain is a blessing from God, for the crops will grow greener because of it."

"And all our fortunes prosper," said Lord Geoffrey, who rode at the count's left hand. Alain glanced at him. Was his tone sour, or was that only Alain's imagination? Geoffrey was usually scrupulously polite. "You would have been better served, cousin," continued Geoffrey, "to tend the gardens at court more assiduously. There are many factions to be watered."

"I see no point in gardening where I have no skills. The king supports me. That is all I need to know."

"The king, God's blessing on him, will not live forever. There was a rumor at court that the king means to name his bastard son as heir after him. But Princess Sapientia has her own adherents, and they will not stand by and do nothing if that comes to pass."

"The king has favored me with the reward I most wished for. Now I will toil in those fields that God cherishes most: to make sure my fields and my folk prosper."

"Is that what God most cherishes?" asked Tallia. "God wishes us to cleanse ourselves of the stain of darkness that has corrupted all earthly creatures, all save the blessed Daisan."

"Even the blessed Daisan labored in the fields of earth, my lady Tallia. Is He not also known as the shepherd who brought us all into the fold? What if there were no women spinning and weaving, no men smithing or toiling to grow crops, and no lady and lord watching over them as God have ordained each to her own station? Then what would become of those good church-folk who pray for our souls and for their prayers are given wax and wheat and cloth as their tithe?"

"Why, then, they would shed their earthly clothing—which is nothing but a burden—and ascend to the Chamber of Light!" she replied, looking surprised.

That twitch of the mouth signaled irritation. Alain recognized it, but not even the count of Lavas dared criticize a woman who, although now his daughter-in-law, outranked him. "So they would," he agreed curtly.

Lavastine had sent most of his men home before him, after

Gent, but Tallia had brought an impressive retinue of her own, one provided for by the king's generosity. They rode home like a victorious army.

"Do not be seduced by the pleasures of the court, Alain," Lavastine added. "What use to fly about in the train of the king? For his pleasure? His favor?"

"The favor of the regnant is nothing to sneer at," retorted Geoffrey, stung. "It is no sin to enjoy hunting and the pleasures of court."

"So I have observed," said Lavastine in his quietest and most scathing voice, "that you have acquainted yourself well with hunting, hounds, horses, and hawks, but rather less with fabric-making, blacksmithing, agriculture, commerce, and medicine."

"I have a wife, and she has a chatelaine and a steward.'

"So you do, and so she has. I also have a chatelaine. But what captain can expect to win a war when he makes merry in his tent while battles are fought outside? No matter how sweet his songs. Nay, cousin, we gain greater favor by pleasing God as I have described."

"We gain God's favor by prayer!" said Tallia stubbornly.

"So we do." He always agreed with her. Then he smiled. "And I pray God that my house is blessed soon with the fruit of your marriage to my son."

"Indeed," said Alain with feeling. "May God so bless this house."

Tallia blushed scarlet, glancing at him and then away. A few of their attendants chuckled. Lord Geoffrey smiled thinly.

The road crossed into forest, and for a while they rode in silence, making good time on the smooth dirt path that cut through the trees. Even the wagons rolled swiftly, unjarred by ruts. Now and again the woodland opened into a meadow where flowers bloomed. A doe bounded away, followed by a half-grown fawn. A buzzard soared above the trees.

They came to a village at midday, and children ran up to watch them ride by, only to scatter at the sight of the black hounds. At the village well they stopped to water their horses at the trough. Once Alain had secured the hounds, the village householders came forward to pay their respects. One old woman had a wickedly sharp cider that brought tears to Alain's eyes and made him a little giddy, and he thanked her, amused by her laughter at his reaction.

Yet it wasn't just the cider. The sight of Tallia, in such sun-light, made his head spin. She had covered her hair with a shawl, neatly folded and tucked, but even so wheat-colored strands of hair curled free. She had a way of standing, hands lax and mouth slightly parted, that made his heart ache to comfort her. Offered a cup, she took it—to refuse was unworthy of a noblewoman of her consequence—and sipped at the cider. Alain envied the humble wooden cup, whose plain surface in this way met her lips. When she had finished, she gave the cup to her attendants to drink from, and when it was refilled, they handed it to the servants. After this, Tallia waited by the well while the house-holders brought loaves, cakes fried of flour and honey, and a pungent cheese. These offerings were modest, but they seemed to please her more than any feast.

"Will the young lord take an egg?"

It was a rich gift for such a village, offered by a young woman no older than Tallia. She had dirty blonde hair pulled back in a braid, a face hastily washed with dirt still smearing her neck and patching one ear, and an appetizing shape that her clothing did little to disguise. She had a pretty smile, and she opened his hand so she could roll the egg onto his palm. It was warm, roasted, and her fingers were warm as well. Alain was suddenly terribly glad that their party wasn't spending the night here. He flushed, she thanked him, and abruptly Tallia came over to stand beside him.

Someone laughed. The village girl retreated, not without a backward look. Tallia had a high stain of color in her cheeks, and, daringly, she took hold of his hand right out there in pub-lic.

It was a tiny victory. He squeezed her fingers, feeling tri-umphant—truly hopeful—again.

"God will only favor our sacrifice as long as we both remain pure," she murmured.

His reply stuck in his throat. He felt like he'd been kicked. She let go of his hand and went over to her horse as soon as Lavastine's steward called the servants to order, leaving him standing there. He didn't have the heart to eat the egg himself. He peeled it, broke it in half, and fed it surreptitiously to Sor-row and Rage.

They had ridden not an hour out from the village when an outrider clattered up to tell the count that an Eagle had been sighted, riding after them. Lavastine obligingly pulled the party aside and soon after a weary-looking Eagle rode into view. He had a remount on a lead behind him, rings of dust around his eyes, and hair that would have been red if it hadn't been so dusty from riding.

"Count Lavastine. I am sent by order of His Majesty, King Henry. This tale came to his ears through the agency of Prince Sanglant." He paused. Alain knew the look of Eagles recalling a message memorized days or weeks ago. " 'Count Lavastine must beware. The one whose arrow killed Bloodheart is protected against magic, and if Bloodheart's curse still stalks the land, then it seeks another.' "

"A curse," muttered Lord Geoffrey.

"Prince Sanglant spoke of a curse before," said Alain. "The Eika, at least, believed it could affect them."

"Yet Bloodheart is dead." Lavastine smiled grimly. "Nevertheless, I value my life as much as any man, and in particular the life of my son. Let men march in a square around the riders, each one a spear's length apart, and let them keep their eyes to the ground and look for any creature that might fit the description Prince Sanglant gave us. Let my clerics pray, and cast such charms as God allow. We must trust in God to see that no harm comes to those who have been faithful to Their commands." He gestured to signify that this was his will on the matter. Terror barked once, and Fear answered. Steadfast and Bliss sat, panting, on the verge. Sorrow sniffed in the brush growing in the ditch that lined the road, and Rage had flopped down on the track in the shade of a wagon.

Lavastine turned back to the Eagle. "Return to the king. Tell Prince Sanglant that I am beholden to him for his warning. I will do what I can should he ever have need of my aid."

Geoffrey hissed out a breath. "If the court divides on the issue of succession, then you have as good as declared yourself for the prince."

"God enjoin us to honor our debts," retorted Alain.

Lavastine nodded. "Eagle, have you understood the whole?"

The Eagle looked uncomfortable. "Matters are troubled between king and prince," he said, choosing his words with care. "There was an altercation at court, and when I left Werlida the prince had retired to his rooms in disgrace. His own dogs attacked the king, he struck a holy frater in front of the entire court, and he has gone against the king's will and claims to have wed a woman of minor family who has in addition had accusations of foul sorcery laid against her." Then, noticing that his voice had risen, he coughed and finished in a more temperate tone: "But he may be bewitched."

"Liath!" breathed Alain. Tallia turned in the saddle to stare at him with a frown.

"The Eagle," said Lavastine.

"An Eagle no longer," said the Eagle before them. "Stripped of her cloak and badge. She is now the prince's concubine. Or was, when I left Werlida."

"She would have done better to come with us. The displeasure of the king is a hard path to walk." Lavastine considered the road in silence. His milites were already moving into their new positions around the riders, and two of his clerics had lit censers to purify the road before and behind with incense. "Tell King Henry that if this disgraced woman has no other place to go, the count of Lavas will take her in."

"Are you sure that is wise, cousin?" demanded Geoffrey.

"I am sure it is prudent, and farsighted. I know danger when I see it, and she is no danger to us. There is something there . . ." He trailed off, drawn away down an unknowable path; a moment later, blinking, he shook himself. "Who holds her holds a strong playing piece."

But as the Eagle rode off and their retinue lurched forward again into their new marching order, the words Tallia had spoken on their wedding night rang in Alain's ears as though she had only spoken them moments before:

"I am merely a pawn, nothing more than that. As are you, only you do not see it."

2

AT the palace of Werlida, Queen Sophia had commissioned a garden to be built in the Arethousan style. Shaped as an octagon, it had eight walls, eight benches, eight neatly tended garden plots that bloomed with brilliant colors in spring and summer, and eight radial pathways leading in to the center where stood a monumental fountain formed in the shape of a domed tower surrounded by eight tiers of angels, cavorting and blowing trumpets. According to legend, the fountain had ceased flowing on the very day Queen Sophia died.

In fact, the fountain had ceased flowing years before that because the Arethousan craftsman who had devised the cunning inner workings had died of a lung fever one winter and no one else knew how to repair it.

But the story persisted, as such stories do.

Now Rosvita made a leisurely circuit of the fountain together with half a dozen of Theophanu's young companions, noble girls who had gravitated around the princess as part of her entourage. Theophanu stood on the lowest tier with her feet on the stone wings of one angel and a hand clutching a trumpet on the third tier for balance. Standing thus, she could get a better view over the retaining wall out to where the road branched at the base of the lower enclosure.

From the garden a magnificent vista opened before them. The land spread out as fields and villages, pastureland and scrub brush and woodland, and finally the distant march of forest. The river wound south, a ribbon vanishing into the haze of trees.

From the gravel path, Rosvita watched as Duke Conrad's entourage reached the branching road and his banners turned south. From this distance, she could only guess which figure was his.

Was Conrad thinking about Theophanu? Did he truly regret that Henry had forbidden the match, or was his anger for the insult implicit in Henry's refusal?

Did Theophanu regret the lost chance for a betrothal, or was she relieved? Rosvita could not tell. Another person might rage, or sulk, or weep. Theophanu either did not have the heart for it, or concealed her heart too well.

"Theophanu!"

Prince Ekkehard marched down a path at the head of a gaggle of boys. The schola had only arrived in Werlida yesterday.

"Are you happy to see Conrad go?" demanded Ekkehard as he scrambled onto the stonework beside Theophanu. "I wanted to go with him to Wayland, but Father says I'm to go to Gent and become abbot of the monastery he means to establish there dedicated to St. Perpetua in thanks for Sanglant's rescue. But I don't want to go to Gent and certainly not just because Father is so mad that Sanglant ran away with that woman. I don't know why he's punishing me for what Sanglant did." Ekkehard talked more than he thought. But perhaps he had stumbled on the heart of the matter nevertheless: the change in Henry's behavior that had come about since the morning they had all risen to discover Sanglant and Liath gone.

Theophanu's inscrutable smile did not change as she answered. "He isn't punishing you, Ekkehard. He's giving you authority of your own. Remember that we are royal children. Father will use us as he sees fit, to strengthen the kingdom."

Was there a trace of irony in her voice? Even sarcasm? Rosvita could not be sure.

The gates into the garden opened again, and their quiet contemplation was completely overset as the king and his courtiers entered in the wake of Ekkehard. The chatter of the mob irritated Rosvita. What had happened to unbalance her equilibrium? Didn't she always pride herself on her cleric's amiability and even temper? Hadn't she gained the love and trust of king and court, not to further her own ambition but because it was her duty as one of God's servants? She had not felt so much disturbance in her mind for many years. Like Henry, she desperately wanted to know what had happened to Sanglant and Liath, but until Henry mentioned the subject, no one else dared to.

Courtiers fluttered around the king, chief among them the Salian and Ungrian ambassadors. Sapientia clearly preferred the elegant Salian lord who had journeyed here on behalf of Prince Guillaime, but Henry hid his leanings and let himself be courted. As he reached the fountain, he turned away from the Ungrian ambassador to help Theophanu down from her perch. Ekkehard leaped down after her.

"Will I get to ride out to hunt with you tomorrow, Father?" he demanded.

"Of course." But Henry was distracted by the sight of Conrad's entourage crossing into the forest. Was he thinking of Sanglant as he watched them go? He drew Theophanu to him, and a moment later he and Villam and several other lords began to discuss the situation in Aosta, leaving Ekkehard to stand helplessly at the edge of their discussion.

"My lord prince. I hope I don't intrude." Judith's young husband Baldwin slid into the vacant space beside Ekkehard. "Perhaps you'll recall that we met last night."

"You're Lord Baldwin, Margrave Judith's husband."

"So I am," agreed Baldwin guilelessly.

For an instant a smirk hovered on the young prince's lips, but Ekkehard had learned manners in a hard school, and he recovered himself. "Of course I remember you."

"I've heard nothing but praise for your singing, my lord prince. Perhaps in the days to come you might honor us with some songs." Baldwin was, truly, an exceptionally handsome young man, and Rosvita watched with some amusement as Ekkehard melted under the combined flame of prettiness and flattery.

"I see no reason to wait! We'll go now. And perhaps you'll ride out to hunt with me tomorrow."

"Of course, my lord prince. I am yours to command."

They strolled away together. Was that Ivar in their wake, looking as sullen as a dried-up frog? She had not been allowed to speak to Ivar, who was under a novice's vows, but perhaps that was for the best. When Judith and her retinue returned east, he would be safely confined to a monastery, where labor, study, and prayer would circumscribe his day and leave him little time to dwell on that which was forbidden him.

Rosvita shivered, thinking of the silence of the convent. No, indeed, she had not truly been at peace since the day the *Vita* of St. Radegundis had come into her hands. The mouse's hunger gnawed at her, unceasing and implacable. She had so many questions, and too few answers.

Where had Sanglant gone? What had happened to *The Book of Secrets?* Had Liath bewitched him with magic, or had the prince overwhelmed the poor young woman with his attentions?

Did Henry's seeming calm only cover a furious heart that would fester and, in time, erupt in some other form?

"Sister." Brother Fortunatus had sidled into the garden behind the king's retinue. She bent close to hear his whisper. "I stood at the lower gate and observed every rider and every wagon. There was no sign of Sister Anne of St. Valeria Convent in Conrad's retinue."

"Sister Amabilia has found no sign of her in the lower enclosure either?"

"No, Sister." She had never before seen him so grim. "She has vanished."

"It is a mystery," agreed Rosvita. "Draft a letter, Brother. We must inform Mother Rothgard as soon as possible."

He nodded obediently and retreated, and his white-robed figure was soon swallowed in the milling mob of courtiers, who had expanded onto all the paths to exclaim over the beauty of the flowers and the grave little sculptures, mostly saints and angels, that populated the garden or waited with the patience of stone in niches carved into the walls.

Judith and the Ungrian ambassador had walked over to the outer wall to watch the last of Conrad's impressive retinue pass from sight. Rosvita moved closer to listen.

The man spoke with the aid of an interpreter. "This daughter he has taken away, she is the granddaughter of the Alban queen, is she not? How does Duke Conrad gain for his wife a daughter of the Alban queen, when he is no king himself?"

Judith had a smile that softened her mouth and made her gaze quite hard. "If you wish your suit to succeed, I would not ask that question of the king."

"So I did not do so," he said, laughing. Cousin to the Ungrian king, he had a jovial face, long, dark mustaches that he greased with oil, and a wispy beard no thicker than that of a sixteen-year-old boy although his own hair had white streaking it. "But it is said that men work as slaves in Alba while women rest as queens, and that no daughter of their ruling house before this one left her mother's side. So I wonder."

"Many have wondered," replied Judith, looking faintly amused. "Duke Conrad traveled to Alba when he was young. Some say he charmed the Alban queen into agreeing to the betrothal. Some say he charmed the daughter and ran off with her when her mother refused his suit."

"But he do not run off with the Princess Theophanu, although the king refuse his suit."

"Alba is an island. Henry will not need a fleet of ships to pursue Conrad, should Conrad displease him."

"Ah, I see much truth in your words." The Ungrian ambassador wore a fine silk tunic of Arethousan design but spoiled the elegance of his dress by draping a heavy fur cape over his shoulders despite the summer heat. He stank of a sickly sweet perfume that gave Rosvita a headache. "Will the king bless this wedding, or will he prefer the Salian prince?"

Judith only smiled coolly. "I, too, wish the Quman raids to end. My lands have been hit hard these last two years, as have yours, and if Wendish and Ungrian armies join together, then perhaps we can strike into the heart of Quman lands and put an end to their plundering. But of course there is the problem of worship, my friend. The Arethousan deacons you keep in your retinue do not adhere to the church practices observed by the skopos in Darre. A Wendish princess cannot marry an Ungrian prince who does not worship according to the correct manner. King Geza must recognize the primacy of the skopos in Darre rather than the illegitimate patriarch in Arethousa if he desires this alliance with King Henry."

"Henry's blessed wife was an Arethousan."

"Blessed by the skopos in Darre."

"As King Geza is willing to be, if Henry offers him this alliance."

Judith shrugged to show that she was helpless in this matter. "Then you have done all you can. The king will speak when the king makes up his mind."

The king did not speak that day, but the next night at the feast in honor of the birth of Sts. Iskander and Dawud, the holy twins, he rose to toast Sapientia and to announce her betrothal. Rosvita's fingers were sticky with honey; it was traditional at the feast of the twins to drink honey mead and eat honey cakes because of the famous miracle of the bees. She licked her fingers hastily and grabbed the cup she shared this night with Princess Theophanu. Henry had not asked her advice as he usually did, but since the debacle with Sanglant four days ago Henry had spent his days and evenings carousing with no apparent thought for serious matters.

There was a pause while the king watched his court hoist their cups in anticipation.

Brother Fortunatus, behind her, muttered to Amabilia. "Have you laid a wager yet? Which worthy prince will the king choose? The civilized Salian or the half-barbarian Ungrian?"

"It is sinful to lay wagers," announced Brother Constantine in a low voice, "and more sinful for clerics to do so than ordinary folk, for God have forbidden us to take on ourselves what only the angels may know."

"I say he will favor the Salian prince," murmured Sister Amabilia, ignoring Constantine as usual. "That will give him an alliance with the Salian king in case the Varren lords rebel again."

"With Sabella in prison? Nay, my dear Sister, he will choose the Ungrian, and if I am right, then I think you will give me those last two honey cakes you have on your platter."

"Gluttony is a sin," interposed Constantine primly.

"You think he will favor the Ungrians? But King Geza didn't even offer his own son but only his younger brother as bridegroom!"

"A younger brother who is an experienced war leader, and who has fought the Quman and other barbarian tribes. With success. Whom better to ally with Sapientia, if she becomes Margrave of Eastfall? Someone who understands the situation there."

"I accept the wager," said Amabilia, "but what will you give me if I am right?"

"I've already eaten all my honey cakes. What else could you possibly want?"

"Your owl quill, Brother. That is the only thing that will content me."

Hush, my friends," said Rosvita, but with a smile. Princess Theophanu's expression remained as bland as those on the sculptures from the Octagon Garden. Her gaze was fixed on her father, who extended a hand to Sapientia and bid her rise.

Sapientia was flushed. Somehow she managed to keep silent while her father spoke. His voice carried effortlessly to the four corners of the hall and even outside where servants and hangers-on thronged at the doors to listen.

"Let the Salian ambassador ride west with one of our Eagles and bring presents to our brother, Lothair, as a sign of our good will and our mutual love. Let the Ungrian ambassador ride east with one of our Eagles, and let him give this message to King

Geza: Let your brother, Prince Bayan, meet my daughter at the city of Handelburg not before Matthiasmass and not after the Feast of St. Valentinus. Let them be wed in the presence of Biscop Alberada, who rules over the souls of the marchlanders and those of the pagans who still live in darkness. After a three-day feast in celebration, let them then proceed to the Eastfall, there to protect and defend the people of Eastfall against the depredations of the Quman raiders. Such is my will."

Theophanu hissed a word, but it was lost in the hubbub that arose, cups lifted, a shout rising from the lips of every person there. Sapientia was still flushed. She glanced toward the Salian ambassador, then the Ungrian one. She did not look displeased. She looked happy.

"Betrothed at last," said Theophanu, taking the cup from Rosvita and draining it. She called for a servant, who filled it again. "Will you drink to my sister's good fortune, Sister?"

"Assuredly." Rosvita drank gratefully. It was hot and stuffy in the hall, and she wished suddenly to be walking alone in the Octagon Garden, where she could hear herself think. But she had no time to think. Theophanu had not done speaking, her voice pitched so low that only Rosvita could hear.

"If Henry means her to rule after him, then why did he betroth her to a foreign husband who cannot expect to receive much support from Wendish courtiers? They say the Ungrians still sacrifice horses at the winter solstice, even if they pray to God the rest of the year. Is that the man my father means to be the next king consort?"

"We know little about Prince Bayan except that he is a renowned fighter who has won many battles," replied Rosvita reflexively.

The Ungrian ambassador called for another toast. He had cast aside his fur cloak and now, with his odd mustaches and thin beard, looked incongruous in his elegant yellow silk tunic. The Ungrians had been raiders like the Quman not two generations ago. They had not lost their barbarian look, not quite, even if they mimicked the sophisticated Arethousan way of dressing.

"They are all blind," said Theophanu sharply.

"Who is blind?" asked Rosvita, taken aback by the unusual passion in Theophanu's voice. "What is it they are not seeing?"

"It matters not." She smoothed her expression and took the

cup from Rosvita, but she only sipped at it. "Not if you don't already know."

"You're thinking of Sanglant."

"My father has thought of nothing but Sanglant these last four days. Can you not tell by his manner, and by the way he never mentions him? I am not blind."

"Blindness comes in many guises." Rosvita watched Sapientia drink in triumph and kiss her father, the king, on either cheek as the assembly roared with approval.

Blindness comes in many guises and a furious heart overflows down unexpected channels. Rosvita had cause the next morning to reflect bitterly on this theme. The king sent for her early.

He sat in the forecourt watching his stewards oversee the loading of wagons, such provisions and in particular gifts of treasure and fine stuffs that Sapientia would present to her bridegroom as the seal of their alliance. Now and again he raised a hand to show that a certain item should not be loaded; now and again, he gestured, and a certain item, held aside, was placed in one of the chests being filled for the dowry.

Courtiers attended him, among them Helmut Villam and Judith.

All three of his children stood behind him. Sapientia looked smug, Theophanu calm. Ekkehard shifted restlessly from one foot to the other, looking for someone in the throng of nobles. He would have been a handsomer boy had he not frowned so much.

"Ah, my faithful counselor." She knelt before Henry and was allowed to kiss his hand. He had a glint in his eye that made her uncomfortable.

"There will be more partings on the morrow." Henry beckoned to Theophanu. "You, Daughter, will ride to Aosta as my representative. Aid Queen Adelheid as you can and if you must."

"Gladly. But surely, Father, I will ride south only after the council at Autun."

"Nay, Daughter. You must ride now if you mean to cross the Alfar Mountains before the passes close. Our cause will be lost if we wait too long. You will start south tomorrow."

"But you know I must testify at Autun at the trial of Father Hugh!"

"I have spoken," said Henry without raising his voice.

"But if I am not there to testify at Autun—!" Red stained her cheeks and she broke off, glancing toward Judith.

Rosvita recognized the look of a campaigner who knows that both her flanks are protected and that her center will hold: Judith wore it now.

"You will ride to Aosta, Theophanu. It is the place of the biscops to judge one of their own, not yours."

"But my testimony—!"

"You may dictate what you wish to the clerics. That way your voice will still be heard at the council."

There was nothing Theophanu could do unless she meant to defy her father—as Sanglant had done. But Theophanu was nothing like Sanglant. She recovered herself, murmured cool words of agreement, and retreated. But the look she shot Rosvita was anything but mild.

"Promise me," she whispered, stopping beside Rosvita, "that you will yourself read my words aloud at the trial. The biscops will listen to *you!*"

"Sister Rosvita." Henry's mild voice wrenched her attention away from Theophanu. "So that my daughter need not negotiate the treacherous paths in Aosta alone, I would send you along with her to advise and counsel her."

"Y-your Majesty." She was too shocked to stammer out more than that.

"Is there something wrong, Sister?" he asked gently.

It took no educated cleric to envision the scene: with both Theophanu and Liath gone, and Rosvita not there to argue their case, the accusations against Father Hugh would carry little weight. Especially not if Judith brought her own witnesses to argue for Hugh's innocence.

Who suspected her? What did Henry intend by this sudden change of plans?

"I have never seen the holy city of Darre," Rosvita said, stumbling, all eloquence lost. She could only register Theophanu's eyes, bright and fevered, and a look on her face that made Rosvita think the princess was about to shriek in frustration.

But there was nothing she could do.

*   *   *

Rosvita took Theophanu's testimony herself that afternoon, wrote it down in her careful hand, and sealed the parchment. Then she wrote a letter and took Sister Amabilia aside.

"Amabilia, I wish you to personally deliver this letter to Mother Rothgard at St. Valeria Convent. Fortunatus and Constantine will come with me to Aosta, and I regret you will not set foot with us in the skopos' palace, as you deserve. But you must serve me in this way. If Mother Rothgard will not heed the words I have written, then beg her yourself to come to the council at Autun. She can give testimony of what she observed when Theophanu lay sick at the convent."

"Surely she will think it strange that Sister Anne has vanished." Amabilia frowned at the letter. "According to Princess Theophanu, Sister Anne witnessed the whole as well, the fever and the ligatura they found. Where do you suppose Sister Anne could have gone?"

"I do not know," said Rosvita, but in her heart she feared the worst.

3

THEY came upon the first signs of habitation in midmorning: a hunter's trap, a lean-to built of branches with a roof woven out of vines, and a ten-day-old campfire. At midday they found the first dead body at the edge of a clearing newly hacked from beech forest. It was a male dressed in Wendish clothing. His head was cut off at the neck.

"Quman raiders." Zacharias knelt beside the bloody corpse, touched his wooden Circle, and began reflexively to speak the prayer for the dead. But he broke off. They were just words, weren't they? They didn't mean anything. "We should bury it," he added, looking up in time to see his companion pick up the ax that had fallen from the dead man's hands. She studied it, grunted, and tied it to the horse, then strode on. He scrambled up, grabbed the horse's reins, and hurried after her. "Shouldn't we bury it?" he demanded, panting, as he came up beside her.

She shrugged. "His people will find him."

"But his spirit will roam if we don't lay it to rest properly. That's what my grandmother always said." Yet she had been a pagan, and the church of the Unities had put an end to the old ways.

"Human spirits haven't the strength to harm me. How can we bury them all?"

"All?"

"Don't you smell the smoke?" she asked, surprised.

He smelled nothing. Not then. Not yet. They walked on through beech forest, following a trail. A day ago they had reached hill country, leaving the grasslands behind, and although he had felt the anger of his Quman master like a spear point pressing against his shoulder blades, they had seen no sign of Quman. He began to believe he had truly escaped them.

When they came to the village, he knew that, again, he was mistaken.

The stench of burning hung over the tiny village like a shroud. The half-built palisade had given little protection to the brave souls who had sought to cut farmland out of the eastern wilderness. The huts still smoldered. A dog lay covered with flies. Some of the corpses had heads. The rest did not.

"They're riding before us." Fear curdled in his gut.

She merely shook her spear. The jingling bell died away into the silence but not before he heard a scuff from the shell of one of the scorched longhouses. "Some remain."

"Quman?" His voice caught on the word and splintered. He knew in an instant he would start to weep.

"Nay, the horsefolk are gone. We go as well."

"Shouldn't we give them a decent burial?"

"It will take too long. Stay if you must. They belong to your kin, not mine." But she didn't leave immediately. A row of open-sided sheds had been left untouched. Their roofs sheltered craftsmen's tools and paraphernalia: a woodworker and a stone knapper had once worked here, together with a leatherworker. Cured skins lay draped over crude sawhorses next to a dozen or more skins strung on frames to cure. She hefted tools, tested their balance, took a few, but it was the leather she found most interesting. She rolled it in her fingers, spat on it, tested its strength over her knee. Finally she took three skins and rolled them up, then scavenged in the half-burned bakehouse and returned with several blackened loaves and two leather bottles filled with cider. He stared, as stunned as an idiot. Wasn't it wrong to take what wasn't theirs? Yet the dead had no need of food. She tied skins, tools, and provisions on behind the horse's saddle without a word, then turned and raised her spear as her gaze fastened on something behind him.

That noise wasn't the wind. It was whispering.

He turned.

"Frater!" Four women, two adolescent boys, and an old man crowded together at the door of the burned longhouse. About a half dozen children huddled behind them. One woman held a baby in her arms. "Ai, God! Good frater! God have sent you to us in our time of need!" A woman stepped forward, arms outstretched as for a blessing. "We thought you was the raiders, come back. That woman with you—" She broke off as her gaze took in the terrible scene, a dozen men of various ages, one young and one very old woman lying dead on bloody ground. "She wears their coat."

"She's not Quman." He was amazed at how hoarse his voice sounded. The words still did not come easily, and this village woman spoke with a thick dialect, a migrant from a different region than his own kinfolk.

"Thank God you are come to us, frater," she went on, taking another step closer. "You can pray with us. You can tell us what to do." The youngest of the women had begun to sob, and half the children followed suit. "We ran with the children, but the others had to stand behind to stop the raiders from coming after us. Ai, God! What did we do to bring God's wrath down on us in this way?"

"Come," said the Aoi woman. "We go." She pulled the reins out of his hand and started walking.

The old man fell to his knees. "You have come in answer to our prayer!" he wheezed. "It has been many seasons since a holy deacon sang prayers in our presence. We begged for God to give us a sign, when we hid from the raiders in the forest."

"Did they come today?" asked Zacharias nervously.

"Nay," replied the woman. "It were yesterday afternoon, late. We didn't dare come back till this morning."

"Then they're not too close, surely," said Zacharias, but the Aoi woman did not look back or wait for him. He gripped his walking staff higher, took a step. The younger women began

wailing like ghosts cursed to wander aimlessly after death. He
hesitated even as the sorceress crossed behind the palisade and
vanished from his sight, moving ever westward. "I can't help
you," he said at last.

"But you're a churchman," cried the woman. "Surely you will
stay long enough to say the blessing over these brave dead ones
so their souls can ascend to God!"

"God have forsaken us." How he hated them at that moment
for their weeping and for the way they looked at him for salvation. He couldn't even save himself. "Pray to the old ones, as
your grandmothers did. Maybe then your luck will return."

He turned his back on them and followed his mistress. Their
cries and weeping followed him for a long time in the quiet forest, even after he could no longer hear them.

4

THREE days after the Eagle had delivered his message, Lavastine's party reached the convent of St. Genovefa. Some playful
soul had carved the gates into the shape of two great dogs, and
this same spirit pervaded the guesthouses as well where every
mantle and beam seemed to hold its share of dog faces or dogs
cavorting or at the hunt or resting quietly as if in expectation
of the martyred saint's imminent return to care for her beloved
comrades. The abbess sent her own servants to wait on the count
and his heir and cousin, and after they were settled invited them
to dine.

The abbess was startlingly young, scarcely older than Tallia.
Second daughter of an ancient and noble house, Mother Armentaria had been invested into the church as abbess at age
twelve. Her mother's great-aunt had founded the convent and
been its first Mother, and a woman of that family had always
served as abbess. She had the habit of command, and the insti-
tution over which she reigned was a prosperous one. In sweet,
haunting voices, her nuns sang praises to the Lady which the
young abbess had herself composed in praise of God in Unity.

"Holy Mother, you who have brought life,
Blessed Thecla, you who have witnessed death,
In this female form God have brought us the highest blessing,
Let us praise you and rejoice in you."

But she was still eager for news of the world.

"I heard that the king of Salia has offered one of his sons as consort and husband for Princess Sapientia. Will King Henry take this alliance? Some of the lands under my rule lie in the borderlands between Varre and Salia, and there has been trouble there, with Salian lords claiming the rights to those lands although I have charters that prove them mine. Such a marriage might bring these troubles to an end."

"It is possible that the king will look east for such an alliance," said Lavastine. "Report has it that the barbarians have increased their raids in the marchlands."

"He has two daughters," observed the abbess. "And two sons, even if one is a bastard. He may make as many alliances as he wishes, up to four, to benefit those of us who serve him."

"Do you not serve God?" Tallia asked sharply.

Mother Armentaria's reply was sharper still. "Will you not pray with us this night at Vigils, my lady Tallia? Then you may judge for yourself how we honor God."

"I will pray gladly, and with a full heart, and for the entire night. And there is more, that you may wish to hear."

Lavastine looked at her in surprise, but he could not object. Nor could Alain. When they left the table, Tallia escaped him, again, as she always seemed to be escaping him: into prayer. He could not follow her into the cloister reserved for women.

Lavastine took him into the garden out of earshot of Lord Geoffrey and the rest. The hounds followed meekly. Under the shade of an apple tree, he set a hand on Alain's shoulder and regarded him sternly. "Is she pregnant yet? I fear that only a child will cure her of these ravings."

"N-nay, Father. Not yet. She is so—" He stammered out syllables that even he could not understand.

"A stubborn nut to crack, so the wits would have it. But fruitful within that hard shell."

Alain began to stammer out an apology.

"Nay, Son, you have done as well as any man. She only begins to trust you, and I fear that she takes after her noble mother

in having a stubborn nature and after her noble father in being
simple in the mind."

Alain didn't know how to reply. "Surely it's her holiness, not
her simplicity, that makes her what she is." Fear padded away
from them down a lush row of greens, turnips, and radishes not
yet harvested. A bee wandered among roses. Sorrow and Rage
had gone over to sniff at comfrey. Steadfast licked Alain's hand.
The bell rang to summon the nuns to Vespers.

"If it were holiness, then why would she cling to this heresy?"
objected Lavastine. "And if her words held any danger to those
of the faith, then Mother Scholastica would not have released
her out into the world. Or they would have threatened her with
excommunication. But they do not fear these delirious speeches
she gives. Therefore we have no reason to fear them either."

"But she is so set on it. I don't know what to do!"

"She clings to it because it gives her comfort. As she comes
to rely on you, she will come to you for comfort. You must win
her trust as a mason builds a keep: one stone at a time. The
more careful your work, the stronger the foundation and walls.
A few months more will make little difference except to harm
your alliance with her if you move too hastily and set her against
you. You can breed many children whether you start having them
in ten months or twenty."

In the field beyond the garden, geese began squabbling. Bliss
stood suddenly, watchful, and padded over to the archway that
opened onto the field. The geese had foraged so diligently before; now they hissed and honked—as Aunt Bel would say—as
if they meant to frighten off the Enemy. "But what of the curse
that Prince Sanglant sent warning of?"

Lavastine whistled Terror over and stroked his ears. "Bloodheart is dead. If his dead hand still holds a weapon, then we
must be ready to meet it." He smiled grimly. "And we must trust
in God's mercy."

The hounds went mad. Fear bolted toward the archway, barking furiously. Bliss had already vanished out onto the field. Geese
scattered. Sorrow and Rage bounded away through the garden,
leaves flattening under their heavy stride. Steadfast gripped
Alain's hand in her mouth and dragged him after her. Only Terror stood his ground, hackles up, growling fiercely as he stuck
beside the count.

Alain ran to the arch. Out in the field the hounds converged, then Rage split off, cutting sideways, and Sorrow leaped the other way. Their barking came fast and furious. Was that a flash of white along the ground? Sunset bled fire along clouds that had streamed out to cover the western sky. In the east, a few stars winked into view between a patchwork of clouds. From the church, he heard the first high voices raised to God. Vespers had begun.

> "Lay down beside me, O Lord, sleep beside me.
> Protect me from all harm.
> Let my Mother watch over me and sing me to my sweet rest
> as You watch over Your children.
> Lord, have mercy. Lady, have mercy."

Bliss bowled over, tumbling, righted himself, and began to dig. Dirt sprayed out behind his forepaws. Steadfast, Fear, Sorrow, and Rage converged on him and soon they dug furiously and with a hellish cacophony of barking.

"What means this?" asked Lavastine, coming up behind Alain, but Terror was already there, biting down on the count's wrist and trying to tug him back into the garden.

A shuddering thrill ran through Alain. He touched his chest, where hung the tiny pouch that concealed his rose. It seared his fingers with cold through the linen of his summer tunic.

"Let me go," he said. By then others had come out to investigate. Reluctantly, Lavastine let Terror pull him back into the garden into the circle of his attendants.

Alain ran forward into a blizzard of dirt.

"Peace!" he cried, but they gave him no peace. Dirt stung his eyes and coated his tongue and lips. They were in a frenzy, barking so frenetically that he could no longer hear the nuns' singing over their deafening noise. A tiny body, white against the earth, darted, spun, and leaped.

Bliss' jaws snapped shut over it.

The other four hounds stopped barking instantaneously and formed a circle around Bliss, who swallowed. Then he slewed his great black head up to look at Alain. He pressed a dry nose into Alain's hand, snuffled there for one moment, and as suddenly turned away and broke into a ground-eating lope toward the woodland that lay beyond the fields.

Alain chased him, but the other hounds got in his way, mob-

bing him. Their weight threw him to the ground, and there he
lay with Sorrow draped over on his chest, and Fear and Rage
sitting on his legs. Steadfast trotted after Bliss but stopped at
the wood's edge, like a watchman. The geese had clustered at
the distant end of the field and, settling now, they waggled off
to glean between rows of barley and spelt.

"What is going on, Alain?" Lavastine arrived, sword in hand.
Four men-at-arms bearing torches and armed with spears attended him.

But when Alain tried to describe what he had seen, none of
it made sense.

"Come," said Lavastine to the men-at-arms. "I've had enough
of curses and superstition. Get a dozen more of your fellows
and we'll search for the hound."

"But, Father—"

"Peace!" snapped Lavastine. Alain knew better than to protest.

He walked with Lavastine into the forest, never leaving his
side. The good sisters of St. Genovefa Convent had long since
cleared out most of the underbrush and dead wood for kindling
and charcoal. The open woodland gave sparse cover. There was
enough of a moon to guide their feet, and the torches gave Alain
heart, as if he could thrust the flame into any curse that tried to
fly at him out of the darkness.

But the five hounds padded quietly along, content to let them
search, which they did for half the night at least. They found
no sign of Bliss.

When he stumbled at last into the chamber set aside for himself, Tallia, and their servants, he had to pick his way carefully
over their sleeping attendants. It was black in the chamber, and
he was too tired to undress, so he simply lay down in his clothes.
With a hand, he searched the bed, careful not to wake her. But,
like Bliss, she was gone.

Faintly, he heard voices singing Vigils, the night office. She
had hidden herself away beyond the cloister walls. If only he
could heave himself up off this bed and go in search of her,
who was everything and the only thing he had ever wanted.

He slept.

*He weaves his standard himself. From two spear hafts bound
into a cross-shaft he strings up the bones of his dead brothers—
those that can be recovered—and when the wind blows, they*

make a pleasant sound: the music of victory. Certain items—five hand bells, an ivory-hafted knife made of bronze, needles, a gold cup, iron fishhooks, and a thin rod of iron—he laces in among the bones to give variety to their song. He binds the five braids of his dead rivals at the top, ties strips of silk and linen torn from the bodies of Bloodheart's enemies below them to make streamers, and weights each dangling line of bone and metal with a pierced round of baked clay.

The entire tribe has assembled to watch this ceremony on the dancing ground of the SwiftDaughters. He stands facing the long slope that leads down to the beach where the ships are drawn up. Behind him stand the dwellings of his brothers and uncles, marching up the long valley toward the fjall. On his left lie the storehouses held in common by the tribe, and on his right the longhall that belongs to OldMother, built entirely of stone and thatched with sod. The doorway gapes open, but he sees nothing stirring within its depths. SwiftDaughters stand in a semicircle in front of OldMother's hall. They have finished the long dance whose measures tell the story of Rikin's tribe all the way back to the dawning of the world.

That song has been sung, and his victory acknowledged: Fifth Son of the Fifth Litter will become chieftain of Rikin tribe.

He binds off the last strand of his standard and jams its sharpened base into the dirt so that it stands upright. From the ground he picks up a stone scraper and with it scrapes the residue of paint off his chest—the paint that marked his kinship to Bloodheart, who is now dead. With his fingers, dabbing in tiny pots of ocher and woad, he paints a new pattern on this chest, his pattern: a circle with two lines crossed inside so that they touch four points on the circle, one for each of the winds; north, west, east, and south.

"On these winds my ships will sail," he cries. They all listen. They are his tribe now, his to mold and use as a weapon. "On four winds to the far shores of the world, all the regions of the earth that are known to the WiseMothers."

A murmur arises among the soldiers, who kneel with that particular combination of patience and tension that mark them as wary of his reign. He has yet to prove himself before them. But they also do not truly understand—not yet—what he intends.

The chieftain's chair—which he alone had the foresight to salvage from the disaster at Gent—is brought forward, and he seats himself in it. *"Come forward, each one, and bare your throat before me."*

He extends his claws, and they come forward one by one. First the soldiers who followed him even through his disgrace stride up, confident, proud, ready to serve his will. They believe in his strength. After them the others come forward, some with reluctance, some with curiosity. A few he smells fear on, and those he kills at once. But Rikin's tribe is a strong one, and few among his uncles, cousins, and brothers have survived Bloodheart's campaigns by showing weakness.

It takes most of the day for each soldier to submit, but he minds it not; this is not a ceremony which should be hurried.

The sun sinks in preparation for a longer night than last night, each night waxing, each day waning, toward the midpoint that Alain Henrisson calls the autumn equinox and the Wise-Mothers call The-Dragon-Has-Turned-Her-Back-On-The-Sun. From the shore he hears the lap of waters stirred by creatures out in the depths. Have the merfolk come to witness? Have they come to pledge themselves to his rule?

He cannot yet leave his chair. There is other business to transact.

"Where is the priest?" he asks, and the priest shuffles forward, mumbling and chanting and humming in his reedy flute voice. *"Do you have what I need, priest?"*

"Do you hold safe what I most hold dear?" retorts the priest.

He smiles. *"It lies safe in a place you will never find, Uncle. Do you have that which I demand in return for its safekeeping?"*

"Must I not now walk many journeys?" the priest complains. *"Must I not now trek on many fell paths? Do you think it will bind itself easily into my power and thus yours?"*

"I will be patient a while longer," he answers.

Movement eddies at the back as the SwiftDaughters ready themselves to come forward, to escort him to the chair of Old-Mother. But he is not done yet. He gestures, and out of the shadows walk his slaves, in tidy lines, obedient to his wishes. They are not beasts, like the other slaves, but even so the tribesmen murmur in surprise and with distrust.

"What means this?" some of the RockChildren cry. And others: *"Will we follow after the one who wears the circle of the*

Soft Ones and who lets these slaves walk in his train like honored warriors?"

"Challenge me if you wish," says Fifth Son, *softly to show threat but loudly enough to carry.* *"But I am far ahead of you on the path, Brothers. I have defeated my rivals and walked without harm on the nesting ground of the WiseMothers. Can any of you say the same? Come forward and challenge me if you dare."* *He does not raise his voice or bellow, as Bloodheart would have. He does not rise, to make of his stature a challenge. He does not need to.*

They fear him because he is different.

And they are not fools. They will wait, and measure him and run in his tracks as long as he walks the path of victory. Only a weak leader needs to look back over his shoulder; a strong leader need only scan the ground ahead, because he knows that his troops are faithful and that they run eagerly at his heels.

"Come forward, those who are born of human kin and who serve me."

They come hesitantly through the glistening obsidian spears and the gleam of claw, but they come, although he can smell fear on all of them except one. They dare not refuse him, and some have even become bold enough to hold their heads high. The chieftain and OldMother among them kneel before him, as he has taught them to do; he has seen this form of obeisance in Alain Henrisson's dreams.

The deacon Ursuline, like any OldMother, does not fear him—she alone of her tribe. She lifts her eyes to meet his gaze. *"I have done as you asked, and you have no cause to be displeased by my service to you. What of our bargain?"*

Said boldly, among those who could cut her throat in an instant. He bares his teeth to remind her of his power, but she has the serenity that walks with those who themselves walk hand in hand with the gods, even if it is only her circle god, whose footsteps he has never seen mark the earth.

"You have served me well. In this way I reward you: All the slaves of Rikin fjord may walk free of the pens and build longhalls, as is the custom of your kind. This they may do, as long as they submit to the will of their masters in all other ways. As long as they serve our purpose, they may live, and as long as there is peace among those who walk free of the pens, they may live. If there is not peace, then justice will be swift." *He curls*

his fists toward his chest so that his unsheathed claws shine bright before him, slender blades of killing sharpness grown into his body. "Do you doubt me?"

"I do not doubt you," *she answers gravely.* "What of the other matter we discussed?"

The other matter. It takes him a moment to recall it, but it was the one she most desired. She would have left her kinfolk in the pens in exchange for this one thing. That he gave her both in exchange for her service is a mark of the generosity he has learned through his dream: That the chieftains and Old-Mothers of the human kind use gifts to keep their tribes together.

"With your own hands and such tools as we allow you, in your own time as long as it does not interfere with the tasks set for you by your masters, you may build a church for your circle-god and worship there."

She bows her head. In this gesture he sees both submission and respect.

But he is not altogether sure whether her submission is for him, her master, or for the circle-god whom she considers God of all Creation.

Yet, truly, he cares not which it is as long as she serves him on this earth. Where her feet will take her after death is no concern of his.

At last the SwiftDaughters come forward. Their hair shines in the sharp afternoon light, with gold like that of the sun, with a silver-white as pale as the moon, with the copper and tin and iron veins of the earth. No son of the tribe may enter OldMother's hall without her invitation, and her invitation comes only to those sons who will lead, breed, or die.

He might still die. OldMother may find him unworthy. But he doubts it.

He crosses the threshold and walks into OldMother's hall, into a darkness dense with the scent of soil and rock, root and worm, the perfume that marks the bones of the earth. The floor turns from beaten dirt to cool rock beneath his feet, a transition so abrupt that his head reels and he has to pause to steady himself. Air breathes onto his face, stirring like a great beast, and from where he now stands he gains the impression of a vast space opening out before him. He feels as though he stands on the edge of a vast abyss. Behind him, although he has made no turn, although no wall has come between his back and the wall of the house, the door has vanished. He stands in utter darkness.

Above, impossibly, he sees stars.

And below, too, beyond him and spread out like so many pinprick watch fires, he sees stars, glittering, bright and unattainable.

"Who are you, Fifth Son of the Fifth Litter?" He cannot see OldMother, but he feels the whisper of her dry breath on his lips, feels her weight, that which makes her formidable, that which reveals her as a child of earth. *"By what name will we call you when we dance the measure of our tribe? When we sing of the life of the grass, which dies each winter, and the life of the void, with lives eternal?"*

Long ago, months ago as the human kind measure the passing of days, he met the youngest WiseMother on the path to the fjall. There, she spoke to him: *"Let be your guide that which appears first to your eyes."*

He believed then that she meant the funeral he saw on his way down the valley, because it was the first event he witnessed after leaving her. But he dreams, and in his dreams he listens when Alain Henrisson speaks of his dreams. Like the serpents on the shields carried by his soldiers, he and Alain are interlocked, wound each into the other, with no ending and no beginning.

In a dream he heard Alain speak: *"It wasn't the funeral at all. It was his own hand."*

His own hand.

Bloodheart did not trust his own strength, or his own cunning. In weakness, he sought the aid of magic. But magic is only bought for a price, and it is never something you can truly possess: That is the lesson he learned from his father. He knows better than to rely on magic.

He can rely only on himself, his own strength, his own cunning.

He bares his teeth, what the Soft Ones would call a smile. He holds up the hand with which he laid the offering on the palm of the youngest WiseMother. He cannot see it, even so close before his face; that is how dark it is. But he does not doubt that OldMother can see, for her sight is not like that of her children.

"Call me by this name: Stronghand.*"*

He hears her movement on the rock, as heavy as the groaning of the earth beneath the weight of mountains. "Let it be done. Let the WiseMothers speak of it, and let this name be known through all the fjalls."

"And farther," he murmurs. "Let it be known to the four corners of the earth."

Her reply, like the knife she wields, is sharp. "Their voices are heard farther away than you can know, my son. Now go. Stronghand will rise or fall through his own efforts."

Thus is he dismissed.

Where rock turns to beaten earth, he pauses, blinking, as the door appears before him out of nothing. Enough light trails in that he can turn and look over his shoulder. The chamber behind him, the long hall of stone and sod, lies empty. He sees no heavy chair, no sign of OldMother at all, only raked dirt, dim corners, and the rough topography of the stone walls.

Not even his footsteps mark the dirt.

Alain woke at dawn. In the distance he heard Lauds being sung, and as he lay in the bed with one hand outstretched onto the cold space where Tallia had not lain the night before, the voices celebrating Lauds finished, paused, and began the service of Prime for sunrise. Was that Tallia's voice among them? He could not make her out among so many. Of her, in this chamber, there was no trace.

He heaved himself out of the bed and staggered outside to find Lavastine already up. Geoffrey, looking bleary-eyed, gave orders to men-at-arms and servants. Lavastine talked with foresters brought in from the nearby lands which lay under the rule of the convent, and now glanced up. "You are awake, Alain. We'll go out again. He can't have vanished utterly."

They went out again, lines of men beating the undergrowth and walking in staggered groups so that every stretch of ground near the convent was covered. Alain was exhausted; he stumbled on fallen logs and upthrust roots, saw a heap of houndlike leaves that scattered every which way when he dug through it.

By midday they still had found no sign of Bliss.

Lavastine called them in for their meal, but Alain could not give up, not yet. He stayed out with a handful of servants, Sorrow, and Rage. They backtracked to the field where the geese had first set up the alarm, and he tried again to follow Bliss' trail into the forest. The hounds were no help at all. They barked at every squirrel and bird that crossed their path, or gulped down beetles, or dug holes in the dirt.

At last, by midafternoon, he had mercy on his exhausted serv- ingmen, and they trudged back to the guesthouse. He was so terribly tired, perhaps more from heart's pain than actual bodily exhaustion. What had Bliss gulped down, out there in the field yesterday? Why had he run off like that afterward? Why hadn't he returned?

Sorrow and Rage followed him back to the chamber set aside for Count Lavastine and his servants. Two servingmen crouched outside in the corridor, but they jumped up at once, seeing Alain, and let him in. In the small room he found Lavastine asleep on the bed. The shutters stood open to let in light and air, and the sunlight lay in a bright patch over the lower half of the bed so that the folds of the blanket had two tones. Lavastine's head lay in shadow still; his sandy-blond hair had slivers of white in it. His eyes were shut and he breathed evenly while Terror, Stead- fast, and Fear lay on the flagstone floor around him, his faith- ful attendants. Terror snored lustily, sprawled on his side, while Steadfast dozed with her head cushioned by her paws. Fear kept watch.

Alain sat on the bed. Moved by impulse, he reached to brush hair out of Lavastine's eyes. Sun, wind, and age had taken their toll on the count, chapping his face and hands; tiny wrinkles perched at the corners of his eyes, little crow's-feet, but in many ways his face had remained smooth. Lavastine was a man who offered both smiles and frowns sparingly, and thus those ex- pressions had not left their tracks on his face.

He was not a big man, like Prince Sanglant, but although he was slender and not particularly tall, he was made strong by the power of his will and mind. He was a man like most men, bet- ter than many: steady, practical, even-tempered, prudent and sharp. He was not formed for the strong emotions he had named his hounds after but rather for the day-to-day work of the world.

Alain smiled softly, flicking away a fly. Not old yet, not even as old as the king, still he was no longer young. He might be a grandfather soon.

Alain flushed, hot all through his face and elsewhere. Only the women and men of the church kept themselves pure like the angels. In that way they made of themselves vessels whose purity would bring them closer to the immaculate light of God.

But God had created desire so that humankind could grow and prosper. Hadn't the Lord and Lady conceived the Holy Word between them, by joining together in lawful congress? Wasn't the Earth and the entire universe Their creation? Was it wrong of him to delight in the world? To think of Tallia and of their joining in the marriage bed? To think of making Lavastine a grandfather? For Lavastine, a grandchild, heir to his heir, would be the triumph he desired most. Alain meant to give that to him.

Sorrow whined at his knee. He reached out and patted the hound, and Sorrow set his great muzzle on Alain's knee. It reminded him suddenly and blindingly of little Agnes, Bel's youngest, when she was just a little girl and would drape herself over Alain's leg for comfort on a winter's evening. How did Aunt Bel fare? Did Henri think of him at all? Did he still hate him?

Even now the memory of that last meeting with Henri was so painful that Alain could not bear to think on it for more than a moment. To be accused of lying, and for his own selfish gain! As well to have stabbed him in the heart as to have said that.

Terror grunted in sleep. Rage barked and set his paws on the sill, and like the claws of the Enemy's minions sorting through a troubled heart for weakness, a shudder ran through Alain, a sudden cold chill.

Something rustled in the bush outside the window.

He leaped up and bolted to the window, leaning out. Sorrow roused and followed him over. None of the hounds barked. Terror and Steadfast slept on. Lavastine stirred, snorted, and turned over.

It was only a bird, a spotted thrush that scolded Alain for disturbing it before it flew away with a berry in its beak. But he cold not stop shaking.

What was the curse of the nestbrother? Fifth Son had spoken of it in his dream, and the priest had sung of turning it onto another—*"Let this curse fall on the one whose hand commands the blade that pierced his heart."* Liath's arrow had killed Bloodheart. But Lavastine had led the army among whose number she rode.

Alain knelt beside the open window, head bent until it rested on his clasped hands. Terror snored peacefully on the flagstones and Lavastine on the bed. Steadfast and Fear had settled down by the door, heads on paws, eyes closed. Rage and Sorrow kept him company as he prayed.

A wind stirred the leaves in the bushes outside. A woman laughed. The hammer of a blacksmith rang distantly and, farther away yet, a horn shrilled. Against his chest, the Lady's rose throbbed like the echo of the blacksmith's hammer, the striking of his own heart.

It was only a heathen curse, after all. God were stronger than Eika magic, weren't they? If he prayed with a pure heart, then surely God would protect his father.

5

ALAIN woke suddenly, startled by the wood thrush, who had come back for another berry. His neck ached, and he realized that he had fallen asleep where he knelt with his hands and head resting against the window ledge.

He stood, stretching. Sorrow watched him. Rage had padded over to the door and looked up expectantly. Lavastine still slept, and he didn't want to disturb him.

He opened the latch quietly—thankfully the good abbess' servants kept the mechanism well oiled—and stepped outside with Sorrow and Rage at his heels. When he eased into his own chamber, he saw, for a miracle, that Tallia had come back. She had fallen asleep draped over the bed, her hands curled into fists, head resting on her knuckles. Like him, she had been caught by sleep in the act of prayer.

Tenderly, he lifted her onto the bed and arranged her limbs so she could rest comfortably. She did not wake, only murmured in her sleep, shifted, and sighed. He lay on the bed beside her, head propped on a hand, elbow bent beneath, and studied her. Because he had dozed off, because he had been up half the night searching for Bliss, he was now too tired to remain awake but too wakeful to go to sleep. She was so pale, like finest linen. Her lips had the faintest pink tincture, as delicate as rosebuds.

A wooden cup had touched those lips. Was he to be less blessed than the humble cup? Surely he had as much right—the right of mutual obligation, the oath made by a wedded couple to be fruitful.

He leaned over her, felt her breath as a light brush on his cheek. Surely she must feel a stirring of desire. He need only coax it from her. She, like every other human soul on this earth, was not formed out of stone. There had to be answering fire within her.

He brushed his mouth over hers. She stirred slightly, as at the kiss of a butterfly, and that tiny movement brought her hip up against him. That touch alone, the feel of her body through the heavy cloth of her long tunic, the tilt of the bed under their weight that seemed to draw them together, all of this blinded him. He couldn't see, he could only feel. All the hours and days he had waited, the night's search for the missing hound, the utter obliteration of every sensation but that of desire, all of this consumed him.

He pressed against her, stroked her chin, bent to kiss her again, just to feel that touch, the pliant curve of her mouth.

Her eyes opened, and she whimpered in fear.

He jerked back.

"All night I prayed for a sign," she whispered, "so that God through my agency could reveal the truth of the Redemption to the abbess. And God answered me. Do you mean now to defile what has been made holy by God's touch?"

She opened her hands. The skin of her palms had begun weeping blood again.

He bolted. He no longer knew what he was doing, but he ran with Sorrow and Rage at his heels and confusion buzzing in his head like so many gnats. He reached the wood and still ran, floundering through clumps of undergrowth, running to no place, without reason.

He simply could not bear it any longer. He could not be patient. Was the flaw his, or hers? Did it even matter? He could not think of her, even with her wounded hands, without feeling the full flush of arousal. He would never escape it, and why should he? Didn't women and men partake of God's holy act of creation by making children in their turn?

He caught himself on a tree, leaned there, but the fit did not pass. He was sweating, hot, all on fire. He could not endure it any longer. He would go back and make her yield to him. Ai, God, but doing so would destroy any trust she had given him thus far.

He began to weep in frustration, and at the same time his body clutched the tree closer, thrusting his hips against it as if to make love with it. Appalled, he spun away.

On the edge of a meadow he saw a thicket of nettles and briars.

He stripped, flung aside tunic and leggings, and threw himself into the thorns and stinging nettles. Sorrow and Rage began to bark, but they did not follow him in. He rolled back and forth until his skin wept blood and his whole body was a mass of welts. Only then did he crawl to his knees and stagger out.

On the leaves, on the cool forest floor, he bent double, convulsed with weeping and pain. Sorrow and Rage crowded him, licking his skin to ease him, but the fire burned so violently, the scratches stung like so many lashes, that they brought no comfort.

But he could think of Tallia with a calm heart.

Much later, he pulled on his tunic, although he could not bring himself to bind his leggings on over his inflamed legs. Every shift of the tunic on his shoulders as he walked back through the wood brought fresh pain. But he could think of Tallia with a calm heart.

Mercifully, Lavastine said nothing after Alain stammered out an explanation of going out in the woods to search for Bliss and thinking he had seen the hound in the middle of a nettle patch. An ancient nun came from the convent to spread a soothing ointment over his skin, all the while clucking her tongue. But even she did not ask how a man fully dressed could have gotten welts and scratches on every part of his body.

Bliss did not return that evening, and Lavastine, at last, declared that they would have to travel on. In the morning, the count gave an offering of silver plate at the chapel. Alain knelt beside him and was blessed by the abbess, who sang the service in front of a carved wooden altar brimming with faithful dogs. Tallia prayed beside him, and with his skin still stinging and sore, he could smile calmly and speak softly. Temptation had poisoned him, but pain had scoured him clean.

When they set out on the road, five hounds padded alongside, and the shadow of the sixth in his heart.

6

"WHY do you call them fixed stars," Sanglant asked, "if they
always move? They rise like the sun and set like the sun. In
winter different stars shine in the heavens than do in the spring
or summer or autumn. So they must move or we would see the
same ones all the time."

"We call them fixed stars because they don't move in relation to each other. The planets we call wandering stars because
they move through the fixed stars along the ecliptic, along the
path through the stars that we also call the world dragon that
binds the heavens. Or the zodiac, because it's a circle of living
creatures set into the heavens."

Sanglant was the kind of person who liked to touch. Right
now he had an arm draped over her shoulders, and she loved its
weight and warmth. After he had settled the horses for the night,
he had searched her out and found her here where she had retreated to practice certain tricks Anne had taught her to control
calling fire. But it was such a beautiful night that the stars had
distracted her. The Queen stood at zenith, trailed by her Cup,
Staff, and Sword. The Lion set west with the Dragon in pursuit,
and the Serpent wound in sinuous splendor along the southern
horizon while the Archer rose behind it with her bow nocked
and ready. Of the planets only Mok was visible on its slow climb
through the Lion toward the Dragon, which it would reach—she
tried to calculate—in another month or two.

They had passed a tiny monastic estate a few hours ago but,
as usual, had not stayed there for the night. Instead, as usual,
they found more isolated accommodation. Behind them at the
fringe of wood stood an old traveler's hut built out of brick in
the Dariyan style. It had fallen down in disrepair, but the ma-
sonry walls were still strong and half the roof remained. The
door stood ajar because it was too warped to close. A single

light burned within, the magelight of Sister Anne who was now mediating or at prayer.

Even after twelve days on the road, Liath could not easily call her "Mother."

"Then if the stars are fixed, how do they move?" Sanglant demanded, laughing.

"It's like a turning wheel. See." She held up a hand, cupped it so the knuckles pointed up and the palm made a curve like a dome. He couldn't see well on a night when there was no moon, but he had his own ways of seeing: he let his free hand explore the shape of hers by touch. Which was very distracting.

After a while he remembered that he had asked her a question. By this time they were lying down. "What's like a turning wheel?"

"The heavens are." He had one arm under her neck and she had to shift to get comfortable. "Imagine a wheel with many sparks *fixed* on it. Now curve that wheel into a dome and join the dome with another dome so that it becomes a sphere. Those sparks are fixed to the inner surface of the sphere, so they don't move, but when the sphere moves, if it rotates in a uniform circular motion, then if you stand at the center of the sphere, the stars move because the sphere moves."

"What are you standing on there in the center of your sphere?" He still seemed amused. The truth, as she had come to learn, was that he was curious but also skeptical and quick to get bored by such talk, and that sometimes irritated her.

"You're standing on the earth, of course! The universe is a set of nested spheres, one inside the next with the earth at the center. Beyond the seventh sphere, which is the sphere of the fixed stars, lies the Chamber of Light—where our souls go after we die."

"Has any scout walked up through these spheres and returned to report on what she saw?"

"A blasphemous thought." Anne's voice, cool and yet perhaps faintly amused, came out of the dark.

Liath sat up at once and moved slightly away from her husband.

Husband! The word still staggered her.

Yet something about Anne's presence made her feel unclean for the physical feelings she had for Sanglant. It was frustrating to be newly wed while traveling with a woman who thought you ought to remain as pure as the angels, so frustrating that at times Liath toyed with heretical thoughts. God were male and female. Why should angels not be as well, and if they were, then where did infant angels come from? If God had joined in harmony to create the universe, why shouldn't angels join as well? In which case, there ought to be no shame for humans to join so.

She could have asked Da. But she didn't have the nerve to try out this argument in front of her mother.

Sanglant got to his feet to show respect. "Your knowledge is vast and impressive," he said lightly. Anne didn't daunt *him*. "But it makes no sense to me."

"Nor should it. You have your place, Prince Sanglant, as we have ours. You need know only that God have created the universe we stand in. That which they wish to make known to you they will reveal to you, Liathano." She turned away from him. "Come inside."

Liath hesitated.

"Go on," said Sanglant softly. "I must tend the dog."

The old hut had a mosaic floor, river stones pieced cunningly together to make an image of partridges picking up seeds in a thicket. Magelight illuminated the floor, which was chipped and worn and, at the end where the roof no longer covered it, broken and coming to pieces. Anne sat on a canvas stool. A fire burned in a stone hearth, newly swept out, and their cook pot bubbled with a stew that smelled so good that Liath's mouth watered. Along one wall, an insubstantial shape wavered, slipped like the antithesis of shadow toward the door, and vanished into the night. Anne frowned.

"They're afraid of me." Liath blurted it out, although she hadn't meant to. Although it was the truth.

Anne regarded her evenly. "It is time to eat our supper."

There were two bowls. Liath obediently dished out stew for Anne, then took some for herself and sat on a stack of bricks that served well enough as a bench. She blew on the broth to cool it. It had a savory odor, rabbit, leeks, herbs. They ate in silence, as always. It needed only a sister to read aloud from the Holy Verses for the atmosphere to match that of the convent.

When she was done, she went back to the cook pot to ladle out Sanglant's portion.

"Nay, child," said Anne softly. "We will talk first. You can bring him his supper later."

Annoyed, Liath set bowl and spoon on a hearthstone to keep it warm, and sat down on the brick bench. She had learned caution. Anne was nothing like Da. She seemed more a force than a person, like the hand of God reaching below the moon to touch mortal spirits. One did not speak rashly to the hand of God.

"Your education in the basic knowledge necessary to the mathematicus is sound. I am pleased with the answers you have given me these past nights."

"You said you would answer my questions when you had finished. May I ask them now?"

The fire had such a constant glare that Liath knew its flame arose from an unnatural source. Two logs lay within the stone hearth, but although fire licked them and curved around their sides, they were not consumed. Were those salamander eyes blinking in the depths of fire? Blue sparks winked and dazzled in the flames.

"You may."

Liath started up, suddenly aware that she had been staring into the fire like a madwoman. "How did you find me?"

"The spell Bernard concealed you with has worn away strand by strand since his death, just as this hut and indeed the great network of roads and towns and way houses built under the rule of the Dariyan empresses have all worn away with the passage of time and with none to care for them each day or month as is necessary. Until then, you were hidden from me."

"After Da died, I would sometimes hear a voice calling my name, but there was never anyone there. Was that you?"

"At times in remembered sorrow I spoke your name. You may have heard me. The link between us runs deeply, and could never be fully severed."

"But if Da knew you might be looking for us, why did he hide us? He thought you were dead!"

"If he thought I was dead, then he could not believe I was looking for you."

"But what about the creature that killed Da? What about the daimone I saw, and the demons that chased me on the road?"

The magelight sharpened, as if it reflected Anne's thoughts. A moth fluttered in through the door and danced along the ceiling, trying to get close to the light. "You must tell me precisely and in detail about each of these incidents."

She told of the voice of bells, Da's death, and the white

feather. Of her encounter on the Osterwaldweg with the daimone and the glasslike feather it had left behind on the road, and of how she had sat so still that it had walked past her without seeing her. Of the creatures that dusk had spun out of the shadows, who had pursued her down the road beside the Bretwald and how she had hidden in a stone circle.

"How did you escape them?"

Words caught in her throat like stones. Finally she said: "I saw an owl." She could not lose her habit of caution. She did not mention the gold feather given to her by the Aoi sorcerer.

The stone circle, and the owl. That was all.

Anne watched her without expression. "An owl is a common creature to see in the night. Such creatures as you describe would not be halted by mere stone."

"T—they didn't see me," she stammered. "They passed me by." The horror of it struck her, and her next words came out harshly enough, because they at least were not half-truths. "There were other travelers on the road. They stripped them down to the bone but left their clothing and gear untouched. I'd never heard of such a thing before. I didn't know such creatures even existed, or what they're called."

"The minions of the Enemy walk on this earth in many guises," replied Anne with her usual calm. "But there are certain signs, and portents. . . . Certain disturbances touch the fabric of the universe, of God's creation, and when that happens, gateways appear like rents in a cloth. Creatures who were once confined in other planes of existence can cross through." Now her forehead furrowed, and she frowned the kind of unforgiving frown that the Lady might turn on an apostate. "Or be called."

"I thought daimones were called down from the spheres above the moon."

"They can be. Each sphere is home to unique kinds of daimones. Those in the lowest sphere are weakest while in each ascending sphere, they grow in power and aspect. Yet, in addition, there are other bridges, other lands that exist close by ours, even other ways of existing in the universe that we do not fully understand."

"You know so much." The easy way Anne spoke of these matters seized her twofold: awe at her knowledge, and violent curiosity because she wanted to understand the natural world herself, from the rocks and stones all the way to the highest sphere.

"Much knowledge has been lost. It is like this land we travel through now. We make our way on roads paved long ago by the ancient Dariyans, whose merchants and soldiers and administrators traveled widely and swiftly. How far we have fallen!"

"But they were heathens."

"That is why they fell. However, we are all tainted. It cannot be otherwise as long as we live on this earth, here where the hand of the Enemy lies most heavily. Nevertheless, they had great knowledge that is now lost to us, just as we have let their great works and buildings and roadways fall into disrepair and ruin."

From the mosaic floor, a partridge's eye gleamed up at Liath, a brightly-polished agate. Its beak was missing, although the rest of the bird lay intact surrounded by a depiction of grass and sedge. The realism of the scene enchanted her. She could practically hear the birds rustling through the thicket, seeking seeds and insects. Wind sighed over the roof, and she glanced up to examine the two beams that still spanned the chamber.

That after hundreds of years such a humble structure still stood was astounding, of course, but the ancient Dariyans were said to have used magic in their architecture. These days, the roads had little enough traffic, and she knew from experience that on a rainy night the best a traveler could hope for was to find a village with room in the stable or, with luck, a humble monastic guesthouse. The prouder monasteries and convents were hesitant to admit common travelers, and Da had always hated to attract notice to himself.

"My tongue is the pen of a swift writer," continued Anne. "Let me tell you a story. Long ago, soon after King Taille of Salia—he who would become the Emperor Taillefer through the grace of God—came into his crown and his power, his blessed mother Bertrada brought to him a woman of noble family and told him that she had seen in a dream that these two should wed. The woman's name was Desideria, the daughter of King Desiderius and Queen Desideria of the Lobardian people, who had a custom of naming their royal family all of the same name so that the power of the name would not pass out of the family. It was also said of them that they married sister to brother, but the chroniclers of Taillefer's court may have desired to slander that tribe because of the great trouble they caused the emperor. However, what matters to my story is that this noblewoman, Desideria, was known as a haruspex, which craft is anathema to humankind. She foretold the future by means of sacrifices and mirrors, and she had used certain of her arts to bewitch the dowager Queen Bertrada into pleading her cause because Desideria had seen through her forbidden auguries that King Taille would become Emperor Taillefer, the greatest regnant known to humankind.

"Now in those days in Salia where old customs still flourished, women could not rule the great houses. Despite these ancient pagan practices, men still understood the reverence and respect due to a mother, so Taille bowed to his mother's wishes and wed the woman, and in this way she became queen, as was her desire. But within the year King Taille had seen what manner of foul sorceries she used to get her way. He dismissed her and sent her back to her kin. As soon as she was gone, he married a princess of Varingia."

"Was that St. Radegundis?"

"No. This was his second wife, who was called Hiltrude, and who was in all ways a most noble woman. Now Desideria was furious at her humiliation, and she plotted her revenge in this way. When Hiltrude's first child was born, it died soon after of a fever, and the second child suffered in this terrible way as well, afflicted by the minions of the Enemy who made it turn bright red and howl for five days straight before God had mercy on it in its agony and took its soul up to the Chamber of Light. These were the only two legitimate male children born to Hiltrude. Afterward, in revenge for his lost heirs, the king invaded the Lobardian realm and defeated them utterly."

"But Queen Hiltrude bore him legitimate daughters, did she not?" objected Liath. "Any one of them surely could have ruled after Taillefer had the Salians recognized queen regnants as every other civilized people do."

"Did I say that those were the only legitimate male children born to Taillefer? Nay, listen to my tale and you shall see how far Desideria's fury carried her. Later Hiltrude did indeed give birth to three daughters, Tallia, Gundara, and Berthilde. Of these, Tallia was the jewel of her father's house. Because he was unwilling to part from her, he named her as biscop of Autun, the city he most often visited and where he built the great chapel that still stands today. At the fall of the fortress of King Desiderius, Desideria escaped the conflagration by dressing as a humble deacon. Then the malignant woman came to court to avenge her family's disgrace and destruction. But Tallia was so cunning and so blessed that she recognized Desideria although she had never before seen her. Desideria fled to a convent and there took refuge, and after this a report came to the king that she had taken ill and died. Soon after this event Queen Hiltrude died of a wasting sickness, and the king married a woman of good family called Madalgard. However, she was barren, and although the king felt affection for her, she begged him to put her into a convent since God had clearly meant for her to live as a *monacha,* as they called nuns in those times. After this he took a concubine whose name was not recorded, who bore him the illegitimate son who later claimed the throne and was killed for his daring, and after this he married the Svalabian princess Farrada." Anne broke off to take a sip of cider. She looked no worse for the wear after twelve days on the road, every bit as much the regal noblewoman here as in the fine chamber at Werlida where Liath had first seen her.

"But let us skip this part of his life, when he became emperor, because it has no bearing on what I mean to tell you for your instruction." She cleared her throat, considered, and began again. "The emperor summoned certain wise churchwomen and men to his court, so that they could undertake to educate him and his children. Of his children, Tallia was the most precious of his possessions. She excelled at all her studies, and in particular she applied herself to the study of mathematics. With this knowledge she traced the course of the stars with utmost care until at an early age she knew as much as her teachers. At this time, a certain deacon arrived at court who claimed to understand the most veiled of the arts of sorcery. Princess Tallia was eager to study with her, but not a year had passed before the young princess fell gravely ill. At that time she was attended by a young bondswoman named Clothilde, who was as clever as the princess although of low estate. Clothilde came before the emperor and pleaded with him to dismiss the holy deacon from his service, since a miasma of evil clung like the stench of the pit to the woman. She was sent away, and in this way Tallia's life was saved, and she went on, as I have previously related, to become biscop of Autun. There she continued to study the

arts of the mathematici and there, with her companions, she revealed manifold secrets of the heavens.

"But her skill made her enemies among some of the church-
folk. Later, a deacon came to the skopos' palace in Aosta and
laid charges against Biscop Tallia, saying that the biscop had in-
dulged herself in base sorcery. This deacon claimed to have
taught the young Tallia, and testified that she had been forced
to flee when she discovered the terrible practices of murder, au-
gury, and blood sacrifice that Tallia and her companions used to
work their will upon others, even upon the emperor. By this time
Taillefer had put aside his later concubines and married the young
Radegundis as his fifth wife. Although he was still hale and
hearty, he was quite old. The young queen pleaded with him to
let their marriage be like that of the angels, fulfilled in mind
only, but in time she became pregnant and her body was irre-
trievably stained by the touch of the Enemy, which is mortality."

"But how do we know that angels feel no desire—!"

"I have not yet done." Anne did not need to raise her voice.
Liath bent her head obediently, but anger burned inside her. Of
all the things she had done in the two years since Da's death,
marrying Sanglant was the only one that rang utterly right in
her heart.

"You are young," added Anne, "and Bernard's influence still
weighs heavily on you, as do the temptations of the world and
the flesh. Let me continue, and if you will be patient, you will
see that I am almost done." She had to pause to recall her place.
"At this time the skopos, under the influence of the deacon, was
alarmed at these tidings of sorcery and malifici at the court of
the powerful Taillefer. She went herself with an embassy to inquire into the truth of these accusations, and soon after they arrived in the company of the aforesaid deacon, the great emperor
fell ill. Everyone feared for his life, and Biscop Tallia hurried
from Autun to be at his side. There, in the sight of all, she un-
veiled the deacon who had brought the charges against her as
the very same Desideria whose plots and contrivances had long
plagued the emperor and his family. She had gone unrecognized
because of the peculiar youth which still resided in her face.
Some said she had used magic to keep herself young, but when
she was brought before Biscop Tallia she claimed only that hate

had kept her young. In this way, she came into Tallia's keeping as a prisoner.

"However, at that time the skopos, the third Leah to take the title, had no love for the family of Taillefer and in particular little love was lost between Mother Leah and Biscop Tallia, who was not overly proud of her learning and her blood but might seem so to those who envied her all that God had given her. Taillefer died, and the vultures flocked round to despoil his empire. His young queen feared for her life and fled the palace with her handmaiden Clothilde, the same one who was once bondswoman to Tallia. The skopos took Desideria away and not two years later this same Desideria testified at the Council of Narvone about the practices of Biscop Tallia. At that Council, under the influence of Mother Leah, the assembled biscops outlawed the practice of certain sorceries, including that of the mathematici, and Tallia herself was placed under a ban and no longer allowed a seat in the church council. After that testimony, Desideria vanished, and no one knew what happened to her. Although no one could prove it, there was no doubt that by poisoning Taillefer, Desideria had in the end revenged herself upon Taillefer for the insult given her when he set her aside in favor of another woman. In this way her spiteful rage, wielded so unremittingly, brought an end to the reign of Taillefer and his descendants in the kingdom of Salia."

She smiled slightly, but only as a gesture to show she had finished. "Both Desideria, who wanted dominion over the world, and the skopos Leah, who wanted dominion over the arcane knowledge of sorcery but could not master it herself, envied those who had what they most desired. Desideria poisoned Taillefer in the body, and Mother Leah poisoned Tallia in the church. That is why desire is a sin, because it allows the Enemy to hook claws into our skin and drag us down. We cannot ascend to the Chamber of Light as long as we are burdened with desire. Do you understand what I am saying, child?"

Irritated, Liath said nothing, but started up, surprised, when a new voice answered.

"You say that Desideria ended the reign of Taillefer and his descendants. But there's one question you yourself asked that your story didn't answer."

Liath grinned sheepishly and sat back down. She had been listening so intently that she hadn't noticed Sanglant lounging at the door at the borderland between cool magelight and the black of night.

Anne responded coolly. "What question is that, Prince Sanglant?"

"'Did I say that those were the only legitimate male children born to Taillefer?'" He ducked his head under the lintel and came inside, but was careful not to sit next to Liath, although he could not have distracted her any more than he did whether he sat a hand's breadth or a chamber's breadth from her. She was so painfully aware of him, his physical body, his presence, the way he flinched at unexpected noises and tried to cover his reaction, his habit of scenting, like a dog, as he scouted out the lay of the room. He found the half-warm bowl of stew, settled down cross-legged, and set the bowl on his knee.

"I've heard the tale of Desideria. I've heard the glorious *Life* of Taillefer sung in court. In all those stories the poets lament the terrible fate of Hiltrude's two sons. But never have I heard them speak of other legitimate male children. His third wife had no children, so the poets say, and the fourth had only one daughter. But I've always wondered about St. Radegundis."

"What is it you wonder?"

He took a long look at the congealing stew, as if trying to decide whether to bolt it down right now or to be polite. After a moment, manners won out over hunger, and he merely toyed with the spoon's handle as he answered. "All the stories agree that Queen Radegundis was great with child when she knelt for hours beside Taillefer's sickbed and prayed for his release. But no story that I've ever heard relates what happened to the child she carried. She enters the convent, and there she lives her saintly life. Surely someone would have remarked on the fate of the last child born to Taillefer."

Anne regarded him with maddening tranquillity. "I do not speak aloud of everything I have learned or that I suspect. That would be foolish, and especially here, on the road, where all manner of creatures might overhear us."

Abruptly, Sanglant laughed and began to eat his stew.

"Pray excuse me." Liath went outside. She paced along the side of the old hut down to the sagging double doors that marked the entrance to the lean-to. They had used it as a stable, and she heard from inside the snuffling of the Eika dog and the soft noise of the horses at rest. She leaned there, shut her eyes, and breathed.

Ai, Lady! She did not regret coming with her mother. They'd had no alternative in any case. But it was so hard to understand her. Understanding was like a gulf of air she had to leap, but she didn't know how—and she wasn't sure she liked the lay of the land she glimpsed on the other side, where she was meant to go.

A thread brushed her cheek, and she started up to see one of the servants hovering in front of her, exploring her face with its translucent fingers. It skittered away like a leaf and came to rest in the shadow of the trees, a thread of light with a vaguely male shape, nothing she could pinpoint to distinguish it from the other servants except that the other two seemed vaguely female.

"Liath." Sanglant approached out of the night, and she hugged him, hard. This, she understood: that he was solid, and present. Her shield.

"It makes you wonder, though, doesn't it?" he said into her hair.

"What makes you wonder?" She could have stood here forever and remained content, but he was restless. He was always restless, could never quite be still, even in sleep, like a dog aware of a threatening scent in the air.

He touched his neck, the old habit. Both scars—the chafing left by Bloodheart's iron slave collar and the cut left by Hugh's knife—had healed to leave a band of lighter skin and a thread of white, a neck ring of scar tissue. But then, strangely, he curved a palm around her neck, the pressure of his thumb at her throat.

"Why does your mother wear a gold torque?"

VII
INSTANTIA

1

THE rats came out at night to gnaw at the bones. He heard their claws skittering on stone, heard the dogs growling as they crept close enough to clamp their jaws down over his throat, and he bolted up—

Awake.

He was sitting, arms raised to strike, as out of breath as if he'd been fighting. The bed of leaves he'd laid down yesterday at twilight shifted under him. Stars glittered above. The Eika dog whined softly. Liath stirred, murmuring his name.

"Hush," he said softly. "Go back to sleep."

She tugged the blanket over her hips, pillowed her cheek on an arm, and was out, that quickly. He knew he would not sleep again.

"Ai, God," he whispered. "Lord protect me from my dreams."

He eased away so as not to wake her. He did not bother to pull on his tunic, but he grabbed his sword belt. A hazy night stillness lay over everything except for the faint rustling of wind in leaves, not enough to dispel the weight of summer's heat. Nearby he heard the chuckling stream at which they'd watered their horses that evening. This night they had camped in woodland just off the old Dariyan road they followed southeast into

lands more wilderness than cultivated. This night no intact
Dariyan way house had appeared at the expected mile marker,
only a ruin torn apart long ago by scavengers. The servants had
lashed branches together to make a small shelter for Sister Anne,
but Sanglant was used to harsher conditions than these from
campaigns. He was happy to collect leaves and, with the dragon
sigil quilt thrown over all and a blanket atop, make a bed of
them on the ground by the fallen way-house wall.

He was happy . . . or at least content. The day-to-day rhythms
of the journey kept him moving, and when he moved, he didn't
think. If he stayed still for too long, the old nightmare clawed
up, as it had this night—and most nights—in his dreams.

He touched his throat, realized he had done so, and shook
his hand violently as if to shed the chains that had once shack-
led him. He was free. But the memories still weighed as heavily as the chains ever had. He had been Bloodheart's prisoner
for a long time.

Something rustled in the trees, and he spun and growled,
caught himself. Froze.

A wolf padded out into the clearing. Its amber eyes gleamed
softly as it stared at him. A second wolf, lighter, emerged from
undergrowth beside the first. He drew his sword. Its ring, coming free of the scabbard, drew an answering bark, crisp, short,
and clear, from the lead wolf. A third ghosted into the clearing
a short way from the first two, and halted.

How many more were out there?

"Liath," he said softly.

She stirred but did not wake.

He eased a step sideways, toward her. The Eika dog slept on,
too, and it usually woke at once if any danger threatened him,
but it had remained terribly weak since Werlida.

A fourth wolf, black enough that it seemed more shadow than
body, arrived in the clearing. It growled softly, and he, that fast,
unthinking, growled in reply. The lead wolf barked again, like
an order. Two more wolves loped into the clearing and halted.

"Liath!" he said, more sharply.

She stirred, yawned sleepily, and murmured his name on a
question.

"Get your weapons," he said without varying his tone of
voice.

Three of the wolves broke away to circle them. Liath sat up, grabbing her bow.

Light streaked off the shelter, a silvery thread more thought than form. It bore human lineaments, but in the darkness it shimmered. It slid under the nose of the lead wolf, evaded a snap, and a moment later was joined by one of its comrades. Together, they pulled on the tails of the wolves and otherwise pinched and teased them until the entire pack turned tail and vanished into the forest. The servants disappeared after them, their laughter as soft as the wind.

"Cover yourself."

Sister Anne emerged from the shelter with the third servant hovering at her side. Liath yanked the blanket up to her shoulders. Sanglant ignored her and went to the edge of the clearing to listen, but although he stood there for a long time, he heard no trace of wolves.

When he turned back, Anne had gone inside. He sheathed his sword and knelt beside Liath, kissed her, then recalled that Anne was, presumably, still awake. He sat back on his heels.

"What happened?"

"Wolves. The servants chased them away. Go back to sleep. I'll stand watch."

"I thought my mother said that the servants would stand watch."

"And so they do, but I can't sleep now." But he didn't tell her it was more because of dreams than wolves. The servants had done a better job of dispelling the wolves than he ever could have. She hesitated, then lay back down, a sumptuous curve under the blanket. For an instant he was tempted—but two of the servants had gone into the wood and had not yet returned. He pulled on his tunic and bound up his sandals, then dragged a fallen log close to the old, ruined way house, midway between Liath's bed and the shelter, and sat down.

As he sat, he watched the stars. He tried to imagine fixed stars and wandering stars, spheres and epicycles, all these words that Liath used so easily—but it only made him impatient. He got to his feet and began pacing; he couldn't sit still although he knew full well that a sentry needed to be still. But when he was still, the weight of chains seemed to settle on him, whether Bloodheart's chains or the chains his own father wanted to bind him with.

King and emperor, with every prince and noble going for his throat.

He shuddered, spun to walk back the way he had come—

They had returned without him noticing.

He stared.

He had seen enchantment while under Bloodheart's rule. As a child, he had seen certain small creatures hidden in the shadows, peeking out from bushes, half-hidden among the leaves of the deep forest where children weren't allowed to play, but he had explored there nevertheless. He knew magic lived in the land, and although he hated the thought of it, he knew some part of it lived in his blood, his heritage from his mother.

This was enchantment of a different order, creatures from another plane of being—*from a higher sphere,* Liath would say.

They danced on the grass, hands interlinked and perhaps even melded in some inhuman way, because they were made more of light than of flesh. They sang an eerie, angular melody that had no words but only a kind of keening throb. Their dance was at once joy and sorrow, braided together until they could not be unwoven one from the other.

If they knew he watched, they gave no sign of knowing. They only danced.

He neither saw nor heard nor smelled any trace of the wolves.

He watched the servants for a long time, until the predawn light made gray of tree trunks and the servants faded into the light of the coming day and vanished from his sight except where light played along the branches of the shelter, corresponding in no way to the sun, which had not yet risen above the treetops. He heard a giggle at his ear, felt fingers tweak his earlobe and a breath of wind tickle his cheek. Laughing, he went to saddle the horses.

Despite the encounter with the wolves, Anne led them deeper into woodland and lightly settled territory. The next day at about midday they came to a crossroads. It was a lonely place at the base of a rugged hill made forbidding by an outcropping of stone halfway up the steep slope. Someone had cut back the trees to make a clearing, but one huge old trunk had been left.

"We'll turn east here," said Anne.

"Not south?" Liath glanced at her mother, surprised.

"East," repeated Anne.

They reached the actual crossing of paths, and as he came up beside the huge old stump, Sanglant saw that carvings decorated the wood: stag-headed men, women with the heads of vultures, a wolf. Oak leaves, all dried up and crinkly now, littered the base, and someone had piled a cairn of stones on top. Those stones had red stains on them, blood long since dried.

"Sacrifice," said Anne harshly. "And worse things." She dismounted and walked over to the stump. Without expression, she took apart the cairn stone by stone. At its base, half sunk into the rotting center of the trunk, lay an amulet, somewhat decayed. She swept it off the stump with a branch. "This is the work of the Enemy."

Sanglant watched her with interest, waiting to see what would happen. Perhaps it was true that the Enemy prodded weak-willed souls to work harm in the world in this fashion. But he had seen men resort to stranger rites before battle, and of them, as many who prayed to the gods of their grandmothers were as likely to live as those who prayed to God. Nevertheless, it was true that such displays displeased the Lord and Lady, and they had to be eradicated.

Anne turned to where Liath sat on her horse. "Burn it."

Liath paled. She did not move or reply

"The gift of fire is in your nature. Burn this place, where the minions of the Enemy have set their hands."

"No. The people hereabouts only do it to protect themselves and their animals from harm on their journeys, or to guarantee good weather while they're on the road. Why should we harm them when what they've done gives no harm to us?"

"This is Bernard talking through your lips. He traveled too much and was too lenient in his judgments."

"Da always said we should leave well enough alone."

"I left you with him for too long."

"Which way do we go?" answered Liath stiffly. She looked furious.

"You will not do as I ask?"

"I will not. You don't understand what you're asking me to do."

"I am one of the few who do understand." Anne glanced toward Sanglant. He saw the air shimmer around Anne, and suddenly he heard the servants, whispers cutting at the high end of his hearing: words about fire, and burning, but what they used of language was too distorted for him to understand more.

"I say we should ride on," he said. "Surely there is a deacon hereabouts who will deal with these old superstitions in a fitting manner. Isn't that why God have ordained some to dedicate their lives to the church, to be weapons devoted to God's working in the world?"

"Many were conceived and born to be weapons, Prince Sanglant, and yet have no knowledge of their destiny."

"Spoken like my father, Sister Anne. But I am not such a one. And neither is my wife."

She measured Liath a final time. "The iron does not know what it will become until it has been hammered in the fire."

"Let us ride on," he said again. Liath urged her horse forward, taking the right fork.

Anne remained behind. "It would be going against God's will to leave such a shrine behind as a temptation to the unfortunate and foolish people who may be lured to pray and give offerings here only because it exists."

"We'll wait for you ahead." Sanglant rode on, following Liath. The Eika dog padded listlessly beside him. Up the road, Liath had halted in the shadow of the rock outcropping.

"I don't understand your mother's position in the world. Is she sworn to the church, or is she a great lady with many estates under her rule? Who are her kin?"

"She won't tell me," she said, so caught up in her own anger that for an instant it appeared she hadn't heard him, until he realized she had just answered his question. "I asked her why she wears the gold torque, but she wouldn't answer me. She doesn't want me to know my own kin!"

"Or she has reasons of her own for keeping you ignorant. What *does* she want you to know, Liath?"

"The art of the mathematici."

" 'The iron does not know what it will become—' " he murmured, then faltered, smelling smoke. He heard the *clip-clop* of Anne's mule, and a moment later she appeared around the bend.

That afternoon clouds blew in, and gusts of wind shook the trees and threw branches every which way. It began to rain so heavily that they were forced to take refuge at the first village they came to, and there they had to stay for two more days while storm raged and howled around them.

2

AS they climbed the last long slope, Lavas tower gleamed in the distance, all freshly whitewashed and with a new thatch roof. They topped the rise to see Lavas Holding spread out before them. From here, Alain could see the river curling away through lush fields, the little church, the neat houses in the village, the enclosure, and the tower and great hall, all looking prosperous and busy. By the gates, a large crowd had gathered, and at the sight of Lavastine's banner a great cheer rose up. At once, the people waiting by the gates lurched forward into an ungainly procession, coming out along the road to greet their lord.

"Chatelaine Dhuoda has made ready for our coming," said Lavastine.

"Your fields look well tended," said Tallia. "And your people clothed and fed."

"That they are," he replied, not in a smug way, merely stating a fact.

"The church is small," she added.

"But richly furnished, as is fitting." He glanced at Alain, then back at Tallia. "There is also a chapel in the tower where we pray each day."

They rode down to an enthusiastic greeting. Many of the gathered servants and villagers reached out to touch either Lavastine or Alain on the foot as they rode past. Alain noted a number of unfamiliar faces on the fringe of the crowd, people dressed in ragged clothes and with expressions drawn taut with hunger, watching, hopeful.

"Your people love you," said Tallia. People called out her name and prayed for God's blessing on her womb. "When we rode through Arconia, the folk would gather to watch us go by. But they feared my parents, they did not love them."

Lavastine held court in the great hall, an assembly that took all afternoon. He distributed certain items he had obtained on the king's progress to his chatelaine, his stewards and servants, and the village folk: inks and parchment, iron tools, a bull to be used in common by the villagers to breed their cows, a dozen stout ewes, cuttings from quince, fig, and mulberry trees, and vine cuttings from one of the royal vineyards. There were harness and leashes for Master Rodlin, cooking pots for Cook, and javelins, spears, and knives for the men-at-arms.

"We have an unusually great number of laborers this season," reported Chatelaine Dhuoda. "We hear rumor of a drought in Salia. Many have come in hope of harvest work."

Tallia did not even wait to see the tower and grounds but walked out at once with her attendants to give comfort as she could among the poor. Dhuoda led Lavastine and Alain upstairs to show that she had followed the orders sent ahead by the count. A new bed had been built and placed in the chamber the count used as his study.

"This will be my sleeping room," he told Alain, gesturing to the study. They took the curving stairs up to the sleeping chamber that by custom belonged to the count of Lavas and which he and Alain had shared before. Now the bedspread marked with the combined symbols of Lavas hounds and Varren roes brightened the room, and Tallia's chests had been moved into place. "This will be yours. In that bed all the heirs of Lavas have been conceived."

"Even me?"

Lavastine sighed, frowned, and absently patted Terror's head. By his expression, he looked a long way away—in time, if not distance. "Even you, Son. But God are merciful, and They forgive us our sins as long as we do our duty on this earth."

Alain walked to the bed, set a hand on the bedspread, and looked back at Lavastine. Walking had been agony twelve days ago when every step meant that his clothing rubbed against his blistered and raw skin, but he had healed, and the nettle blisters had even gained him some sympathy from Tallia. More importantly, they had allowed him to get through the rest of the journey without any further rash incidents that might turn her against him.

But coming home had lifted both impatience and despair from his heart. As Aunt Bel would say: *"If you want to start a fire, you must chop wood for it first."*

He had not forgotten the *Life* of St. Radegundis, which they

had listened to while on the king's progress and which Tallia
had so admired. So as quiet day succeeded quiet day, as crops
ripened and came to harvest, he walked with her every morning among the poor laborers who had come to Lavas in hope of
work and bread. When she spoke of founding a convent in honor
of St. Radegundis, he encouraged her. Together with her favorite
lady, Hathumod, they spent many pleasant hours with the builder
she had brought with her, a cleric educated in Autun, who discussed the traditional design favored by St. Benedicta in her
Rule as well as certain modern innovations devised by the brothers at St. Galle.

At night, when they lay down together, he remembered the
nettles.

"What of the old ruins the people here speak of?" Tallia asked
Alain one day. "Wouldn't it serve God to build over an old temple and reconsecrate the ground for holy purposes? My attendants tell me that the servants here say there is an altar stone
there where terrible sacrifices were performed. They say you can
still see the stains of blood."

She looked so eager at the mention of sacrifices. When she
was in this mood, she would often touch him, brush her fingers
over his hand, lean against him, all unconsciously. He wanted
to encourage that, and yet it would be a lie to agree with her
when he simply didn't know. "It's laid out with defensive walls.
I think it was a fort."

"But they must have worshiped their gods there. Such people always do."

"We'll go ourselves. You can make your own judgment of
whether the old ruins would be suitable for a convent."

The next few days he spent with Lavastine overseeing the
harvest. It was usual for the lord to bend his own back to cut
the first sheaf of grain in each field, for luck, and Alain did not
mind the work. It reminded him of his childhood. But Lavastine never let him labor in this fashion for long; that was not a
lord's place.

The expedition was set for the feast day of Raduerial, the
angel of song. By the time servants, attendants, and grooms assembled, Alain felt as if they were going on progress, not just
a short way up into the hills. Tallia's ladies chattered excitedly.

Lavastine observed their laughter and gossip with a shake of
the head. "I do believe," he said to Alain, "that King Henry se-

lected only those girls who were as empty-headed as possible. If they have brothers, I expect they think of nothing but hunting, hawking, and whoring."

"Lady Hathumod is not like the others."

"True. She's a sober girl, but she came from Quedlinhame with Tallia. I suppose they rid themselves of her because of the heresy. She's the only one who can pray for as many hours as can your wife."

"Prayer to God is never wasted," retorted Alain, a little stung.

Lavastine whistled back Terror, who had gone to investigate a fresh pile of horse manure. "I am more inclined to believe that God values good works above prayer, but let us not argue this point, son. Lady Tallia is generous to the poor. The king chose wisely when he picked these girls to serve his niece. Tallia will make no useful alliances here."

Lavastine signaled to the grooms, and they set off. They followed a broad path through the fields and up into woodland heavily harvested by the villagers for firewood, small game, and herbs. In late summer the sun seemed to bleed until the air itself took on a golden sheen. Pigs scurried off into the brush. They flushed a covey of partridges, and the huntsmen ran off in pursuit. Alain had to whistle Steadfast back when she loped after them. The path branched, narrowed, and they climbed onto steeper slopes into old forest untouched by human hands. Tallia's deacon entertained them with a story as they rode.

" 'At that time, the savage Bwrmen marched west on the rampage that eventually led them to the great city of Darre, then called Dariya.' "

"Didn't the Bwrmen destroy Dariya?" asked Hathumod, who was inclined to ask questions.

"They did, indeed. Laid it waste, burned it, killed every male above the age of twelve, and made all the women and children their slaves. But the reign of Azaril the Cruel lasted only five years, for God's mercy is great and Their justice swift."

"But what about the visitation of the angel?" Tallia spoke quietly, but Alain was by now so sensitive to every twitch she made that he could hear her as clearly as if she rode beside him.

"Let me return to my story." Cleric Rufino was as bald as an egg and had ruddy cheeks from working so many hours out in the sun supervising construction. "As they marched west toward Dariya, the Bwr army besieged a town called Korinthar.

Now the people of Korinthar had been visited by St. Sebastian
Johannes of Eisenach in the course of his holy travels, but although he sang the mass most sweetly, the townsfolk had not
heeded his preaching. Instead they mocked him, and when the
Bwrmen approached, these same townsfolk thrust him outside
the gates into the path of the Bwr scouts. In this way God granted
St. Sebastian Johannes the glorious martyrdom he desired. Meanwhile, the people of Korinthar readied themselves for the final
battle with the savage Bwrmen. Although they knew they would
lose, they believed it better to die fighting than to beg for mercy
from an enemy they hated. But the angel Raduerial visited the
chamber of young St. Sonja, who alone in that town had heeded
the preaching of St. Sebastian Johannes. The angel blessed her
with the gift of song.

"St. Sonja offered herself at the gates in the hope of saving
her people, even though they ridiculed her for her faith. Because
of her youth and beauty, she was taken to the tent of the cruel
king, Azaril, where she sang so sweetly that his heart was softened. He spared Korinthar and all those people who lived inside its walls. At this sign of God's grace, the entire town wept
and prayed at the tiny church built by St. Sebastian Johannes
with his own hands, and pledged from that time forward to follow the faith of the Unities."

"What happened to St. Sonja?" asked Hathumod.

"No one knows," admitted the cleric. "Some say the Bwrish
king took her captive and later had her killed when she refused
to become his wife."

One of the girls squealed. "But it's said that the Bwr people
aren't people at all but—"

"I beg you, my lady!" From such a mild-mannered man, the
retort bit doubly hard. "It would be abomination to speak more
on that subject. That's only a tale concocted to tempt men and
women into improper thoughts. Most agree that she walked of
her own accord into the dark lands inhabited by the Bwrmen,
to bring the Light of the Unities to their tribes. She was never
seen again. But in any case, she left Korinthar and did not return."

"Look!" Tallia jostled her way to the front of the procession
and now emerged first into the wide clearing. Alain rode up beside her. The ruins lay sprawled below them. She stared, pink
staining her cheeks, and as he surveyed the walls, he wondered

if there was a Dariyan road hidden here, now covered by grass and moss.

While the rest of the progress fanned out to explore, Tallia dismounted, and he followed her into the ruins where she exclaimed over the carvings on the stone: spirals, falcons, people with human bodies and animal heads. "We must tear all these walls down! We can chisel these evil images from the stones and use them to build a convent where our prayer will glorify God."

She grabbed his hand to tug him along. Inside the altar house she knelt beside the white altar stone—still holding Alain's hand—and with her free hand traced the pattern of four spirals that led into a fist-sized hollow sunk into the center of the pale stone. She shuddered ecstatically and drew Alain against her. "We will build the church right here! The chapel, with the Hearth, right over this very stone!"

Her shoulders were so thin. She was still quivering. The feel of her body against him swept such strong feelings through him that he tried to disengage his hand from hers so he could step back. The memory of nettles was not helping.

She stood so close he could easily tilt his head down and brush her mouth with his own. She stared up at him with her lips parted and a breathless urgency in her gaze. She did not shrink away when he gathered her more closely against him.

"Do you see?" she whispered. "God has given us this opportunity to build a chapel, to honor Her, and Her Son, as is fitting. We can build a place to worship Mother and Son, to bring the true faith to those who have been lost in the false word of the church."

Dazzled by the flush in her face and eyes, he would have agreed to anything as long as it meant she stayed this close. Sorrow yipped from the shadow of the doorway. A moment later Lavastine appeared at the threshold, ducked inside, and registered their embrace.

"I beg your pardon," he said quickly, and made to turn and go back outside.

"My lord count!" Tallia broke away from Alain, who stood there shaking as he struggled to control himself. "Now that the harvest is almost in, there are many laborers hereabouts who can serve my builders."

"To what purpose?" Lavastine came over but only to touch the altar stone.

"To build a convent dedicated to Mother and Son! And a chapel, where they may be worshiped properly, and where the image of the sacrifice and redemption of the blessed Daisan, Her holy Son, can be painted so that people can learn the truth!"

"Certainly not!" Lavastine plucked several weeds that had grown up around the stone, as if such untidiness offended him. "The counts of Lavas have always been on good terms with the church, and I do not intend to change that now."

"But you must wish to see the truth brought to light in the world!"

"I wish for no disruption in my house! My lady Tallia, that you hold close to your heart beliefs that the church has named as a heresy troubles me, but I acknowledge that only God can judge our hearts, and so I leave you alone to pray as you wish. But I will build no monument on these lands to a heretical notion condemned by the skopos. And neither will my son!"

The flush that stained her cheeks now was brighter and hotter than any brought to her skin by Alain's presence.

"However." Lavastine surveyed the curving stone walls and the tiny carvings of snails and rosettes that adorned the altar stone. "You may found a convent here with my blessing, one dedicated to Edessia and Parthios."

"You are mocking me." Her bright flush had faded to the pallor of anger.

"Not at all. That the holy Edessia and Parthios, wife and husband, brought the blessed Daisan into the world is not mockery."

"He is the Son of God, not of mortal creatures!"

"So we are all the children of God, according to the teachings of the church. But the blessed Daisan was born out of the womb of the holy Edessia. Unless there is another way for children to come into the world, of which I am not aware."

She sucked in air loudly, prelude to an outburst. With her head thrown back, chin raised, she looked every bit a king's niece, aware of her power and willing to use it. But instead she burst into sobs and rushed out of the building.

Alain jerked round to follow her, but Lavastine's voice stopped him. "I beg your pardon, but I refuse to offend the church merely to indulge her misguided whims."

"You must not apologize to me. I didn't expect her to want to build a chapel to her heresy."

Lavastine sighed. "Perhaps her anger at me will make her confide in you. You must follow up any advantage, as I see you were already doing. Let her oversee the building here. Cleric Rufino may know of relics of the holy parents which we can bring here. It will do her good to be reminded that even the blessed Daisan's parents married and were blessed with a child by God's grace."

Alain hurried outside. Tallia was snuffling noisily while her women gathered around her like so many flustered chicks.

"Tallia." They parted to let him through, and he took Tallia's arm firmly and let her aside out one of the gates into the wild field of grass and withering flowers. At once, she began to blurt out all her grievances, her thwarted heart, her desire to honor the Mother and Son. "No one ever listens to me! My mother never spoke to me except to tell me what to do and how to act, and my father is an idiot and he always used to spit up and pee in his pants and fondle the servingwomen and try to mate with them just like a dog right in front of everyone!"

She was so frail he feared that all this trembling and sobbing would shake her to bits, but it did not. After a while she wiped her nose with the back of a hand and they wandered along the stream without speaking. He knelt where the stream pooled, caught behind a bank of rock, and she sat down on the grass beside him. A few tears still rolled down her cheeks.

He leaned over the pool. A flicker of movement among the trailing weeds caught his attention. Barely breathing, he waited with one hand sunk in the cold water so long that his fingers began to go numb. But his stillness at last brought out a little green frog hidden among the rushes. It swam, fetched up against his hand, and he slowly lifted it out from the water, cupping his other hand over it to shield it from the sun.

"Look," he whispered.

She bent, peered—and shrieked, jumping away. Birds fluttered up. The frog leaped and vanished into the stream.

"Such creatures are minions of the Enemy!" she cried. "They give you warts!"

"I was only trying to cheer you up!" He jumped the stream, slipped and got his feet soaking wet, and strode away from her. His heart thumped wildly, and a moment later Sorrow and Rage ghosted up beside him, silent shadows. He realized he was clenching his left hand and loosening it, clenching and loosening, to an erratic rhythm. He was furious, stung, insulted. Rage snapped at a butterfly. Lady Hathumod called his name, but he ignored her and tramped down to the forest's edge.

Stumbled on rock.

He swore, a string of oaths heard long ago from the men who worked the quarries. Aunt Bel would have tweaked his ear hard to hear him speak so. But she wasn't his aunt any longer. His stubbed toe hurt, and being cold and wet made it hurt more. Sorrow snuffled along the ground. Alain crouched to rub his toe, and his fingers brushed stone.

Here, concealed by grass, lay the broken paving stones of the old road, leading east into the forest. He pulled up grass until he had uncovered an entire paving stone. When he set his palm on it, the surface was cool and strangely smooth. An ant scurried across the stone. He shut his eyes. Long ago, Dariyan soldiers and merchants had walked on this roadway, their hearts lying elsewhere surely but their heads full of plans and dreams. The rose burned at his chest. Tiny legs—the ant—tickled the base of his thumb. And he fell . . .

Waves slap the side of the ship as they emerge from the sheltered fjord into the wind-chopped sound. Islands lie everywhere around them, some of them merely slabs of rock, some gently-rounded curves and green slopes. Goats scramble up from the beach, startled by their silent approach. The sky lies clear above, absolutely blue; the distance bleeds to a whitish haze as if the horizon is fading into the light. Sunlight glitters on the waves together with the scalloping ripples of the wind.

The sails go up, and wind fills their bellies. His standards flutter at the stem of each ship, a crest on the dragon-head which blazes their path through the seas.

Let others rest. Let others believe that Rikin will fester in disorder, hopelessly weakened by the collapse of Bloodheart's hegemony. Any of his brothers, had they won, would have wasted their chance in a frenzy of bloodletting and useless petty revenges.

He stands at the stern, shading his eyes against the sun, and counts his ships. Out of what remained to him, he mustered fourteen. In their wake, other movements eddy. A slick back surfaces, and dives.

No one will expect Rikin's tribe to strike so soon.

*   *   *

. . . and caught himself, reeling. The ant had reached the first
knuckle of his hand. Without looking up, he heard the noise of
horses, of distant laughter. For some reason the ant fascinated
him. It scurried out along his thumb, crawled onto the stone,
and was lost in the grass. But where his thumb lay on the stippled stone, in the shadow made by his body, he saw a tiny carving cut into the stone like a mason's mark: a delicate rosette.

The rose, seen everywhere in this ancient ruin, was drawn in
the stylized manner the Dariyans had used: seven rounded petals
around a circular center. He pulled on the thong around his neck
and pulled out the pouch, opened it. Although he reached in
carefully, he still pricked his finger on a sharp thorn as he freed
the rose from its leather hiding place and drew it out so he could
look at it. It gleamed, and the blood welling up on his thumb
was no darker than its petals.

His pulse beat time in his ears like the steady march of feet,
soldiers in formation striding away. He could almost see them
on the road, shadows flowing around him as they marched onward to some unknowable destination. A great plumed standard
waved at the head of the line, turning in the wind, and wind
whipped the stiff horsetail crests on the soldiers' helmets. They
had grim faces not unlike that of Prince Sanglant, high, flat
cheekbones, a cast of feature unknown in Wendish and Varren
lands. But among them marched more familiar faces, broad-
shouldered men with pale hair, a tall woman with skin the color
of pitch, a man with flaming red hair, and a stocky woman with
scarred hands and eyes pulled tight at the corners. A woman
rode along the line, calling out orders, or encouragement, or
news. She, too, wore armor, polished to a high sheen. A hip-
length red capelet trimmed with black fur concealed her back,
and a short sword swung by her thigh. She carried a staff in her
right hand which she raised as she called out. The short staff
had a silver gleam to it, a sinuous dragon twining up its length.
She, too, had the look of Sanglant, descendant of the Lost Ones.
She shifted in the saddle, turned her horse, and light glinted on
her painted shield, a red rose on a silver field. He blinked hard,
half blinded.

The shadows passed. It was only Rage, looming over him to
lick his face. He spluttered, sat back as he wiped saliva from
his face, and looked around. Long shadows drew the print of

ruined walls far across the clearing. Everyone else had left. He
had no idea how long he had knelt here alone. He put the rose
back in the pouch.

When he stood, two servants ventured cautiously forward,
keeping well away from Sorrow and Rage. "My lord Alain, the
count told us to escort you back."

He nodded, still dizzy. They brought the horses, and he had
to shake cobwebs out of his mind before he could remember
how to mount. Where had Tallia gone? Had she just deserted
him? Anger still burned, dull but nagging. Why did she have to
be so stubborn? Why couldn't she just love him?

But was that what God ordained when they decreed that there
be harmony between female and male? That one should bow to
the other's desire? Would he truly be any different from Father
Hugh, who had used his power to force Liath to lie with him?
He remembered Margrave Judith's handsome young husband. *He*
had not looked particularly happy. Was that what he wanted for
Tallia? That she merely acquiesce to *his* desires?

No. There was no other way but to coax her to do what was
right, to change her mind. But that task was proving far harder
than he had ever imagined it could be.

He and the servingmen reached Lavas Holding at sunset, and
as they passed through the gates a lone rider came up behind
them.

"My lord!" he called. "I bring a message from Varingia."

The voice sounded strangely familiar. For an instant Alain
saw a stranger, a young man with broad shoulders and a light
brown beard. Then he recognized him. *"Julien?"*

The young man blushed and stammered. "M-my lord Alain!"
He said it awkwardly, as though he had practiced words he'd
known would be difficult to say.

"I didn't think to see you here," said Alain stupidly.

"I'm a man-at-arms serving the duchess of Varingia."

A man-at-arms. He had a horse, a leather coat, a helm slung
over his shoulder, a shield bearing the stallion of Varingia hanging from his saddle, and a spear. Bel would never have outfitted Alain so; Henri had promised his foster son to the church.
Then he laughed suddenly. How could he possibly be so foolish as to envy Julien, or begrudge him his good fortune?

He clapped Julien on the shoulder. "Well met, cousin." He
was a count's heir now; he could afford to be magnanimous—

and ought to be. "How are Bel and Henri? How does everyone fare?"

Julien was still flushed and clearly uncomfortable, but after they left the horses at the stable he gave a halting account of the family: Bel and Henri were still strong; Stancy's youngest had died of a fever, but she was pregnant again; Agnes' betrothed had come to live with them, although they wouldn't marry for two years yet; he himself had his eye on a young woman but he had to have Duchess Yolande's permission to marry.

They walked to the hall where the evening's supper had just commenced. The servingman had gone ahead, and a steward came forward to show Julien to a seat.

"Not ale and porridge!" said Alain at the sight of the humble meal set before Julien. "Bring something from the count's table!" God Above! He would not have Julien reporting to Aunt Bel that Alain had treated him like a common servant, and fed him no better than this! He lingered long enough to see that Julien was brought wine, fowl, and other savories from the kitchen such as usually were reserved for the count's table. The he took his place beside his father, let a servant wash his hands and face, and gratefully gulped down a cupful of wine.

"Who is that," asked Lavastine, "to whom you show such marked favor?"

"My cousin Julien—not my cousin, I mean. He's the eldest son of Bella of Osna village, the woman who fostered me. He always treated me as a cousin."

"Why is he here?"

The shock of seeing Julien had driven everything else out of his head. "He serves the duchess of Varingia. He's come on her business. I don't know what it is."

Tallia tugged on his sleeve and when he leaned toward her, whispered in his ear. "You were taken by a fit. You shouldn't have touched the frog! I begged your father to let the deacon sprinkle holy water on you and exorcise you with prayer, but he refused!"

"My father knows what he is about." It wasn't right that Tallia criticize his father, when she understood nothing of the matter: That Lavastine deliberately kept churchfolk away from Alain when he was struck by visions. With a flash of irritation, Alain turned away from her and picked up the wine cup again, sipping at it to stop himself from saying something rash.

As soon as Julien cleared his platter, Lavastine called him forward to deliver his message.

Julien acquitted himself well enough. Alain had no cause to feel embarrassment at the association, and why should he? Bel had made sure that all of those under her charge were raised with good manners. "My lord count. My lord. My lady." He nodded to Lavastine, Alain, and Tallia, in turn. "I ride at the bidding of Yolande, Duchess of Varingia. She bids you greeting, Count Lavastine, and sends greetings to her cousin, Tallia of Varre. Within a fortnight she will pass this way to offer these greetings in person and to bring gifts in honor of the wedding of Lady Tallia and Lord Alain. It is her devout wish to celebrate Matthiasmass with her cousin, so that they may pray for peace."

Cousin. Julien was his cousin no longer. He truly understood it now as Lavastine told Julien that in the morning he would ride back to his mistress and let her know that all would be ready for her arrival. Julien did not hesitate as he returned to the lower end of the hall, where men-at-arms and servingwomen gathered cheerfully around him to hear news of far-off regions. It was not a place Alain belonged any longer. He would only be in their way, should he try to speak to Julien again.

"So it begins," said Lavastine softly. He wore his thinnest smile. "Now the jackals will gather round, because we have the prize."

The prize.

It had never meant anything to Alain before, prizes, alliances, the ties of blood. But now it came clear: Tallia's blood and rank would draw them to Lavas like flies to honey. Tallia had called herself a pawn because more powerful hands moved her where she did not want to go, but he had learned the rules of the game called chess this past year. The pieces called Lions were also called pawns because they were men-at-arms, common-born and expendable—like Julien. But Tallia was not a pawn. She was the granddaughter of kings and queens.

In the game of chess, that made her a Regnant.

3

THE journey on roads fallen into ruin was hard on the horses. Anne directed them down the wrong fork in a maze of woodland paths and they had to retrace their steps only to find after much confusion that the pavement of the old Dariyan road had lain hidden by debris and moss. A chance-met forester, surprised to see them, told them that the village of Krona lay some miles ahead, and Anne nodded, seeming to expect this. Not four miles after, as twilight lengthened, one of the pack mules collapsed and died, worn beyond endurance.

They camped that night out of sight of the corpse, but Anne set a servant to watch over it. They had been dogged by miserable weather, and it drizzled now. Liath had twisted her ankle when she'd slipped while dismounting, but she dealt with her misery by becoming increasingly silent. In truth, Sanglant was glad of it. He'd known soldiers who suffered loudly and those who suffered silently, and although he knew God enjoined humankind to feel compassion, he preferred the silent sufferers.

Right now he crouched over a fire that he coaxed to stay alive despite the rain. Earlier he'd gathered comfrey along the banks of a stream. Now it steeped in boiled water. Anne came up behind him. She had an odd step, decided, as if she knew where she was going, but not at all heavy, as if she meant to treat lightly so no footprint would be left behind. Her robes smelled of rose oil. "You are learned in herb lore, Prince Sanglant? I thought you merely a fighting man."

"I know a little," he said cautiously. "It's always wise to observe, to learn what's useful. I can treat wounds and a few illnesses, such things as we see on campaign."

She asked him a few questions, and he was astonished to discover that he knew more than she did about herbs. Her knowledge of them seemed all secondhand, as if she had spent time with someone who knew herblore but had in that time never truly listened to that wisdom. It did not interest her. If anything, what interested her was the extent of his knowledge, not the lore itself, which he had gleaned over many years by watching, listening, and asking questions of wisewomen and conjuremen and such healers as traveled in the train of armies.

Later, when Liath sniffed at the poultice, she said "comfrey" in a choked voice, then shut her eyes and sucked in air as he pressed it gently over her ankle. He settled down behind her so that, back against back, they braced each other. It had stopped raining but now and again drops sprayed his face, spilled on a gust of wind. The dog snuffled along the ground, then flopped down beside him. It was so thin, and it never seemed to get any stronger. Sometimes he felt as if he were the thread drawing it forward, that otherwise it would simply lie down and die.

"Da always said comfrey for sprains and aches," murmured Liath. "People would come to him when they were sick. I never paid attention to how much he knew."

Sanglant shut his eyes. He was comfortable with her as counterbalance against his back. His fingertips brushed the dog's ears. Its hide had such an odd texture, not at all comforting like a real dog's coat but dry and rough. Still. It grunted and whined, tail thumping as he scratched its head. He felt himself dozing off, his awareness like the thread that bound the dog to him just as he was bound to his father by an intangible cord that gleamed as softly as starlight. Yet that connecting thread wound farther back, beyond, to a place unremembered but felt in the pulse of his heart, so faint that he had to smell it and hear it more than see it, a binding made by the pull of blood.

A woman walks along a forest path. Shadow and light makes her clothing appear strange, unearthly: a jacket like that worn by the Quman, a ragged skin skirt made of a thin, pale leather. Feathers and beads decorate her hair. A rough-looking man walks behind her, leading a horse. She pauses as if taking a scent, then lifts her stone-pointed spear, shakes it once, twice.

He grunted, coming awake to see a fire snapping brightly a body's length from them.

"I'm better at controlling fire," she said. "It helps that it's wet. The damp is like a shield—"

Such a bitter regret washed over him at the thought of the

soldiers he'd left behind at Werlida that he winced, then struggled up to his feet.

"What is it?"

"I have to walk."

He walked back to where the dead mule lay at the side of the old road. Its gear had been stripped and taken forward to the campsite. It had collapsed beside a mile marker, a small granite post barely poking out above the litter of forest fall. With a finger he traced the number carved there. Lichen had grown into the chiseled lines. Moss made a little hat on the flat top of the marker, damp and soft. The dead animal had a faint putrescence, and the sheen of light that marked the presence of one of the servants hovered round it, inquisitive, as if it had never seen death before and did not know what to make of it.

In the morning Anne had the servants transfer the baggage from the dead mule to her own, and she insisted on walking even when Sanglant offered her Resuelto.

It was hard going. Roots had torn up portions of the old pavement; water and ice had shattered others. Liath stayed on her horse and didn't complain. Eventually the woodland opened out, and beyond a river they saw a thread of smoke marking a village. The old bridge had fallen to pieces, planks lost or gaping. Sanglant scouted the shore but could find no boat, and in the end he volunteered to lead the horses and mules across one by one. In some places he had to shove planks together. In others, he simply laid his shield down over the gaps so they could get across. In this way they made it to the other side. Of the servants he saw no sign, but one of them blew in his ear teasingly.

The old road forked one last time before the village, and here Anne took the fork that led away from the first strip of fields.

"We are not going to the village," said Anne when he objected. He was tired, damp, hungry, and wanting a fire. But they pitched back into woodland again, trudged up through rugged country torn by rock falls. The old road thrust gamely along, finding purchase through a series of switchbacks and supporting arches. Long after midday they reached a ridge. Wind blew incessantly and broke the cloud cover into a patchwork, ragged clots of blue among the gray-white clouds. They struggled along the exposed road for what seemed hours. The footing was terrible, loose rock, pebbles, slick moss. To the right lay a deep and narrow valley, thick with trees. At last the road skirted a hollow sunk into the ridge, and there, in the hollow below, stood nine stones, one of them listing badly. The other eight were squat and square, dark-grained, colored by lichen. It had long since stopped raining, and most of the cloud cover had blown on to the northwest, but the wind cut wickedly here on the height. Anne slipped back her hood and started down where a path cut away from the road and curved down the slope to end as a dirt ring around the stones.

They made camp outside the crown of stones, somewhat out of the wind. Liath winced as she put weight on her foot, but she could walk on it now. Sanglant diligently applied another poultice. He loved touching her, even if it was just rubbing ointment on her swollen ankle. It was quiet except for the wind. Too quiet.

He looked up suddenly, stood, and listened. "The servants are gone."

"They cannot enter the halls of iron," replied Anne. "They will return by a different road. *We* must wait for night. That is the measure of the darkness which taints us as long as we exist on this earth: that we can only see into the world above when nights lies over us."

"I don't understand what you mean."

"The arts of the mathematici," said Liath abruptly. She had barely spoken to her mother since the incident at the crossroads. She closed her eyes and got that look on her face that meant she was remembering, "seeking in the city of memory," she called it. "'The geometry of the stars,'" she said slowly, as if quoting. "'Through their shifting alignments the mathematicus can draw power from the highest spheres down below the sphere of the moon.' The stone circles are gateways that were built long ago, even before the Dariyan Empire. Da spoke of such pathways. But we never used them."

"He did not have the knowledge, or the strength," said Anne. "He was not patient enough." She seemed about to say something else, but did not.

"They were too dangerous," retorted Liath. "They can find you there, just as in the vision seen through fire."

"Who can find you?"

"Anything that's looking for you. If there is a gate, then anyone who can see it can also pass through it. Isn't that right?"

"Many creatures walk for a time upon the earth, it is true, and some have the ability to pass through into places where humans cannot wander. These crowns are gateways, but not just for creatures who are made of a different substance than we are, and not just for those of humankind who have struggled to master the arts of the mathematici. There are yet others who know sorcery and practice its secrets for their own gain, because these gateways open into places far distant from here, even beyond what we understand of earth itself. Did Bernard never tell you of what else has sought to use these gateways for their own ends?"

"I found out for myself when I saw a daimone," she said bitterly. "I heard its voice calling me—" Then, abruptly, her expression changed; she had thought of something else, not daimones at all, something she did not want to speak of. She had never mastered concealing her thoughts; to him, she was transparent. It was one of the things about her that he found so attractive, the impulsive way she had, as if she could never help herself.

"The Lost Ones," said Anne. "They seek the gateways." She turned away from Liath. "So, Prince Sanglant. Will you walk with us when night comes and we open the gate?"

"The Lost Ones," he repeated, dumbfounded, and knowing he sounded like a fool. "But they're gone. They vanished long ago, even before the old Empire. The old Dariyans, the empresses and emperors, they weren't even true elves, they were only half-breeds."

"Like you."

"Like me," he said harshly. "But nevertheless the Aoi went away so long ago that maybe they're just a story."

"Except for your mother?"

He closed his mouth on an angry retort. On such a field, she would rout him. He knew when to shut up.

"Where did they go, then?" asked Liath. Abruptly Sanglant understood what she concealed with her expression: She didn't want her mother to know that she had spoken with an Aoi sorcerer, that she had passed through one of the gates and returned. Where had she traveled on that journey?

"Where, indeed," said Anne, echoing Liath's question. "In Verna, where we have some measure of protection, you will see what answers we have come to."

Twilight came and, with it, stars, like exclamations, each one unseen, unspoken, and then suddenly popping into view. Anne rose, shook out her robes, and took the reins of her mule. Sanglant made haste to get Resuelto and the other mule while Liath brought up the rear. Just before entering the stones Anne knelt and began to diagram in the dirt, using her staff to draw angles and lines. After a bit she rose and considered first him and then Liath.

"This may damage your eyes," she said at last, and she found cloth with which to blindfold them.

"But I want to learn—!"

"In due time, Liath. You would not want to go blind, would you?"

Liath fumed, but Anne waited until it became obvious that they would go no farther this night unless they acquiesced. Sanglant had to crouch for Anne to reach him, to tie the cloth over his eyes. The procession made a complicated skein: one pack mule at the front where Anne could reach it, he behind holding Resuelto with Liath mounted on the gelding, holding in her hands the lead for the other mule and the reins of the mare. In this way he waited. He heard Anne's staff scratching in the dirt. A thrumming rose from the ground. The dog whined, ears flattening. The horses stirred nervously, although the mules merely stood with stubborn patience, waiting it out. Even through the cloth he thought he saw light flickering.

Without warning, the mule started forward. He kept one hand on its girth and the other on Resuelto's reins and managed to move forward into the stones without stumbling. The ground shifted under his feet, disorienting him. The night air had a gentle touch, like spring. His ears buzzed, and it took him a moment to realize that he was *hearing* voices, like the servants' voice, but many more and all in a jumble.

Shapes brushed past him. Fingers pinched his body. At once, he tore off the blindfold. The night sky shone clearly with no trace of cloud except for huge dark shapes that were not cloud at all but mountain. Three figures were walking up a path to greet them, but he could not see their faces. Anne walked down to speak with the people below, who had halted on the path. He saw now the shimmer and dance of aery spirits flocking around him, and shying away from Liath.

"She drew down the power, from what she read in the heavens, and opened a pathway," breathed Liath. She had also pulled down her blindfold. "Da spoke of it, but he never attempted it. Sometimes I thought it was just a story he made up. But it *is* true. There *are* threads woven between the souls of the stars. The sage Pythia said that if you listen closely enough, you can hear the song made by the spheres as they turn. Each one striking a different note in relation to the other, always changing. An endless melody."

"Hush," he said softly. "I hear them."

"The music of the spheres?" She strained, listening, but obviously heard nothing, probably only faint sounds of wind and small animals rustling in the leaves.

"The servants."

She had dropped the reins of her horse, leaving it to explore the luxuriant grass, and now she touched his elbow, began to speak as she peered around her, trying to see them. But he touched a finger to her lips to still her.

And he listened.

Slowly their voices came clear, or perhaps only the ones that had traveled with them had modulated their tone enough that he could now begin to understand them.

"Where are we?" he whispered.

But they only answered. *"Spring."*

They were very excited, clustering close, shying off, always coming back. They circled round in a dance that was not a dance, half seen against night and blazing stars.

Suddenly it all became clear, not in words precisely but in the way they fluttered in and out, venturing to touch Liath but frightened of something about her, cautious, yet curious, pulled by that curiosity in the same way that the servant had hovered around the dead mule. They were attracted to something never before experienced and strange to them, who were not formed of earth.

He laughed with a sudden wild happiness and pulled Liath against him to whisper in her ear.

"They say you're carrying a child."

4

ZACHARIAS poked at the skinned and spitted squirrels and watched clear fluid dribble down. "We can eat."

This night they had made camp beside a stream, within the shelter of trees grown up among a tumble of boulders: shelter, defense, and water. For the first time in days, she had allowed Zacharias to make a fire while she snared squirrels. They had seen no sign of Quman raiders since the burned village, uncounted days ago. Once, as a churchman, he had kept track of the days and always known which saint's praise to sing at Prime and Vespers. Now he watched the sun rise and set, that was all. Today had been a day like any other summer's day, made more pleasant because he had not yet been killed and beheaded by his enemies.

She crouched beside him and took the larger portion of the first squirrel, as she always did. He did not begrudge it to her. "You are always looking over your back," she observed. "Are you a prince among your people that the Quman should pursue you so? You do not seem like a prince to me."

"I am a freeholder's son and grandson," he said proudly, "not a lord."

"Then why do the Quman want you?"

"Among the Quman I was a slave, but I publicly mocked the war leader of the clan who owned me, the one called Bulkezu. I mocked him in front of the *begh*—the chieftain—of a neighboring tribe, in front of his wives and daughters. Bad enough for a man to do it, but for me—Bulkezu cannot let the insult go unavenged."

She licked her fingers and sat back on her haunches. "You are not a man?" Fat dripped from the cooking meat and sizzled on the coals beneath. He did not answer, "Ah," she said suddenly. "You are missing the man-thing. The man part. I do not know what it is called in this language."

Was that the heat of the fire searing his face, or his own shame?

When she saw that he would not reply, she shrugged and busied herself tallying the provisions that remained to them: three hard black loaves, five strips of dried meat, two pouches of beans and withered peas, a hand-sized block of salt, and turnips that had a rancid smell.

"You've never told me your name," he said, in a burst of anger. "You know mine. I offered it when we met. But you've never given me yours in exchange."

She had a way of smiling that displayed threat as much as amusement. "In exchange for what?"

"My service!"

"No. That you gave in exchange for your life, which I saved from the one you call Bulkezu." She hoisted one of the leather bottles looted from the burned village, the last that still held hard cider. Unstoppering it, she poured a little on her hand and lapped it up, made a face, but she took a draught anyway and passed the bottle on to Zacharias. The backwash of its heady flavor made him light-headed and bold.

"It's true I have nothing to offer you except—" His gaze lit on her skin skirt, and he shuddered, went on. "—except my knowledge of the Wendish people. That's worth nothing to you, since you've traveled among them before, so it seems. But it would be simple kindness to offer me your name, after we have traveled so far together."

"*Kindness?* What is *kindness?*"

"It is the custom of my people to exchange names," he said finally. It angered him that she held more of him than he did of her. But they could never be equals, no matter what.

The woman put all the provisions back in the pouches, keeping out only one loaf, which she broke to show a moist, thick, dark interior. She tried it, nodded, and broke the loaf into equal portions, handing one to Zacharias, then sat back on her heels as she chewed. Zacharias eased the second squirrel off the spit and they ate in silence while the fire guttered and sank to coals.

She answered abruptly. "I am known among my people as The-One-Who-Is-Impatient. The Wendish people knew me as The-One-Who-Is-Not-Like-Us."

"What can I call you?"

She had grease on her thumb, and she drew the thumb down

one seam of her skirt so that the fat soaked into the skin, darkening it.

Who had once lived in that skin, and how had he lost it? Her eyes had the hard green glare of emeralds. "The-One-Whose-Wish-is-Law."

"You have no real name?" The profusion of titles puzzled him.

"A name is only what other people call me. Since I am a different thing to each one of them, I have many names."

"What do you call yourself?"

She grinned. She had remarkably beautiful teeth, white, and straight. "You I will call More-Clever-Than-He-Looks. I do not need to call myself because I am already in my body. But if you need a title, you may call me *Uapeani-kazonkansi-a-lari,* or if that is too much for your tongue, then Kansi-a-lari."

This challenge at least he could meet. He had always been proud of his clever tongue. "Uapeani-kazonkansi-a-lari." He stumbled over it, said it a second time, then a third after she corrected his pronunciation. By the fourth he could pronounce it well enough to please her, and she laughed.

"Well, then, More-Clever-Than-He-Looks, build up the fire."

Brush and deadwood littered the area and was easy to collect. Twilight had barely deepened to night when he laid on more wood and watched the fire blaze. She rocked back and forth on her heels, palms out. Flames built, leaped, and melded into an archway. And through it:

Fire.

Nothing else, only fire. No figure of a man, such as they had seen before.

Kansi-a-lari muttered words, like a curse. She wove her fingers together, making a lattice of them, and through this lattice she looked at the fire again, as through a screen. Zacharias saw only fire, as seen through a veil. She spoke another word. Dim shapes flickered to life in the fire. A lord rode on a handsome horse at the head of an impressive retinue. He had silvering hair and beard, a man in his prime. Standards flew before him: eagle, lion, and dragon.

"The king!" breathed Zacharias in amazement, not because he had ever seen the king but because he recognized his sigils.

But she frowned at this image of the king, seeking someone else.

"*Sawn-glawnt,*" she said, more commanding now, but the image faded and fire danced and blazed. She spoke another word, and shadows appeared within the fire, sharpening into visions:

A dead dog lies tumbled in leaves. Its ribs glare white against decaying black fur. A gaping hole sags in the flesh of its belly where something has eaten it away from without—or within.

A man dressed in cleric's robes sits in a shuttered room. He has the clean chin and short hair of a man sworn to the church, and his hair is starkly gold, as if a sorcerer had spun it out of pure metal. His hand trembles as he reaches to touch writing on a sheet of parchment that lies on the table before him. The vision is so clear that Zacharias can read the words: "To Mother Rothgard of St. Valeria, from the hand of Sister Rosvita of Korvei, now in the king's schola, this message delivered to you by my trusted companion Amabilia of Leon. I beg you, Mother, to travel with Sister Amabilia to Autun. You are needed to testify to the events—*The man smiles, revealing a chipped tooth—the only flaw in his beauty. He folds the parchment up. Underneath it lies a bronze Circle of Unity. Dried blood stains it. The man lifts it and spins it by its chain, and the vision spins and folds in on itself and becomes something else. . . .*

A strange bronze-colored man hugs his knees to himself. He is shaped like a man, mostly, but he looks like no man Zacharias has ever seen. His hair gleams like polished bone, his skin has the scaly texture of snake hide, and he goes naked like a wild person except for a scrap of cloth tied around his bony hips. He holds in one hand a staff. With a sliver of sharp-edged obsidian he carves marks along the length of the wood, then dips a feather in little pots of ocher and paints the marks a dull red. Many small items he weaves together, rolls up, and stuffs inside the hollowed-out staff. Now and again he rocks back on his heels and throws his head back—Zacharias hears nothing—and howls, in triumph or in pain. A ripple crosses this vision, the shadow of great stone figures and a circle of smooth sand . . .

. . . and they are flying above the grasslands, deep in the borderwild where griffins dwell. The grass grows taller than a man, even than a chieftain's wife with her elaborate headdress. But as they skim down, a figure parts the grass, a face patterned green and white peers out with a great bulk of body behind. Wings flutter. An arrow flies, sharp, killing, aimed true at his heart.

* * *

"Hai!" cried Kansi-a-lari, leaping back and clapping her hands once, twice, as if the sound could shield her.

The fire whoofed in and collapsed upon itself. The night birds had fallen silent. The moon shivered on the waters of the stream.

She stood. Even in the pale moonlight he saw that her expression was more than usually grim. "He has vanished from my sight." Then, eyeing him as a hunter eyes the deer that will provide her supper, she took a step back, touched her knife as she balanced for speed and striking—then seemed to change her mind.

"Tomorrow we travel west. To *churendo*."

"What is *churendo*?"

"The palace of coils." She spun and walked out into the night.

The quiet lay like death around him. Of all the usual night noises, he heard only the stream's babble. Finally he knelt and reached forward to stir the fire with a stick, but turned up no burning sticks, no red embers. Puzzled, he put his fingers into the pale remains, rubbed substance between his fingers. .

It was dead ash, as if it had ceased burning days ago.

5

IVAR had never seen so many biscops and presbyters in one place. King Henry had convened the council on Matthiasmass, but it had taken two days of fractious arguments over precedent and rank—who would enter first, who would sit where—before the council could even be seated. Now they entered the hall on the fourth day of the proceedings, led by Biscop Constance of Autun, the king's younger sister. After her walked a haughty presbyter whose arrogance was legendary; he was said never to speak to any person whose mother was not at least a count. Then came several biscops and presbyters whose cities and names Ivar couldn't keep straight, followed at the end by an elderly presbyter named Hatto who had not minded praying beside Ivar at the service of Lauds three days ago and, finally, by young Biscop Odila of Mainni, who had only recently taken up miter and crosier.

The assembled biscops and presbyters took their seats in a semicircle at the head of the hall, facing the king's throne. Once they had settled into their cushioned and gilded chairs, horns blew to announce the king. Every soul in the church knelt—except for the seated churchmen and women, whose dignity was too great to bow before mere worldly power. King Henry came in, robed and crowned in splendor.

But what did earthly splendor matter when the only person you had ever truly loved walked away from you without a backward glance? And into the arms of another man! Even Hanna had left him. And Lady Tallia had been taken away. Ai, God. What did earthly splendor matter when their eyes remained closed to the truth? He clutched that thought to him as the king called his Eagle forward and had her recite the charges: an accusation of sorcery against Hugh, abbot of Firsebarg, countered by an accusation of sorcery against one former Eagle, called Liathano. Usually the regnant left such matters solely in the hands of the church. But everyone knew that King Henry had cause to hate the woman who had stolen away his favorite child.

Biscop Constance rose, lifted a hand in the sign of peace, and the restless audience quieted expectantly. Ivar supposed sourly that some few people cared that justice be served and malevolent sorcery banished from the king's progress. The rest just wanted the lurid details.

The young biscop's strong alto carried easily over the throng. "In the three hundred and twenty-seventh year after the Proclamation of the Holy Word by the blessed Daisan, the matter of sorcery was brought before the assembled biscops and presbyters at the Council of Kellai. In their wisdom, these elders proclaimed that the Lord and Lady do not prohibit what is needful, and that therefore benevolent magic may be practiced under the supervision of the church. But the council also proclaimed this: that it goes against nature for humankind to attempt to look into the future, and all such practices are condemned."

"Is it true you leave for Gent tomorrow, my lord prince?"

The whisper distracted him. Annoyed, he glanced back to see Baldwin and Prince Ekkehard as thick as thieves and quite disinterested in the council.

"It is true. I'm to ride out with twelve novices who'll enter the monastery with me, and with that awful old Lord Atto to watch over us, as if we can't command ourselves! Alas that we should part so soon, Baldwin, for I much prefer your company to any of the others."

"You honor me, my lord." Baldwin had a habit of smiling prettily when he wanted something. "Court will seem a dreary place without you. What shall we do for singing? None of the court poets have your lovely voice, and perfect ear." He brushed a finger along the lobe of Ekkehard's ear, and the prince's eyes widened. Baldwin leaned closer, whispered something, and Ekkehard looked even more startled. Baldwin caught Ekkehard's hand in his and drew him away toward the entrance. He beckoned to Ivar, but Ivar shrugged angrily, turned his back on him, and tried to wriggle forward into the crowd. How could Baldwin *also* desert him, just-when Liath's fate was at stake?

"We are each granted liberty by God to do or not to do what we will," Biscop Constance was saying. "We are not merely an instrument set in motion to do God's will but rather equal to the angels. Yet the flesh is often weak, and temptation as certain as the rising and setting of the sun each day. Certain members of the church could not resist the blandishments of the Enemy and so delved into the darker arts. At the Council of Narvone a hundred years ago such practices were roundly condemned: the arts of the mathematici, the tempestari, the augures and haroli and sortelegi, as well as those more horrible arts of the malefici, whose names I will not utter out loud. Be sure that the Enemy still tempts those who are weak in spirit. Be sure that we in the church will root them out. Let the accused be brought forward."

Ivar hissed in a breath when he saw Hugh. His heart thumped madly, like a hammer. Ai, Lady! How meek Hugh looked, barefoot and dressed in a humble robe fit for a novice undergoing his final vigil. But the plain brown robes rendered him no less elegant. Some penitents shaved their heads as an offering to God. Hugh had not touched a single strand of hair upon his handsome head except to trim it. He knelt humbly before the biscops, golden head bowed just enough—but not too much. A margrave's son could not be too servile.

A cleric read aloud from a parchment. "These are the charges laid against Father Hugh of Firsebarg Abbey, formerly of Austra." The cleric had a deep voice that rolled across the hall like thunder. "That he has trafficked in malevolent sorceries. That he has harbored unclean texts in his possession. That he has attempted to murder by sorcerous means Princess Theophanu—"

A murmur rippled through the crowd, spread and faded. There hadn't been this good a show at court since Sanglant's defiance. As people stirred, Ivar used his elbows to press closer to the front.

"—and further, that he laid certain ligaturas upon her body to bring the elf-stitch down on her as a fever which nearly killed her." He then read, out loud, three documents: the testimony of Princess Theophanu as dictated to Sister Rosvita, the testimony of Sister Rosvita, and a letter written last spring by Mother Rothgard of St. Valeria's convent to Sister Rosvita. Finally he described a sketch of a brooch molded in the shape of a panther and twined with certain unmentionable signs and sigils, which had been a secret gift from Hugh to Theophanu.

"What answer do you make?" Constance asked when the cleric had finished.

Hugh's voice was low, but by now Ivar was close enough to hear. He had such a beautiful voice. "I am guilty of a grave sin. I have let myself be tempted by that which is forbidden and now I kneel before you and ask you to pass judgment. When I was young I attempted certain spells—" With a shake of his head, as at a painful memory, he went on. "But I was justly punished and sent into the north to do penance by working among the folk there, many of whom still worshiped the old gods. There, alas, I was seduced." He drew in a rasping breath and for an instant could not go on. Brother Hatto leaned forward intently. Biscop Odila looked nervous, and the wizened biscop of Wirtburg looked as if she had just discovered that underneath the savory platter of fowl laid before her writhed a nest of maggots. The silence in the hall was absolute as Hugh struggled to control himself.

"God forgive me. I still dream of her every night." Tears leaked from his eyes as he looked up beseechingly at the biscops and presbyters. "I pray you, Brothers and Sisters, release me from her spell."

How could he be so beautiful and so hateful all in one? Ivar would gladly have leaped forward and run him through in that instant, if he'd only had a sword.

They began to ask Hugh questions, and he answered haltingly. He had first met Liathano in Heart's Rest. Her father

Bernard was commonly supposed to have been a monk who had lapsed in his vows and fled the church. Her mother was deceased. That her father was a mathematicus no one now doubted. Certain witnesses came reluctantly forward, Eagles, Lions, servants, to note that she often gazed up at the heavens and could name the constellations and track the movements of the wandering stars. Even Hathui came forward and, with a frown, testified that Liath had carried a book with her which she had tried to keep hidden.

"Sister Rosvita says you stole the book from the woman called Liath," said Constance. "Where is it now."

Hugh's eyes widened with innocent alarm. "Sister Rosvita! I tremble for her soul, Your Grace. By her own testimony she betrays how she, too, was seduced by the maleficus, and yet she does not realize it."

"What do you mean?" demanded Biscop Odila. It was the first time she had spoken. "What are you accusing Sister Rosvita of? No one has ever had any cause to reproach her for her service!"

"Does that not prove my point? By her own testimony she states that she knows of the book because she stole it out of a chest my own servant guarded! Ai, God, that she should come to this! And did she steal for herself, because she loves evil? No, indeed. She returned it to the very sorceress who had wrapped her spells around her!"

The biscops murmured among themselves.

"Did this Liathano bespell Princess Theophanu as well?" Constance looked skeptical. "She must have been very busy, if she had. Otherwise why would the princess make such accusations against you?"

He bowed his head, refusing to answer. It was his mother who called forward a number of servants who had, in the way of servingfolk, noticed every small and out-of-the-way interaction. Princess Theophanu had been jealous of her sister, and they had seen certain signs that she had formed an unnatural passion for Hugh, which he had delicately attempted to turn aside. Assigned to Sapientia, the aforesaid Liathano had made no secret of how much she had disliked her royal mistress; she seemed to hold herself as high as the royal sisters; she had odd habits and a way of being secretive; she looked different; she could read and write and had a strange and troubling treasury of knowledge. Sister Rosvita had made overtures to her, and seemed interested in her well-being. Prince Sanglant was obsessed with her. Most men who saw her desired her, as if she had cast some kind of spell on herself to make men helpless before her.

Through it all the king watched and said nothing.

"What of the incident in the forest?" demanded the haughty presbyter. "No one questions that arrows were shot at Princess Theophanu."

Some who had witnessed the incident came forward. All noted how strange it was that the Eagle had cried out a warning when no one else had seen anything amiss, how she had been first to reach the fallen princess. Was it a sign of her innocence? Or of a plot gone awry?

"What possible reason would an Eagle have to murder Theophanu?" asked Constance.

"What possible reason would she have to burn down the palace at Augensburg?" asked Hugh softly.

The king stirred. "What do you mean?" he asked sharply.

"It is so terrible a story that I hesitate to speak. But I must." Hugh glanced at his mother, who stood silent and severe next to Helmut Villam and certain other of Henry's favored companions. She nodded curtly. "I confess that I have at times been tempted by the flesh. I am not a saint, to battle temptation and win every time. My soul is stained with darkness, and there have been times when worldly lusts have overpowered the will of my soul. When Princess Sapientia on her heir's progress rode by Firsebarg and spent a night at the abbey's guesthouse, I admit freely and with shame that that night became a week and that week a fortnight. It would be a lie to say that I was never tempted by the thought of worldly gain in the matter, as well as her—" He chose his words very carefully, considering that her father sat near by. "Princess Sapientia is impulsive and charming. Perhaps I was proud to be the one she chose, even if I ought not to have succumbed. But it was done, and I returned with her to the king's progress. I believed myself free, then, of the spell that had imprisoned me in Heart's Rest, but I was mistaken. *She* was there. And her anger was like a spear, for that is the way she had, that once you had been spelled by her you were to love no one else. But when she saw that my respect and affection for the princess could not be shaken, she took more drastic measures."

The king rose from his throne. "Go on."

"She wished to rid herself of Sapientia and of the child that was the mark of my affection for the princess. At Augensburg, she spelled the inhabitants of the palace into a sleep and although I struggled with her, although I tried desperately to stop her, I was still in this matter a slave to her power over me. I could not stop her. She brought fire. Ah, terrible! Terrible!" He faltered and the entire hall stirred and rustled like the distant murmur of flame. With a palpable effort, he went on. "It was enough that we saved the princess and most of those in the palace, although I regret bitterly the lives that were lost. Yet I can never stop thinking of this: what if the entire court had been there that day? What if the king himself had been in residence in that terrible hour? What then?"

An exhalation hit the crowd, many people shocked and too stunned even to whisper to their neighbors. Henry walked right out into the middle of the hall and stood looking down at Hugh, his expression sharp and furious. "Why did you not testify before me at Augensburg? Why was this kept a secret?"

Hugh buried his face in his hands. "I could not," he cried. "I could not! You can't understand the power she held over me!"

Henry's mouth twisted. He lifted a clenched hand, held it at his heart, and stared unseeing at Hugh's golden head. But he made no reply, only turned to look at Biscop Constance, as if expecting her to pass judgment.

Constance shook her head in the way of a woman who doesn't like what she is hearing. "But why would Princess Theophanu and in particular Sister Rosvita accuse you, Father Hugh, rather than the Eagle, Liathano? Sister Rosvita is both wise and cunning. Why does she speak against you? There is also the matter of this Sister Anne from the convent of St. Valeria who vanished without a trace."

Something sparked in Hugh's expression, a lightning flash of anger as swiftly gone. "Sister Anne of St. Valeria Convent vanished when Liath returned. Who can say if she found the good sister a threat and disposed of her? I cannot, but I fear the worst."

"Sister Anne had the panther brooch in her possession, and it vanished with her," retorted Constance. "Surely it would be in your interest, Father Hugh, to make sure such a ligatura disappeared, so its existence would not condemn you."

"That is true," he agreed. "I would never dispute your wisdom, Your Grace. But others had access to my personal belongings. I am not the only person who could have woven a ligatura from a brooch whose very shape would have betrayed its owner, since the panther is well known as the sigil of the marchlands of Austra. Isn't it also true that a message was sent to St. Valeria Convent? Yet Mother Rothgard has sent no representative to testify against me. There would have been time for such a person to reach Autun had Mother Rothgard deemed her testimony against me necessary." He turned from Constance to Henry, and he looked as innocent as an angel. "As for Sister Rosvita, I do not know what her relationship was to the sorceress, or how she might have been influenced by her. If only I could have protected her—" His voice caught on the word and then, with difficulty, he went on. "But I was helpless, God forgive me."

Helpless! The humble word stuck in Ivar's throat like a stone. He knew with sudden sick certainty why Margrave Judith looked so cool and calm. He knew as if he had seen it through the veil of time, through the forbidden arts of the sortelegi who seek knowledge of future events, how the rest of the council would unfold. Sister Rosvita always traveled with the king. Her voice carried weight. Why had she been sent south to Aosta with Theophanu?

It was all so clear now. Hugh would win again.

"He's lying!" Ivar thrust his way forward until he stumbled out where everyone could see him. "I was there in Heart's Rest! He abused her beyond what is rightful. He trapped her, stole her books so she couldn't make the debt price and only because he wanted her for himself. *He* wanted *her*, not the other way around. Everyone in Heart's Rest knew he coveted her since the day he first saw her."

Hugh winced with apparent pain. "The books! Ai, yes, I took them from her in a vain attempt to save her soul." He turned to the biscops. "Isn't it the duty of those of us who serve God to take all such tokens of forbidden sorcery into our hands, to send them to the skopos? But Liath was so young. How was I to know that she was already so thoroughly corrupted by the Enemy—?" Here he broke off. He reeled slightly and such a sick look of despair crossed his face that for an instant Ivar felt pity. "Ai, God," murmured Hugh. "And that she should have taken Prince Sanglant."

Ivar saw the king's face in that moment when Hugh spoke the fateful words. An instant only, but a cold fear swept through him and out of an old memory borne forward on that wind he recalled a line from the *Gold of the Hevelli.*

"Her doom was laid down like the paving stones of a road before her, where her feet were meant to walk."

"Why else would Sanglant have ridden away from everything I offered him?" murmured Henry.

"But it isn't true!" cried Ivar.

"He loved her, too, poor boy," said Hugh, looking up at Ivar with such sincere sympathy on his face that Ivar faltered. "He, also, was one she snared."

Wasn't it true that Liath had only seemed to love him? That she hadn't honored the pact they made at Quedlinhame? She had said that the man she loved was dead and that she would never love another, and yet had turned around and ridden off with the prince.

But even if he hated Liath for abandoning him, he hated Hugh more. He hated Liath because he still loved her. Hugh had never offered him anything but scorn and insult. "I called her a sister," he said hoarsely now. "And I would have married her if I could have, but not because she cast a spell over me."

"What is your name, my son?" asked Constance, coming forward.

He shook under the weight of so many eyes. Judith glared at him. Baldwin had reappeared and made frantic fluttering hand signs, as if to send a message, but he was too frightened to read the gestured words. "I—I am Ivar, son of Count Harl and Lady Herlinda of the North Mark."

"A novice poisoned by heresy whom I'm delivering to the monastery of St. Walaricus in the marchlands," added Judith in a loud voice.

Constance lifted a hand for silence. She had cool features and stunningly bright eyes. Her mouth had a displeased curve to it, as at a sour taste. "You were not among those brought forward to testify. What do you know of this matter in Heart's Rest?"

"I remember when Liath and her father came to Heart's Rest. I befriended her, and so did Hanna, my milk sister. She's an

Eagle now." Sapientia's Eagle, flown with the princess to the east—and thereby another witness who could not testify.

"Is it true, as Father Hugh claims, that her father was known as a sorcerer? That people came to him for diverse spells and certain potions and amulets?"

"He never did any harm! No one had a bad word to say of him!"

Then cursed himself, because they all looked at each other as if to say: "So, there is all the proof we need." Even kind Brother Hatto sighed and sat back in his chair, the way a man reclines after he's made a hard decision and wishes to rest a moment before he takes action on it.

"Her father was a sorcerer, one who had turned his back on the church," said Constance softly. She frowned. "It may even be true he meant no harm."

"Bernard was a good man, if misguided," said Hugh abruptly. "He loved his daughter too well. He let her know too much too young. Ai, God, I fear she did not begin this way but that the promise of power was too much for her. The first step on such a journey may be made with the best of intentions." He concealed his face with a hand. His shoulders shuddered.

The king spun, hand still clenched, and strode back to his throne. There he sat.

"Sisters and Brothers," said Constance to the assembled council, "have you any other questions you wish to ask, or is it time now to confer on our judgment?"

They had no further questions.

"We must pray," said Constance. "Clear the hall. Our judgment will come when God make the truth manifest to us."

The speed with which two of Judith's burliest soldiers caught Ivar by the arms and led him out took his breath away. They hustled him out of the hall and through the biscop's palace to the suite where the margrave had taken up residence.

She came in with her attendants, her husband, and her disgraced son at her heels, and the first thing she did was to hit Ivar so hard across the face that he reeled back, but only into the hard grasp of his escorts. At a sign from her, they beat him, and when he dropped to the floor whimpering and crying and begging for mercy, they kicked him in the stomach and the shoulders and trod on his hands until he could only bleat like a wounded animal.

After a while they stopped.

"How dare you speak out of turn, you who have eaten at my table and traveled in my train?" She towered over him in a cold rage, drew her boot back to kick.

"Mother." Hugh knelt beside Ivar, shielding him with his own body. "The poor boy couldn't help himself. I saw the way she wrapped her spells around him—"

"I'll hear no more from you! Go and pray with just humility, which is all you're fit for!"

He didn't move. "He's been beaten enough. He won't forget this lesson."

"Hush! I'm sick to death of your mewling, Hugh. It was done well, and I have no doubt the girl bewitched you in an unseemly way, but don't think that I haven't kept clear in my mind the incident in Zeitsenburg all this time. But you remain my son, and I will protect you as long as you obey me. I have my doubts as to how God would judge the matter, but I know perfectly well that the king hates the girl for stealing his son and in any case he knows how much he needs my support. The council knows well enough which way the wind is blowing."

"They'll condemn Liath to please the king?" gasped Ivar.

"Put him in the stables!" she said with disgust.

They hauled him away, and since he could barely walk, they dragged him along without caring that his shins bruised on steps and his head banged into corners. He was dizzy, dazed, and weeping when they dumped him onto a pile of straw and slammed shut a stall door. There he lay, stunned and aching, for the longest time.

He got very thirsty after a while. His face had swollen, and it was hard to see, or maybe that was twilight sinking onto the earth. His heart ached as much as his body. Why had Liath deserted him?

But he must not think of her. He must remember Tallia's preaching, for she was the only one who had stayed. The others could not see the truth because they were blind, their sight had clouded just as he could barely see because of his injuries. That was the life granted to humankind, to be battered and bruised and left to rot in the stink hole of earth. Only in the sacrifice and redemption could salvation be found.

A light swam into his vision, bobbed there. He heard whispers, a giggle, the shuffling of feet down to the other end of the stables, and painfully he got to his knees just as the stall door was unfastened and flung open.

Was it an angel, gleaming in the soft light of a candle?

"Ivar!" It was only Baldwin, sagging forward to embrace him, but even that embrace hurt and he yelped in pain. "Dear God," swore Baldwin. He soothed Ivar's face and hands with a cool cloth. "Come, come, my heart. We haven't much time. We bought the whore for the night, but I don't think the sentry will stay away from his duty for too long even for that." He got an arm around Ivar's waist and grunted, tugging Ivar to his feet. The movement made Ivar sneeze, and the jolt made him hurt everywhere. His left knee throbbed. His right hand felt broken.

"Come on," said Baldwin impatiently.

"Where are we going?" He could barely get the words out of his throat. Pain had lodged in his belly and wouldn't go away.

"Hush." Baldwin brushed his hair with his lips. "You just don't understand how much I love you, Ivar."

Outside, the night wind hit hard and made him shiver convulsively. After a while, stumbling over stones and with Baldwin murmuring an explanation that Ivar couldn't quite register through the throbbing pain in his head, they came to an alleyway. At once he felt more than saw the presence of others.

"Your Highness," said Baldwin.

"Ah, you got him. Good!"

Ivar sucked in a breath in surprise and then coughed violently, and that made his ribs hurt so badly he almost vomited. But he dropped to his knees. He had recognized the voice. "Prince Ekkehard!" His voice sounded like the rasp of a file on a dull blade.

"Milo and Udo will smuggle you and Baldwin out of Autun tonight and hide you along the road," said the young prince briskly. "Tomorrow, when my entourage reaches your hiding place, we'll smuggle you into one of the wagons and take you with us."

"Baldwin?" croaked Ivar.

"She'll do it to me next, beat me like a dog, when she's forgotten how much she lusts after my face. I hate her!"

"And you love me," said Prince Ekkehard with sudden passion.

"Of course, my lord prince. I will love you and serve you as you deserve." Ekkehard laughed happily, recklessly. He was so

young, not quite fifteen, and the young men around him were
no more than boys, really. But they had opened the gate to freedom.

Ivar did not resist as they bundled him aboard among chests
and draped a blanket over him and Baldwin. He hurt too much
to resist, and anyway, he didn't want to stay, not with Judith,
not anywhere near Hugh, not by the king, and nowhere where
his heart would bleed for Liath. But his heart would always
bleed. It was the sacrifice he would make day in and day out,
like the sacrifice made by the blessed Daisan, flayed and bleeding at the foot of the empress of all Dariya. Heart's blood blooming into roses.

"Stop talking," whispered Baldwin. "You're delirious. We'll
be safe as soon as we get outside the gates."

Rough wood planks scraped the side of his face as the wagon
lurched along the streets. After a while, through the veil of the
blanket, he saw the hazy glare of torchlight. They passed under
the gates of Autun. He smelled the tannery first, then the slaugh-
terhouse, sharp with blood and entrails and death. Once they got
beyond the environs of town, he smelled fields and dirt and the
dust of harvest. It was quite cold, but Baldwin, feeling him
shiver, curled around him and breathed softly into the back of
his neck, warm, sweet breath that stirred the hairs at his nape.

"Liath," murmured Ivar.

"They branded her with the mark of outlaw. And excommunicated her. I thought you'd want to know. She was named as
a maleficus. That's very bad, isn't it?"

Very bad.

"But Hugh—"

"They're sending him south to pray under the eye of the skopos, to do three years penance. I'm glad. I hope he's made to
kneel for days and days and that his knees bleed."

The wagon hit a pothole and threw Ivar against a chest. He
grunted in pain. Blood trickled down his lower lip where it had
cracked and begun to bleed. There were still tears, even though
it hurt to cry. Everything hurt.

"Hush," said Baldwin. "It'll be an adventure, you'll see."

6

WHEN the hunting party came crashing through and erupted into the clearing, they flushed not boar or partridge but a ragged covey of poor. Dirty, sore-ridden men, pale women, and children as thin as sticks and filthy with grime fluttered away from their makeshift huts and came to rest in the fringe of the trees. Not one of them had shoes or even cloth to wrap their feet in, and an early frost had rimed the ground with a sparkling coat, pretty to ride over and horribly cold to walk upon.

But Alain sat in the saddle, and he wore boots, gloves, and a fur-lined cloak.

"Who are these?" demanded Lavastine, coming up beside one of the foresters.

The foresters did not know. They had scouted out this ground ten days ago, thinking to lead the count and his retinue on a hunt in this direction, and found no one here.

"They'll have chased off any game hereabouts. Cursed nuisances!" Lord Amalfred spat as he reined his horse aside. "Let us ride on!" The young Salian lord had arrived with Duchess Yolande's retinue, and given any choice in the matter Alain would much rather he had never arrived at all.

Lavastine surveyed the clearing with frown. The people huddled under the trees looked too exhausted to scatter and run. They simply cowered. Alain nudged his mount sideways to get a better look at the huts. These hovels scarcely deserved the name of shelter: They had been built hastily, with gaps in their walls and roofs that couldn't possibly keep rain out. Fire burned in a hearth ringed with loose stone. Someone had made a shelf of logs inside one of them, and withered greens lay there, together with acorns and a skinned rabbit.

Beyond the huts, in the shadow of the trees, lay five fresh graves, two of them smaller than the others. A sixth lay half dug, a crude wooden shovel abandoned beside it.

Finally one of the women edged forward. She held a bundle

in her arms; it was so still that Alain could not tell if it were a child or a bolt of cloth. Her hands were white with cold and her skeletal feet whiter still, and there was fear in her eyes and in the pinched pale grimace of her lips. "What will you do with us, my lord?" Her voice was more cough than words, and she coughed in truth after speaking, and that woke up the child— because it was in fact a child—in her arms, which whimpered, stirred, and fell quiet again, too weak to protest.

"You must move on," said Lavastine. "Our harvest is past, and we have no room for more supplicants. You may have better luck to the south." ·

"We come from the south, my lord. There wasn't enough at harvest, and no work to be found. We will bind ourselves into your service if only you will pledge to feed us and give us work."

"We have as many as we can feed," repeated Lavastine. He gestured to a steward, who hurried forward. "See that some bread is given them, but then they must be off these lands."

Several of the adults dropped to their knees and blessed him for this bounty, as little as it was. The children merely stared, their eyes as dull as wilted leaves.

"Pray you, my lord, may we stay at least long enough to bury my child?" Another fit of coughing seized her, and this time the child in her arms only mewled softly and didn't stir at all.

Alain dismounted and strode over. She shrank away from him, but stopped, frightened more of disobedience and the spears of the huntsmen than of what he himself might do to her. Her breath stank of onions and her breathing had the rattling lilt of a lungfever coming on.

"Let me see," he said gently. He flicked back the thin blanket that covered its face.

The child might have been any age between three and six. Sores blistered its mouth, and at the sound of his voice its eyes flickered but were too swollen to open, ringed with a sticky yellow pus. A fly crawled along the lid. It was naked under the blanket, wasted and pale, and the blanket itself had worn almost through. He could see its toes. He took off a glove and brushed his fingers over its forehead. It burned with fever.

"Poor child," he murmured. "I pray you will find healing and shelter and food, pour souls. God will walk with you."

She began to cry noisily, hopelessly, coughing hard.

"Alain," said Lavastine, both warning and command.

He began to step back, could not. The children—about ten of them—had crept forward so silently that he hadn't noticed their coming, and now they trapped him, pressed so close that one ragged child—impossible to tell if it were boy or girl—reached out and touched his boots as if they were a holy relic. Another brushed the hem of Alain's cloak and exclaimed something that might have been a word or only a bubble of amazement.

He could not bear it. He unpinned the cloak and swung it off his own shoulders to drape over the stooped shoulders of the woman, so that it covered the child as well. At once the others grasped at it and tugged, trying to get it into their own hands, fighting over it.

"Stop!" ·

They shrank back, even the one he had gifted. The child in her arms lay still and silent. For all he knew it had already expired.

A sick despair settled on him, a weight far heavier than the cloak had been. He shuddered in the biting autumn wind, spun, and hurried back to his horse. A groom was there to lace hands under his foot and hoist him up.

"God save us from beggars!" cried Lord Amalfred as the hunt made ready to leave. Harness jingled, horses snorted, and his leashed hounds lunged toward the children, who scattered with screams and cries. Amalfred laughed and gathered his companions around him as they plunged into the trees. Foresters vanished into the wood before them, and far away they heard the solitary bell of a hound marking a scent.

"It isn't right to mock them," said Alain to the count, who had come up beside him.

Lavastine did not speak until they had left the clearing behind. "You can't clothe them all."

"Poor creatures. I would have given them my boots, but then I saw how they would fight over them and it would only be worse. Ai, Lord! What suffering."

"It is a mystery, indeed."

"What is a mystery?"

"Why God allows suffering in the world."

"The deacons say it is a just punishment from God for those who have sinned."

Lavastine grunted in a way that suggested he was not convinced. "I have listened to the Holy Verses, and it seems to me that they have not heeded the words of the blessed Daisan. Some things are within our nature. Just as lions eat meat, sheep eat grass, and scorpions sting, we eat and drink, sleep and wake, grow up and grow old, are born and then die. But wealth and sickness, poverty and heath: these things are brought about purely by the decree of Fate. Not everything happens according to our will. Yet we also have liberty to choose our own actions, as you did just now by giving that poor woman your cloak. She has liberty to make use of the gift or to cast it away, and the others with her may steal it, or leave it in her hands. That is the measure of our worth to God: how we act with what we are given, and whether we chose to obey God's law whatever our circumstances."

Hounds belled, and their belling blossomed into a sudden rash of barking. The young lords attending Lord Amalfred whooped and cheered and raced ahead into the forest, leaving Alain, Lavastine, and some men who by reason of age or prudence chose to ride at a slower pace with their host.

Alain had lost his appetite for the hunt. "But surely sometimes desperation may drive you to sin," he objected, watching branches whip and still as the forward party vanished into the trees.

"It is true that we aren't made guilty by those things that lie outside our power, but certainly we aren't justified by them either. Evil is the work of the Enemy. It is easier to do what is right."

"You were laid under a compulsion. What you did while under that spell was no choice of your own."

"And that, my son, is why the church must keep her hand closed tight around all matters pertaining to sorcery."

All five black hounds broke into a chorus of barking. Steadfast and Fear bounded away into the brush. Lavastine pulled up and began to dismount, but suddenly Terror was beneath him, nudging him with his head as if to keep him in the saddle.

"I'll go look," said Alain quickly. Sorrow and Rage bristled, hackles up. They had coursed silently around to place themselves between Lavastine's horse and the undergrowth where the other two hounds thrashed and barked within a thicket that rattled and swayed as if a wild wind had been bound into the spot.

"My lord count." Several servingmen rode forward, but Alain pressed past them, dismounted, and with his sword out forged into the brush, batting aside branches, getting a mouthful of dry fern leaves as he shoved through. Sorrow followed him, still barking. Rage stayed behind with Terror. Steadfast and Fear had cornered something in the densest corner of the thicket strewn with brier and fern. He saw it, a flash of dead white darting here, and then back, seeking an exit. Dread hit like the blast of cold wind, making him shake.

"Alain!" called Lavastine.

"Don't follow me!"

It darted past Fear's snapping jaws. Alain cut. His sword hit loam, sprayed bits of leaves. Steadfast leaped past him. Sorrow pounced. A creature scurried away under the leaves. He saw it again where leaves parted and it darted into a screen of briers, that unnatural white gleam like bone washed clean and polished by the sea. He stabbed again at it but only got his hand scratched by thorns.

There it was again. He stabbed. And missed.

The *thing* scuttled past Fear. That fast, it turned to bolt toward the horses. Sorrow snapped. Alain jumped after it. Beyond, he saw movement among the trees, horsemen closing in.

"Don't dismount!" he cried, but no one could hear him over the clamor of the hounds barking. Steadfast dove headfirst into a bush. She yelped, and then, abruptly, everything was still except for the distant blare of a hunting horn.

Terror growled, and Rage joined him, and then Sorrow and Fear as well, a shield wall of hounds at Steadfast's back. The sound crawled up Alain's spine like poison. His neck prickled, and he spun round, sword raised. A flutter in the leaves. He hacked at the bush, but a wren struggled away, broke free, and flew off.

That ragged breathing was his own.

"Alain?" Lavastine forced his horse into the brush. "What is going on?"

Alain dropped the sword into the forest litter, caught Steadfast by her collar, and dragged her back. Blood swelled from her right forepaw and even as she licked it, whimpering, the wound began to swell strangely.

"We must get her back home. I fear—" He broke off and glanced up at the servingmen, who had clustered around and all gawped at him. He gestured as Lavastine would, and the servants moved away. Alain continued in a low voice. "I saw it again, the size of a rat but without any color at all. I even thought Bliss had simply eaten it, taken it into himself to save you, but I must have been wrong. Ai, Lord! It's the dead hand of Bloodheart, the creature Prince Sanglant spoke of. It's followed us this far."

Lavastine considered him in silence, then shifted his gaze to Steadfast. A leaf spun on the wind and settled to earth. "Put her over my saddle. It would be prudent to return now and let the others hunt as they will."

There were many things Alain wanted to say on the ride back, but he could not make them into sentences that made sense. It was a long, quiet ride with Steadfast draped awkwardly over the neck of the nervous horse, but Lavastine kept a firm hand on the rein and the other on the hound's back. At the stables, they handed over the horses to Master Rodlin and Lavastine himself lugged the hound up to his chamber, leaving Alain to venture into the hall where the women had settled for the day.

They had taken over the upper half of the hall, and he paused by the door, hesitant to enter, as he watched them laughing and talking. Even Tallia engaged in the debate with an eagerness she rarely displayed for Alain. Set in the pride of place, as befit her birth, she shared a couch with the stout, handsome young woman who called her "cousin."

Duchess Yolande made him nervous. Halfway through her second pregnancy, she was far enough along that she didn't care to go hunting, and if she did not go hunting, then no other woman in her train would go either. But neither were any men welcome to spend the day with the ladies, whom she had organized into a symposium in the Dariyan style, with couches and wine and certain intellectual questions to be debated.

"The Dariyan physician Galené clearly states that males are like deformed creatures," she was saying now. "But I suppose it is not their fault that they are the product of weaker, more sickly seed. That is why they cannot develop wombs, as females can."

"But She who is Mother to us all chose to voice the divine word through the lips of a man," objected Tallia.

"A man gave voice," corrected the duchess, "but a woman

witnessed. It was the holy Thecla's testimony which gave rise
to the church."

"Even so," insisted Tallia, "men can also aspire to become
like angels."

"Who are formed in the shape of women."

"Better to say that women are formed in the shape of angels," corrected the duchess' deacon, who seemed by turns to
rein the young duchess back and then egg her on.

"But we are all of us capable of being like the angels in purity of purpose and the sincerity of our prayer, if nothing else."
Tallia remained stubborn on this point.

"Your beliefs, my lady, are well meant," chided the deacon
but in the most delicate manner possible, "but the church ex-
plicitly condemned as heresy the wrongful notion of the sacrifice and redemption at the Council of Addai. You must pray for
God's intervention in this matter."

"And so I have!" retorted Tallia defiantly.

"Nay, let Lady Tallia speak as she wishes. I am most intrigued by God our Mother and Her only Son."

"My lady—!"

"I will listen to such tidings if I wish! Do not silence her."
A servingwoman bent to whisper in the duchess' ear and she
looked toward the door. "Ah!" she cried with a smile that made
Alain want to bolt outside. "Here is Lord Alain." She rubbed
her belly reflexively and then gestured for him to sit between
her and Tallia on the couch. Compared to Tallia, she looked vast
and ruddy, the kind of woman who would produce many healthy
babies and live to see her grandchildren. "Alas that I did not negotiate with your father for your hand before you were stolen
away by my dear cousin."

"My lady," remonstrated the deacon, "think of your husband,
so recently lost to you."

"Ah, poor Hanfred! I am truly sorry an Eika spear got him
through the guts. But you will admit, cousin, that your husband
is far more pleasant to look upon than my old Hanfred ever was,
may his soul rest in peace in the Chamber of Light."

"Is he?" asked Tallia, staring at Alain as if she had never
seen him before.

"You pray too much, cousin! Come now, sit here beside us."
Alain did not budge from his station by the door. That she was
rather free with her hands, knowing him a married man and

therefore in her words "ripe for the sampling," made him even less inclined to sit within her reach.

"I beg your pardon, I must attend my father. I only came to pay my respects. Some portion of the party has ridden on, and I doubt they will return before nightfall."

"Lord Amalfred among them, I trust?" Yolande had a hearty laugh. The riches heaped on the platter she shared with Tallia would have fed the entire flock of starving souls they had stumbled across earlier. Alain wondered with sudden violent loathing how much of that food would be thrown to the pigs, although certainly the pigs, too, were deserving of food. "I would be sorry to hear he had returned early. He's hoping I'll marry him, and I confess that hearing that he shot an arrow at our dear cousin Theophanu thinking she was a deer inclines me to think well of him, but dear God he is such a bore."

"Why *have* you come back early?" asked Tallia suddenly, as if accusing Alain of ruining her day by thrusting so indelicately into the pleasant female companionship she was now enjoying.

"Steadfast was injured."

She lost interest at once. No longer terrified of the hounds, still, she did not care for them at all. She dismissed him with a wave of the hand mimicked from Duchess Yolande, and that stung him, to be treated like a servant; but she wore the gold torque of royal kinship and the Lavas counts did not. She might be his wife, but Duchess Yolande had not journeyed this far to see the count of Lavas but rather the woman who was the granddaughter in the direct female line of the last Varren queen.

That was the game being played here today, and he was not part of it. He was a man, and according to Duchess Yolande men were suited for the hunt, not the hall. While men might excel on the field of battle, the true dance of power took place where alliances were sealed, rebels brought to justice, and gifts exchanged.

Upstairs, Lavastine sat on his bed and stroked Steadfast's head where she lay, breathing heavily, on the coverlet beside him.

"But her *father* was duke before her," said Alain, sitting on the other side of Steadfast.

Lavastine glanced up. "You have fled the redoubtable duchess, I see. Well, her mother is of Karronish kin, and it is well known that they do not let men rule there unless no daughter, sister, or niece can be found to take up the staff. Her father Rodulf had the duchy because he had no sisters, and he devoted himself to the battlefield and let his wife administer his holdings as well as her own. She was a difficult woman. No doubt he was happier in the field."

"But it's true, isn't it, that the ancient physicians wrote that male seed was weaker and that females are formed more like to the angels than are males?"

"That is what the learned deacons report. If you and Tallia have a daughter, I will be well pleased."

"Ai, God," whispered Alain. Steadfast lay still, eyes open and fixed on Lavastine as he curled his fingers around her ears and stroked them softly. Her right paw was hot and swollen and had an odd, grainy texture rather like stone at the very tip. "Just like Ardent."

Lavastine grunted. "If it is true that some creature stalks us, then we must post more guards and sentries. But if we do so, then Duchess Yolande may feel we do not trust her, and she may take offense."

"Why has she come?"

"Her father followed Sabella, and he was not bespelled as I was. Sabella still lives—"

"As a prisoner in the care of Biscop Constance, in Autun."

"But nevertheless alive. And Tallia is her daughter, of age, and married—so she will in time produce an heir."

Alain found a burr in Steadfast's coat and busied himself worrying it free.

"But I don't believe she plots treason. I think she is merely paying court. Prudence dictates that she ought to. Henry is not overly pleased with his three legitimate children. Tallia has as much right to the throne as any of them do."

Suddenly the only noise Alain heard was the pounding of his heart and the slow wheeze of Steadfast, drawing in a labored breath and letting it out again. "The *throne?*"

"You must be ready for anything." Lavastine stroked Steadfast's head. His frown was fleeting but more frightening because of that. "This wound is exactly like the one inflicted on Ardent. Three incidents, taken together, suggest a pattern, and while Prince Sanglant acted strangely after his rescue, still, we all heard rumors about Bloodheart's enchantments. There is also the testimony of your dreams. Dreams are often false, but I think yours

are true visions. It is better to assume we are threatened by a
curse than to do nothing."

Ai, God. It was like the battle of Gent all over again; watching your faithful retainers fall one by one as they protected you.
It made Alain sick at heart to see the hounds suffer so. "The
deacon must bless this hall, and place an amulet over every
threshold."

"I dislike resorting to sorcery. Yet . . . Send a mage to kill a
mage. We must speak to the deacon about this matter, and send
word to Biscop Thierra. She may have certain clerics among her
schola who can drive out demons and other creatures molded in
the fires of the Abyss."

"What about guards?"

"It would be wise, I suppose. But we are better protected by
the hounds."

"They always know," said Alain. "They can smell it."

"You must not go out alone, Alain. *You* must be careful."

"It's not stalking me—"

"How can we know? Curses are driven by hate, not intelligence. I will not risk you, Son. We must behave as if any person who marched to Gent is under attack." He sighed suddenly
and reached to tweak Alain's sleeve straight. "You will need another cloak. Here, now, open the shutters. Give her some light.
Perhaps if we soak the wound, and draw out the poison—"

But in the end it mattered not. It took her six days to die.

7

RAIN poured down in torrents. It had been days since they
had seen the sky or even the steep ridges around them as they
struggled through the Julier Pass on their way to Aosta. The road
had washed into mud, and Rosvita had given up riding on her
mule and now, like every other soul in Princess Theophanu's
army, she picked her way along the path one foothold at a time.

"Beware!" The shout startled her.

Ahead, the horrible ripping sound of sliding rock made her

stop dead. She clutched the reins of her mule and muttered a prayer. Arms waving, Brother Fortunatus slipped from the path in a cascade of mud and gravel.

"Brother!" she cried, but she had learned not to move. She had seen a pack mule and drover lost that way, walking where the ground had just poured over the path. But God were merciful this day. Fortunatus fetched up a man's height below them, and once the mud had stopped moving, the men-at-arms threw down ropes to drag him up. He had lost his mule the day before when it had gone over the cliff, caught in yet another avalanche of mud and shale.

"I hear we're almost at the top!" Fortunatus cried cheerfully after he had caught his breath. "It certainly looks farther down to the rocks than it did yesterday!" He was coated with mud, but then, they all were.

"But isn't it easier to climb up than to climb down?" wailed poor Constantine, who looked truly frightened, more like a little boy than a young man. "We'll never live to get there!"

"Hush, now, Brother," said Rosvita. "We must go on and trust that God will see us through safely." She gave Fortunatus a hand and helped him struggle to his feet, no easy task on a path washed slick with endless rain. But at least it hadn't starting snowing.

"We ought to have waited in Bregez," cried Constantine, "and crossed next summer!"

Fortunatus snorted. "With a royal bride and all of Aosta within our grasp! You can be sure that the Aostan lords won't bide their time through winter and spring."

Rosvita set a hand on Constantine's shoulder. He was trembling. "We have come this far, Brother, and it is only the first week of autumn. We've just had ill fortune with this rain. There is nothing we can do but go on." Were those tears in his eyes or was it only the rain?

The day passed, one slow step after another. By midday they had reached an exposed side of the mountain where rain battered them, but word came down the line that the princess deemed it better to forge forward even in such terrible conditions than to try to make camp where they would be at the mercy of the elements. For the first time, as they floundered forward on the narrow path with a sheer cliff rising up on the right and a rugged drop-off plunging down to their left, Rosvita heard the men-at-arms grumbling.

"We should have turned back." "Why didn't we wait until summer?" "Our luck is run out." "Do you think we'll even reach Aosta or all die at the foot of these cliffs?"

"They won't last much longer," said Fortunatus to Rosvita when the entire line came to a halt while they waited for a wagon in front of them to get unstuck. "They don't trust her, not like they would the king or Prince Sanglant."

"Why does everyone speak so lovingly of Prince Sanglant?" demanded Constantine. His hood kept getting swept back from his face and by now his hair was plastered to his head. "He's no better than a dog. He behaved so strangely."

Fortunatus laughed bitterly, and for once his inexhaustible store of humor failed him. "You didn't know him before, you young fool. Now shut up!"

A crack like thunder shuddered in the air. A man screamed. Not twenty paces forward the road collapsed and a wagon, two oxen, and the driver plunged down the slope. Everyone screamed and shouted at once, men cursing, others shouting orders that no one heeded as the wagon crashed down the cliff only to lodge in a fissure. The driver clung to the wagon as it creaked. Scree poured down around him and rain battered the wagon as its contents slid away into the misty vale below. One ox lay limp, its weight dragging the wagon inch by inch out of the fissure; the other fought madly until it worked free of the harness and, with a last bellow, vanished into the mist.

"Ho, there, lads!" cried a captain, coming up alongside Rosvita on his horse. "Throw down the ropes!"

"But it's too dangerous to go up to the edge," shouted one of the servingmen. It was the only way to be heard above the rain. "We'll never get across. We may as well turn back now!"

"Hold your mouth! The princess is ahead of us. We can't abandon her."

"Why not?" demanded the man. "We've no cause to be following her."

The captain raised a hand to strike, but a new shout came from the other side of the scar torn out of the road. "Make way! Make way!"

If a heart could be said to lodge in a throat, Rosvita's did so now. Theophanu's figure was instantly recognizable for her height and broad shoulders and the fur-trimmed cloak she wore, but also because she rode her light gelding, Albus, a most intelligent and levelheaded horse.

Now, despite shrieks of fear and protests behind her, Theophanu urged Albus forward over the broken road where the least misstep would cause her to fall to her death. The slope plunged down in jagged bursts, so steep that only a few stunted trees had found a foothold. Theophanu did not hesitate as she crossed the washed-out gap, even when wind gusted and her cloak swept out like the wing of an eagle, billowing over empty air.

As everyone stared, she came clear of the breach and calmly reined up beside the captain. "Captain Fulk, throw ropes down to that man. The wagon is lost to us, but we need not lose him as well. And have the servingmen get shovels. The pack mules and foot soldiers can cross the fall, but we'll need some bracing for the wagons." She appeared oblivious to the rain, immune to it—unlike the rest of them. Then her gaze caught on Rosvita. "How did you come to be toiling back here, Sister? Ride forward with me."

"We are needed here, Your Highness."

Theophanu looked startled. Her gaze flicked over the waiting soldiers and servants, all standing as still as statues under the pounding rain—all except those who had thrown ropes down to rescue the driver. Another crack snapped the air, and the wagon lodged in the fissure shuddered, lurched, and crashed downward, shattering into bits.

Theophanu frowned. She urged Albus closer to the edge, and Fulk began to object, then faltered. "Ah," she said, "they have him." Under her cool eye they hauled the driver up. He appeared to have a broken arm and many bruises, but was otherwise whole. "As you wish, Sister Rosvita," she finished coolly. "Attend me this evening."

Without another word, she turned, crossed back over the washed-out area, and vanished into the rain and mist that shrouded the road before them.

"She's got courage, I'll give her that," said the captain in a loud voice, meant to carry.

"She's got no heart," objected one of his men. "Not like our—"

"Hush! Now get on with it."

Mercifully, the rain slackened to a drizzle, and after about an hour's work they were able to get wagons over the cut in the road. On they went. The wind cut through layers of damp clothing and only the endless trudging walk gave any warmth.

Late in the afternoon they came upon a village perched in a high valley as an eagle perches in its aerie. The villagers were tough, squat mountain people, and not even the presence of a royal princess could awe them. They demanded an exorbitant rent for the use of their stables. While Theophanu's stewards haggled, Rosvita found blessed shelter in the shed which Theophanu's servants had commandeered for their mistress. It stank of mildew and pigeon droppings, but it was dry, and a fire burned merrily in the stone hearth.

"Sister Rosvita!" Theophanu was weathering the journey well, but she had her father's stamina and rude good health. She had chosen her attendants—young noblewomen all—for the same qualities; they laughed, drank ale, and chatted as if they had just finished an exhilarating hunt instead of a struggle through a downpour on a dangerous road. "Sit next to the fire. Leoba, let the good sister take your stool for a while."

Rosvita sat down gratefully and warmed her hands at the fire. "You took a great risk today, Your Highness. I must advise against such—"

"Nay, Sister, do not take me to task. They don't love me. If I fell to my death, half the men in this army would shrug their shoulders and then march on to Aosta and win the throne to hold in readiness for my brother. Have you heard about Captain Fulk and his men?"

"No, I have not. He's a steady man."

"So he is, and a loyal one."

"I saw that today."

Theophanu's lips quirked up as at a joke only she knew. "Indeed. They came and pledged service to me—pledged service, I should add, because my brother Sanglant had told them to do so. They offered to ride with him into exile, but he told them that where he meant to go they could not follow, and he bid them follow in my train until such time as he returned! It's odd, though. They said there was another woman with him besides the Eagle. Do you know anything of that?"

"I do not! I heard the tale as everyone else did: that he and Liath rode off alone, no one knew where."

"You may question the good captain if you wish. I'll have

him brought here." She sent a servingwoman out into the drizzle.

The captain seemed grateful to stand by the fire while Rosvita asked him questions. He had observed that the woman was of noble rank, dressed in robes. "I thought she was a cleric, perhaps. And—well, I recall it now. The prince called her 'Sister Anne'."

"Sister Anne!"

They heard a shout at the door, and a moment later an Eagle crossed the threshold and knelt before the princess. He was wet through, even with a cloak tied over his shoulders, and his silver-white hair lay plastered against his head.

"Wolfhere!" exclaimed Rosvita, standing out of sheer surprise.

"My father's favorite Eagle," said Theophanu with a glint in her eyes. "What news do you bring us, Eagle? Where have you come from?"

"From Aosta." He looked first at one, then the other. "But I am surprised to see you here, Your Highness. Sister Rosvita."

"You thought to see my brother?" asked Theophanu. "He left the king's progress in disgrace."

Rosvita did not know Wolfhere, of course, but she knew of him; he had been a fixture of King Arnulf's court, the kind of man people whispered about. No one knew why Arnulf favored him, but many guessed. When Henry had come to the throne and made it clear he was no longer welcome on the king's progress, the rumors had only gotten worse. What secrets did he hold locked within him? He was only an Eagle, and yet for all that, he was not the kind of man one could simply ask such questions of.

His grimace now concealed more than it revealed. "What of Liath?"

"It seems everyone has an interest in her," remarked Theophanu lightly. Her little court gathered closer to hear; even the youngest members of the king's progress had heard gossip about the mysterious Wolfhere, a man whom the king hated but would not lift a hand against. "But I will take pity on you, Eagle. She left with Sanglant."

"But where did they go?" he demanded.

"No one knows."

"They must have gone to the convent at St. Valeria," said

Rosvita suddenly. Why else would Sister Anne have been with them? "Surely, Eagle, you know that is a good thing."

He did not reply. He seemed distracted, discouraged.

"You had a special interest in her," Rosvita continued, her curiosity wakened by his grim expression. "What did you mean to do with her?"

"To *do* with her?" he exclaimed indignantly. "I meant to help her. I freed her from that terrible situation—"

"Hugh," breathed Theophanu.

He looked at her, startled. It was rare to see the old Eagle surprised. "Oh, yes, and Hugh also, of course." His hands were in fists, and then he recalled himself, drew off his gloves, and fumbled at his belt pouch with fingers made stiff by cold. "I rode in haste, Your Highness, and crossed the mountains some weeks ago with this message from King Henry to Queen Adelheid, pledging his support." The rolled-up parchment had water stains on it but was otherwise intact.

"But you have not delivered it," observed Theophanu.

He held it out to her, and after a moment she took it from him, opened it, and smoothed a hand over the finely-written letter. Rosvita recognized the hand as Sister Amabilia's. Had she reached St. Valeria Convent in time? Had she escorted Mother Rothgard to Autun for the council? Had she crossed paths with the prince and his concubine?

"I could not," said Wolfhere finally, starting back as if his thoughts had wandered again. "I found Queen Adelheid, but I could not reach her. She sits besieged in the citadel of Vennaci. John Ironhead, lord of Sabina, had settled his army outside the walls and his intent is to capture her, make her his wife, and crown himself as king over Aosta. But he is not alone in this wish, he is only the one who reached her first."

"It is good you found me, Eagle. Now we know where we must march. Is there aught else we should know of the road ahead?"

"Your Highness, Lord John's army is far larger than yours."

"Well, we shall see. Queen Adelheid must have an army within the citadel. We can catch him between two pincers."

"If you can find a way to get a message to her. Lord John has sealed all ways in and out up tight, or you can be sure I would have gotten in."

"I feel sure you would, Eagle. It is well known that you are as cunning as the serpent, and you have had many years to hone your wisdom."

His smile was brief but true, and he seemed about to chuckle, but he did not. "As for the road, you have crossed the worst of it. I had better weather than this, and if the rain stops, you will be well on your way."

Theophanu had her captains summoned, and Wolfhere went on, then, to describe in detail the number and disposition of the lord of Sabina's army as well as what information he had gleaned about the citadel itself and the various factions in Aosta, all of whom seemed set on fighting with each other for this prize like dogs over a bone. Rain had started up again and pattered noisily on the roof. It was getting smoky inside, and a servingwoman opened the door, which seemed to have little effect beyond letting in a blast of cold wind that eddied the smoke from the hearth into every corner of the shed.

Rosvita let herself out as the last downpour passed, and as she walked through the village searching for her clerics, a few last spitting drops wet her cheeks. Brother Fortunatus had found refuge in a stall, and she was relieved to see that their pens, ink, and parchment had come through the day unscathed. The *Vita* of St. Radegundis, wrapped in oilcloth, was dry, as was the incomplete copy that Sister Amabilia was still working on, and her own *History*. Now that the rain had stopped, they all trooped outside where the village folk had built a fire and there they took turns trying to dry their clothing.

She noticed the wink of a tiny fire away from the village. Even after the hardships of the road, she could not resist the prick of curiosity. Because the sodden ground cushioned her steps, she got out away from the village and was able to come up behind him without him noticing she was there. By the fire back in the village, soldiers laughed and began to sing.

The old Eagle sat on the ground, on his cloak, and stared into a small campfire with such intense concentration that he might not have noticed her even had she called out to him.

"Lady have mercy," he said in a soft voice. "I am so weary."

At first she thought he knew she was there, and that he had confided in her. His shoulders sagged, and his real misery cut her to the heart. She took a step forward—

The fire hissed. She stopped dead.

There were shadows moving in the fire.

She almost shrieked, but she had honed her control over many years in the king's schola, and the fear skittered over her like a thousand bugs crawling on her skin and then faded as her vision sharpened—as she began to understand what she was seeing.

"I have failed," he added, speaking to the shadows within. He sounded close to tears. A slow drip, drip, drip of water serenaded them where moisture seeped off an overhanging rock. Beyond it, she could hear a distant waterfall—or was that the crackle of the fire, a whisper. . . .

"Do not worry, Brother, you have done your part well."

Ai, God! Old secrets hoarded by certain Eagles, the ability to see through fire or stone, an old trick that had, so it was said, fallen into disfavor after the Council of Narvone. But such a trick remained useful to the regnant, kept secret among the Eagles by their pledge of loyalty to each other and to the king. How else could they bring their messages so quickly, know where they were going so clearly, and bring such exceptionally valuable intelligence when they arrived?

Wind moaned through the rocks. Within the fire the shadow moved, shifting like a person swaying before a large fire. A tiny light bobbed impossibly behind, a candle caught within the flames—or only the image of a candle, seen through fire.

"You discovered the one whom we all thought dead, who may yet be a threat to us. Armed with this knowledge, we can act. And despite everything, Brother, you found the girl."

Wolfhere shook his head impatiently. Rosvita could not see his face, but everything she needed to know she heard in his tone. "Found her, and then lost her again."

The wind tugged at her robes, as cold as winter, and she shuddered. Flames shivered in that wind, and for an instant she thought the branches and coals would be scattered. Then, inexplicably, the wind died. Wolfhere rested his forehead on his fists. In the silence Rosvita heard the voice clearly; not young, not old, it was without question female.

"Fear not. She is back in our hands."

8

WAVES chop the hull of the ship as they drive north along the landward side of the island of Sovi. Oars beat the sea in a rhythm as steady as the drum of his heart. He shades his eyes against the glint of sun on the waters. Is that movement in the sound ahead? Or only the hump of a rocky islet?

"Ships!" cries the watchman. "To the north, near the fjord's mouth!"

He had hoped to skate in down the long fjord waters and take them unawares, but Skelnin's chieftain is no fool, and not unambitious on his own account. He has scouts, he has ears. He will not go down without a fight. He may even believe he can triumph this day—and it is possible he will. But unlikely.

The watchman tolls off the number: one, four, nine, twelve, fifteen longships in all, and a number of fishing skiffs that no one bothers to count. His own forces number only fourteen longships, but Skelnin's ships come at him like sheep, bunched without order. They will fight with no plan beyond killing.

At his shout, his own ships are lashed together, three abreast like islets on which Skelnin's warriors will run aground, with five to guard his flanks and strike at will where there is an opening. The cauldrons of hot oil are readied; stones moved; spears lowered.

He himself stands in the stern of the middle ship in the middle raft. The captain of each ship looks not at Skelnin's ships but on Rikin's chief. As the ships close the gap, he lifts his standard as a signal.

In each ship two poles are raised, each one capped with an iron hook. Each hook holds a cauldron filled with oil bled from the ocean leviathans and mixed with certain powders that intensify its burning. At his order, brands are lit from the fire boxes set by the lowered masts, and when fire touches the oil within the cauldrons, black smoke boils forth.

A rain of arrows showers down, and his own men loose a

sheet of arrows in answer. A few warriors drop, those who have not tucked under their shields in time; one spins and falls over the side to vanish in the gray seawaters.

The first of Skelnin's ships reach the platforms, grinding along broadside. Shields are locked and spears bristle to repel boarders as others knock away grappling hooks. The Skelnin RockChildren jeer and cry as they try to leap the gap, but he only watches; he can hesitate one instant more as two more ships move in against his own and as his other ships, too, are attacked.

He won this battle when the cauldrons were lit.

The first rocks fly, crashing against wood. The prow of his ship with its glaring dragon stem clashes with the proud boar's head stem of the Skelnin chieftain's ship. Now they are surrounded on three sides. He lifts the standard a final time.

The cauldrons swing out and a searing waterfall pours down upon the enemy. It spreads into the enemy ranks, spattering on flesh and wood like the wet hot heart of the earth itself, as fierce as the molten rock that runs in the veins of the earth. As the ships scrape each other, his own warriors press the attack where panic erupts among the enemy.

One ship begins to burn. The shield line breaks, and Skelnin's warriors scatter as his own press their advantage, leaping across the gap and striking with their axes to clear the ship. The dead and wounded are thrown into the sea, as he had promised: when he surveys the waters, he sees the ripples that have followed in his wake boil to life as the merfolk net the feast he has promised them.

So the battle runs. Three of Skelnin's ships blaze into fiery death; four are cleared and taken; three try to bank away into flight, but his own ships, those left to guard his flanks, race after them. Four fight on as though courage itself may bring victory.

But he knows better. Fortune favors the bold, and the cunning.

The last of Skelnin's ships are grappled in by three of his own ships, and their crews overwhelmed. The ships of the fisherfolk are of little account. Most have fled already and those that attempted to join the melee were sunk with rocks. But caught in the middle of the battle, Skelnin's chieftain roars on, his own picked warriors fighting beside him with the blind fury of berserkers. That they will lose is evident to all. Now the last dozen of them press forward, and with a great roar of hopeless rage they beat down the shields on the steerward side of his own ship, thrust somewhat out before the others by the tide of the battle. With a stunning leap the hugest of them—Skelnin's chief himself—forces his way over the side. The ship rocks wildly behind him, tipping one of his own men and one of Rikin's into the water. Their heads bob, white as tiny icebergs, and suddenly Skelnin's man is dragged flailing into the depths.

Skelnin's chief shrieks out his fury and knocks aside two of Stronghand's crew as though they are feathers. With a curse on his lips, he charges Stronghand.

Such strength is a weakness. Reliance upon it makes one's mind weak.

As Skelnin's chief bashes his way toward the aft of the ship, clubs and spears and axes rain down upon him. His boar-tusk helm shatters, and the bone of his head shines through his torn scalp like snow upon a peak, but he still comes. Is it possible that fury can transcend the limits of flesh? Poised in the stern, hand upon his own iron-tipped spear, Stronghand watches with interest as Skelnin's chief staggers on. But in the end even the greatest will bleed, and flesh becomes dust just as the great cliffs that loom over them will become sand in the end to be scattered in the breeze—or so the WiseMothers say.

Struck behind the knee and pierced through his throat, Skelnin's chief collapses a spear-length from Stronghand's feet.

A roar of triumph lifts from his warriors, a shout that shudders the air and echoes off the distant dark cliffs. Now they will believe in him. Now others will flock to follow his standard. He surveys the carnage without pleasure, but also without pain. This is the way such things are accomplished. For other tasks, other methods will prevail.

Those of the wounded who seem minded to surrender, and to live, he lets pledge loyalty to Rikin fjord. Those of his men who flounder in the sea are fished out, untouched—it was the bargain he made. Most of the dead they tip into the water, as he promised, but he lets his own dogs, now unleashed, tear Skelnin's chief to pieces.

The clamoring of dogs ripped Alain out of his dream. He half fell off the bed. The rug had slipped and the cold floor against his bare feet brought him fully awake.

Tallia stirred. "What is that noise?" she murmured, a soft complaint.

He wore his shift, as he always did to bed—unnatural in a marriage bed, but it was Tallia's wish. Now he fumbled for his sword and sheath and bolted for the door, where servants rolled aside, coming awake themselves as they scrambled to get out of his way. An amulet wrapped the latch, and he got his fingers around the cord and yanked it free. He flung the door open so roughly that the ligatura—blessed and bound by the deacon— that hung from the threshold rained onto him, dried herbs and parchment scraps inscribed with verses from the holy book. He brushed his hair free of them as he ran down the stairs to the level below. The walls stank of incense from the nightly rounds the deacon made with her censer, swinging it back and forth to drive away evil creatures from within the walls. A smoky light permeated the curving stairs from below—the fire of torches.

Fear clutched his heart.

It had been so quiet for a month after Steadfast's death. He had begun to believe that they were free, that the curse was nothing but ravings spun into being by the prince's disordered mind.

The door into Lavastine's chamber was latched from the inside, and servants already crowded there. Several bore torches aloft to light the others, who were slamming their shoulders into the heavy door to force it open. Alain stumbled onto the landing, slipping on the litter of pine needles that had been strewn on the floor to drive away evil. Even through the heavy wooded door the noise of the hounds was deafening.

"Let me through!" The men parted before him, but he grabbed two of the stoutest and all together they hit the door with their full weight, hit it again as inside hounds went wild. One of them yipped in pain, a high yelp, followed by a furious crescendo of barking.

"Terror!" It was Lavastine's voice.

"Father!" cried Alain. With servants on either side, he slammed against the door again. It shuddered, creaking. A ligatura had been laced above this door as well, fastened more tightly, but now its component parts began to drizzle down on them: sage, withered dill, oak twigs, and linen strips written with signs, smelling faintly of cypress.

"Alain, don't come in!" shouted Lavastine. "It's in here."

"Again!" His shoulder was numb, so he turned to use the other. They hit the door, and it creaked again, but did not budge.

"My lord!" A soldier came panting up the stairs, carrying two axes. He was followed by another soldier carrying a torch.

Alain grabbed one and set to work with a will, out of his mind with fear, hacking madly as the hounds scrabbled and barked on the other side; so close, so impossibly far. He could not hear the count, except for a string of curses. Ai, God, if the thing had gotten into the room, then his father could not risk a dash across the floor to open the door. He was alone in the dark, helpless except for the hounds.

Wood shattered under the blade. Beside him, the soldier wielded the other ax with the trained strokes of a man who has seen battle many times, and indeed the torchlight gave enough clarity for Alain to glimpse the man's face: one of the veterans of the Gent expedition.

"Is it an assassin?" a servant wailed.

"Nay, an evil curse!" shouted another. "The dead hand of the Eika, avenging hisself on the count for his victory at Gent!"

Haze made the landing yellow as Alain chopped. Wood splintered, and his blade cracked through, hung up in the wood. The hounds fell silent except for a whimper coming from one of them.

"Hold!" Lavastine's voice came abruptly, from the other side of the door. "Stand back."

They all obeyed without thinking. The latch moved. The door creaked, shifted, grated.

"It's stuck," said the soldier, and he and Alain got their shoulders behind it and shoved. It gave way all at once, and Alain fell into the room, staggered, and caught himself, blinking. The shutter lay wide and the thinnest gray streak of light blurred the horizon. Servants crowded in behind him, but the silence was frightening, and intense.

Lavastine stood barefoot, in a shift, on the stone floor. In his right hand he held his unsheathed sword, in his left a knife. Sorrow and Rage growled at the men until Alain bade them hush. They were so tense that even then they growled, but they sat. Terror lay on the floor licking one of his hind legs, and Fear crowded directly behind Lavastine, a headless bulk.

The torchlight made shadows dance crazily in the room as the servants moved forward, muttering, afraid.

"Father!" Alain found his voice and stumbled forward to grasp Lavastine's wrist. His skin was terribly cold, but his face was flushed. "Ai, God! What happened?"

Lavastine opened his hand and the knife fell to the floor with a thud. Fear growled, a rumbling in his throat. He moved around Lavastine, and Alain had a brief glimpse of something white dangling from his jaws before the hound opened his mouth to drop a sickly white ratlike creature at Lavastine's feet like an offering. It looked quite dead.

But it was too late anyway.

Alain's gaze, drawn down, stopped at the count's bare feet, pale, well-groomed, and clean . . . except for two spots of blood on his ankle, set close together. Lavastine said nothing, only set a hand on Alain's shoulder for support and with Alain beside him limped back to the bed, where he sat down.

But his expression was perfectly calm. "Call the deacon," he said. "I have been bitten." The servants wailed aloud, all clamoring at once, but he raised a hand for silence. "Nay, God is merciful."

"Merciful!" cried Alain, aghast. He did not want to look at the creature that lay exposed on the plank floor, but one of the soldiers poked it with the haft of its ax, and it did not stir, made no movement. It was completely lifeless.

"Now it is dead and cannot harm you, Son." Finally, one of the soldiers hurried away down the stairs. Lavastine touched Alain. His fingers seemed as cold as marble. "See that it is burned, but out away from the village where the smoke cannot poison anyone."

Across the room, Terror whimpered, and suddenly the count's cool expression faltered, and the shadow of death flickered in his eyes. "Ai, God. My old Terror. Most faithful."

"Here, now," said Alain brusquely, "sit there, Father." He grabbed the knife from the floor and cut a cross over the wound, then set his own mouth to it and sucked, although Lavastine began to protest but gave up. His blood tasted as bitter as hope. Alain spat it out on the floor, sucked again, and again, and then did the same for Terror while the servants hurried to get hot water, cloth to bind the wound, and a shovel to carry away the dead creature. The deacon came as the sun rose. She busied herself making a poultice, and Alain sent a messenger to the monastery of St. Synodios, asking them to send their Brother Infirmarian at once.

Lavastine sat throughout as calm as stone, and never once cried out in pain, never cursed the Eika enchanter, only waited, stroking Terror's head, and watched with that least smile, the one that denoted his approval, while Alain ordered the servants and then, finally, because there was nothing else to do, knelt beside him and prayed.

PART TWO

THE TURNING WHEEL

VIII
THAT WHICH
BLINDS

1

"HERE comes the young lord!"

Alain heard the shout rise up as his entourage rounded the forest path and came to a halt in a clearing. Ten huts stood along the path with narrow garden strips stretching out behind each one. A score of cows grazed along the forest's verge. Fields of winter rye sprouted beyond the village. He dismounted and gave his reins to a groom.

"This is the disputed land?" he asked his steward, but already the village folk swarmed forward and in the old tradition began clamoring all together to get his attention.

A steward brought his stool, and he sat down, although that did nothing to mitigate the outcry. So he just sat, calmly regarding them with Sorrow on one side, Rage on the other, and Fear flopped down at his feet, and after a while one and then another stopped shouting and gesticulating as, one by one, they realized he did not intend to speak until there was silence. In time, because he was patient, they all stood respectfully before him and waited.

"It has come to the attention of my father, Count Lavastine, that certain disputes have disrupted the peace of this village and that several mèn have been injured in fighting. It is my father's will that no feuding be allowed on his lands, so I have come to settle the matter. Let those with an interest each come forward— No!" He had to raise his voice as several crowded forward at once, arms raised to get his attention. "Each person will have opportunity to speak, no matter how long it takes."

Their testimony took a while to give, and it was cold work, especially since he was obligated to sit still and listen under a chill autumn sky. But he had a fine, fur-lined wool cloak, and, in addition, he never wanted for hot cider brought to him by the village children. He listened, because he was good at listening, and after a while as the village folk saw they would truly each be heard, a certain temperance settled over their speech and they began to accuse less and explain more. Once he had sorted through their complaints of each other and the petty injustices and quarrels over the meadowland, grazing rights, division of rents paid to their lord out of the common rye fields, how to parcel out the remaining fallow lands, and how often to let the fields lie fallow, he lifted a hand for silence.

"This is the root of what I hear you say: that you have all prospered so well under the rule of Count Lavastine that there isn't enough land for your children to inherit so they can each have a portion as large as the one you have worked in your time." They dared not quarrel with his opinion, but he saw the idea take hold in their minds. Once he had seen the pattern emerge, he knew how Lavastine and Aunt Bel would answer it, and he wanted to do the best he could. In truth, he could have sent a steward to deal with the problem, but with Lavastine ill he needed to be seen. And anyway, staying busy kept his mind off Tallia.

"It is my will as heir to these lands that you be rewarded, not punished, for your hard work, but it is also necessary that these disputes end. Therefore, in the name of my father I will allow you to cultivate clearings within the forest, which has up to now been reserved for foraging, pigs, and hunting. But you must take only two harvests from any field there, and then move on to clear new fields, and you must not return to any field previously cleared for at least ten years. For every five measures of grain reaped, one shall be given to the count's granary. For one plowing a year you shall have the use of an iron-sheathed plow from Lavas Holding. In the name of my father, and in my own name, I have spoken."

They were satisfied. He saw it in their expressions as they bent their knees to him, as they said, "Bless you, my lord." No doubt details remained to be worked out, but those could be left to the stewards. Quarrels would still erupt because they always did. But he was content that he had done his best.

"What of our good Count Lavastine, my lord?" called one of the elders. "We heard he'd taken ill."

Any satisfaction he felt drained from him in an instant. "Pray for him," he replied. "Pray to God for Their healing grace."

They returned to Lavas Holding by early afternoon, and as Alain followed the hounds up the stairs to Lavastine's chamber, he heard a woman's muffled weeping. He entered the room to see Tallia kneeling beside the count's bed in prayer, her shoulders trembling and her cupped hands covering her face.

"I pray you, Son," said Lavastine, seeing Alain as he chained Fear and Rage to an iron ring set into the wall close beside the bed. The expression that crossed his face was clearly one of relief. "Escort your wife to your chambers. She has prayed over me all morning, and I fear she needs rest."

Alain paused to caress Terror; by Lavastine's order the old hound had been allowed to lie on the bed beside him, and there he rested, quieter each day but somehow still alive. He whined, pressing his hot, dry nose into Alain's hand. He could not thump his tail, or move his legs, but he kept his dark gaze focused faithfully on his master.

"Come, Tallia." She did not resist as Alain took her elbow and raised her up. Behind, servants helped the count sit up in bed, then flinched back as Fear jumped up onto the bed to lie across Lavastine's dead legs. Alain looked away and hurriedly led her upstairs. Sorrow followed him as far as the threshold; then, whining, she turned back into the room to remain with the count.

Upstairs, Alain sent Tallia's servingwomen from the room. She was still sobbing softly. Her sorrow for Lavastine touched him deeply. He thought he had never loved her as much as he did now, when her compassion was made evident by her tears.

"Don't despair, beloved," he whispered into her ear. She was limp with sorrow; he held her close.

"How can I not?" she said faintly. "He remains stubbornly

blind. That's why he's turning to stone, because he refuses to accept the true word, the holy death and life of the blessed Daisan, who died that we might all live unstained in the Chamber of Light. He will fall into the Abyss. If only God had given me the strength to make him see!"

He was too startled to reply. This was not what he had expected.

Then she looked up at him; a spark of passion lit in her eyes, a hundred unspoken promises. It dazed him, torn with grief and sorrow for Lavastine, yet wanting her so badly. He sighed and gathered her closer, waiting for what she would say to him while she allowed him to hold her so intimately.

"After he's dead, you will let me build a convent, won't you? You'll put no obstacles in my path, I know it. It's only *he* who is trapped by his old allegiances to the word of the false church. We can build together a church dedicated to Mother and Son, and we'll dedicate ourselves there, in perpetual virginity, in Their Names. In this way we can free ourselves from the burden of mortality! We'll bless any children we might have had by never condemning them to the prison of existence on this earth!"

"No!" He flinched, let go of her as he recoiled. How could she talk like this when every soul in this holding mourned their good lord who lay dying? "You know Lavas County must have an heir. You know it! It's our duty."

"Nay, it's our duty to break the chains of this world, to escape the flesh that traps us." She shuddered. "Everything that is most distasteful, all that binds us to the Enemy, darkness, desire, bestial mating, all that pumping and panting—"

Was she mocking him? Out of patience, he grabbed her shoulders. "But we must make a child, Tallia! *That's* our duty." She tried to pull away, but he was too angry to feel compassion for her fear, if it was fear at all. Maybe it was only selfishness.

"Never! I'll never defile myself so! I've dedicated myself to—"

"Do what you will, build what you will, dedicate yourself as you will—*after* you've given Lavas County an heir!"

She swayed, eyes rolling back, and fainted.

He stood there stupidly with Tallia limp in his arms as her servingwomen crossed into the chamber, alerted by their raised voices. They stared at him like frightened rabbits. With a cry of frustration, he surrendered her into the care of Lady Hathumod;

the only sensible one among them, and fled to the chapel. He knelt before the Hearth, but although the frater who attended the chapel touched his lips with sanctified water from a gold cup, still he could find no words. After a while, the frater left him alone in the silence of God's chamber, and as he knelt there, he thought he had never felt more alone in his life. He wanted to weep, but he had no tears. He wanted to pray, but he had no eloquent words. Yet did good God ever demand eloquence? How many times had Aunt Bel told him that God preferred an honest heart to a clever tongue?

Finally he gripped the tasseled end of the altar cloth in one hand and pressed the cloth against his forehead. "God, I pray you," he whispered. "I beg you, heal my father."

For the longest time he listened, but he heard no answer.

"I beg you, come, my lord," said the frater quietly, reentering the chamber. "The count is asking for you."

He followed the frater quietly, and so quietly did they come that he paused at the threshold to Lavastine's chamber without at first being noticed. Fear still lay on the bed, and Sorrow and Rage sat within reach of the count's hand, should he wish to pat them. As unnaturally still as Terror, they ignored the folk crowded around the bed, and Alain did, too. He could not take his eyes from Lavastine.

No casual observer could possibly have guessed that the count was anything but a late riser, sitting comfortably in his bed with a hand on the head of his favorite hound as he disposed of the business of the day before getting up to go hunting or hawking. No casual observer could possibly have guessed that the legs hidden under the blanket now felt like stone, and that the bed had already been reinforced once underneath to take the extra weight.

Was he terrified as the poison crept inexorably day by day up his body?"

"Be sure that the second best bedspread goes to your daughter, Mistress Dhuoda, for her dower. Of my second best tunics, be sure that one goes to the captain's window for her eldest son and the others to each of my loyal servingmen." The slightest of smiles graced his mouth as he nodded toward a rotund steward who waited at the foot of the bed. "Except for Christof, here, for I fear he would need two to cover him." There was a hearty laugh from everyone in the room, but Alain could see the tears in their eyes; in every eye, except for Lavastine's. "But there is a good piece of linen in the weaving house that should be ample for him, I trust."

A frater sat at the table, writing everything down as Lavastine went on. "Once the weaving house is done with the new tapestries for the hall, I wish the ones hanging there now to go to Bativia."

"But haven't you assigned that manor to your cousin's daughter?" asked Dhuoda from her seat beside the bed.

"To Lavrentia, yes, when she comes of age. I will not have it said that I left her with scraps. Those tapestries will do very nicely there. It's a small hall but well built and warm in the winter. Has there been any word from Geoffrey yet?"

"No, my lord count," said Dhuoda with a frown. She looked at the frater who had come in with Alain, but he only shrugged.

Lavastine followed the direction of her gaze rather more slowly, as if his neck was stiff and it was hard to move. He managed to lift his right arm to beckon Alain, but it clearly took some effort. "I want Lord Geoffrey's sworn word that he will support my son in every way he can once I am gone."

Several servants drew the Circle at their chests. Alain threw himself down beside the bed.

"You won't die, Father! See how slowly it grips you—you'll recover. I know you will!"

Lavastine struggled to get his arm up and with a grimace of satisfaction rested it on Alain's bowed head. Already it weighed far more than it ought to. "The poison creeps higher every day, son. I can only imagine the creature had expended most of its poison upon my faithful hounds and so had little enough for me. I suppose it is possible that the poison will only paralyze me, but I do not feel any such hope in my heart. Do not despair. I am at peace with God, and I have left precise instructions." He looked toward the table where the frater had paused in his writing, then back at Alain, his gaze cool and calm. "My wishes and commands are clear in this matter. You need only to prove your worthiness by producing an heir."

2

ALL the Ungrians smelled funny, but they looked powerful and warlike in their padded coats, fur capes, and tasseled caps as they assembled for the wedding feast in the great hall of the biscop of Handelburg's palace.

Prince Bayan was a man in his prime, stocky, sun-weathered, with a fair bit of silver in his black hair and a habit of twisting the drooping ends of his mustaches. He had brought his mother, but she remained concealed in a palanquin, hidden by walls of gold silk. Four male slaves—one with skin as black as pitch, one as ice-blond and fair as Hanna, one golden-skinned with strangely pulled eyes, and one who looked much like the Ungrian warriors surrounding them—braced the litter on their shoulders so that it never touched the ground. The feast had started at noon and yet by late afternoon not one platter of food had passed behind the concealing silks.

Princess Sapientia had made up her mind on the long trip to Handelburg to like her betrothed, but in truth he was an easy enough man to like.

"When Geza beloved of God is still the prince, not the king yet, then he fight the battle with the *majariki*—" He turned to his interpreter, a stout, middle-aged frater who had only one hand; where the other should be he had a stump ending at the wrist. "What they call in Wendish? Ah, the Arethousans. Yes?" He spun the tail of one of his mustaches between fingers greasy from eating meat. "Gold hats and much strong smell of perfume, the *majariki*."

"Prince Geza defeated the Arethousans in battle?" Sapientia asked.

"So he become king of the Ungrians. He fight against his uncles, his mother's brothers you would say, who say they must be king, not he. They ride to *majariki* and promise no raids and bow to *majariki* God if *majariki* army fight on their side. But Prince Geza beloved of God win this battle and he is king."

"God do not favor those who pray to Them only for their own advantage," observed Biscop Alberada from her seat between Bayan and Sapientia. As Henry's illegitimate, and elder, half sister, she had taken the biscopric allotted her with a firm hand and always supported her brother here on the eastern fringe of his kingdom.

"Did you fight with him, too, against your uncles?" asked Sapientia, less concerned about spiritual matters than glorious stories of battle.

"They not my uncles," Bayan explained. "I am son of third wife of King Eddec, our father. I am still young in that day, sleep in my mother's tent."

A new course was brought, served by his warriors and certain clean-smelling clerics from the biscop's staff. Biscop Alberada presided over the carving of an impressive haunch of pork. As robust as her legitimate half brother in health, in looks she evidently resembled her mother, a Polenie noblewoman who had been taken captive in some nameless war and become Arnulf the Younger's first concubine before his marriage to Berengaria of Varre.

After the meat was distributed, Alberada regarded Prince Bayan with a sour gaze. "I believed that the Ungrian people had ended their custom of a man marrying many wives when they accepted the Holy Word of the Unities. According to the Holy Word, one woman and one man shall cleave each to the other in harmony, and exclusivity, in imitation of God Our Mother and Father."

The biscop's speech had to be translated, and Bayan listened intently and then nodded enthusiastically. "This my brother proclaim when he take the circle of God. I follow his rule. I put aside my wives when I come to marry Princess Sapientia." He grinned at her. He had one tooth missing but otherwise a strong mouth, although his teeth were somewhat yellow, perhaps from the copious cups of steaming hot, pungently-scented, brown-colored brew that he downed after finishing each cup of wine set before him.

"You had other wives?" asked the biscop.

"All at once?" demanded Sapientia.

"Many clans wish alliance with house of Geza and send daughters as gift. Too many for him and his sons to marry, so some come to me because I am only king-brother alive. It make

insult to send them back." Then he leaped up suddenly, lifting
the cup he shared with Sapientia, and called out in his own language, gesturing with the cup. A young man outfitted in a gaudy
tunic trimmed with gold braid jumped up, answered him, and
drained his own cup of wine, then sat down. Bayan took his
seat. "That one is younger brother of my second wife. She very
angry to be turned away, but I give her much gold and let her
marry prince of Oghirzo." He laughed. "I tell her he make better husband."

"You are not a good husband?" But Sapientia had a glint in
her eye, and after a moment Hanna realized with some astonishment that Sapientia was actually *jesting* with her betrothed.
She would never have jested with Hugh.

Prince Bayan found the comment uproariously funny, and he
leaped again to his feet, called every man in his retinue to stand,
and led them in a toast to his bride. One table of men, still on
their feet, sang a boisterous song while the rest kept time by
pounding their cups on the tables. After this, Bayan declaimed
in his own language a long and tedious paeon to his new bride,
punctuated by the translation of the interpreter:

"She is as beautiful as the best mare. As robust as the rabbits in wintertime. Her grip is as strong as an eagle's, her sight
as keen as a hawk's, she is as fecund as the mice," and so on
until Sapientia burst out laughing.

"Your Highness," whispered Hanna, bending low over her.
"If you give offense—"

"You do not like my poem?" cried Bayan, plumping down
in his chair. "It is my own words I craft, not speak another
man's."

Sapientia choked on her laughter and turned red. "I am sure,
Prince Bayan, that it is only the words your interpreter gives to
those you crafted in your own language—"

"No, no!" he cried cheerfully. "Always I make these poems
that others say is no good, not like the true poets. But I do not
mind their laughter. These words is from my heart."

"Ai, God," said Alberada under her breath. "A bad poet. It
is as well he is a good fighter, Your Highness."

But Sapientia was glowing. "You crafted that poem yourself,
for me? Let us hear it again!"

He was happy to oblige, and this time was not interrupted
by the princess' laughter. The poem had some kind of refrain,

and each time it came around, the Ungrians would all jump to their feet, cry out a phrase with one voice, and drain their wine cups. While this went on interminably, Hanna ate the scraps off Sapientia's platter, shoved forgotten to one side. She was terribly hungry, although now and again Sapientia would offer her own cup to drink from. The hall stank of wine, and urine.

The poem was followed by a display of wrestling, clearly meant to inflame female desire because the young Ungrian warriors stripped down to less clothing than Hanna had ever seen on a grown man in such a public place, just breechclouts covering their groins, and then oiled their skin until they gleamed, all moist and slippery. Did the curtains of the palanquin part slightly? Did she see a hand, fingers studded with rings, part the silk, and a suggestion of movement behind, someone peeking out to observe?

She leaned down to speak into Sapientia's ear. "I wonder if you ought to offer to share food with Prince Bayan's mother, Your Highness. I haven't seen a single platter taken to her."

Sapientia seemed startled by this oversight. "Will your mother not take supper with us, Prince Bayan?"

He changed color, kissed the tips of the fingers of his right hand, and made to throw something invisible over his left shoulder. "Not proper." He glanced nervously toward the palanquin and the sheet of gold fabric that concealed the woman within. "My mother a powerful sorcerer, I think you name it, of the Kerayit peoples, very strong in magic they are. They are the enemies of the Ungrian people, that is why my father marry her. In our language we call her a *shaman*. For her it is not allowed to share meat with people not of her kin."

"But you and I are to be wed! That makes me kin to her."

He grinned. "Not wed until man and woman join in the bed. Yes?"

She flushed. "That is the custom in my land, yes."

"Has your mother accepted the Holy Word and the Circle of Unity?" asked the biscop tartly.

He blinked, surprised. "She a good Kerayit princess. Her gods will take her power if she do not to them give the sacrifice. That is why she cannot be seen in this company."

"A heathen," muttered Alberada. "But you worship at the altar of God, Prince Bayan."

"I am good worshiper," he agreed, glancing at the frater as

if to be sure he had said the words correctly. The man leaned down and whispered into his ear, and Bayan nodded, then turned to the biscop and spoke again, more emphatically. "I follow the Holy Word of God in Unity."

As if these words gave a signal, men lit torches and set them into sconces along the walls. The biscop rose with regal grace; although not tall, she had a queenly breadth of figure. Like her illegitimate nephew, Sanglant, she wore the gold torque that marked her royal kinship, although, like him, she could not aspire to the throne—unless the rumor was true that Henry himself conspired to place his illegitimate son on the throne after him. Hanna was not a fool: she listened, and she observed. Why would Henry marry his daughter to a man who, although renowned as a strong fighter, was unlikely to command respect and loyalty in Wendar itself? Only Sapientia seemed unaware of the implications of her father's choice for her marriage partner. Face bright and eyes glittering, she rose to stand beside Alberada as the biscop called the company to order.

"As night falls over this hall, let God's will be worked in this matter."

There were the usual pledges, an exchange of marriage portions: a disputed border region made over to Prince Bayan, a tribe whose tribute would henceforth grace Wendish coffers instead of going to the Ungrian king, many precious vessels from King Henry of Salian and Aostan manufacture, and from the east two wagons heaped with gold that Bayan's men pulled into the hall. Hanna had never seen such an astounding display of pure gold, not even on Henry's progress. It gleamed with a muted, almost ominous presence, heaped up like so much casually discarded debris.

The biscop spoke words of blessing over them, and there were toasts to their health, to Bayan's virility, and to Sapientia's womanly strength.

" 'Let us contest with swords not with words,' " cried Bayan, " 'and if not in battle with worthy opponents then in the bed of a handsome woman.' " He laughed as he tossed off another cup of wine. He had an amazing capacity to drink and had only had to leave the table twice to pee. He turned to his betrothed with a grin. "These words is teach to me by your brother, the famous warrior Bloody Fields, who makes the land to run red with the blood of his enemies. But you name him differently in your own tongue." He spoke to the frater, grunted, and tried the word on his tongue but could not make it come out like anything intelligible.

"Do you mean Sanglant?" demanded Sapientia. "You have met Sanglant!"

"Hai—ai! We fight the Quman together these five years past. It is a good battle! They run, and do not to come back. He is alive still, your brother?"

"He is still alive," said Sapientia curtly, and seemed about to say more when shouting rose from the far end of the hall.

"Make way! Make way!" Two men in soiled clothing came forward and knelt before the high table.

"What is this?" asked the biscop. "Is the news you bring so urgent that it cannot wait until morning?"

"I beg your pardon, Your Grace," said the elder of the two. He had a reddish beard and a scar above his left eye. "We have had news of several raids beyond the town of Meilessen. There have been more than a dozen such raids, villages burned, many people killed and some beheaded, so it is said. It is hard to know how long ago this began, twenty days or more, but the raiders are moving west. We thought it best to tell you as soon as we entered Handelburg."

The frater had been translating, and now Prince Bayan got to his feet and gestured for a servant to take wine to the two men. "Who does this raiding?" he asked, but he seemed already to know the answer.

"It is the Quman, my lord," said the man, startled as he now took in the assembly of Ungrian warriors mixed together with Wendish folk.

Bayan set his teeth in a vicious smile, an expression quite at odds with his usual jolly demeanor. "What mark do they bear, these Quman?"

The spokesman consulted with his companion, then looked toward the biscop for permission to speak. Sapientia stirred restlessly, then rose, too, a pallid echo of Bayan's movement. The spokesman acknowledged her with a bow, but it was obvious he did not recognize her as Henry's eldest daughter and putative heir.

"They wear the mark of the claw's rake." The messenger took his three middle fingers and made a raking gesture down his arm. "Like so."

Bayan spat on the floor, then leaped up onto the table with raised cup. He shouted out a name, and the hall rang with the shatteringly loud reply of his assembled men as they, too, all cursed a name and spat on the floor in response. He cried out again, and they answered him, then all drained their cups dry to seal their bargain.

"The snow leopard clan," translated the frater. "Bulkezu, son of Bruak."

Bayan had launched into another one of his poems, which Hanna recognized by its distinctive cadences, and by the awkward translation of the frater, who no doubt did what he could to make the words pleasing.

" '. . . Hard rides the fighter. Strong are his sinews. Many days in the saddle . . .'."

"What is the snow leopard clan?" demanded Sapientia, still glaring at the messengers, who, poor souls, looked quite taken aback at being surrounded by a host of shouting Ungrian warriors who were most likely still half heathens themselves—and pungent ones at that. She beckoned to the frater, who faltered, stopped translating, and answered her.

"The snow leopard clan is one of the many Quman tribes."

"There is more than one Quman tribe?"

The frater looked at her with ill-concealed surprise. "I know the clan marks of at least sixteen Quman clans. They are numberless, and as merciless as any of the tribes who live out beyond the Light of God."

"Are they the ones who took your hand?" she asked.

He laughed. "Nay, indeed. They'd have taken my head."

"Who is this Bulkezu they all speak of, and spit at?"

"The war leader who in battle killed Prince Bayan's only son, eldest child of his first wife. She was a Kerayit princess like Bayan's own mother."

"And these Kerayit—" Sapientia pronounced the word awkwardly. "They are a Quman tribe as well?"

"Nay, Your Highness. They live far to the east, beyond even those peoples who pay tribute to the Jinna emperor. It is well enough that his first wife is dead, for she'd not have given him up. She'd have hexed you."

"Hexed me!" Sapientia pressed a hand over the gold Circle of Unity that hung at her throat, and glanced sidelong at the palanquin. The gold silk walls did not stir. There might have been no creature inside at all, only air.

He bent closer. His breath smelled of exotic spices. "They are terrible witches, the most unrepentant of heathens." He bent his elbow to display the stump of his right wrist. "They thought writing was magic, so they cut off my hand." He faltered, glanced like Sapientia toward the motionless palanquin as if he thought that the hidden mother could hear his words even at such a distance and over the howling of Bayan's warriors as they called out the refrain. "That is how I came to Prince Bayan's service. He is a good man, Your Highness, I have nothing but praise for him."

"Is he truly faithful to God's word, Brother?" asked Biscop Alberada, who was not afraid to listen in to her niece's most private conversations.

"As faithful as any of the Ungrians can be."

"And his mother?" asked Sapientia without looking again toward the palanquin. But the frater only gave a tiny shake of his head. "She is a powerful woman. Do not anger her."

Hanna could not help but look, but the palanquin remained undisturbed both from within and from without. How the slaves could stand for so long without staggering amazed her. And wouldn't the woman inside begin to feel cramped, closed up in a sitting position for so long? Hanna wasn't sure she could stay still for such a long time. Even waiting on Princess Sapientia, she had freedom of movement; she could excuse herself to go out to the privies, could pace, laugh, sing when appropriate, and eat and drink what the princess herself did not want. The leavings off a princess' plate were far better fare than anything she had eaten in Heart's Rest.

No, indeed: being a King's Eagle was a good life, even with the dangers involved. Danger walked beside every woman and man no matter what their circumstances. It wasn't often that you could walk through life well fed, well shod, *and* with new things to see 'round every corner.

Prince Bayan was still going on, stamping one foot for emphasis with each line of verse; cups and platters rattled. As the volume of noise in the hall increased, the frater had to bend close to explain: "He is singing the death song of his son, to remind his men of the boy's glorious death, and of the unavenged spirit that still walks abroad."

"A heathen belief," observed Biscop Alberada.

"To get to any place, Your Grace, we must still take one step at a time."

She chuckled. "Brother Breschius, you have gained wisdom in your time among the heathens, despite the suffering they have caused you."

"I have learned to be tolerant, which comes to the same thing. God will be victorious in the end. We need only be patient and trust to Their power."

"War!" roared Prince Bayan, a word echoed by his men in their own tongue. "Swear to this battle we will ride!" he called out, then repeated himself in his own language.

His men clamored in answer. Hanna had to clap her hands over her ears.

That quickly, they drained their cups and with a flood of movement the hall began to empty.

"Where are they all going?" demanded Sapientia. Biscop Alberada had also risen, watching the milling crowd intently for any sign of trouble. Drunk and excited young men were likely to get into fistfights, or worse; Hanna knew that well enough from evenings at her mother's inn.

"We ride in the morning," cried Bayan enthusiastically. He jumped down from the table, still remarkably agile for a man who was close to Sapientia's father's age. "Now, to bed we go!"

Sapientia smiled sharply. Their escort to the bedchamber set aside for them this night was ample: fully thirty people of various stations, but in the end Hanna found herself together with two servingwomen alone in the room with Sapientia, Prince Bayan, and a single male retainer, a sleek, unbearded young man who wore a thin iron torque at his neck that looked suspiciously like a slave collar.

Bayan drew his sword, and for an instant Hanna grabbed her own knife while Sapientia stood, frozen, at her side of the bed.

"No woman," proclaimed Bayan as he laid the sword down the center of the bed. "I swear before my men to have no woman until I kill a man in battle. This the men of my people swear, to give ourselves strength. If we break the oath, then we lose our luck. If it is hard with you to have no man, I have this one—" He gestured to his manservant. "He is one of these *majariki* men who have no, what do you call it? They have the man part but not the seed. They can give you this pleasure without the seed, for now that we are betrothed, you may take no seed but that I give to you. Yes?"

What glinted in his gaze belied the pleasant smile on his lips and the congenial tone. It flashed, a bone-deep core of unforgivingness, startling to glimpse in a man who seemed as easy going and pleasant as the warm glow of the summer sun—until you were caught out under its heat for too long.

"Your children will be my children. Yes?"

"That is the agreement!" retorted Sapientia, looking affronted. She reached across the bed to touch the sword, caressing the blade. It was a handsome piece of metal, slightly curved; letters had been carved into the blade, but Hanna could not read them. Gold plated the hilt. "But I am a warrior, too! I will swear no less an oath than you do!"

"Then you and your fighting men will ride beside me when we go in the morning, to hunt these Quman raiders?" The unforgiving glint had vanished. He laughed out loud. " 'Strong is my woman. She is hunter like the lion queen!' Together, we ride to war!"

3

PRINCE Ekkehard's servants managed to conceal Ivar and—more importantly—Baldwin from old Lord Atto for ten days during which Ivar had either to trudge alongside the wagons with a cowl over his head like a comman laybrother or be jolted about in the back of one of those same wagons. In a way, it was a relief to be discovered, despite Lord Atto's explosive reaction.

"Lord Baldwin must be sent back to Autun at once! What were you thinking, my lord prince? This is a grave insult to Margrave Judith. Feuds have destroyed whole families on lesser grounds than these!"

Ekkehard did not quail before this onslaught. "She need never know, and I and my people certainly won't be the ones to tell her." He did not really have the stature to stare down Lord Atto, who had the burly physique of a man who has fought in many battles, but he was free of the schola, young, and out on his own for the first time. "Baldwin stays with me!"

"He'll be sent back in the morning, my lord prince. It's what your father would command."

But Lord Atto wasn't as young as he used to be, and his left leg and right arm had sustained enough damage over his years of fighting that no one thought it particularly odd when, in the morning, he slipped while mounting. Maybe the mild paralysis that sometimes afflicted him chose that moment to reappear. Ekkehard and Baldwin hurried over to assist the poor old man, fussing around him and his horse, and by the time anyone thought to check the saddle, the girth was good and tight.

Atto was left at the manor house to recover from the fall, with two servants in attendance. Prince Ekkehard rode on with his party otherwise intact and Baldwin riding at his right hand. No one mentioned the matter again. But they rode at a good clip, always aware that the news would get back to King Henry eventually.

Yet such a pace couldn't tire them. They were young, and reckless, and happy to be free of restraint. Happy, that is, except for Ivar.

At first he didn't join in at their nightly revels at whatever manor or guesthouse put them up. They drank heavily, wrestled, sang, and entertained themselves with whatever young female servants were on hand and more or less willing; if no women were available, they entertained themselves with each other.

Ekkehard took to calling him "my prim frater," and it became a joke among them that of all of them, Ivar stayed "pure," just like a good churchman. But Baldwin was always pestering him, and on those nights when Ivar and Baldwin shared a blanket for warmth, Baldwin had a discomforting way of rubbing up against him that aroused thoughts of Liath. He was tired of thinking of Liath. Sometimes he hated her for the way her memory surfaced again and again in his mind. Maybe Hugh was right: maybe Liath had cast a spell over him. Why did the thought of her grip him bodily with such violence? He could hardly think of her at all anymore without embarrassing himself, and then they would all notice. They would all know he wasn't any purer than they were.

But he wasn't pure. No one was, nothing could be, trapped in the impure world. Alone, he couldn't even find the courage to preach the True Word, and he resented Baldwin—now free of Judith, after all—for not joining him in prayer. There wasn't any satisfaction in praying alone. Indeed, after enough days in their company, he began to wonder why he should stay sunk in pain and grief when he might as well be as careless and fickle as they all were.

A terrible rumor greeted them when their party rode into Quedlinhame: Queen Mathilda was dying. Ekkehard's steward found Ivar and Baldwin lodging in the house of a Quedlinhame merchant, since they dared not risk them being recognized at the monastery itself, where the prince would stay with his aunt. But the merchant spent all his time at the town church praying for the health of the old queen. They had no fire, and it was cold and miserable with an autumn drizzle shushing on the eaves above them.

"I hope the prince doesn't take long." His teeth chattered. He had been shivering all day, and knowing that the prince and his official retinue would be better housed, and given more than lukewarm gruel for their supper, only made it worse.

"He must do what is proper, for his grandmother," retorted Baldwin primly. He had a mirror and was checking his face to see if his shave was clean enough. "Come under the blanket with me, Ivar. It'll be warmer."

"I won't!" he said with more heat than force. "You know I've taken vows as a novice. It wouldn't be right."

"Prince Ekkehard and all his companions have taken vows as novices. That doesn't stop them."

"But I don't want to be like them," retorted Ivar. Yet he wondered in his heart if the person he most despised was himself. Baldwin sighed and went back to his shaving.

That evening bells began to toll, the somber roll of the Quedlinhame cathedral bell blending with the lighter ring of the town bell.

"Someone's died," observed Baldwin wisely. "Come on!" He tugged on his cape and pulled the hood up to conceal his face.

"But if we're seen by someone at the monastery who knows us—"

"Why should they look if they think we're townsfolk? I can't abide staying shut up here any longer." Like the wind, Baldwin had enough energy to pick Ivar up like a leaf and carry him along with him outside and into the crowd.

"The queen is dead." The wail started on the edge of the crowd as they flowed up the steep road that led to the monastery gates. By the time they reached the gates, the crowd had an edge of hysteria, weeping and wailing, a wild noise like beasts gone mad.

"They'll never let us in," Ivar shouted. It would be better so. The walls of Quedlinhame monastery scared him. He'd escaped once; if he went inside again, maybe he'd never get out.

But laybrothers did open the gate, and crossing that threshold had a miraculous effect on the crowd. Once they stepped through onto holy ground, they calmed. A baby squalled, but otherwise the huge crowd—hundreds of people, more than he could count—went forward in as much silence as so many shuffling footsteps and smothered sobs could grant it. Many of them clutched Circles and prayed soundlessly. As the crowd filed into the cathedral under the watchful gaze of half a dozen elderly nuns who looked as fierce as watchdogs, Ivar kept his hood pulled forward so that no one would see his red hair. Baldwin used his elbows, hips, and one well-placed pinch to squeeze them forward and in the end they found room just inside the door, far away from the altar. The stone pillars, carved with dragons, lions, and eagles, loomed over Ivar. Once he had prayed under their vigilant eye. He began to shiver. What if they bore some magic within them, what if they could see and recognize him for what he was? Hadn't he betrayed the church by running away from Margrave Judith? Hadn't he rebelled against the very authority of the church by listening to Lady Tallia's preaching?

Baldwin put an arm around him to warm him. Townsfolk stamped their feet and rubbed limbs leached of heat by the rain. The smell of so many unwashed winter bodies gave off its own heat. His fingers hurt as warmth flooded back.

When the nuns and monks marched in, all the townsfolk knelt. The stone floor was, predictably, hard and cold; his knees hurt. In an awful silence frayed only by a child's cough and the whispering of cloth as people shifted position to see better, the body of Queen Mathilda was carried in on a litter. She was tiny, frail, and shrunken, dressed in the plain robe granted to the humblest sister of the church. But she wore rich rings on her fingers, and a slim gold coronet circled her white hair. Mother Scholastica and Prince Ekkehard walked behind the bier, and once the dead queen was laid in state, the abbess came forward to kiss her bare feet. Then Prince Ekkehard, too, was allowed this privilege. The novices filed in silently to kneel at the base of the stairs that led to altar and bier. Ivar stared, hoping to pick out Sigfrid among their number, but their hoods and bowed heads concealed them too well.

Mother Scholastica stepped behind the altar. At her side, Brother Methodius began to chant the opening prayer for the Mass for the Dead.

"Blessed is the Country of the Mother and Father of Life—"

"Lies!" On the steps a slight figure leaped up to address the townsfolk caught in the opening cadence of prayer, at their most responsive before the flow of the liturgy lulled them into a stupor. "You have all been made blind by the darkness spread over this land because of their lies. The true course of Her miracle and Her Holy Word has been hidden away. For God found a worthy vessel in the holy Edessia. God filled her with the blessed light, and in this way she gave birth to the blessed Daisan, he who partakes both of the nature of God and of humankind. He brought God's message to all of us, that he would suffer and die to redeem us from the stain of darkness that lies within all of us—"

A shriek of frustration burst from the schoolmaster. Three monks leaped up, scuffled with the young novice, and hauled him away while he still shouted, his words muffled by a hand pressing his mouth closed. Ivar stood stunned while around him people burst into frenzied talk, pointing and questioning.

"That was Sigfrid," whispered Baldwin. "Is he gone mad?"

"That's what's become of him without us to protect him."

"We'll have to get him free."

"How can we get him free?" Ivar's laugh left a bitter taste. He dragged Baldwin back by the elbow. "Let's go. What if they find us here?"

He knew that look on Mother Scholastica's face as, slowly, the multitude quieted in the face of her anger. She looked mightily displeased as she spoke to Brother Methodius. He nodded, knelt by the bier, kissed the dead queen's robe, then left the church by a side door.

Mother Scholastica lifted her hands. "Let us pray, Sisters and Brothers. Let us pray that God forgive us our sins, and that through prayer we may follow the example of the blessed Daisan, he who was the child of God brought forth into this world through the vessel of St. Edessia, he who through his own efforts found the way to salvation that we all may follow. Let us pray that we may not be stained by those desires which the Enemy casts upon the ground like jewels, tempting us to pick them up for they glitter so brightly and their colors attract our eye. Let us be humble before God, for Their word is truth. All else is lies."

"We must stay and listen!" hissed Baldwin. "Prince Ekkehard will be able to get Sigfrid free. His aunt can't refuse him anything."

"Do you think so? I know better." He was bigger and stronger, and he was shaking with fury and helplessness as he hauled Baldwin backward.

"We'll look more suspicious if we run away!"

At the threshold, the people who hadn't found room inside pushed forward, trying to see what had caused the commotion, and those disturbed by Sigfrid's outburst or by the squeeze inside pressed outward. Ivar followed their tidal flow, two steps forward, one back, two forward, until they came out into a drizzle and the finger-numbing chill of a mid-autumn day.

Baldwin pouted all the way down the hill. But for once Ivar wasn't minded to give in to his pretty sulk. The only thing worse than abandoning Sigfrid was to be caught themselves. Mother Scholastica would not be merciful.

They stumbled down the road churned muddy by the crowd, slipped more than once until their leggings and sleeves and hands dripped mud. They had nothing to wash with, and so huddled in the loft while mud caked and dried, then crumbled with each least movement. Baldwin sulked with the only blanket wrapped around him. Ivar paced because he could not sleep, and it was too cold to be still.

Why had Sigfrid done it? Had he bided his time all this while only to burst like an overfull winesack at the sight of so many willing ears? Would he, Ivar, have done anything as courageous—and so blindly stupid? Was he brave enough to act on what he believed, to preach, as Tallia had, as Sigfrid had, and accept the consequences?

It was an ugly truth, but it had to be faced: He was nothing but a cold, miserable sinner.

"Oh, Ivar," said Baldwin. "I'm so cold, and I love you so much. I know you're just shy because you've never—"

"I have so!" he retorted, face scalding. "That's how my father always celebrated his children's fifteenth birthday. He sent me a servingwoman—"

"To make a man of you? It's not the same. You were just using her the way Judith used me. You've never done it just for yourself and the one you were with. That's different."

"I did after that, when I—" *When I thought about Liath.* And she had thrown him away.

"Just doing it once won't matter. You'll like it. You'll see. And you'll be a lot warmer."

It really didn't matter, did it? That it did matter was the lie he'd been telling himself all along: look what had happened to Sigfrid. At least Baldwin cared for him, in a way Liath never had. He dropped down beside Baldwin and, cautiously, nervously, touched him above the heart. Baldwin responded with a sudden, shy smile, the touch of a hand on his thigh, sweet breath at his ear.

And then, after all, it proved easier to live only in sensation.

In the morning, Milo arrived out of breath, nose bright red from the cold. "Go out of town now," he said, "and wait on the road to Gent."

Beyond the gates they walked a while to warm themselves; as the traffic along the road began to pick up, Ivar got nervous. He used a stick to beat out a hiding place within the prickly branches of an overgrown hedge. There, with the blanket wrapped round them, they waited.

"We could have done something for Sigfrid," muttered Baldwin.

"Just like you could have done something when Margrave Judith came to fetch you? We're powerless against them. Or do you want to go back to your wife? It was certainly warmer with her!"

Baldwin only grunted.

Wagons passed, then a peddler on foot and, later in the morning, clots of pilgrims dressed in rags, weeping and wailing the name of Queen Mathilda. No doubt word had already been sent to King Henry, by horse, but these humble pilgrims would spread the news among the common people in return for a bit of bread and a loft to sleep in.

Something stirred in Ivar's gut, a feeling, an idea—or maybe just hunger.

"Look!" Baldwin jumped up, got his hair caught in the hedge, and swore as the branches yanked him to a halt. By the time Ivar had freed him, Prince Ekkehard's cavalcade had come up beside them.

"How did you get so muddy?" said the prince with a frown for Baldwin.

"We had to walk here, my lord prince. What news of our friends?"

Prince Ekkehard had a habit of blinking two or three times before he replied, as if it took him that long to register words. He was all sun and light when happy but as sullen as a rainy day when annoyed. Right now he glowered. "It is no easy thing to question my aunt, I'll tell you that. That comrade of yours is quite mad, and disrespectful, too. Imagine treating my grand-mother's memory in such a way! I didn't like him, and my aunt said there's some terrible punishment in store for him, so it's no use to pine over him. He's lost to us."

"But you promised—"

"Enough! There's nothing I can do." Then he grinned. "But I got in a good kick to my awful cousin, Reginar. I told my aunt that the abbacy of Firsebarg has come free now that Lord Hugh is being sent to the skopos for punishment, so she's sending him there. He was so grateful that he promised to do me a favor, so I told him there was a novice there called Ermanrich whom I'd seen in a vision, and that I wanted him to come to Gent to serve me." His young attendants giggled. "Come now, fair Baldwin." He turned coaxing, seeing that Baldwin still pouted. "I did what I could."

"You could have got Sigfrid as well."

"There's nothing I could do against my aunt when she was in such a rage! He'll deserve whatever punishment she metes out. What a terrible thing—" The young prince faltered, seeing Baldwin's expression. "But I did everything else just as you wished, Baldwin. You do love me, don't you?"

"Of course I do," said Baldwin reflexively, then muttered, "as long as you keep me away from Margrave Judith." Ivár kicked him, and he startled like a deer seeking cover. "I am grateful, my lord prince."

"As well you should be. Come, ride beside me, Baldwin."

A horse was brought. Ivar found a seat in one of the wagons, and there he brooded as he jolted along, listening to the chatter of the prince and his loyal retainers. He had heard the refrain often enough: That young men were reckless and feckless and untrustworthy by reason of lacking a steadying womb and the knowledge that they would give life to daughters, who would inherit after them. It was no wonder that women, like the Lady before them, held the reins of administration while they tended the Hearth. What could they expect from feckless men? Headstrong Prince Ekkehard? Pretty, spoiled Baldwin?

Was Ivar, son of Harl and Herlinda, any better? Trapped by desire for a woman who had never even wanted him. A coward, unlike Sigfrid, who however stupidly and disrespectfully had at least shouted the truth out loud, no matter the cost to himself.

He wept, although the day was bright.

4

"WHITE-HAIR! Snow woman!"

A dozen Ungrian warriors sat cross-legged on the ground, sharpening their curved swords, but they had all paused to look up as Hanna passed. She had almost grown used to being the center of attention whenever she walked through camp, on account of her blonde hair and light skin. Except for Prince Bayan, the Ungrians knew no Wendish, but it seemed like every soldier in his retinue had all learned these few phrases, and they were completely unashamed when it came time to call them out to her in their atrocious accents.

"Beautiful ice maiden, I die for you!" cried one young man with black hair and a long, drooping and exceptionally greasy mustache. He had sweet eyes, and was missing one of his front teeth. Like all the other Ungrians, he wore a padded leather coat over baggy trousers.

"My greetings to your wife, my friend," she called back in Ungrian. They all laughed, slapped their thighs, and began to talk volubly among themselves—probably about her. It was disconcerting, and tiring, being the object of so much attention.

Beside her, Brother Breschius chuckled. "Softer on the 'gh,'" he corrected, "but otherwise it was a creditable attempt. You have a better head for languages than your mistress."

Hanna let this gentle criticism pass unremarked. "They flirt terribly, Brother, but not one has propositioned me. I feel perfectly safe walking about the camp."

He grunted amiably. "For now you are safe. When they swear an oath, they keep it, and they are still barbarians in their hearts, which means they are superstitious. They truly do believe that if they waste their strength on carnal play before a battle, they will surely die at the hand of a man who did not waste himself in such a manner."

"But some who hold to that vow will die anyway."

"True. Such is God's will. In their minds, such deaths will be blamed on other things they did or did not do: stepping on a shadow, the chastity of their wife a hundred leagues away, a fly that landed on their left ear instead of their right. They profess to worship God in Unity, but they have not yet given their hearts fully into God's care. You, too, come from a land only recently brought into the Light, I believe, my child. On the first day of spring do you place flowers at a crossroads to bring you luck in your journeys for the rest of the year?"

She looked at him sharply. Then she grinned, because she liked him, with his missing hand and his tolerant heart. "You have traveled widely, Brother. You know a great deal."

He chuckled. "We are all ignorant. I do what I can to share God's Holy Word with those who live in night. But mind you, Eagle, be cautious after the battle. It is the custom of those who survive to behave wildly. At that time I advise you to remain close to your mistress."

She glanced up at their destination: a stone tower set on a ridge overlooking the long valley of the Vitadi River. Half a palisade of wood had been built a generation ago and then abandoned. Now, at Princess Sapientia's order, a levy of men from the surrounding settlements labored to complete the fort.

Men dug out a trench, hauled logs, swore, and sweated as she and Breschius climbed the path that led to the palisade gate and then inside, up a trail hacked into the rock face of a cliff, through a roughly-hewn tunnel where she had to duck her head, and into the fortress itself.

Within the inner rock wall she heard Prince Bayan's jovial laugh echoing among the stones. He stood at the threshold of the tower, laughing with the Wendish captain who commanded the fortress. Turning, he saw Hanna and beckoned her forward.

"The snow woman arrives!" he exclaimed. "Soon winter comes in her trail." He had a pleasant habit of wrinkling up his eyes when he spoke, and even when he didn't smile, his eyes laughed. Life was good to Prince Bayan because he made it so. "To where is my royal wife?" he asked.

Hanna glanced toward Brother Breschius who, mercifully, saved her the awkward reply. Lady Udalfreda of Naumannsfurt had arrived with twenty cavalry and thirty-five foot soldiers, and Princess Sapientia felt obliged to entertain her fittingly.

In truth, Hanna suspected Sapientia, for all her love of fighting, did not have the stomach for what she had sent Hanna to witness in her stead.

Bayan merely shrugged good-naturedly. The Wendish captain led the way down a narrow flight of stairs to the root cellar. It was very cold down here. Water dripped along the rough-hewn rock and made puddles for unwary boots. Beside the cellar door a brazier glowed red with coals; a soldier thrust an iron rod in among the coals to heat it. In the dankest corner, lit only by a dim lantern, lay a savage so heavily chained, wrists to ankles, that he had been forced to lie in his own filth. He stank. Two soldiers grabbed him by the shoulders as Bayan entered the room and jerked him upright. He only stared at them with stubborn eyes dulled by pain. A weeping sore marked his cheek. When he saw Bayan, he spat at him, but he could make no fluid pass his lips.

"This is the one we captured when they raided here two days ago," said the captain. "We burned him with an iron rod, but he would only speak in his language, and none of us understood him."

Jovial Prince Bayan had vanished somewhere on those stairs. The man who stared down at the Quman prisoner frightened Hanna because of his merciless expression. He dispensed with his crude Wendish and spoke directly to Breschius, who translated. "Bring me a block of wood and an ax." When that was done, he had them unchain the prisoner's left hand and haul the man forward. The prisoner had no weapons, of course, but he still wore his armor, which resembled nothing Hanna had ever seen before: small pieces of leather sewn together to make a hard coat of armor, and a leather belt studded with gold plackets formed in the shapes of horses and griffins. A small object swung from the belt, resting now on his bent legs, but she couldn't make it out. He wore a strange harness on his back, a contraption of wood and iron and, strangely enough, a few shredded feathers.

Hanna was beginning to feel sick to her stomach. Waves of stench accompanied the prisoner. He made no sound as the Wendish soldiers held his left hand, fingers splayed, against the block of wood. Prince Bayan drew his knife and with one sharp hack cut off the man's little finger.

A sound escaped the prisoner, a "gawh" of pain caught in as blood flowed. Bayan addressed him in a language Hanna did not recognize, but the man merely spat again in answer. Bayan cut off the next finger, and the next, and then Hanna had to look away. She thought maybe she was going to vomit. Bayan questioned the prisoner in a calm voice that did not betray in its tone the torment he was inflicting; she hung on to that voice, it was her lifeline. The man screamed.

She looked up to see him lolling back, handless now as blood pumped from the stump of his wrist. Thrown back as he was, she could see clearly the object that hung from his belt: black and wizened, headlike in shape with a dark mane of straw hanging from it, it had one side molded into the grotesque likeness of a face. Then the hot iron rod was brought forward to sear the wound, and as he screamed, she stared and stared at that ghastly little thing hanging from his belt so that she wouldn't have to watch his agony and after forever she realized that it was, in fact, a hideous little human head, all shrunken and nasty, with a glorious mane of stiff, black hair.

"I'm going to be sick," she muttered. Brother Breschius moved aside just in time and she threw up in the corner while, apparently oblivious to her, Prince Bayan got back to work on the right hand. He broke the fingers first, one by one, then cut off the little finger, then the next, then the middle finger; but the prisoner only grunted, stoic to the end.

Bayan finally cursed genially and slit the man's throat, stepping back nimbly so that he wouldn't get any blood on him.

"Once sword hand crippled, he never speak because he have nothing to go back to in his tribe, because he no longer a man," he explained. He shrugged. "So God wills. These Quman never talk anyway. Stubborn bastards." Then he laughed, an amazingly resonant and perverse sound in the stinking cellar. "That a good word, yes? Taught to me by Prince Sanglant. '*Stubbornbastards.*'"

He chuckled and wiped at his eyes. He did not even give the corpse a second glance. It meant as little to him as a dead dog lying at the side of a road. "Come," he said to Hanna. "The snow woman must wash away this smell and be clean like the lily flower again, yes? We go to the feast."

They went to the feast, where Bayan entertained Lady Udalfreda and her noble companions with charming and somewhat indecent tales of his adventures as a very young man among the Sazdakh warrior women who, he claimed, could not count themselves as women or warriors until they had captured and bedded a young virgin and then cut off his penis as a trophy. Hanna couldn't touch a bite, although Brother Breschius kindly made sure that she drank a little wine to settle her stomach.

In a way, she was relieved when two scouts came in all dustblown and wild-eyed with a report of a Quman army headed their way.

The Ungrian warriors slept, ate, and entertained in their armor. They were mounted and ready to ride so quickly that they made the good Wendish soldiers in Sapientia's train look like rank, newcomers, awkward and fumbling. Even the colorfully painted wagon of Bayan's mother rolled into line and waited there like a silent complaint long before Princess Sapientia finished arming, and mounted.

"Prince Bayan's mother will ride with us?" demanded Hanna
Breschius nodded toward the wagon, his gaze alert. With its closed shutters and curtained door, it resembled a little house on wheels, and it would have looked rather quaint except for the clean white bones hanging from the eaves like charms, although they were, mercifully, not human but animal bones. At the peak of the roof a small wheel decorated with ribbons turned in the wind, fluttering red and yellow and white and blue as it spun. "The shamans of the Kerayit tribe do not carry their luck in their bodies as the rest of us do. Their luck is born into another person, someone born on the same day at the same time. It is

said that Bayan's mother's luck was born into the child who later became Bayan's father, a prince of the Ungrian people, which is the only reason she agreed to marry him. But he died on the day Prince Bayan was born, so by their way of thinking her luck passed from father into son. That's why she must stay close by Prince Bayan, to watch over him." He smiled as if laughing at himself. "But she is in no real danger. Not even the Quman would harm a Kerayit princess, for they know what fate awaits the clan of he who touches a Kerayit shaman without her consent. You will see. She is useful."

They rode out at last, and Hanna was grateful to leave the stone tower behind. The chill autumn air and the dense odor of grass and brittle scrub brush drove the last vestiges of that terrible stink out of her nostrils. But an image of the hideous shrunken head seemed to ride with her, burned into her mind's eye.

They forded the river, running low here after summer's heat and autumn drought. The cold water on her calves made her breath come in gasps. Sapientia rode just ahead of her, beside Bayan, and the princess laughed merrily as they came splashing up the shoreline, more like a noble lady riding to the hunt than to a battle. Behind, the oxen drawing the wagon forged stolidly into the water, led forward by two of the handsome male slaves. And it was very strange, and most certainly a trick of the light running over the water, because it seemed to Hanna that the river receded somewhat, that the waves made of themselves a slight depression around the wheels of the wagon so that no water lapped into the bed. Behind the wagon marched the Wendish infantry; without horses, they were soaked to the hips, joking and laughing at those among them who showed any sign of sensitivity to the cold.

Soon everyone had crossed, and their army—perhaps two hundred soldiers in all—made ready to move on. Hills rose from the valley floor about half a league north of them. They turned east to follow the river. Clouds moved in from the east as the wind picked up. The Wendish soldiers began singing a robust hymn.

A sudden shrilling call rang down the line and, with it, that tensing of line and body that presages battle. The Ungrians shifted position, flanks spreading out, Bayan moving to take up the center as he called out orders to his men in his strong baritone. About half the Ungrian riders broke off from the main group and swung away into the hills. The Wendish infantry fell back to form a square on a rise.

A strange whirring sound grew in the air, building in strength. It seemed to come from nowhere and everywhere at once: eerie, troubling, like the sensation of a spider crawling up one's back. Hanna's horse shifted restlessly under her; she reined it hard back to its place beside Brother Breschius where they waited behind Sapientia and Bayan, and leveled her spear. Bayan's soliders began to keen, like a sick wolf's howl, but even that noise was better than the awful disembodied whirring. She squinted eastward, trying to make out the source. Clouds darkened the eastern horizon. In the distance, a rumble of thunder rolled away into the hills. Even above the dust kicked up by the army, she could smell rain.

Abruptly Prince Bayan turned around, saw her and Breschius, and snapped an order at them. Sapientia objected. Husband and wife exchanged perhaps four tense sentences, Sapientia all white fire and Bayan utterly focused and without any patience.

Abruptly, Sapientia gave in. She turned. "Go!" she called to Hanna. "You and the frater. Go, and observe all that occurs!"

Riders made way for them as they rode back through the line.

"What is that awful sound?" cried Hanna above the din of thrumming and howling.

Breschius smiled but did not reply as the outer line of foot soldiers parted to let them through into the center of the infantry square. Here, beside the painted wagon, Hanna turned her horse just as the Wendish soldiers let out a great shout of alarm and surprise, which the Ungrians answered with a howl of glee as they charged.

She saw the Quman, then, beyond the Ungrian line, advancing along the river plain with dark clouds scudding in their wake. They weren't human after all. They didn't have faces, and they had wings. Feathers streamed and pulsed, shuddering in the air, flickering shadow and light in the huge wings that curved forward over their heads. Beneath helmets, their flat, metal faces shone with dull menace as the westering sun broke through the cloud cover and lit the Wendish and Ungrian army with a mellow glow. The Quman warriors made no sound except for the spinning and singing of their wings as they rode.

The Ungrians charged, all disorganized in uneven lines like

a pack of starving dogs gone mad at the sight of fresh meat. Their shrieks and whoops almost drowned out the thunder of hooves and the whir of wings. Even from a distance Hanna had no trouble seeing Sapientia waiting impatiently beneath her banner. The princess began to move out after the Ungrians, but Bayan stopped her by resting the length of his spear across her chest as he waited and watched his own men ride rashly and without order at the enemy.

"They'll be picked apart!" cried Hanna, suddenly wondering what would become of the Wendish after their allies foolishly threw away their strength in this manner. Breschius smiled with the calm of a man who has long since made peace with God and no longer fears death.

A curtain made of beads rustled as an ancient, yellowing hand pressed a few strands aside, peering out. Hanna glanced there, surprised, but she saw only deeper shadow within. She heard a hiss, soft words in an alien language, and then a single puff of white was blown out from between two strands of amber beads. A feather of goose down drifted lazily to earth.

"Ho, there!" cried one of the infantrymen. "They come!"

The Quman charged in good order toward the attacking Ungrians, closing the gap.

The mad Ungrians suddenly wheeled around and shot so many arrows into the Quman ranks that the whistle of arrow flight hummed in tandem with the whirring wings. The eastern sky darkened with rain as the Ungrians fled back toward the Wendish line all in disorder, some lagging, some way out in front. The entire center around Bayan swayed, shifted, and began to disintegrate. Bayan cried out something unintelligible from this distance as the Wendish line, too, fell back, retreating toward the infantry square. Only Sapientia tried to pull her cohort forward, shouting to her men, trying to rally them.

Again, Bayan intervened ruthlessly by placing his spear between her and her sword, and suddenly the entire center collapsed and all of them fled back in a complete rout.

Beside Hanna, Breschius grunted.

Hanna stared in horror at the debacle. She couldn't speak. On the plain behind the Quman army, rain pounded the ground to mud, and yet where she stood, where Bayan's soldiers fled in disorder, the sun still shone and it was dry. The plain ran with movement like ants whose nest has been trampled. An Ungrian soldier, lagging behind, went down with an arrow in his back, and his body vanished beneath a score of hooves and whistling, winged riders.

At that moment, she knew she was going to die. The knowledge burst within her like a flower opening, a transforming beauty imbued with the fleeting perfume of mortality and the revelation of God's eternal presence.

The strong Quman line began to dissolve as some of the young warriors couldn't contain their impatience and broke forward. As they split away from the rest, she saw them clearly for the first time: not winged creatures at all but only men wearing wings strapped to their back in imitation of birds. Even the flat, metal faces were only part of their helmets.

And then, of course, the Ungrian flank that had ridden away into the hills thundered in to hit the Quman flank, which was now all strung out in pursuit of the retreating banners. A shrill hooting cry rang out along the retreating Ungrian line and as tautly as if they were all pulled by the same string, they wheeled around again and in almost perfect formation charged back at the Quman center.

"Haillilili!" cried Hanna exultantly, in echo of her mistress. She watched as Sapientia's banner followed and then caught up to Bayan's, as together prince and princess plunged into the fighting. Caught between two hammers, the Quman didn't have a chance. Those who finally broke and tried to flee got caught in the soggy ground farther east along the river plain.

Bayan withdrew from the melee back to his mother's wagon and, from that vantage, he surveyed the scene with a frown, not troubled, merely measuring. He did not seem to notice Hanna, but he called Brother Breschius to attend him. At intervals one or two of his men would ride up and speak to him, or hand him a scrap of cloth, or a knife, or a broken feather, or, once, a trampled face mask broken off from a helmet. Each item he examined with care and then he would resume watching as the Wendish and Ungrian armies set upon their enemy.

They killed until it was too dark to see.

At last, lanterns were brought from camp. Sapientia emerged from the slaughter with her face bright with excitement and her sword dripping blood. A lantern hung from her banner pole, lighting the banner that now rippled in a wind blowing from the west.

"Haililili!" she crowed, saluting her husband. "A victory! We have brought them to battle and defeated them soundly!"

Bayan lifted his own sword in answer. It, too, was stained with drying blood. "I have killed my man!" he cried. "Now, I bed my woman!"

Sapientia laughed ecstatically. She had a kind of thrumming energy about her, like the charge in the air just after lightning strikes. Indeed, as the entire army gathered around the lantern-lit rise, Hanna felt the tension rising within them, more danger-ous, perhaps, than that which had come before the battle.

With banners flying ahead and torches surrounding them, Bayan and Sapientia moved down through the army and back toward camp. Hanna made to follow them, but Breschius stopped her.

"Touch the wagon," he said sternly. "Do so!"

Hesitantly, she touched the corner of the wagon. It felt like plain wood to her, nothing magicked about it. A moment later, it jolted forward, following Bayan, and she obediently followed in its wake with Breschius beside her. The army rode in for-mation alongside, and she felt now that many of the men in the Ungrian army watched her, stared at her, ogled her. The Wendish soldiers no doubt did so as well, but to them she was a King's Eagle. They knew her oaths, and they understood that she had the king's protection.

"You are safe beside the wagon," said Breschius. "When we return to camp, you must stay close to me."

"What do you think might happen?"

He shrugged.

But her mother hadn't raised a fool. Her heart had stopped pounding so hard, and she could think more clearly. "That wasn't really a battle," she said finally. "It was more like slaughtering pigs there at the end."

"That wasn't an army. I have seen a Quman army and it is a fearsome sight, my child. That was a raiding party. Those were young, restless men sent out in advance of a real army to gather glory to themselves, or act as a warning flag to those behind them if they do not return. You saw how they fought. They were foolish enough that they couldn't see before their noses a trick as old as these hills. I think it likely they had no older, wiser head who could prevail when they got the killing fever in them."

"The way Prince Bayan intervened to stop Princess Sapientia from getting herself killed."

He glanced at her, but she couldn't read his expression in the dim light. A lit lantern had been hung from each corner of the wagon, and these lanterns swayed seductively as their party splashed back over the river and climbed the opposite shore. Oddly, the river ran more shallow now; Hanna's boots barely brushed the water on this crossing. Ahead, in the torchlit camp, she could already hear singing, cursing, and half-wild laughter. Around her, men drank heavily from the leather pouches tied to their saddles, some kind of potent brew. Its fermented scent permeated the air as they cried out and howled to each other, sang snatches of song, or danced in lines to the twanging accompaniment of odd-looking lutes. They were overexcited, flushed with easy killing, and ready to get into trouble.

"My grandmother once told me that to kill is only half the act," she said finally.

"A wise woman, your grandmother," replied Breschius. "What did she say is the other half of the act?"

She smiled nervously under the cover of night. "Ah, well. My grandmother still worshiped the old gods. She said that if you take blood, you owe blood, but that most people forget the old law when they kill in war or in anger. But then that blood still stains their hands and curdles in their hearts."

"Indeed. When you sunder spirit from body, there is energy left over. If it is not contained by means of prayer or forgiveness or even an act of creation or a gift of commencement, then the Enemy may creep into the heart of the one who did the killing. That is why many terrible acts accompany war, and why those who have partaken in battle should always be cleansed by prayer afterward."

"Will you lead a prayer here, tonight?"

"For those who choose to attend. But, alas, my master and most of the others still live in their bodies in the old ways, even while with their tongues they praise God in Unity. Prince Bayan will consumate his marriage and in this way cleanse himself, although the church does not approve of such ancient methods. But do not stray far from Princess Sapientia's tent tonight. Her presence in camp may not be enough to protect you from any insult offered your person by one of these young men who are drunk on both wine and blood."

"I will be cautious," she promised. They came then to the royal pavilion. Bayan and Sapientia still stood outside, toasting their followers, but it quickly became apparent that Bayan had only waited for his mother. Her wagon rolled to a stop about twenty paces from the pavilion, and at once he deserted his guests to go to the wagon. He waited, head bowed, as four steps were unrolled from the tiny door. The three old, wrinkled handmaidens who attended the Kerayit princess clambered down the steps, carrying with them the usual trays and leavings of food and a covered chamberpot. Then an astoundingly beautiful young woman emerged through the bead curtain, which shimmered and danced behind her as she descended the steps. She had creamy skin a shade darker than Liath's, sensuous lips, broad cheekbones, bold eyes, and hair like black silk. Her gown might have been spun of sunlight. She wore laced at her waist at least a dozen gold chains, and a profusion of gold necklaces draped from her neck. A gold ring pierced one nostril, and she wore three gold earrings in each ear, shaped as dangling bones. Every finger bore a ring, each one studded with precious gems.

"Who is that?" Hanna whispered, amazed. In the days since the wedding feast, she had never seen nor even suspected the existence of this woman. She had only ever seen the three old handmaidens come and go from the wagon.

"I do not know her name," said Breschius softly. "She, too, is a princess of the first degree among the Kerayit peoples. She is the apprentice to the old woman. She hasn't found her luck yet, which is why she can still appear before people who are not her blood kin."

Prince Bayan climbed the stairs and ducked into the wagon. Sapientia tried to follow him, but the young Kerayit woman set an arm across the threshold. For an instant, Sapientia began to protest, but the other woman simply stared her down, not threatening, just flatly negating, and at last Sapientia made a show of deciding to step back to the pavilion to wait. The Kerayit princess watched her go under heavy-lidded eyes, like a modest woman watching her beloved.

Ai, Lady. There was something about her . . . something familiar in the way Liath had always seemed familiar to Hanna, some kind of inchoate power she could not name but which Liath had held like a captive eagle inside her, waiting only to be freed—

Breschius hissed as the Kerayit woman swept her gaze over the assembly. He began to tremble. Hanna could feel his apprehension, he who had stood straight at the battle without a trace of fear. Every soul there, even to the drunkest, rowdiest young soldier, quieted in deference to her measuring eye; she possessed the imperious indifference of the sun, which never questions its own brilliance because it simply is.

In the silence, Hanna thought for an instant that she could hear the murmuring of Bayan's voice and, in reply, the cricket-like whisper of another person. Then she met the gaze of the young princess, and the woman's beautiful almond eyes widened in surprise as she stared at Hanna. Fair hair, pale eyes; Hanna knew how different she looked out here on the frontier. Few of the Wendish soldiers were as startlingly light as she was and, anyway, they were even more dust-covered from battle.

Prince Bayan shook the beaded curtain aside and clumped down the stairs, laughing. "Now! To the bed!" he cried, and everyone cheered, and when next Hanna could look past the people who suddenly swirled around her, the young Kerayit woman had vanished. The steps into the wagon had been drawn up.

"Eagle! Hanna!"

She had to go. She attended Sapientia to her bed, waited with the others until the covers were drawn back. As Eagle, she had to witness that husband and wife were put properly to bed together. Then, with the others, she discreetly withdrew.

She had a blanket, and it seemed more prudent to her not to step away from the awning that night. It was hard to sleep because it was so noisy, laughter and grunting and pleased exclamations from the tent within, singing, drumming, shouting, and, once, a scream of terror from the camp without. Breschius also had a blanket, and he snored amiably beside her, all rolled up *and* comfortable on the old carpet laid out beneath the awning. A few other servants slept peaceably as well over to one side.

She was cold and restless. She was waiting, but she didn't know for what. At last, she dozed off.

And she had the strangest dream.

All the clouds have blown eastward to harass the Quman, to bleed away the trail left by their young brothers who rode out to find the enemy but never returned. The stars stand so brilliantly in the heavens that they shine each one like a blazing spark of light, the souls of fiery daimones who exist far beyond the homely world of humankind. Stars have never shone as brightly as these, as if they have somehow bowed the great dome of the heavens inward by the force of their will, because they are seeking something lost to them, fallen far far below onto the hard cold earth.

At night, the wagon of the Kerayit shaman blazes with reflected light from the stars, and only now does the magic shimmer in its walls: marks and sigils, spirals and cones, an elaborate tree whose roots reach far below the earth and whose branches seem to grow out of the roof itself and reach toward the sky. A glimmering pole more light than substance thrusts heavenward from the smoke hole at the center of the wagon: seven notches have been carved into its branchless trunk, and the top of the pole seems to meld with the North Star around which the heavens revolve.

Beads clack and rustle as the steps unroll from the wagon's bed. The young princess steps out, and she beckons to Hanna. Come to me.

Hanna sheds her blanket and goes. The lintel of the tiny door brushes her head as she ducks inside. But inside is not as outside. The wagon is tiny, and yet inside she seems to be in a pavilion fully as large as that in which Bayan and Sapientia now sleep. The walls ripple as if stroked by wind; there are two elaborate box beds, a low table, and beautifully embroidered pillows on which to sit. A green-and-gold bird stirs in its cage, eyeing her. She sits on a pillow, and one of the ancient handmaidens brings her a cup of hot liquid whose spicy scent stings her nostrils.

"Drink," speaks a cricket voice, and then Hanna sees Bayan's mother sitting veiled in the shadows, the suggestion of a face visible behind translucent silk. A tapestry hangs on the tent wall at her back: the image of a woman standing on earth and reaching toward the heavens where hangs a palace that magically glides in the aether: from the woman's navel stretches a cord which attaches to a tree in the courtyard of the floating palace: an eagle flies between, and two coiled dragons observe through slitted eyes. "What comes from earth, returns to earth," says the old woman as Hanna obediently drinks. "What have you brought me, sister's daughter? She is not my kin."

Gold flashes, and the young princess steps forward. "I have found it at last," she says. "My luck was born into this woman."

"Ah," says the old woman, the exclamation like the rasping of crickets. There is another noise from outside, a keening moan that sends shudders down Hanna's back, and Hanna thinks that probably they aren't in camp anymore, they have gone somewhere far away where dangerous creatures stalk the night grass because it is in the nature of dreams that one may travel quickly a long distance without moving.

"Ah," repeats the old woman. "She will come with us, then."

"No. She will not come with me yet. She must find the man who will become my pura, and then she will return to me, with him."

The young princess turns to look at Hanna, and Hanna thinks maybe she can see through the dark irises of those beautiful almond eyes all the way back to the land where the Kerayits live and roam, among grass so tall that a man on horseback can't see over it, where griffins stalk the unwary and dragons guard the borders of a vast and terrible desert strewn with grains of gold and silver. There waits a woman in that place, not a true woman but a creature who is woman from the waist up and from the waist below has the body and elegant strength of a mare. She is a shaman of great power and immense age, with her face painted in stripes of green and gold and an owl perched on her wrist. She draws her bow and looses an arrow spun of starlight. Its path arcs impossibly through the North Star, and with a high chime it pierces the heart of the young princess, who gasps and falls to her knees, a hand clasped to her breast.

Hanna leaps up at once to aid her, but as soon as she touches the young woman, she feels the sting of the arrow in her own breast, as though a wasp has been trapped inside her. It hurts.

She woke up suddenly as a hand touched her, brushing her breast. She sat up fast, and hit heads with the man who bent over her. Then her eyes adjusted to the graying light that presages dawn.

"Your Highness!" she exclaimed, scooting backward as quickly as she could.

Prince Bayan smiled charmingly as he rubbed his forehead. He wore his rumpled trousers, but nothing else, revealing much of his strong, attractive body. She smelled wine on his breath. "Pretty snow maiden," he said winningly, without threat.

"Bayan!" Sapientia appeared at the entrance to the pavilion, clad only in a shift.

"She is awake!" cried Bayan enthusiastically. He staggered back inside and, after an annoyed glance at Hanna, Sapientia followed him.

Several of the servingwomen had woken and now hastened in to assist their mistress. They came out moments later, giggling, carrying the chamber pot, and Hanna felt it prudent to go with them down to the river. They washed among the rocks, finding safety in numbers, but in any case with the morning the carousing had died down, and about half of the soldiers seemed to be sleeping it off in a stupor while the other half had returned to the battlefield. When they returned to the tent, Brother Breschius asked Hanna to accompany him, and she did so reluctantly, only because she liked the old priest. In the hard glare of morning, the battleground was an ugly sight: vultures and scavengers had to be driven away, and the bodies were beginning to smell. More and more soldiers arrived to loot the enemy, but Hanna couldn't bear to touch them even when she saw a good iron knife stuck in the belt of one dead man. He, like the others, wore slung at his belt one of those ghastly tiny human heads.

A buried detail was organized. Wendish soldiers dug mass graves, stripped the bodies, and rolled them in as Brother Breschius blessed each dead soul. But what the Ungrians did to their own honored dead was hardly less awful than the disregard with which they looted the enemy. Every corpse of their own kin was mutilated before being buried: a finger cut off, a tooth pried out of the jaw, and a hank of hair hacked off. These treasures were carefully wrapped up and given to certain soldiers, who carried them away together with the salvaged armor and weapons.

"Why do they do that?" Hanna asked finally as she and Breschius returned to camp. "Aren't they given a proper burial and laid to rest as is fitting?"

"Oh, yes, as you saw. But they also believe that some portion of the spirit resides after death in the body, and each year at midwinter they burn the remains of their relatives in a bonfire. They believe that in this way the spirits of all those who died in the previous year are sealed away into the otherworld so that they can't come back and cause mischief in this world."

"But don't they believe that their souls ascend to the Chamber of Light? How can they worship God if they don't believe *that*?"

Breschius laughed kindly. "God are tolerant, my child. So should we be. This is all Their creation. We are sent to this earth to learn about our own hearts, not to judge those of others."

"You aren't like most of the fraters I've ever met." Then she flushed, thinking of Hugh. Beautiful Hugh.

Breschius chuckled, and she had a sudden feeling that he could read her heart well enough but was too humble a soul to judge her for what she knew was a foolish and sinful yearning. "Because we are none of us the same, we must each learn something different in our time on this world."

"I had such a strange dream," she said, to change the subject. "I dreamed I went inside the wagon of Prince Bayan's mother, and that the young princess said that her luck had been born into my body."

He stopped dead and his face blanched.

She felt suddenly as if a butterfly fluttered in her throat, captive, never to be free again.

"But it was only a dream. It had to be a dream. I could understand what they were saying."

"Do not discount their power," he said hoarsely. "Do not speak of it again, ever. They will know."

"How can they know? What if I'm a thousand leagues away from them?" He shook his head stubbornly. Such a change had come over him, he had become so tense and troubled, that she, too, felt frightened. "Will you answer one question, then? What is a *pura*?"

He flushed. Sweat broke on his neck and forehead although it wasn't warm. The camp swarmed with movement in front of them; behind, the river murmured over smooth rocks in the shallows and on the far bank a line of soldiers reached the ford and set out across.

"A pura," he said in a hoarse voice, "is a word in the Kerayit tongue for a horse."

"Then why would the Kerayit princess say in my dream that I would find the man who would become her pura?"

He shut his eyes as though to shut out—or to see more

clearly—some dim and ancient memory. "A horse can be ridden. It can carry burdens. If it is male, it can be bred to mares. Its blood, drunk hot from a vein, can strengthen you. A fine, strong, elegant horse can be a source of pride and amusement to his owner. A pura means also a young and handsome man who serves any young Kerayit princess who has been called to become a shaman. The shaman women of the Kerayit tribe live in utter seclusion. Once they have touched their luck, they may never be seen in front of any person who is not their own kin, or who is not a slave, whom they do not count as people. Shamans do not marry, as do their sisters. Prince Bayan's mother did so only because—well, I have spoken of that before. You do not take your luck as your pura. A pura is not a real person, but only a slave."

"Then why do these women take a pura at all?"

He had recovered enough to look at her with amusement lighting his eyes. "You have sworn oaths as an Eagle, my child. But do you never look at young men with desire stirring in your heart? Even Prince Bayan's mother was young once. A Kerayit woman chosen by their gods to become shaman is young, and her path is a difficult one. Not all survive it. Who would not want a horse on such a long road?"

His flush had subsided, and for the first time she really looked at him as a woman looks at a man. The ghost of his younger self still lived in his lineaments. Once he had been a young and handsome man, a bold frater walking east to convert the heathens. It was easy to imagine a Kerayit princess taking a fancy to such an exotic young man.

"And are puras set free," she asked, "once their mistress no longer needs them?"

"Nay," he said softly. "No shaman willingly gives up her pura."

Had she misunderstood? "I beg your pardon, Brother. I thought by your words and expression that perhaps you had once been—" Now she was too embarrassed to go on. "I did not mean to wrong you. I can see you serve God faithfully."

"You have not wronged me, Daughter." He touched her fleetingly on the elbow. "She did not willingly give me up. She died. I was blamed for it because I was teaching her the magic of writing. It was her aunt, a queen of her people, who cut off my hand. Later, Prince Bayan came to hear of my captivity because that queen was his wife's aunt's cousin, and he asked for me as a present. That is how I came into his service. God forgave me for my disobedience, for the truth is I loved Sorgatani freely and would have remained in her service for the rest of my life. But it was not to be." He smiled wryly, without anger. "So now I serve God's agent, who is Prince Bayan, whatever his other faults. Do not think ill of him, child. He has a good heart."

Hanna laughed, at first, because she hadn't been scared or felt at all in danger in the predawn chill when Bayan had accosted her. But then she sobered. Liath had suffered terribly, pursued by Hugh. Hanna did not relish spending her nights fending off the attentions of a prince far more powerful than she would ever be, and especially not when she remained so very far from the king who was her only protection. Prince Bayan wouldn't be blamed for the seduction of an Eagle; *she* would be, and lose her position in the bargain. And she wanted to remain an Eagle. Maybe that, more than anything, made it hard for her to understand Liath's choice. How could Liath walk away from the life offered those who swore the Eagle's oath to their regnant? Hanna could no longer imagine being anything other than an Eagle. It was as if she had been one person before Wolfhere arrived in Heart's Rest that fateful date and another person after, as if she had simply been waiting her whole life up until then for him to offer her an Eagle's badge and cloak.

"I'm an Eagle," she said out loud. "And I want to remain one. Advise me, Brother. Will it happen again?"

He could only frown. "I don't know."

Bayan and Sapientia emerged just before midday looking well satisfied. Brother Breschius led a prayer service for the living and a mass for the dead. A war council was called, and the disposition of forces discussed, what signs seen where of activity beyond the border, where the Quman had last attacked, and how big a force might be lurking, waiting for opportunity. The sentries reported that they had killed half a dozen lurking Quman warriors in the night. Lady Udalfreda confided that at least ten hamlets out beyond her town of Festberg had been burned and refugees fled to the safety of her walls. Other Wendish lords and captains gave similar reports, and the Ungrians had other news as well, tribes driven southwest by drought or fighting, raids along the border with the Arethousan Empire, certain portents seen in the midwinter sacrifice that presaged disaster.

Sapientia called Hanna forward. "There has been much rumor of a large force of Quman moving in these marchlands, and now we have confirmation that it is so. But we do not have the forces to withstand an invasion, should it come. You, my faithful Eagle, must return to my father, King Henry, and report our situation. I beg him to send troops to strengthen the frontier, or else it is likely we will be overwhelmed."

Prince Bayan watched Sapientia proudly, as any praeceptor regards with pride his pupil as she makes her first steps by herself. But he also glanced now and again at Hanna, and once he winked.

"Eagle, I would speak in your ears a private message." Hanna had to lean forward to hear the princess, who dropped her voice to a murmur. "I like you, Hanna. You have served me faithfully and well. But I remember what happened with that witch who seduced Father Hugh. You knew her, and maybe she made some of her glamour rub off on you, even though I'm sure you would never try such witcheries yourself. You must go. When you return, my husband will have forgotten all about this morning."

Yet Hanna wasn't so sure.

The truth was, she wasn't sorry to be going. Yes, he was an attractive man, charming and good-hearted. No doubt he was a pleasant companion in bed. But she would never forget the cold, casual way in which he had tortured that Quman prisoner and then, afterward, casually mentioned that he'd known all along that the man wouldn't tell them anything. What was the point, then, except that he hated the Quman? He was getting his revenge for the death of his son, one man at a time.

At dawn the next day she took her leave of the princess and said farewell to Brother Breschius, who blessed her and said a prayer for a good journey on her behalf. She hesitated beside the Kerayit wagon, but she had seen no sign of the shaman and her young apprentice since the night of the battle. Even now, the door remained closed. Did the bead curtains sway, parting slightly so someone inside could look out? Maybe they did. She raised a hand in greeting, and farewell, just in case.

Then she rode west, with the rising sun at her back. It was a good day to be riding, crisp, clear, and pleasantly chill. As she

left the camp behind, she began to sing, and her escort joined
in with her in good harmony.

> *"I will lift up my eyes to see the hills,*
> *for Their help shall come to me from that place.*
> *Help comes from the Lord and the Lady*
> *They who made Heaven and Earth.*
> *The Lord shall preserve us from all evil.*
> *The Lady shall preserve our souls."*

But she couldn't help thinking of the Kerayit princess. Had
it been a dream?

The wasp sting burned in her heart.

5

IN the evening, Alain left the chapel in the pause between Vespers and Compline to walk through the silence until he reached
the great hall. Sorrow and Rage padded after him. At the other
end of the hall, two servants swept rushes out the door. They
jabbed their brooms at the ground outside, shaking off straw,
and because they had their backs to the hall they did not see
him but spoke together in low voices as they shut the doors behind them on the bitter gloom of an autumn twilight.

Some light was left him, as little as the hope left him. The
hall had been set in order, tables and benches lined up neatly,
but nevertheless he banged his shins on a bench and bruised his
hip on the corner of a table before he stumbled on the first step
of the small dais behind the high table. He hit his knee on the
second step and cursed under his breath. Sorrow whined. He
groped, found one leg of the count's chair, and hauled himself
up, then just stood there feeling the solid square corners under
his hands, the scrollwork along the back, the arms carved like
the massive smooth backs of hounds, each ending in a snarling
face.

Not even rats stirred in the hall. He heard the whisper of

Compline, muted by distance, stone walls, and the ripening comprehension of the Lavas clerics.

This morning, for the first time, Lavastine had not been able to be sat up in his bed. His body was now too heavy to move. Prayers and physic, all to no avail.

For the first time, Alain sat in the count's chair.

The hall lay shrouded by twilight, but it was easier to test this seat in private, without the stares and bows, the expectations and petitions, that would greet him later when everyone assembled to see him take the seat of power. This way he could get used to it slowly—if he could ever get used to it.

He started up guiltily out of the chair as a procession entered the hall: Tallia with several attendants. They lit her by torchlight so she could cross to his side unmolested by benches and table corners.

"You didn't stay for Compline." She had certain secretive habits left over from her childhood, and now, touching the count's chair, she leaned closer to him in the manner of a thief planning mischief with an accomplice. "I prayed for this . . . for God to strike him dead as an unbeliever. You see, don't you, that it is best this way? God answered my prayers in this way because She wishes me to build a chapel in Her honor." She faltered, pressed a hand over his as if to seal his approval.

Alain could only stare. Behind, a servingman hurried into the hall.

"My lord Alain!" The servant was weeping. "He's very bad, my lord. You must come quickly."

Alain left Tallia to the ministrations of her fluttering attendants. He took the steps two at a time. A servant held the door open as he strode into the chamber where Lavastine lay in his curtained bed as still as stone. Fear kept watch at his bedside.

Alain knelt at his side and took hold of one of the count's hands: it had the grain of pale granite. It stirred only because Alain lifted it. Lavastine's eyes moved; his lips parted. That he still breathed Alain knew because he still lived: His chest gave no telltale rise and fall, God's breath lifting and descending to feed his soul.

A musky odor permeated the room, fleeting, gone. He looked up to see Sorrow, Rage, and Fear cluster around Terror, who lay at the foot of Lavastine's bed.

Lavastine murmured words. His voice was almost inaudible,

a thin wheeze, but Alain had spent many hours beside him these past fifteen days, and he could still understand his few, labored words. *"Most faithful."*

It struck Alain as sharply as any blow had ever shuddered his shield in battle: Terror was dead, had died in the last hour, passed beyond mortal existence. That was why the others sniffed at him, seeking the smell of their father-cousin and not finding it. His spirit had fled. Ai, God! Lavastine's would soon follow.

He pressed a hand to the count's throat, but there was no warmth, no pulse.

"Alain." By some astounding force of will he still lived, although he was by now completely paralyzed. *"Heir."*

"Father. I'm here." It tore his heart in two to watch Lavastine's suffering, although in truth it wasn't clear he was in any pain. His brow remained as unlined as ever, even as it took on that grainy, stonelike cast, as if he were transmuting into an effigy carved from rock.

But Lavastine was nothing if not stubborn, and determined. Had he had more expression left him, he would have frowned. One eyebrow twitched. His lips quirked ever so slightly. *"Must. Have. Heir."*

From the chapel in the room below, the clerics began to sing a hymn from the Holy Verses: "A remnant restored in an age of peace."

> *"On that day, say God, We will destroy all your horses among you and break apart all your chariots. We will raze the cities of your land and tear down your fortresses. We will ruin all your sorcerers, and no more augeres shall walk among you to part the veil that allows them to see into the future. We will throw down all the works made by your own hands. In anger and fury will We take vengeance on all nations who disobey Us."*

Alain was weeping, He could not bear to let Lavastine go in hopelessness. "She's pregnant," he whispered, too softly for anyone else to hear. Hearing himself speak, he said it again more boldly. "Tallia is pregnant."

Was that a stirring in Lavastine's face, the breath of an expression across skin made marble by poison? Was that a swallow at his throat, a spark of joy in his eye? A smile on his lips?

Surely God would forgive Alain the lie. He only meant it to make his father happy, in his last hour.

"We're to have a child, Father," he continued. It got easier as each word slipped out. "There will be an heir, just as you decreed."

"Children of Saïs, you shall shepherd your foes with the sword, the sacred pillars shall be raised from their ruins, and all who hate you shall be destroyed."

A breath escaped Lavastine, a last shaping of words. *"Done. Well. My. Son."* As Alain watched, his eyes began to glaze over, a stippling, granules speckling the white of his eye as his iris turned to sapphire. After the long struggle, it was all going so quickly now, but perhaps his soul had been tethered to faithful Terror, and with Terror gone, he sped, too, on the final journey. Perhaps he had only waited for news of this.

Silence reigned.

Alain wept bitterly. His tears soaked the coverlet and ran like rain off stone down Lavastine's arm. The hounds growled softly but did not interfere as several servingmen came forward, and the steward pressed a finger against the count's cold lips.

"God have mercy," the steward said softly. "He is gone."

Alain leaped up and grabbed a candle, held it before Lavastine's lips. The flame stirred, the merest flicker.

"He still lives!" he cried. A servant took the candle from him gently. He flung himself down beside the bed, still weeping, still gripping the cold hand, and prayed with all his heart in it and his own hands wet with tears. "I pray You, God. Spare my father's life. Heal him, and I will serve You."

"My lord Alain. Come away. He is beyond us now. He has gone to our Lord and Lady."

"The flame moved. He still breathes."

"That was your own breath, my lord. He is gone."

He shook off the hand impatiently, and Sorrow growled, echoing his mood. The servants moved back as he bent to pray. Surely God had power to heal any poison, any injury. This was only a trifle, compared to Their power. "I will do as Tallia wishes, or as You wish. I will swear my life to the church, forever, gladly, if only You heal my father, Lady. If only You give my father back his strength and his life, Lord. I will sire many strong chil-

dren if that is Your will, or remain celibate, if You so choose,
but please, I beg you, God, heal him. Don't let your loyal servant die. Give me a sign."

The tapestry on the wall rippled lightly as though a wind had
stirred it, except the shutters were closed up against wintertide.
It shuddered again as if a hand shook it and, shaking, shook
him. His vision had gone all tight until he could only see the
scene depicted in the tapestry: *A prince rides with his retinue
through a dark forest. A shield hangs from the prince's saddle:
a red rose against a sable background.*

*And there: hidden in the shadows of the tapestry. Why hadn't
he seen them before? Black hounds trailed alongside, a trio of
them, dark and handsome. He could hear their footsteps padding
on the earth, could hear the creak of harness and the steady
clop of horses' hooves. Wind made the branches dance, and because it had just rained, they were showered with drops from
the leaves like the tears of watery daimones. He rode among the
servants, innocent, invisible because he was one among many.
He felt protected by the darkness and the shadows, by the wall
of forest that towered on either side of the road. It made him
bold, and he pressed his horse forward. As he came up beside
the prince, he saw with a shock that it was no prince at all but
a woman dressed as a man, as if in disguise. She was older than
he had first guessed, with a cold, stubborn expression. The brooch
that pinned her cloak shut was a fine jeweled replica of the red
rose painted on the shield hanging at her thigh. What noble
house bore the red rose as its sigil? She turned, unsurprised to
see him ride up beside her, and said: "How fares the child?"*

*But there is torchlight coming up beside him, blinding him
for a moment, and he no longer rides along the forest path but
instead rocks in the breeze that is not a breeze but rather the
timber of a ship beneath his feet, swaying gently on the water.
Headland blots out the stars along the eastern horizon. Along
the dark shore torches bob, massing, darting forward. He hears
the schiiing of metal ringing against metal as a skirmish spreads
up the twilit vale toward the great house built two generations
ago by the famous chieftain Bloodyax of the Namms tribe.*

Another war leader has arrived at Namms Dale before him.

*A small boat ties up alongside his ship, and a scout—Ninth
Son of the Twelfth Litter—scrambles on board to give his re-*

port. "It is Moerin's tribe, nineteen ships, come to settle an old feud against the Nammsfolk."

"Moerin's chieftain is old Bittertongue, is he not?" asks Stronghand, still staring at the unfolding battle made bright by the last gleam of the sun on trusting spears and the flowering of torches all along the path of the fighting.

"Nay, old Bittertongue died in a raid last spring. There is a new chief who has taken advisers from the island known to the Soft Ones as Alba. He has named himself Nokvi in the style of the humanfolk."

"Look!" Tenth Son of the Fifth Litter stands at Stronghand's side, one of his standard bearers by reason of his sharp eyes and unusual strength. He raises an arm and points up into the darkening vale. "Where the great house stands. Look there."

Flame flowers into life as bold as fire can be when let loose. Stronghand sets a foot up on the lip of the uppermost plank and leans out, staring into the twilight as the great house goes up in a towering blaze of fire. Torches ring the burning hall. He smells oil, quick to flame. "Listen!" says Stronghand, and all the men within sound of his voice quiet and listen.

Nokvi, chieftain of the Moerin tribe, has trapped Namms' war leader and his fighting men inside the hall, coated the hall with oil, and set it alight, burning them alive. Not even the tough hides of the RockChildren can withstand such an inferno.

"Do we attack?" asks Tenth Son.

"With eight ships?" Stronghand cuts down sharply with his left hand, to signify "no." "I came to make an alliance with the Nammsfolk, not to fight them. We must learn more of this 'Nokvi' before we fight him. Winter is coming on, and soon no ships will sail. But there are other ways to gather our forces even against a leader who has allied with the humans of Alba."

He hates to turn away without that alliance he came for. It smacks of cowardice. But he is not a fool. He is not blinded by the lust for glory. He seeks something harder, and colder, and longer lasting than the brief if brilliant flare of battle glory.

He lifts the warhorn to his lips and blows the retreat.

The sound brought Alain sharply back to himself, a mewling that seemed remotely familiar and yet utterly strange.

"My lord count!"

Alain bolted up to lean over Lavastine, but the count might

as well have been a stone statue. He didn't move. He didn't breathe.

He was dead.

A weight nudged against Alain's leg and abruptly he remembered the chamber he stood in, and he realized that Sorrow, Rage, and Fear had collapsed to the ground and lay beside Lavastine's deathbed like helpless pups, whimpering. It took him a moment longer to register the waiting attendants, who all stared nervously at the hounds, awaiting their reaction. The steward who had just spoken had not been addressing Lavastine.

"My lord count. Come away. There's nothing you can do."

The words struck like the tolling of a bell. But it *was* the bell, which had begun to ring at the old church, tolling the dead soul up through the seven spheres to the Chamber of Light. He stood, although his legs did not really feel like his own legs.

There was nothing he could do. He rested a hand on Lavastine's cold forehead, then bent to kiss it. He might as well have been kissing stone. He touched the eyes, to close the eyelids as was customary. But he could not close them. They were frozen that way; hardened open, perhaps. Ever vigilant, even in the grave.

There was truly nothing more he could do here. The servants parted before him, a whisper of movement away as the hounds heaved themselves up and fell in behind him, who was now their master. But they did not growl or even seem to notice the servants around them. They walked at his heels as though they were sleepwalking, as meek as lambs.

He walked silent, down the tower steps and along the dark corridor to the great hall. Where a door opened to the courtyard, a breath of crisp air stung his face, and the taste of it brought him a vivid and painful memory of autumn afternoons toiling outside Aunt Bel's longhouse with his foster father, Henri, making rope or repairing sailcloth. But that life had fallen behind him. God had marked him out for greater things. He walked past the open door and into the dense and anticipatory silence of the great hall.

There he sat in the carven chair reserved for the count of Lavas. Sorrow, Rage, and Fear sat at his feet.

After a while, Tallia ventured into the hall with her attendants. With lips drawn white and hands shaking, she took her seat beside him.

Slowly, from hall and hut and stable, from village and kitchen, from field and courtyard, servingfolk, soldiers, farmers, and attendants gathered in the hall in ranks alongside the tables. Torchlight made their expressions fitful, shadowed now by hesitancy, lit now by respect, made constant by a certain wariness toward the hounds and, perhaps, toward him. At last the bell finished tolling.

"My lord count," said their spokeswoman, chatelaine of this holding, Mistress Dhuoda.

For an instant he did not reply, waiting for another to answer. But that voice never came.

"Come forward," said the count of Lavas, "and I will honor your oaths, and make my own to you in turn."

IX
A NEST OF MATHEMATICI

1

THEOPHANU made cunning use of the information they had gained from Wolfhere: She used the lay of the hills around Vennaci to conceal the numbers of her troops and in this way pretended to lay in a countersiege with a large force that, so it appeared, surrounded the force mustered by John Ironhead.

He quickly called for a parley. Theophanu went in state with twenty attendants; Rosvita served as interpreter, since the language spoken in Aosta was intelligible to any person who understood Dariyan.

Ironhead was blunt and impatient. He no sooner had his servants bring round a chair and wine than he started in. "King Henry wants to marry Queen Adelheid himself."

Theophanu eyed him over her wine, which she sipped at her leisure under the shelter of a fine canopy woven of scarlet cloth. "God be with you, Lord John," she replied finally. "The weather is very fine here in the autumn in Aosta, is it not?"

Once out of the mountains, the rain had stopped and the skies were cleared. The light was so bright that at midday every person and thing, the tents, the banners fixed to spears, the rank of guards, the distant line of tethered horses, seemed sharpened in outline.

"I see no point in pleasantries, Princess Theophanu. I have reinforcements coming. The lords of Aosta support me. They do not want a foreigner to rule over them."

"Yet you are not the only prince of Aosta who wishes to marry Adelheid. It is obvious, Lord John, that the man who marries Queen Adelheid can lay claim to the vacant kingship."

Ironhead had a face as blunt as his tongue, undistinguished except for the scar on his cheek, and his prominent Dariyan nose. The depth and brightness of his dark eyes saved him from being ugly; certainly he looked determined, and he stuck stubbornly to the topic that interested him most. "Henry wants to marry Adelheid himself," he repeated.

Theophanu replied before Rosvita translated, since she could understand somewhat of his words. "No, indeed, that is not the intent of King Henry."

"Then why are you here?"

"Merely to pay my respects to Queen Adelheid. If you will give me an escort through your lines, I will enter the city and leave you alone."

"Impossible. I cannot allow it."

"Then we are at an impasse, Lord John."

"So we are, Princess Theophanu." A servant refilled his cup as he waved forward a captain who had come up at the head of a group of soldiers chained together as prisoners. Most of the prisoners were short of stature, broad through the shoulders, and even darker in hair and face than the Aostans.

"These are the ones?" Ironhead asked of his captain.

"Yes, my lord, the very ones captured yesterday when they attacked out the eastern gate."

Ironhead looked them over contemptuously. His own soldiers, rough-looking men who wore a ragtag assemblage of tabards and armor that they had probably scrounged off many battle-fields, spat at the prisoners.

"Well, then, take care of them, but be sure it is within sight of the walls, as usual."

"What will be done with these prisoners, Lord John?" asked Theophanu. "Surely they have served their mistress faithfully. That is no crime, not in Wendar, at any rate."

He snorted and called for more wine. They had not, pointedly, been offered food, but it was possible that the siege weighed as heavily on John's supplies as it must on those besieged within the city's walls. "These are mercenaries from Arethousa, not faithful retainers. We all know what a bloody-minded, vicious people the Arethousans are, as well as untrustworthy." He smiled without taking the sting from the words. Did he know Theophanu's mother was an Arethousan? Was the bait meant for her? Theophanu merely regarded him with a cool stare. "There are a fair number of these Arethousan flies buzzing 'round Adelheid's honey, and I see no reason to encourage them to stay. Take them off!" he shouted to the captain. "Use your knives wisely. Don't cut too deep."

The soldiers in attendance all laughed heartily, not kindly.

"You're going to execute them?" Theophanu demanded, startled. "I will certainly pay the ransom price to free each man among them."

"And enter them into your army? I think not, Princess Theophanu. Everyone knows the Arethousan emperor desires eunuchs, so I have been sending him many more with my respects, and today he'll receive another twenty or more for his pleasure."

"This is barbaric!" muttered Theophanu.

"I advise that we retire, Your Highness," murmured Rosvita in return. "I fear we'll get no satisfaction here." .

"Then how can we reach Adelheid, or even let her know we are here?" whispered Theophanu. "Lord John has thrown up more obstacles than I thought possible."

As the prisoners were led away, there came a sudden commotion from the road that led to the north gate, which John's encampment faced. A young woman had entered the camp, but she staggered, shrieking, with her hair unbound and all in a tangle. When she saw the lord under the canopy, she wailed more loudly still and scratched at her cheeks until blood ran. An infant slept in a sling at her hip, and the blood dripping from her face stained its tiny legs like a sudden blooming of the cowpox.

"Bring that woman to me," cried John. Hustled forward with more haste then courtesy, still, she did not flinch when she was flung down to kneel before Ironhead. "What is the matter with you, woman? All this crying and wailing makes my ears ring."

"What kind of mighty warrior makes war on women who have no weapons? Some among our sex do truly take up arms, and to them I commend your violent ways, but the rest of us have heeded the words of Our Lady and we use only the tools given us by the Queen of Heaven. But now I see you have decided to make war upon those of us who have sworn to do our Lady's work on this earth."

He looked affronted. "I do not make war on any woman except those who have taken up arms like a man, like the Sazdakhs of old."

"Is it not a war you make upon us when you deprive us of what is ours by right? You took my cattle a month or more ago, and never once have I complained of that. But now you seek to take from me that which can never be regained once it is lost." She gestured toward the prisoners. Ironhead shrugged, as if to say he did not understand her. "You will castrate them, as is your habit, my lord, but by what right do you take from them that member which does not belong to them?"

"Well, then, to whom does it belong, if not to them?" he demanded as the soldiers around chuckled. More had gathered; a siege was boring business, and any distraction was welcome.

"Why, to their wives, of course!" she retorted indignantly. "What else keeps us warm at night? What gives us the children we so dearly desire?" She set a work-roughened hand on the sleeping infant. Drying blood stained her course fingernails. "Take what else you will from me, my lord, but not that which is most important to me!"

At this, the soldiers all began to laugh uproariously and even John guffawed. "I can't defend myself against such an argument," he cried. "Very well, then. You may have your husband back unharmed. But tell me, woman, I must have some means to discipline those who take up arms against me. If your husband fights me again, what may I remove?"

The young woman hesitated only a moment. "He has feet, hands, a nose, eyes. Take what you will of the things that belong to him, but I pray you, leave to me that which is mine."

This speech sent the soldiers into another great round of laughter. Theophanu, too, smiled slightly as the woman's husband was unchained from the rest of the wretches fated to go under the knife. "I hope her husband is worthy of such a clever wife," she said as woman, man, and baby were escorted away.

But Rosvita bent lower, to speak more softly. "I am thinking," she said slowly, "that if one woman can come out of the city, then another can get in."

*   *   *

"I am against it," said Brother Fortunatus. "What if you are caught?"

"I am a cleric," insisted Rosvita. "Lord John is unlikely to harm me. It he takes me prisoner, I will appeal to the skopos in Darre."

"Then let me go with you."

Rosvita indicated the pallet on which poor young Constantine lay moaning, clutching his belly. He had foolishly drunk from standing water and now had a flux. "You must safeguard the books, Brother," she said to Fortunatus, "and care for young Constantine. Even if he were well, he's still too young and inexperienced, and I couldn't trust him to watch over things as you can."

The arduous trip over the mountains had stripped Fortunatus of both bulk and humor. He frowned now. "Sister Amabilia could have talked you out of this."

"Nay, Brother. She would have insisted on coming with me."

That forced a laugh from him, but their leave-taking was somber.

The sun had not yet risen; mist muted the edges of camp and made the tents into hulking beasts hidden by cloud. From among her women Theophanu had chosen Leoba, who was tall, strong, and a trifle reckless, to accompany Rosvita. Too many sent together would attract notice; one deacon alone might attract mischief. With her face and figure concealed in a cleric's robe and hood, Leoba waited for her at the edge of camp together with the two guards who would escort them through the lines. The dawn mist robed them in secrecy as they passed through undergrowth, crossed a narrow stream, and then left the guards behind at the farthest sentry post on the lip of the flat plain. The hill on which the gates and towers of Vennaci stood shone in mist and the first glimmer of the sun. They walked across empty fields to one of the old paths on which laborers had once made their way back to the safety of the city walls at night.

The trail lay dusty and level as they walked along, following the path of an irrigation ditch half overgrown with weeds. Everywhere she saw the legacy of conflict: ripe barley unharvested, fallow fields that should have been sown with winter wheat instead grown waist-high with weeds, a distant herd of cattle trampling through a stand of oats. Adelheid's people could not come out; Ironhead either had sufficient supplies, or he chose to leave the fields to rot as a message to the people trapped within the walls.

The young noblewoman said nothing as they walked, kept her hood down over her face to disguise her Wendish features. The loose robe disguised her body but could not hide her height. Even here, alone, she kept silence: practiced it, Rosvita supposed, for the time when Rosvita's skill at dissembling would see them through the lines or find them exposed and taken prisoner.

John Ironhead might be merciful and take a ransom for them, or he might be stubborn. Rosvita knew better than to dwell on such thoughts. Yet she was glad enough of Leoba's silence and the careful way she concealed herself from view. As they walked, Rosvita rehearsed her speech, trying quietly on her tongue the slurs and lisps with which these northern Aostans disfigured the clean sounds of Dariyan.

Ironhead's main encampment lay to the west. Here along the northern wall where only a postern gate opened along the river, his guards had set up watch posts. They had been here long enough that some had built shacks, and there was a brisk business with prostitutes who now left those same shacks in twos and threes to slip back into town, hands clutched over coins or gripping scarves wrapped around bread and cheese. A few vendors had come from town, too, cloaked by night, and now here at dawn they packed up their wares, gorgeous silks, linens, silver spoons, such luxuries that, in the face of dwindling food supplies, might not seem so important when children cried with hunger.

"Here, Sisters! Where have you come from?" The guard who stopped them had greasy hair, and a thread of meat had caught in his yellowed teeth.

"Which kind of sisters?" cried another guard, snorting with laughter as he grabbed roughly at their hoods. He yanked back Rosvita's hood and they all exclaimed over her northern paleness; then, with a stick, he prodded back the hood that concealed Leoba.

Rosvita's heart curdled with fear. It was not Leoba at all. Yet surely she should have known what would happen when the princess acquiesced so graciously as Rosvita insisted that it would be too dangerous for Theophanu herself to attempt to slip through the lines. If Ironhead's men caught them, he would have a noble prisoner to ransom and a sharp blade to hold over her father's head. Obviously her words had fallen on deaf ears. Theophanu neither flinched nor showed any expression as the guards poked at her with their sticks. Clearly they had not been in Ironhead's camp yesterday: they did not recognize her.

The thought hit her at random, like the voice of the Enemy whispering of betrayal: no person seeing Sanglant for the first time could mistake him for anything but a king's son. But without her retinue, it was impossible to know how exalted Theophanu's status was.

"Mayhap we should turn these over to Lord John," said the greasy guard.

"We are good deacons of the church, as you can see," said Rosvita coldly, slurring and lisping her words as much as she could manage. The anger she did not need to feign, and if she spilled it out on them, then perhaps she would manage not to betray her anger at her lady for putting herself in such jeopardy. "We have come all this long walk from the archbiscop's palace at Raveni because we heard that many women have fallen into disrepute due to this siege, which disturbs God's peace. We mean to lead them back onto the path of righteousness."

"Is there much bread on the path of righteousness?" demanded the greasy guard, and this jest earned him a round of laughter from his companions.

"There is no bread sweeter than God's forgiveness," retorted Rosvita sternly. "Will you pray with us, Brothers?"

Bu they didn't want to pray; they were satiated, and bored, and saw no threat in two deacons crazy enough to want to enter a besieged city. But they were alert enough to argue.

"We've orders not to let anyone go in. You'll bring them news."

"Oh, hell, Aldericus, the whores take news in every day. You can't tell me that you don't squeal out bits of gossip before, during, and after. Half those whores are spies for the queen."

"Lady's tits, for all we know, one of them whores *is* the queen! That's a hot line of women, they say, going back to old Queen Cleïtia when she ruled Darre. They say she took no less than six husbands and made every new presbyter prove himself to her on her couch and the ones she liked best were forced to satisfy her again and again and again until she tired of them or a handsome new face come along. It's no wonder she warred with the skopos, who in those days was of a similar mind. That's all women think about!"

They all snickered and guffawed, but some watched her and Theophanu closely. Rosvita could not hide her scorn, but Theophanu had the Arethousan gift of showing no emotion; her expression remained guileless and haughty.

"There is much sickness in the town." Rosvita had brought silver with her, but she wondered now if a bribe would seem too suspicious. "Both my young Sister and I are healers, and God have spoken to us and told us to come minister as we can among the sick and the sinful. And we shall wait here, praying, in this camp and tell each of our sisters in sin that they must turn aside from the path of folly and uncleanliness, for every day and every week as long as you are here, my brothers, until we are allowed to go inside to help those who are in need."

As a threat, it worked well enough. None of the guards wanted holy sisters praying publicly and attracting attention to the illicit activity taking place under the shadow of the siege.

"Go on! Follow the whores! You'll get less pleasure from them than we did, I'd wager!"

With laughter and mocking calls at their backs, they crossed the no-man's-land, the empty stretch of ground that marked out a bow's shot from the walls, and came to the postern gate.

The city guards were thinner, and less cheerful, and didn't want to let them in in case they were spies sent by Ironhead. Rosvita had to bribe one with silver to get through the gate, but after he'd palmed the slender bars, he took her despite that to the guardhouse. The stone barracks built up against the wall stank of filth and excrement, and most of the soldiers lounging on the cots or on the floor were sick with colds or open, raw sores. But they did not look dispirited. The stone walls wept moisture; it stank of mold and unwashed sweat. Rosvita sneezed, and their escort murmured reflexively: "Health to you, Sister. May the Enemy's creatures all flee your body and leave you whole."

The captain had his own windowless room at the base of the guardhouse. There was no door, only a ragged cloth hung across the threshold. A rash covered one side of the captain's face, and his nose wept mucus. The soldier set the silver bribe down on the table before him while he sipped at a cup of wine and eyed them with the resignation of a man who has heard it all.

"I tolerate the whores and the peddlers because every scrap of bread they bring in gives us a brief reprieve on our stores of grain. And because they bring us news. But I have no patience for spies, even ones robed as clerics."

"And I have no patience with fools," said Theophanu, coming to life at last. She had remained silent for a long time. "I am Theophanu, daughter of King Henry of Wendar." As if she knew he might doubt her claim, she pulled her robe away from her neck to reveal her gold torque.

That was all it took.

The captain jumped to his feet. "Your Highness! I'd heard that a force had come from the north, but I thought it was just a rumor. People will say anything to get a scrap of bread, and Ironhead's men aren't idiots. They know to feed us lies. If this is true—"

"If it is true," Theophanu pointed out coolly, "then you had better escort us to Queen Adelheid at once."

Their escort led them through winding streets to the heart of Vennaci: a huge open square fronted on four sides by the cathedral, the town hall, the marketplace, and the palacio. There they were handed over to the care of a steward. The servants who haunted the palacio corridors, like the soldiers, looked thin, but nowhere in the streets or among the soldiery or the citizens of Vennaci did Rosvita see panic or the flush of desperation which precedes defeat. There was enough water, and obviously someone was doing a good job of administering the food supply.

But the grain stores couldn't hold out forever.

A steward dressed in a rich indigo tunic led them to the courtyard that lay at the center of the stately palacio, the heart of hearts, the pulse of the city. Flowering vines made the arcades a riot of purple flowers. Bees hummed. Noblewomen sat on ornate benches, petting monkeys and little dogs who wore gold chains as leashes. Servants swept clean brick pathways shaded by plum trees. A gardener watered a bed in lavender, lilacs, and brilliant peonies with a ceramic pitcher so finely made that a noble lady would not have felt disgraced to use it for refreshment in her chamber. A hedge of bay lay soberly along the south prospect. There the courtyard, enclosed on three sides by the palacio, gave way to a vista of the plain below. Ironhead's army lay encamped on that plain, tents and banners seen from here in distant, muted colors like a fresco laid on against the sky.

There was no throne, no central seat, only benches laid out at tasteful intervals among the planting beds: rosemary, rue, sage, and roses. But among the many souls populating the garden, Rosvita recognized the queen at once, although she had never seen her before. She sat on a bench like any other of the noblewomen, and was dressed no more richly than they without the crown of regnancy or the gold torque of royal kinship common in the north. Draped at her feet lay, not a little pug dog or a chittering monkey, but a spotted leopard, lithe and handsome, with lazy eyes and a tense curve to its shoulders. It purred, more of a rumble, as she rubbed it with one slippered foot as casually as if she did not realize it could take off that delicate foot at the ankle with a single bite.

She was interviewing three of the whores, who knelt somewhat nervously an arm's length away from the big cat, and in her quick movements and flashing, sudden changes of expression, Rosvita read the habit of command. The steward bent to whisper in her ear, and she dismissed the prostitutes by giving them each a coin, then rose and strode over to her visitors. The spotted leopard uncoiled gracefully to pad after her. The timbre of the pleasant courtyard atmosphere changed utterly with her movement: Everyone watched to see what she would do.

She halted before them, looked Theophanu up and down, and said boldly, in terrible Wendish: "You my cousin? I learn this tongue for to speak with the king."

"Cousin, I greet you," replied Theophanu in the Aostan way. Then she switched to Wendish and let Rosvita translate. "I greet you, Cousin, and bring you greetings from my father, Henry, king of Wendar and Varre." The princess towered over Queen Adelheid; she stood a good head taller, and her handsome features had that strongboned cast that lasts through old age. Adelheid was formed of different matter: She had the kind of lush, youthful prettiness that fades with age into the respectable authority of a stout matron.

"Come," said Adelheid in Aostan, acknowledging Rosvita with a nod, "we will take wine and food, but alas we can waste no time with pleasantries, as would be proper. You must tell me how many troops you have brought, and if you are willing to use them to drive away Ironhead." She continued talking so rapidly that Rosvita was forced several times to ask her to repeat herself as they left the courtyard, passed down a shadowed colonnade, and were shown onto an airy balcony shaded by a massive grape arbor where servants laid out a table with various delicacies: a platter of fruit, gold dishes filled with plum cakes and poppyseed bread, and a decanter of wine whose rich bouquet flavored every bite they took.

"You have seen," Adelheid began when the worst pangs of hunger were assuaged, "how dogs fight over a bone. The good people of Aosta are my children, and they are obedient, but the lords are scavengers. I can trust none of them. If one throws out Ironhead's army, it will only be to take his place. They say Ironhead had his wife poisoned before he marched here because she refused to take the veil and enter a convent to leave him free to marry me."

"He did not seem a merciful man." Theophanu took another bunch of grapes from the platter and neatly plucked the ripe fruit from the stalk. "But I do not have sufficient strength in troops to drive him away alone."

"If we coordinate our attack? You attack as my own forces sally out of the walls?"

"It is possible. Before I left, I agreed on certain signals with my captains. They are ready to attack if need be. But what is the number of your forces? How many may you rely on?"

They discussed the option, but dismissed it finally, with reluctance. Ironhead still had too great an advantage, even if they attacked on two fronts.

"How long can you withstand the siege?" Theophanu asked. "I could return to my father and assemble a larger army. Nay. Even if we can still cross the mountains, we couldn't return until spring."

"By then our stores will be exhausted." Adelheid gestured toward the table. "The palace gardens cannot feed everyone, and the sentries on the wall have told me that Ironhead has already set engineers to work to try to dam the river. Nay, cousin. This morning my clerics brought word to me that guards at the north gate saw a vision in the night sky, of an army made of flame. Surely that sign was the herald of your arrival. I believe this is part of God's plan. Now is our last, best chance to act."

"Ironhead will soon know the disposition of my forces," added

Theophanu, "and then he will know that I dare not fight him. At that point, I will be forced to withdraw."

"He won't let you go. You are at risk here as well. He would as gladly marry a Wendish princess as another woman, if he cannot have me. His first wife he took by force as well, after he'd murdered her husband. She came from the south, although her family's lands are now in the hands of the Arethousan generals. Thus she was of no more use to him. No, there must be some way out."

"Perhaps you can escape in the same way we got in, disguised as a cleric, or as some other sort of woman."

Adelheid laughed. "As a whore? I know what they say of me. It might work, I alone with one other might be able to get away, but I will not leave my loyal subjects in Ironhead's hands, especially not my good soldiers. You see what he will do to them. No, but still I must get to Henry. Is it true his queen is dead and he has not yet remarried?"

"It is true, Cousin. My mother, Queen Sophia, died three years ago. Indeed, I will not conceal from you the wish of my father's heart." Theophanu paused, and a sly smile graced Adelheid's pretty red lips as she waited for Theophanu to finish. "That you will marry his son."

"His *son?*" Adelheid flushed red. "He must be very young, no, this prince?"

"No, Sanglant is certainly five and twenty by now, and rich in reputation as a warrior and a captain—"

Adelheid jumped to her feet, and the leopard, who had seemed asleep, sprang up so quickly that Rosvita let out a yelp of alarm. "This Sanglant you speak of, he is the bastard, no? *I* will marry no bastard! Is Henry crippled? Is he too old to sire children, or too sick to ride to war?"

"No, Your Majesty," replied Rosvita, not waiting for Theophanu. "He remains strong in every way."

"Then what would a woman like me want with a young man when I can have a man in his prime, who is still strong, and who has proved he knows how to rule? Let us only come free of this place, and make our way safely to his court, and I will offer him my hand and the king's crown of Aosta. Do you think he will turn me away?"

Even subtle Theophanu was taken by surprise by this outburst. But Adelheid was magnificent in anger and distress, and she offered Henry what he had wanted all along. Sanglant had disgraced himself by refusing such a rich reward. Why should Henry turn away from it, now that circumstances were so changed?

Theophanu rose, walked to the balcony's edge, and leaned against the balustrade to look down the steep side of a hill covered in olive trees. Between each tree lay a squat beehive. Farther down lay an orchard whose trees grew all the way to the inner wall. "My father is not a fool, Cousin." She stared downslope for a long time until Adelheid grew curious, or impatient, and crossed to stand beside her. Rosvita was careful to keep her distance from the spotted leopard, who stood alert by the young queen's side, tail lashing, as the queen stroked its head absently.

"What are you thinking, Cousin?" Adelheid asked finally, breaking the silence.

Theophanu smiled, cool and almost mocking, as she cupped her chin in a hand and surveyed the olive grove and the beehives. "I am thinking that I have an idea. We have other allies if only we think to use them. Tell me, Cousin, do Ironhead's horses wear much armor?"

2

THERE was no reason for the tree to fall at that moment, and from that direction. His keen hearing saved him: a creak where he should have heard nothing, the first splinter of a tree's weakened stump as it groaned into a fall, the alarmed whispering of his ever-present companions. One tweaked him, hard, on the thigh, and he jerked sideways, then leaped out of the way as a huge ancient fir tree crashed down through the forest cover and smashed onto the spot where, an instant before, he had been standing. Branches and coarse needles scratched him as he spun away out of their reach. The shuddering noise of its fall echoed off the surrounding cliffs.

Sanglant was so stunned that he actually stood gaping among the firs and spruce and scattering of ash that covered the hillside, ax hanging loosely from his hand, as the branches of the fallen tree shook, quivered, then quieted, and the last echoes rolled away. There was no sign of disease along that vast length, no brown in the dense coat of needles, no infestations riddling the bark. His breath came in clouds in the air, here on the highest slopes at the fringe of the enchanted valley, where winter could reach. Snow dusted the ground, fading on the slopes below into grass and spring flowers.

Healthy trees do not fall by themselves.

He shook himself out of his stupor and whistled to the dog. It raced down the length of the fallen fir, lost itself in a thicket, and yipped wildly, came racing back with whip-tail tucked between its legs. After the incident with the soup, he had taken to carrying his sword with him. He leaned his ax against the trunk of the tree he'd meant to fell, scarred now by his first half dozen strokes, and grabbing up the sheath, drew his sword. It had good balance, although it was a little light to his hand now that he had put on weight and gained strength working with Brother Heribert on his construction projects.

He growled softly, scenting the air. One of the servants flashed by him, strange because she had no scent but rather a texture, in the way cloth has texture, a difference felt by touch, not seen or heard or smelled. Others crowded around, until he felt smothered by their presence.

"Hush, I beg you," he said, to still their chattering. They quieted. He listened, but heard nothing. He followed the tree to its base. The huge trunk had been cut away, a wedge taken out of it so smoothly that as he ran his fingers along the severed stump he knew no ax had hewn this. It looked more as might an apple sliced by a knife. He got down on his knees and sniffed along the ground, but smelled nothing.

"What has done this?" he asked the spirits. They would not answer, only crowded together. He did not smell their fear, precisely; it was more like a weft woven through the pattern of their being, abrupt, rough, and startling, they who were not creatures of earth at all but some kindred of the daimones whose natural home was the airy heights below the moon, or so Liath had told him. Easy to catch and enslave, these airy spirits served the five magi who lived at Verna.

Just as, in cold truth, he and Brother Heribert served them by building and hewing. Indeed, it was particularly irritating to see that someone in this valley had the means to fell trees with far less effort and time than he had to expend and yet was unwilling to share that knowledge with him and Heribert, the ones who had to perform all the hard physical labor of building decent living quarters for everyone. A king's son ought not to serve others in this way, no matter how exalted their rank, and yet for the time being, and with Liath's pregnancy and studies advancing, he was willing to bide his time. He was willing to work and eat and enjoy this interlude of peace.

But the surreptitious attempts on his life were beginning to get annoying.

He explored the forest briefly but, as he expected, found neither sign nor trail of his assailant. He did not expect another attempt today; whoever didn't want him here was a little clumsy, as witness the incident with the soup, someone unused to murder, perhaps, or someone who consistently underestimated him. Obviously no one in this valley knew of the curse his mother had laid on him, or they wouldn't have bothered to try killing him.

He went back and felled the tree he had come for, then set to the tedious work of trimming branches off the trunk of the great fir. He paused only to take bread and cheese and ale in the midafternoon, and several times to sharpen his ax, but even so, as dusk neared, he had only cleared half of it. His back ached, and his tunic was clammy with sweat. He slung the sheathed sword over his back and headed downslope on an animal track.

Firs and spruce gave way to oak, to beech and ash, then to orchard. He paused at the vineyard to pluck a few ripe grapes and, savoring these, went on. Shadows drew long over the dilapidated stone tower, the old sheds, and the newly-finished hall, so raw that it still seemed to gleam. Heribert worked at the sawhorse, stripped to the waist with his robes tucked into his belt. He had the slight elegance of a cleric, wiry now with muscle, and the callused hands of a carpenter. He was planing smooth a plank.

"Peace, Brother," said Sanglant, laughing as he came up. "You'll shame me if you don't stop working and join me at the pond." Heribert grinned without looking up from his work. "Some day," Sanglant observed, "I expect an avalanche to wipe out this entire unnatural valley, but, by God, while the rest of us flee to safety, you'll stand your ground and be swallowed up under it because you damned well are determined to get a last corner curved just so."

Heribert chuckled, but he continued to work. His ever-present helper, a robust creature who seemed as much wood as air, blew wood shavings off the plank as quickly as they flew up from the plane. Sanglant sat on a neat stack of unfinished planks that he and Heribert had sawed out of logs over the last week, and several servants settled around him like so many contained whirlpools of air. He had become accustomed to their presence. While Heribert finished the plank to his liking and touched up the corners, the prince watched two of the magi, one old woman and one young one, who sat outside the stone tower on a crude bench arguing in a language he didn't know. They were too far away to hear him and Heribert, and as usual did not appear to notice them.

"I dearly would like to see our Sister Zoë naked even just one time, for I think she must be a rare sight to behold under that robe."

Heribert snorted as he measured the corners with a square, then grunted, satisfied with the proportions.

"But I fear me," continued Sanglant, "that she despises the male kind."

"Or the male member." Heribert shrugged the sleeves of his cleric's robe back on and retied the rope belt at his waist. The servant made the odd noise that signified "farewell," and slipped away into the uncut logs piled nearby. "She was married very young to a man who used her cruelly, so I've heard. She killed him with a spell when she was sixteen, after three years of abuse in his bed."

Sanglant shook his head. "If only she'd done it sooner! How came she here?"

"She fled to her aunt, who was a nun at St. Valeria. By one means and the other they ended up here."

"Ah," said Sanglant. "But which is the aunt?"

"Dead, now, so they say." Heribert had started to put away his tools. Now he paused. "Do you think Sister Zoë is the one trying to kill you?"

"Who can know? Sister Zoë and Brother Severus prefer not to speak to me at all. They despise me, I think. To Sister Meriam, I am an object of complete indifference. To our fine and mighty

Sister Anne, I do believe I am only another tool, one she hasn't yet discovered a use for." He gestured toward the older woman who sat next to the voluptuous Zoë. "Only Sister Venia treats me kindly."

Heribert colored. "The more subtle they are the more fair they appear. Do not trust her."

"So you have said before, and since she is your aunt, I suppose I must trust your judgment since you surely know her far better than I do. A fair face can conceal a foul heart." He grinned, thinking of Hugh. Although it was certainly no Godly sentiment, he liked to remember how he'd last seen Hugh, bleeding and beaten on the ground, at the mercy of the dogs. But thinking of the dogs made him think of his father, and he sighed. Two of the servants brushed against him, their light touch like balm on his scratched-up skin.

"You'd think Sister Anne would put a stop to the attempts to kill you," Heribert was saying as he tied up his tools in a cleverly-sewn pouch of his own devising.

"Maybe it's a test. Or perhaps she doesn't know."

Heribert laughed sharply. "I don't believe there is anything she doesn't know. But surely Liath might have some insight into her mother's mind that we lack. You should confide in her."

He considered, but finally shook his head. "Nay. It would worry her needlessly, and she would insist we leave—and that, I fear, would cause more problems than it would solve in every way. She needs to be here, at least until the child is born and she has recovered her strength." Then he smiled wryly. "And in any case, Heribert, I haven't found that she can keep secrets very well, although she thinks she does. If she gets angry, she'll blurt it all out and accuse everyone just because she is so indignant on my behalf. I like knowing that they don't know that I know."

"Unless they do know that you know, and, knowing that, know that you believe that they don't know that you know, so that this is only a more convoluted game than even you perceive, my friend."

"Ah, but you forget that I was raised on the king's progress. Certainly I have seen almost every knot that can be tied when it comes to intrigue."

Heribert hesitated, looking troubled. "You must be careful, my lord prince," he said, using the title as he always did when he meant to tease, or to be serious. "A nest of mathematici is a nest of dangerous creatures, indeed."

"Why do you stay, Heribert?" asked Sanglant suddenly.

Heribert's smile was mocking. "I fear leaving more than I fear staying. I'm not a brave man, as you are, my lord prince. I'm not a warrior in my heart, as many churchmen are. I'm afraid of what they'll do to me if I try to go. In any case, there *is* no way out except through the stone circle, none that I've ever found. I don't know the secrets of the stone." He put his leather tool pouch away in the shed he and Sanglant had built beside their working ground, where Heribert now slept. "Truth be told, I'm content here. I was never given a chance to build before."

"Well, my dear friend," replied Sanglant, standing, "it's a handsome edifice you've built. But right now I want to be clean. Shall we go?"

The servants swirled around him as he rose, tickling his chin and tweaking his ears. He had enough natural quickness that he could pinch them in turn, a form of teasing they delighted in because he could do no harm to their aetherical bodies. Laughing, he chased them until they scattered, their delicate laughter chiming on the breeze. Heribert only shook his head and, together, the two men went to the pond to wash themselves free of the sweat and dust of an honest day's work.

Sister Venia, formerly known as Biscop Antonia of Mainni, watched her illegitimate son and his companion vanish into the dusk. Perhaps it was inevitable that the two men, thrown together under such circumstances, would become friends. Whatever his virtues, Prince Sanglant was uncouth, uneducated, and only half human, scarcely a fit companion for a young man who had been molded carefully from childhood on to become the ornament of wisdom and the shining vessel of God's grace. Still, the prince could hardly fail to be uplifted by the company of such an astonishingly fine young cleric.

"I don't like the way he looks at me," said Sister Zoë abruptly. "He has a lewd eye."

"Brother Heribert?" cried Antonia, astounded by the accusation.

"Heribert? Nay, I speak of Prince Sanglant."

"Ah, yes. He is much attached to the flesh, I believe."

Zoë shuddered.

"None of us can escape the flesh." Brother Severus emerged from the tower, lantern in hand. "Not while we still walk on this earth, at any rate. He's a bad influence on the girl. As long as he is around, there is no hope she can learn with a focused mind. Pregnant!" He said the word with distaste. "She is not what we were led to expect."

Zoë shuddered again. "It's disgusting. I can hardly stand to look at her, with that swelling belly. It's a deformity of the clean flesh she might have, had she kept herself a pure vessel."

"Who among us has been given leave to cast the first stone?" asked Antonia mildly. "Not one of the women in this valley is unstained, even Anne, who gave birth to the girl, after all. For the men, of course, I cannot speak." But she often wondered about Severus, the old prune. He had the kind of self-important arrogance that in her experience might cover a multitude of sins, now since conveniently forgotten.

He only raised an eyebrow. "That is of no matter. We expected a pure vessel, but now we receive one that is broken. It is not just this carnal marriage that has made her so, but her entire association with that creature. The prince is a danger to everything we've worked for. See how the servants cluster around him when they ought to be engaged in tasks for us."

"Better under our eye than where he can work mischief hidden from us," retorted Antonia.

"An argument Sister Anne has used. It may even be true. But it seems to me that we could simply rid ourselves of him once and for all time, and that would be the end of it."

"He is not so easily killed," said Sister Anne, emerging from the tower with Sister Meriam walking slowly behind her, "although I am in agreement that his influence on Liathano works counter to our purposes."

Meriam had become increasingly frail over the past several months, and her voice was scarcely more than a whisper, thin and dry, but her mind had not lost any of its penetrating strength. "We were all young once, and the young are most susceptible to temptation. I sometimes think that only our absent Brother Lupus may have remained faithful to his vows."

"A commoner!" Severus looked toward the hall, now lit by

wands of light that glowed as softly as will-o'-the-wisps. "Hardly the creature such as we ought to measure ourselves against, Sister Meriam."

"We had a saying in my country, Brother: that a rich man might as easily become a slave as a poor man might, if God so wills it. Fortune is fickle, and a poor man might become rich, or a slave become a general, by God's design."

"The sayings of infidels can be of little interest to us," retorted Severus coolly.

"Let us go in to supper," said Zoë, standing hastily. "Then perhaps we may eat our fill before the dog returns. I hate having to watch him eat."

"You must strive for detachment," said Sister Anne in a calm voice. "What disturbs you is not his presence but some lingering touch of the Enemy within your own soul."

Zoë flushed. Since the arrival of Sanglant, Zoë had begun habitually, and no doubt unconsciously, to smooth her robes down against her body whenever she spoke of the prince. She did so now, brushing white, soft hands never marred by manual labor along the azure linen of her robe. In a way, it was a relief to Antonia; Heribert might have noticed Zoë's lush charms, but it was now manifestly obvious that *she* had never noticed him. His purity was safe from her, at least. He noticed Liath, of course. Antonia had observed human nature for many years, and she had known at once that Liath had the unconscious warmth of beauty that attracts males as moths to the flame that will kill them. But Liath was pregnant, and her husband hovered at her side in all his bestial glory. Heribert would not interfere there. Males were easily led precisely because of their inclination to submit to any one of them who seemed stronger; that was why God had chosen women to administer Their church, because women were more rational.

"He has brought discord in his wake," said Severus, "but that, I suppose, is the legacy of his mother's blood."

Poor Sister Zoë was a passionate being, despite her wish to live the contemplative life. Still flushed and flustered, she set off for the hall. Antonia could smell roasted lamb and freshly baked bread. Anne glanced toward the open door to the tower, made some internal decision, and followed Zoë. Severus waited only long enough to accompany Sister Meriam at her slow pace. For once, Antonia missed Brother Marcus, who for all his haughtiness had more conversation than the rest combined and was not afraid to speculate on the goings-on in the world outside, but he had left weeks ago to travel to Darre.

A light still burned within the lower chamber of the old stone tower. Antonia glanced inside to see Liath seated on a bench at the new table recently built by prince and cleric. That they should set themselves to carpentry was appalling, of course, but on the other hand, the old table had been atrocious, gapped, listing, rotted at one corner. The new tables they had built for tower and hall were a great improvement.

Liath was reading, her finger tracing words across the vellum page, her lips forming the words as she read but rarely uttering an actual sound. She was the quietest reader Antonia had ever seen, uncannily silent:

"Ah," Liath said suddenly, to herself. "If all things fall toward the center at an equal pressure, and if therefore the universe as a whole would be always pressing against the Earth on all sides and of a uniform nature, then the Earth would need no physical support to rest at the center of the universe."

"What are you reading?" asked Antonia. Liath was a strange creature; although she was Anne's daughter, there was something unnatural about her, not least that she was capable of reading in such dim light.

Liath started up, surprised, banged her thighs on the table, and muttered a word under her breath. "I beg your pardon, Sister Venia," she said politely, closing the book. "I hadn't realized it was dark. I'm reading Ptolomaia. I never had a chance to read the *Syntaxis* before, only excerpts from it. I see now that although I've read *On the Configuration of the World* there was a great deal hidden in its words that I never fully understood."

Antonia had never heard of a book called *On the Configuration of the World,* but she was not about to admit it to this ignorant child who still dressed like the common Eagle she once had been and who did not have the decency to conceal her unattractive passion for the crude creature she called "husband." It was tremendously hard to see her as the daughter of Anne, who was arrogant and cold and in all other ways everything one would expect from the scion of a noble house. Just which noble house Anne was from Antonia was still not sure, because her compatriots had not yet taken her fully into their confidence, but she was not stupid: she was beginning to see the pattern that had been woven here.

Liath wrapped the book in its leather binding and put it away in the cupboard, then frowned for a moment at the tablet on which she'd been writing, mathematical calculations drawn from an ephemerides, a collection of tables which showed the daily positions of the heavenly bodies. She hesitated, fingered the stylus, then made a correction to her calculations. "What do you think?" she demanded imperiously, thrusting the table out for Antonia to look at.

It was immensely irritating that this callous young woman should grasp so easily what was for Antonia the most excruciatingly difficult part of the education of a mathematici. No wonder the church had condemned such arithmetic as the scratches of the Enemy's fingers when they had sat in judgment on Biscop Tallia, an adept of the art and the daughter of Emperor Taillefer, at the Council of Narvonne one hundred years ago. "That is for Sister Anne to correct," said Antonia sternly. "I came only to tell you that it is time to go in to supper."

"Is Sanglant back yet?" demanded the girl. She had no respect for the dignity due her elders. She seemed quite unconscious of the elegant manners that Heribert, for instance, wore as unthinkingly as his robes.

"He has gone to cleanse himself, I believe."

"Oh! I'll go fetch him to supper."

Antonia began to reprove her, but she already slipped past, quick even with the early belly of pregnancy on her. Poor Sister Anne. The child had been poorly brought up. It must, indeed, be a daily affront to Anne to see her own daughter behave with the manners of a commoner and the thoughtless insolence of a petty prince. Sanglant might be uncouth, but even his manners, court-bred as he was, were better than Liath's. Like a dog, he was trainable.

Antonia followed her through the twilight, past the orchard and the vineyard, to the grassy meadow where a pond lay nestled against a slope, almost swallowed in darkness. She heard the two men laughing with that easy companionship common to the male kind, feckless creatures that they were.

Then Sanglant called, suddenly, in the kind of voice that carries over the clash of battle: "Liath! God forbid you come any closer or you'll despoil our chaste cleric, who stands here quite as his mother made him." There was a loud splash.

Alarmed, Antonia moved closer to see the moon's light illuminating the water, where Heribert's slender figure stood waist-deep, hands on his hips. Sanglant came spluttering up from the water next to him and burst into merry laughter as water sluiced off his chest and back and head. He had been dunked.

"Don't think me weaponless," retorted Heribert in a bantering tone unlike anything she had ever heard from him before, "since I have the sword of wit at my service and you, alas— well, I'll say no more."

"I just came to say that supper is waiting for us," called Liath plaintively from the darkness.

Sanglant emerged from the water quite immodestly and shook himself all over like a dog, then patted himself dry with a tunic. He dressed hastily while Heribert remained discreetly in the water; when he was dressed, he vanished into the trees. There came murmuring, too indistinct to make out but with the timbre of love words.

It was a puzzle, but like all puzzles it could be solved or, at worst, bludgeoned until it gave up its secrets: two children born out of mothers who were, if all accounts of Sanglant's mother were true, powerful magi. No matter what the others suspected the Aoi of, no matter if they suspected the Aoi were not truly lost but only somehow hidden to the world of humankind, for all their knowledge they were fools to wish to kill Prince Sanglant. He had power writ large in him; he had been blessed by God with the power to lead. She knew what reputation was worth in the world. She had owned it once herself and had not given up her hopes and dreams. Her sojourn here in Verna was only a way station to something larger, something she could control with the knowledge she would gain from the mathematici here. Brother Severus was wrong: it was not God's will that all Their chosen ones should let go of the world but rather that the wisest among them should rule it rightly. She was one of those chosen ones.

"We'll meet you there, Brother!" called Sanglant to Heribert.

Antonia listened as their footsteps moved away in the direction of the hall. His usual throng of attendants—any of the servants who had not been commanded by Anne to various tasks—followed in his wake. It was uncanny how they clustered around him.

By now the pond was gray and Heribert only a grayer shadow as he got out of the water and dried himself. How much had Liath seen of him? Surely the twilight had covered his nakedness, and if it had not, well then, that was a small price to pay while he unwittingly ingratiated himself with the prince who might someday prove of great use to her.

3

THE beekeepers of Vennaci had a special kind of smoke they burned to make the bees go to sleep. In the night they moved the hives up to the ramparts on either side of the great eastern gate, and made ready with small catapults.

Adelheid's army had assembled the day before and with a single sortie at dawn out of the eastern gate, in force, had done damage to Ironhead's camp before his superior numbers forced them to retreat back into the city. Many had been captured; some had been killed. In the wake of their attack Theophanu had broken through the lines with a small escort and returned to her army, leaving Rosvita with Adelheid as a sign of good faith.

Now, from the ramparts by the eastern gates, Rosvita watched the survivors assemble again before dawn, ready for a fight in which many would perish. She was impressed by their loyalty: Adelheid knew the secret of rulership, that as ye give, so shall ye receive. She was generous and she looked after her own. That was why they were willing to risk so much to win her the freedom to escape north.

Ironhead had not been idle. He had drawn his forces up before the eastern gates for an assault, and as the sun rose, he brought his cavalry forward to repel a second sortie if it came.

"Sister, I pray you, we must assemble at the north gate." One of Adelheid's clerics drew Rosvita away just as, from the hills to the north, she saw the first thick clots of smoke begin to rise: the signal from Theophanu. They hurried away through the quiet city. The citizens of Vennaci had either retreated into their houses to hide or now waited outside with such belongings as they could carry, hoping to flee in the wake of Adelheid's escape. It was so quiet in the town that Rosvita heard the first clash of arms, as distant as a bell ringing in a church a league away. Theophanu's army had attacked Ironhead's camp, or so they hoped.

At the north gate an armed escort of some one hundred soldiers surrounded Adelheid. Behind them came her train, wagons, servants, and livestock by now bawling and mewling. There came a shout from the eastern gates.

Queen Adelheid sat on a fine black mare. Rosvita mounted, beside her, on a gray gelding, and just as she got on the horse, she heard a maddened roar erupt from the east.

Adelheid laughed out loud. "They have thrown down the bees into Ironhead's cavalry!" she cried as her soldiers cheered. "Come. Let us ride!"

The north portal was flung open as her archers began shooting from the walls. Infantry clattered out to carve a path for the cavalry behind, and soon Rosvita was moving with them. It was horrible and exhilarating at the same time to ride out into battle armed only with prayers.

An arrow whistled overhead. She ducked, felt taut muscles pull, cursed herself for age and infirmity. A spasm tore through her back, but she felt no blood. Her horse faltered as she gasped, and then a soldier came up beside her and grabbed the reins out of her hands. He yelled something at her that she couldn't understand; sound roared in her ears, but whether it was the cacophony of battle or only her own fear and discomfort deafening her, she could not tell. She let him lead her, and set her thoughts to that task that had been drilled into her in the convent: praying.

They trampled the line drawn up beyond the north gate, where three days ago she and Theophanu had crossed words with Ironhead's bored and satiated guards. Now, Adelheid's soldiers crossed swords with those same guards, cutting them down as their heavy horses thundered past. Wagons rumbled in their wake. Shacks crumbled under the weight of their charge, and then they were out on the plain. From this angle, she could see the cloud of battle before the eastern gate, observed only from this distance as a churning mass of maddened horses, thrown riders, smoke along the rampart, a seething struggle fading into a haze of dust. They pounded over abandoned fields, leaped irrigation ditches, skirted ranks of trees set up as windbreaks, and without further incident the front rank of cavalry with Adelheid at their head reached the first crumpled line of hills.

They paused there, looking back. Dust obscured the plain around Vennaci, all but the high towers. The soldiers cheered. Adelheid stared at the city she had left behind, her profile stark against the autumn-gold hills behind. She wore men's leggings under her gown, which was hitched up over the saddle, and a cunningly worked leather coat fitted to her small frame with a capelet of light mail over her shoulders and red leather flaps reinforced with metal plates draping down over her hips. On her head she wore only a conical helm with a scarf wound 'round her hair for padding. The ride and the wind had uncurled the scarf and now it rippled behind her, making of her the banner which her men followed. She was young, and in that moment on the hillside with battle raging behind her and only a fugitive hope of escape ahead, she was beautiful in the way of saints and God-touched generals.

"We're not out of danger yet," she said abruptly.

"There should be sentries here." Rosvita recognized the steep-sided little valley through which she and Theophanu had walked those three days ago. Her back still ached, but as the pain subsided, she realized that she had only wrenched it. As she watched the stragglers come up behind them, she knew she had been lucky. Horses arrived without riders. Of the wagons and servants, only one clattered up—Adelheid's treasury, richly guarded by an escort of twenty armed riders of whom four had weeping red wounds on their bodies. Adelheid surveyed this remnant with an expression of fierce defiance.

In their wake came a captain, gloriously outfitted in mail and a tabard whose rich indigo was not muted by dirt. The crest on his helm had been knocked askew. "Your Majesty! Ironhead has rallied his forces. Soon they will understand our purpose. We must ride on now. The rest are lost to us."

"Then we will wait no longer," she said stoutly. "May God watch over and protect those who have served me faithfully."

Captain Rikard took control of the troops, and they plunged into the hills with the wagon lurching and rattling behind them. A shout tore the air, coming from far behind, then they heard screams and the clash of arms. A rider appeared, vanished where the ground dipped, and reappeared. He wore Adelheid's colors. The captain sent a trooper back as the rest pressed forward, and as soon as the trooper reached the messenger, they both turned to follow the rest. Soon their shouts could be heard: "Ironhead has sent a large force in pursuit!"

They came to a landmark Rosvita recognized, a forked tree at the meeting of two paths. As the captain began to direct the queen straight ahead, Rosvita hailed him. "The path toward Princess Theophanu's encampment is this way!" she cried, indicating the path that ran to the right.

Rikard shook his head. "If the Wendish forces are engaged with Ironhead, then we'll be caught between his flanks. We must ride north. There are nobles faithful to the queen in Novomo."

Five soldiers split off and rode down the path that led to the Wendish camp. For an instant, Rosvita considered riding after them. But she did not. She had been charged with aiding Adelheid, and Adelheid would not be safe until she reached Wendar. Some truths taste bitter: like most second children, Theophanu was dispensable. Was that why Henry had sent Theophanu to Aostà instead of Sapientia, after Sanglant had refused him?

The winding path broke through bracken and swathes of grass turned brownish gold. They pressed higher, each turn of the path taking them up in switchbacks until they had to get off and lead the horses. The midday sun made the rock outcroppings shimmer, but only Rosvita seemed to suffer under its heat although the soldiers, too, were sweating. On one rocky stretch the wagon finally broke an axle. A great wailing arose among the servants as Adelheid surveyed this calamity with a frown. Anger sparked in her eyes, but not for her servants.

"We must keep the royal insignia and the crowns and the tribute lists at all costs," she commanded. "But leave what we can't carry of the rest of the treasure. Gold will be of little use to me if I am locked away with it all in my lap in a prison of Ironhead's devising."

"If we could hide some it off the road, Your Majesty," said one of the stewards, "then perhaps we could return and find it."

"Look!" Captain Rikard had sought out a vantage point, the ruins of an old tower somewhat above the main track. As Rosvita rode up beside him to look down at the rugged hills up which they had come, helmets bobbed into view far below. "Ironhead's men," he told her, pointing. From this ancient site, soldiers of another race had surveyed the southern approach with ease, as Rosvita did now, shielding her eyes from the sun's glare as she squinted south. Vennaci's towers lay small and dust-hazed far beyond, no taller than her hand measured from this distance. She searched to the west, where Theophanu had set her camp—

"There!" cried the captain.

There! Fire ravaged the Wendish camp, tents ablaze. Smoke obscured the struggle raging below, and in any case they were too far away to truly make sense of what they saw. Was Theophanu routing Ironhead's troops, or being routed in her turn?

"They are closing," said the captain, and all at once Rosvita realized that he cared so little for the Wendish camp that he wasn't looking there at all: He was still measuring the progress of Ironhead's soldiers. A helm winked in sunlight, then was lost to shadow as a score of soldiers vanished up a switchback, riding in the vanguard. Below them, a banner appeared, colors Rosvita could not quite make out but which the captain recognized.

"Ironhead himself dogs us." Hurriedly, they made their way down to the main path, where Adelheid and the others waited. "Your Majesty, we must leave those on foot behind or you will surely be captured. Ironhead has learned of the trick. He himself leads the party that pursues us."

She said nothing for a moment that seemed to drag out into infinity and yet comprised no more than ten heartbeats. But her servants, quickly understanding the situation, threw themselves onto their knees among dirt and stones and begged her to go on. She blessed them and, with tears in her eyes, abandoned them to the mercies of Ironhead's men.

"Was I wrong, Cleric?" she demanded finally as they picked their way down a defile: the queen, a dozen courtiers, six servingwomen, four clerics, Rosvita and about eighty soldiers. Her servants followed en masse, for here on the roughest part of the trail it was no hardship for them to keep up with the horses. "Was I wrong to believe that it was time to make my escape? Should I have thrown myself on Ironhead's mercy? Should I have maintained the siege through the winter and prayed for deliverance? Was the vision seen in the sky of an army marching in flames a sign sent from the Enemy, not from God?"

"Only God can know, Your Majesty. Their plan remains a mystery to those of us of mortal kin. You did what you thought was right at the time."

Adelheid glanced at her sharply. "What of your lady, my cousin Theophanu? Perhaps this plan of ours has resulted in her death. Was it foolish to try?"

"God have given us free will, Your Majesty. It is in our nature to take risks, to press onward, sometimes foolishly into disaster, sometimes recklessly into unexpected success. I cannot answer. I can only say that we can be no more than what we are."

For a while the path led smoothly alongside a stream flowing down the length of a narrow valley otherwise inhabited only by scrub trees and grassy slopes. Here they made good time, leaving the mass of servants behind. Once they heard a shout, carried on the wind by an echo. But soon the trail turned rough again, pushing up and over several ridges. They came to a stony patch of ground where the path plunged down into a defile, then took a steep turn upward, only to descend again in the next valley, where rocky outcroppings formed fantastic shapes along the steep valley walls, sculpted by a millennia of wind and rain.

"Our road to Vennaci was much smoother than this," said Rosvita to one of the clerics, a lean, unsmiling man called Brother Amicus.

"You came on the road through the Egemo Valley," he observed. "We move west and north into the country of the Capardian ascetics. It is harsh country, and will be hard enough for us to cross. But it will be harder for Ironhead and his men to cross because they have more horses to water and men to feed. It is possible we can hide there until he gives up the chase."

Would Ironhead turn back to take Theophanu prisoner? Or was she already in his hands, or dead?

The horses struggled along on stony paths that in some places were little more than goat tracks. Toward dusk, one went lame. Its rider threw off his armor and took to the countryside, hoping to escape Ironhead by hiding in the hills. The rest pressed on. By this time Rosvita's robes were covered with dust, her lips chapped, her face burned by sun and dry wind. Her back still ached, and she was hungry. But at least her horse remained sound and strong. Slowly, her world had shrunken until the health of her horse and the blessedly empty path behind encompassed her entire world.

Water had collected in the shadowed depths of the next defile, a trickle that fed into a pool and then drained away into rocks. Here they stopped to drink and to water the horses. They were not well provisioned; food and clothing had been lost with the wagons, but the soldiers carried with them dried meat and yesterday's bread, made palatable by keen hunger and by the knowledge that Ironhead was better armed, better provisioned, and probably gaining on them. There were enough oats for the horses for three days at most. After that, they would have to forage in an increasingly harsh countryside.

Twilight had lowered over them suddenly, but a waxing gibbous moon shone strong enough to light their way as they walked, leading the horses. It was very quiet except for the sound of their passage. Leather creaked. A man whispered to his companion. Brother Amicus coughed. Water trickled down a stony rock face, and after horses and people had drunk their fill, Rosvita took handfuls of it to bathe her face. Grit smeared on her cheeks. One of the combs holding up her hair had come undone, and tendrils of hair stuck to her neck, pasted there by sweat and grime.

They walked on, leading the horses, until the moon set and they had to catch what sleep they could alongside the path with sentries set to watch before and behind. Rosvita dozed fitfully and dreamed of Brother Fidelis' book.

The opening lines of the *Life* of St. Radegundis burned in her mind as if they had been set afire, lines of flame on shimmering, unearthly vellum. *"The Lord and Lady confer glory and greatness on women through strength of mind. . . . One of this company is Radegundis, she whose earthly life I, Fidelis, humblest and least worthy, now attempt to celebrate. . . . The world divides those whom no space parted once."* There was more, but it was not from the *Vita* at all. It was a scrap recalled from a florilegium which she had read years ago before the words made sense to her, but she could not now remember where, only that the words swam to the surface of her mind in the way of such thoughts, a shoal of minnows darting along the shore.

"In this way the mathematici read the past by means of that ancient record we can comprehend through the uniform movements of the heavens, which God have left as their record book, which hides nothing from the scholar who has learned the secret language of the stars. All that has happened may be read there, and all that will happen, and she who masters this language may find revealed to her even the most ancient hidden

*knowledge of the Lost Ones who vanished off this earth long
years ago by means of powers beyond our understanding."*

The burning words flashed with sparks as bright as stars
falling to earth like angels fleeing God's justice, and she heard
a voice in her dream, completely unfamiliar and yet as clear as
if she had heard it yesterday:

"And they called that time the Great Sundering."

She woke suddenly, shivering. Ai, God! What had happened
to the book? What of Brother Fortunatus and poor, ill Brother
Constantine? Had they died in the conflagration? Had Ironhead
taken them prisoner? Had he tarnished the book? Had it burned?
Had it been lost, and the copy so painstakingly made by Sister
Amabilia lost with it, all of Brother Fidelis' knowledge, his *Vita*
of the blessed saint, obliterated in a flash of lust and greed?

Without the moon to dim their light, the stars shone with the
brilliance of a thousand fiercely burning lanterns. The River of
Heaven spilled westward, brimming with the souls of the dead
as they streamed toward the Chamber of Light. A horrific fit of
certainty overtook her: Amabilia was dead, lost to the world.
Her soul flowed overhead in the great river, one of those myr-
iad sparks of light.

She wept a little, and weeping, shifted her seat on the cold
rock. Her back flared, hot pain that made her wince. Sparks of
light shivered in front of her eyes, only to vanish, then reappear, then vanish again into the hazy distance.

She heard whispers, abrupt and intense. Around her, the company readied to move, although it was still night. The inconstant
lights resolved themselves and became will-o-the-wisps and then,
with a shudder of fear, she realized they were lanterns carried
along the trail.

"Sister!" Brother Amicus knelt beside her, more felt than seen.
"We must move quickly."

She could not rise by herself. Two soldiers had to hoist her
up, and every least movement sent an agony of pain lancing
through her back.

"I can't walk!" she whispered. She almost begged them to
leave her, but she heard a sharp challenge, words exchanged,
and a blessedly familiar voice.

Joy can ameliorate pain.

The parties mixed, melded, although there were few enough

of the Wendish. She fought her way to Theophanu's side and kissed her hand repeatedly.

"Your Highness!" She was aghast to hear what a croak her voice was, sanded away almost to nothing. "How have you come here?"

"These good Aostan soldiers led us on your trail," said Theophanu. "My most valued teacher!" She kissed Rosvita on either cheek. It was too dark to see her expression, but her grip was strong, even passionate. "I feared you were lost, like so much else."

"Sister!" From out of the darkness she heard Brother Fortunatus' voice, rather wheezy but wonderfully real. "Sister Rosvita!"

They were separated by the press of the crowd as Adelheid came forward to greet Theophanu, as whispered commands raced through the company and they made ready to leave. Somehow she found her horse and, with the aid of an Aostan soldier, mounted, giving the reins into his care. Perhaps it would have been better to walk. She gripped the saddle and prayed; each least shift in the saddle made her back burn; she became quite light-headed. After a long while she realized that she could see the countryside in the gray light of early dawn.

They came to a forking of paths. Rosvita had somehow gotten to the head of the line. She heard a great deal of discussion behind her, and she desperately wished to look behind, but each time she tried to turn in the saddle so much pain tore through her back and shoulders that she literally could not move, and she finally gave up and just sat hunched there, enduring the pain and the awful curiosity, not sure which was worse. At last they moved on, but she could hear at her back a party moving off away from them.

After a while, Brother Fortunatus drew up beside her. "Are you well, Sister?" His expression betrayed his anxiety. "You are not wounded?"

"It is only the infirmity of age, Brother. I'm not accustomed to riding in this rash manner. My back is all a knot."

"I have a salve that should help you, Sister."

"What have you saved from the camp?" she demanded. "Where is Brother Constantine?"

He looked too tired to cry. "Brother Constantine took a turn for the worse after you left, Sister. I believe—I *must* believe—

that the worst was over, that he was recovering, but he was simply too weak to be moved when—" Now he faltered. "We had to leave him behind. But I trust that Aostans respect the church and will care for him as God wish Their servants to be cared for." He pressed a hand against the dust-coated saddlebags draped over the mule's back, his only possession besides the robe he wore. "But I have your *History,* Sister, and the *Vita* of St. Radegundis, and Sister Amabilia's copy. Such salves and ointments as were near at hand, and your eagle quill pen, neatly wrapped. Everything else we had to abandon."

"Bless you, Brother."

"Nay," he said impatiently. "I was of no use. Princess Theophanu remained calm throughout the disaster, but it is only because of Captain Fulk and his men that we escaped with our lives. They did not let the passing days lull them into somnolence, as the rest of us did. Ironhead's men are merciless. It is clear to me now that they had long planned to attack our encampment without warning. Indeed, we are lucky that Queen Adelheid chose to lead her escape when she did, or we would all of us have been lost, because I do believe Ironhead had made plans to wipe us out entirely. Only because of the queen's gambit was he forced to pull many of his forces back to the city. He had already placed men beyond our lines in readiness for a night attack."

Abruptly, above the ringing of harness and the steady clip-clop of horses and the whine of wind through the rocks, they heard the unmistakable clamor of battle joined.

"What is happening?" Rosvita exclaimed.

"Captain Rikard stayed behind with half of his men to ambush Ironhead and perhaps kill him, if God should favor them. That will buy us time."

"At the cost of their lives."

Fortunatus merely shrugged. They pressed on and soon the sounds of battle faded. Rosvita's awareness contracted to the agonizing throb in her back and the presence of Brother Fortunatus at her side. She stopped seeing the landscape through which they rode. She did not dismount when they came to a spring but gratefully drank the water brought to her by a Wendish soldier in his upturned helmet. The water was warm and the helmet slick with sweat, but she minded neither of these things: it was moist and it gave relief to her dry throat. She was past caring about anything else.

War was a sport for the young. Or was it sport at all, but only the physical manifestation of discontented ambition and youthful boredom? Old women rarely had the energy or the compulsion to ride to war: that was why God had placed them in positions of authority, to rein back the dangerously high spirits of those ruled by lust for material power and wealth, all that which is made of flesh and earth and thus tainted by the hand of the Enemy.

For a long while, as the sun rose higher in the sky, she simply shut her eyes and hung on, accompanied only by the sound of their passage through a ringing, empty countryside. It was hot for autumn. She thought perhaps her throat had become so parched that she would never talk again, but that surely would then allow her to retire from court and, at last, to finish her *History* of the Wendish people which she had promised to Queen Mathilda so long ago. Was it really five years ago she had made that promise? Had she been so occupied in Henry's court that she had accomplished so little? Would she ever finish?

"Sister!" She started, gasped at the pain, and became aware that she had dozed off in the saddle. Brother Fortunatus stood beside her, propping her up. "Are you fainting, Sister? Can you walk?"

A soldier stood beside her holding a hunk of dry bread and that same helmet. She had to soak the bread in the water to make it edible, but in the end she got it down and was able to look about, counting their much reduced company: Queen Adelheid, Princess Theophanu, some three dozen Wendish soldiers commanded by Captain Fulk, an equal number of Aostan soldiers, and an assortment of noble companions and clerics and servants numbering about three dozen. Slowly, she became aware of consternation eddying through the ranks. It took her a moment to understand its origin: in the last hour, eight horses, including the queen's, had come up lame, and they now did not have enough mounts. Two scouts had been sent back down the path to seek news of their pursuers, but neither had returned. They still had oats for the horses but no more food, and for water they were now entirely dependent on such springs and rivulets as they could find.

The bread had given her a bit of strength, and she now saw

how cruel the countryside looked, a reddish, crumbling stone warped by wind and time to make great pillars worn smooth into striations as even as if God's Hand had painted them there and soft cliffs eroded with a hundred tiny cavelets along their faces. There were no trees. Grass and scrubby bushes huddled like lost souls along dry streambeds.

"No!" Adelheid's voice rang out. She looked as bold as a lioness. "I have lost too much now to give in to Ironhead. He has made it a duel between him and me, and I refuse to surrender or to give up! A short way from here we will leave this path and turn north into the wilderness of Capardia."

"He will see our tracks," objected Theophanu, without heat. Rosvita had to admire her. As dusty as they all were, as exhausted, as bereft of hope, Theophanu remained composed and upright, coolly assessing their desperate situation.

"So he will," replied Adelheid. "But where we will go, it will make no matter because he cannot follow us. Who among you is brave enough to follow me into the haunts of those long dead?"

A sentry waved a flag from the ridge behind them, and word was ferried down from man to man until it reached Adelheid. "He sees Berto riding in our direction, at a gallop."

"Then one of our scouts returns to us," said Adelheid with satisfaction.

But suddenly, the sentry left his post and came scrambling down the hill himself at a run, men scattering around him. "Ai, Your Majesty!" he cried. "Berto's shot in the back by an arrow. I see Ironhead's banner, and his men. We haven't much time."

"And how much time do we have?" asked Theophanu as calmly as if she were asking for a second helping of meat at supper.

"They'll be on us within an hour like to that sung by the clerics at sunrise."

They looked then, all of them, to Adelheid, not toward Theophanu.

"Come," she said decisively. "Brother Amicus knows this country well, for he was fostered here. He will lead us to the convent of St. Ekatarina. There my mother sent me when I was a child and my elder sister had just been abducted and killed by a prince not unlike Ironhead. I lived there in safety for a year while war killed my three older brothers. The nuns won't turn me away. Come, then! We must hurry!"

Several of them were forced to double up in the saddle, including Rosvita. As they rode in haste along the path, Rosvita sat behind Fortunatus and simply laid her head against his broad back, bonier now, but still substantial. She drifted off; started into wakefulness when they left the main path and headed up into a landscape so weird that for a hallucinatory while she thought they had passed through a magical portal into another world entirely, inhabited by fantastical creatures from another plane of existence: basilisks and dragons, griffins and giants molded from stones. Eight riders remained behind to brush away the mark of their passing and to go on along the main path as a decoy. Brave men, each one. But wasn't that the way of the soldier? If he served his lady faithfully, he would be rewarded with earthly prosperity if he lived, and when he died, as all must in time, then with a place among the loyal retainers in the Chamber of Light.

She was dizzy with hunger and pain, and everything seemed so strange to her. Her lips burned as with words unspoken.

"What was the Great Sundering?" she asked. But no one answered, and she closed her eyes to blessed darkness.

A long time later she swayed as on the ocean, and the gulf of air opened beyond her so that if she inhaled deeply enough, she could breathe in the entire universe and all the stars which lay within reach of her hand, there beyond the chasm. She saw ground far below and a cliff at her shoulder, rubbed by the huge basket in which she sat all curled up. She was jerked upward, fainted again, and then there was rock beneath her feet and hands to lift her up. Many voices echoed around her, and it was terribly dark, as dark as the Abyss, into which none of God's light shines, for it is not the presence of the Enemy that is torment as much as the absence of God.

But the air was sweet, and she was laid down on a soft bed and water soothed her skin and then an ointment eased the terrible pain that had gripped her back and shoulders and she was fed a gruel so soft and mildly warm that it slipped down her throat like a salve for the dolorous heart.

But no one had yet answered her. A face swam into view, as blurry as a shifting shoal of minnows underwater. It was ancient, wrinkled like an apple left over from the last autumn's harvest.

"What was the Great Sundering?" Rosvita asked, surprised to hear her own voice, such as it was, coarsened by pain and the hardship of the journey and their failure. Why was she asking this question? Where had it come from?

The ancient crone smoothed a salve onto her cheeks. For a moment it stung, then faded. "You are suffering from a lack of water, and a surfeit of sun and pain and anxiety, my child," she said in a voice made reedy by age. "Who has spoken to you of the Great Sundering?"

"I don't know," said Rosvita, marveling. Her eyes had adjusted. Two slits in the rock chamber let in air and light, and she realized that she lay on a pallet in the middle of a circular room hewn from rock. The plastered walls were entirely covered with frescoes that had long since cracked and peeled with immense age. People—nay, not people, but creatures like to humankind—stared at her with jade green eyes and skin now discolored to a greenish bronze. They wore plumage more than clothing, bold feathers, crudely cut skirts sewn of leather and furs, cunningly tied loincloths, shawls woven of shells and gold beads and precious stones. There was some narrative written into these paintings, a lush land torn by invasion, a desperate, overwhelmed population, the workings of magi each of whom held a staff carved out of black stone. A man of their kind was flayed alive, and his blood gave birth to warriors. Great cities of a vast and intricate architecture burned and toppled. And there was a crown of stars: a stone circle set out under a night sky brilliant with stars. Only one constellation was picked out in jewels above the stone circle, that of the Child who will be Queen; she reached for the sparkling cluster of seven stars, itself called the Crown, that lay directly above Rosvita at the height of the curved dome that was the ceiling of the stone chamber.

"Where am I?" Rosvita whispered.

"We are here in the convent of St. Ekatarina, she who prayed and fasted in the desert for many days until in the heavens she saw a vision of titanic battles and of dragons flying in the sky. And a voice said to her: 'All that is lost will be reborn on this earth because of a Great Unveiling like to that Great Sundering in which vanished the Aoi.' Then she came to this place. Here she found these paintings which spoke to her of that terrible time when the Lost Ones ruled mortal lands. Here she established a convent, and so we few have followed after her in caring for what God have preserved."

"Are these relics of the Aoi themselves?"

"Who can know, child? These were painted long ago. Perhaps they represent the last testament of the Aoi. Perhaps they represent the memories of those humans who lived in that long ago time, before they had the means to record their remembrances in writing. But you must rest now. You must sleep."

"The others?"

"They are safe."

She left, and Rosvita was alone, yet not alone at all because of the creatures who stared at her from the walls, accusing, plaintive, proud, and angry. *They are not like us.* They looked hard and cruel, arrogant and cunning and unforgiving. What was it the church mothers had written of elvenkind? *"Born of the mating between humans and angels."* With all the cold beauty of angels and the bestial passions of humankind.

Sanglant's mother had looked so. Rosvita had seen her one time, when she was herself a very young woman newly come to King Arnulf's court. The elven woman had called herself. "Alia," which means "other," in Dariyan; no one had ever known her real name. She had wanted something, and everyone had first thought she wanted the child, but then she had abandoned him soon after his birth.

What had Alia truly wanted? Would they ever know?

Beyond the fresco depicting the stone circle and an assembly of Aoi magicians, a painted obsidian knife seemed to cut away the narrative told on these walls, as if to end it. Beyond the knife-cut lay only a scene of sharp sea cliffs and shoreline and the cool expanse of empty sea. All the elves, and their cities, and their troubles, and their enemies, had vanished.

4

LIATH didn't like being pregnant. It made her feel stupid, and ungainly, and trapped in an odd way that she had never before experienced, as if before she could have stepped off the earth into the aether without looking back and now she was anchored to the earth by the creature growing inside her. It also made her tired, and cranky, and weepy, and distracted. Her feet hurt. And she had to pee all the time.

But except for that, she was utterly and enchantingly happy. Right now, with a contented sigh, she sank down to sit on the edge of the bed. It had, of course, been the first thing Sanglant had helped Heribert build when they arrived at Verna four months ago. Sanglant tumbled into bed behind her and stretched out with one hand propping up his head and the other splayed over her belly, feeling the beat, so he always said, of their child's heart.

"Strong and clear," he said into her silence. "What is it, Liath?"

She had been absently scratching the head of the Eika dog, curled up half under the bed, but his words startled her into blurting out the thoughts, all chopped up and half-formed as they were, that crowded her mind with such pleasant chaos. "When I calculate the movements of the planets in the heavens into the months and years to come, I keep stopping at midnight on the tenth day of Octumbre in the year 735. On that day I see great signs of change, of powers waxing, the possibility of power and of change. Three planets at nadir, and two descendant, and the waxing crescent moon is beneath the horizon in the sign of the Unicorn, although it will rise in the early hours of the morning. Only Aturna is ascendant, rising at midnight in the sign of the Healer, well, really, right at the cusp of the Healer and the Penitent."

"Is this soothsaying?" asked Sanglant. "I thought one could not read the future in the stars, and surely we have not yet reached the year 735. Or have we?"

"Nay, nay." She reached for her wax tablet and toyed with the stylus tied to it, then, distracted by the round of cheese sitting on the table, cut off a wedge and ate it. "This year is 729, and it will soon turn to 730. But the movements of the wandering stars are constant, so we can predict where they'll be at any date in the future. But when I calculate the chart for that day, I feel that I'm missing one thing. That if I had that one thing, all the portents would make sense."

Sanglant groaned in mock pain. "Perhaps while you think you can find all the aches in my back and arms and legs. I've never seen such a mighty fir as the one that fell—" He broke off, rubbed at a welt on his left hand, and continued. "As the one I felled yesterday. I have hacked at unyielding wood all day and been scratched by needles, and now I itch horribly, and my back hurts." But he said it with a laugh; he never whined. He moved closer so that he curled against her back, a hand stroking her. "Is it too much to ask for an hour of simple comfort?"

She and Da had lived without much laughter, but with Sanglant, it was easy to laugh. "I never get an hour of simple comfort anymore. Why should you?" He kindly did not reply except to roll onto his stomach, displaying his fine, muscled back in the light of the single lantern that hung from the crossbeam above them.

With Heribert's help he had cleaned out an outlying shed, closed up the gaps in the walls, rethatched the roof, closed off the fourth side, and hung a door in the threshold. The bed had been the first piece of furniture, four posts, a lattice of rope, and a feather bed into which they sank each night with pleasure. He had also built a chest on which to sit, and in which he kept his armor, which he oiled and polished once a week. Over the last months he had made free with Sister Meriam's herb garden and on a shelf fixed high on the wall above the chest an entire shelf of oils and salves and pouches of dried herbs lay ready.

He closed his eyes while she rubbed ointment into his back and dabbed a poultice mixed of the pulped root of carrot onto the scratches on his hands and lower arms where his tunic had not protected him from the sting of fir. The aroma of pine resin melded with oil of ginger.

It was absorbing work, the feel of his skin under her hands, the slope of his body, the half smile of contentment caught on his face. He lived so easily in the world, in the present moment, purely in the realm of senses. Sometimes that irritated her, but other times she admired it. She could never be like him. Even now, her thoughts spun off as if caught in the whirl of the heavens, ever-moving.

Was it the heavens that moved, east to west? Or was it the Earth, revolving west to east? Both Ptolomaia, writing centuries ago, and the Jinna astronomer al-Haytham, writing only ten years before, believed that physical law and observable fact proved that the Earth remained stationary at the middle of the heavens while the heavens rotated around it. But more ancient authors had argued otherwise. Indeed, the fact that no one truly knew the answer made the questions all that much more interesting to her.

Sanglant grunted as she worked through a knot in his back. God knew he didn't truly belong here in this nest of mathematici. And yet, why not? He needed a refuge, too. He needed to rest; he needed a place where he could be at peace. He had fewer nightmares now, and he didn't act quite as much like a dog as he had before. But sometimes she worried that he would grow bored with nothing to do but fell trees and help Heribert build things. She wasn't ready to leave yet. There was so much to learn that it hurt sometimes, knowing that she had finally come to a place where they would let her learn without punishing her for what she was.

And yet . . .

She stroked his cheek gently. "Why do I never feel I can trust them?" she whispered, leaning to his ear. The servants curled and hid everywhere, and she never knew what they reported to Anne, who controlled them. "Why don't I trust my own mother?"

But he had fallen asleep.

In truth, maybe he would never know the answer. Maybe he could never know it. He couldn't do everything for her. Nor could she let him.

She kissed him, slipped on her sandals, and left. She trod the accustomed path, worn smooth now, to the pits out beyond the settlement. The night lay cloudy and cool around her, but she had no trouble seeing in the dim light; she never did. With her pregnancy, she had given up wearing leggings because it was so inconvenient and wore only her old tunic, belted loosely now so it draped over her swelling abdomen and fell to her calves. None of her companions ever said anything out loud, but it was clear to her that they disapproved of the casual way in which she and Sanglant dressed—she like a commoner, he like a soldier. Yet although the magi themselves wore robes of the finest cloth, that cloth was now worn threadbare; they cared little for such trivial considerations as clothing—or so they claimed. And anyway, Da had always said that, "Fine feathers don't make a duck, swimming does."

But their censure made no difference in any case. She had no cloth for new clothing, and no way to get any unless the servants could weave a robe for her from stray beams of light or the silk of spiders or the veins of leaves. No doubt they'd do it if they could, if only to please Sanglant. She could just see a dozen or so twined around the jutting eaves of the old shed, but as she walked down the path to the stone tower, only one servant followed her. It was always the same one, a femalelike daimone with the texture of water, flowing, translucent, yet it wasn't truly interested in her but in what grew inside her, as if the fact of her pregnancy had laid a compulsion on it to remain by her side. The others still seemed to fear her.

She pushed open the tower door, found a lantern on the table, and opened its milky glass door. Licking forefinger and thumb, she touched them to the wick. Light flared, oil caught, and the lantern burned steadily. Anne had taught her this trick, had schooled her in the habits of mind that allowed her to control such insignificant amounts of fire, like to a child learning her letters so well that she need not think consciously of them to know them instantly on sight. The servant flicked away from the fire, frightened of it, but the creature did not leave the chamber, only hovered nearby like an anxious nursemaid. Liath set tablet and stylus down on the table and unlocked the book cupboard where the ephemerides lay stored among other such treasures, the repository of centuries of knowledge hoarded and saved from the ravages of time and ignorant men. So Anne always said.

Her hand touched the spine of the well-worn ephemerides, but instead, distracted, she drew out Ptolomaia's *Syntaxis*. She opened it to the second chapter where the esteemed author set down the six hypotheses. One, that the heaven is spherical in shape, and moves spherically; Two, that the Earth is spherical; Three, that the position of the Earth is at the middle of the uni-

verse; Four, that in size and distance the Earth has the ratio of
a point relative to the sphere of the fixed stars; Five, that the
Earth is at rest, not experiencing motion from place to place;
Six, that there are two motions in the heavens, one daily motion that carries everything from east to west, and the motion of
the Sun, Moon, and planets along the ecliptic from west to east.

She rose again and stepped outside. Was it pregnancy that
made her restless, or the sudden infusion of knowledge, the constant studying, the pressure of her five companions in the arts
whose expectations pressed on her endlessly? They wanted so
much from her. She wanted so much from herself. Only Sanglant
expected nothing of her, and yet that wasn't true either; his expectations were only different than theirs, less open and force-
ful but perhaps more insidious.

Wind off the peaks had torn up the clouds and she saw stars,
quickly covered again. The sphere of the heavens revolved from
east to west, and so, seen from a motionless Earth, the stars rose
in the east and set in the west. But maybe the heavens were at
rest and it was the Earth which revolved from west to east, as
the long-dead Arethousan astronomers Hipparchia and Aristachius
had suggested. That would create the same effect, wouldn't it?
Or perhaps both heaven and Earth moved around the same axis,
preserving their observable differences by rotating at differing
speeds.

She picked up a rock and threw it into the air, put her hands
over her head. It landed with a thunk beside her. Surely if the
Earth were in motion, then if she threw a rock with enough force
straight up into the air, the motion of the Earth would carry her
away from it before it fell to the ground?

Ai, God, she had to pee again. And by the time she had done
with that, her mind had swung back to the most nagging question, the only one that clung to her all the time: Why didn't she
trust them?

Night was not a good time to work through such a complicated tangle of thoughts. And she was tired again; exhaustion
always came on suddenly. But she had left a lantern burning
and a book out, so she returned to the tower. All was peaceful
there, just as she had left it, the lantern burning quietly and the
book resting open on the table, a moment suspended in time
that roped her thoughts back to where they had been. Certainly
she couldn't throw a rock with enough force to test the theory

of the Earth's rotation. Compared to the heavens, the Earth was tiny, but that didn't mean that to a human walking its surface it could be quickly traversed. She had seen ships come up over the horizon, sails and masts emerging first; that suggested not only a spherical Earth but one of immense size compared to a single human stride. It seemed to her that she need only find a place where the summer solstice sun at noon cast no shadow when measured against a stick stuck vertically in the ground as a marker. Then she could walk north along that same longitude, measuring her path, and on the next summer solstice sun she need only measure the shadow cast by another vertical marker at a different location. If there was again no shadow, then the Earth wasn't spherical; but if there was, then she ought to be able to calculate the circumference of the Earth by multiplying the degree of the angle with the distance in leagues between the two points. In *The Book of Secrets* Da had written of a town far to the south, in sun-raked Gyptos, where St. Peter the Geometer had dug a well so exactly situated that on the summer solstice the Sun's rays touched its bottom. If she walked north from that point . . .

"Your thoughts are far from here."

She jumped and gasped aloud, almost comically, and was relieved to see Sister Meriam standing just outside the threshold, walking stick in her right hand. Liath helped her over the threshold.

"I saw a light," said Meriam. "You have not woken Brother Severus?"

Liath looked toward the ladder that led to a trapdoor set into the ceiling. "I have been quiet."

"That is well," replied Meriam. She placed a gnarled hand on Liath's belly without asking permission, but she had the authority of the ancient: Liath could not really be offended by her blunt speaking or intrusive manner. "You are growing as you should be. Where is the prince?"

"He's sleeping."

"So many knots."

"What do you mean?"

Meriam removed her hand. Age had sucked her dry; she was so small that Liath felt like a giant beside her. "I mean what I say: so many knots in the threads that bind the life of humans one to the next."

"Where do you come from?" asked Liath suddenly. "How did you get here?"

"I come from the east," said Meriam wryly, indicating her dark skin.

"I know that!" Liath laughed, then caught herself and glanced up, guiltily, knowing that Severus would not take kindly to being woken. He didn't like looking at her; her pregnancy disgusted him. But his disgust only made her wonder why a man with so much knowledge would even be bothered by such a common thing. What did it matter to him? "I mean," said Liath, "where in the east? How did you get here?"

"I came as a sacrifice."

"A sacrifice!"

"An offering." She had an accent blurred by time and age, a hint of exotic spices and brutal sun. "I was sent as a gift by the *khshāyathiya* to the king of the Wendish people, but the king had no use for me, so he gave me to one of his dukes. When I flowered I was brought to his bed. Some time after that, I gave birth to a son."

"Are you saying," said Liath slowly, astounded, "that you are the mother of Conrad the Black, duke of Wayland?"

"So I am."

It seemed impossible to Liath that this tiny woman could have given birth at all, let alone to as robust a person as Duke Conrad. "But you have estates to administer. A child to watch over. Grandchildren! Why are you here?"

Meriam was too old to take offense at impertinent questions. "That I bore one living child and three dead ones did not change the path laid out for me. It only delayed it. Once my son came of age and gained his dukedom and a wife, then I had the freedom to retire. He no longer needed watching over."

Liath choked back a snort of laughter.

"You have met him?" Meriam asked without smiling, but with the simple pride of a mother who knows the worth of her child.

Liath considered what to say, and chose caution. "He is hard to forget."

"You are not at all like him." Meriam brushed dry fingers over Liath's arm. Despite her age, her hands bore no calluses; she had lived a noblewoman's life from infancy to this day, never humbling herself with the day-to-day labor of living. Liath's own hands bore calluses, the legacy of her life with Da, and

Meriam's light touch explored these briefly as well, as if Liath's skin revealed her entire history, all from the brush of a finger. "You are not of Jinna blood. Who are your father's kin? From whence comes this complexion?"

"All I know of my father's kin is that he has a cousin who is lady of Bodfeld. But might it not come from my mother's kin?"

Meriam looked at her strangely. "Has Anne not spoken to you of this?"

"Of what?"

"Then it is not my place to do so."

When Meriam spoke with that tone of voice, Liath knew that it was useless to try to influence her to say more. Not even Brother Severus in all his arrogance could bully her. In the intimacy of a private meeting in the middle of a peaceful night, Liath couldn't help but ask one more question. "You said that your path was laid out for you, but delayed. But you never really answered my question. Why are you here, Sister Meriam?"

Wind creaked the door. Shadows curled along the beams, a servant settling down to listen, or to sleep—if they ever slept. In the dim light it was easy to forget how old and frail Meriam was; her voice still had the strength of youth. "I was taken from the temple of Astareos, He who is Fire Incarnate, where I was to have been an acolyte in His service, a priestess of the Holy Fire. I had already learned enough then to know my task in life, for certain priestesses there had the gift of prophecy. That my fate led me elsewhere for a time is only another knot in the tangle of life."

"The you were always meant to be a magi, the way I was?"

Meriam chuckled, age amused by youthful blindness. "Nay, not as you were. I came here to save what I can."

"Save it from what?"

" 'When the crown of stars crowns the heavens . . .' Ah. But you haven't completed your calculations yet."

That casual remark threw Liath again, like a flung stone falling to earth far from its original resting place. Those damned calculations. What had she overlooked?

"You will know it when you see it," said Meriam, answering a question she hadn't asked.

"Why must you all make it like a puzzle?" demanded Liath. "Why can't you just tell me what I'm looking for?"

"Because you won't truly understand what it is we work toward until you have discovered it for yourself." Liath began to protest, but Meriam raised a hand for silence. "It is all very well to protest that because you have seen a horse ridden, you know how to ride. But you don't know how to ride until you have yourself ridden. Isn't that true?"

"I don't see—"

"You don't see because you persist in thinking that the art of the mathematici is like a story, something you can understand equally well whether it is read to you or you read it yourself. But the art of the mathematici isn't a story, it is a skill, like riding a horse, or fighting, or administering an estate, something that takes time and effort to master. Would you set an apprentice weaver to weave the king's royal robes? Ask a novice to illuminate the Holy Verses? Trust your life to a pilot who had never before sailed through these shoals? You, of all people, must understand fully."

"Why?" Then Liath laughed, having picked up the habit from Sanglant. "Never mind, Sister. I know what you will say. You will say that when I understand fully, then I will also understand why I must understand fully."

"There lies the beginning of understanding." Was Meriam amused? It was hard to tell. She was too ancient to be easily read. Like all the magi, she held layers within layers in herself, none of which were readily peeled off.

"Is that why you're here, to understand?"

"Nay," she replied so quietly that a hundred misgivings congealed into a dreadful foreboding in Liath's heart, and the night no longer seemed so tame. "I am here to save my child and my child's children from what will come."

Sanglant woke abruptly, was on his knees on the bed ready to lunge for his attacker before he realized that it was dawn and that Liath had just closed the door behind her on her way out. He shook sleep and fear and memory out of his head.

Sometimes he thought the dreams of Bloodheart would never end. Sometimes he remembered that one night out of two he slept in peace and didn't dream at all.

He had woken in the night when Liath returned, and they had

had a long conversation that he didn't recall with any clarity now except that in addition to eating all the cheese and bread she had gone on about not being able to trust this nest of mathematici into which they'd been thrown. Maybe he hadn't really been awake. Sometimes he didn't know when Liath's sudden attacks of foreboding were just shadows woven out of her own fears or real premonitions of a truth she only glimpsed. He knew better than to trust a nest of mathematici, especially ones as powerful and as hidden as these. Especially knowing that at least one among them wanted to kill him. Perhaps Liath only suffered because she wanted to trust them. She wanted them all to have her open delight in knowledge, to want to know things for their own sake. She wanted them to be simple, and honest, and pure.

But he had lived for a long time in court. He had fought in more battles than he cared to count, and he would fight again if need be and pray to God afterward for peace. He had seen a lot of people die. Truly, there were some people who could be trusted, some open, honest souls like his poor, dead, faithful Dragons, or even some old, wily ones, like Helmut Villam, who would hold fast at your back when you were fighting for your life. There might even be some pure souls in this world, but he doubted it.

Most people in this world, he had found, were agreeable—as long as you treated them agreeably in your turn—but they were far from pure. Even after a life of running and hiding, Liath could be remarkably naive.

But with God as his witness, he had never desired a woman as much as he desired her. And he had desired, and consorted with, a lot of women in his time.

He grinned, dressed, rousted out the dog, and went outside to find Liath shooting arrows at herself.

At first he gaped stupidly as he saw her out in the meadow beyond their hut: He had never before seen such a display of idiocy. She aimed directly above her head as if shooting at the heavens, drew, and loosed the arrow.

"Liath!" he shouted, bolting for her.

She had her back to the sun, and to him, and she had thrown her head back to watch the arrow fly up and up and up, and then, as any fool knew it would, slow, tumble, turn, and fall back to earth. At her. She took a step back, caught her foot in a hole in the ground, and fell down hard just as the arrow whoofed into flame above her head and showered to earth as ash, sprinkling her hair.

"Liath!" he cried, kneeling beside her, but she was laughing and rubbing one hip where she'd landed hard.

"I didn't see the hole!" she said cheerfully.

"You would have seen it if you'd kept your eyes on the ground and looked where you were going!"

"But then I couldn't have watched the arrow's flight!"

"Ai, God," muttered Sanglant, helping her up and, for good measure, taking the bow out of her hand. He rested a palm on her abdomen to listen for the child. Its heart beat steadily, quickening as it stirred, slowing as it settled again. No harm taken. "What on God's Earth were you doing?"

"Just that. I'm trying to see if the Earth rotates. Because if it does, then surely an arrow shot high enough would land some distance away from the archer. That's because the archer, standing on the Earth, would have moved as the Earth rotates in the time it takes the arrow to reach the height and fall—"

"On your head!"

"Not if you have sufficient height or speed of rotation." She winced, kneading her bruised hip again, then rubbed the remains of the arrow into the grass with one sandaled toe, looking thoughtful.

The rising sun shone behind her, struggling up over the mountain peaks. She hadn't rebraided her hair yet, and wisps of it trailed around her face, curling delicately along her neck. How often did he catch himself just admiring her, as if nothing else existed in that moment? It was as if a part of her had settled down inside him, taken up residency in his soul, long before he had realized she was there. He was more her captive than he had ever been Bloodheart's, and yet in this case the chains were of his own making, and they weren't truly chains at all. That which bound them remained invisible and yet no less strong because of that. It was at moments like this that he felt blinded by happiness.

She glanced up to see him watching her, then smiled brilliantly and indicated her bow, which he now held. "Do you want to try?" she asked brightly.

It was at moments like this that he thought he would probably never understand her.

X
IN PLAIN SIGHT

1

SORROW, Rage, and Fear woke him this morning as they did every morning, with dog kisses, sloppy tongues licking his face. They didn't cease pestering him until he rolled out of bed, washed his face and relieved himself, and let a servant bring him tunic and hose. He led them down the stairs and outside, where they ran, tucking their tails and tearing around like wild things, barking with pleasure, snapping at garlands of ice on low-hanging branches. It hadn't snowed yet, although Candlemass, the first day of winter, was only a week away, but every morning the ground sparkled with a coldly beautiful frost.

When the hounds had run off their high spirits, he whistled them back, and they followed him meekly to the hall. He seated himself in the count's chair, and his people came forward as they did every day, wary of the hounds who lolled at his feet but otherwise respectful: this week so many apples had been pressed and laid aside into barrels for cider; goats had gotten into winter wheat at the Ravnholt manor, and the man who worked the field wanted the woman who owned the goats to pay him a fine for the damage they had caused; a laborer up by Teilas wished for the count's permission to marry at the new year; the shepherds had cut out fifty head of cattle for the Novarian slaughter, those animals deemed unworthy to be wintered over; his clerics wished to know which grain stores should be opened next for the distribution of bread to the poor. Duchess Yolande had sent a messenger to say she would arrive to celebrate the Feast of St. Herodia with her beloved cousin. They had, therefore, about six weeks to make preparations to house and feed her entourage. The falcons and merlins must be flown. There was hunting to do, both as sport and for meat to smoke against the lean months of late winter and early spring.

He took something to eat at midday and then, as always, he climbed the stairs to the chamber where Lavastine's corpse lay as cool as stone, without any taint of decay. Terror lay on one side of the bed, Steadfast on the other, two faithful attendants seemingly carved out of granite. Here beside the draped bed Alain prayed every day, sometimes for an hour or more as the fit took him, but today he merely laid a hand on Lavastine's cold brow, feeling for the spirit buried deep within. It was difficult to believe his spirit was flown when he lay here so perfectly hewn as by a master sculptor, in death as in life. Alain wept a little, as he always did, out of shame for the lie.

Ai, God. Tallia had not been visited by her monthly courses since the death of Lavastine over two months ago. Everyone said she was pregnant, and Tallia herself had begun to murmur about holy conception and a shower of golden light visiting her while she was at her prayers, which these days took up most of her waking hours. Alain could not help but hope against hope even though he knew what Aunt Bel would say: "No cow will calve without that a bull covers her first." It was one of her ways of saying that work wouldn't get done unless someone did it, and he was bitterly aware that he hadn't done his work.

But he was simply too tired to fight past Tallia's resistance. It was hard enough to get her to eat more than a crust of bread each day. It was hard enough to get up each morning himself and sit in the count's chair and ride the count's horse and speak with the count's voice; he kept expecting Lavastine to walk into the room, but Lavastine never did.

But as Aunt Bel would say: No use for the child to cry over what's been spilled; she's better off cleaning it up and getting on with it. Lavastine would have agreed with her. Alain shook himself, kissed the granite brow, and left.

Aunt Bel was much on his mind as he walked to Lavas Church

with three clerics and two stewards in attendance, to oversee the
work going on there. In the spring he and Tallia must go on
progress through their lands, to show themselves, to receive oaths
and give oaths in return. How would he be received at Aunt
Bel's steading? With surprise? With the respect due his position?
Or with scorn and anger? He could not bear to think of Henri;
it still hurt too badly, even after all this time. It infuriated him
that Henri, of all people, would believe that he could lie and
cheat to gain advantage in his life. Maybe it would be better
simply to ride on by and not see them, not now. He could wait.
There was always another year.

But that was the coward's way.

The stone workers sat outside the church in the sun eating
bread and cheese. Strangely, Tallia's attendants also waited outside the church, clustered like a flock of lost doves on the entry
porch.

"My lord count." Lady Hathumod came forward hesitantly.
She looked troubled. "Lady Tallia asked to be left in solitude to
commune with God."

"So she shall be. I'll go in alone." He signaled his own attendants to wait outside, and the hounds flopped down at the
threshold.

He hadn't seen her since yesterday and, pausing in the nave
of the shadowy church, he didn't see her at first as his eyes adjusted. Light from the east-facing windows fell on the altar. Midway along the nave, the stone bier was rising slowly, dressed
stone by dressed stone, to make a fitting resting place for Lavastine's corpse.

Her slight figure knelt on the steps before the altar, shoulders hunched and shaking. He walked forward so quietly that
she didn't hear him, and as he came up beside her, he heard her
grunting softly with pain.

"Tallia?" He gently touched her on the shoulder.

She cried out and jerked back from him. In that moment, he
saw what she had been doing: scraping at the wounds on her
palms and wrists with an old nail. Blood oozed from the jagged
cuts. Pus inflamed the gash on the palm of her right hand. Seeing his horrified expression, she began to weep helplessly.

He did not know what to do, except to take the nail away
from her.

Finally, he coaxed her back to their chamber. He settled her

on their bed and chased away her servingwomen, even Hathumod. She only stopped weeping because she was too weak to
cry for long. Her face was sunken, almost skeletal, her skin so
translucent that the veins showed blue. She hadn't washed in a
long time: he found dirt behind her ears and a collar of grime
at her neck. Her feet were filthy, and her knees scabbed and
scaly from all those hours of kneeling. Her wrists felt so thin
he thought he might have been able to snap them in two were
he angry enough.

But, strangely, he wasn't angry. He was just very tired.

"Tallia," he said finally in the tone Aunt Bel might have used
after she'd sat up three nights running with a deathly ill child
who, past the point of danger, had now begun to whine that she
didn't like her gruel, "you are not well. You will remain in bed,
and you will eat gruel and bread pudding every day, and greens
and meat, until you are strong enough that you don't forget yourself in this way again."

She began to whimper. "But God must love me. God will
only love me if I suffer as did Her beloved Son. It is through
our suffering that we become close to God. Then I can become
close to God, too. I wish you would let me build a chapel. Then
God would love me more because I was so obedient."

"I love you, Tallia," he said, without passion. He felt astoundingly tired. The nail weighed in his hand as heavily as a
grievous sin, and maybe it was. He did not wave it in her face,
or accuse her. Maybe the first time *had* been a miracle.

But she was still going on about God's love and a shower of
golden light and a pure vessel molded as Her Son's bride, who
would be clothed with the odor of sanctity granted to all saints
beloved of God when in fact—even in a chamber strewn with
dried lavender and honeysuckle to sweeten the closed-in scent
of winter and sachets of hyssop and mint to drive off fleas and
vermin—he could smell her, an odor like milk gone sour.

"You haven't washed," he said. He rose, fetched cloth and
pitcher, and sat beside her on the bed. He was too exhausted to
coax her, but he knew what had to be done. "Give me your
hands."

She complained in a weak voice as he washed her hands, her
elbows, her neck and face, and her filthy feet and knees. Because he ignored her and simply did what needed to be done,
she finally acquiesced to his attentions.

The water was brown when he finished. He turned the nail through his fingers, examining it, but it told him nothing except that blood stained its point. The nail could not speak. Then he looked at her to see that she was staring at the nail in her turn, eyes as wide as if she'd seen an adder resting in his hands. He sighed, pulled the pouch out from under his tunic, and drew out the rose. Its petals lay cool and sweet in his palm. A thorn pricked his finger and blood welled.

She whimpered, staring at him, or the rose, or the nail, or his blood, as if these were signs of the Enemy. Or perhaps she was just afraid he would betray her secret, and her sin.

"Lie still," he said firmly, and, amazingly, she lay still as he stroked the delicate petals along the ugly gashes on her palm, the stroke an hypnotic rhythm as he rocked

as they rock, riding heavily on the waves as they leave the still waters of the fjord behind and come into the sound. He stands in the stem of the ship, holding an empty wooden cup in one hand and a small chest in the other. The waters part before him, stream alongside to form a frothing wake behind. Heads bob in the surf, his ever-present companions.

With eleven ships he races south toward North Jatharin, because a messenger has come from Hakonin saying that their outlying lands have been attacked and halls burned by Eika gone raiding out of Jatharin. Many slaves have been taken, or killed, and worst of all, a nest of eggs was stolen. This insult must be avenged, and in a way, it is a kind of test. If he cannot protect those who are sworn to ally with him, then one by one his allies will sail away on dawn waters seeking a stronger ally. Seeking the one who has named himself Nokvi, Moerin's chief, friend to the Alban tree sorcerers.

He turns, finally, and beckons to the priest, who shuffles forward holding what looks like a spear completely wrapped in saffron-dyed cloth.

"You have returned from your journey," he says.

"Have I? Where do you think I have been?"

"North and east, south and west," he replies. "Above and below. These are all mysteries which only the wise can fathom."

"Who is wise, and who is foolish?" cackles the priest.

"We shall see," he answers. "What have you brought me?"

The priest chants nonsense in reply, as priests are wont to do. "Falcon flies, nightwing dies. Raven calls, ash tree falls. Yoke of gold, song of old. Serpent's skin, tooth within. Dragon's wing, wolf's heart-string. In flute's breath, magic's death. Where he stands, lives the land." As he chants, he unwraps the cloth to reveal a man-high half of painted wood adorned with feathers and bones, unnamable leathery scraps, the translucent skin of a snake, yellowing teeth strung on a wire, the hair of Swift-Daughters spun into chains of gold and silver, iron and tin, beads of amethyst and crystal dangling by tough red threads, and several bone flutes so cunningly drilled and hung that the breeze off the water moans through them.

"Did I not travel over sea and land, under the water and through mountains, above the moon and even to the fjall of the heavens, to find these things?" wheezes the priest. "Did I not bring you what I promised?"

Stronghand grasps the haft. It hums against his palm as though bees have made their hive inside the wood—and maybe they have, although he can see no opening. He examines it all around, and except for the humming that emanates from the half it appears to him as any standard that marks out one chieftain's followers from another's, little different from that he himself made when he triumphed at Rikin's fjord. It is only an object; it cannot speak to him to tell him the truth.

"This will protect me from magic?" he asks. "What of those who follow me?"

The priest rattles the pouch of bones at his skinny waist. With effort he focuses his cloudy eyes as if he is trying to see only in this world, not in the many worlds, as priests are rumored to do. He speaks in true words instead of riddles and questions. "I have labored many months to devise this working. I am wise in the threads that weave magic. This amulet is your banner. Bear it with you, and it will protect you and yours from magic as far as you can spread your arm of protection."

He smiles, holding out the cup in his other hand. "I have a strong hand. In it I can hold many."

"What of our bargain?" wheedles the old one. "How will you give me freedom from the OldMothers?" He almost shivers with excitement. His skin is like a leathery old purse slipped loosely over scrawny bones. Stronghand wonders how old he really is. How many winters has he seen? How did he stretch the span of his years beyond that natural for a son of an Old-Mother's nest?

But he is resigned to never discovering the truth. Perhaps some truths are better left unspoken.

"It is easy enough to give freedom from the OldMothers," he replies.

He signals, and his warriors grab the priest's arms to restrain him as Stronghand flips open the chest. The scent of blood and power are strong, but he does not hesitate. He plunges his knife into the priest's pumping heart. The old creature thrashes, jerking, trying to call down a curse, but the amulet protects Stronghand and his followers from magic. Blood spurts freely from the priest's mouth, and Stronghand catches it in the cup.

Only in death is there freedom from the decrees of the Wise-Mothers, who, like the rock, live for uncounted generations. Their children are like the rain, touching rock briefly before they flow away into the river, into the fjord, into the sea.

As the cup fills to the brim and blood spills over the side, he sees the priest's spirit swirling in the greenish-copper liquid. He hears a disembodied howl: "No, no, no, I have been tricked!"

As the body ceases its thrashing, as the last blood pumps in sluggish jerks and slows to a trickle as the body sags, the priest's spirit reaches with threadlike mist fingers, trying to find a house for its dying spirit; but everyone there is protected by the amulet. It expands in widening circles, seeking, groping, and once it leaves the cup, he takes one swallow of the priest's blood and then passes it around to his soldiers, who each take one swallow. In this way the priest's essence will be diluted among the many, and his vengeful spirit cannot return.

Suddenly, the mistlike hands find the thread that links his body to that of his brother in blood, the one he sees in his dreams, and it races down that thread like a spark of fire as Stronghand takes the empty cup to the railing.

"Throw the body into the sea," he orders, and it is done. Merfolk surface to circle the sinking corpse. Behind him, the chest and its now desiccated heart are placed in a brazier. The smoke of their burning stings his nostrils. He leans on the railing and turns the wooden cup in his hand. The last drop of blood beads on the lip of the cup and falls. As the drop shatters in the waves, a last, faint howl of fury and defeat vibrates that thread that binds him to Alain Henrisson, and then it is empty. The *priest's spirit has dissolved. Waves slap the ship. The oars are pulled in, and the sail is hoisted. Wind batters it; they come round, tacking.*

From far away he hears a seagull's mournful cry. Surf pounds on unseen rocks.

Casually, he lets the cup roll off his fingers. It falls, hits water, and vanishes into the sea.

The nail rolled out of Alain's fingers and he jolted up, clutching the rose in his other hand.

"No, no, no, I have been tricked!"

Who had spoken? But there was no one in the chamber.

Tallia had fallen asleep.

He picked up the nail and hid it in the pouch, nestled together with the rose.

2

EVER since Rosvita had been given the *Vità* of St. Radegundis, she had had strange dreams. Voices whispered in her dreams in a language she could not quite understand. So many people were staring at her, and yet they weren't people at all, they were strangers who had once walked these roads and then vanished; they had been lost a long time ago, but they had left a message if only she could read it. But the words swam close and then skittered away until she could not tell where one left off and another began.

"Are we safe?" she asked, but she was very hot, sweating until the walls seemed to run, bleeding away bright murals of an exotic landscape into white.

"Rest, Sister. You are ill." She thought perhaps it was Theophanu who spoke to her, or it might have been Fortunatus, or else the ancient nun who had spoken of the Great Sundering, the one who rubbed salve into her aching chest when it was an effort simply to breathe. It was easier to sleep, and to dream.

A golden wheel flashed in sunlight, turning. Young Berthold

slept peacefully in a stone cavern, surrounded by six attendants whose youthful faces glowed in a shifting glamour of light. A blizzard tore at mountain peaks, and on the wings of the storm danced moon-pale daimones to a melody of envy and mystery and fear. A lion stalked a cold hillside of rock, and on the plain of yellowing grass below this escarpment black hounds coursed after an eight-pointed stag while a party of riders clothed in garments as brilliant as gems followed on their trail.

The lost ones surrounded her, crowding her with their jewel eyes and barbaric clothing, whispering secrets in her ears: "I did not protest as long as I saw that our lord father preferred his firstborn, for that is the way of things, and as one of those who came second I did not mind waiting behind the first, because I saw that he was worthy. But what good is my high birth if our lord father marries again and sires younger children whom he loves more and sets above me? Why should I serve them, when I came before them? Is that not why the angels rebelled?"

She woke up.

"Sister Rosvita." Princess Theophanu sat on a stool beside her. She looked as robust as ever, if a little pale. Was that anxiety that swept her face? It was hard to tell, and the expression vanished quickly. "I brought you porridge and wine. And news."

"Let me eat first, I beg you, Your Highness."

Rosvita lay on a cot in a small monastic cell cut out of the rock. The whitewashed walls seemed so stark compared to the strange and compelling frescoes that had decorated the other chamber, that haunted dreams made rich by a lung fever brought on by exhaustion. For a long while they had despaired of her, but once over the worst of it, she had been moved away from there and into this cell, which lay close to the refectory.

A servingwoman brought forward a tray with a wine cup and bowl, then retreated to the low archway cut into the stone that led into the corridor beyond, out of earshot. Theophanu waited patiently, hands folded in her lap; a thin beam of light from the smoke hole illuminated her face. By this means alone Rosvita knew it was daytime. At the convent of St. Ekatarina, time held no purchase. One day slipped into the next here confined in the rock walls, shrouded from the world outside, and the only constant was the round of prayer, the canonical hours that slid one into the next, Vigils becoming Lauds becoming Prime becoming Terce becoming Sext becoming Nones becoming Vespers becoming Compline becoming Vigils again. And on and so on, like God in Unity, the circle which never ends.

As soon as Rosvita finished, Theophanu leaned forward to gather tray, cup, and bowl from Rosvita's lap and set it on the floor. The movement covered her whisper, as quiet as that of the Aoi in Rosvita's dreams. "Perhaps I should give myself up to Ironhead in exchange for letting Adelheid go."

"Is our situation so desperate?"

In the dim light it was hard to see Theophanu's expression clearly. Was that anger or anguish that flashed across her cool Arethousan features? "It is desperate enough. The good abbess has been generous with her stores. But we are seventy-five people and fifty horses in a convent that houses nine. There cannot be more than a week's worth of food and fodder left. We have taken everything that the nuns have, and won no advantage against our enemy. If I give myself up to Ironhead, then we would not leave the nuns destitute."

"A noble gesture, Your Highness. But we know what kind of man he is. He would make a poor husband."

"He would make a husband. I have been patient, Sister. I despair of my father ever agreeing to marry me to any man, or even to the church. Ironhead is ambitious and ruthless. Am I any better in my heart? I would rather have a husband like Ironhead than wait for my father to marry again and displace me with younger children who please him more."

"It is your words I heard in my dream! I thought it was another voice—"

Was that color in her cheeks? "I beg your pardon, Sister. I should not have spoken so rashly. The Enemy troubles my thoughts."

"Be patient, Your Highness. Surely in this harsh land Ironhead is having trouble maintaining an army of three hundred men."

"So we have hoped. But Ironhead is not stupid. I have other news." Some tone in Theophanu's cool voice made Rosvita dread what would come next. "You must come with me, Sister. You must see. I am not sure I can trust my own eyes."

Such a statement could not help but kindle Rosvita's curiosity, always a flammable thing. She rose and was pleased to find her legs steadier today than they had been yesterday. Theophanu called her attendant in from the hall to help Rosvita dress. Then they made their way down a tunnel carved out of stone that led to the refectory. Light poured in through seven windows carved into the rock high up in the wall, revealing a single trestle table, enough for the nine women who made their home here, and the tall loom at which Sister Diocletia knelt, having just thrown newly-measured warp threads over the crossbar. She acknowledged them with a nod, then grabbed a handful of loose threads and deftly began tying them to a loom weight.

Beyond the refectory a terrace opened out. Rosvita heard the sounds of Ironhead's camp: mallets and hammers pounding in a ragged rhythm, captains calling out orders, men grunting and cursing. Their cries carried easily, echoing off the monumental rock face of the huge outcropping into which the convent was carved. The terrace was a commodious slab of south-facing rock high up on the cliffside. The sun spread such a pleasant light over the terrace that it was hard to believe it was winter, two days after Candlemass. At a shallow basin hollowed out of the rock, Teuda, the stout lay sister, hunched over, grinding grain into meal. Pots of grain soaking in limestone water sat beside her, next to a basket for the freshly-ground barley. A spacious garden filled the rest of the terrace, cut into quarters by walkways raised above the soil and handsome interlaced screens that served as windbreaks. No doubt the dirt had been drawn up basket by basket from below. Sister Sindula was weeding mint; she was quite deaf, and intent on her task, and did not notice them. But the other lay sister, young Paloma, knelt a few strides away, watering herbs. She set down her ceramic beaker, stood, brushed the dirt on her robe back into the plot, and crossed to them. No older than Theophanu, she already had a withering look to her like that of her elderly companions, as if the wind sucked them dry on this isolated height.

"Come." She led them to the railing from which they could look down.

Off to the right on a lower terrace, a dozen of Fulk's soldiers stood guard over the winches. The smaller winch had been damaged in the last attack, one of the support legs smashed by a rock from a catapult. The larger winch held the big basket in which she had been hoisted up on that day six weeks ago, although she recalled it now no more clearly than she would a dream. According to Theophanu, Captain Fulk and his soldiers had devised a broad strap to replace the basket so that they could winch up the horses rather than lose them to Ironhead. She traced with her eye a series of drops and shallower ledges, the ladder path; all the ladders had been drawn up and taken inside. There were also several steep staircases lower down, and an abandoned winch, burned in the first assault. Cliffs loomed above them, broken into giant stair-steps that ended in a small tabletop plateau marked by a stone crown: from this angle she couldn't count the great stone slabs set upright at the flat height, nor could she imagine how anyone could possibly have carried them up this massive outcropping that was almost too steep to climb.

"For a holy place," remarked Theophanu, "it is certainly defendable."

"No doubt the ancient mothers who hollowed out the convent here were well acquainted with the imperfections of humanity."

The scaffolding being built by Ironhead's soldiers now reached about halfway to the lower terrace, with a broad base, reinforced sides, and plenty of dampened hides to protect the timber. Ironhead had even allowed his troops to cut down the dozen mature olive trees growing at the base of the cliff. No one seemed idle. Ironhead's banner flew from the central tent, well out of arrow shot of the lower terrace and almost out of sight where the gully cut away to the left. She did not remember riding down that gully on their last gallop to safety, but she could see it was the only path to the convent.

"Is there something new you wished me to see?" She saw it just as Theophanu pointed to a banner fluttering atop a small traveling pavilion half concealed behind Ironhead's palatial white tent: red silk with an eagle, dragon, and lion stitched in gold.

"Isn't that the sigil of Wendar?" asked Paloma. "Does that mean the king of Wendar has come?"

Rosvita almost laughed, imagining the king confined to such a paltry tent and with no sign of his elaborate entourage. "Nay, child. A party riding on King Henry's business and under his safe conduct would carry such a banner. There, at the tip, is a gold circle. That signifies an embassy led by a cleric from the king's court."

"They arrived yesterday at dusk, escorted by Ironhead's soldiers," said Theophanu.

"Can it be that your father has heard of our plight?"

"You shall see," said Theophanu. She turned to the young lay sister. "Paloma, you know the route." The young woman nodded. "Gutta," she said to the dark-haired girl, "go see what work awaits you in the kitchens."

Paloma led princess and cleric back through the refectory, down a side tunnel that banked into stairs, and through a hanging that concealed a smaller tunnel ventilated by air holes. Soon it grew too dark to see except by touch, and they crept forward as quietly as wolves nosing up on unsuspecting prey. Then, abruptly, dim light filtered through a screen carved so cunningly out of a thin sheet of rock that they could see into the lit chamber beyond without their own shapes being revealed. Rosvita eased in beside Theophanu and together they gazed into the whitewashed guest hall. Rosvita had come to that hall four days ago to see Brother Fortunatus who, like the soldiers and male servants, could not venture into chambers consecrated as a holy convent. Now she saw only soldiers standing at nervous guard over a pair of Aostan clerics. A red-haired Eagle stood off to one side, expression shadowed.

"It still seems incredible to me," one cleric was saying to another in Aostan. "I've crossed St. Vitale's Pass in Aogoste and met blizzards. I don't see how his party could have made it over the pass this late in the year and then brag of fine weather." He dropped his voice. "What if it was weather sorcery? Yet none of his escort will utter an ill word of him. It's as if he's bewitched them all."

"Or was wrongfully accused."

"You know as well as I that normally St. Vitale's Pass is closed from mid-autumn to early summer. I've never heard of any party crossing a week before Candlemass!"

The other man shrugged. "It's been a mild winter. They just had good fortune. The soldiers I spoke to said that as they came down the last few leagues it had begun to snow behind them."

"That proves nothing. It could still have been weather sorcery. What about those other tales we've heard? What about those lights we saw from the height of the rock last night? You heard screaming, too."

"Hush," said his friend, glancing toward the soldiers. "We're here to see that he keeps his word to Lord John, nothing more. What matter if there *is* sorcery at work? Sometimes I wonder what harm there is in sorcery, if it can be used for good. I'm sick enough of this siege and these rations that I'd not care if magic were used to persuade Queen Adelheid to surrender, so we could finally go home."

"Dominic!" His friend drew the Circle of Unity at his chest, like a ward against evil.

Theophanu tugged on Rosvita's hand, and Rosvita followed her into a passage so narrow that rock rubbed her shoulders, then her head, and she had to kneel and walk forward on her knees like a penitent approaching the altar. The path dipped, Theophanu let go of her hand, and she touched a stair-step and, farther up, Theophanu's sandaled feet. She pulled herself up beside the princess in a cupboardlike space scarcely large enough for both of them. A hazy veil more mist than light screened one side of the space, but it took her a few moments to understand where she was.

They crouched together crammed inside the altar carved into the chapel. The light that burned without, veiled by a screen of cloth, came from two lamps hanging from iron racks set on either side of the tiny chamber.

A man knelt before the altar, head bowed, hands clasped as he prayed. She could not see his face, but she did not need to see his face. She felt Theophanu trembling beside her like a doe caught in a net. She knew the set of those shoulders, that golden sheen of hair, the perfect posture, neither too humble nor too proud as he knelt before God's altar and prayed in his mellifluous voice.

"Lord, my heart is not haughty nor my eyes lofty;
neither do I exercise myself in things too high for me.
Lady, surely I have behaved and quieted myself.
My soul is like that of a weaned child clinging to its mother.
Let us put our hope in God, for ever and ever."

A cleric straightened up after ducking through the archway that led back into the guest hall. "I beg pardon for disturbing you, Lord Hugh."

He looked up. It was truly amazing how perfectly the light framed his features even when he could not know that someone watched him. His expression was somber, his eyes kind. "Brother Dominic." He smiled gently, not quite enough to reveal the chipped tooth. "Speak, Brother. Tell me what troubles you."

"Has the mother abbess replied to your request yet, Lord

Hugh? Will she see you and allow you to speak to Queen Adelheid?"

"I have heard nothing yet. But I trust in God, as must we all."

"Some have wondered if you volunteered to negotiate with the mother abbess only to escape Lord John's captivity. After all, you are safe from him up here. You might hope for rescue and watch from safety while those who brought you this far suffer below."

"I am humbled by your accusations, Brother, but I would be first to acknowledge that I deserve them." As he spoke, his features perfectly composed, he toyed with a red ribbon twined in his left hand. "I bear no ill-will toward the clerics and soldiers who were given the duty of escorting me to the skopos. Lord John's soldiers should not have taken us prisoner and brought us here, and once Lord John learned of our destination, he should have freed us to continue on. But I understand that he is an ambitious man and hopes to make use of us as hostages. If I fail here, then I will join my companions in a martyr's death. If I succeed, then we will ride on to Darre and I will present myself to the skopos as I was bidden at the Council of Autun."

Brother Dominic grunted, as if himself displeased. "Your words are reasonable, Lord Hugh." He hesitated, and finally spoke in a voice as low as that of a man plotting against his master. "It is hard to believe that any council could condemn you."

Hugh bowed his head. "God know the truth."

Brother Dominic shuffled nervously, as if he feared he had said too much. "I will leave you to your prayers." He retreated.

For a long while Hugh knelt there, head bowed, unmoving, saying nothing. Rosvita scarcely dared breathe. Her gaze was caught by the painting on the wall opposite, faded now but still perfectly legible. The images depicted a party of Aoi dressed in feathers and short capes and not much more passing through a burning archway that led into a circle of standing stones. Beyond the stones lay a second and smaller stone crown, about a quarter the size of the first circle, situated within a cluster of buildings of a strange and wonderful design; a party of travelers, painted proportionately small, emerged from the second stone crown out of an arch of flame.

Hugh's movement pulled her back. He drew out a small chest

that had been concealed by the fall of his robes. A blood-red ribbon wound like ivy through the clasp that locked it tight. He untied the ribbon, raised the lid, and lifted out a sprig of juniper and a rectangular shape muffled in linen. Unwrapping it, he revealed a book.

Rosvita jerked back, hitting her head against rock. She caught a gasp in her throat. How had he regained *The Book of Secrets?* He began to read out loud.

> "When the Moon is full, the studious one can by means of the threads woven by the planets and the heated air engendered by the Moon's waxing coax down to the Earth the daimones of the lower air, those who live beneath the Moon's sway. It is well known that men who are perverted and greedy for earthly gains are more susceptible to their influence, and the studious one may gain what she desires in this way: If she wraps the threads of the heavens neatly around these daimones and speaks the charms and the seven names of the holy disciplas and burns the smoke of juniper and fennel to cloud and chain their spirits, then they will do as she bids them. By certain unseen ways they insinuate themselves most subtly and marvelously into the bodies of humans because their own bodies have little corporeal substance but partake of the air and fire of heaven, and through certain diverse and imaginary visions they mingle their own thoughts with those of their hosts until one mouth may utter what another mind whispers."

Ai, God, what had happened to Liath at the judgment at Autun? Her head throbbed.

Theophanu nudged Rosvita, and with Paloma they backed up along the tunnel until they emerged into the main corridor. She had to rest because her legs trembled and ached as if she'd just climbed the rock itself, but when she had recovered her strength, they walked in silence past the chapel where hump-backed Sister Carita knelt in prayer. Beyond the chapel lay the tiny library whose vertical shafts gave enough light that Rosvita could see all the shades of color in the soft rock, gray and pink and cream, that striped the walls. Sister Petra sat at the scribe's lectern, situated so that the light from the ventilation shafts striped her work. With practiced strokes, she drew her quill across parchment. Rosvita paused. Weeks ago in the throes of the worst of her fever, she had asked Mother Obligatia to continue the copy Sister Amabilia had been making of the *Vita* of St. Radegundis. Was Sister Petra copying Brother Fidelis' work?

Theophanu and Paloma had gone ahead, so she hurried after them instead of going in to ask. Many hands had worn the walls smooth, and the ground slid like finest marble under her slippers, burnished by the passage of many feet over the centuries. They descended stairs and here, deeper in the rock, they came to a landing so dim that they almost ran into Sister Hilaria, who emerged from the broad stairs that led down to the well. Two full buckets swayed on the yoke set over her shoulders and a third balanced on her head on a base of rolled-up cloth. She smelled of water and dripping rock. Behind her, two of Adelheid's servingwomen staggered onto the landing and set down half-full buckets as they caught their breath and shielded their eyes from the light.

"A good day to you, Your Highness," Sister Hilaria said, seemingly unwinded by her climb. "Sister Rosvita, it is good to see you on your feet."

They stood aside to let her pass before them into the kitchens. Smoke stains decorated the walls above the kitchen hearths where huge ventilation shafts let in light and let out smoke. A fire burned on the middle hearth, tended by poor Sister Lucida, who was not only crippled but not quite right in the head. At the single table, Gutta and another woman kneaded dough, in flour to their elbows. Gutta wore a crude burlap apron to protect the queen's fine gown. Two other servants made themselves busy, stirring a thin soup flavored mostly with horse fat and patting out flat cakes.

Sister Hilaria emptied the water into a barrel. She patted Sister Lucida on her shoulder, and the crippled nun bobbed her head happily and said a few slurred words which Rosvita could not understand. Sister Hilaria laughed. "Nay, I shan't let you have all the onions. You're a glutton for onions, and I won't be the one to lead you into sin!" Lucida honked out a laugh, and with a cheerful grin Hilaria set yoke and buckets over her shoulders for another trip to the well just as the other water-bearing women finally made it to the barrel. "Just one more trip, friends!" Hilaria cried enthusiastically, "and we'll be done."

"For this hour!" groaned one, but Theophanu and Paloma had already gone on, and Rosvita hastened after them. She was still weak and didn't trust her legs, so she went cautiously down a steep ramp that rang with strange echoes. It grew dark quickly, and because the nuns had no oil to spare for lamps they had to feel their way. Rosvita noticed the change: a yeasty scent, a roughening of the walls under her seeking fingers. She stumbled on the lip of a little ditch dug into the rock, and Theophanu took her by the elbow to steady her. Groping, Rosvita discovered a millstone set on its side, rolled away into a recess cut into the rock.

"Careful," said Paloma. "It can be rolled across the passageway to block it."

"In the event of an attack," said Theophanu. "The nuns who built this place surely had little trust in human kindness."

"Oh, no," said Paloma with surprise. "The nuns didn't carve these chambers. They've always been here, so the story goes. The nuns and Teuda and I just live here. Even Mother Obligatia doesn't know how far into the rock the labyrinth goes. I've taken a candle and gone down to explore, but there's never time to get far before the candle burns low. Come. It's just around this corner."

It took Rosvita a moment to identify the sounds echoing around her as music, and then they rounded a corner and came into a cavern so high that she couldn't see its ceiling for darkness. A single lamp burned, revealing Queen Adelheid seated at her ease while soldiers entertained her. One had a battered lute, decently tuned, and he strummed a cheerful tune while a companion played the tune on a pipe. A trio slapped out drum patterns on their thighs and another man trilled birdcalls as a counterpoint to the melody. At the edge of the light, half a dozen soldiers stamped and spun in intricate little turns, dancing. It was odd to see Queen Adelheid smiling and clapping as if this rustic display pleased her as much as an elegant court entertainment. Her noble companions stood behind her, some enjoying themselves, others looking strained and tense. Adelheid saw Theophanu and beckoned to her, indicating a chair next to hers. As soon as the soldiers saw Theophanu, they faltered and ceased their playing.

Theophanu removed the pillow from the chair and set it on the floor. "Sit here, if it pleases you, Sister."

"I thank you, Your Highness. Your Majesty, where is Mother Obligatia?"

"She is still with the wounded."

"If I may attend her for a moment?"

Both queen and princess assented. A soldier came forward to escort Rosvita to the side chamber where the wounded lay, and as she ducked under a low arch carved into stone, she heard the music begin again behind her, echoing weirdly in the great cavern.

Weeks had passed before Rosvita had understood that the ancient nun who was tending her through her sickness was Mother of the convent. Now, by the light of a single lamp, Mother Obligatia knelt beside a fair-haired man who had been wounded fighting off one of Ironhead's fruitless attacks. She was carefully rewrapping the poultice at his shoulder.

"Bless you, Mother," he murmured as Rosvita came up beside them.

She said a blessing over him before bracing herself on a stout walking stick as she struggled to her feet. Before Rosvita could move forward to aid her, Captain Fulk appeared at her side to help her up.

"How may I assist you, Mother?" Rosvita asked.

"Stay beside me a moment, Sister. I am done except for this poor soul, but I fear there is nothing I can do for his wounds."

One man rested apart from the others, and he lay silent except for a ghastly whimper that escaped him at intervals, sometimes followed by a string of hoarse words that made no sense until she realized he was speaking in Aostan, not Wendish: "no beginning no end cold sting in my heart falling the stone it hurts Lord protect me Ai God! the eyes!"

The shadows were a merciful cloak. His injuries had festered. Skin peeled away from his mouth, exposing teeth and gums, and one eye seemed seared shut with silvery threads impressed into the curve of his skull. A faint metallic scent stung her nostrils, a flavor like iron filings that she could almost lick from the air. Then Mother Obligatia undid the wrappings that covered his chest. Rosvita gagged at the stench of decay and had to step back.

A hand steadied her: Captain Fulk. He murmured an apology and hastily stepped away. The soldier holding the lamp shut his eyes.

From the pool of darkness outside the lamplight, Brother Fortunatus ghosted into view to take his place at Rosvita's side.

"You are well, Sister?" The murky light made his face seem unnaturally pale, or perhaps it was only the poor soldier's suffering.

"You are too anxious, Brother," she said fondly. "I am recovering well for a woman of my years. I have nothing to complain of. Dear God, how could I?" She gestured. "What has happened to this poor man? Is he one of Queen Adelheid's soldiers?"

Mother Obligatia dabbed a sharp-smelling ointment on his wounds, and the soldier began thrashing, moaning horribly. Rosvita had to look away as Captain Fulk knelt to hold the man down.

Brother Fortunatus shifted nervously before he spoke in a whisper. "There is magic here, Sister. It has been hidden from us until now."

"You cannot believe that Mother Obligatia or any of these good nuns indulge in sorcery?"

"There is a secret hidden here," he insisted stubbornly. "Look at him. He was brought in last night, just before Vigils. It seems odd to me that their attack should come only hours after Lord Hugh begged leave to speak with the queen."

"What do you mean?"

The man gasped out a strangled croak, an unintelligible word, and then passed out. The threads of silver burned into his face gleamed, pulsing as if to the beat of his heart.

"He is one of Ironhead's soldiers. A party of a dozen or more climbed the north face of the outcropping last night. They reached the stone crown at the summit at dusk. I suppose from there they meant to drop down upon us from above."

She felt abruptly weak, shaken with memories of uninterpretable dreams. The ground seemed to rock beneath her like a boat shifting on the waters, and her stomach ached. "I must have been asleep."

Fortunatus caught her elbow. His voice trembled. "You were very ill, Sister. I despaired of you."

His concern steadied her. She could look at the poor man lying unconscious on the ground; Mother Obligatia worked efficiently. "What became of the other soldiers, then? Were they taken prisoner?"

"Nay. Some creature haunts the stone crown. It killed them. This man was the only one to survive, and he will not live long."

Mother Obligatia rose with Captain Fulk's help and stepped away from the dying man. "There is nothing else I can do," she said to Fulk. "Has he taken any water?"

"He cannot keep it down, Mother." Fulk's expression was grave.

Obligatia nodded and at once made her way, hobbling slowly, out of the little side cavern with Rosvita, Fortunatus, and Fulk in attendance. Captain Fulk brought her a stood, and she sat between Adelheid and Theophanu, gesturing with a hand to show that the musicians should finish. Rosvita settled herself on the pillow at Theophanu's feet, and Fortunatus in attendance behind her. When the soldiers' song was done, Mother Obligatia turned to Rosvita.

"Sister Rosvita, I am pleased to see you looking so strong. You have seen our visitor?" Mother Obligatia was sharp without being proud, wise without being serene, and generous without being kind. As always, she came straight to the point. "He was sent by Lord John to negotiate an end to the siege. His companions from Wendar are being held as hostage for his good conduct. Do you know who he is?"

"Hugh of Austra," said Theophanu in a tone as cool as if she were reciting the list of crops to be planted, "illegitimate son of Judith, who is margrave of Austra and Olsatia as well as a valued companion to my father, King Henry."

"You are acquainted with him," said Mother Obligatia.

"If I may speak," said Rosvita quickly, and Theophanu nodded. After six weeks subsisting on Mother Obligatia's charity, Rosvita saw no point in sliding around the truth. "I believe that both Princess Theophanu and I were sent south to Aosta so that we could not testify when Father Hugh was brought before a church council last autumn in Autun. He was accused of sorcery."

Adelheid sat forward, expression bright and curious. "Would you have spoken for him, or against him?"

In the dim light, Theophanu looked more than ever like an ancient queen caught in paint on some ancient church wall, gilded with gold leaf, eyes darkened with kohl. She replied without emotion. "We have reason to believe that the charges laid against him were true. We must not trust him, whatever promises he makes."

"Strong words," observed Adelheid.

The ancient mother toyed with the polished walking stick laid across her thighs. Behind, half lost in shadow, Captain Fulk and the soldiers had hunkered down to listen. "It is difficult to know whom to trust when charges of sorcery are at hand," she said.

"Have you had experience in these matters, Mother?" asked Rosvita.

"I have seen things I wish I had not. But nevertheless, in a week our stores will be depleted. It is time to make a decision. I am perfectly willing to starve for a point of honor, but I cannot ask my nuns to do likewise."

"Then it appears we must speak to him," said Adelheid. Her smile flashed like laughter. "My soldiers say he is a remarkably handsome man. Is that true, Cousin? I haven't yet seen him."

But Theophanu would not be drawn. "You must make up your own mind on that score, Cousin."

"Then it is agreed that we will speak with him?"

"I am against it," said Theophanu coolly. She glanced at Rosvita; they all did.

Rosvita sighed. "In truth, Your Highness, there is no choice. I am no more eager than you, given what we have seen and experienced, but under these circumstances we must see what he has to say."

"I will not go to Ironhead without a fight," said Adelheid. The fierce lift of her chin and the ringing trumpet she made of her voice contrasted baldly with Theophanu's inscrutable calm, and by no means did Theophanu come off the better.

Captain Fulk stepped forward. "If I may speak, Your Majesty? Your Highness? Mother?" When they assented, the soldier went on. "We must take action soon, one way or the other. Both food and tempers grow short, trapped as we are. We've already lost a quarter of the horses. After last night there are rumors of a goblin haunting the stone crown. My men are afraid of stable duty, because those halls lie so close to the summit. Some are fearful that now that the creature has tasted blood, that it will stalk them. Some would rather surrender than die in such a terrible way."

Everyone quieted, and Rosvita realized now how much tension had ridden the air. The yellowy gleam of the lamp gave scant protection from the darkness. But Mother Obligatia showed no sign of nervousness. "A daimone does indeed haunt the stone crown at the height of this rock, but it is not more dangerous than the goblins that lurk in the hearts of those who are discontented with their lot in this world. My predecessors and I have guarded this convent since the days of St. Ekatarina, four hundred years ago or more. We have not been troubled by the creature trapped above, nor felt its claws."

"Where did it come from?" Theophanu asked. "Why does it haunt this place?"

"It has always been here. That is why I forbade your party to explore the crown."

"You said it was a consecrated place, forbidden to any who are not sisters in this convent," objected Adelheid. "You did not say it was haunted by such a creature!"

"Now you see why it is forbidden. We do not tell everything we know. Nor do we need to."

Even a queen could look abashed. Adelheid did so now. "I beg your pardon, Mother. I'm sure you know better than we do in such matters."

"Ancient knowledge must be guarded lest it fall into hands made rough by ignorance or ambition. Do you think we want a man like Lord John suspecting we have secrets hidden within these walls?"

"Like the knowledge of the Aoi," murmured Rosvita, but Mother Obligatia had keen ears and now swung her walking stick off her thighs and rapped it once, sharply, on the floor. The sound rang with echoes in the cavern, and men jumped, startled. A murmur, a ripple of nervous chuckles, spread and settled.

"With old secrets it is better to be cautious. I would rather you not have known, because an ancient secret is like a great stone. Resting on the shore undisturbed it remains silent. Uprooted and cast into a still pond it creates strong ripples that alter the very fabric of the water and may even overset or wash away the net of life that flourished there."

"I give you my word, Mother Obligatia," said Adelheid. "You have shown us much generosity. I will never reveal your secret."

"If any of Ironhead's soldiers escaped after their attack last night, they will have a tale to tell. So be it." She settled her stick over her thighs as if to indicate that the matter was closed. "Captain Fulk. Have a dozen of your men escort our visitor here. Be sure to blindfold him. What he does not know he cannot reveal to Lord John."

Captain Fulk chose five men and went himself with one lamp. Because they had so little oil left them, Mother Obligatia suggested they wait in darkness, and no one was eager to object. With the lamp snuffed out, the darkness in the cavern was so profound that Rosvita could not see her hand held in front of her nose. She felt the chill of the stone as intensely as the fever of curiosity as she sat in the blackness with the rustle of nervous soldiers around her. What would Hugh say? How had he come to be here? How had he gotten *The Book of Secrets*? What was the creature that haunted the stone crown? Was it truly a daimone, and if so, what did a daimone look like? They were creatures of the aether who lived above the sphere of the moon, so how had it become trapped here below the moon? With what power had it killed the soldiers? Would it come in search of the rest of them, or did the crown itself contain it? And if the crown did contain it, then what property inherent in the stones could confine a creature of such power and unearthly provenance? And if so, did all stone crowns hold within themselves intrinsic magical properties? Was it even possible that poor Berthold had somehow been imprisoned within the stone crown above Hersford, instead of killed by a fall or a cave-in, as she had assumed? Was there truth in her dreams?

Theophanu shifted in her chair. Fortunatus coughed softly.

"Perhaps a song," said Adelheid in a voice that the darkness made startlingly bright, like a sudden shaft of light that makes the eyes sting.

Tentatively at first and then more forcefully as the sound filled the echoing space, the soldiers began to sing: *"To the Lady and to the Lord both light and dark are one."*

"I have been reading your *History,* Sister Rosvita," said Mother Obligatia as the soldiers continued with a quiet tune composed of more secular sentiments: a lost love, a long journey.

"I fear it is incomplete. Had I time, and with your permission, I would consult your library to see what I could learn from any chronicles you may have here. Yet here in Aosta there is no reason why chronicles would contain records of the doings of the Wendish. No doubt my people are still considered barbarians to those who once ruled as part of the glorious Dariyan Empire."

"Then it is well you are writing their history, since no one in Darre will do so. I came here from the North."

"You have surprised me, Mother. I hear no trace of the North in your speech."

"I was raised from an infant at a convent in Varre, but when I was fourteen I was taken from there to St. Radegundis' convent in Salia. Indeed, I came to her convent not six months after St. Radegundis passed out of this world and into the Chamber of Light."

"That is incredible. Surely you have looked at the *Vita,* then?"

"Sister Petra has been copying it diligently these last six weeks. You yourself in your delirium mentioned that this manuscript is the only copy in existence. Such a precious document must not be lost to us." Her voice had the familiar quaver of age, as fragile as stalks of flowers torn by a gale. The company had stilled, and it was silent as Obligatia spoke as a biscop might, reading from the scriptures to edify her congregation. " 'The Lord and Lady confer glory and greatness on women through strength of mind. Faith makes them strong, and in these earthly vessels, heavenly treasure is hid. One of this company is Radegundis, she whose earthly life I, Fidelis, humblest and least worthy, now attempt to celebrate so that all may hear of her deeds and sing praise in her glorious memory. The world divides those whom no space parted once. So ends the Prologue.' "

Something in the abbess' tone made Rosvita's skin prickle, like a mouse nibbling cheese down to the fingers that hold it.

"How did you come by the book, Sister Rosvita?"

"I received it from Fidelis' own hands—" She broke off, hearing Mother Obligatia gasp, as at a pain.

"His own hands! You must have been very young."

"Not at all, Mother. He lived to an incredible age. It was not two years ago that I received it from him."

"Two years! How can that be? He was already old—"

The ring and echo of soldiers' voices and of boots tramping on stone cut through the old woman's reply, and light rose just quickly enough that Rosvita caught the end of Mother Obligatia's gesture: wiping a tear from her cheek.

Then Hugh came among them. It was impossible to know how he could walk so gracefully, blinded by cloth bound over his eyes. Steered by Captain Fulk, who kept fingers pressed to Hugh's arm, he knelt before the three women, whom he still could not see. Rosvita hitched the trailing edge of her robe sideways, half afraid that if any part of him came in contact with it, he would know of her at once, that he would know everything about her and all that she suspected, all her loyalties and weaknesses.

"I had hoped to be brought before Queen Adelheid or the blessed Mother of this convent," he said in his beautiful voice. The soldier holding the lamp stood behind him, which had the effect of giving a halo, the crown of saints, to his golden hair. "I am Hugh of Austra, son of Judith, margrave of Austra and Olsatia. I beg you, let me speak if that is your will."

"I am Adelheid." She rose, though she knew he couldn't see her, but surely he heard the change of position because his head shifted slightly, an odd questing motion like that of the great cats Rosvita had seen in the menagerie in Autun, lifting their heads when they heard the sound of the gate being opened and closed as a deer was driven into their enclosure. "How did you and your party come to be here, Lord Hugh? This convent lies on none of the main roads."

"Your Majesty." He did not precisely incline his head, but he had mastered the art of shifting his shoulders to show respect: as proud as a nobleman, he was not too proud to acknowledge her greater rank. "We had crossed St. Vitale's Pass and were riding south to Darre when we were accosted on the road by Lord John's soldiers and brought against our will to this encampment. We still wish to ride on to Darre. That is our only goal."

"Then why did Ironhead send you up here, if you are his prisoner? What of the other people in your party?"

"Alas. Lord John is an ambitious man, Your Majesty. I will tell you truthfully that he was suspicious of our reasons for traveling. He suggested that we must be agents of King Henry of Wendar. He believes that we have messages for the skopos from King Henry regarding the fate of Aosta. He was blunt, Your Majesty." He paused as Adelheid laughed. "He said that were *he* Henry, he would send a message to the skopos offering protection and gold if she were to support him as king of Aosta."

"Is that the message that you and your company are bringing to Darre?" asked Adelheid sharply.

"Nay, Your Majesty. I have been accused of sorcery, and I am being sent before the skopos to be judged." How easily the words came out of his mouth, so easily that for an instant it was impossible to believe that he had been anything but falsely accused. "Lord John sent me to persuade you to surrender in return for letting my party go. That is all."

"Or in return for letting you go free, so that you can escape the skopos' judgment!"

The cloth blindfold did not conceal his beautiful mouth. He smiled now, not quite enough to reveal the chipped tooth. "I do not intend to persuade you to surrender, Your Majesty. I intend to reveal to you how you can make your escape. After that, I will convince Lord John to release me and my party so that we can continue on to Darre."

Adelheid laughed delightedly, and Rosvita realized that she was enjoying the match, like two swordsmen playing at an absurd battle. "What loyalty do you have for me and my followers?"

"I have no loyalty toward you, Your Majesty, although I hope you will not take offense from my plain speaking. I am a loyal subject of King Henry. If Lord John captures you, he will force you to marry him and use that claim to establish himself as king of Aosta. King Henry has ambitions in Aosta as well."

"Does he?" asked Adelheid coyly. "I am not altogether sure what it is that Henry wants in Aosta." She glanced at Theophanu but did not address her directly. Theophanu sat unknowable in her silence.

Hugh seemed caught by surprise. "King Henry sent a force south to find you, Your Majesty, but perhaps you did not meet them. That would account for this terrible situation you now find yourself in. Therefore I beg you, Your Majesty, let me act as King Henry's ambassador: he seeks to aid you, who are the rightful queen of Aosta. He will aid you with an army, if need be."

"Yet I have heard he seeks to marry me to his bastard son, Sanglant, whom he intends to become king beside me."

There it was: a change in his expression as startling as a peal of distant thunder ripping away the calm of a hazy summer day. Then it was gone. "Why give to the son what the father deserves?"

"Do you think Henry wishes to marry me?" asked Adelheid.

"He would be a fool to turn away from a woman of your rank and quality, Your Majesty."

Theophanu came alive as a painted figure might stir, cracking its shell of paint, to walk out into the room. "My father's

wishes cannot be known to you! He hopes that Sanglant will
marry Adelheid."

"Your Highness!" He was startled. He shifted, marking her
place. "I did not know— This blinding cloth has disoriented me,
or surely I would have been aware of your presence—"

"And changed your tale?" demanded Theophanu. "But I am
here, and I have listened. How do you intend to aid Ironhead in
his plans?"

But he was more in control than she was. "No man can serve
two masters. To aid Ironhead for my own gain would be to betray King Henry." He had the elegant speech of a courtier, graceful and pleasing, but for the first time Rosvita heard a different
timbre ring underneath that elegant tone, one as unyielding as
granite. "I have done things I am not now proud of, I have been
made to see how shamefully petty ambition can ruin a man of
promise. But I have never acted in any way against my regnant." He almost seemed to be daring Theophanu to suggest otherwise, but she did not reply.

"I wish to hear Lord Hugh's proposal," said Adelheid.

"Is the Mother of this convent here?" asked Hugh. "Her permission must be gained, for what I propose might not meet with
her approval."

Theophanu's grunt was itself a comment.

"I am here, Son," said Mother Obligatia. "Speak freely before me."

"There is a crown of stones atop this rock. It is possible to
travel long distances quickly through gateways created by the
architecture of these stone circles."

"To travel?" demanded Adelheid, then laughed as at a particularly fine joke. "You must explain yourself, Lord Hugh. I do
not understand you."

"When we travel by ship, Your Majesty, we make landfall
not at any cliff or coastline but at harbors suited to putting
ashore. Think of the stone crowns as harbors, and the road traversed between each crown not as land or sea but as the aether,
the element of the seven spheres, all that lies above the moon."

"How can this be possible?" cried Adelheid. "Isn't it blas-
phemy to suggest that we can travel the aether while we are living? Only the souls of the dead ascend through the seven spheres
when they journey toward the Chamber of Light."

Hugh turned his head toward Mother Obligatia; despite his

protestations about the blindfold, he could distinguish where each of the speakers sat. "Even the wall paintings in the guest chapel reveal the real purpose of the stone crowns. I cannot say if there are other paintings hidden away within this convent which reveal other secrets. But the painting I saw confirms that the ancient Aoi knew how to use the stone circles. Perhaps they even built them, for in the old stories they are portrayed as great magi."

"Can this be true, Mother?" asked Theophanu in a low voice. "Surely this is only the raving of a deluded mind. You don't believe him? Do you?"

Mother Obligatia was silent for a long time. Then she said only, "Go on, Lord Hugh."

He inclined his head to show respect and obedience. "Yesterday at dusk I observed strange lights emanating from the summit of the hill. I heard horrible screams. I even smelled a strange scent like that of lightning that has just struck, and I wondered. Can it be some creature resides there, guarding the crown? I have seen other crowns, but they are not so haunted, not any that I saw or heard tell of."

"Indeed, Son, you have guessed correctly. A daimone is trapped within the crown, by what agency I do not know."

"How long has it been trapped there?"

"Our records always speak of it dwelling there. St. Ekatarina founded this convent over four hundred years ago. So if it is possible to travel through the crowns, and I admit I am not sure I can believe such an incredible claim, then in any case ours is closed to such traffic because of the daimone which haunts it. It will kill anyone who comes too close."

He knelt with head bowed for a long time, and Rosvita watched those watching him. Adelheid leaned toward him as toward a tawny leopard that she wanted to stroke and yet remained unsure whether it might bite off her hand. Theophanu's gaze was fixed on Hugh as if he were a snake about to strike. Mother Obligatia merely watched him.

At last he lifted his head and spoke. "What if I can bind that daimone, and free you from its shadow on this convent? Then Queen Adelheid, Princess Theophanu, and their followers can escape through the crown, and Ironhead can do nothing to stop them."

Adelheid sat back, face shining as if she had discovered that

the leopard was vicious after all, and was pleased to have such
a wild creature in her menagerie. "And you would come with
us, leaving your party in Ironhead's hands?"

"Nay, I would remain behind. I will not abandon my escort.
They are good men, and do not deserve such a fate."

"If you succeed at this plan, Ironhead will murder you for
betraying him. You have met him. How can you believe otherwise?"

"I recognize the kind of man he is. My mother is the same.
I know how to handle Lord John."

"Surely, Cousin, you would not put your life in this man's
hands," said Theophanu with soft fury. "How can we agree to
be aided by the very sorcery for which he was condemned by
the church? He himself admits that he was sent to be judged by
the skopos for his crimes! How can we trust him? He could as
easily send us into the crown to be killed by this creature—!"

The soldiers and courtiers all began to talk at once, a disturbed buzz that Captain Fulk did nothing to silence. Adelheid's
noble companions afflicted the queen with a flood of questions
while Theophanu's stouter companions were quieter but no less
agitated as they whispered to each other, pulling on sleeves and
pointing and gesturing. Hugh did nothing but listen, and Rosvita
was abruptly afraid to breathe, as if he could hear the distinct
quality of her breathing and by that means identify her. Had he
known Theophanu was there all along? Was he only playing with
them? Yet the annoying suspicion plagued her that in speaking
of his loyalty to King Henry, he was speaking truth.

The servants huddled in the darkness caught the fever, and
soon the noise lifted until it echoed in the cavern.

Mother Obligatia rapped her walking stick three times on the
floor, and there was a sudden numbing silence punctuated by
two coughs and a sneeze. "That is enough," she said without
raising her voice. "We have heard what Lord Hugh proposes.
Captain Fulk, escort Lord Hugh back to the guest hall, where
he will await our decision."

Captain Fulk gestured to the escort. Hugh rose gracefully, as
acquiescent as a tamed fawn.

"I pray you, Mother, let his blindfold be taken off before he
goes," said Adelheid. "I would like to see if he is as handsome
as everyone says."

Mother Obligatia merely turned her walking stick in her hands.

"In the convent of St. Radegundis, we worshiped at mass on either side of a screen that ran down the center of the nave so that we could not look one upon the other, female upon male. For as St. Radegundis herself was recorded as saying, 'The Enemy knows many ways by which to tempt women and men away from their holy path.' I have held to that rule here, and I do not let my nuns look upon men once they make their oaths as novices. But I know that custom is different in Wendar, and that clerics of both sexes mingle freely in God's work."

"I am no nun in any case, and not desirous of becoming one," said Adelheid.

"Even if that were the only way to save yourself from becoming Ironhead's bride?"

The question slipped out with deceptive smoothness. Theophanu's eyes widened, and she looked abruptly thoughtful. But Adelheid flung her head back, laughing, as if passion and price were things to be rejoiced in and embraced, the soul of her existence. "I will be queen in my own right, or dead, Mother. You know I mean no disrespect to the church."

"So you will," agreed Obligatia, and Rosvita could not interpret the emotion in her voice. "Very well. Let him be unmasked for a moment."

At Adelheid's order, a lamp was lit. As Captain Fulk untied the cloth, Rosvita scuttled backward to hide herself in the shadows behind Theophanu's chair, and as Theophanu's remaining ladies shifted forward to see better, she was further hidden by their skirts. She could not see, only hear, as Hugh spoke in a gracious and amiable tone.

"Your Majesty," he said. "Your Highness. Mother."

Rosvita imagined him punctuating the greetings with an elegant bow, suitable to the humble yet melodious tone.

"Handsome enough," said Adelheid while her companions whispered and giggled among themselves, "but one young pretty husband was enough for me! He was always at the poor servant girls, and I've always wondered if it was one of them who pushed him down the stairs the night he died, Lady forgive him for his faults."

"The Lady and Lord know our faults well," said Mother Obligatia, "and They are merciful. Captain, blindfold him and return him to the guest hall, then come back here."

It was done. Hugh was led away.

Rosvita slipped back to Theophanu's side. No one had time to comment on her odd behavior since Adelheid stood immediately to address abbess and princess.

"I say we chance it."

"We can't trust him!" cried Theophanu. "He'll drive us into the crown and let this terrible creature murder us all. Then Ironhead will be rid of us."

"Ironhead needs me! I am the last surviving member of the royal house of Aosta. Our kin has ruled here for fifty years. He can legitimately claim the throne only through me."

"Not if you're dead," retorted Theophanu. "Then the field is open."

"Not to him! His mother's father was a mercenary who made his fortune fighting with the Jinna and who later sold his daughter as a concubine to the lord of Sabina. But *she* was known to have had many lowborn lovers, and one of them is commonly supposed to have sired Ironhead."

"How came he to the lordship, then?" asked Theophanu.

"Ironhead murdered his half brother and married the widow, who possessed noble birth, lands, and treasure. But he sired no children on her, and the Arethousans now occupy her lands. No one knows if he murdered her or banished her to a convent. Do you think the nobles of Aosta will kneel before *him?*" Her anger cooled abruptly, and she turned to the abbess. "I beg your pardon, Mother. This is not our choice, is it? If you forbid it, then we cannot act."

Obligatia smoothed her hands down the length of her walking stick. "I will not interfere if you choose to accept Lord Hugh's aid."

"Do you think it possible the crown can serve as he says it can?" asked Rosvita, startled.

"When my predecessor was on her deathbed, she spoke to me privately and passed on to me knowledge that has been in the keeping of the abbesses here since the days of St. Ekatarina. I have no proof, I have seen no evidence myself, but there are stories of crowns being woven into gateways that can lead a traveler to distant lands."

"An old magic now lost to us," mused Rosvita. "Yet, Your Highness," she added, addressing Theophanu, "did we not see the painting on the wall of the guest chapel? It could signify a way of traveling that humankind has long since forgotten—or never known."

"I am against it," replied Theophanu stubbornly. "I cannot do anything but speak against it, because I believe now and always that he tried to murder me by means of magic. But you have not yet said what you think, Sister Rosvita. Do you agree with me, or do you agree with Adelheid?"

"Is it right to accept aid from one who has already been censured for the act we would demand from him? And yet, a man like Ironhead who would cut down mature olive trees and castrate his enemies' loyal soldiers is not wise enough to make a good regnant. And if he is not of noble blood, then he is not worthy—" But strangely, she thought of Hathui, and she did not finish the comment. "In any case, Your Highness, we must act to benefit your father, whom we know to be a just and wise regnant." Yet she could only shake her head, burdened by the sudden weight of it all. "Nay, I cannot make a decision quickly when the matters before us are so grave. I must have time to think it over."

"Very well," said Theophanu, all cool strength again. "I will abide by your decision, Sister Rosvita. I will agree to whatever you choose."

"I pray you, Your Highness!" cried Rosvita, almost laughing, for the burden seemed doubly weighty now.

"Nay, I have spoken. I will agree to whatever you choose, Sister, because in this matter I trust your judgment better than I trust my own."

Ai, God! Theophanu trusted her to see Hugh in a reasoned light, where Theophanu could only view him through a veil of hatred and, perhaps, thwarted desire. But Rosvita was not sure she could judge Hugh and his offer with any greater wisdom, not given her own prejudices in the matter. She was not unbiased; she might yet be proved wrong about Liath.

Yet judge she must. The fate of a queen and a princess and the future of Aosta itself rode on her shoulders now.

Everyone was waiting on her. She found her voice at last. "If I might have some solitude to reflect, Mother?"

The abbess nodded. "As you wish, Sister. Paloma can escort you to the library."

It seemed a fitting place for a woman of her inclinations to make what might prove to be the most difficult, even damning, decision of her life.

3

IVAR woke disoriented. His head hurt, and his mouth tasted like rotten fish. After a moment, he realized he was not alone. Someone who was very warm, rather damp, and quite naked pressed against him on the lumpy bed. From elsewhere in the dim hall, he heard whispers, giggles, grunting, and a moan that trailed off into a gasp of sudden pleasure.

The person beside him stirred. "Are you awake, my lord?" She had a high, breathless voice, like to a woman in the throes of carnal ecstasy. Last night at the Feast in honor of Candlemass, that voice and her body had inflamed him past endurance; that, and the wine, of course. But it was like this every night, here in Gent in the newly built dormitory hall of the monastery of St. Perpetua, Lady of Battles and patron saint of the chaste and of barren women. Every night Father Ekkehard ordered a feast laid out and buxom young women brought in from town to serve food and drink, and after dicing, and singing, and dancing, and wrestling, and a great deal of wine, some of the girls left, and some stayed.

Someone flung open a shutter, and he shut his eyes. The light made his head pound. The girl slid off the bed and peed in the corner; he heard the quiet splash of it on the juniper boughs strewn on the floor. A moment later she sat down heavily next to him and stroked his loins unenthusiastically.

"We can ride that horse again, my lord," she said. "You know how I do love to ride."

In the sour grip of morning, her voice didn't sound quite as sincere as it had the night before. She sounded tired and frankly rather bored.

He fumbled under the mattress, found a few coins, and thrust them into her hands. "Nay," he said. "Go on, then."

"Ah!" For the first time, he heard real passion. "That's so generous, my lord."

He only waved his hand. He had to pee, and he wished mightily that she was gone. Yet as the girl shrugged on her clothing and left amidst sounds of other women leaving, someone vomiting, and the roll and scatter of a dice game starting up, he wished even more that he could fly away with her. But not *with* her, precisely; he didn't care any more for her than he had for the woman he'd bedded before her, or the one before that, or perhaps it had been the same woman several nights running; he wasn't sure. But Ekkehard never seemed to tire of their nightly feasts, and since Ekkehard was prince, and newly ordained father of the monastery of St. Perpetua on the Veser, they followed where he led.

"Darling Ivar." Baldwin plopped down beside him, as naked as the girl had been. He was all sweaty, his hair was rumpled, and someone had dumped the dregs of the wine pot over his head. He was still the handsomest man in the hall. "We're off to hunt. New game's been sighted in the eastern woods. Get dressed!"

Ivar groaned.

"Ridden to exhaustion!" Baldwin laughed. "Foundered! Or is he?" He nuzzled Ivar's neck far more passionately than the young woman had, and Ivar felt the familiar stirring of lust between his legs. Most anything could rouse it these days; most everything did.

"Not yet lamed!" Baldwin let his hands stray as he lay down beside Ivar on the narrow bed. And why not? There wasn't anything else to do here, day in, day out. At least Baldwin really loved him. The woman had just wanted the coin. "Dear Ivar. How was she? Tell me about it, everything you did with her. Did she touch you like this? Did she remind you of Liath?"

Ivar bolted up, lust banished. "I have to pee." He practically fell off the bed in his haste to get away. The movement made his head swim, and his stomach curdle. He threw up into a corner, and began to weep, and after a bit he realized that Baldwin crouched beside him, a steadying hand on his back.

"There, now, I'm sorry," said Baldwin. "I promised you before not to talk about her anymore."

"I hope she's dead," said Ivar furiously. "She abandoned me. She never cared for me at all."

"That's right, agreed Baldwin. "Here, lie down again. You look ill." He whistled sharply, and one of the servingmen hurried over. "Get him some wine. And get my clothes."

"I don't like it here," muttered Ivar. His head throbbed. "But there's nowhere to go, and no reason to go, and nothing, nothing, nothing! And I don't much like the prince," he added, hating himself for whining.

"I don't either," confided Baldwin. "But he got us away from the margrave, didn't he?" The serving man returned with a cup of wine and Baldwin's clothing. "Come now. Where's that sweet smile?"

Ivar couldn't muster up any smiles, sweet, grumpy, or otherwise. He flung an arm over his eyes and lay there, hating himself and everything around him, except maybe Baldwin.

Must his head pound so? A moment later, the door into the dormitory hall was shoved open so hard that it banged on the wall behind. Baldwin leaped up. The ill-named Brother Humilicus appeared in the door like the wrath of God, glowering, with a frown so deep that it seemed permanently chiseled into his handsome features. He had been set in charge of the new monastery by King Henry; it was his precise and orderly rule that Ekkehard had, upon arriving, overset completely.

But Ivar didn't like Brother Humilicus either. In fact, Ivar no longer liked anyone, anywhere, anyhow. Except maybe Baldwin and Ermanrich and Sigfrid, because they had suffered with him at Quedlinhame. Except Lady Tallia, but he didn't really *like* her; one didn't like or dislike a saint. Saints lived beyond crude emotion. They simply existed to be venerated.

Yet he had done nothing but drown himself in wine and carnal lust.

Baldwin got a strong grip on his arm and yanked him to his feet as the other young novices stumbled up to show respect to Brother Humilicus, their senior in every way.

Including piety.

Prince Ekkehard sprawled on his bed, staring sulkily at Brother Humilicus but not bothering to rise. His bed was set somewhat apart from the others and, as was usual for him, he had two girls with him, one on either side. Milo lay curled like a dog at the foot of the bed, snoring loudly. One of the girls dressed hastily as Brother Humilicus stared at her with disgust. The other, Ekkehard's favorite, was a pretty, dark-haired woman at least five years older than the prince. Her slender body already showed signs of pregnancy. Carrying a royal bastard had made her proud, and she took her cue from the prince: She stretched insolently, displaying swollen breasts and belly.

"You have missed morning prayers, Father." Brother Humilicus felt obliged to say this every morning.

"So I have. Here, Milo." He nudged Milo with a foot, and the boy snorted awake. "Get me my hunting clothes. Dear Brother Humilicus, please see that the horses are ready. Will my cousin Lord Wichman be coming with us?"

"As you wish, Father," replied Brother Humilicus tonelessly. He withdrew without further comment.

Ivar pulled on his tunic, stumbled outside, and washed his face in the cistern. Although winter's chill stung the air, no ice had formed over the water. In the last month or so snow had dusted the ground two or three times and melted off, and it had rained a few times, nothing more. As he stood breathing in the cold air, the ache in his stomach subsided, but nothing could ease the ache in his heart. He didn't want to be here in Gent; he didn't want to go back to Heart's Rest or Quedlinhame, and he couldn't anyway. There was no reason to be anywhere. He had had a good life before Liath. He had been happy then, almost. It was all her fault.

"Maybe she did witch you," said Baldwin, coming up behind him and resting a hand companionably on his shoulder.

Ivar began to weep, hated himself for weeping, and got angry instead. "What was the point of seeing the miracle at Quedlinhame? Why would God torment us with seeing Her handiwork so close up, and then abandon us?"

Baldwin shrugged, found a ceramic pot on the ground, and used it to sluice water through his hair. When he straightened, he set the pot down and wiped water from his eyes and lips. A bead dripped from his nose. "God never abandoned us. The miracle is still with us in our hearts, if we let it be. Maybe Liath was really an agent of the Enemy, like they said at the council. The biscops and presbyters wouldn't condemn her for no reason, would they? Maybe she shot a poisoned arrow into your heat, Ivar, and that's why you're so sad and angry all the time. Prince Ekkehard has noticed it. He's not sure he wants you among his companions if you won't drink and laugh and sing with the rest of us."

"And whore and be drunk every night and never pray and do nothing but please myself? That's hardly God's work!"

Baldwin picked a spray of wilted parsley, chewed on it, then spat it out. "How can we know what God's work is? I just do what I'm told."

"You don't! You ran away from Margrave Judith."

"I had to," said Baldwin solemnly. "God made me. God whispered to me that Margrave Judith sent her last husband into a battle where she knew he'd be killed, because she wanted to marry me. God warned me that she'd do the same to me in four or five years, when a younger, handsomer boy came along."

Ivar regarded Baldwin in the fine light of a pleasant winter's morning. "Baldwin, there isn't a handsomer man than you, not in this entire kingdom."

"She might still get tired of me. She might sell me to the Arethousans, and they'd cut off my cock. They like eunuchs there. That's what Father Hugh told me. Anyway, I don't like her and I never will. I don't want to be married to a woman like that. She treated me like a horse! Just something she would use and then keep around until she needed it again!"

"Is there a woman you *would* like to be married to?"

Baldwin considered this for a long time. "One who treated me well," he said finally. "But meanwhile, I'm free of *her*. If I had to be Prince Ekkehard's whore before and his flattering courtier now, so be it. If I have to embrace his leftover whores because he thinks that's funny, so be it. I don't mind, as long as they don't smell. Why should I mind it?"

"Because it's boring."

"Boring!" Baldwin's perfect features registered astonishment. "A woman or two every night, or a friend, if you wish that instead. Hunting almost every day. Good food and the best wine. Singing and dancing and wrestling. Acrobats to entertain you in every way. Poets singing tales of ancient battles. How can that be boring?"

"Ai, God!" The notion, once conceived, took root fiercely in Ivar's heart. "But it's just the same thing over and over again. In the end, you've nothing."

"The same thing! You can't tell me you weren't as amazed as the rest of us by those acrobat women and what they could do. Lord Wichman would have made them stay a month if he could have."

"But they didn't stay a month, did they? None of them wanted to." Ivar recalled the acrobats vividly. The lithe, half-naked girls who had done rope tricks were zealously guarded by the men of the troupe, even to the point of offending an amorous Ekkehard, but two of the older women had performed in other, quite astonishing, ways for the men. But the troupe had left as soon as their pockets were filled with coin and gifts. *"They didn't like us.* No more than you liked being Margrave Judith's husband. Animals eat and drink and hunt and rut, Baldwin! How are we different from the beasts, as we are now?"

Baldwin blinked at him. A sudden burst of color and noise erupted from the dormitory hall as Ekkehard and his companions emerged into the cloister, laughing and chattering. The few monks who still labored under Brother Humilicus' rule scurried away into the church, which was the only place Ekkehard never profaned with whores.

"Come!" the young prince ordered. "Baldwin! We go to hunt!"

Baldwin grabbed Ivar by the wrist. "You've got to humor him," he muttered, "or he won't protect us!" He tugged Ivar along in the prince's wake, and Ivar let himself be led: After all, there was nothing else to do. At the monastery gate they were met by Ekkehard's cousin, Lord Wichman, who paced with furious energy. Looking up, he saw Ekkehard.

"You're late abed, little Cousin!" he cried. "We should have been out an hour ago. I won't wait for you again!" It had taken Wichman months to recover from the wounds he had received at the battle for Gent last summer, and he still limped, but he was otherwise hale and restless and, as Count Harl often said of such restless young men, ripe for trouble. He had made himself de facto lord of Gent in the absence of any other claimants, and he ruled by turns leniently and intemperately. He laughed now. "And I won't have to! I've received news that there have been Quman raids in the East. My companions and I are going to ride east to fight the barbarians!"

"I'll go with you!" cried Ekkehard.

"You've no experience fighting. You'll just slow us down and get in the way."

Ekkehard had a pretty face and a mulish way of thrusting out lips and chin when he was crossed. "How can I get experience fighting if no one will let me ride into the field?"

"You're an abbot now." Wichman laughed again, not particularly kindly. Ivar didn't think Wichman liked his young cousin; he tolerated him because he was bored. "You have spiritual fields to tend."

Ekkehard did not back down easily. "But just yesterday you got a message from Duchess Rotrudis that you were to return to Osterburg to get married. What about that?"

"I burned the message." Wichman shrugged. "I'll tell my mother I never received it."

"I won't tell her that," said Ekkehard slyly. "I'll write to her myself and tell her all about your disobedience."

Wichman scratched his beard, shifting off his bad leg. "Very well. But it's your head that'll hang from a Quman belt, not mine, Cousin." He didn't say the words fondly. "You and your companions can ride with me, but I warn you, you must abide by my command. I won't have you getting the rest of us killed because you're foolish."

Ekkehard thought about this, but he wasn't stupid. "Very well," he agreed. "*Now* can we go to hunt?"

One of Wichman's companions stepped up and whispered in the lord's ear. "Ah." He beckoned. A ragged-looking person was brought forward from the rear of his troop. "I've a gift for you, a fish my guards netted at the gates last night. He demanded to be let in, said he'd come all the way from Firsebarg in Varre at your express order. But it's just another monk, and a fat one, at that. I don't think your lemans will think much of him." Then Wichman laughed with a sharp grin. "He's not pretty like the other ones."

And there he was, looking tired but still stout and untroubled. His bare feet were a mass of sores, and his hair was ragged and grown long, but he was happy to see them.

"Ermanrich!" Baldwin pounded Ermanrich on the back and then led him before Prince Ekkehard, who allowed Ermanrich to kiss his hand and then dismissed him. He was of no further interest.

"Come, Baldwin," said the prince. "I got you what you wanted. Now we'll go hunt."

"I'll stay behind and make sure he's tended to," said Ivar quickly, and Baldwin gave him a quick look, a silent gesture of approval.

Permission was granted. In truth, the young prince cared not one whit whether Ivar stayed or followed. Horses were brought;

the prince and his followers mounted and rode away all in good cheer.

Ivar led Ermanrich to the infirmary, empty at this hour except for the infirmarian. That good man regarded Ivar suspiciously and signed Ermanrich to lay down on a cot. He rubbed Ermanrich's feet with lavender oil, then clipped and combed his tangled hair. After that he left, no doubt to inform Brother Humilicus of this new arrival. Ivar regarded Ermanrich's feet with awe: the skin on the soles was cracked and dry, as thick and tough as horn. "Did you walk the whole way? Barefoot? In this cold?"

"It took me two months!" cried Ermanrich cheerfully. "And what a fine road it was!" He rolled onto his stomach and tugged up his robe to display his backside. A mass of old welts and stripes marked his rump and back. "The prior at Firsebarg himself whipped me every day because I wouldn't recant! But I knew God would hear my call." He let his tattered robe drop and heaved a sigh of relief. "Then Lord Reginar came from Firsebarg and released me to come here, to Gent. I knew God had called me!" Ivar handed him ale and bread, and as he bolted his bread between sloppy swallows of ale, the chanting of monks in the church serenaded them. Ermanrich broke the silence finally. "Do you chant mass at all hours here? They only did that at feast days at Firsebarg."

"Nay. You heard that Queen Mathilda died?"

"So we did, may she rest in peace. We prayed for a whole week. Then Lord Reginar let me go."

"The queen bequeathed her computarium to Prince Ekkehard. So the monks here pray for the souls of the dead written into that book—all her dead kinfolk and, oh, as many other people as gave fine gifts to Quedlinhame or did some other service. All those prayers take up most of the day."

"But I saw Prince Ekkehard ride out to hunt. Isn't he father here, over the monks? He should be praying, not hunting. The queen's own computarium! How can he treat it so lightly? Isn't it his duty to pray for the souls of his dead kinfolk, as she did, so that his prayers here will help lift their souls to the Chamber of Light?"

"I see Brother Ivar has chosen to hold firm to his vows this fine morning and stay here to pray." The door darkened as Brother Humilicus entered, followed by the infirmarian, who wrung his hands. Humilicus' dry words always made Ivar wince. "What is this? Another stray taken in by our holy father? But he speaks with good sense. Do you seek to serve God, Brother?" he asked Ermanrich.

Ermanrich jumped to his feet and bowed respectfully. "So I do, Brother. I greet you in the name of God, Our Mother, She who delivered Herself of a child born of mortal parents who yet partook of no stain of the Enemy. This child She named Her Son, and through His suffering and redemption we ourselves can be saved." Then he squared his shoulders stoutly, waiting for the rod of martyrdom, or at least a switch across the buttocks.

"A heretic," said Brother Humilicus mildly. "I should have known. But, alas, we have fallen so far that I find I prefer a heretic who serves God with devotion than an abbot who mouths the truth but serves only himself. What is your name?"

"I am called Ermanrich, Brother." He made the sign of respect to Humilicus, and knelt obediently. "I see you are engaged in God's work, even if you are misguided. If you do not yet believe in the truth, then I will pray that God will lead you to the truth in time."

Brother Humilicus merely glanced at the infirmarian, who busied himself brewing some kind of drink over by the cupboard where he kept his herbs and simples. "These are the days when all things are turned asunder. Abbots use the cloister as a whorehouse, and novices lecture their elders. Still, it is an odd coincidence. Biscop Suplicia came to me only yesterday to complain of certain paintings fashioned by the Enemy, telling the tale of this heresy, that have appeared here and there on walls in the city. It's a foul hand that appears fair to the eye but conceals beneath its skin only maggots and worms."

They endured a lecture from Brother Humilicus on the evils of heresy and disobedience, but Ermanrich's presence had bolstered Ivar's heart. For the first time in weeks, he felt hope stir. Perhaps all was not lost. Perhaps life was not a meaningless round of eating and shitting and whoring and vomiting after all.

Who was painting pictures in Gent?

In time, even Brother Humilicus had to leave off. He grudgingly allowed Ivar and Ermanrich into the church to pray at the service of Terce. But Humilicus had a monastery to supervise which he ran on a tight rein in Ekkehard's absence. He did not like Ekkehard's boys, as he called them when the prince wasn't around, and he made no effort to include them in the daily round of monastic life. It was easy enough to slip out the servants' gate and trudge alongside fields of winter wheat and rye, then cross the stone bridge into Gent. Because they were still novices, their hair hadn't yet been cut in a monk's tonsure, so they could pass for young fraters. Fraters passed aplenty through Gent on their way east to convert the heathens or to preach among the newly-converted tribes, the Rederii, the Salavii, the Polenie and the horse-sacrificing Ungrians, the red-haired Starvikii and the warrior clans who called themselves Rossi. Some of these fraters stayed a night at the guesthouse in the monastery, and sometimes Ivar would sneak away from the feasts in the dormitory hall to listen to them converse with Brother Humilicus about their adventures among the flat-faced Bodinavas who ate, peed, fought, fornicated, and gave birth all in the saddle, the dreadful Quman who took human heads and wore wings on their bodies, the Sazdakh warrior women who killed any man who set foot in their territory, or the mysterious Kerayit whose witch women were so ugly that one glance from their eyes would turn you to stone. They all knew tales of other fraters, their brothers in the church, who had been granted glorious martyrdoms among the savages, and they spoke of these blessed events in marvelous, gory detail.

"Look!" murmured Ermanrich, shaking Ivar and pointing to a whitewashed wall. Color crept out over the long white wall, an unfolding tale told with pictures: God reigns in heaven upon her high seat, holding the entire universe in Her hand; into the body of the blessed St. Edessia She miraculously places a holy child who partakes both of human nature and of God's nature; he grows to be a man, and receives in a dream the Holy Word; he preaches, and followers come to him, chief among them Thecla, Matthias, Mark, Lucia, Johanna, Marian, and Peter; he is arrested on charges of sedition by the officers of the Dariyan Empire; he appears before the Empress Thaisannia, and when he refuses to honor her with sacrifices, she condemns him to a criminal's death; he is flayed alive and his heart is torn out of his body, but where his blood falls on the earth, roses bloom.

They stared, and as they stared, Ivar became aware that townsfolk passed by the wall to point and whisper. Someone had placed a withered garland of autumn flowers below the painting that depicted Daisan's suffering at the hands of the empress' executioners.

He moved forward to cautiously touching the painting. The colors already cracked and peeled; a few storms would erase it, as though it had never been. But the images would remain in people's hearts.

Who had done this?

"Stop, friends!" Ermanrich was saying behind him. "Gather 'round! I can tell you of this mystery, which has been hidden from you. Here is the truth! Listen!"

Ivar began to turn round, to silence him—and bumped into a girl of perhaps twelve years of age. She was stout, well-formed, with the golden-blonde hair common to these parts and a peculiar cast of skin, a kind of reddish, nutty brown. She grabbed his elbow and looked him right in the eye, as if trying to see into his heart. Dirt smeared her chin but she was otherwise clean. A well-polished wooden Circle of Unity hung at her chest.

"What is it, child?" he asked, in the way of fraters. She tugged on his elbow, then signed, "Come," in the sign language used by churchfolk. Ermanrich was well launched into a sermon, and townspeople gathered to listen, some with interest, some with scorn, some no doubt because they had nothing better to do.

The girl pulled at him again, and signed again.

"What do you want?" he demanded.

She didn't reply, but she pointed at the pictures and made stroking movements, as with a brush. Abandoning Ermanrich, he followed her.

She walked quickly, ducking into an alley. A stray dog nosed through trash. A broken pot had been abandoned in a shadowed corner under overhanging eaves. They emerged onto a street and walked alongside the wall of the palace compound from whence Lord Wichman lorded it over the town; he had topped the walls with bright banners, red and gold, black and silver, that fluttered in a wind off the river. The girl tugged on Ivar's hand, and they cut through a courtyard where a dye-pot bubbled over an open fire and a delicately-formed girl-child of some four years played with a doll sewn out of scraps of cloth. She looked up and babbled meaningless syllables at them, but Ivar's companion only made the sign of "silence" toward the girl before pulling him on. Beyond well and cistern stood a small door; Ivar had to duck his head to avoid hitting it. They came into an alley made dark by houses built out over the narrow lane until they almost touched walls above. Rounding a corner, he blinked away the sunlight.

There, alongside a freshly plastered compound wall, a crowd of about fifteen people had assembled to stare. The girl tugged him forward, and when the townsfolk saw that she came attended by a frater, they stood aside to let Ivar through.

Beyond them, working feverishly, a slight, robed figure drew figures on the wall and filled them in with dyes: pollen gold, willow purple, cornflower blue, juniper brown. *The blessed Daisan, released from the mortal clothing of his skin, rises to the Chamber of Light to rejoin his Holy Mother. His disciplas, below, weep tears of joy—*

The painter turned to dab at a pot of ink, and Ivar saw his face.

"Sigfrid!"

He jerked up, spilling the pot, turned full to face his accuser. His thin face looked sweetly familiar, but there was something wrong with the set of his jaw.

"Ai, God! Sigfrid! What are you doing here?" Ivar leaped forward and grasped him by the arms, then hugged him. "How did you come to leave Quedlinhame?"

Sigfrid wept a few tears. His gentle face shone with joy as he embraced Ivar in his turn. Then, with ink-stained hands, he pointed to his feet and signed, "Walk." His feet, like Ermanrich's were sore-ridden, callused, and filthy.

"We were there, Sigfrid, at the death of Queen Mathilda. Baldwin and I were in hiding because we ran away from Margrave Judith, and we escaped with Prince Ekkehard, but we couldn't stay in Quedlinhame Convent with the prince because we thought they might recognize us but we went to the church anyway and we heard you, we heard you jump up and start preaching. They dragged you away. Did they throw you out? How did you come to be *here?*"

Sigfrid didn't answer. That supple, sharp mouth merely smiled softly, betraying the intelligence that lit his being. Sigfrid was alive in a way the rest of them weren't. Once he believed, he believed with all of him, every particle. Ivar saw it shining from his face, and for an instant he was seized by the ugly claws of jealousy: Why should Sigfrid be granted such certainty while he spun in this agony of doubt?

But wasn't that only the voice of the Enemy, seeking to make him hate his friend?

He grabbed him by the shoulders. "Sigfrid, speak to me."

Sigfrid indicated the wall, and his hands and then opened his mouth.

They had cut out his tongue.

"God's mercy!" cried Ivar. "Who did this to you? Was it bandits on the road?" Sigfrid shook his head, all the time regarding Ivar with an expression brimming with unspilled joy.

Ivar felt his breath coming in gasps as the awful truth dawned. "They did this to you at Quedlinhame?"

Sigfrid signed, "Yes."

Simply enough: Mother Scholastica had ordered it done, but Sigfrid showed no sign of anger, of hate, of sorrow. God's will had been done: They had cut out his tongue, but they hadn't silenced him. Speaking with the tongue was only one way of talking.

It all flowered then, like the rose blooming from the blood of the blessed Daisan. Sigfrid had given up his tongue because he was not afraid to speak the truth. But Ivar still had a tongue. *He* could still speak, just as Ermanrich preached a few blocks away.

God had chosen them to witness the miracle. In their turn, they must give testimony. After all, it was that easy, God's will made plain. He saw now how everything had led him to this moment, and where they would go from here, riding east with Prince Ekkehard and Lord Wichman into those lands where the hand of the false church did not grip so tightly.

Ivar faced the crowd, now some two dozen in number. The mute girl stared at him, eyes wide, waiting.

The whole world was waiting.

"My friends," he began.

4

IN the hours between Sext and Nones Rosvita sat in the library with the chronicle of St. Ekatarina's convent open on the lectern before her. Most of the entries were innocuous enough: *In the year 287: There was a great plague among the birds. In the year 323: The queen sent her youngest daughter to become abbess over us. In the year 402: A blizzard came untimely in Cintre and all the grapes withered. A party of clerics from Varre stayed three weeks in the guest hall. In the year 479: Certain omens were seen in the villages, and there was a comet that blazed in the southern sky for two months, and after this there was an earthquake. Many villagers came to the ladder to beg for bread. The king died in Reggio.*

Would the chronicle record Queen Adelheid's death? *In the last months of the year 729: The queen starved to death at the convent of St. Ekatarina.* Or there might be other outcomes. *In the year 731: The queen was strangled by her husband, John Ironhead, after a child was born to her who had a legitimate claim to the throne. Ironhead named himself regent for the infant.*

Could they trust Hugh? Would they condemn themselves by trafficking in magic, even to save their own lives? Could his claims possibly be true in any case?

Was history merely a record of one bad choice made in place of a worse one? They had so few options left, and all of them desperate. Yet did it have to be so? She had searched in many chronicles, had learned to read between the lines and in the marginalia so that she wouldn't discover too late things that she ought to have known, that needed to be woven into the story so that her history of the Wendish people would be complete. There was always something that had been left hidden, something that had been forgotten.

What is in plain sight is hidden best, as the old saying went.

The pattern developed slowly and increased markedly over the last one hundred years, after the death of Emperor Taillefer. They began as marginalia but soon appeared within the main body of the text, listings that made no sense but mostly were linked with a comment about a noble entourage that had sheltered unexpectedly in the guest hall: Hersford in the duchy of Fesse, seven stones; Krona in the duchy of Avaria, nine stones; Novomo in the county of Tuscerna, eleven stones; Thersa in the duchy of Fesse, eight stones.

Mice scratched in the walls. "Sister Rosvita. I hope I do not disturb you?"

She started, slapping a hand down over parchment, then

chuckled as Mother Obligatia hobbled in. "I thought you were mice, and then I remembered there aren't any mice here." She rose hastily and drew forward a bench so that Obligatia could sit.

"There are mice, surely enough. Most of us are mice, creeping along the halls of the powerful. If we do not stay out of their sight, they will crush us."

"Strong words, Mother."

"Surely the ways of queens and princes are no mystery to you." She rested a hand on the *Vita* of St. Radegundis, which lay closed on the second lectern next to the almost finished copy, abandoned these hours by Sister Petra, who had gone to help carry water. "Have you found your answers?"

"Nay, I have only found more questions, Mother. I am too curious. It is the burden God have given me. What am I to make of entries like this one: 'St. Thierry in the duchy of Arconia, four stones.' The convent of St. Thierry is near the seat of the count of Lavas, is it not?"

"So it is," said Obligatia, not looking at the chronicle. "I was raised in the convent of St. Thierry, although I never saw Lavas Holding myself. Who rules there now?"

"Count Lavastine, son of the younger Charles, grandson of the elder Lavastine. His heir is a well-mannered and serious young man, Lord Alain, although I must note that he was born a bastard and only accepted as Lavastine's heir about two years ago."

"You are a true historian, I see. Lavastine had no legitimate heirs?"

"He was given no child born in legal marriage. Here is another entry, a place I have visited, above Hersford Monastery." She touched the entry. "Seven stones, just as it says here. Ai, God, Villam lost his son there, who had gone to play among the stones."

"The boy died?"

"I do not know. Young Berthold vanished with six companions. No one knows what became of him, but I had always assumed that he crawled too far in the darkness and fell, and was killed. Now I'm not sure what to believe. Poor child. He had the making of a good historian. He should have been put in the church."

"Ah. It is always a terrible thing to lose a beloved child."

"These are all stone crowns, are they not? When Henry was still prince, he lost his Aoi lover at Thersa, the one who gave him his son, Sanglant. She, too, vanished among the stones, so the story goes." She turned another page, searched it, and read out loud. "Brienac in the lordship of Josselin in Salia, seven stones. Here, another with seven stones, in the ruins of Kartiako. I did not know there were so many stone circles."

"No one can know, unless they look. That which is in plain sight is easily hidden."

"But they were built a very long time ago, even before the Dariyan Empire. The chroniclers of that time mentioned them as being ancient then, and they wondered if giants had once roamed the earth. No one knows who built them."

"Who do you think built them?"

"Giants, perhaps. But if it were giants, then why have we never found the remains of palaces fit for giants? I think Lord Hugh is right, that the Aoi must have built them." It was difficult to say; giving Hugh any truth undercut her desire to condemn him utterly. "If that's so, then their secret was lost."

Within the walls of the convent, wind did not blow, only a faint whine heard as down a far distance. No oil burned in the library, and with the sun no longer overhead to pierce down through the shafts, it had become quite dim. Rosvita only noticed it now as she looked at the convent chronicle and had to squint to read the letters; the change had come so gradually.

"I do not want my secrets to be lost," said Mother Obligatia. Her fingers brushed Rosvita's like the flutter of a moth's wings, moved on to the *Vita*. "I have held them close to my breast for many years. But this book is a sign." She opened the *Vita* at random and read aloud.

"'When the women of the court came to Baralcha, they brought the finest clothing sewn of Katai silk and embroidered with thread beaten out of gold and silver, but the blessed Radegundis would not wear the garments of earth, however splendid they might be. She would not come before the emperor dressed in gold and silver but only in the robes of the poor, which she had herself woven out of nettles. And the women of the court were afraid. They feared the displeasure of the emperor would be turned on them, who brought her to the holy emperor dressed like a pauper instead of a queen, yet in her beggar's robes the blessed Radegundis so outshone the multitude in their rich clothing that even the emperor's fierce hounds bowed before her in recognition of her holiness.'" Her voice failed, and she shut her eyes. Like all old women, it was hard to judge her age. Her skin was wrinkled but otherwise soft and white, that of a woman who has spent much of her life indoors. She had a noblewoman's hands, unmarked by the calluses brought on by hard labor but still strong.

"Brother Fidelis ended his days at the monastery at Hersford," said Rosvita, seeing that his book had uncovered a deep well of emotion in the abbess. What had brought it on? "He must have been almost one hundred years old when I spoke to him. He gave the book to me just before he died. It was his last gift. It was his testimony."

"Indeed, it was his testimony." Her breath came a little ragged, as though she had been running. "That after all these years I should again touch something he once touched—"

"You speak in riddles, Mother." She spoke in her calmest voice, but her heart was aflame.

"I think I fell under a spell that summer. He was old enough to be my grandfather, full fifty years of age, and I was perhaps fifteen. He worked in the garden, and because of that I thought he was a lay brother. But he was kind, and sad, and I had always been lonely and alone in the world. We girls at the convent of St. Thierry were never allowed outside the walls. Then I was uprooted from the only place I had ever known and brought to Salia, where I scarcely understood the language. I had taken a novice's vows because I knew nothing else in life, but I found those vows were easy enough to forswear."

"'I have sinned once, and greatly,'" murmured Rosvita, recalling the scene: the door made of branches lashed together, his refuge a poor hovel so crudely made that the winter winds must have whistled through its gaps day in and day out. The butterfly whisper of his voice. "'For lying with a woman.'" The thought was almost too blasphemous to utter, but Rosvita had never shied away from wells and ditches when her curiosity led her through rough country. "You were his lover, the one he sinned with."

Obligatia went white, as if she had been slapped, and then she chuckled. "You are well suited to history writing."

"I beg you, I meant no insult! He said he still thought of her with affection."

A single tear budded at the corner of her eye, but it was so dry that the air wicked it away. Obligatia went on with perfect composure. "We did not sin. He did not touch me until he forswore his own vows as a monk, until we spoke the pledge of marriage before a witness, under the eyes of God. We should have left to start a life elsewhere. But we were both foundlings. We had known no place but the cloister. He thought we could remain on the estate as laborers. I see now how innocent we both were.

"Of course it was all discovered when my pregnancy became advanced. The abbess was furious, because she wanted no stain to mar the sanctity of the convent founded by the saintly queen so recently deceased. Ai, Lady, the pain of my labor was as nothing to the pain of being separated from him. They took the child away from me as soon as it was born, but not before I saw that it was a girl. They never spoke of the child again. I never saw Fidelis again either. He was sent away, or locked away. I never knew. I was so terribly alone. Solitude is always worse once you have known companionship.

"I was taken to a convent in Wendar and placed under a vow of silence in a hermit's cell, but I ran away from there because my heart had broken and I could not bear to be alone with my thoughts as one day ran into the next. I could no longer hear God even in the songs of the birds. I wandered destitute for a week or more, eating berries and onion grass. I finally came to a manor house at an estate called Bodfeld. I was taken in because they wanted someone to teach their daughters Dariyan. The nearby convent dedicated to St. Felicity was run by an abbess from a family they had long feuded with, so they refused to ask her help in finding a tutor, but I had enough education to teach the girls how to read and write and figure.

"There was a nephew, the son of the lady's dead brother. He became infatuated with me. I was like any plant starved for water. Events progressed as they will with the young. He insisted on marrying me, and because they were kindhearted and had a plot of land somewhat away from the main house, because he mattered little in terms of their succession and I had the manners of a noblewoman and the education of a nun, they let us marry. In time, I gave birth to a boy-child. We called him Bernard, after my husband's dead father. Then both my husband and his aunt died, and her sister came into the estate. She did not like me. She took the baby from me and gave it to a monastery to raise, since she didn't want the expense of feeding us."

"How cruel," murmured Rosvita, but Obligatia went on steadily, as if she were afraid she would not get it all out of her heart, confined there for so long in silence as she had herself been confined within the rock walls of this convent.

"I was forced to retire to the convent of St. Felicity; but I was ill-treated there because they resented the work I had done at Bodfeld. God willed that an educated man, an Eagle who was the favorite of King Arnulf, sheltered one night at the guest-house of the convent. It was my duty at that time to bring food for guests, although I had to slide it under a screen, for I wasn't allowed to see them. But I was curious, and he was talkative. Four months later the abbess received a letter from the king's schola, requesting that I be sent to study at the schola in Mainni.

"I studied at Mainni for one year. Then that same Eagle came by the schola on his way to Darre with a party of clerics. I was taken south with them so that I might come to the attention of the skopos. I was badly injured in a fall on the passage over St. Vitale's Pass and the party brought me here to recover. Mother Aurica took me in with the promise to send me on once I had healed. But poor Sister Lucida was left as a foundling at the ladder not two months later, and I was given the care of her, such a small, sickly child. I could not bear to leave her, and I no longer trusted the world. Mother Aurica agreed to the de-ception: We sent word that I had died of blood poisoning. I gave up the name Lavrentia, given me by the abbess at St. Thierry, and I took the name Obligatia, to show that I understood that God had forgiven me for my sins by giving me a child to care for. That was forty years ago."

The story was so incredible that Rosvita could not fasten on it all at once, and in the way of such things got hold of a small detail, almost lost in the retelling. "You must be speaking of the Eagle Wolfhere."

"Ah." Her face lit, as at an old toy rediscovered. "That was his name! I had forgotten it. Stranger yet, I saw him a year ago, at the palace of the skopos in Darre. He is an old man now, cer-tainly, but not one whose face I would forget, for he rescued me from misery."

"Why were you in Darre?" Rosvita found herself compulsively stroking flat the slightly curled edges of the parchment and at once clasped her hands and set them firmly in her lap.

"It is customary when the abbess of St. Ekatarina dies that her chosen successor travel to Darre to be blessed by the skopos. I waited in the palace guesthouse for a week before I was granted an audience with our blessed Mother, Clementia, in her audience chamber. I was there when the Eagle arrived, sent by King Henry of Wendar. I heard him tell his story of Biscop Antonia of Mainni and the accusations of sorcery laid against her. I heard Mother Clementia lay down the punishment of excommunication, and I will tell you honestly, Sister, that I feared for my daughters, the nuns who remained here while I ventured forth. What if we were accused of sorcery because of the creature who haunts the stone crown? Because of these chronicles so conscientiously recorded over the years, that take note of stone circles? What might they accuse us of, for as you have seen yourself, there are secrets hidden here. So I returned, speaking nothing."

"Yet you are willing to countenance Hugh of Austra working sorcery."

"I know what it is to be kinless and unprotected, at the mercy of those who have more power than you. Adelheid sheltered here once before, many years ago. She was a sweet, brave child, always cheerful. I would aid her if I can."

"But Hugh will know your secrets as well. He can use that knowledge against you."

Obligatia extended a hand to touch the library wall, here washed white and painted with lozenges inside lozenges, like puzzle pieces stacked one upon the next. Rosvita could not imagine living forty years within such walls, even if one learned to let the spirit fly free. A corner, a shadow, or a wall always broke the line of sight; only on the terrace did a vista open up, and then the view never changed. She had grown used to the view changing, like life, a journey where no scene is ever truly repeated, no river ever crossed twice because every river is always a new river from one hour to the next.

"He knows them now in any case," Obligatia said quietly. After a moment, she went on. "Last summer a lone frater begged leave to spend a night in our guest hall. It is unusual for us to receive guests, as you can imagine. If travelers over St. Vitale's Pass must leave the main road because of rain, then sometimes they will wash up here, but otherwise we live an isolated life. It is what we seek, each for our own reasons."

"Yet when guests arrive, it seems according to the testimony of this chronicle that you ask them if they know of any stone crowns."

"Few of us are immune to curiosity. So I asked our traveler that question. He called himself Brother Marcus. And then he did a strange thing: He called me by my old name, the one I had given up when I chose life as a nun here. He called me 'Lavrentia.' How could he have known that name was once mine, for he was younger than I?"

"Who knew in any case that you were last seen alive entering this convent?"

"The Eagle, Wolfhere."

"Who may have seen you at the skopos' palace. Yet there must have been other people in the party that you traveled south with forty years ago."

"In all these years, I have seen no other person I recognized. Mother Aurica is long since dead. My nuns know me only as Mother Obligatia. The Eagle is the only link, and it suddenly seemed strange to me that he had made such an effort to remove me from St. Felicity all those years ago. Why would this other man come and ask for me by my old name? What of my secrets did he know?"

"'She is back in our hands,'" murmured Rosvita, recalling the scene before the fire high in Julier Pass. "Wolfhere was banished from the court by King Henry years ago. In the time of King Arnulf it was said that he knew more than a man ought. I have myself seen that he can speak through fire. Yet that power is also known as the Eagle's gift. Did this Brother Marcus give any reason why he wanted to find you?"

"Nay. But I admit freely, Sister, that I was frightened because I feared the woman who removed me from St. Thierry when I was a girl. I had nightmares that she still pursued me. It seems odd to me now that in Salia, in a monastery where women and men were so strictly separated, I managed to find my way into a garden where a monk worked."

"Hindsight is a marvelous thing. It might have been an accident."

"I no longer believe it was, and yet I have no proof. Did I

not say who came to fetch me in Varre, what person took me away from St. Thierry? It was Sister Clothilde."

"The same Clothilde who was St. Radegundis' handmaiden and· later her companion in the convent?"

"The same one. I never doubt that she was loyal to Radegundis. I believed then and believe now that she would have smiled kindly and cut the throat of any person who crossed her. No one ever crossed her."

"Except you. For a novice to have carnal knowledge of a monk, both of them under her care, in the monastery—"

"Nay, Sister, she knew of it. She was the one who witnessed our pledge of marriage. She allowed it to happen. That is why I am telling you this. When I was young, I was too passionate and too starved to think clearly. But Brother Marcus asked questions that woke my memories, and now I can see patterns that I could not read then. You are a historian, Sister. I am sharing my secret with you because I think there is an answer to be found. I think now that they left me alive because I was ignorant."

"Or because they thought you were dead."

Mother Obligatia smiled bitterly. "You have a mind for this, Sister. But I am now determined not to let my secret die with me. I lost my first two children because I had no power in the world, no· kin to protect me. I now rule as Mother over a tiny convent of six nuns and two lay sisters. That we guard a mystery within was the charge given to the mothers here centuries ago, but I wonder if the skopos and her advisers have forgotten its existence."

"You have honored me with your confession, Mother."

"Nay, I have only given you another burden. You have a keen mind and a level heart, Sister. I beg you, find out why a man calling himself Brother Marcus came to our guest hall last summer and asked for me by the name Lavrentia, which I abandoned long ago."

The rock had a muffling effect, close and confining. On the king's progress Rosvita had grown accustomed to the shouts of the wagoneers, the neighing of horses, the fall of rain, the heedless song of birds, the smell of the stable, and the laughter of wind on her face. Here, she couldn't even hear the mice. Lord John and his men might labor a hundred miles away, for all that their work lay invisible and inaudible beyond rock walls. No vibrations, no cracks within the stone brought her any hint of the man who bided his time in the guest hall. Was Hugh still praying? Would God ever forgive him for his sins? Would God forgive her hers?

"There is so much to find out." Rosvita turned the pages of the *Vita* to the end. Fidelis had mastered the art of script; even Sister Amabilia had found nothing to criticize in his precise hand. He had spoken of such peculiar things. "The birds sing of the child known as Sanglant," she said, remembering his words. "Have you ever heard of the Seven Sleepers, Mother?"

"Of course. St. Eusebë tells the story of the Seven Sleepers in her *History*."

"You have heard no other tale that mentions them?"

"I have not. Why would the birds sing of this Sanglant? What sorcerer understood their language?"

"I do not know." Her eye followed the writing and her lips shaped the words, and then a thought occurred to her and she spoke out loud. " 'The world divides those whom no space parted once.' Do you suppose, Mother, that Fidelis was thinking of you when he wrote those words? I assumed he was writing of St. Radegundis. He lived on the men's side as a monk for the entire span of St. Radegundis' life there, almost fifty years. Until her death, he would never have known a world without her in it."

"Surely he wrote this *Vita* long after I had gone from his life. He must have repented if he went back to the church and became a hermit."

"Or he felt he had no choice. But he wandered far from Salia in his later years. He was a curious man, the one flaw they could not smooth off of him."

Mother Obligatia smiled as at a fond and distant memory. "He was a curious man once his interest had been roused." The light of youth shone in her briefly, a glimpse of the fifteen-year-old girl who had captivated a fifty-year-old monk. Then she recalled who she was now, and she sighed. "God willed that I should spend my life in prayer. But sometimes I wonder what became of my two children. God forgive me, Sister. I am still afflicted with selfishness. In a way, I care nothing for your immortal soul or whether you condemn yourself by trafficking with an accused sorcerer. I want you to escape so that you can find out the truth, and I fear that if you surrender now, Lord John will imprison you and everyone in your party and hold you for ransom. You might be in his prison for years. You might die in Aosta. How then can you find out the truth? If there is no one to aid me, how can I be sure that no harm will come to those who live under my care?"

"Do you think it possible that the stone crowns are harbors, gateways from one to the next? That we can actually travel between them?"

"I do not know, but I know what my predecessors thought. They believed it." She drew a finger over the pages of the old chronicle delicately, as if she feared it might dissolve at her touch. "That is why they recorded the stone circles here. They thought there was a pattern, hidden in plain sight if they could learn to read it."

A hand bell rang, the call to prayer.

"What have you decided, Sister Rosvita? Will you counsel in favor of Lord Hugh's plan, or against it?"

"I don't know. I must pray for God to give me counsel."

Rosvita closed both books and left them on the lectern as she assisted Mother Obligatia to rise. She offered her arm to her, and although Obligatia braced herself on Rosvita's elbow, her touch was so insubstantial that it seemed more like a memory than an actual presence.

With Theophanu and Adelheid and their noble ladies in attendance, the chapel was crowded. Its walls curved up into a dome, laden with symbols painted onto the whitewashed wall: St. Ekatarina sits in the center, arms extended to either side, palms out in the gesture of an open heart and complete surrender to God in Unity; a pale crown composed of stars burns at her brow, the mark of a saint; above her, twin dragons twine through hoary clouds, engaged in the fiery battle that denotes the conflict inherent in a creation stained by darkness; beyond that, as if seen from the mountaintop, a palace gleams in the sky, no doubt meant to represent the Chamber of Light where all souls return when the robes of darkness have at last been lifted from their spirit after their ascension through the seven spheres after death.

In deference to the several crippled or old sisters, railings had been set in rows so that, when they knelt, they might lean on wood. The dark grain was well polished, as if over the decades many of the nuns had needed a little such help at their prayers.

After so many hours, Rosvita found herself exhausted. She, too, needed the compassionate support of the simple wood railing.

She had been ill for a long time and recovering for a much shorter one, and now she felt flashes of heat, sweat breaking on her forehead and down her spine. The hair at the nape of her neck was damp, and her palms slick.

Ai, Lady, she was tempted. Could Hugh bind the daimone? Could she see it done? She had never seen a daimone, of course, and the intense desire to see what she had never seen before and would likely never see again scalded her heart.

They sang from the *Sayings* of Queen Salomae the Wise, who had lived long before the birth of the blessed Daisan.

> *"Do not follow the path of evildoers. Turn aside. Avoid it.*
> *For the evil man cannot sleep unless he has done wrong.*
> *The evil woman cannot sleep unless she has caused someone's*
> *   downfall."*

Yet she and Theophanu would become accomplices to Hugh's misdeeds and his terrible acts if they accepted help from him, if they allowed him to aid them with that same sorcery they had been so eager to condemn him for before.

> *"For although the lips of the sorcerer drip honey*
> *and his speech is smoother than oil,*
> *yet in the end he is as bitter as wormwood*
> *and as sharp as a two-edged sword."*

Could she stain her own hands, even for a good cause? Yet she knew herself no saint, willing to die rather than compromise her own honor. If Adelheid died rather than submit to Ironhead, then Aosta would suffer. If Theophanu surrendered, then she and everyone in her party would endure imprisonment and possibly death at Ironhead's hands.

Surely under these circumstances God would forgive them for setting foot briefly on the path known otherwise only to the wicked. Yet when did the end ever justify the means?

Mother Obligatia led the daily lesson in her frail voice. "Let us sing this day the hymn of creation, in honor of the feast day of St. Eulalia, she who was midwife to St. Edessia. Her hands brought forth that which is life to us, the blessed Daisan, who brought the Divine Word from heaven unto Earth."

"Everything is placed upon nothing.
In this way the universe came to be.
Yet something streamed out from the Father of Life
and the Mother became pregnant in the shape of a fish
and bore him; and he was called the Son of Life.
As his soul descended through the seven spheres
he partook only of pure things.
He took into his spirit nothing impure as he descended.
But we know this to be true, that the world is impure.
We know this to be true,
that the impure world separated him from the Father and Mother
in whom he once dwelled without separation."

It came to Rosvita in that moment, unasked for, unexpected, a bolt from heaven not seen before it struck and shattered earth.

"The world divides those whom no space parted once."

What if Fidelis was Radegundis' son?
Then the enormity of it slugged her. She was suddenly unable to catch her breath. The railing seemed to shift under her like the earth when a tremor wrenches the ground on which you had once stood firmly.
What if Fidelis was Taillefer's son, his rightful heir?

"For God measured it and laid it out,
the Father with the Mother by Their sexual union they founded it.
They planted it with their descendants.
To the Garden of Life, which is the Chamber of Light,
all souls return."

If it were true, then why had Queen Radegundis not proclaimed abroad that Taillefer had a living son? Her silence had brought about the end of Taillefer's great empire.
Why had she not spoken?

"Yet out of necessity Love compels us.
It is completely impossible for a solitary one

> *to bring forth and to bear,*
> *therefore he was the child that was produced by two,*
> *both Mother and Father, who together make life."*

"What are you, Eagle?" Rosvita had asked Liath that night last summer when she had given the young Eagle *The Book of Secrets,* which she had stolen from Hugh, because she had believed Liath and not Hugh. And Liath had replied: "I am kinless."

"I lost my children because I had no kin to protect me," Mother Obligatia had said not an hour before.

Taillefer's legitimate son would have reigned after him *if* Radegundis could have found support among the Salian nobility for enough years to raise an infant to manhood. Salian princes often killed their rivals for the throne, even if those rivals were blood relatives, even if they were children. Radegundis was a woman without family to stand behind her. Her kin had all been murdered when she herself was only a child. Why should she have trusted the Salian lords?

> *"And he answered us, he said:*
> *You shall come to that paradise if you act rightly,*
> *if you heed the Word of Our Lady and Our Lord."*

Radegundis had not wanted to be queen. Perhaps she chose to remove the child from the temptations of worldly power. Or perhaps she only wanted to protect the child from his enemies. How better to do so than to give him as a foundling to the very convent in which she served?

What is in plain sight is hidden best.

Theophanu glanced at her and made a question with her expression, as if to ask if she were well. Rosvita shook her head, to show that she needed no help. To negate these disturbing thoughts. It was too incredible. She couldn't believe it.

And yet it was so unbelievable that she had no choice but to believe it.

> *"And he said to her, 'When will we see your wedding feast,*
> *you who are the blush of the earth and the image of the water?*
> *For you are the daughter I set upon my knee and sang to sleep.*
> *We all came to be because of the union of Father and Mother.*
> *The road to purification arises out of conception and birth.'"*

Mother Obligatia had unknowingly given birth to Taillefer's legitimate granddaughter forty-five years ago. What had happened to that child?

As she knelt, the sweat cooling on her neck, the trembling in her hands subsiding, she was reminded again of words from the *Holy Verses: "The beginning of wisdom is this: gain understanding, although it cost you all you have."*

She had to escape, even if it cost her everything she had. She could not risk being held prisoner by Ironhead, even if it meant the greater risk of trusting to Hugh's sorcery, even if it meant her own complicity in that sorcery.

She had to find out if it were true. She had to find out what happened to the child.

She had promised Mother Obligatia, and it was obvious now that someone else had discovered the old woman's secret and sought her out, hoping to find the only descendant of Emperor Taillefer, if she still lived. She had a duty to aid Adelheid and Theophanu. She owed loyalty to King Henry and his ambitions.

But mostly, she was just so damned curious.

Yet the song of Queen Salomae the Wise rang in her ears as the congregation knelt in silence and the rock walls of the tiny chapel breathed dust and the weight of uncounted years into the musty air:

"Do not let your heart entice you to stray down his paths: many has he pierced and laid low. His victims are without number."

So be it.

She had long known that curiosity would be her downfall. She would find out the truth, no matter where the path led her.

5

"TONIGHT," Hugh had said when they told him they would accept his aid, and now she found herself buffeted by the flood of activity as they made ready to leave. She was a leaf torn and floating on an uncontrollable tide. She had to find Mother Oblig-

atia and speak to her before they left—there had been no time
before, everyone had conspired to drive them apart as soon as
it became clear that they would risk what ought to have remained
forbidden.

And yet, she was exhilarated.

"Sister Rosvita, I beg you, wake up."

For a moment she did not recognize the brown hair and broad
face of the woman staring down at her. Had she kept her suspicions to herself? How long ago was it that she had been shaken
by revelation?

"May I help you rise, Sister? We must go now or we will be
left behind."

She had fallen asleep in the library, slumped over the lectern.
She had even drooled a little in her sleep; one corner of the
chronicle was moist. Lady Leoba briskly put both the *Vita* of
St. Radegundis and the copy so lovingly penned first by Sister
Amabilia and then by Sister Petra into the sturdy leather pouch
that contained Rosvita's unfinished *History*.

It was hard to stand. She felt weak and tired, and she ached
everywhere. Her neck had stiffened, and her spine crackled with
pops and creaks as she straightened. Her left knee hurt, and her
knuckles felt swollen. This was the burden of age.

"Let me carry this for you, Sister," said Leoba, graciously
shouldering the pouch.

"Where is Mother Obligatia?"

"She is with the princess."

"I must speak to her before we leave."

"As you wish, Sister. Princess Theophanu is waiting for you."

By the light of a single lamp held aloft by young Paloma,
they made their way to the cavern. It was empty, eerily so: not
one scrap of leather remained to show what a great party had
sheltered here, only a fading and somewhat putrid scent.

"That man died," said Paloma. "The one who was touched
by the creature. Will you all die, too, do you think?"

"I hope not, child," said Rosvita. Leoba shuddered, but she
was too sow-headed a woman to voice her fear, if she had any.

Paloma led them past an odd array of side chambers carved
out of the rock. Tunnels curved off on either side, descending
and ascending.

"Was this a city once?" Rosvita wondered aloud as they
reached a ramp that sloped upward, curled around a huge wall

of rock, and narrowed abruptly where a groove was cut into the earth. Another millstone lay on its side, slotted into the rock, ready to be rolled shut in the event of attack.

"I think it was a refuge," said Paloma, "just like it is now. They built ways to block the path behind them if they needed to flee upward to the stone crown. Here, careful—" She lit them over a plank that bridged a ditch, whose steep sides vanished into darkness below. "It's too far to jump. Can you smell the horses?"

Rosvita could smell them, and soon enough could hear nervous whinnies, the mutter of men, and the restless undercurrent of an entourage making ready to leave. Light bled in through cunning shafts angling sunlight down through the rocks. Paloma doused the lamp, and they climbed steps over a low wall whose sides were stippled with squares of light.

"Those holes make arrow slits, so defenders in the stables could shoot anyone coming down this corridor."

Two sharp corners brought them to the low, lit caves used as stables, high up on the rock where several more terraces gave light and air and room for exercise. Nevertheless, she saw several heaps of bone and offal, burned and swept to one side; six weeks under these conditions had been too much for some of the horses already weakened by the grueling ride from Vennaci.

Ahead, the retinue gathered in marching order, lined up and stretching out of her sight on a path that curled out onto a terrace and then on up around the rock face. Wind blew steadily; it was night, but the sky was clear and the moon bright and perfectly round. They dared use no lamps for fear of alerting Ironhead to their desperate ploy, and yet it was possible that his sentries might see them anyway, silhouetted by moonlight against the huge outcropping. Looming above, she saw the black mass of the summit and beyond it, the garden of winter stars, their brilliance dimmed by the glare of the full moon.

Leoba used her elbows as well as a few choice phrases, some polite, some coarser, to press their way forward through the rearguard and then the main party. Rosvita had to pause briefly to reassure Fortunatus, who was trapped in a clot of clerics and wanted desperately to join her. To salve his distress, she gave the pouch of precious books into his keeping. Then she went on to the front where Queen Adelheid and Princess Theophanu stood beside their mounts. Captain Fulk and a dozen soldiers made up the van.

"Where is Mother Obligatia?" Rosvita asked after she had paid her respects.

"She has gone ahead with Lord Hugh," said Adelheid. "The rest of us will remain here until we hear the horn. That will mark that it is safe to proceed."

"If it will ever be safe," murmured Theophanu. But she stood resolutely beside her mount, as calm as ever. She had accepted Rosvita's decision without objection, almost without reaction. The groom holding the reins of her mount looked nervous, shifting his feet as he stared up the path cut into the rock. It vanished around a curve in the rock, leading toward the summit. Was that a glimmer of light there, or only the trick of her eyes?

"I must speak with her alone," said Rosvita. "Let me go up."

"Nay, Sister!" said Theophanu sharply. "I will not lose you!"

"Mother Obligatia warned us not to follow her until she knew it was safe," said Adelheid. "What if Lord Hugh cannot bind the creature? It might turn its killing gaze on you as well, Sister. And you are innocent."

"No more innocent than that soldier who died," said Rosvita. "Nay, Your Highness. I pray you, do not attempt to stop me. I will be cautious. But I must speak to her."

Theophanu said nothing, neither to give permission nor withhold it, so Rosvita walked on. Wind bit at her face, and she chafed her hands together to warm them as she kept her gaze fixed on the ground, always aware of sheer cliff dropping off to her right and the distant tiny campfires of Ironhead's encampment far below. But the path unrolled before as broad and easily negotiable as the apocryphal road that leads the unwary and the foolish and the wicked to the Abyss.

She labored up the slope and where the path cut left through a series of squat pinnacles, it gave out suddenly onto a flat summit. The standing stones blotted out the stars at even intervals. A faint tracery of white slipped between them like mist blown on the wind. Littered among the circle of stones lay putrefying bodies, a dozen at least, mangled, arms outflung, faces blackened, weapons broken and lying askew.

She staggered back from the sight, heard a warning whisper. A hand caught her elbow.

"You must go back, Sister Rosvita. It is dangerous for you to stay here."

"Someone must witness." Understanding had freed her: she was risking not just her body but her immortal soul, and she intended to see all there was to see.

"I have taken responsibility to witness," whispered Mother Obligatia. Rosvita felt the old woman's walking stick pressed against her hip, and she marveled that the abbess had strength enough to walk so far on her crippled legs. She could not leave her alone.

"I will stay with you. I must speak to you of what I have discovered—"

She saw him then, walking forward in plain sight, tall and glorious in moonlight as he crossed toward the circle of stones and halted about three paces in front of the first gaping archway of standing stones and lintel where an oval patch of sandy soil turned the ground white. A translucent figure darted forward through the stone circle, curling around the lintel sparking with the reflected glint of starlight. Hugh began to sing, hands lifted with fingers outspread. The wind died, and such an unnatural stillness settled over the height that she could hear his voice as clear and sweet as that of the angels.

> *"Matthias guide me, Mark protect me, Johanna free me, Lucia aid me, Marian purify me, Peter heal me, Thecla be my witness always, that the Lady shall be my shield and the Lord shall be my sword. Sanctify me, God, and destroy all that is evil and wicked. Free me from all attacks of the Enemy. Let no creature harm me. May the blessing of God be on my head. God reign forever, world without end."*

Rosvita smelled burning juniper, a sharp incense underlaid with a second, sour scent. Still singing, Hugh knelt to place nine small stones on the ground in the same layout as the greater stones that made up the stone circle and, with a polished walking stick much like that on which Mother Obligatia leaned, he traced a pattern of angles and intersections between those stones in the sandy oval. Rosvita blinked rapidly, thinking surely that her vision was distorted, because as he drew the lines on the oval patch she thought that these same angles and intersections glimmered into life among the stones, like a huge cat's cradle of faint threads woven in and out between the monoliths.

Light flashed within the stones with the pulse of lightning, and she heard a wail. She expected Hugh to fall, stricken, and she clutched at Mother Obligatia's arm, to drag her backward to safety if she could, but it was not Hugh who had cried out. For an instant, the creature swelled until it towered over them, and she saw it clearly: It had the delicacy of blown glass and the sharp glitter of a drawn sword. Its wings, encompassing half the sky, seemed feathered with glass. Was this how the angels appeared?

"What are you?" said Hugh, more command than question.

It had a humanlike form, but perhaps it was only imitating Hugh's figure or the form of the soldiers it had destroyed. It cried out again, a dissonant lament, and now Rosvita saw that it writhed against the threads woven through the stones, as if they trapped it. "Lost, lost," sang the creature in a vibrant bass tone that had the resonance of a bell.

It danced and leaped like flame within the pattern, its aetherical shape growing and shrinking according to an unseen tide, and Rosvita felt a chill boiling off it so deep that the backwash made her fingers and cheeks burn with cold. She could actually see through its figure into the sky and the stones.

"The path is closed behind me and before me. I only stepped down to see what had opened when the earth exhaled, oh, that was not a moment ago, or has it not happened yet?" The creature sang more than spoke in such a melange of language that Rosvita thought she was hearing Wendish and then Dariyan and then Aostan and then Arethousan, or all of them together or none of them, as if the human speech it drew over its utterances was a cloak patched together from many scraps of wool.

"What are you?" said Hugh. "From whence do you come?"

"Lost, lost," it wailed. "The road is closed before me and behind me. The air lies heavy here. It breathes with a foul wind full of dying things. Why have I been trapped below the moon? I should have followed them upward for they escaped this place, they above us, and I am below and lost here."

"I can only help you if you can speak sense to me," said Hugh coaxingly.

The creature flared suddenly, as if in anger, and Rosvita threw up a hand to protect her eyes from the blinding light. As the glare faded, she peered out between her fingers to see clearly the cage of insubstantial architecture that surrounded the daimone: lines and angles and intersections lancing up from the earth toward the heavens, each one glittering as if a thousand thousand dewdrops of pure and brilliant aether clung to it, delineating its length in the same way a line of lit candles delineates a path in a garden sunk in night. Each scintillant thread shot as straight as an arrow's flight up into the dome of heaven, and each thread pulled taut against a star. Two threads, thicker than the others, more powerful, had hooked planets: the hard blood-red glare of Jedu, the Angel of War, and the honey gleam of wise Aturna. A thread as gauzy as uncombed wool touched the moon as if its substance had been grabbed and pulled and stretched.

This was sorcery, the art of the mathematici who could bind the heavens to their will and weave its power to alter earth. Or so she had heard whispered. Even the most lenient of the church mothers had condemned it, and a hundred years ago as powerful a churchwoman as Emperor Taillefer's daughter, Biscop Tallia, had been censured for studying it.

But it was beautiful.

"What are you?" said Hugh again, still patient, still sweet. "From whence do you come?"

"Lost, lost," sang the creature in its bell voice, and then it curled and shifted and writhed closer, imitating the coaxing lilt of his voice, thrown back at him. "Unbind me, and I will give you all that you desire."

Hugh laughed. "You cannot give me what I desire, for you cannot control that whose genesis lies above your own."

It writhed and wailed and moaned in thrumming, agonized tones. "Lost, lost. Open the road."

"I do not know how to open the road, fair one," he said reasonably. "But you will serve me because I have bound you."

He withdrew from his sleeve the red ribbon he had used to bind closed the chest in which he kept *The Book of Secrets*. Dangling that ribbon over the pale patch of ground, he lowered it until one end brushed the central point of the small oval, where all the lines converged. Then he let go, and it slithered down to land in an oddly elegant spiral, twined around that center point. He clapped his hands once, clapped them twice sharply, and then three times clapped. The sound reverberated like the crack of rock splitting, and the daimone vanished from the stone circle.

He bent to pick up the ribbon. It seemed to writhe and curl in his hand like a snake as he tucked it back into his sleeve. The daimone had vanished. Then he stood in silence for a moment, studying the gleaming threads woven through the stones. Had Hugh's sorcery made manifest the invisible structure that overlay the cosmos, that vast heavenly architecture created by God?

He began again to sing softly; the wind had come up, and she could not make out the words. But she could see him in the moon's light as he took his staff and used it almost like a shuttle, actually used it to reweave the threads into new patterns, ones that made the lines begin to pulse and thrum as if down their spun length she could hear the distant music of the spheres.

A thin light bled from the stones, blossoming suddenly into an arch of flame surmounting the nearest lintel.

"I beg you, Mother!" cried Hugh, sounding as out of breath as if he'd run a league to reach them. "Call them."

Rosvita took the horn from Mother Obligatia and blew: the sound arced, and sputtered, and then she tried again and this time it grew low and deep, resounding off the rocks, until she ran out of breath and it stuttered and failed. She heard an answering horn at once, and they waited.

Hugh strained to hold the lines in their new configuration, and yet as the entourage rumbled up the path and the moon slid along its night's road, some lines fell into place while others had to be nudged back into the pattern.

Captain Fulk and his soldiers came into view with Adelheid and Theophanu directly behind them, lamps raised to light their way, and they halted in astonishment as Rosvita and Mother Obligatia quickly stepped off the path.

"Quickly," said Hugh, almost panting from exertion although he hadn't moved from his kneeling position. His face was hidden; only the lines of his back and neck and the catch in his voice revealed his tension. His hair gleamed like gold. "You must go through now while the heavens—while the heavens are in this conjunction. Quickly. The path will close."

"Dear God," said one of the soldiers, and Captain Fulk told him to hush.

"But I don't know—" Hugh went on, almost hoarse from ex-ertion.

"You don't know what?" cried Theophanu sharply. Like Adel-heid, she was now mounted; her groom walked beside her with one hand on the bridle of her horse. The others crowded up be-hind them, horses whickering, servants and companions nervous and mumbling.

"—where you'll come out."

Adelheid laughed. She spurred her horse forward, past the soldiers, past Captain Fulk, skirting Hugh, to pass under the gleaming arch, where she vanished. Just like that.

Whether Theophanu hated to be shown up or suspected as cowardly, or had simply handed her fate into Rosvita's hands without thought to the consequences, Rosvita could not guess. "Captain!" Theophanu called now, and Captain Fulk shouted the marching orders. His soldiers started forward with the grim ex-pressions of men who have been ordered to march off a cliff for the good of their lady.

"Ai, God!" said Rosvita as Theophanu passed her, looking only at the frighteningly beautiful lattice shining in the night in front of her. "Mother Obligatia! I must speak to you."

"I never thought—" Obligatia's whispered words were almost lost beneath the tramp and creak of the entourage moving for-ward.

"Listen to me! I've no proof, and if my suspicions are true then the knowledge will be dangerous to you and to those in your charge—" A horse brushed close, knocking her off-balance, and she had to catch herself against rock, scraping her palm.

"Steady, child." Mother Obligatia used her stick to fend away a straying servant who looked ready to bolt. "Knowledge is al-ways dangerous. Come, Daughter. Move away where we won't be jostled." She drew Rosvita out of the way, hard up against a pinnacle. Moonlight made alabaster of her face, made her young again, an innocent maiden used and discarded.

Rosvita found she was breathing heavily and that she had broken out into a weeping sweat. Her stomach ached, and she was so tired. But she had to hurry. "I think Fidelis was Queen Radegundis' lost child. That he was Taillefer's last and only le-gitimate son. If that's so, then you gave birth to Taillefer's grand-daughter, conceived in and born out of a legal and binding union. If I'm correct, then it's not surprising that there are folk abroad in the world who seek you out, now that they know you are still alive, now that they may wonder how much you know. If I'm correct, then it means that Wolfhere is far more than what he seems. It cannot be coincidence that he appears so often in your tale."

"Well," said Mother Obligatia with the kind of smile a queen gives when she is finally handed proof that her best companion and adviser has been plotting treason all along, "that is a great deal bluntly said, Sister."

"Sister Rosvita!" The cry came from the retinue, and she looked up to see Brother Fortunatus waving frantically at her even as he was pushed and prodded along. He tried to get out of line, to join her, he gestured and called to her, but he was forced along as the main party pressed on after the queen and the princess, the most reluctant thrust forward by the most loyal. A horse balked and had to be whipped. She could not see Hugh, for the path into the crown lay between her place and his. Threads of light still drew taut between the heavens and the earth, twined among the stones, and the stars seemed to pulse—or maybe she was so exhausted that she was seeing things.

"I was the only novice Clothilde ever brought to St. Radegundis' convent," said Obligatia suddenly. "Does that not seem strange to you? Doesn't it seem strange that she looked the other way when Fidelis and I met? That she herself witnessed our pledge of consent and, because she witnessed, gave legitimacy to our union?"

"She must have desperately wanted Taillefer's legitimate son to sire an heir in his turn."

"But if the Eagle's part in this tale is no coincidence, then Clothilde's actions must be equally suspect. If this is all true, then she must have known who Fidelis was. She must have agreed to keep his birth secret. But why wait so long, then, for his marriage? Why not sooner, before all those who might have supported him were dead and a new lineage established on the throne of Salia? Why wait until he was full fifty years of age?"

The answer came in an instant. It was obvious, if you believed the fantastic premise. "She waited until Queen Radegundis was dead."

" 'Radegundis swore to marry no earthly prince.' And swore the same for her son, perhaps. Ai, God, poor Fidelis. He was a man with a full heart. If that's so, if Queen Radegundis wanted to spare him the chains of worldly power, then Clothilde did not serve Queen Radegundis as well as the tales sing, did she? Yes I can well believe it, having suffered her attentions."

"From this distance we cannot know what was in either woman's mind."

"To randomly pluck a foundling girl from an obscure convent and carry her so many leagues and across two realms on such a subtle conspiracy that in the end came to nothing. It seems incredible."

"But it didn't come to nothing. Where is your daughter? What happened to her? I mean to find out."

The last of the horses had crossed, and the rearguard, fallen into a robust drinking song perhaps to lend themselves courage, marched two abreast into the archway.

"Hurry, Sister!" cried Mother Obligatia, clutching Rosvita's hand briefly, then thrusting her forward. "Find out what you can!"

Rosvita hurried forward with her heart pounding like a hammer and her breath short and painful and her knees ready to give out. The dirt was all churned and scuffed, and she kicked fresh manure in her haste, but the pungent scent exploded and gave her strength somehow to hasten on as the last soldier vanished through the shining archway. A leather pouch lay discarded on the ground just beside the glowing arch. She bent to pick it up and felt the familiar lines of the *Vita* together with the unbound pages of· her *History*. Fortunatus had taken the copies and gone on, had left these for her, and with a gladdened heart she hastened after him only to hear her name,

"Rosvita,"

voiced as softly as a whispered curse, behind her. Light flared as she turned to look back, standing with one foot within the circle and one outside it on night-soaked earth, hoping to see Mother Obligatia, but she only saw Hugh. He stood with his staff dangling from his hands, staring after her with an unreadable expression as the threads burned and tangled and the swelling moon bloated like a dead thing until it encompassed the entire sky.

Ai, God, what had she done? She had agreed to let him proceed with his plan. She had persuaded Theophanu to allow it to happen. With her complicity, at her urging, she had caused forbidden sorcery to flower in this holy place. Horrified, she stepped backward and was instantly awash in light, disoriented, pathless.

But Sister Amabilia met her there in the light, smiling although her throat was cut and blood ran down the front of her cleric's robes.

"Dear God, Sister," cried Rosvita, hurrying to embrace her. "Where have you been?" But she could not catch Amabilia in her arms; no matter how close she came or how fast she hurried after her, Amabilia remained always the same distance away.

"I am murdered, Sister. They came upon me out of the forest and slew me and my escort, but they took nothing but the letter I carried for Mother Rothgard and the Circle of Unity I wore at my heart. I thought I would live to be as old and wise as you, Sister, but it was not to be. Yet do not mourn for me, for I have been granted God's embrace. Only beware, Sister. You are in danger as well."

"Ai, God, Amabilia! Can this be true?" She wept, and her tears became slivers of ice in the cold wind. "No one writes as beautifully as you do. How can I work without your jesting and your kind heart beside me?"

"Guard yourself, Sister. Guard those we love. Stay on the path."

Amabilia was gone. There was no one there. It had only been a vision, and no doubt a false one at that, and the road was gone as well, only her tears turned to ice beneath her feet that burned and pierced her, each step an agony. The leather pouch tucked under her arm grew hot, blistering her skin, and she swung it out and away from her and drew out the *Vita* to save it. But it was the book itself that cast off light and heat. Sigils woven into the cover of the book ignited like coals come alight, magical bindings and protections sewn into leather and into the parchment itself, strange symbols and familiar ones, the signs representing the planets and the sun and the moon, the Circle of Unity, Arethousan letters and other ones she did not know, peeping here and there from within Fidelis' meticulous hand.

Who was Fidelis protecting himself against? From whom was he hiding?

And then they loomed above her, manifesting out of the light, resplendent and terrible, spirits burning in the aether with wings of flame and eyes as brilliant as knives, and when their gaze struck her, it was like being struck by lightning.

"Where is the child?"

Their voices rolled with the searing blaze of flame torn from the Sun. She was no longer on earth, she knew that then, and she was lost because the road had vanished before her and behind her. She covered her eyes but she was already sightless, blinded by their refulgence, and desperately she staggered backward, hoping to escape.

But she fell. She fell and the wind rushed past as though she had fallen and was falling and would fall for a thousand thousand years. Darkness swallowed her, and she saw no moon and no stars. She knew then which road she had followed: She had taken the last step over the precipice and now she was plunging forever into the bottomless pit, where her sins had led her.

XI
THE PALACE OF COILS

1

HAD Zacharias known how far away lay the palace of coils, he might not have followed her. They walked west through the marchlands that summer, and then, as the autumn rains and storms came and went, they walked through Wendar, tramping down the paths and old roads of the duchies of Fesse and Saony, on into the old queendom of Varre which now lay under the rule of Wendish kings. They came close enough to see the towers of Autun, but never did they enter any city or town. They hunted game and gathered herbs and reeds and flowers in the forests and wild lands. The horse did well enough on grass and weeds.

Sometimes at villages he traded pelts which he'd skinned or baskets or magical charms woven by Kansi-a-lari in exchange for flour or salt or cider. Once, they traded a charm for fertility to a barren householder in exchange for a length of cloth. The young farmwife's monthly courses had ceased just after her marriage, but no child had ever come. Kansi-a-lari's interest in this problem amazed Zacharias. She had so little interest in the doings of humankind, but for this barren woman she interrupted their trip for fully four weeks while she plied her with hazelnut porridge, marjoram tea, and various oils and potions out of blind nettle or jessamine. Zacharias watched her carefully; he had a good memory, and she knew things that were forbidden by the church. As if by a miracle, the young woman's courses resumed for the first time in five years. The grateful householder sewed them tunics out of the cloth, and that made the trip easier, because now Kansi-a-lari could wear something other than the skin skirt and Quman jacket and he something other than his torn frater's robes, something to make her look a little less foreign and him look more like a man. With these disguises they could even work for bed and board at outlying farms when their supplies ran low.

At Candlemass they paid two copper coins and a charm against warts to the ferryman who took them over the Olliar River, and when they stepped onto the opposite shore, they stood on Salian soil. Zacharias discovered to his surprise that Kansi-a-lari spoke Salian better than she spoke Wendish.

Here in Salia, it rained perhaps one day out of ten, never snowed, and even in the mornings no more than a film of ice coated such puddles as laced the ground. It was fine weather for traveling, but he sensed a tide of desperation in the countryfolk as they surveyed their sparse winter crops and their wasted woodlands. If the rains did not come soon, there would be no spring flowering. Because of their fear, the countryfolk wanted no outlanders in their villages, so he and the Aoi woman took to camping in the woods every night. It was no great hardship. They wore tunics, now, and leggings and cloaks made of fur. He missed ale and cider, but there were running streams aplenty to drink from, and he rarely suffered from the stomach complaints he had been plagued with while living as a slave among the Quman.

They came at last to a country rich in rocks, and here their path led them to the edge of the sea. Zacharias had heard tell of the sea, but he had never seen it, a river so broad the far shore lay beyond view. Waves pounded on the shore below at the base of a rugged cliff. Farther along, the cliff gave way to a crescent of sand where spume lay in pale arcs at the highest reaches. A stream poured down through rocks and cut a channel through the sandy beach to reach the sea. Salt stung his dry lips, and he wept tears of astonishment and exhaustion as he stared at the horizon and the westering sun. The ceaseless motion of the waves made him dizzy.

"Soon we will be there," she said, shading her eyes against the sun. She licked her lips, as though tasting the salt in the air, then pointed west—to the horizon where the setting sun gleamed on surging waters. Or was that gleam the sun? Something else lay out there, so far away that it flickered bright against the dull waters and vanished, then reappeared as the angle of the sun brought it back into view.

"*Churendo,*" she said. Behind them, two goats had ceased their grazing along the rocky verge to examine them suspiciously. A tern waded along the crescent shore below, head dipping into the water, and out, in and out. Another joined it, then a third. Clouds brushed the sea to the south.

"We wait," she said, "until the round moon returns."

They camped in a hollow where weathered driftwood had collected. He built a rough shelter while she wove walls and roof from the tough sea grass. There they waited as the crescent moon waxed to full, and in long hours of observation he learned the sea's rhythm as the tides rose and fell with uncanny regularity. The stream gave plentiful, sweet, cold water. They caught and ate the goats, netted some fish, and scraped off the inner bark of pines for bread. Zacharias even found a few shrunken radishes, which they threw together with withered leeks to make a stew.

On the day of the full moon, she insisted that they bathe. The water was desperately cold and the day no warmer, but she was adamant: to approach the churendo, they must be clean. They had become intimate in the way of companions on the road, and she was not afraid to examine his every crevice, his ears, his nostrils, the folds behind his knees, the place where Bulkezu had mutilated him, the skin between his toes. She used her knife to clean dirt out from under his finger and toenails. He felt like an animal being prepared for slaughter; when he was very young he had seen his grandmother wash a lamb for the spring sacrifice in this very way, checking it carefully for imperfections. But since Kansi-a-lari prepared herself in the same way, he thought maybe this was just part of some other ritual: one does not approach the holy places of the gods with unwashed ears and dirty toenails. He knew now that she had long since stopped considering him a man because she washed in front of him and allowed him to wash and check those places she couldn't reach or see. He felt desire for her, for she was

beautiful in a strange and uncomfortable way. Bulkezu had not
mutilated his brain, after all. His skin flushed, and his heart beat
faster, and the familiar hand of the Enemy reached into his gut
to stroke at him temptingly. But there was nothing left to respond.

She let him wear tunic and leggings but no sandals, and on
his hands and feet she painted white circles, like a slave's man-
acles. Her own tunic and their cloaks and sandals she stored in
the horse's saddlebags.

It took her all afternoon first to oil herself and then to dress
herself. From her five-fingered pouches she drew tiny gourds
and cunningly carved nuts capped by equally tiny lids of leather,
which contained seeds and dyes. She painted herself in strange
swirling colors to match the tattoo that ran from shoulder to
hand: burnt orange spirals on her belly and breasts, four-pointed
yellow lozenges on her hips, small red circles on her buttocks,
and harsh blue zigzags on her legs. On her hands and feet she
painted white marks like leopard's claws. She put on her skin
skirt, tied tasseled bands around her ankles, calves, and knees,
and around her neck she hung two necklaces made of polished
mandibles. Into her hair she braided beads and into this beaded
headdress she stuck a slender needle of bone, and three feathers: one as gold as the sun, one as green as the spring earth,
one as black as the pit. She garlanded her spear with ribbons,
and to the base of it she tied on the bells that she had stored
away.

At dusk, they drank their fill of the sweet stream water, and
she filled two leather bottles. After that, she gave him three seeds
to eat, one dry, one bitter, one sweet. Then she led him and the
horse down to the crescent beach. The tiny melody of the bells
accompanied them, and every fifth step she shook the spear hard
to make them sing loudly. There was no wind, but it was still
bitterly cold. The tide was out, far out, as if the sea had been
sucked away into the maw of some great monster who lived in
the nethermost depths. They walked out on the crescent beach
beyond the ridgeline of vanished breakers and then farther yet
as the waters seemed to recede before them and the land behind
them. On they walked, the sand gritty beneath his feet but amazingly firm. He turned once, to look back, and saw the cliffs so
far behind that for an instant terror blinded him.

Long ago, he had known how to swim; a child in the marchlands learned early, just as he learned how to fish and weed and cut wood. But he had lived among the nomads for a long time, and they never entered the water because it was bad luck. Maybe he had forgotten how. Maybe the surging waves would sweep him away—

And then where would he go? Would his soul ascend through the seven spheres to the Chamber of Light? Nay, he was no longer welcome there. Would he fall endlessly and eternally in the Abyss? And yet, what did he have to fear from the Enemy? Who was the Enemy to *him*, since he no longer feared and loved God?

She knelt to draw markings in the sand, then prayed in her language, making certain gestures first to the north, then to the east, then to the south, then to the west. From her pouch she drew pebbles, and she laid a green one to the north, a reddish-orange one to the east, a dull brown one to the south, and a white one to the west. Sand glistened under the full moon. Rivulets of water coursed toward the hidden sea, a hundred fingerlets probing west through the seabed.

Were they getting wider? Was the tide coming in?

"We stand halfway," she said, rising. She unstoppered one of the leather bottles and allowed him three swallows. "We must walk quickly."

The horse snorted nervously. A wind touched his cheek. Then it was still again. They walked on.

"Teach me how to pray to your gods," he said suddenly.

After a long time, she said, "My gods are not your gods, and we do not pray to them as you pray. If you will not pray to the heaven god of your people, then you must find another god to pray to. You tell me before that your grandmother is a wise woman. Pray to the gods of your mother's mothers. Then you will be happy, and maybe they will protect you."

A narrow channel of water lay before them. She waded in, and he followed. The water was only ankle-deep, but beyond it lay a second channel, then a third, each one deeper than the last. They slogged over yet another sandbank to a fourth channel, and here she had to hike up her skirt to her hips to keep it from getting wet.

Unseen fish nibbled at his legs. When he turned to look behind, he saw only a dark line marking the shore. The horse grew more skittish. Water stirred and coiled in eddies like a nest of

snakes coming awake. Wind breathed on his neck. The great
monster was exhaling: the tide was coming in.

"How soon?" he asked hoarsely.

"There," she said.

There. It loomed before them out of the seabed. Looking up,
he stubbed his toes on stone. She led them up a shallow-sloped
stone ramp that emerged seamlessly from the sea floor as from
a forgotten city buried beneath the sand. As they walked, the
water swirled in around them, swallowing the glistening sands
and the narrow channels, all of it subsumed until only they on
the stone ramp walked dry-footed as the sea returned and with
it the night wind. The moon rode high in the sky, drowning the
stars.

His grandmother had named the moon "the Pale Hunter," she
who watches over the life and death of animals, and at full moon
her strength was greatest.

"I pray you, Great Hunter," he murmured, trying out the
words, feeling awkward, "give me strength. Lend me some of
your power."

An island rose steep-sided before them, a stone fort with
gleaming marble walls. They climbed until the ramp ended at
the base of an ebony gate. A path paved with black stone curled
away on either side, a wall rising sheer on one side and cliff
dropping away sheer on the other.

She led them to the left, deocil, along the path as the waters
rose along the base of the hill, slowly submerging the ramp.

"What if it comes up higher?" he asked nervously. She did
not answer him, only walked forward on the black path that circled the island. He tried to remember the prayers his grandmother had spoken, but the words had fled long since, leaving
only the memory of her, old and gnarled but hale, with a wicked
sense of humor. She had after many years agreed to pray before the altar of the Circle God, and the frater had rejoiced and
given the entire village a great feast to celebrate her conversion,
and his parents had wept with joy that she had walked at last
into the Light. But he had seen her hide a carved wooden figure of The Fat One, the bringer of wisdom and plenty, in the
skirts of the hearth; every time she knelt and prayed before the
holy image of the Mother and Father of Life, she was really
praying to The Fat One.

They walked forever on the black path, but when they returned to the ebony gate, the waters lapped the stone ramp two man-lengths from them. It was still rising.

"Now we are outside," she said. She drew her knife and drew the blade over her palm. She smeared her blood over the ebony surface of the gate, then cut Zacharias' hand in the same manner, and nicked the horse on the shoulder; this blood, too, she smeared on the gate.

Her fingers probed the shadows beside the gate, caught a lever, and pulled. The door swung open outward on silent hinges. She stepped over the threshold, and he followed her only to find that he stood in a narrow lane that ran parallel to the black stone path outside. High stone walls rose on either side. The horse balked, but when seawater lapped the threshold to drown its hooves, it bolted inside.

She tugged the gate closed against the rising tide. He glanced up anxiously: were the stone walls high enough, and watertight enough, to keep them safe from the waters? But when he knelt to brush the ground, it was as dry as bleached bone racked by a summer of rainless heat. She began to walk to the right, widdershins, and he followed her. After about the time it would take to sing the service of Terce, a short hour, they returned back to where they had started, at the ebony gate.

"Now we are inside," she said.

His hand smarted. He was very thirsty, but she offered him nothing to drink. He was abruptly so tired that, trembling, he leaned against the stone walls—

"Grandson."

He jerked back. "What is that?" he demanded. "There's something alive in the stone. It's speaking to me in my grandmother's voice."

"There is nothing alive here," she said firmly. "We have entered churendo, the palace of coils. Here the three worlds meet. Do not be surprised by what you see and hear."

"What are the three worlds?" he asked, but she had already started walking left, deocil, and he had to follow her with the horse in tow. "What's the use of walking around again?" he demanded of her back. "Isn't there a path that leads up?"

She stopped abruptly and turned. Her stare shut his mouth, and when she began walking again, he followed silently, humbled.

They walked the dusty path, grit scuffing and slipping under his toes. They circled the hill deocil, as they had outside, but when they returned to the ebony gate it was no longer ebony; it was no longer the same gate but rather a gate of palest rose stone. He gazed out to see the sea surging and rising below. Craning his neck, he could even see the corbeled entrance that marked the ebony gate, now half underwater below them. Then he saw the moon. They had been walking for a scant hour yet the moon lay low on the horizon, almost swamped by the sea, a waning quarter moon surely a good six days past full. Feeling dizzy, he swayed and caught himself, bracing a hand on the stone. But when he touched the stone, he saw through rose quartz onto a different sea, not a sea at all but a river snaking up through sharp-spined hills.

Ships ghost up the river, slender and predatory. The prow of the lead ship is long and lean, carved into the shape of a dragon's head. Creatures like men but not men stroke at the oars and sometimes, as they skate the shallows, their oars break through a skin of ice. Stone and metal spearheads gleam as sun catches them, rising low over the northeastern hills. Ahead, the river swirls white around a series of posts; someone has staked the river so that ships can't sail up it.

But the creatures in the ships merely anchor their ships to the stakes and from this base they harry the countryside, burning and killing. Halls and cottages blaze under the pale light of a sun that never rises more than halfway up the sky. Soon night falls, gray and icy. Fires dot the slopes and valleys like an uneven procession of torches. Late into the night they gutter and fade as a storm sweeps in. There is only darkness.

She vanishes around the curve of the lane, still winding up deocil. He grabbed the horse's reins and followed. He did not want to be left behind. He felt the ground slope under his feet, growing steadily steeper. They were climbing.

The next gate shone with a pale iron gleam. The tide was low. Dawn's light rimmed the eastern horizon, a sullen gray along the rocks. Stars gleamed fiercely above. He saw no moon. Was that its reflection in the torpid waters below? He leaned forward, pressing a hand against the gate.

*　　　*　　　*

A woman sits in a chair carved with guivres. She wears the gold torque of royal kinship at her throat and a coronet on her brow. Her hair runs to silver, and her face is lined with old angers and frustrations. Her tower chamber is elaborately and richly furnished, but the two guards standing just on the other side of the door betray its purpose: it is a prison, nothing more. She lifts a hand and beckons forward the messenger who has come, a nondescript woman dressed in the robes of a cleric.

"What have you brought me?" she asks in a voice too low for the guards to hear, and in any case they are bored and at this moment chatting with an unseen comrade out on the stairs. "You are certain Biscop Constance knows nothing of this?"

"Nay, Your Highness," replies the cleric. "The biscop had a new cote built, but this pigeon came to the old one. That is how I came to know of it, through certain faithful of your servants who do not approve of a Wendish biscop being set over them as liege lord and biscop both."

"Give it to me," orders the woman. The cleric obediently hands it over, and the woman unrolls a thin strip of linen, rather dirty and damp, marked with letters. She returns it to the woman. "Read it to me."

The cleric puzzles over it for a while, since some of the letters are stained and blurred, but at last she reads aloud. "To she who is rightfully queen over Varre and Wendar. Hold fast. Do not despair. There is one who has not forgotten you and who will return to aid you in time."

"That is all?" demands the woman.

"Yes, Your Highness."

"What of the mark, there, at the end?"

"It is some kind of sigil, but I cannot make it out."

The woman grunts, then, and gestures toward the fire. "Burn it."

A shutter has been taken down to admit air. Through it, he sees the dawn sky and the distant moon: the last sliver of the waning crescent moon setting below trees that range alongside a broad, noble river.

"Pale Hunter, protect me," he gasped as he shoved himself away from the gateway and staggered backward, colliding with the massive wall behind. There was no way up, no way down, except the way he was going. But maybe he shouldn't be pray-

ing to the Pale Hunter at all. Maybe he should be praying to the
Hanged One, who killed himself for wisdom, hanging nine nights
and nine days under an ash tree while ravens fed on his liver.
But he doesn't remember. That was a long time ago, and his
grandmother's ways were a curiosity to him; he already believed
in the Circle of Unity and the Mother and Father of Life because his parents believed, because he obeyed them, because he
liked the sermons given by the frater and later because the words
written in the Holy Verses rang so sweetly in his ears that he
memorized them, every one.

Now, standing alone with the horse in the narrow lane, he
couldn't recall a single word of all those psalms he had once
known by heart; he could only remember his grandmother's
prayers. She hadn't been blessed with beautiful words or elegant phrases, but she had known how to get straight to the point.

"Oh, Fat One, here are the first leeks from the garden. They're
a little small, but very sweet. Please let my daughter have the
second child she longs for. Here are some apple pips I saved
over from last harvest. The fourth tree on the left didn't produce well this past autumn. If you choose not to honor it with
fecundity this year, then I'll have my son-in-law cut it out and
we'll plant a nice hazel tree instead in your honor. I've a nice
sapling down by the river in mind for you, a good strong one
that's not yet too big to be transplanted. I'll lay a stick of it
here, next to the pips, so you can smell how holy it is."

That next winter, he remembered, she had had his father cut
out the apple tree and planted the hazel instead; his mother had
borne a strong, healthy daughter, whom she had named Hathui.
Hazel tree and Hathui had flourished together, and every autumn
his grandmother secretly set out an offering of the first hazelnut porridge before The Fat One's altar, by the spring in the hills
behind their holding. He always went with her; he never told.

She was gone.

She was long dead. And his companion had vanished up the
path, away around the curving walls.

He shook himself free of memory, terrified of being left behind in this place of visions and shadows. The horse plodded
stolidly behind as he hurried forward, and his legs burned as he
hurried to catch up. At last he caught sight of her. She seemed
so high above him, and the air shimmered strangely as though
they pressed through another substance entirely, something out-

side of air, beyond air. His knees hurt. His throat burned. The sun shone with a light as pale as the marble walls.

The third impossible gate appeared, a sudden azure like river waters frozen and set upright between two stone pillars. Beyond the gate, the sea boiled and lashed under a cloudy sky, torn by storm. Foam sprayed the rock walls. He could not see the distant land at all. He stepped back, ready to walk on. He didn't want to lose sight of Kansi-a-lari again.

But she had paused by the azure gate. "Who is there?" she asked, and in answer, she placed her palm against the pale blue gate.

Banners fly outside a fine wood hall, and servants rush hither and thither carrying wood and chests and cloth and shovels and bags of bread so fresh that he can see the steam rising and rounds of hard cheese and a cage full of brightly-colored songbirds. Snow dusts the ground. As the sun rises, the full moon sets. Horses are brought 'round, breath steaming in the cold, and suddenly people burst from the hall like chickens erupting from their henhouse to escape a fox.

That is the king. Anyone would know the king, even if, like Zacharias, he had never seen him before except in a vision. His courtiers swirl around him like the tidal currents, some in, some out. Messengers come and go as he waits for his horse to be brought forward. A woman in an Eagle's cloak stands with her back to the king, listening to one of her comrades, who looks as if he has just ridden in. She turns, then, a tall, hawk-nosed woman who is so astoundingly familiar that he can only gape as she speaks her comrade's message into the ear of the king.

"Your faithful Eagle Udala has come from Varre, Your Majesty, with news from Biscop Constance that all remains quiet in Autun despite rumors of witchcraft in the lands to the west. There is drought in Salia. Udala also brings a message from Lord Geoffrey, cousin of Count Lavastine. He has heard that the count died not two or three months ago of evil sorcery. He begs you to come to Lavas Holding, for he accuses the man who claimed to be Lavastine's bastard of using witchcraft to dupe Lavastine into naming him as his heir. He begs you to come when you can, to pass judgment on this matter."

Zacharias stares, astounded, as the king scratches his beard thoughtfully, not angry, merely considering. He would never have

known her by her face alone, for she has changed over the years
since he last saw her, grown up and filled out. But the memory
of her voice lies forever lodged in his deepest heart; so much
of what he remembers is words and voices.

Who would have thought it? She was such a bold, scrawny
girl. It is his sister, Hathui, wearing an Eagle's cloak and stand-
ing at the right hand of a king.

The king's horse is brought up. He mounts and rides away.

"Ah," said Kansi-a-lari beside him, the same sound a person
might make who has finally pulled a thorn from her foot. She
set her right hand on her left shoulder as though to say, "I greet
you," as though to say, "I am resigned to my unhappy fate."

She walked on, and he walked beside her. The fourth gate
had the luster of amber, but because she did not hesitate, he did
not stop; he did not want to be left behind. The steep lane became stairs, steepening as they made their way up the hill. He
understood now, finally, that the path was a spiral one, curling
in toward the top.

The fifth gate surprised him. It gleamed like amethyst, washing the scene behind it of sea and night sky with a brush of
palest violet. There was no moon. He couldn't make sense of
the stars, all topsy-turvy and in the wrong place. Disoriented, he
stumbled and fell against the horse. Jostled, he braced himself
against the rock, but his hand slipped to the slickly damp surface of the gate just as Kansi-a-lari cried out a warning.

"Do not look!"

But he was already gone.

A young woman with hair as black as obsidian, almond eyes,
and the broad cheekbones and dark complexion of the eastern
tribes kneels on grass like a slave instead of the princess she
obviously is. She wears a gown woven of gold thread so sump-
tuously rich that it shimmers as she shifts. Her head is bowed,
but her gaze, looking up at the creature that stands before her,
is bold.

The creature is like nothing he has seen before, but he knows
what it is, one of the Bwr people, the fabled ones who live in
the deep grass. She is a woman, or a mare; she is both, and
neither. She wears her coarse hair in braids, and a coarse pale
mane runs down her naked back, and it is also braided, twined

*with beads and tiny mice bones. Her face and upper body are
striped with green-and-gold paint. Her body below the waist is
that of a fine mare with a coat so magnificently gray that it almost seems silver.*

*"Come back to me," the creature is saying, "when you can
bring to me these things. The claws and grease of a bear. Mole's
teeth. The bones of a mouse, with none missing. Threads from
a dead man's shroud. A dragon's scale. The shed skin of a snake.
The ashes of a fire that burned on the night of a full moon. Two
coals, still burning, from the hearth of a pregnant woman. One
amber bead. Lapis lazuli carved in the shape of a god. An owl's
feather. The shell of a—"*

*She breaks off and at once he understands that she is aware
of him. She moves her left arm out of shadow to reveal an owl
perched like a falcon on her wrist.*

"Go," she says to the owl. It takes wing abruptly and silently.

Kansi-a-lari wrenched him away so painfully that he gagged,
gasping for breath. Spasms racked his stomach, just under his
rib cage. His left elbow throbbed.

"You will ruin everything," she said harshly. "Do not look
through the gate of Shagupeti again."

They climbed on. The path was all stairs now, winding up
around the hill with the towering walls on either side, the endless walls, he never saw any break in them from this side, no
trace of dwelling places or ladders or paths or halls or wells or
of any kind of animal or bird, not even ants and spiders. The
fort was empty, except for the three of them, she, he, and the
horse; except for the visions.

The sun shone, but he could not see it as he trudged up stair
after stair. He tried to count them but could not. He was too
thirsty to count. She gained ground on him, impatient with his
sluggish pace, and got out of his sight, but he was just so tired
and his knees hurt and he knew he would catch up to her in
time because there was nowhere else he could go.

When he came at last upon her again, she stood motionless
before the sixth gate, both of her palms pressed against the
gleaming green banded stone, like malachite worn so thin that
it had become no thicker than a veil.

She spoke and, speaking, received an answer. He crept closer
to listen.

"Be cautious, Cousin," said a voice through the veil. *"We are not the only ones walking the paths. New gateways have opened, although this was not unexpected. Walk cautiously in the world of humankind. You are a long way from home, and the paths grow increasingly more unstable. Do not take too long about your errand, or you will not be able to return."*

As he came up beside her, she pulled her hands from the gate and turned to regard him evenly. "Come," she said. He had to follow her. He didn't dare pause to touch the gate, to see what she had seen. To whom was she talking?

Now each stair step was like one carved by titans, knee-high, and the poor horse had to scramble like a mountain goat from ledge to ledge. But it was a hardy creature; like all Quman horses, it had never received any pampering. Those who couldn't keep up were killed and thrown into the stew pot. It was a strong little horse, fit for a chieftain like Bulkezu to ride, it had the heart of a prince, and no damned stairs were going to keep it from following.

He was out of breath and had to stop to get his wind back when they came to the seventh gate. He had to stop to lift a hand over his eyes, because the sight of the gate blinded him, all blue-white fire, not stone at all, not wood, but some substance that was as bright as a blacksmith's forge and yet as cool as the winter air. He feared it, and he stayed well back, but he could not help but stare because he knew in his gut that beyond that gate lay a place no man had ever before seen, that no man could ever see.

He saw movement, coming closer, the flutter of wings within a burning fire as though some terrible creature were about to emerge out of the brilliant gate to engulf him.

He screamed. And then something dark and hot and heavy shadowed his eyes.

"Quickly," she said, dragging him forward by the elbow.

He whimpered, struggling, and finally yanked off the creature that shrouded him. She had thrown his cloak over his head.

"Do not look back," she said. "The veil is thinning. They have become aware of that which lies far below them, and they are terribly dangerous. If they touch you, you will be burned to ashes in one blink of an eye."

"Was there truly something there?" he gasped. "What was it?"

"I think in your tongue you call them 'angels.'"

All at once, the path cut sharply to the right. They passed under a corbeled archway topped by two massive stones carved to look like lionesses, fierce and protective. His ears rang to the sound of three deep thunderous notes, and blood trickled from his nose. She let go of his arm, and he staggered in her wake out into an oval plaza paved entirely with marble and ringed with hip-high marble walls cut so perfectly that when he knelt and ran his finger along the thin crack that joined two, he found no mortar within, only the perfect fit of two blocks of masterfully-dressed stone.

The wind cut unmercifully up on this height, and he was glad to have the cloak to swing over his shoulders as he regained his balance and stood. It was a cloudless, cool night made stinging by the wind's roar. Sea ringed the island, shushing rhythmically at the base of the rock. No clouds concealed the heavens. The Queen's Sword, Staff, and Cup glimmered in the east; the light of the bloated moon, now setting, had washed away the western stars, all but the brightest ones. He knew the boldest of the stars and constellations. Any child did who stared at night up at the heavens, hoping to see an angel.

Had he seen the shadow of an angel, there at the seventh gate?

"Zacharias."

She hobbled the horse by the gateway and strode to the wall to lean out. Her body shone with an uncanny glamour, like polished bronze. The skin skirt swayed around her hips and thighs, and the fold of her arms concealed her chest. A gold chain curled loosely over her wrist. She inhaled deeply.

"Can you smell it?" she said. "Day and night are in balance again. Spring has come. The world between is rich with growth. How long it has been since I have smelled such richness!"

He stared at her, bewildered. How could it be spring? They had reached the sea a few weeks after the winter solstice, no more. It had only taken them one night to cross the sands and climb the island fort. Hadn't it?

The gleam of dawn twilight edged the eastern land on the far horizon as the moon sank below the western waves. She pushed away from the wall and raised her spear, shook it once, twice, three times. "Come. Follow in my steps."

From the archway she walked in a straight line toward the center of the plaza. He followed her, but the closer he moved toward the center, the more he felt that the ground began to melt beneath him, that he was walking first on stone, then on mud, then through sludge that dragged at his feet as it soaked away his strength. A shallow pit lay at the center of the oval, and here Kansi-a-lari knelt. He had to crawl to get there, pressing through air that seemed more like water pouring against him, a channel opening out of the pit. At its edge, he felt forward and suddenly he was falling, sliding, spinning, until he fetched up with a bump against Kansi-a-lari, who stood at the center of the shallow incline with her feet braced on either side of a depression just large enough to hold a human heart. His forehead ached from the impact. Her closeness made him dizzy, something overwhelming in her scent, or her power, or the air. He looked up.

"Pale Hunter," he breathed, but he could no longer see the sky, only a kind of pure hazy light that emanated from all places and no place. Beyond that light, as through bubbled glass, he saw a golden ladder striking up from the center of the shallow pit right through Kansi-a-lari herself and beyond her, reaching into the sky. It receded into the heavens far, and farther yet, until it became a thread. He thought he saw figures ascending and descending through a rainbow of colors, rose, silver, azure, amber, amethyst, malachite, and blue-white fire, but they were of such various pale forms and they moved with such slippery grace that he thought maybe he was just hallucinating. He passed a hand over his eyes, and looked down.

Far below, down through the rock itself, so far beneath that it seemed impossibly far, as far as it might take a man to fall in a day or ten days or a year, he saw the restless, surging waters, as black as tar, topped with white foam.

But when he touched the shallow curve of the pit, he only felt cool marble under his fingers.

"What is this place?" he whispered. He hardly had any voice left. Maybe she meant him to die of thirst. Maybe it was a kind of sacrifice to her gods.

"This is churendo," she repeated, somewhat impatiently. "The palace of coils. Here meet the three worlds, the world above, the world between, and the world below."

"Ai!" he whispered fearfully. "What lies below us? Is it the Abyss?"

"I know not this 'abyss' you speak of," she answers. "Below

us lie the waters of chaos. Above us lies the sea above, which you call in your tongue, 'heaven.' That is where our ship sails, and we must bring it home to its harbor. But all is not yet ready for our return, and yet we cannot delay, because in the world between the days pass regardless. They do not wait for us. Ai, Sharatanga protect me! I cannot find him looking through the world of earth, but in the palace of coils, nothing is concealed to our sight. Where has he gone?"

She turned to the north and lifted her spear, shaking it four times. She spoke first in her own language and then, as if respecting his presence, in Wendish. "Jade Skirt, here is my blood." She drew a fine needle out of her hair and carefully pierced her tongue. Blood dripped onto the marble and slid away into the fist-shaped depression. "Ask your sister to hear my words." She turned to the east and lifted the spear, shaking it three times. "Flower Skirt, here is my blood." It dropped, still, from her tongue, beads of it scattering, sliding, into the bowl carved out of the marble paving. "Ask your sister to hear my words." She turned to the south and lifted the spear, shaking it two times. "Serpent Skirt, here is my blood. Ask your sister to hear my words." She turned to the west and lifted the spear, shook it once. "Lightning Skirt, here is my blood. Ask your sister to hear my words."

Last, she looked heavenward, raising the spear without shaking it, so that the bells only rustled but didn't ring. "Kerawaperi, here is my blood. Hear my words. Show me what is concealed to my eye." She squatted over the fist-shaped pit. She did something under her skirt with the needle; blood dripped down, swirling and melding in the small depression.

Still squatting, she untied the five-fingered pouch and took out an acorn. She twisted the tiny cap free and tipped the acorn over. A black, viscous liquid like tar oozed from it, elongated, then fell, sizzling when it hit her blood.

"The waters of chaos," she said. "Take these as an offering."

She cast away the acorn and searched in the bulgy teats of the pouch, brought out another. This one, uncapped, produced a liquid more gold than water, so light it seemed to drift upward slightly on the air before it floated down to meld with the others in the depression. "Five drops from the sea above. Take these as an offering."

She clucked her tongue once, twice, and twice again quickly, and beckoned to Zacharias. Fear gripped his belly. But he crawled forward. Now she wanted him. This was to be the sacrifice, his own heart puddling beneath her feet.

"It is better from the male part," she said, "but you have none left. Stick out your tongue." She held the needle lightly in her hand.

Ai, it hurt. He squeezed shut his eyes and prayed to the Hanged One for courage. When his blood flowed and she began to speak, he opened his eyes to look.

"Take this, the blood of a creature who will live and die on the world between. Let the three worlds be joined here." Finally, she stood, uncapping one of the leather bottles. He gasped. Thirst had congealed his throat. Now, suddenly, his heart pounded as fiercely as with any desire he had ever felt for her body. He could smell the water, sweet clear, and strong.

She poured all of it into the fist-shaped depression, and as it spread and spread, backed up while she stayed with her feet in the water. She plucked the feathers, one as gold as the sun, one as green as the spring earth, one as black as the pit, and let them fall.

When they struck the water, a steam rose from it, a mist that eddied, then cleared. Within the mist he saw a vision so lifelike that he felt he ought to be able to reach out and touch the woman within.

A young woman with skin the color of burned cream reads by candlelight, lips moving but making no sound. Her right hand turns the pages, one by one. Her left hand rests on her hugely pregnant belly.

He heard a hiss, sharp, between clenched teeth; a moment later he recognized it as Kansi-a-lari's breath, her voice. "He is nearby. I can feel him."

A man moves into the room cautiously. He is tall, broad-shouldered, graceful in the way of big men who are at ease in their bodies. There is a glint in his eyes that might be fury—or laughter. This man he has seen twice before in visions.

His companion breathed out a Salian word, sharply, on an exhalation: "Sanglant!" She stamped her foot three times, and shook the spear threateningly toward the sky with a high cry like that of a hawk.

The vision vanished together with the water and tinctures she had poured out on the marble floor. Wind cut the mist into tatters and the sun rose on a bright spring morning full of promise. They stood alone on an oval plaza; the sea huffed and murmured below. The Aoi woman had a grim, satisfied smile on her face. She handed him the other leather bottle.

"Drink now. After that, we will eat what is left of our stores. We will rest here for a day, and begin our descent tomorrow at dawn."

He would have gulped it all down, but he had too much respect for his good companion, the horse, so he poured water into his palm and let it snuffle it up. Only then did he sip himself, three swallows, then three more, sparingly.

When he had his voice back, he turned to her. "Who was the young woman? She was beautiful."

"I don't know." She sat at her ease by the shallow pit, eating the last of the dried goat's meat.

"Who was the man?"

She shredded the tough meat to tatters and ate each string of it, then licked her fingers before she finally replied.

"That is my son."

2

TALLIA whined and complained, but in fact once any order was given firmly enough, she obeyed it. It was the tack he ought to have taken all along. He understood that now, finally. She certainly outranked him, but birth wasn't everything; she was weak, just as Lavastine had said. He remembered Duchess Yolande's hints and intrigues about crowns and thrones. Yet Tallia wasn't even strong enough to rule herself. How could she be expected to rule a queendom?

It took her a long time to recover because she had come so close to starving herself. For a while she lay ill, often feverish. Certain foods gave her the flux. Others she vomited up. At first she refused food from any hand but his, so he had to feed her minuscule portions six times a day like the invalid she was. But growing up in Bel's house he had spent time caring for sick children, he knew how to handle them, obstinate one moment and malleable the next. Eventually she became accustomed to eating normally again, and after some weeks she began to gain strength. The Feast of St. Herodia came, and went, the month of Askulavre wept to its chill conclusion, and Duchess Yolande did not arrive.

In the last days of Askulavre, heavy gray clouds covered the sky and for two days it snowed industriously. For weeks they could travel no farther than the river and the little convent dedicated to St. Thierry. It had been established by Lavastine's grandfather, Charles Lavastine the Elder, the year his mother, Countess Lavrentia, had died giving birth to her second child, Lord Geoffrey's grandfather, who had also been named Geoffrey.

St. Oya's Day came, and Tallia proved strong enough to sit beside him as he welcomed the girls who in the year past had been blessed with their holy courses. She garlanded them with wreaths of juniper and holly, since the snow precluded the customary violets. At church that day, the girls so recognized were allowed to sit on the women's benches in recognition of their new status. But St. Oya's Day released nothing in Tallia's womb. Her breasts did not swell, as they would if she were pregnant. No holy blood stained her thighs as the moon waxed and waned. Several gnarled wisewomen from the village examined Tallia and said that because of her illness her womb had withered and needed time to become fertile again, time together with various teas steeped in blind nettle and dittany, or a potion of Lady's Mantle, every woman's cloak against illnesses of the womb. Given time and a diet strong in meat and beans, they said, her womb would swell again and be ready to grow a child. But they warned him that, until then, he and she must not resume the marriage bed.

He was cautious with her, but he made it clear to her that once she had recovered, they would, they must, make a child between them. She only stared at him with those huge, delicate eyes.

Like a bitter joke, Rage came into season. He penned up Sorrow and let her run with Fear, but she didn't settle. As with Tallia, he would simply have to wait.

Fevrua was understandably known as the month of hardship, with winter stores run out and spring not yet arrived. But under Lavastine's stewardship, there were provisions enough for his own people, and Alain managed well, leaving to Chatelaine Dhuoda that which she did best and for his own part judging disputes: a rock wall had fallen and now the two householders quarreled over the exact boundary line; a young man had gotten a young woman pregnant and they wanted to marry, but his parents had already arranged a good match for him and they wanted the pregnant girl's family to either desist in their claims or else provide an equivalent dowry; a laborer had murdered one of his comrades, but they had both been drunk; mold had ruined a precious store of rye and the farmer in question accused his neighbor of working a charm against his grain because she was mad at him for not letting her son marry his daughter, even though in truth her son was a good-for-nothing slut. Winter disputes, Aunt Bel always said, had a flavor of boredom about them, petty and sullen. He did his best to resolve these disputes with common sense and a clear eye.

By the Feast of St. Johanna the Messenger, Tallia had recovered sufficiently to walk out among the poor who came and went in the shantytown built in the woods to the west of Lavas village. Many of them had trudged north away from Salia in the hope of finding shelter here. Every ragged family gave a different story, drought, famine, fighting among lords, Eika raids, and in truth none of them really knew what was going on, only that in Salia there was suffering, no work, and nothing to eat.

There was not enough for everyone. There never would be.

Often he wept at night, having seen another tiny corpse. It seemed so horrible. It seemed so unjust.

Often he set aside a loaf from his own platter, little enough, and himself passed out those loaves late in the evening when he took the hounds out for their last run. And those poor souls had so little that the next day they might speak of one loaf having become twenty, enough to feed forty people; and then some few of his own people might grumble, hearing such rumors, saying he wasted their living on strangers while others would retort that his own folk had plenty and it was the sign of a generous lord who didn't hoard what he didn't need.

Often he prayed by Lavastine's stony corpse, but he never received an answer.

Come Mariansmass and the first day of spring, the snow melted off, violets bloomed in profusion, and the bier in the church of St. Lavrentius was at last complete. It seemed appropriate to lay Lavastine to rest on such a fine day, with a nip in the air that, like his cool way of showing approval, refreshed one's heart, and with a sky evenly composed of high, light clouds and blue heaven, neither too dark nor too bright.

It took all morning to get the body down the stairs on a sledge. Instead of rigging up horses, they simply tied stout ropes to the sledge and a dozen men gladly volunteered to haul the body to the church. A short walk under normal circumstances, it took an hour to drag the heavy corpse to its resting place, while in the church the deacon led the congregation in the Mass celebrating the martyrdom of St. Marian the discipla. The congregation looked on in silence as workmen used a combination of levers and ropes, stones and pulleys to hoist the body onto the bier. Afterward, they placed Terror at his feet and Steadfast above his head, to accompany him in death.

Then, with Alain and Tallia kneeling beside the bier, the deacon sang the mass for the dead, and led the congregation in hymns. The bells rang to conclude the service, and as the assembly filed out, each one of them touched one or the other of Lavastine's feet before leaving the church. Tallia went away with her servingwomen to see about the funeral feast being readied in the kitchens.

Alain found it hard to leave. Somehow, leaving Lavastine alone in here meant he was truly, finally, dead. "Ai, God," he prayed, "let him not lie in darkness. I pray you, Lady and Lord, let hope arise out of sorrow." He touched the cool forehead, as hard and as smooth as granite. "I promise you," he whispered, "that I will see your rightful heir installed as count after me."

"My lord count!"

For an instant he didn't reply, waiting for another voice. Then he brushed a finger over the pale stone lips, turned, and acknowledged one of his stewards.

"A messenger, my lord! Duchess Yolande arrives today with full forty folk in attendance!"

The snow had melted, but a blizzard of activity met Alain when he hurried back to the hall. He had little enough to do but wait: his people knew their jobs, and he allowed them to perform them without interference.

In the late afternoon, after the service of Nones, the retinue marched into view, fine banners and polished spears, bright tabards and merry songs. For a moment he forgot himself, recalling that time—so long ago—when he had first seen a noble retinue, when he had seen Lady Sabella's progress. It had seemed like a vision sent from heaven to him, then; now, he could not help but calculate how many days they would stay, how much meat and bread they would eat—leaving less to distribute among the poor—and how much mischief they would cause with their gossip and intrigue.

The cavalcade wound its way to the gate amidst much laughter and shouting. His own people lined the road to stare as he waited on the porch of the hall with the westering sun on his face, Tallia at his side, and Sorrow, Rage, and Fear sitting obediently at his feet.

"What do you these long faces mean?" cried Duchess Yolande as she dismounted to kiss Tallia's cheek. She looked stout, well-fed, and cheerful. Despite her weeks of recovery, Tallia looked thin and sallow beside her. "It is spring, and we should rejoice. Ah, Count Alain. See whom I met on the road! I have brought him to you so that you may celebrate spring together."

Riding at her side as if he were her kinsman was Lord Geoffrey. He greeted Alain with dutiful politeness, kept carefully back from the hounds, and paid his respects to Tallia. By then, Yolande had heard about their day's work, and she insisted on being taken to see the bier.

She chattered on as they walked. "I meant to come earlier, indeed, but I was brought to bed early with this child. Thank God he has proved strong despite his small size." Alain had seen no sign of the child, who seemed to be in the care of a nurse back with Yolande's entourage. "So we rested a while at Autun, where I was brought to bed. I was so grateful for the prayers of the biscop that I named the child Constantius, in her honor. He's quite dark-haired like his father, more's the pity. Ah, well. But Autun was quite the maze of gossip. I would hear one thing one day and then quite the opposite the next. Henry is discontented with his children. He banished Sanglant from court for consorting with one of his own Eagles, but then the Eagle was excommunicated and outlawed for malevolent sorcery. It seems she cast a spell on the prince because Henry meant to set the bastard up as king after him and she wanted to be queen. But Sanglant was such a womanizer anyway that I wonder if it can be true. More likely he seduced her than the other way around!"

"I pray you," interjected Alain, startled by these tidings. "What was her name?"

"Whose name? Meanwhile, the king is marrying Sapientia to some barbarian, and sent her east to fight the savages. That can't bode well for her chances at the throne. He would never have married her to an Ungrian had he meant her to rule after him. He sent Theophanu south to Aosta, so perhaps it's her he favors, but she's so coldhearted. She never shows her feelings like a true person. It's her mother's blood that marked her, I swear to you. The boy he sent off to Gent to be abbot. What make you of these tidings, Cousin? It seems to me that Henry thinks none of his legitimate children are fit for the throne."

Tallia started, flushing. She had a way of listening without listening; Alain recognized it now. Yolande's talk had flowed over her like water over a stone, and she hadn't even realized how all of it was directed at her.

Finally, with a nervous glance, she responded. "What of my mother?"

"I was only allowed to see Lady Sabella with Biscop Constance in attendance." Yolande laughed bitterly. "For my father's crimes against Henry, I am still not trusted. But she is well. Your father has taken vows as a conversi at Firsebarg. They say he is content there. Your mother is not so content, although she knows well enough to hold her tongue. I told her of your vision of Our Holy Mother, who is God, and Her Blessed Son."

Tallia came alert, like a hound to the scent. She was so beautiful when she was passionate. Yet the nail weighed against Alain's chest, the heaviest burden he had ever carried—except for the lie he had told Lavastine and the oath he had broken to his foster father, Henri. "What did my mother say? Did she embrace the True Word? Does she understand the miracle of His sacrifice and redemption?"

Yolande shrugged casually. "She said that the one who is regnant can use her power to influence the church."

"Oh!" Tallia glanced at Alain, then away. Her color was high; her slender hands twitched as if she held the leash of an excitable dog. "I hadn't thought of that," she said softly, and then abruptly shut her mouth and stared fixedly at the church porch as they came in under its shadow. They waited inside the nave for a moment to let their eyes adjust. Then, in a group, they went forward to the bier.

"Ah! I misunderstood," continued Yolande. "I thought you said that Lavastine himself was laid to rest today. What fine workmanship this is! It is very lifelike. I swear I have seen nothing like it even at the chapel in Autun. There is a stone statue of the great emperor himself, lying in state, rather like this, but I swear that the workmanship is not so excellent."

Tallia whispered. "It was a curse."

"I beg your pardon?" asked Yolande sharply, glancing at Alain. Geoffrey had come forward and he ran a hand over one stone shoulder, then pulled his hand back quickly as if he had felt something disturbing.

"God cursed him for not letting me build a chapel in honor of Our Mother and Her Son," said Tallia. "That is why he died. But everything will be different, now."

"So it will," murmured Yolande, glancing at Geoffrey, "if you make it so. What of an heir? Are you pregnant yet?"

Geoffrey's head came up. Stillness settled so profoundly over the group that Alain heard dust falling from the eaves and mice scrabbling in the walls. Tallia took in breath to speak. The last lance of sunlight through the western windows made a path along the stone floor, trembling, as brief as a human's lifespan, one passing tremor in an angel's wings.

It flickers, a pale rose curtain in the air, light trembling in the sky and then fading. Was that the passage of an angel's wings? Nay. He knows better. The WiseMothers say that the curtain of light seen sometimes in the winter sky is wind off the sun, blown to earth. He supposes they are correct; they see much farther than he does. But on such a night as this, he wonders if it is not wind at all but a kind of water, some deep inexplicable tide that drags back and forth, rising and falling, between the earth and the heavens. Here he stands, caught in the current, waiting.

The air breathes around him with the slow exhalation of earth, warmth rising into the chill night sky as heat fades off the rocks. He waits in a crater, a bowl of stone on the high fjall. He waits alone, because he alone was marked by the spoor of Hakonin's OldMother. Because he defeated Hakonin's warriors five seasons ago, because he earned a name by becoming chieftain of Rikin tribe, because he drove off Jatharin's raiders who harried Hakonin's outlying farms, because of all this, he was chosen by Hakonin's OldMother to enter the nesting cave deep in the rock. The ways are hidden from all but the SwiftDaughters, traps and pitfalls await the reckless, those who seek what is forbidden, the secret of the nests.

He walked through rock halls and along the phosphorescent gleam of tunnels, following the faint chime and scatter of the golden girdle of the SwiftDaughter who led him. She brought him here, up stairs carved into the rock, to this bowl of stone open to the air, stung by the wind off the fjall. Here, he waits.

He perceives it first as a tickle along the back of his neck, a penetrating pain at the base of his spine. All at once the scent blooms as sharp as obsidian's edge.

Hakonin's YoungMother has spawned.

The smell hits him hard. Pain rips through his belly. He is torn in half, eviscerated. All of his senses reel under the onslaught. As with a needle, a thread is sewn through him, woven into him, so there is no ending to what he was before and no beginning to what he is now. When the tide comes in, the strand is helplessly engulfed; when a waterskin is filled too full, the water bursts and spills over because it cannot contain more than what it is: when a smoldering fire catches dry tinder, it rages.

He is in the grip of it. He is lost to it, a mass of feeling. The smell of moist nests freshly expelled stings him like a rain of arrows showering down on him, each one piercing him to the bone.

Pity poor Alain. For him, every day is as this day, scarred by the pitiless and bottomless maw of emotion.

Hakonin's YoungMother emerges from shadow, a graceful, massive shape like to the most beautiful granite. She watches him steadily, the weight of judgment in her gaze. Beyond her, fresh nests glisten in shallow pools, masses of tiny globes whose colorless membranes are bathed rose-red under the curtain of *heavenly light dancing above, the wind off the sun. Their complex perfume tangles with the thread grown into his body to make him part of the weave. Down by his groin, a sac buds and swells, ready to erupt. Others follow.*

He is no longer his own creature. For this night, he belongs to Hakonin's Mothers, and he will serve their purpose, which is the life of the tribe. He staggers forward, hating this, reveling in this as his last rational thoughts are obliterated by the raw red hunger of a thing he cannot name in his own language but only in the language of Alain, which is "desire."

The stripe of sunlight shivered and vanished as the sun set in the west. He felt her breathe beside him, the merest tremor as she let out the breath she had taken in a moment ago; ages ago. Her fingers brushed his; she flinched and shied off, like a butterfly, as beautiful, as fragile. He remembered it all, then. All of the desire he had ever felt for her swept him as does a wave the shore. She was even more beautiful now, the palest rose color in her cheeks, her hair washed and clean and as fine as the tawny stands of wheat under the summer sun. Her neck had the supple grace of a swan's. She had put on enough weight that her breasts pressed against her gown and her hips swelled under the fabric, a resting place for loving hands.

She did not look at him, but she flushed, the color of a woman who sees her beloved for the first time in the intimacy of the bedchamber. Was it not obvious that she loved him, he who was surely not worthy of her, the granddaughter of queens and kings?

At last, she spoke in as firm a voice as he had ever heard from her. "God has heard my prayers. I remain a virgin. I am not pregnant."

Geoffrey let out a sharp, satisfied breath, turning to Yolande. "Did I not predict this? God have made him impotent! It is a sign. If he was the rightful heir, he would have gotten her with child by now."

Ai, God. His own desire had blinded him. Tallia stared at him defiantly. Finally, he stammered out words. "Say what you mean, Lord Geoffrey."

"I mean," said Geoffrey, warming to his subject, "that you duped my cousin Lavastine. You are a fraud. I knew it all along. I have already sent a message to King Henry asking him to judge this matter."

"King Henry has already judged this matter," retorted Alain. "He himself sealed my father's claim. *I* didn't ask to be acknowledged as my father's heir. Lavastine himself took me forward before the king before I knew what he meant to do!"

"So you say now. But everyone knows Lavastine was ensorcelled at that time. I was loyal to King Henry all along. But you consorted with that Eagle, the one who was outlawed and excommunicated for sorcery. You gave her gifts. Who is to say you didn't ensorcell my cousin Lavastine? That you convinced him of what was never true? He was taken by a fit, that is all, a fit brought on him by witchcraft. That is why he named you as his heir."

Duchess Yolande watched him with the weight of judgment—and opportunity—in her gaze. Hadn't her own father ridden with Sabella, against Henry? Who could know where her loyalties lay? Tallia had a legitimate claim to the throne. Geoffrey had a wife with powerful kinsfolk, and an infant daughter whom he had, until last spring, expected to install as count of Lavas. And Yolande had an infant son, second child, who—if he lived—would need to marry a powerful noblewoman.

Ai, God! No wonder Lavastine had had little patience for court. Intrigue was nothing more than a palace of coils, all tangles and knots, and once you wandered in, it was impossible to find your way out. There you would starve, and the scavengers would eat you, flesh and blood and bone.

Alain turned to Tallia, but she only smoothed her hands down over her virgin womb. She would not even look him in the eye. And that, of course, was what hurt worst of all. She might as well have scoured *his* hands with the nail as her own. The pain wouldn't have been as great as this.

He whistled, and at once the duchess' attendants scattered as the hounds bounded in, growling, and ringed him. Tallia began to cry, Geoffrey took five steps back and set a hand on his sword. Duchess Yolande called to her guards, but they hesitated at the door, afraid to come any closer.

"Then what of the hounds?" Alain demanded. "If you or your daughter are the rightful heir, then why do the hounds obey *me*?"

"More of your sorcery!" hissed Geoffrey. "It wasn't *my* grandfather who was cursed by the hounds. He was only the younger brother of Charles Lavastine, he who became count after his mother died. Ai, God, don't you know the story? Countess

Lavrentia had only the one child, the boy she named Charles
Lavastine. They never liked each other. She prayed every day
for a girl, who would take precedence over the son, but she
didn't became pregnant. Not until Charles Lavastine was eighteen. Everyone was surprised that a woman of full forty years
was carrying a child. Her husband died in a hunting accident
while she was still pregnant, and then she herself died in childbed.
Some say she died of disappointment that she had given birth
to another boy instead of the girl she longed for. Some say
Charles Lavastine murdered her to make sure she wouldn't get
pregnant again. But he was count now, and it fell to him to name
the infant. He called the baby Geoffrey—my grandfather. He
founded a convent at St. Thierry and scoured the countryside for
foundling girls to become nuns, so they could pray for his
mother's soul. That's where he laid his mother to rest. But it
was right after she died that the hounds came to Lavas County,
that he began to hunt with them and go everywhere with them,
as though they were his bodyguard. No one knows how, or why,
or where they came from. But everyone said it was witchcraft,
that he had traded something precious for the hounds. Ever after
those hounds obeyed only him, and then his son the younger
Charles, and then *his* son, the younger Lavastine."

"And now they obey *me*," retorted Alain softly. Ai, Lord and
Lady! He was furious, and yet the anger lay muted, red-hot coals
banked by ash. Geoffrey had concealed his plans all this time.
Had Lavastine suspected? No doubt he had. That was why he
had wanted Geoffrey to appear at his deathbed, to swear an oath;
Geoffrey hadn't come.

"But if it was witchcraft all along, then you could have
witched the hounds as well. You have no other proof that he
sired you. I'll call every soul in this county forward to swear to
what they saw, or didn't see, eighteen years ago when that servingwoman was brought to bed with the child she claimed was
his bastard. Any woman can lie. Or you could have lied, hearing the story, and pretended you were what you are not. God
Above!" Geoffrey turned to Duchess Yolande, as though pleading to her. "How can we trust the testimony of these hounds?
They're creatures of the Enemy. Everyone knows that these very
hounds killed my cousin's wife and infant daughter, ripped them
to pieces."

Tallia whimpered and shrank against Yolande, whose eyes

had widened with appreciative interest. "If this is true," said Yolande, "then how could Lavastine tolerate such beasts in his train afterward?"

"She lied to him," said Alain hoarsely. "The child wasn't sired by Lavastine but by another man."

"So he said," replied Geoffrey. "So he said to cover his own guilt. No one spoke of it, no one accused him, because they feared him."

This was too much. "His own people trusted him because he was a good lord to them and looked after his own!"

"Who will look after them now?" Geoffrey turned again to Duchess Yolande. "The hounds are a curse, not a gift. But the curse was laid on my great-uncle Charles Lavastine, not on my own grandfather. The curse passed from the elder Charles to the younger Charles and then to Lavastine, who was swayed by sorcery and duped by this boy. But *my* line is free of the curse, and my daughter is healthy. *She* was named by Lavastine as his heir on the day she was born. She is the rightful heir to this county, not this—this—" He did not look at Alain, merely gestured toward him as toward an animal about to be led to the slaughter. "This common-born boy who defames all of us by pretending to be of noble birth."

Fear lunged.

"Peace!" cried Alain, but the damage was done. Fear bowled Geoffrey over, knocked him flat, and would have torn off his face if Alain hadn't leaped forward to grab his collar and yank him back.

"If there are any besides me to whom you should owe allegiance," said Alain furiously to the straining hound, "then go to them now!" He let go of Fear's collar.

Fear bolted for the door. Guards jumped out of the way, frantically hacking at the great hound with their spears. Yolande shouted a command and they formed up, belatedly, making a wall to protect Yolande, Tallia, and the prostrate Geoffrey. Outside, retainers scattered and shrieked.

Rage growled but did not stir. Sorrow stalked forward two steps, and halted, shuddering, when spears lowered to graze his big head.

"Peace," said Alain, more softly, although his voice trembled. The two hounds sat obediently.

Geoffrey climbed to his feet, brushing him off. "So you see," he said to Yolande. "The hound went." He no longer looked at Alain; he turned his back on him.

"The king must judge what you have laid before me," said Yolande. "Come, Cousin," she said to Tallia, who was as white as death and scarcely more mobile than a corpse. "You must lie down. Be assured that I will protect you until I see that justice is served."

They moved off together, strength in numbers. Tallia didn't even look back once.

It was quiet in the church. Lavastine lay still in death, a statue in all but truth. Did his spirit mourn, hearing Geoffrey tear his hopes asunder? Or did he already rest in peace in the Chamber of Light?

"Ai, God." Rage nosed his hand, then licked his fingers. He started, recalling himself and where he was. Two of his stewards remained, looking restless and troubled. Sorrow whined softly and padded over to the door, ready for his nightly run. Alain led the hounds outside. Some of his servingmen had waited for him outside; some had left with the duchess.

He looked for Fear in all his usual haunts: the kennel, the bedchamber, Lavastine's empty chamber where only the musky scent of stone remained and the track of the sledge they had used to drag Lavastine's stone corpse over the floor. But Fear had vanished.

In the morning he looked again, but he found no trace of him even with Sorrow and Rage hunting at his side. Then he went to take the noon meal with Duchess Yolande, in the chambers allotted to her.

"Where is my wife?" he asked her, seeing that Tallia did not appear for the meal.

"She is not feeling well," said Yolande smoothly. "But have no fear for her well-being, Count Alain. She rests under the care of my physicians."

"I would like to see her, my lady duchess," said Alain stubbornly.

"Alas. She is sleeping, and I think it best that she not be disturbed, don't you? I will let you know when she wakes."

But she didn't let him know. He visited her chambers eight times that day, and Tallia remained indisposed, resting, asleep, or under the care of the physicians, whose work couldn't be disturbed. Had Yolande made a pact with Geoffrey? Had they planned this abduction all along, for it seemed like an abduction to him. If he could only speak with Tallia, surely she would return to his side. But he didn't know the protocols; he could scarcely call out his soldiers to attack the duchess and her retainers. In truth, he didn't know what to do.

Duchess Yolande left the next day, and Tallia went with her, concealed in a wagon tented over by a strong canvas roof embroidered with the stallions that were the sigil of Varingia's power. Geoffrey rode east to his wife's holdings, but he left his banner behind to mark his claim.

"King Henry will come." It was more threat than statement.

The count of Lavas held court in his hall and rode progress through his lands, avoiding Osna. News travels fast. When he rode out in the fields and forest, he saw them whispering and pointing. A few were too quick to bend a knee while others were guardedly insolent. And while most of them remained genuinely respectful, he hadn't been heir and count long enough that he couldn't tell what they were thinking, what he would have been thinking in their place: Whom will the king favor? How will the king judge? How can we prepare for what will come?

They were waiting and watching. Chasms had opened. Doubt had been seeded. That was enough; it was what Lavastine had feared all along.

Fear never returned.

3

"MOTION is the primary cause of change," said Severus in his dry, arrogant voice, "and the lower spheres are governed by the laws of celestial motion. Power emanates from the aether, that element which is closest to God and thus unstained by the touch of the Enemy." Liath could not see his expression, but she could deduce it from his tone of voice. He insisted on hanging a blanket between them when he tutored her so that he would not be forced to look upon her. "This effluence from the aether affects all things. In movement lies harmony, but in movement also lies power. As the celestial bodies move, they weave threads of power out of the aether depending on the angle and confluence of their relationship each to the other."

At this moment, the only effluence Liath could concentrate on was that the fetus in her womb was pressing on her bladder, but she dared not interrupt Severus. He had once scolded her for asking to pee in the middle of a lesson and had refused to teach her for two weeks until Anne had finally soothed him.

"Ptolomaia discusses the positions of the planets and stars in the heavens according to their motion." At this point, Anne or Meriam would have insisted that Liath recite passages she had herself read in the *Syntaxis* or in al-Haytham's *Configuration of the World,* but Severus never sought to discover what she already understood. Like the aether, he simply emanated. "She states, 'The celestial bodies are at their most powerful at the zenith,' and we have also discovered that their power waxes along these angles and threads when they lie at midnight, at the nethermost depths, opposite zenith. But she continues in this fashion, 'Further, they are in their second most powerful position when they lie on the horizon, or just below it, about to rise.' Descending stars and planets create a different flux in the pattern, one which can be used, or countered, depending on your purpose, but never disregarded. All movements must be taken into account. The whole must be seen, not the parts. In this way the mathematicus can understand and harness the power immanent in the heavens. Therefore, position and motion. Let these act as your guide."

The fetus stirred, pressing upward against her stomach. Liath stifled a burp. The hall smelled of the fresh wood shavings that had been littered over the floor that morning. Severus never allowed them to sit outside when he lectured because, he said, the natural world distracted her—yet another instance of her degeneration, no doubt. A breeze brushed her cheek, curling in through the front doors, which were thrown open. It was another fine day. In the distance, she heard steady ax chops fading into silence at intervals. Sanglant would be out on the valley slopes, out in the sun and wind and fresh air. Able to pee when he pleased. At moments like this, she envied him.

Severus went on. "Now. Let us pass over the question of variation of force with distance and consider instead the celestial bodies. Most of the ancient scholars agree that the stars are fallen angels cast out from the Chamber of Light. But in what relation do they stand to the daimones who dwell in the upper spheres? Are the daimones slaves to their motion and their will, or are daimones creatures with free will, as we are?"

Liath shifted in her chair, hoping he was almost done. He tended to mix theology liberally with astronomy, and theology bored her; she would rather calculate the motion of the planets or observe the natural world than ponder God's will or dissect some obscure point glossed over in the Holy Verses.

"So we are fallen," he continued with a sigh more of disgust than longing. "This is the tragedy of humanity, that our pure souls have fallen through the spheres and lodged in a corrupt body, here into the cruel and transitory world of generation. Could we only lift ourselves closer to God—"

He broke off. She heard, as clearly as if it were a bell ringing, the barking of a dog. But it was not Sanglant's dog. Then she heard a shriek.

Severus moved beyond the blanket. She grunted, heaving herself up, and waddled after him, thrusting the blanket aside and stepping carefully over the threshold, blinking as she came out into the sun.

At first it was hard to make sense of the scene before her. She cut around the corner of the hall and there, out of sight, squatted to pee while shrieks, growls, and shouts serenaded her. She got herself up again and lumbered back around the corner just as a huge black hound lunged toward Sister Zoë. Liath grabbed a stick, but by the time she reached the scene Heribert had come running, brandishing his saw ineffectually, and Zoë had retreated to the tower where she sobbed from the safety of the doorway while Sister Meriam comforted her. Sister Venia had retreated with Severus, but now she cried out a warning. The hound lunged for Heribert and bowled him over just as Liath whacked it on the hindquarters. It slewed round, growling, but the sight and smell of her caused it to whine and slink away.

She heard a howl. A moment later Sanglant came at a run, his Eika dog loping ahead of him. The black hound leaped forward, and the air became charged with the expectation of blood and death as the two dogs closed and Sanglant sprinted to reach them before they ripped out each other's throats.

"What is this noise?" demanded Anne, pushing past Zoë and Meriam and striding out to place herself beside Heribert, who scuttled backward, crablike, to get out of the way. "From whence comes this creature?"

As if pulled by an irresistible thread, the black hound broke away, circled back, and padded over to sit at Anne's feet. There it rested, tongue lolling. Sanglant whistled his own dog back, and it slunk along at his heels, still growling, as he came up beside Liath. He brushed her shoulder to make sure she was all right. She was breathing hard, from the rapid movement or from fear, she wasn't sure which, but she only shook her head to show she'd taken no harm. He went over to help Heribert up off the ground, and Sister Venia hastened up to brush off the young cleric as solicitously as if he were a three-year-old. They all stared at the black hound who sat submissively at Anne's feet.

"What means this?" demanded Anne. She lifted up the hound's ears to look for ticks, opened its mouth to examine its teeth, and checked its paws for thorns and sores. "Where did it come from?"

Zoë still would not come out of the tower, but she answered in a breathless voice. "It came out of the circle of stones. Then it went after the goats, and then it chased *me*. You saw the rest."

"I see no reason for this intrusion to interrupt your work any longer." Anne snapped her fingers at the hound. "Come." It followed her meekly to one of the sheds, where she bade it lie down. There she tied it up and left it, after bidding the servants to bring it water. "It will have to be fed," she muttered.

Severus came over to her, keeping well out of reach of the hound, and began speaking in muted tones that excluded the others. Sanglant had come back to Liath and now he frowned at her.

"It could have hurt you," he said.

"But it didn't, and it looked as if it were about to rip Heribert's face off. No harm came of it." She caught hold of his elbow and with a light pressure drew him closer. "But doesn't it look to you very like one of Count Lavastine's hounds?"

"So it does." He took in a breath. "And smells like one of Lavastine's hounds."

He was silent for a long time, listening, and she said nothing, only watched him. He had filled out, had lost the haunted expression that had chased him after Gent; his tunic now fit him without the swathes and folds of extra fabric draped over an overly-thin body. He was handsome not because his face was pretty but because he was bold and full of life, the way she had first seen him before the disaster at Gent. She sighed happily and leaned against him. Without taking his gaze off Anne and Severus, he pressed his palm onto her belly and, as if in answer, the fetus rolled, some uncanny communication of movement and pressure between father and child.

"They're speaking in Dariyan," he said finally, in disgust, "and I can't follow more than one word in ten. It's something about that hound, I swear it, as if they recognize it, or know why it's come. But why would they be talking about Emperor Taillefer?"

"Hush," she said, glancing toward the others. Meriam and Zoë had gone back into the tower, and Sister Venia was still fussing over Heribert, who appeared eager to free himself from her attention. Anne and Severus remained oblivious, deep in their profound debate. Servants clustered near Anne, pale shapes curling in the wind. Liath's constant attendant, the watery nymph, had sidled closer to brush up alongside Sanglant. Liath hissed at it, and the creature slid away quickly. "Come," repeated Liath. "Let's see what we can see."

No one seemed to mark them as they walked away from the cluster of buildings: the new wooden hall, the old stone tower, and the half dozen sheds and shelters. They passed the aromatic pits, crossed the orchard, and skirted the meadow and the pond. Beyond the pond an animal trail cut upward through forest to a clearing bounded on one side by a sheer cliff. Here the valley ended, blockaded by a fall of boulders.

An old hovel lay abandoned in the clearing. It looked rather like an old way station, long since fallen into disuse. But the floor was sturdy enough; she and Sanglant had tested it several times before she got too pregnant to be energetic. It was one of the only places they had any privacy, although in truth, with the constant presence of the servants, they never truly had privacy. But they still liked to come here, since none of the magi ever did.

A ring of stones under a sagging thatch roof constituted the cookhouse, and she crouched here, knees wide to accommodate her belly. He sat cross-legged beside her, the dog at his back. The water nymph slithered through the rafters and curled around one beam, peering nervously out at them. None of the other servants had followed them, still drawn to the confusion below.

Sanglant had laid in a store of firewood, and with kindling

and small logs she built a simple edifice in this primitive hearth.
Then she called fire. She was aware at first of the servant fleeing to a safe distance. Sanglant glanced up, marking its swift,
fluid motion with his gaze.

Liath touched his hand. "Look." She said it every time, even
though it did no good. She fashioned an archway in the flames
and looked through it, seeking— "Count Lavastine's not there,"
she murmured. "I can't find him."

The fire flickered, then leaped higher, casting shadows through
a narrow cavern that resolved itself

*into the nave of a church where a young man kneels, pray-
ing beside a stone bier. His head is bent and his hair hangs forward to conceal his face, but she knows him at once. She would
know him anywhere even without the two black hounds sitting
beside him, his faithful attendants.*

*"Alain," she whispers as heat sears her face and he falters
as he prays as if he has heard the echo of her voice in his heart.
He looks up, but it is only to mark a servant entering with a lit
candle. The inconstant light falls on the bier, and there she sees
Count Lavastine at last, silent as he rests, until she realizes it
is not him at all although it could as well be him, the image is
so astounding lifelike. For an instant she feels a profound amazement, respect for the unknown craftsman who has carved this
monument in stone; then, curiously, she feels sorrow, as she
might for a kinsman.*

"He's dead," she says.

*But the words spin her away and she slips through a second
archway, the familiar one that draws her always into its grip
like desire. Through the burning stone she stares at the empty
glade and dying trees. An azure feather lies discarded in the
dirt. The Aoi sorcerer is gone.*

"Liath!" he said sharply, hand on her wrist as he tugged her
back.

Her face burned, and for an instant she couldn't speak, she
couldn't remember where she was.

"Hush," he said. "You're crying!"

She remembered him and who he was and what he was to
her, and for a while she only rested her face against his chest

while she sniffled. But it was so uncomfortable, with her huge belly always getting in the way.

"Ai, God," she muttered, half laughing. "I'll be glad to get this child out of me!"

He kissed her on the forehead and released her. "What did you see?"

"You didn't see it?" she demanded, as she always demanded, no matter how many times they tried. "I thought your mother's blood tuned you to magic."

"So it might have," he said with a half grin, "but it still doesn't make me able to see through fire, nothing more than shadows. Did you see Lavastine?"

"He's dead," she said, and Sanglant replied with a gusting sigh, an "ai!" of despair. "Lord Alain has become count in his place. But he only had two hounds beside him. Maybe the others were in the kennel."

"Ai, God. We should have followed him. I'm sure it was Bloodheart's curse that killed him."

"The curse that was meant for me," she murmured.

"Peace, my love. What's done is done. It was God's will, or it was an accident, but there's no undoing it now."

"Nay," she agreed, wiping tears from her cheeks. "It can't be undone. He's dead. I saw Alain praying by his bier. Ah!" She grunted, legs smarting, all pins and needles, and got to her feet. Sanglant went with her to the cliff and she ran a hand lightly along the stubbly grain of rock as they walked alongside. The grass grew to the very foot of the sheer rock wall that then abruptly disintegrated into boulders, hulking things like monsters crowding the clearing. It was odd how they sat poised there, all jumbled up and yet with no sign that any had fallen farther to roll down onto the grass. It was as if an invisible hand had halted them and held them steady, there at the verge of the clearing. Snowflakes spun out of the air and lit on her cheeks. She smelled winter, but it didn't touch her.

"I'm sure it's one of Lavastine's hounds," said Sanglant finally. He licked a snowflake off a finger. "I know their smell."

Snow swirled around them, dissolving in the brook that gurgled down from the stones past their feet, powdering daisies and snowdrop and vetch and then melting away into the green grass like the tears of a child who's just been given a new toy. Be-

yond cliff and rock wall, winter engulfed the mountains while
they stood here in eternal spring.

"But if that's true, how did it get here?" she asked. "Why
did it come?"

Sanglant said nothing, only brushed his fingers over his neck,
where he had once worn the gold torque of royal kinship.

4

SHE dreamed.

A golden wheel flashed in sunlight, turning. A withered hand
scraped at the latch of a door made of sticks bound together,
and slowly the door opened; she would see Fidelis' face at last.
Would it resemble that of Emperor Taillefer, which she had seen
carved in stone? It was so dark inside the hovel that she could
only make out the shadow of a man, frail and ancient, and then
the dream slipped through her mind like a fish twisting out of
her hands, and as she stooped forward to enter the hut, she
walked into a cavern whose walls gleamed as if they had been
plastered with molten gold. Young Berthold slept at the base of
a burning pillar of rock, surrounded by six attendants whose
youthful faces bore the peaceful expression known to those angels who have at last seen God. The flames leaped heavenward,
and she could actually see through them into another landscape
so vivid that in an instant she was there, standing on a blanket
of ice. A blizzard tore at mountain peaks, clouds streaming off
the high rock summits, and the scream of the wind almost
drowned the voice that spoke in her ear:

"Sister, I beg you, wake up."

Her neck was cold and her shoulders were damp, and as she
groped for purchase her hands slipped on dewy grass. A bee
buzzed in and out of her line of vision. As a breeze came up,
grass swayed into her face, tickling her nose. She sneezed.

"Sister Rosvita!" With exaggerated care, Fortunatus helped
her sit. "You fainted. Are you well?" A rising sun glinted in her
eyes, and she had to shadow her face with a hand.

"I'm very confused," she said feebly. "Where are we? Is Sister Amabilia here?"

"Hush, Sister." He was smiling stupidly and he patted her hand more in the manner of a man soothing a nervous hound. "We are safe. Here. Let me help you up."

Even with his help, she trembled as she stood. She had pressed too hard after her illness, and it was all hitting now. The scene was so impossibly strange that she knew she was still dreaming. But she heard the bee clearly enough, humming about its business, and her nose tickled most realistically, stung by pollen, and she sneezed again.

"God bless you," said Fortunatus.

Perhaps she wasn't hallucinating.

She stood on a grassy knoll sprinkled with sweet cicely, milk-white snowdrops, and the poisonous blue of wolfsbane, such a lovely flower that anyone might be forgiven for thinking it had some fine virtue when in fact it was deadly. Behind her, where the hill leveled off into a flat summit, a circle of standing stones crowned the height. Before her, the entourage had scattered down the hill like children at play, making for a ribbon of road worn into land below. Their spirits were infectious; they whooped and laughed and called out, and Fortunatus actually clapped her on the shoulder and pointed to the vista before them.

"Do you see it?" he cried. Beyond, nestled at the opening of a steep valley that cut up into high mountains, lay a walled town. "Brother Amicus says it is Novomo, fully a hundred leagues or more from the convent. One step has brought us this far! We are saved by a miracle!"

"No miracle," she said hoarsely, "and more likely damned than saved. Is this truly the winter we left behind us?"

But he hadn't heard her, he was laughing, and slowly the warmth of the day and the high spirits of the others melted into her and warmed her. The memory of poor Amabilia faded, as did the horror of the pit. She had chosen to seek aid from Hugh, knowing what he was, like a desperate woman using a tincture of wolfsbane to treat a child's raging fever knowing that the ointment was as likely to kill as cure. But they had lived; they had even escaped. For that, for now, she would be content.

As their cavalcade straggled toward Novomo they gained an escort of curious farmers and a handful of soldiers who had has-

tened out to see who they were and sent a message back to their
lady. On the ride, Adelheid could speak of nothing but their mysterious journey.

"Only imagine if we can harness this power! Armies could
move swiftly. We could always be a step ahead of our enemies."

"I beg you, Your Majesty," interposed Rosvita. "It is dangerous to rely on those who have gone against the church in
order to learn such skills."

"Are you sorry we escaped?" demanded Adelheid.

Theophanu watched Rosvita, saying nothing. She seemed distant, preoccupied.

Rosvita sighed. "Nay, Your Majesty. But our situation was desperate. I would hope never to have to make such a choice again.
It may be that we were lucky this time, and might be lost on a
second attempt. Nor is it clear to me that such a gateway could
accommodate an entire army. Can it be held open indefinitely?
Do the gateways only accommodate small retinues? What if clouds
cover the sky? In any case, I wonder if we have truly come through
unscathed. Doesn't this landscape seem strange to you?"

"Those are the Alfar Mountains. Beyond Novomo lies St.
Barnaria Pass. To the south the road leads to Darre, not more
than ten days' ride. None of this seems strange to me, Sister."

"Not the flowers, or the warmth? What happened to winter,
Your Majesty?"

That stilled Adelheid, and when an elaborate escort, alerted
by the scouts, rode out from the city to greet her, she made no
mention to them of the mysterious gateway through which they
had traveled.

"Your Majesty!" The lady of Novomo dismounted and made
her bow. She was shaken by Adelheid's appearance, and at once
she began to look nervously around her at the copses of trees
and the fields where dutiful farmers broke the ground for sowing. "God is merciful, Queen Adelheid. We heard that you were
dead."

"Dead!" cried Adelheid.

"You have not heard? The skopos crowned John Ironhead
king of Aosta over one month ago, in Darre."

"King!" cried Adelheid.

"We have been betrayed," said Theophanu coolly.

But Adelheid was not ready to bow under at the first sign of
adversity, not after their astounding escape. "I am not dead, as

you see, Lady Lavinia. I can march on Darre to take back what is rightfully mine!"

Lady Lavinia was an older woman with keen brown eyes and the sharp wariness of a lady who has learned to brew her own potions so that her enemies will have no opportunity to poison her through her own laziness. She gestured now toward the raggle-taggle retinue, all strung out behind queen and princess. The horses looked appalling in the clean light of day. Three were already bloating from a surfeit of fresh grass, and one had broken its leg, bolting after it came through the stones, and been put down. Most of the servants were on foot, and even some of the noble companions limped along, their once elegant clothing as filthy as six weeks under siege with only enough water for drinking and cooking could make them. No doubt they all stank, and would have been horrified at their own smell if they hadn't become accustomed to it.

"I beg your pardon, my queen, but with what army will you march on Darre? Once Ironhead hears that you are still alive, he will send his men to capture you. His spies are everywhere. Indeed, Your Majesty, I cannot march with you because my eldest daughter has been taken to his court to live as a hostage for my good behavior. You will find, I fear, that Ironhead has gathered many allies to him in this same manner. You must free them from their fear for their children before you can count on their loyalty. Many would willingly rally round you, because we know what Ironhead is, but in truth, there must be a chance of victory or we will all lose our lands."

"If I can raise an army?"

Lady Lavinia only lifted her hands helplessly. She indicated her own escort, handsome enough in their bright tunics, with spears and helmets and a line of clerics carrying incense in polished censers. "Your kinfolk are dead, Queen Adelheid, may God grant them rest. Ironhead possesses your treasure, all the gold and silver and weapons you left at Vennaci. How will you raise an army great enough that the rest of us can trust our lives and land to your cause?"

Adelheid could not be daunted. Perhaps that quality made her shine. She raised an arm to indicate the mountains rising to the north. "I will lay my case before King Henry!"

A ragged cheer rose from Fulk's soldiers and was caught and echoed by her own retinue.

Lady Lavinia looked honestly relieved. "A wise decision, Your Majesty. I will do my best to shelter you, and I will gladly supply you with fresh mounts and provisions. I have always honored you and your kin, and I would not have you made Ironhead's prisoner—or his wife. But I cannot offer more than that, not now. My hands are chained."

"They will not remain chained forever," declared Adelheid. Less ragged than the others, she had worn her mail capelet for their flight, although a servant now carried her helmet. "Ironhead will never dare pursue us into Wendar, and I know that King Henry will not let this injustice go unpunished. Let us only shelter over the winter with you, Lady Lavinia, and we will cross into the mountains as soon as the passes open in late spring."

Lady Lavinia got a puzzled look on her face, and her clerics, those within earshot, whispered one to the next. "You have wandered far in the wilderness, Queen Adelheid. Spring and the new year came more than a month ago. Have you no clerics among you to calculate the days? Today we celebrate the Feast of St. Peter the Gatekeeper."

The third day of Avril!

Rosvita felt dizzy, quite out of her head for a moment until Fortunatus, walking beside her, reached up to steady her where she sat on a placid and bony mule. But she recovered fast enough. She had always had a good head for calculations, and this one took no great skill in any case, not with the signs all around them.

They had stepped into the circle of stones on the third day of Decial, at the full moon. Somehow, in that one step, they had spanned one hundred leagues . . . and four full months!

5

THAT'S it!" cried Liath. She hadn't been able to sleep, and she'd been sitting on the bench by the open door, reading with her uncanny night vision under the unexceptional light of a waning quarter moon. "'At this point it would be well to keep in mind that all bodies have three dimenstions: longitude, latitude, and altitude.' Ai, God! How could I not have seen it before? That's what I missed!"

Sanglant bolted up from the bed as she swore, a soldier's curse he hadn't even known she knew. She clutched at her belly, bit her lip, and grimaced.

"Ah! Ah! Ah! No, no, I don't need help." She waved him off, although her other hand still pressed against her abdomen. He held down the bench, which rocked as she rocked with the pain. "It's passing."

"Is the baby coming?"

"I don't know," she said disagreeably. "Ai, Lady. I don't want the baby to come now! I'm so close to the answer!" She groped for and found her sandals. "I'm going to walk over to the tower. I just need one more evening—" She cursed again and tossed the sandals aside in disgust, unable to reach her feet to bind them on.

"I'll come with you," he said as she heaved herself up, evidently having decided to go barefoot.

"Very well." She walked outside without waiting, still muttering to herself. She was in the grip of something larger than he was, the mystery she pursued, or the mystery of childbirth, or both together. Sanglant had seen women in the grip of labor become oblivious to the world as though all of life and the universe had squeezed into a cord that linked them, a solitary daughter, to the holy Mother of Life, She who had given birth to the universe.

He dressed hastily. The Eika dog trotted at his heels. Servants whispered around him, pinching his ears and teasing his hair, but when he didn't respond, they hung back at a distance and then vanished into the night to their revels. Only the watery nymph whom he had started calling "Jerna" dogged him, slipping along in his shadow as if to keep out of Liath's sight. The creature's shape had changed noticeably and disturbingly over the last months. He wasn't sure if both daimones and humans wore as their material forms a dull likeness of the angels, or if the servants, more essence than substance, merely copied human form while they were imprisoned on earth. But that vaguely female form she had worn was filling out, breasts, swelling, belly rounding in imitation of Liath. Why this yearning on her part? Didn't the daimones conceive and give birth in

the same way as humans did? In truth, her presence had begun
to bother him in other ways, just as his eye strayed to Sister
Zoë more often than it ought.

It was easy to catch Liath on the path as she waddled along.
He touched her on the arm and when she looked up at him in
surprise, as if she'd just then realized he was following her, he
kissed her. Momentarily distracted from her purpose, she leaned
against him, smiling softly, gaze lifted to his face.

In the paddock, Resuelto stood sleeping, one leg cocked. The
mules bunched somewhat apart, one resting his neck on another's
withers. It was very peaceful.

"Look," she said, lifting a finger to touch his lips and then
move his chin so that he had to look where she was looking:
not at him at all, but at the heavens. "At dawn it will be the
sixth day of Avril, and right now, at midnight, we see the same
sky that in summer we'll see at dusk and in winter we'll see at
dawn. There is the Dragon. There. Look. You can see red Jedu
leaving the Scales. On the seventh of Avril, she enters the Serpent. The seventh is a day full of power and fluctuation in the
heavens, because bright Somorhas and fleet Erekes also shift,
moving from the Child into the Sisters. A time of strong be-
ginnings."

"Where are Somorhas and Erekes?" He could identify many
of the constellations now and all of the wandering stars. After
so many months with Liath, he could scarcely have failed to
learn their names and histories.

"They can't be seen right now because they're still wandering too close to the sun. But Somorhas should return as evening
star on the seventh, when she moves into the Sisters. Erekes is
harder to see. But if we stood beneath the north pole, or at the
equator, this sky on this night at this same time would look different. Longitude, latitude, and altitude."

"It would?"

She took his hand as she started walking again. "The ancient
Babaharshan magi and the Aoi sorcerers who taught them lived
far south of here. As the observer moves south, the celestial
equator moves higher in the sky. So does the plane of the ecliptic. To be at zenith, to 'crown' the heavens, means that a star
stands directly above the observer at the highest point in the celestial dome." She stopped again. "Look there. The Queen's Bow
stands almost at zenith."

"She's hunting the Dragon."

"In another few hours, the Queen herself will stand at zenith, and at dawn her Cup and Sword will follow through the zenith behind her."

"Because of the turning wheel of the stars," he observed, and was gratified at the sudden, sharp smile she gave him, staggering in its heat.

"Exactly. Which brings us back to the tenth day of Octumbre in the year 735. Five years and five months from now." Liath opened the door into the tower quietly, and Sanglant glanced up at the beamed ceiling as they entered, but he heard nothing. Severus slept upstairs, and woe to anyone who disturbed him. "Autumn's sky at midnight is the Child's sky, she who is Heir to the Queen. The Guivre swoops down upon the Child as she reaches for the Crown, but the Child is not defenseless. She is attended by the Queen's Eagle, by the Sisters, who are her aunts, and by the Hunter who is also a prince. The Falcon flies before her, and behind her trails her faithful Hound."

"And even if the planets change over the course of the years, the stars always rise at the same time."

She hesitated, then laughed. It was such a bright sound that he had to laugh with her, and then he snorted, seeing her glance upward with exaggerated apprehension.

"Come, my love, if you'll protect me from the fates woven into the stars, I'll protect you from Brother Severus, no matter how grumpily he descends."

"Ai, God." She stiffened suddenly with a hand clasped to her belly. He felt the pain ride her, but she said nothing, only panted to let some of the pain out as he stroked her lower back. The nymph darted out of the night to stroke Liath's belly, but Liath did not notice, and as she relaxed with an exhalation, Jerna slipped back into a pool of protecting shadow.

Recovering, Liath kneaded her belly with the heels of her hand, chuckling weakly. "I was only going to say that the fixed stars don't always rise and set at the same time. It's called the precession of the equinoxes, but the cycle takes place over such a long time, thousands of years—"

"Ai, Lady," he groaned. "Five years is enough for me. God Above, Liath, just tell me this secret you've discovered so we can go back to sleep!"

She found a lantern, brought fire to the wick with a touch;

the ease with which she brought fire was never less than startling, although he ought to have gotten used to it by now. Pregnancy had not dimmed her beauty, although certainly she tired quickly these days. Her face was softer and rounder, but her eyes were as brilliant and as fierce and her hair just as likely to escape in curls and wisps from the braid he made of it each evening.

She took the ephemerides out of its cupboard and opened it to the back. He recognized where the precise writing of an unknown scribe ended and Liath's began, full of ink blots, blurred letters, and sudden breaks.

"If we look at the progression of the planets through the ephemerides . . ." She turned, pointed, even though she knew the marks were meaningless to him. "On the thirteenth day of Cintre of the year 735, four of the planets will be in retrograde, moving backward along the ecliptic: fleet Erekes at the cusp of the Dragon, both sage Aturna and bold Jedu in the Lion, and stately Mok in the Penitent. This suggests lines of force moving in the universe against established patterns. Only bright Somorhas, shining as the Evening Star, moves forward and on this day enters the Serpent." Her finger moved off the precise and rather fussy hand of the unknown scribe and onto the pages she had herself filled in over the last seven months. "But by the eighteenth day of Cintre, Erekes and Aturna and Jedu will reverse themselves and travel forward again, as if restoring the universe to its rightful order. Yet in the month of Setentre, two months later, bright Somorhas will go into retrograde, followed in early Octumbre by fleet Erekes. It all culminates on the tenth of Octumbre in the year 735. Aturna and Jedu will stand at the cusp of the Lion and the Dragon while Somorhas and Erekes move in retrograde through the Serpent and Mok slides in retrograde along the cusp of the Penitent and the Healer. The waxing crescent Moon, which by midnight will have set below the horizon, will be in the sign of the Unicorn. The Sun at midnight sleeps at the nadir of the heavens in the sign of the Serpent, the harbinger of death and change who shucks one skin only to live again newly reborn in another." She lifted both hands, palms out to mark a point flatly made. "But we live in the northern latitudes. In the latitude where the Babaharshan magi lived in their ancient cities, on the tenth of Octumbre in the year 735 at midnight, the Crown of Stars will crown the heavens."

"But that's exactly what Wolfhere—" He broke off. Through the open door he heard the night breeze sighing through trees and, half hidden in the rustle of leaves, a scuff like that of a large animal moving along the ground. Mice skittered in the walls behind the open cupboard where the magi stored their apparati: an astrolabe packed in velvet in a rosewood case, an armillary sphere that showed the motions of the heavens, a celestial globe with the stars marked out as pinpricks of silvery paint. A shutter creaked. "That's exactly what Wolfhere said to me."

She had to brace herself on the table either from another wave of pain or from the shock. "He lied to me," she whispered. "He must have known she was here all along."

"Liath—" He lifted a hand to warn her. A footstep pressed the earth outside. Jerna, hovering near Liath, suddenly darted away and folded itself into the metal bands of the armillary sphere until it became only a shimmer among shadows.

"You are wakeful," said Anne as she crossed the threshold. She did not ask what Liath was doing; she did not need to.

"We commonly reckon a year by the return of the sun," said Liath, not looking up. She still breathed hard, as after a footrace, and her gaze seemed fixed on some sight beyond the book that lay open in front of her. "The Babaharshan magicians reckoned a year by the precession of the equinoxes, when all the stars would have returned to the same places from which they had started out and by this means restored the same configuration over the great distances of the whole sky. One of their 'years' would count as tens of thousands of years as we reckon years."

"You have been reading Cornelia again," said Anne.

"But there might be other ways to reckon a year. By the cycle of bright Somorhas every eight years, for instance. Or by the Crown of Stars crowning the heavens." Liath finally straightened. She looked tired, and anxious, and triumphant. "Some people say the Aoi were always here, before humankind built cities. Others say that long ago the Aoi sailed to these shores in beautiful boats woven of gold and silver reeds, and that they ruled over the villages of humankind and in time offered to teach some of them the arts of sorcery."

"To their everlasting regret, when human magi turned against them," said Anne. "When humankind outbred them and filled the countries the Aoi ruled with unmatchable human armies.

When humankind brought disease to their masters, which they could not combat."

Liath frowned. "According to the *Book of Chaldeos,* the emperors and empresses of the Dariyan Empire reckoned years as we reckon years, by each return of the sun. But they also imitated the Aoi, whose calendar recognized a Great Year equal to fifty-two of our years. Even Chaldeos didn't know how the calendar of the Aoi worked. That was lost with them two millennia ago. But their year began and ended when the Crown of Stars crowned the heavens. They lived far south of us, or came from a land far south of where we live. They must have looked at the sky differently than we do." Liath closed the book and set a hand on it, as if to keep it closed. Now she looked at Anne directly. "Who did the calculations in this book?"

At first, Sanglant did not think Anne meant to answer. But instead she walked forward and turned the book to the opening page of calculations. There was no preface, no explanatory note or signature, only the numbers. "Biscop Tallia."

"The daughter of Emperor Taillefer."

"The same one. She understood that some deeper secret underlay the mystery of the Lost Ones. So she calculated all the way back two thousand seven hundred years to a day when the Crown of Stars crowned the heavens. On that midnight, the portents, as read in the lines of force woven through the heavens, opened the world to change, bringing the breath of the aether which is untainted by the touch of the Enemy into the air we breathe here below the Moon. . . ."

"When portals open between the spheres. When great power can be unleashed for good or for ill. You said there are ways to reach between the spheres and even beyond them——" Liath grunted as another wave hit her. He caught her as she staggered, held her.

Anne watched him with a gaze so open and clear that it was like the cut of an ax: nothing subtle about it.

Sometimes, when he was tired or preoccupied, his mind would stop working for a while, like a stream suddenly clogged with leaves and dirt and stones that backs up, and up, until the accumulated force of the trapped water finally and abruptly drives a passage through the debris. "You're talking about that great conspiracy of my mother's people in which Wolfhere implied I was an active participant. But she abandoned me when I was barely two months old. If I am so deep in their confidences, then explain to me why I was left behind, and left ignorant."

"It is a puzzle, truly. But you cannot deny what you are, Prince Sanglant."

"*I* am a bastard. I can fight, and lead men in battle. If there is aught else you know of me which remains hidden to me, then please tell me now."

Anne's smile was slight. "You are not unversed in the art of the courtier, which some call intrigue. In some ways you are cunning, Prince Sanglant, but in most ways you are not, for like your dog that waits outside you show what you are on the surface. There is little else to know."

"No onion, I," he retorted, laughing again.

"He's not—" began Liath hotly, defending him, but he touched her on the hand, and for once she shut her mouth on an imprudent comment.

"But a cup made of gold shows the whole of its substance on the surface as well," continued Anne as if Liath had not spoken. "That makes it no less precious. You are here for a reason."

"You are the thread that joins Aoi and human," said Liath. "But for what purpose?"

Anne smiled, watching Sanglant as he watched her, opponents who had not yet drawn swords. "For as was written in the *Revelation* of St. Johanna: 'And there will come to you a great calamity, a cataclysm such as you have never known before. The waters will boil and the heavens weep blood, the rivers will run uphill and the winds will become as a whirlpool. The mountains shall become the sea and the sea shall become the mountains, and the children shall cry out in terror for they will have no ground on which to stand.'"

"Chapter eleven, verse twenty-one," said Liath automatically.

Anne continued. "Some say Johanna was speaking of a vision she had seen of a great cataclysm that would on an ill-fated day in the future overtake the world. But others claim that she recorded in her *Revelation* the words of one who had experienced in her own time such a cataclysm."

"But you think St. Johanna wrote of the future," said Liath, toying with the pages of the book, running a finger over the old writing as if the ink itself could reveal secrets.

"Nay," said Anne. "I think she wrote of both past and future, of what happened two thousand seven hundred yeas ago, and of what will happen in five years if we do not stop it in time."

This time, he felt it hit her before she moved, eyes widening, jaw setting hard as she reached almost blindly and grabbed his arm. Through her skin he felt the pulse of her heart and, distantly, a second pulse, fine and faint and swift, that slowed as the pain peaked and then quickened again. As the wave passed, Liath spoke in a whisper that carried no farther than the good wool of his tunic. *"I have been to the place the Aoi now live."*

"Not lost at all," he said aloud, amazed that he hadn't seen it before. Had he not really believed her stories of the Aoi sorcerer? Or had he dismissed them as something inexplicable? "How could they have been lost if my mother could walk on earth? What if they were only hidden—?"

"We know that the Aoi vanished from earth long ago, leaving only their half-breed children behind," said Anne. "It was those half-breed children who founded and built the Dariyan Empire."

"The Aoi are not utterly vanished from the earth," objected Liath. "There are shades in the deep forest."

"Are these shades truly of earth, or are they only trapped somehow between the living and the dead, between substance and aether, doomed to live as shadows?"

Like the servants, doomed to live in bodies that only mimicked those of humankind. But he did not voice the thought out loud. He knew better than to challenge an opponent in an open battle when he was outnumbered and held inferior weapons. He wasn't desperate yet.

"You have not listened carefully, Liath," scolded Anne. "Biscop Tallia was the first scholar we know of since the days of the Dariyan Empire who gained enough knowledge to calculate the message written in the heavens. For the heavens do not lie. They only record God's creaticn. She discovered that on the date that you mentioned, great forces might be unleashed. From ancient records pieced together out of the archives of the old Dariyan Empire, she discovered that we have enemies lying in wait to destroy humanity. For this service to humankind, Biscop Tallia was humbled by the church at the Council of Narvonne, because they envied her."

When neither of them responded, she went on. "But Biscop Tallia did not let her knowledge die with her. She passed it on through her companion in the arts, Clothilde, who in her turn made sure that there would always be others to follow her. We are the ones who seem to be sleeping while the world wakes around us, only we are in fact waiting here in our hidden place to save humanity from that which threatens it. Seven is our number, because we are in number like to the seven planets: the Sun, the Moon, fleet Erekes, bright Somorhas, Jedu, who is the Angel of War, stately Mok, and sage Aturna."

"The Seven Sleepers," murmured Liath. "I've been so blind. Ai, God, here comes another one."

He let her clutch him, fingers digging into his arm. There was nothing else he could do.

"You should not have allowed yourself to become distracted from your true purpose," said Anne coolly, not moving to touch Liath as the wave came and went. "It is Bernard who is to blame for this weakness in you."

Liath made a sound halfway between a cry and a gasp. But it wasn't from physical pain. "You have no idea what we went through! Da *died* to protect me." Suddenly tears came, unbidden, unexpected, as if all of it, the memory, the fear, her utter helpless despair at losing him, had finally crashed down with the weight of the heavens. Sanglant had never seen her weep over her dead father. Now it overwhelmed her.

The storm was brief but tempestuous, and Anne waited it out without any response except to carefully take the old book from her and close it so that the pages wouldn't get damp. She locked it away in the cupboard, flicked a finger toward the ceiling, and the servant fluttered down and vanished.

"Sit down, Liath. You are overwrought. The servant will bring you something to drink to restore yourself."

Liath sat obediently, shoulders shuddering under the weight of that old grief. Sanglant did not sit. He, too, had lost a parent and never cried for that loss. "Where did my mother come from?" he asked now.

Anne seemed as usual unsurprised by the question. "Henry found her in Darre, but she had before that been in Salia, or so we assume, because Salian was the tongue she spoke best. From whence in Salia she came no one knew or could guess, and she revealed nothing."

" 'There will come a moment,' " said Liath in the steady voice she used when she quoted from memory, " 'when all the power that churns through the universe, the force that moves the spheres themselves, can be touched by human hands. When it can be drawn down and manipulated for the greater good by those who have the knowledge and the will to risk themselves in such an undertaking.' That's the art of the mathematici. Which was learned from the Babaharshan magicians, who learned it from the Aoi long ago, so the stories say." She grimaced, shifting awkwardly, and for an instant he thought another pain was coming, but she was only uncomfortable. If God willed, the child would come soon and without incident. That would truly be a blessing. Liath looked up at Anne accusingly. "That's what you've been hiding all along. You believe the Aoi manipulated the power in the heavens to remove themselves from earth."

The servant returned and set a tray with three cups of cider on the table, then skittered away into the eaves. Anne glanced at the tray, surprised by the cider or by the number of cups; he wasn't sure which. He handed Liath a cup and made sure she drank before he drained his own. Anne had already begun to speak.

"There is much we do not yet comprehend about the universe, but we know that there are many interstices within the fabric of the universe that may be traversed by those who know how to do so. We call that cluster of stars that the Child is reaching for a 'crown of stars,' yet don't we also call the great stone circles which we find through the land 'crowns'? Magic built those circles long ago, and I believe that it was the Aoi who built them, at the height of their power. I believe that those were the mechanisms by which the Aoi hurled themselves elsewhere. Did you and Bernard ever travel to the cliffs of Barakanoi, southeast of Aosta?"

"Yes, we did. I'll always remember them because they were so sharp, the way the shoreline ends and the waters begin. I remember telling Da that I thought it was like someone had cut it clean with a knife." But she faltered, looking up at Sanglant. He only shrugged. He had never been there. "There was a city there, and it ended, too. As if it had been cut away. I always thought part of it must have fallen into the sea. But it couldn't have. There wasn't any sign of ruins in the sea below. It ran deep there. There weren't even any shoals, that's what Da told me."

Anne nodded. "Those of us born out of the earth must have

earth to stand on. Even magi such as the Aoi could not exist in the aether as do the daimones and the angels."

"Are you suggesting," demanded Sanglant, "that they used their magic to literally take a part of this earth with them into their exile?"

"What does it matter, anyway, if they're gone now?" muttered Liath, rubbing her belly. "If they don't walk on the Earth any longer, then they can be no threat to us."

Anne had not looked away from Sanglant since he had entered the chamber, just as one does not take one's eyes from the poisonous snake with whom you share a cozy patch of ground. "An arrow shot into the air will fall to earth in time. Any great power unleashed in the universe will rebound someday in proportion to its original power and direction. What has been accomplished once may be accomplished again, and if a channel has already been dug, how much easier will the river flow back through where it is dry?"

"Are these riddles that I'm supposed to answer?" asked Liath irritably.

"No," said Sanglant. "I think she is saying that the Lost Ones will return."

"On the tenth day of Octumbre, in the year 735, at midnight," said Anne, "when the paths between the spheres open and the crown of stars crowns the heaven."

Liath pressed both hands against her abdomen and shut her eyes with the kind of sigh that a person lets out when she knows that the toil before her is bound to be much harder than that which she just finished. "Why do I feel like a puppet dancing to the jerk of someone else pulling the strings?"

"If they left because humankind had driven them to such desperate straits," Sanglant asked, "then why would they *want* to return?"

"For the same reason, Prince Sanglant, that they would want a child born half of Aoi and half of royal human blood." She gestured toward him. "To take back what was once theirs: sovereignty over this world."

Wind rattled the shutters. An owl hooted in the night, and Sanglant heard the shriek of some poor creature caught in its claws. Anne shifted to look at Liath, who at that moment gripped his wrist and braced herself as another wave of pain washed over her, harder than any of the ones that had come before. She seemed to fall so far away from him, all her attention drawn inward, that it was as if she herself had been briefly cut away from him and from any part of the world beyond her womb, where the child now struggled to be born onto this earth.

"Sister Meriam should be woken," said Sanglant. "She said she would act as midwife."

Anne simply waited until Liath stopped panting. "That is why you are so important, Liathano. Why everything else in which you have engaged does not matter, and cannot matter." A little sweat beaded on Liath's forehead as she lifted her head and regarded Anne as much with annoyance for the interruption as with curiosity or awe for the solemn pronouncement being invoked.

"They have bided their time in safety hoarding their power and their magic. Now they mean to rule over us again as they once did millennia ago. They are strong and unmerciful. They will make cruel masters. They will sunder the world in order to take it back, for their return to this Earth will cause such a cataclysm as no creature alive has ever seen. 'For the mountains shall become the sea, and the sea shall become the mountains.'"

Anne moved forward until the lantern light limned her. The gold torque gleamed at her throat, and like any queen or empress, she shone with that confidence which is called power, the ability to turn others to her will.

"The only one who can stop them, my child, is you."

XII
A BLESSING

1

SANGLANT had not realized how much he disliked Sister Anne until he spent the rest of a night, a day, another long and exhausting night, and perhaps the most agonizing day of his life at the side of his laboring wife as she struggled silently, suffered silently, and weakened inexorably. The pains came and went in steadily heightening waves, like the tide coming in, but the baby did not come.

Heribert tended the fire, brought hot cider for Sister Meriam and Sanglant and wine for Liath to sip when she could get it down, and fretted over the birthing stool he had constructed to Meriam's specifications a month before. When Meriam needed to rest, Sister Venia sat at Liath's side and chafed her hands and kneaded her back.

"I remember what it was like for Heribert's mother," she said with feeling.

Zoë and Severus stayed away, which was no doubt for the best, but Sister Anne, too, ignored the sweating and straining in the hut, had no words of advice to give and no comfort to offer. She was too busy to attend, or she didn't want to see.

"Doesn't she remember what it was like?" demanded Sanglant finally, but Sister Meriam merely grunted. She was examining

Liath again, one hand probing the shape of her belly from the outside and the other from within the passageway.

"My daughter-in-law had easier births than this," she commented. "So did I. I fear the child is breech."

"How much longer can she go on?" he asked in a low voice, but after two nights and two full days of laboring, Liath was too tired to hear him. Sister Meriam merely shrugged.

Dusk came, and with it came the evening star, a beacon above the horizon. He hadn't seen it for weeks. According to Liath it had been hiding behind the sun, but now it shone reassuringly from the safe harbor of the constellation known as the Sisters, protector of women.

Something shifted then, a last gasp, an unloosening, or perhaps it wasn't Somorhas' influence at all, perhaps it was the infusion of wormwood that Meriam got down Liath's parched throat. Meriam greased her hands with pig's fat and felt up the passageway, got a grip on something. By this time Sanglant was holding Liath up bodily on the birthing stool. She was too weak to sit on her own, and her entire weight sagged against him.

"Come, my love," he said. "Push."

The baby's feet came first, then a rump, then a body all smeary-white. Liath barely had enough energy to bear down to get the head out. After that she fainted and she bled, and he thought maybe he would faint, too, not at the sight of blood but out of fear. He had never been this afraid in his life.

Meriam handed him the baby brusquely. "Wash it," she said, and she set to work kneading Liath's flaccid belly until the afterbirth sluiced out with another gush of bright red blood, Humming, the old woman bound a poultice over Liath's groin as if that might stem the bleeding.

"Mind the baby!" she said sternly, for he had been staring in horror at his unconscious wife all this while. Jolted into obedience by her curt tone, he looked down into a pair of eyes so startling a green that he thought for an instant that they weren't eyes at all but chips of emerald. He went outside, unsteady on his feet but with a good grip on her, as tiny as she was, and washed her in a basin filled with cold spring water.

She squalled mightily.

"Good lungs," said Heribert, who was dancing from one foot to the other, trying to get a good look. "She sounds strong."

"She's a blessing," murmured Sanglant, kissing the tiny creature on its wrinkled forehead.

"What will you name her? It's your right as her father to name her."

He looked up then, surprised. One of her tiny, perfect hands found his little finger and clutched it. She had the stubborn grasp of a warrior born. "I just did," he said, knowing the words as truth. " 'Blessing.' "

Liath was too weak to nurse the infant. Meriam tried nettle tea and parsley, but after a few beads of clear fluid welled up on her nipples, she went dry and no matter what Meriam tried, fennel, strips of meat mashed into a soft pulp, an infusion of vervain or of chaste tree, her breasts produced nothing more. She slept almost constantly and sometimes it was hard to rouse her even to get her to take wine and porridge. At times she burned with fever; at times she lay as cold as death except for the slight exhalation of her breath.

When she burned, she was incoherent, tossing and turning and babbling at intervals, lost to him. "The heavens run swifter than any mill wheel, as deep under the Earth as above it. But they and their creatures are eternal. The Earth is mortal. Yet, behold, she departeth very suddenly. What is this ribbon of light running through the heavens, disturbing them? It has only one side, and it never ends. It only returns again to its starting place."

Sometimes, when she raved, unlit candles would come alight, or lamp wicks snap into life that hadn't been burning before. At these times the servants fled from the hut, frightened. Only Jerna, who was braver now, would stay in the hut, always hovering near the baby, stroking it, blowing its black cap of hair into wispy spikes and then smoothing it out again. She even curled around the baby's cradle at night, an unearthly guardian, when Sanglant caught such sleep as he could, although his sleep was disturbed constantly either by the baby's crying or by Liath's sudden restless fevers.

Now and again Liath tried to show interest in the baby, but she would drift off at the exertion of letting it lie on her chest or, worse, break into a wheezing, weak cry because she couldn't feed it. Then the crying would exhaust her and she would slip into a cold sleep, her hands like ice.

The baby squalled and squalled. Sanglant carried her in a

sling against his chest, or on his hip, or settled in a rocking cradle that Heribert had devised, and everywhere he went the servants crowded round, trying to touch Blessing, so wildly curious
at this apparition that they neglected their labors and Severus
complained peevishly that his bread was burned, his porridge
cold, and the blankets left in disarray on his pallet when they
ought to have been neatly folded after he rose in the morning.

At Meriam's suggestion, Sanglant milked the goats, and they
tried everything they could, heating the milk and dropping it in
her mouth bead by bead, soaking the corner of a cloth in goat's
milk and putting it between her lips, molding a nipple out of
sheep's intestine for her to suck on. But she would only take a
minuscule amount before turning her head away. Squalls turned
to mewls and mewls to whimpers.

"Ah, well," said Anne four days after its birth, observing the
baby with equanimity. "It will die. That only goes to show that
it was never meant to be born."

He felt the growl slip from him, enough that his Eika dog
stood and barked, enough that Anne's new attendant, the black
hound, growled and lunged for him.

"Sit!" said Anne, and the hound sat. She had not yet named
it, nor did she seemed inclined to do so. But she only smiled at
Sanglant, and it seemed to him that she was mocking him, waiting to see him fall apart in a rage as he watched the life leach
out of his precious daughter.

But fear and desperation had healed him somewhat—he hadn't
had nightmares since the day Blessing was born—and now fury
banished the old instincts. He set a hand on the head of his dog
to calm it and looked Anne straight in the face.

"Do you have so little feeling that you would stand by and
let your own granddaughter die?"

"God's will is unknowable."

"Then if you have so little love in your heart, think instead
of the gold torque you wear at your throat. Don't you have a
responsibility to your kin to keep your lineage alive?"

Now she was far more interested than she had ever been in
the child. "What do you mean, Prince Sanglant?"

"Since the day we met, I have wondered to which royal lineage you owe your blood. If I'm right, then it makes no sense
to me why you would not make every effort to keep this infant

alive. Is it possible that you *aren't* Emperor Taillefer's grand-daughter?"

"What makes you think that I am?" she said, but he saw that he had surprised her, and by that reaction he saw that his blow had hit true.

"Who else could you be? You aren't of Varrish kin because they're gone except for my aunt Sabella, her daughter Princess Tallia, and her poor, idiot husband who isn't fit to rule. You're not of Wendish blood because I know all my kin. All the Salian princesses whether married or unmarried or given to the church were discussed by my father's council after Queen Sophia died, from the eldest old crone of sixty to the girl of nine, because they wondered if there was one suitable for him to marry. A woman of your age and appearance was never mentioned. In Karrone they dare not wear the gold torque. Nor do the royal houses of the eastern realms decorate themselves in that way. The Alban queens wear armbands, not torques, to show their breeding. I admit you might be Aostan, but according to every rumor the royal house of Aosta was wiped out except for Queen Adelheid." He smiled a little, thinking that if not for Liath, he might have been bedding Queen Adelheid now. Yet if not for Liath, he would still have been chained to Bloodheart's throne, a madman. "Who else can you be? St. Radegundis was pregnant when Taillefer died. No one knows what became of the child born to her. But you do."

She said nothing.

Blessing stirred and whimpered, head turning to the side, rooting at his breast, but he had nothing for her. Ai, God, he was so angry at that moment, feeling the tiny body cupped between forearm and chest that he could have lashed out and strangled this regal woman who regarded him with the cool stare of an empress surveying that which ought to be beneath her notice; ought to be, but is not, because he had piqued her by guessing the truth. He had pierced her smooth shell, and now he knew Liath's secret.

Ai, Lady! He knew Liath's secret, and he knew triumph. What was Queen Adelheid's lineage compared to this? Henry would have to approve of the marriage now. Indeed, Henry surely would welcome this match, his own line bred and sealed with that of the dead Taillefer, greatest emperor the Daisanite world had ever known. If Henry sought for legitimacy beyond brute force to restore the Holy Dariyan Empire, this child was the one who would give it to him.

"Help me save my daughter," he said, and this time his voice broke. He knew Anne would interpret it as weakness and would seek the soft opening so that she could plunge the dagger in. He understood at that moment as he faced her that she was always and had always been waiting to kill him. She was just more subtle than the rest.

"No," she said.

"Have you no heart at all?" he demanded. "Were there no bonds of affection in your youth? Ai, Lord, who raised you?"

"A woman named Clothilde."

"St. Radegundis' handmaiden." He recognized the story, although it was not at all clear to him how St. Radegundis' lost child had managed to create a child in its turn.

"It is true Clothilde acted as Queen Radegundis' handmaiden, but in all ways and in all her actions she was the loyal servant of Biscop Tallia. She did what had to be done, to face the greater threat. And I will do what has to be done, just as she taught me."

"How does letting this child die aid you in your cause?"

"Because she is your child, Prince Sanglant. She is blood of your blood, and I am sworn to see that your blood never again flourishes on this Earth. They have nurtured their strength out in the aether, where they exist closer to the Chamber of Light, from whence all strength flows. They mean to return to this world and rule it with a hand of iron and with their gruesome sacrifices. They mean to obliterate the Light of the church and blanket the world in the darkness of the Enemy, for they are creatures of the Enemy."

He shook his head irritably. "Liath once told me that the Lost Ones were born of fire and light, and that if they are tainted by darkness it is only because all things that exist in this world are tainted by darkness. How am I any worse than you?"

"You are their creature, Prince Sanglant," she said coldly, "and Liath is mine."

"She is your *daughter!* Surely she means more to you than just a tool!"

"All of us are only tools, Prince Sanglant, but some of us are agents of God and some are agents of the Enemy. Do not ever believe that a child born of your kind will be welcome on Earth as long as I and my people are here to stop you."

He had known despair once, and bitterly. He knew it now.

Anne left, and he retreated to regroup, to suffer, to struggle as had Liath when she labored with all her strength to bring forth a blessing. Liath might yet die. Blessing might yet die.

But not if he could help it.

He leaned against the corner of the hut, exhausted, drained, catching his breath. The baby nestled against him, still and silent, so small.

Meriam emerged and saw him. "Liath is sleeping." She shrugged. "I don't believe she will die, Prince Sanglant, but it will be a long time before she is well. But I fear there is nothing you can do to save the child if you cannot coax it to take the goat's milk." Then she walked away, not with triumph but with a sigh, a practical woman who has read the signs and is sorry at the pain she sees in the world.

But he was something else. He saw Jerna slip to the door, waiting for him to enter. He saw her truly for the first time in days, it seemed; he had been so preoccupied and she was just one among the many creatures fluttering around, things he hadn't the energy to take careful note of. She had fully taken on the likeness of a woman, a face composed in some strange way of all the faces of the women here in Verna: Zoë's kissable mouth, Meriam's sharp cheekbones, Anne's regal nose, Venia's broad and intelligent forehead, and Liath's hair falling like water to her waist, clear enough that he could see through it to the curtain hanging down over the door that led into the interior. She had taken on the shape of a woman, the gracious curve of ample hips with a modest veil of mist concealing her womanly parts, stout arms and a handsome neck, and breasts as bountiful as any nature had endowed woman with, full and ripe, leaking a clear fluid.

It seemed for an instant obscene, against nature. But then Blessing mewled and stirred in his arms, and he didn't hesitate.

"Jerna," he said softly, coaxing her forward, because she was a flighty thing; they all were, those who labored as servants at Verna under the strict rule of Sister Anne, she who was willing to watch her own granddaughter starve.

But he would fight for his daughter until his last breath.

"Jerna," he said, and she flowed toward him, not a woman but something other, something trying to become a woman. This

act might mark her forever, separate her from her kin, who did
not walk on Earth but rather in the air, below the Moon. This
act might mark Blessing forever, for how could he tell what
nourishment she might in truth be receiving from an aetherical
creature who dwelt closer to God than did humankind and who
was composed of a different proportion of elements? But he had
to try it.

He held out Blessing, and the creature sighed in some satisfied, inarticulate way, and settled the child to its breast. Blessing rooted, found the nipple, and began to suck.

2

AFTER a wet and cold journey of over five months, Hanna
finally caught up with King Henry's progress at Lavas Holding
on the Feast of St. Samais of Sartor. She had prayed that morning at sunrise to the saint who was particularly beloved by servants, for hadn't St. Samais been the washerwoman who had
laundered the blessed Daisan's robes, all that remained of him
on earth after he had been lifted bodily to the Chamber of Light
at the Ekstasis? Hadn't the water in which she washed that
blessed cloth healed the sick and cured the lame? St. Samais
had accepted martyrdom rather than hand over the blessed
Daisan's robes to the minions of the Empress Thaisannia, she
of the mask, for the empress had comprehended that the robes
had miraculous powers which she herself wished to control.

Not, Hanna reflected as she crested a rise and saw Lavas
Holding below, that she sought martyrdom as had the saints of
old, but she was Henry's loyal servant and hoped she could serve
him as faithfully as St. Samais had served the blessed Daisan.
Manfred had died in Henry's service, and she hoped she had
courage and loyalty enough to die as honorably as Manfred had,
if it came to that.

Yet a wasp sting burned in her heart, nagging, incessant, uncomfortable. She still dreamed of the Kerayit princess every
night.

A Lion standing sentry hailed her. "Friend Hanna! How fares it with you? What news of Princess Sapientia?" It was her old friend, Ingo, looking fit and well-fed.

"Princess Sapientia was well enough when I saw her last. She and Prince Bayan won a victory over the Quman."

"God be praised! And you, friend?"

She laughed. "I'm happy to see that I won't be riding any farther today. King Henry moves swiftly. I lost three horses to lameness in the past month alone, and there was so much rain! It seemed as if I'd always stay two days behind him. What news here, friend?"

"You hadn't heard? Queen Mathilda is dead, may she rest in peace in the Chamber of Light. The king received word in Autun. Ai, Lord! He prayed for seven days and nights clad only in a pauper's robe." Ingo sighed and wiped a tear away. "His grief moved every soul there to tears. I still weep, to think of it."

"May her memory be blessed," said Hanna, as was proper. "What then brought you here to Lavas?"

"There's a terrible great judgment being held here." His mood changed abruptly and he spat on the ground in disgust. "Nobles, fighting over land again. Greedy bastards always wanting more for their favorite children. You'd think they'd be content with what they've got, but it's never so. When will it ever end?" He said. "Ai, well. Count Lavastine was a fair man. It's too bad he died."

"I don't recall him seeming old or ill," said Hanna, surprised at this news.

"He was not. God's ways are a mystery, truly." He lifted a hand to beckon her closer, and she had to lean down from her saddle to hear him. "Perhaps it *was* sorcery, as some are saying."

She straightened, struck by the way he had moved her aside from his companions, had regripped his spear, as if fearing an attack. "Everyone seems to be speaking of sorcery these days. What news of Prince Sanglant?" It was an oblique way to ask about Liath.

"You were still with the king when the prince rode off, weren't you? Well, he's never come back nor has anyone heard one word from him. It was your comrade who bewitched him, they say."

"Do they still say that?" she asked cautiously.

"Ah," he said, reading something in her expression she hadn't

concealed. "You hadn't heard the news, then. The council held at
Autun excommunicated her. for trafficking in sorcery."

The blow was a hard one and easier to absorb alone. She
thanked him and went on her way, and as she rode down into
the holding she noticed the tight silence of the local people and,
like its counterpoint, the constant whispering of the court's servants, who seemed to be enjoying themselves rather more than
they ought given the grave nature of the charges and the death
of a good man. Was it in the nature of humankind that they
should take pleasure in another's misfortune?

She handed her horse off to a groom, brushed the worst of
the dirt off her clothing, and made her way to the hall, a fine
timber edifice with whitewashed walls and huge roof beams
painted with tar to keep the vermin out. She had never been here
before, although Liath had visited here a year or more ago and
told Hanna a little of what had transpired between her and Lord
Alain. It seemed now that fate would conspire to keep her and
Liath apart. God alone knew where Liath was now, and in what
condition. And she had forgotten to ask Ingo about Hugh.

Her old comrades Folquin and Stephen were standing on guard
at the door into the great hall, and they clapped her on the back
and whispered greetings, then let her through although perhaps
a hundred people had gathered outside, forbidden entrance. And
no wonder: so many had crowded inside that it was reeking and
hot despite the cool, damp spring weather. Someone had thought
to strew mint in with the rushes on the floor, but the sweat of
so many people overwhelmed any other odor. She had to elbow
her way forward because people were so intent on the scene before them that they took no notice of her Eagle's badge.

It was slow work. Somewhere at the front of the room, people were giving testimony about Lavastine, his first marriage,
the horrible death of his only known legitimate child, and the
mistress he had once slept with who had died in childbirth.

She squeezed past two stewards dressed in fine linen, like
chickens tarted up as swans as her mother would have said, but
fetched up behind a hugely broad nobleman who seemed immune
to her nudging. He was short enough that she could see over his
shoulder and glimpse the dais, where Henry sat on his throne.
The king looked tired. He had lines in his face that hadn't been
there six months ago. Hathui stood behind him; she had mastered the blank face of the loyal servingwoman. His niece Tal-

lia sat to his left, Helmut Villam to his right. On opposite sides sat Lord Alain and Lord Geoffrey, the disputants.

Henry lifted a hand, and a steward called forward the next witness, a heavyset older woman who, by the evidence of her stained apron, had evidently been called in from the kitchens. The nobleman in front of Hanna kept shifting as she tried to press forward, and she just couldn't get past him and by now was wedged between him, a bench, and a table. The atmosphere in the hall was so tense and focused that she hadn't the courage to shout out, as Hathui would have, "Make way for the King's Eagle," even though she had the right to do so.

She shoved her way up on the bench beside a trio of finely-dressed boys and was able to hear as the cook told her story with remarkable self-possession.

"Yes, Your Majesty, that would have been Cecily. She's the girl we all knew was Count Lavastine's mistress, may she rest in peace, but she wasn't the one who gave birth to Count Alain. She gave birth to a misshapen lad, our Lackling. Alas, he died two years ago, poor child. Fell in the river and drowned, we think, for his body was never recovered."

"You don't think he might have run off, that he might still be alive?" asked Hathui.

"Nay, Eagle, he'd never have left here. That's how we know he died. He vanished one day and never come back."

"Did Count Lavastine know that this boy Lackling was his mistress' child?" asked Henry.

She looked nervous then, wringing her hands in her apron. "Nay, Your Majesty. A poor beggar woman was brought in that same night, and both she and her child died, so we said that Lackling was hers and Cecily's babe was the one who died. I don't suppose more than three of us knew the truth, and we all swore never to speak of it, for the young count had just gotten betrothed and his bride was a jealous woman, all full of her own hurt feelings, may God grant her peace. We wanted to protect him."

"So you lied."

"So we did, Your Majesty. I'm sorry for the sin, but I suppose I'd do the same thing again. It's for God to judge the matter, not me."

"Who knew the truth?"

"Well, then, I knew, and Deacon Marian knew, and old Agnes

knew. Deacon and old Agnes attended every birth here, and I helped Agnes when she needed helping, bringing her clothes and water and ale for the laboring women, and so on. They're both gone, now, may God bless them. I'm the only one living who attended those births, for there was four babes born in the space of three nights. One was the poor dead beggar child, may God rest him and his mother. One was Lackling. One was Count Alain. And the last was a tiny little thing, a girl. I never saw again because her mother and father fled with her the next morning though the poor woman was still weak. I think they were afraid, for the other three mothers died. They thought it an ill omen, They were afraid she would die, too, if they stayed."

At these words, Geoffrey made to speak.

"Hold, hold," said Henry, lifting a hand. "If you knew that this child Lackling was the baby borne by Lavastine's mistress, and that the child Alain was borne by a different woman, then why did you say nothing when Count Lavastine named this young man as his heir?"

The old cook looked troubled. "What was I to say, Your Majesty? Was I to tell the count his own business? Was I to rule for him?"

"You could have told him what you knew."

She gestured toward Alain. "There was the hounds, Your Majesty."

Of course everyone looked. A hound sat on either side of Alain. He had a hand buried in each one's neck, as if holding them back—or as if they were all that was holding him up. Yet she could read nothing in his expression except perhaps a kind of resigned calm. His black hair had been recently cropped; his clothes were neat and handsomely fitted. But except for the hounds he sat unattended even by a servant while Lord Geoffrey was flanked by noble kinsmen who, with empty sword belts and arms crossed menacingly, looked ready to solve the problem with their fists. Lord Geoffrey had the kind of red face that comes of too much choler seeping from the blood into the mind. He looked as if he were about to burst into wrathful speech at any moment.

"The hounds?" asked Henry.

"He has the gift with the hounds, Your Majesty. Just as Count Lavastine did, and his father before him and his father before him, may their souls rest in peace in the Chamber of Light."

She frowned at a sight unseen by the rest of them, glanced over her shoulder as if looking at someone in the crowd, then rubbed her bulbous nose self-consciously. "Poor Rose. That's the girl who was Count Alain's mother, for I know she bore him truly enough. I saw him come from her body, just as I saw poor Lackling born out of Cecily, No mixing those two boys up, because Lackling come out of Cecily with his face all bent and legs funny and Alain was as perfectly-formed a baby as I ever saw. Yet Cecily was the good girl, obedient and quiet. She never went to any man but the count, and I'm not sure that wasn't more his choice than hers, begging your pardon, Your Majesty. She always said there was a young man in her village she meant to marry, when she returned home. Rose, now, alas, she was a whore, there's no kinder word for it. Pretty as a rose, that girl. That's where she got the name, for she never claimed to have one of her own. She and her people come up from Salia a year or two before to find harvest work and she hadn't anything of her own, as poor as the mice in the church. They was even too poor to have a lord take them in. The man who called himself her father just called her 'girl,' and we all suspected that he was doing that to her that goes against nature, if you take my meaning, Your Majesty."

People chuckled and whispered around Hanna, finding amusement in this salacious tidbit. Henry frowned and rapped his scepter once, hard, on the floor. Everyone quieted.

"Pray give this woman silence in which to testify."

She rubbed her nose again, which had gotten quite red from the heat of the hall, or of the king's regard. "She were so poor and so poorly treated by her father who was always slapping her and calling her indecent names right out where everyone could hear that it's no wonder she went looking for what she could get wherever she could get it. Everyone knew she made her assignations up in the old ruins. She were always going on about meeting the Lost Ones there, and how a prince of the old people was coming in to her and was going to make her a queen. Who's to say she didn't meet the young count up in the ruins one night? Every man in this holding looked at her with lust in his eyes, she was that pretty and had that kind of way with her that made you know that if you just gave her the right thing she'd, well, begging your pardon, she'd make it worth your while. It's as likely that Count Alain was Count Lavastine's son as any other man's, Your Majesty."

Lord Geoffrey looked ready to burst, and he burst now. "He might have been the get of any man in this holding! He might have been the lowest stable boy's by-blow! Ai, Lord! He's as likely to be the ill-begotten product of an incestuous union between the girl and her father!"

"Begging your pardon, my lord," the cook retorted with astonishing asperity, "but what about the testimony of the hounds, then? Not any man but the counts of Lavas can touch them hounds. They obey Count Alain just as they obeyed Count Lavastine. That was good enough for Count Lavastine, and he was a careful man and a good lord to us. We trusted him and never saw reason to question his judgment. He only did one foolish thing in his life, when his poor daughter was killed, and he repented that the rest of his days."

"Strong words," said Henry. His niece Tallia shifted in her seat as if his voice had startled her, but she did not look up from her study of her knees. She had a pale face, pale hair, and pale hands, was almost colorless, quite in contrast to the plump young noblewoman who stood in attendance on her with her hands folded quietly before her and her serious gaze flicking now and again toward Alain.

"What about this boy, Lackling?" asked Henry. "You seem sure he was Count Lavastine's bastard. Could he touch the hounds?"

"Why, bless you, Your Majesty," she said with a chuckle, "he hadn't enough wits to try, nor would anyone let him. He was misshapen in the body, poor lad, as sweet a soul as you might wish, but he was simple in the head."

"I pray you, Your Majesty, have I your permission to speak?" said Alain. His voice warmed Hanna; she had never heard him speak before, but there was nothing nasty or irate in his tone, nothing to trouble one's heart or scrape raw one's soul. Henry nodded. "The hounds never troubled Lackling."

It was an astounding observation to make in the face of the really awful accusations just thrown at him by his rival. The young noblewoman sitting at Geoffrey's side—most likely his wife because she held a young child on her lap—leaned over to whisper in Geoffrey's ear, and he sat back, looking irritated, but keeping his mouth shut.

"What are you saying? I don't understand your meaning." Henry sat back in his chair, hands curling over the dragon armrests. Their carved tongues licked out between his fingers, and he rubbed them absently as he listened.

"They never troubled him," repeated Alain. "They never lunged at him or tried to bite him, as they would everyone else." He pointedly did not look at Geoffrey.

"Everyone but you," retorted Geoffrey. His face went from red to white in an instant, the complexion of a sinning man, or a fearful one. "Because you're an agent of the Enemy. You used sorcery to enslave them, just as you used sorcery to bind my cousin to your will. We've all heard the story that the elder Count Charles Lavastine was accused of having made a pact with the Enemy to get those hounds. Why would any man want them? We've all seen and heard how vicious they are. They can only be creatures of the Enemy, and if they obey you, it must be because you are a servant of the Enemy as well!"

"Hold!" cried Henry, raising a hand for silence as the crowd began to mutter and stir. The hounds growled softly, but Alain merely touched them on their muzzles and they lay down, resting their great heads on their forelegs. The king paused while Hathui bent to whisper in his ear. He nodded, and she gave an order to a steward, who hurried away. Hanna edged forward on the bench, got stuck again, jammed between a noble lady and her companion. She thought of crawling under the table, but the noble lady's whippets had hunkered down in a pack under the table and not only did they growl at her as she bent over to survey her chances, but they had made a stinking mess of the rushes underneath. She shoved her way back up on the bench as the king began again to speak.

"This is a grave accusation, Lord Geoffrey, not only against Alain but against Count Lavastine, his father the younger Charles, and his grandfather Charles Lavastine as well. Do you mean to imply that all of them were in league with the Enemy?"

At once the young noblewoman and an older man who resembled her leaned over to whisper furiously to Geoffrey while he by turns looked irate and mortified. The child on the woman's lap fussed and was given a fig to chew on to keep it quiet.

The crowd had begun talking and there was a buzz of anger below it, like bees smoked out of their hive, but Hanna couldn't tell who the anger was directed against. Alain did not move except to pat the head of one of the hounds. Tallia glanced at her uncle. She seemed to have eyes for no one but Henry, and even so her gaze was more like that of a rabbit eyeing the hawk that would like to eat it than that of a trusting niece. Hadn't she married Lord Alain last summer? Of course she had! Why wasn't she sitting beside him, then?

"Nay, Your Majesty," said Geoffrey finally. "It is evident that Count Lavastine and his father Charles were innocent."

"Then do you lay a claim against the elder Charles Lavastine and his conduct?"

"No one knows what he got in return for the hounds, but it brought ill luck into his house. The story goes that his own mother died in childbed the day he got the hounds. He himself never had but one child although he married four different women, and his son had only the one living child although his wife was brought to bed ten or twelve times. My cousin Lavastine had only the one child, and not only were she and her mother murdered by these same hounds, but it was rumored that the girl wasn't his get at all, that his wife had committed adultery. Two times more he made ready to marry, and both those women died under unnatural circumstances. And last, that same ill luck brought this liar to Lavas Holding, this man who tempted my cousin and bewitched him. And killed him, too, so I hear. Everyone agrees it was sorcery that killed him, some foul creature of the Enemy. Even those who will speak no ill of this bastard acknowledge that my cousin died in an unnatural way. It's true, isn't it?" he demanded at last, for the first time glaring belligerently at Alain.

"That sorcery killed Count Lavastine?" answered Alain. "Certainly I believe it is true, and I was the first to say so." This calm remark caused so much stir, people bending and talking and gesticulating to their neighbors, that Hanna was able to skip across from one bench to another and thereby move herself so far forward in the crowd that she was finally halfway to the front. "He was killed by a curse set on him by Bloodheart, the Eika chieftain he defeated at Gent."

Lady Tallia flushed, color creeping into her cheeks. Her attendant touched her on the shoulder, as if to signal her, but Tallia made no attempt to speak.

"A clever ploy," said the noblewoman sitting beside Geoffrey. Her voice was as sweet as honey and only somewhat more cloying. "But you have no proof."

"Prince Sanglant would testify that there was a curse. When he was Bloodheart's captive, he saw an unnatural creature brought to life to fulfill that curse. That creature, that curse, is what killed my father."

Hanna winced, and it wasn't until then that she realized that she had fallen, heart and soul, in favor of Lord Alain over Lord Geoffrey, simply by reason of their demeanor here in this hall. Yet what was the mood of the crowd? She was only a common-born girl. The nobles would, no doubt, rally around their own.

Henry looked angry at the mention of Sanglant. "Then there is no doubt in your mind that you are Lavastine's son?"

Alain answered without hesitation. "Perhaps it's true that I am not Count Lavastine's son. I can't know and I don't know; for I never knew my mother. I was raised by free-born merchant folk in Osna village, a sister and a brother called Bella and Henri after the children of King Arnulf the Younger after you and your sister, Your Majesty. They told me only that I'd been born in Lavas Holding to an unmarried woman and that they'd agreed to foster me. It's only when I came to serve for a year here at Lavas Holding that Count Lavastine noticed me. *I never asked to be named as his heir.* But he acknowledged me as his son, and he honored me with his trust. I will obey his wishes and act as rightly as he tried to all his life, because that is the trust he handed to me on his deathbed. I swore an oath to him there to uphold this county and the title of count, as he wished for me to do. Any woman and man in this holding will testify that is true. Many of them witnessed." Around the hall, isolated people nodded, but Henry's noble followers merely looked on. "I know my duty," he finished. "It is up to you, Your Majesty, to judge otherwise if you see fit."

"You admit you might not be his bastard?" demanded Henry, clearly amazed.

"God enjoins us to tell the truth, Your Majesty, and the truth is that I don't know."

Geoffrey's kinfolk stirred and smirked; some looked outraged, and some looked gleeful. Their expressions were mirrored here and there in the hall by courtiers, who surely must now be wondering if a common boy had shown them up and embarrassed them by pretending to be one of them. He had the same fine

proud line in his posture, only his expression was tempered by
a gravity and modesty that was more truly noble than any well-
born man or woman there except for the king. And they would
hate him for that.

But Alain had already gone on. Perhaps he was oblivious.
Perhaps he didn't care. Or perhaps he was really that honest, a
miracle in itself. "My fa— Count Lavastine named me as his
son and treated me as his son. That his wishes should be dis-
honored in this shameful way is disgraceful, but I am well aware
on my own account that we are all tempted by pride and envy
and greed and lust to act in ways that God cannot approve. But
I ask you to consider this, Your Majesty. It is Lavastine's judgment that is being questioned here, not my worthiness."

Geoffrey looked furious. His kinfolk muttered among themselves, annoyed and angry at being lectured, and Geoffrey's wife
sat the little child straighter on her lap, as if it were on display
at a market and she wanted to fetch the highest price for it.
Henry looked thoughtful, leaning over to make a private comment to Helmut Villam. His niece sat as stiff as a statue, looking desperate. Had she been forbidden to speak? What did she
wish for?

Hathui was looking around the hall trying to gauge the reaction of the court, and Hanna, seeing her chance, lifted a hand
to catch her attention. It took a few moments, but Hathui finally
saw her and at once brought Hanna to the king's notice. Stewards moved forward into the crowd, paths were made, and Hanna
was able to come forward and kneel before him.

"Where is my daughter?" asked Henry. "How does she fare?"

"She is well, Your Majesty. She is married—" A general cheer
rang out at this statement, and Hanna had to wait for it to die
down before she could go on. "She and Prince Bayan have won
a victory over the Quman." As there came further rejoicing, she
edged forward enough that she could speak to Henry in a low
voice. "There is more, Your Majesty, but I am charged by your
daughter to relate it to you in a more private setting, if it pleases
you."

Henry sat back, and when the crowd had settled down, waiting for his response, he lifted a hand. "I want my dinner, and I
have heard enough for today." He rose, and the assembly was
thereby dismissed.

But that evening at twilight Hanna stood beside Hathui, and

together they watched the king pacing in the garden as a fine drizzle dampened his cloak. She had given him Sapientia's message, and now she simply had to bide her time together with all the other Eagles who rode in attendance on the king, waiting to be sent out again.

"He still mourns his mother," observed Hathui, "may her soul rest in peace. I tell you, Hanna, the king needs good cheer in his life, not dispute after dispute like this one!"

"Then you favor Count Alain?"

"Thank God I don't have to pass judgment! Lord Geoffrey's accusations are troubling, and hard to disprove. But Count Alain is no fool. King Henry respected Lavastine, and as Alain said, it is harder to pass judgment on the actions of a dead man than on the worthiness of a living one."

"Do you think so? The dead man can't defend himself."

"But a good reputation is its own defense, It's harder to pass judgment exactly because he can't defend himself, because the whole of his life is laid out before you. Who are we, then, to decide we would have acted differently, and that our actions would have turned out for the better?" The rose garden was laid out between the great timber hall and the stone tower, bound on the other two sides by a roofed walkway and a log palisade. A half dozen servingmen lounged under the shelter of the walkway's roof. "I do believe also that Lavastine and Alain will always be linked in the king's mind with his own wishes for Prince Sanglant. For that reason, I think him likely to favor Count Alain over Lord Geoffrey."

Hanna hitched up her hood and held it tight under her chin. The wind shifted, and a mist of rain blew into her face. From the other side of the log palisade she heard the sound of horses being led into the stables after their afternoon's exercise. Grooms called out to one another, laughing and joking.

Footsteps crunched on the path behind them, and they moved aside for Villam to pass. He conversed with the king for a few moments, then went back the way he had come, into the stone tower.

"Is there news of Liath?" asked Hanna softly.

She couldn't see Hathui's expression, but she felt the other woman stiffen and shift a little away from her. "She ran off with Prince Sanglant. Nay, you knew that. You were still with the court then. The Council of Autun found her guilty of the crime of sorcery, and excommunicated her. If you have any traffic with her, Hanna—"

"I'll be excommunicated in my turn. But nevertheless, she is my friend, and whatever she was accused of, I know she's innocent. What happened to Father Hugh?"

Hathui grunted under her breath. "He was sent to Aosta to stand trial before the skopos. Only she can pass judgment on a man of his rank."

"You've heard nothing since from Liath? No word of Prince Sanglant?"

"Nothing," replied Hathui, even more softly. "And I've looked. . . ."

Her tone held a caution in it, but Hanna's curiosity was piqued. "What do you mean, that you 'looked'?"

Hathui glanced around to make sure no one stood within earshot, but the stewards were far away and the king had walked to the farthest corner of the garden, where the curve of the stone tower met the palisade wall. Here a dog rose climbed a fretwork, and he touched a flower, bent to smell it, then, as with a fit of temper, snapped it off.

"You've served the Eagles well and faithfully," said Hathui in a low voice, "but you must wait until Wolfhere returns, for I've not the knowledge to teach, only to see a few shadows."

"I don't understand you."

"There is more than one sight with which an Eagle can see. Wolfhere knows the secret of it, as do a few others. Those of us who can, learn it to aid ourselves and to aid the king. But you must never speak of it to anyone else. It's like our badge. It's part of our oath, sworn to serve the king and to aid each other."

"Serve the regnant and no other," said Hanna, watching the king. He plucked the petals on the rose and ate them, wincing a little at their tartness, then picked a second rose. "Speak only the truth of what you see and hear, but speak not at all to the king's enemies. Let no obstacle stand in the way of your duty to the king. Let your duty to your kin come second, and make no marriage—" Here she broke off, and Hathui finished for her.

"Aid any Eagle who is in need, and protect your comrades from any who might harm them. And last, abide by your faith in Our Lady and Lord."

"I do so swear," murmured Hanna, remembering the night

when she had been given the badge that made her an Eagle, for now and for always. She winced at a flare of pain in her chest.

"Are you well?" asked Hathui, feeling her movement.

It had already subsided, vanished as if she had only imagined it. The king walked toward them.

"Hathui," he called, and his servingmen came running. "Here." He handed the rose to Hanna. "Take this one to my niece. Tell her that it would be well for her to remember that the thorns of those words which mislead without lying are small but persistent, and that the white rose which symbolizes purity is also veined with flaws."

She bowed and retreated as he called for and had brought to him a little whippet puppy which he took on a leash to run in the garden. She had to ask among his servants and discovered to her surprise that Lady Tallia did not lodge with her husband in the count's tower but rather in a pavilion pitched just outside the palisade wall, which she shared with the duchess of Varingia.

The duchess was a ruddy-looking woman with the massive presence of a high-ranking noblewoman. An infant old enough to sit up by itself held court on a gold couch, next to the duchess, who entertained the chortling baby by clapping her hands together and tweaking its ears. Tallia's noble attendant had joined in the play as well, getting down on her knees to shake a gourd rattle for the child to grab. The conversation was nonsensical, conducted entirely by Duchess Yolande who treated Tallia little differently than she did the baby and chattered on in singsong rhymes directed at the baby interspersed with commentary on the dress and behavior of the court folk. Tallia said not one word. The baby was more talkative.

"Isn't he sweet?" the attendant asked Tallia, but Tallia only stared at the baby as if it were a scorpion that had gotten loose among the carpets.

"Your Highness," said Hanna, bowing. "Duchess Yolande." In the lamplight she could better see the flower as she presented it to Lady Tallia: the silken white petals were indeed veined with pinkish-purple lines, so shot through with them that she could no longer see the rose as white at all. "His Majesty King Henry bids me give this to you, Your Highness, with this message: 'Tell her that it would be well for her to remember that the thorns of those words which mislead without lying are small but persis-

tent, and that the white rose which symbolizes purity is also
veined with flaws.'"

Tallia did not move, made no effort to take the rose, only
stared.

"A common whore," she murmured, shuddering. She seemed
to be talking mostly to herself. "That's why he showed me the
nail. He was trying to pollute my faith in God."

There was, oddly enough, a sheen of dirt at her collarbone
as if she had forgotten to wash. She wore a gold Circle of Unity
around her neck together with a sachet, a little bag stuffed with
herbs. The bitter scent tickled Hanna's nose and made her want
to sneeze. Up close, Tallia's pale hair looked limp and stringy,
and she had dark circles under her eyes. Her hands were thin
and white and veined much like the flower's, more blue than
purple.

"Come now," said Duchess Yolande, "it's a terrible blow, I
admit it, but he's a good-looking and well-spoken young man,
and I've met many a noblewoman who was scarcely less dis-
criminatory in what manner of man she let into her bed." She
took the rose from Hanna and danced it in front of the baby.
He grabbed for it, got it, and at once pierced himself on a thorn
and began to sob. "There's life for you!" exclaimed the duchess.
She pried the rose out of the baby's hand, kissed his reddened
skin, and tickled him out of his misery. The rose, dropped to
the carpet, was picked up by the young attendant; she glanced
once around swiftly and then tucked it between her bosom and
her gown, as if it were a precious keepsake.

"Lady Hathumod, you haven't said what you think of this
scandal." Duchess Yolande lifted the child onto her lap as her
own attendants gathered round to coo at him and tickle his chin.
He gurgled happily at all the attention.

"Nay, my lady duchess," replied the attendant in a grave voice,
"I have not."

"Surely after months living here with him you have formed
some notion of his breeding. Do you suppose that one of the
hounds sired him?" Her ladies laughed and laughed, but Lady
Hathumod remained silent. "Ah! You're such a tiresomely serious creature, Lady Hathumod. Perhaps you have some new revelation with which to entertain us?"

Tallia looked up, startled, and then sighed sharply, almost a
hiss between her teeth.

"As you wish, my lady duchess," said Hathumod, but she looked at Tallia. "Your Highness?"

"Yes," said Tallia in a passionate voice, and her shoulders shook like a woman in the grip of a palsy. "We were speaking of it yesterday."

"Go on, speak!" insisted Yolande.

"We were discussing the matter of women's holiness," said Hathumod. "Why would God choose a man as the vessel of Her holiness here on Earth rather than a woman? Why did She send a son to partake of mortality and not a daughter?"

"I thought we had agreed that She chose St. Thecla to be the Witnesser because a woman's word is worth more than a man's."

Hathumod smiled with the radiance of an honest heart. She opened her arms as if to open herself to the heavens. "Women are already the vessels of God. Are we not made in Her image? God in Her mercy gave Her Son to be sacrificed just as men are more likely to give themselves in battle to protect their kin. But we are reminded of that sacrifice by the blood women shed each month."

This heretical talk was making Hanna terribly uncomfortable. She slid back to the door, even coughed a little, but when no one paid her any mind nor seemed concerned to send her on her way, she simply eased backward through the door and made her escape.

She found Hathui with the king in the rose garden. The drizzle had stopped although the flagstone walks glistened, slick with water. The whippet puppy had about as much energy as the baby; it leaped and barked as Henry clapped hands at it, racing away and then galloping back when he whistled. Hathui stood beside the king, laughing with him, but when he gathered up the puppy against his chest and sobered suddenly, Hathui quieted as well. He began to pace again, stroking the whippet's back, while his servants watched from the walkway and Hathui waited on the path nearby.

Would he walk in this fashion all night? Would Hathui watch with him the whole time? A breath of rain spattered on the stones, a gust that passed and quieted. Hanna wiped its drops from her nose. Though it was dark, she could feel the clouds churning and flowing overhead. Out in the unseen grounds beyond the palisade, a dog barked. One of the servingmen sneezed, and a companion murmured a blessing. The king paused beside

Hathui to make some comment which she answered in a murmur, then walked again. Hanna wondered at their intimacy, not anything remotely lascivious but rather far more profound, like head and hand.

Hathui saw her and came over. "Is there a message for the king?"

"Nay." She repeated what she'd heard. "She seemed in a trance. The only time she bestirred herself was when they began to speak of that heresy she's enthralled by."

Hathui grunted. "That's as we've come to expect. It's a strange thing all around, I'd say."

"It makes my skin crawl," muttered Hanna.

Hathui glanced up at the tower, where light still gleamed in the upper room. "Go on, then. No need for you to wait up all night."

"Will you, with the king?"

Hathui shrugged. "He often paces at night, now. As my old grandmother would have said, he needs a bed with something more than feathers to invite him in."

Hanna chuckled. "He's nothing like Villam, they say. Not one mistress since the death of Queen Sophia. Do you think it's true?"

"Hush!" The retort came sharply, surprising Hanna. "None of us have any call to speak disrespectfully of King Henry. Would you like to have to stand judgment every day over cases like this one? He's got a hard choice before him. Lord Geoffrey's a good man at heart despite all the anger he showed today, and he has strong kin behind him and the support of the nobles. Yet Count Alain is a better man, and King Henry knows it. But Alain has got no noble kin to support him, not outside his wife. It will all hang on Lady Tallia's testimony."

"Thus the rose."

"Thus the rose," agreed Hathui. "Now go on. You've ridden a long way. You've earned some rest."

She found the barracks where her comrades quartered, unrolled her blanket among the other Eagles, and enjoyed their companionship as she drank ale and ate cheese and bread. They gossiped about where they'd been and what they'd seen, shared tidbits of news and helpful information, what monasteries stocked the best ale and which villages were most welcoming, where bandits stalked and what forest cut-off was bedeviled by an aggressive pack of wild dogs. The others wanted to know about the east and how matters fared there; she told them details of the wedding and made them laugh when she repeated Prince Bayan's poetry. They speculated in low voices about Prince Sanglant, but no one spoke Liath's name out loud, as if by leaving the Eagles her name had been obliterated from their memory, as if they feared that the sound of it on their tongue might implicate them in her sorcery or scar their lips forever.

But she was comfortable here lying on straw and surrounded by good plank walls. Horses stamped in the stalls below them; their scent and warmth drifted up, and one by one her comrades drifted off to sleep. She slept, and she dreamed.

She is lost, battering her way through a tangle of high growth that scratches her hands and slaps her face. Swordlike leaves taper to points swaying far above her reach, a forest of grass. The sky is turgid with clouds. A strange humming tickles the air, a whistle with more weight than breath in its tone. She stumbles over a hump, trips, and lands with her hands buried in the oozing, stinking innards of a huge silver-furred bear that, eviscerated and hacked into parts, sprawls in death along the ground.

Just then, a heavy shadow overtakes her. She feels the wind of talons swiping at her back and hears a shrill trumpet of disappointment. Wings beat like bellows above her. She bolts, terrified, and flails through the grass, hands weeping blood and effluvia, but the wind of its passage returns, hot and staggering. She cannot see it precisely, she is too afraid to look up, but it is some monstrous creature, and as she cries out, the talons settle on her shoulders, grip her, and in the next instant her feet no longer touch the earth.

She kicks helplessly as they go up and up and the ground drops away so quickly that her head spins, and it is all she can do to clutch her spear tight. She isn't imprisoned by bird's talons at all, but by something more like lion's claws, and yet she glimpses a noble and terrifying eagle's head far above, with tufts for ears and armed with a fearsome beak. Beyond massive hind legs poised below her lashes a golden tail. At the heart of the blinding sheen of iron-gray feathers where she might plunge in her spearpoint, she sees a single pale spot on its breast, but they have made height so fast that she fears if she kills it, and it drops her, she will be dead from the fall.

If it is only a dream, will her death matter?
She doesn't want to find out.

*They fly until her shoulders ache. Unlike its claws, time has
no grip. A day passes, an hour, a minute; she can't be sure. The
landscape changes as she hangs above it. Perhaps she isn't moving at all, perhaps it is the land beneath her that moves while
she hangs unmoving. Liath used to talk about such things—*The
heavens are always turning around us, swifter than any mill
wheel, as deep under this earth as above it, quite round and solid
and painted with stars—*but she never understood them or perhaps it is more correct that she didn't understand why they were
worth wondering about. Yet in the last two years she has seen
a lot of things that have made her wonder and made her head
ache for wondering. The clouds have fallen back behind them,
scattering like sheep until at intervals the sun glares down so
that she has to blink wildly as her eyes adjust to its harsh light.
The bear's blood dries stickily on her hands, a pair of unpleasant
gloves. Trembling, looking at her bloody hands, she realizes that
the bear had no claws.*

*Ahead, grass dies away into hillocks of sand and fields of
rock, boulders tumbled into odd, veined shapes by some ancient
cataclysm. Ahead, the ground gleams all silver and gold. The
creature descends until she sees that the plain opening before
her is a desert strewn with sands that resemble seas of golden
granules interwoven with channels of silver dust. The sun sets,
bathing the glimmering sands in rose light. Abruptly, darkness
comes but for a single light, a campfire. She sees no moon.*

*That suddenly, they dip, and the claws release her. The crea-
ture screams, and she is deafened, she falls with her hands
clapped to her ears and her spear lost, and she hits the ground.
Her knees drive into her chest and she can't breathe, clutching
at anything, finding her spear jammed up against one elbow.
The coarse sand burns on her skin, still hot after hours baking
in the sun. The grains are oddly shaped, unlike any sand she's
ever seen before: they're disk-shaped, flat and round like a baby's
petrified fingernail. What ocean deposited this sand here? Where
is the shore?*

*Firelight illuminates a figure walking toward her, but she
knows that form as she knows her own heart, always, for her,
an easy depth to fathom.*

"I called you," says the princess, giving her a hand and help-ing her rise.

"What was that creature?" Hanna demands as she brushes off the knees of her trousers. *In an odd way, she has become used to these meetings.*

"That was a griffin,*"* says the princess, emphasizing the word as though she thinks Hanna won't understand it even though every word they speak, two who share no common language, is completely intelligible in her dreams.

"Do you control it?" she asks, feeling faint.

"Nay, I only asked for its help. Just as I ask for your help." Hanna sees her clearly now with firelight and starlight and the princess' own shroud of magelight to guide her. Four huge bear claws hang heavily from a leather thong around her neck. Several miniature pouches hang from a belt at her waist, each one cleverly tied closed with thread as fine as spider's silk. Her felt conical hat is missing, and she wears no covering at all on her head; her braids have been tied back behind her neck to keep them out of the way. She has a healing cut across the knuckles of one hand, and her leather coat has a huge rent in it, as though it was recently slashed and mended. Meat is cooking, and fat is boiling. Her nose is smudged with soot.

"How can I help you?" asks Hanna. *"This is only a dream."*

"How can I find a dragon's scale? All the dragons are gone. They vanished when the Lost Ones fled, so the old stories tell us."

Hanna laughs. Maybe in dreams the truth is easier to find because it isn't obscured by waking blindness. She drops to her knees and gathers up a handful of sand, lets the odd golden grains pour down through her fingers. The heat of them soaks her skin in dreamy warmth, like the kiss of magic. *"Couldn't these be dragon's scales?"*

The Kerayit princess laughs out loud, a whoop of joy. For all that her expression and demeanor are exotic and somber, still, she is barely a woman, no older than Hanna herself. She is no different than any other child, gleeful as she turns the trick back on a wily old teacher. In her excitement, she grasps Hanna by the shoulders, not unlike the monstrous griffin, and kisses her on either cheek, then slaps her under the chin with the back of her hand, an odd endearment. Her breath smells of sour milk. Her lips are dark, as if stained with berry juice.

"Hai ai!" she cries. "Stay with me, luck, and we will hunt down the others together. Seventeen items she said I must bring her, and I have five now. So I will prove myself worthy of becoming her apprentice."

A bass rumble vibrates along the earth, felt through the soles of her feet more than heard. The princess suddenly grasps Hanna's arm, and together they sway, only it isn't them, it is the earth that is shaken and they only move with it. The land shudders and jerks as if dragons buried beneath a millennium of shed scales have woken and are trying to dig free.

The tremor drags at her, and she feels the ground slide away under her feet, spun not by sorcery or some monstrous flying creature but by a sudden disturbance cutting through the earth itself. She is torn away, but she is still dreaming. She hasn't left the land of dreams, she has only been displaced.

The earth slides under her and the heavens are black. Neither star glints nor moon shines, but the breath of dawn licks at her face; she can see it in the graying scene unfolding before her, and she knows she has traveled a long way, thrown off course by the trembling earth. She is somewhere she has never been before. She feels another mind and another soul tangling with hers as she dreams, and he has brought her here, unawares, perhaps. No malice oppresses her, but the heart that beats inside her is unlike anything she has ever known, unlike her own simple and apprehensible heart, more cruel than merciful, more just than kind, yet in its contradictions unfathomable.

She walks among them and she falls inside.

Spring came early, as foretold by the merfolk who can taste the weather in the salt of the sea. No pounding storms troubled the fjords over the winter. Now he stands in the stern of his ship and the sea slides underneath as smoothly as melted grease coats a hot pan. The pull of the land is almost enough to draw them in. Scarcely does any oar touch the water.

Victory can be had in many ways, and this victory will be taken at dawn on a foe who lies sleeping.

Nokvi is, no doubt, shrewd and strong, and the magic of his allies can undo many an enemy. But that magic cannot harm the host of Stronghand, and Nokvi's strength will not avail him in the confusion brought on him by a dawn raid.

The ships beach silently on the far side of the land's finger, *where a steep ridge thrusts out into the sound. His warriors disembark as mute as stones; for this raid, they have left their dogs behind. They begin the hike that will take them over the ridge and down into Moerin's vale, where Nokvi rules. As they climb, pine and birch grow increasingly thick about them, and the host speeds silently between the trees until, cresting the ridge, they see the watch fires marking Nokvi's long hall burning crisp and clean below them. All lies quiet.*

As they move down the slope, their noise increases, and he feels a stab of misgiving, but it is already too late. His warriors are beginning to howl, full of their cleverness, ready to slaughter, and as they break from the woods and course over the fields he knows that even with this brief notice Nokvi's people will be easy prey, bewildered by the early hour and the unexpected attack.

Still no movement comes from the hall.

Distantly he hears a shriek, like a raven, suddenly cut off.

They reach the hall in a thundering roar, and it isn't until the first of them strikes down the door and heaves it aside that he understands the worst. Outside, the watch fires burn. Inside, the hearth fire burns but warms no one, because no one stands or sits or leaps up in astonished and enraged surprise. The hall is empty.

"Blow the retreat," he cries to his standard bearer even as he knows it is already too late.

Perhaps this will be his harshest test.

"Set the hall on fire," he calls, "and light every torch we have."

A new force emerges out of the trees, leaping in a wild ecstasy, and their ululations rise like the flames now streaking up the walls of the long hall. They are Soft Ones, but their skin is the color of the night sea and without clothing or adornment save spears and clubs spiked with iron they race toward the Rikin warriors shrieking and laughing like madmen. They plunge forward without fear, and in the instant before they fall upon his warriors, he sees robed humans walking among the trees with staffs upraised: sorcerers. His own staff he grips tightly, but their magic does not afflict his warriors, only their own, who hit the Rikin line with howls first of battle fever and then of agony.

"Retreat!" he cries again, and this time he wrenches the horn

from his standard bearer and blows the call himself, sharp, imperative.

"Nay, nay," his warriors cry, "let us slaughter them. They are weak as calves."

But he drives his troops forward. They know to obey him. They know he is more farsighted than they are. And by now, some of them can see that they have been tricked. With spears and fire they beat their way forward through the throng of naked men, headed for the ridge and the trees. Only the stupidest are left at the hall when Nokvi's troops come racing out of the dark from the other direction. It's a clever plan. Nokvi hoped to catch Rikin's army from behind while it wasted itself killing ensorcelled men.

It is a hard and humiliating run back up the ridge and down to his ships. Only four of the ships are burning so fiercely that the fires set on them can't be stemmed. He kills one of the arsonists himself, a naked human man who gibbers and pokes ineffectually at him with a knife before the creature falls, doubled over, from a thrust to the guts.

Four ships lost, as well as a third of his men. One ship has to be scuttled in the sound, and ten more warriors dumped overboard when they die of their wounds.

But he counts himself lucky. He has underestimated Nokvi and his allies. It could have been much worse.

It is not in victory that you learn how strong you truly are.

Sorrow licked him, and he startled up like a hare bolting and found himself weeping at Lavastine's bier.

It is not in victory that you learn how strong you are.

Ai, God. He could not weep for himself, not truly. He was weeping for what they had done to his father's hopes and dreams, shredded now. Thrown to the dogs.

Not my father any longer.

Nay, King Henry had not yet judged the case. Yet if Henry ruled in his favor, could he ever truly call himself Lavastine's son again without wondering if it were a lie to say so? Couldn't it be true, as Cook said, that Lavastine had lain with the young woman as well? Might he not have walked to the ruins one night and succumbed to temptation as Alain had almost done so long ago with that girl, Withi? How could they ever know one way or the other? How could one tell?

What had linked Lavastine and poor Lackling, who were so unlike that it seemed impossible they could be father and son, even after Cook's testimony? Nothing had linked them, except blood, except perhaps the way the hounds had whined and whimpered at both their deaths.

Geoffrey's blood claim to the count's chair was stronger than Lackling's merely by reason of competence. But if fitness was the only standard, then couldn't he argue that he would be a better steward than Geoffrey? Under his rule, the people would do better than under Geoffrey's rule. Was it pride to think so? No, it was truth. Lavastine had recognized that truth and he had made his decision based in part on sentiment and emotion, certainly, but in equal part on reason, because Lavastine took seriously his duty to the land and people under his rule.

What was blood, anyway? It was everything, all that you had to mark kinship, and yet the bond he had shared with Lavastine was no less real whether or not blood had tied them together. He and Lavastine had been woven together in some way evident to them both.

He loved him still, and he had a bitter intuition that had Cook reluctantly brought her testimony before Lavastine, the count would have smiled in his terse way and told her that it made no difference to *him*.

Nay, the failure had not been Lavastine's. He had always known what he was about. *He had known what would happen, and he had made every effort to prepare for it.*

But Tallia wasn't pregnant. Alain had failed and, worse, he had lied to the man who trusted him most.

The knowledge lay in his heart as bitterly as the accusation that he might be nothing better than the ill-gotten child of a whore and her father, born out of incest and cruel poverty. Ai, Lady. No better than the poor beggars who had sheltered in hovels on his land and pleaded for food for their starving children.

Yet did God love them any less than They did the fine nobles who never wanted for elegant clothing and full platters?

But you're nothing so noble as a beggar's child. The voice scraped at him like a finger picking at a fresh scab. Did God love whores, too? The shame of having it spoken out loud in front of everyone still gnawed at him. It would never cease gnawing. His foster father Henri had protected him from the truth of what she was all this time. He had only ever said one thing about her, that she was beautiful. As if that was all that mattered. And maybe, in God's heart, that was all that mattered.

Rage whined, butting him, and he scratched her around the ears, buried his face in her massive neck as he patted her and she grunted contentedly. What about the testimony of the hounds? Yet where had Fear gone? Would he ever return?

He ran a hand over poor Terror's stone flanks where the old hound lay in death at Lavastine's feet. The curse had marbled as the old hound stiffened and died, so that he looked hewn of a dark stone stippled with white. Lavastine lay peacefully, with Steadfast guarding his head and Terror his feet. The shame of this day did not touch him, for certainly he had atoned for his sins; his soul had ascended to the Chamber of Light. Alain had to believe that.

Beside him, Sorrow stood stiffly, growling, but made no move to plunge forward. Alain clambered to his feet and combed back his hair with a hand.

But he stood alone in the church, just as he had stood alone in the hall.

Then he saw her back by the door, peering nervously out from behind the first square column. "Come forward. The hounds won't hurt you."

Lady Hathumod moved with the hesitancy of a fawn approaching tame lions, innocent enough to trust and yet held back by an ancient caution.

"Have you brought word from her?" he asked eagerly.

She halted three paces from him, head bowed modestly, fleshy hands clasped in an attitude of prayer. "Nay, my lord. She refuses to see you. She refuses to send you a message."

"Then I will go to her! It isn't right that Duchess Yolande keep us apart in this way."

Boldly, she stepped forward to lay a hand on his forearm as if she meant to hold him in his place. Then, as quickly, she jerked back. Her cheeks flushed a bright red. She still wouldn't look him in the eye. "Nay, my lord, please do not do so. You will only humiliate yourself."

"How can I possibly bring on myself any greater humiliation than was heaped on me yesterday?" Bitterness rose in his throat, bile burning up from his stomach. "Tallia trusts me. She only need see that I haven't blamed her for what happened. It isn't her fault that Duchess Yolande dragged her away. I'm sure she didn't want to go, not truly."

"I pray you, my lord." She seemed almost to weep out the words as she clutched her hands together so tightly that her knuckles were white and the tips of her fingers red. "Do not blame Duchess Yolande. No matter what you say, Lady Tallia will not see you. So you must either be seen begging outside her door like a vagrant or breaking into her private chambers like a common thief."

"Since most of the nobles here think I am no better than a whore's son, how will it harm me—?" Knowing it was excessive, he broke off. He simply could not believe that Tallia had abandoned him so callously.

"I pray you, my lord," she said in her soft voice. "Do not waste yourself suffering over that woman, for she is not worthy of you."

Amazed, he watched as tears slipped down her cheeks. "What do you mean?"

"Tallia is the flawed vessel. She is how God has tested our faith, for truth was given to her, but it cracked her."

He was too stunned to reply. How had she concealed this disrespect for her mistress all these months? He had never guessed that Hathumod was anything but an obedient companion, willingly accepting banishment from Quedlinhame in order to remain with her beloved lady.

"I know, my lord, that you do not believe the true word as revealed to us by Brother Agius, to whom God granted the glory of martyrdom. Yet who am I to question God's design? I, too, am only God's vessel."

"Surely the Lady sent you to stand beside Tallia. She needs someone to take care of her."

Her mouth, tightening, gave away the depth of her disgust. "She turned her back on the one who loved her selflessly. I am leaving her service, my lord."

"But where will you go? Back to your family?"

"Nay, they sent me to the cloister because they have too many daughters and not enough land to divide between them. They do not want me back."

"Then where? You can't just strike out on your own. A mendicant's life cannot be for you, Lady Hathumod." He gestured toward her clothing, a good linen gown embroidered with cavorting rabbits; she was almost rabbitlike herself, with a soft round face, someone you wanted to pet rather than kick. She wore bright red cloth slippers, the kind of courtly, delicate shoes that would wear out after a day of walking. Her hands bore no calluses. Her skin was still as soft as a rose petal. "Will you go back to Quedlinhame?"

He recognized the stubborn set of her shoulders. "They won't have me back. It matters not where I go, my lord. I will trust in God's wisdom." Finally, she gained the courage to look him in the eye, and he was startled by her quiet yet passionate certitude. "But I know what I have seen here. I saw what happened with the loaves among the poor. If it is God's will to hide Her servants among us, then I will keep silence."

Then, astoundingly, she knelt before him and kissed his hand as a lady would that of her regnant.

"Nay, you must not!" he cried, embarrassed by this act of devotion. He lifted her gently to her feet, but could say no more, because the king's Eagle came in then, looking for him, and called him to court.

And in the end, when they had all assembled, Alain watched as the Tallia who would not speak to him nor even look at him, the only woman he had ever truly loved, came before her uncle the king.

"Can you swear before this court and by the name of Our Lord and Lady that the marriage was never consummated?"

"Yes," she said, and it seemed to him that she was glad to say it, that she positively rejoiced in that one word that shamed him and ruined him.

A nobleman laughed, a snorting chuckle. Henry looked up from his study of his niece, and it became so quiet that Alain could hear Rage's toenails clicking on the floor as she shifted her head on her paws. Someone nearby had farted ripely. A bee buzzed outside one of the open shutters, and from the distant fields he heard a hoe picking at dirt, someone chopping as if they were bothered and angry.

"By the oath you swore in front of witnesses on your marriage night, you have the right to support him as his kinswoman," continued Henry, almost suggestively. "Will you speak on his behalf?"

"I am not his wife," said Tallia, and the gleam of triumph

colored her thin face. "If it was not consummated, then the marriage never took place."

The faintest scent of a fading dog rose drifted to him, vanished, and he became aware of his own rose hanging against his heart, as heavy as a lump of worthless iron slag. The point of the old nail had shifted, driven against his breastbone as if striking for the heart.

It was her betrayal that hurt the most.

Henry sat back with an obvious sigh. "So be it," he said, sounding more than a little displeased. "No woman or man can rule without kin to support them. Because this man Alain has no kin to support him, I have no choice but to rule in Lord Geoffrey's favor. His daughter, Lavrentia, I name as count of Lavas, to be guided under her father's regency until she comes of age at fifteen."

After that it was all meaningless noise.

And yet, hadn't the judgment been passed a year or more ago? Hadn't his foster father Henri accused him of everything Geoffrey had, excepting sorcery?

Henri's own words had condemned him. *"You don't think I'm Lavastine's son,"* Alain had cried. Henri hadn't hesitated: *"Nay, and why should I?"*

Ai, God, and without Tallia, would he have had the heart for it anyway, reigning as count for years and years, alone as Lavastine had been? No wonder Lavastine had fastened on to the unknown fatherless boy. He had been desperate and lonely. What a fool Lavastine had been! Would he have proved any better, any less foolish, any less desperate after years of lonely rule? Nay, it was all for the best that it end this way. He could have expected nothing else.

But then he shook himself, knowing this for the sin of despair. He would not dishonor Lavastine's memory by giving in to self-pity.

In this way he came to himself as the shouting and stamping feet subsided and Geoffrey leaped to his feet in triumph and anger.

"I beg you, Your Majesty! You must punish him for his presumption. Let the church take him to trial for sorcery!" He had to wipe his mouth because he was spitting, so eager was he to get the words out.

Rage and Sorrow rose, stiff-legged, more threatening in silence than a pack of barking dogs. One of Geoffrey's kinsmen grabbed Geoffrey's arm and yanked him back.

Henry rose and rapped his scepter on the floor three times, and anyone sitting quickly stood. "Nay!" cried Henry, staring Geoffrey down until the poor man hit his knees on his chair and sat down hard, then leaped up, fearful of insulting the king. "Your zealotry does you no honor. I see no sorcery involved in this case, only the error of a man heartfelt on finding a beloved son who had been lost to him."

Even Geoffrey was wise enough to let it go. He stepped back, he bowed his head humbly, and took his little daughter—the new count—in his arms, the symbol of his victory.

Henry turned to regard Alain. Did he look aggrieved? Had his voice caught on that mention of lost sons? Alain was too numb to care.

"You have served God and this throne faithfully, Alain. I offer you this choice, that you walk away from Lavas Holding now and never return to any lands under its watch on pain of death, or that you accept a position in my Lions, fitting to your birth, and serve me."

That fast, he had tumbled down Fortune's wheel. It was simply too stunning to grasp. But he had to act. He had to think. He struggled to clear away enough fog so as not to make a fool of himself. God help him, he would not disgrace Lavastine by making a fool of himself in front of Geoffrey and his smirking family!

But of course, Henry knew what he was about. There wasn't a choice, not really. Had he ever had any place to go except to return in shame to Bel's steading, which he could not do anyway because Osna was under Lavas protection?

He came forward and knelt as, from his seat among the nobles, he had once watched Eagles kneel before the king, as servants had once knelt before him, although those days seemed impossibly long ago. The rose seemed to have sprouted thorns of ice, pricking his heart until he thought he must bleed in torrents all over the floor. He would perhaps have fallen over from the pain, but Rage and Sorrow paced forward and sat on either side of him, their big bodies pressing warmly against his trembling one.

King Henry did not step back, nor did they growl at him.

"I will serve you as you command, Your Majesty," said Alain.

3

PRINCE Ekkehard saw the gold feather lying on the road and, after one of his grooms fetched it for him, he held it up in his cousin's face.

"Have you ever seen anything like this? I think it's pure gold! What luck that I saw it first!"

"Get that thing out of my face, I pray you," said Wichman, shoving Ekkehard's arm back. "It smells."

"It does not!" cried Ekkehard, holding it to his nose and taking a big whiff. At once he began coughing, and Wichman's companions all laughed. Wichman took advantage of Ekkehard's coughing to snatch the feather from his younger cousin's hand, and by the set of his mouth and the frown made by his eyes, Ivar could tell he was intrigued.

"That's mine!" objected Ekkehard as the fit passed.

"So it is, little Cousin, but right now I'm having a look." Wichman handed it to one of his companions and quickly it was passed around among the older horsemen as Ekkehard fumed.

Wichman and his fighting men were not unlike a gang of bandits, Ivar reflected. Ermanrich had taken to calling them Lord Reckless and his noble companions Thoughtless, Careless, Heedless, Senseless, Mindless, Wordless, Useless, the three Thundering brothers, the six Drunken cousins, and of course the infamous Thruster, who had once been discovered doing unspeakable things to a ewe. Sigfrid did not approve of this levity, but he always ended up laughing anyway because Ermanrich had such a wicked ability to mimic.

"It's gold," said Thruster wisely as he twirled it, "and God damn it but I'd like to see those acrobat girls perform dressed in nothing but a skirt of these. I know what I'd do with'em then!" Known otherwise as Lord Eddo, he was the most single-minded person Ivar had ever met.

"Can't be gold," said Thoughtless who, like all the rest of

Wichman's cronies, was a fat-headed, bored young nobleman from somewhere in Saony. "Ain't any birds made of gold."

"Is too gold," said Useless, snatching it from his hand. "'Tisn't a bird feather at all. It's a Quman feather. They have wings, too, you know."

"I've never seen anything like it," said Wichman, which ended the matter. "But I'd like to see what bird it comes from. Here, Father Ekkehard." He handed it back with a smirk. "Perhaps you educated churchmen can make more sense of it. Oh, God!" The groan came from him quite unexpectedly, and everyone started round to stare. He slapped his own forehead. "I forgot all my clerics at Gent!"

It had become a very old joke, but he and his companions still found it hysterical.

Amazingly, Prince Ekkehard had learned to keep his mouth shut at such times. He merely handed the feather to Baldwin for safekeeping.

They had passed the first signs of a village some time ago, woods logged out for firewood and buildings, grazed meadows, a litter of pig bones, and fields left fallow. It had been a quiet ride; there were remarkably few birds in the woods. Now as the sun sank into the afternoon, light filtered mellowly through spring leaves. They rode alongside a flowering orchard. Three half grown boys sprinted out from the cover of the trees to stare.

"Look at them spears!" cried one of them, whose face was at least as dirty as his feet.

"Come you to kill the beast?" cried another, galloping alongside the road until a ditch cut him off. Their friend had already taken off across a side path, leaping a rivulet, and vanishing into a crowd of waist-high berry bushes as if all the Enemy's minions pursued him.

Word flew before them, and when they reached the village, they were met by a delegation of village elders, three old women and two bent men who seemed to have about a dozen teeth between them. What must have been the rest of the village population crowded behind: matrons; men and boys of all ages; little girls. Strangely, there seemed to be no young women of marriageable age among them. Dogs barked, and Thoughtless took a swipe at one scrawny yapper with his spear, nicking the poor creature in its hindquarters. Ivar had seen this scene before as they had traveled at a leisurely pace south and east from Gent:

the village elders would offer a few poor gifts as a transparent bribe and then suggest that the group travel to a manor house or monastic farm farther up the road, one more fit to entertain a party of their consequence. Wichman would refuse because he preferred lording it at villages, where there was inevitably a handier supply of reluctant young women.

"God's mercy," cried the eldest of the sages, an old woman who had to lean on a stick to support herself. She had an odd way of clipping off her words at the end, the local dialect. "Our prayers are answered, my lords. Say that you have come to kill the beast!"

"What sort of beast might that be?" asked Wichman, scanning the huts and outlying sheds. Beyond, long fields tipped with green striped the ground, interspersed with ranks of fruit-bearing bushes and trees. Something pale flashed between two trees, escaping to the safety of the woods: a dog? a goat?

"Ai, a terrible creature not born of earth! Since Margrave Villam and Duchess Rotrudis drove back the Rederii these twenty years and brought them into the Light of God, we've had no trouble here. But now!" Several folk wailed out loud. "Shades in the forest there've always been, but this! First all manner of unGodly lights up in the old stones, and now the beast. Why has God seen fit to torment us?"

"What manner of beast is it?" repeated Wichman. He had his most irritating little smirk on his face.

"A terrible creature never meant to walk on earth. It come from the stones one night, flew out of a blinding light. As big as a house, it is, like an eagle, only it's a monster sent by the Enemy to plague us. Its claws could lay open a cow with one rake. First it only took the deer, but we fear that—"

"Haven't you any daughters but those little ones?" demanded Thruster suddenly. He was rubbing one thigh obsessively, sweating a little although it wasn't very warm.

Every man and woman in the place went still and white. One child, piping up, got a slap on the mouth.

"Eaten!" said the woman in a quaking voice. She had warts on her nose and a stubborn gleam in her eye. "The beast took the deer first, and then our daughters."

"I would have taken the daughters first and then the deer," said Useless, "but this must be some agile relative of Eddo's." They laughed uproariously, including Thruster.

"Hold your tongues!" said Wichman, who hadn't laughed. "Whose land is this?"

"It's our own, my lord. I come with my husband, God rest him, to settle here when there wasn't nothing but savages living here. It were the agreement made with King Arnulf's stewards. We're beholden to no lady but only to the king."

He grunted thoughtfully. His horse, getting restive, danced a little sideways, and he yanked it back. "But I must keep my companions happy, or they won't want to risk their lives. What can you offer us?"

"Food and shelter, my lord."

"I know what you're hiding," said Wichman. "And I want it for myself and my men."

"What're they hiding?" cried Thruster eagerly.

Prince Ekkehard pressed his horse forward. Compared to his older cousin, he looked slight and almost frail, but he held his head as proudly and he was of course dressed magnificently. "I am Ekkehard, son of King Henry," he said in a bold voice. "I have come to save you. I ask no reward for my companions and myself no matter what the risk to our lives, for I know my duty as a prince of this realm. Tell me more of this beast that afflicts you."

In this way, Ivar found himself pressing through grass and chest-high foliage along an overgrown trail, following his guide, a thin and rather frightened boy whose speech was almost unintelligible. As Ekkehard's least favorite companion, Ivar had been sent ahead to scout the stones, the lair of the mysterious and horrible beast, and his guide had evidently been chosen because he was one person the villagers wouldn't much mind losing, poor lad.

Bait, Wichman had said, and his companions had all pounded each other on the back at this witticism and snorted and chortled. Baldwin had looked annoyed and begun to intercede, but Ivar had stopped him. He was proud to go, truly. He wasn't afraid anymore because he trusted in God's plan now even if he did still have uncomfortable dreams of Liath some nights. Anyway, it wasn't fair to make the poor boy go alone.

He hiked up his novice's robes as they forded a broad and shallow stream. Wet to the knees, he clambered out on the other side, keeping up a stream of prayer as he crept on behind the boy. God had a plan, of course, really She did, and he trusted Her, but he still wondered why his stomach couldn't decide between leaping up out of his throat or dropping straight down out the other way, and if he kept his mouth moving he didn't quite have to think so much. How many lost souls had he brought to the truth since his revelation on the streets of Gent? Enough that he could go straight to the hall of the martyrs? He and Ermanrich and Sigfrid had preached among the benighted so pugnaciously for the next week that eventually Brother Humilicus had gotten suspicious, and the biscop had had them hauled up before her on the charge of heresy.

They had escaped only because Ekkehard was leaving with Wichman the next day and, driven by Baldwin's coaxing, he had used his princely authority to yank them out of the biscop's very annoyed grasp. But he hadn't been happy about it. And he still didn't like Ivar.

Had there been enough souls saved in Gent? It was hard to tell, and the villagers they had preached to along the way had been reticent, but at least those humble souls hadn't stoned them or driven them out. They'd listened, and whispered to each other. They'd even asked a few questions.

No one had said the work would be easy. God's plan wasn't all honey and pudding.

At times, Ivar wondered what God had planned for people like Lord Wichman, one of the most useless creatures ever to stalk the earth. Send a beast to kill a beast, Ermanrich had murmured as the expedition had armed and made ready to assault the beast's lair, but he'd stopped giggling at his joke when Ekkehard had commanded Ivar to walk ahead. Ekkehard had given him a small horn, which he now clutched in his right hand, and he hoped he'd have a chance to use it.

"Hsst!" The boy waved him back with a stick, then motioned toward a jumbly dark rise ahead of them, an unnaturally round hill crowned with fallen stones and unpleasantly torn up trees. It suddenly seemed odd to Ivar that all birdsong had ceased. Sun flashed among the stones, but then Ivar blinked, seeing it flash again, seeing it move, as if sunlight had been caught within the ruined stone circle and was trying to break free.

"Uh, uh, uh," grunted the boy in terror, and bolted.

From the heart of the stones the sun rose, although the sun was already midway down a western sky half hidden in the broken clouds. *It* was huge and brilliant, covered in gold. Ivar heard shouts from behind him; the rider had seen it, and anyway, as he gaped as it rose higher and higher, he realized that he had dropped the horn.

It was shaped something like an eagle with a tufted eagle's head and a noble beak, but it was manifestly no eagle. They couldn't grow so large, and eagles didn't have gold feathers, as if they'd been gilded by flying too close to the sun. It was magnificent, with tail feathers that seemed to blaze and eyes that even from this distance sparked and glimmered like starlight. It was the most beautiful thing he had ever seen in his life.

Scrabbling on the ground, he found the horn, lifted it, and blew, but all that came out was a stuttering wheeze.

It trumpeted. The sound boomed around him, as melodious as the voice of angels, too powerful for mortal ears to comprehend. He'd never seen anything cover ground that fast. It was far, rising from the fallen stones, and then it was near, as big as a warhorse, diving for him with talons edged and pointed like swords.

He flung himself flat on the ground. The air heaved and blew as the creature passed over him. The beat of its wings burned his neck, and he was dizzied by a scent as sharp and heady as the incense used in church. He heard a very human shriek beyond him, but he was too winded to move.

Was that the face of the Enemy, so dazzling that it would kill you as you stared at it in wonder? Or was it a precious glimpse of the face of God in all Her terrible splendor?

A bony hand tugged at his ankle, and he yelped, kicking— but it was only the boy, who had come back to get him. Distantly, he heard horses scream and an outbreak of shouting. Wichman's voice pierced momentarily above the chaos: "With your spears, you fools!"

A riderless horse galloped out of nowhere, wild with terror, and Ivar leaped back out of its way, stumbled, rolled, and struck his shoulder on an inconvenient rock. He got to his hands and knees, scrambled behind a prickly hedge, and panted until he could think again. The boy had vanished with the horse, or in its wake. Finally, disgusted with his cowardice, he ran back toward the ford, trying to keep out of sight.

The clamor of a particularly ugly skirmish rang in the air, wounded horses, a panicking man, a huffing grunt like erratic

bellows, someone screaming over and over again about his arm.
Ivar came into sight of the ford. Beyond it, where the wood fell
away into open ground, the great creature beat above a churning clot of riders like a beaked angel shrouded in golden light.
Basking in the glow were seven riders, chief among them Wichman, never one to shrink from a fight. Each time the beast came
near the ground, they prodded and thrust with their spears, and
each time, with great beats of its wings, it would lift out of
reach. With a shout, Prince Ekkehard spurred forward from the
group, trying to get a thrust up from underneath, and for an instant he was out of reach of the others. The beast curled sharply
toward him, uncannily graceful, and its talons caught his shoulders.

The young prince's arms were immediately pinned to his sides
as talons dug deep into shoulders protected by a good mail coat.
His spear fell to the ground, yet he didn't shriek, although blood
began to run. With strained wing beats it tried to raise him into
the air. The horse bolted out from under him, and he kicked,
flailing helplessly, as if trying to reclaim his mount although the
horse had already bolted into the woods. His helm, knocked
loose, spun to earth.

He struggled on, pumping and swiping with his feet, as the
beast flew low toward the ford where Ivar stood frozen, quite
unable to think or act. Wichman and the other five riders pounded
after in close pursuit. Shouting and whooping, more came riding from the woods, calling out the prince's name. As the beast
closed, still beating low, Ivar could see Ekkehard's face, white,
grimacing as he twisted, and yet in an odd way almost exulted.

The wind off its wings blasted Ivar as it came right in over
his head, still unable to gain height. Without thinking, he leaped.
Springing from a crouch to the air in two steps, he caught hold
of one of Ekkehard's flailing legs.

At first he thought both he and the prince would be borne
away as his toes left the ground, but in the next instant his feet
were dragging in the water as the beast banked to one side, borne
down by the extra weight. He heard Wichman shout, felt the
press of horses nearby, driven in against their will. He didn't
see the blow, but he felt it shudder through Ekkehard's leg, heard
a grunt from the prince, a groan forced out between gritted teeth.
The beast trembled, and all three of them fell to the ground. The

slow strained beats had become the frantic fluttering of a wounded wing, splashing in the stream.

Letting go, Ivar rolled over to see hooves slashing air above him. A shower of iron points and wooden shafts whistled past, cutting the sky into ephemeral ribbons. The cruel beak struck a hand's breath from his bare foot, and water sizzled from a weeping cut under one radiant eye; its blood scalded his toes. He threw himself sideways, rolling and rolling through the shallow water, gasping for breath and gulping more water than air until he was in the middle of the stream and outside the frenzied circle on the bank. He could see nothing but men and horses and spears, a frenzy of spears rising and falling like hammers beating death from life.

Gold feathers as delicate as anything crafted in the finest goldsmith's hall and that pale viscous blood drifted in a spreading smear from the bank. The steaming blood stung, burning his skin where it flowed over and around him, and he scrambled and scraped over pebbles and slimy stones and heaved himself out on the grassy bank just as a shout rose from the men.

They had themselves become the beast, howling over their defeated prey.

Sigfrid ran up beside Ivar, dropping to his knees. He was weeping, signing frantically: "No! No!"

But it was too late.

The glorious creature was dead.

Ivar staggered up and tottered over to the ravening crowd of celebrating young men, and of a miracle Wichman's cronies made way for him. They didn't even tease him or pinch him as they would otherwise have done as he pushed through them to the side of the beast. In death, it only looked grotesque, not sublime. It was just a monstrous dead thing with shining feathers and dull, lifeless eyes.

Baldwin was helping Prince Ekkehard to stand.

"Damned fool idiot," Wichman was shrieking as Ekkehard tried to move his arms. "I *told* you to stay back. No charging in like a glory-mad fool. Just get out of my way next time!"

Blood leaked through chain mail, and the prince swayed a little as Baldwin held him up and his other young companions clustered around, with their bodies widening the distance between him and his massive cousin. Then he saw Ivar.

"I owe you my life," said Ekkehard irritably. "What reward do you want in return?"

"Burn it," said Ivar. Sigfrid had come up beside him, wiping fresh tears from his face. Ermanrich stood on the other bank, mouth an "o" of astonishment. "That's all I ask, Your Highness. Just burn it."

When the boy came in, leading the bolted horse, he was sent to the village with the news. Wichman ordered half his men to seek out the rest of the lost horses. Poor Mindless, the only casualty, was dying fast of blood loss and trauma: the beast had ripped his arm from its socket. They didn't bother to carry him anywhere, only made him comfortable on the ground and, squirting wine from their wineskins down his throat, got him drunk to kill the pain. Those who remained pulled feathers from the beast as well as they could, but they had to give up their looting because its blood blistered them even through gloves. When the villagers finally paraded in with cries of triumph and a garland of fireweed and pansies to drape around Prince Ekkehard's bruised neck, they had brought flagons of ale and a lit lamp.

Ekkehard still couldn't lift his arms, so he merely nodded when the old village woman offered him the lamp. "It injured you more than us," he said magnanimously. "Let the one of you who lost the most livestock set it on fire."

"But none of us lost any livestock, my lord," she said. "It were so cruel and fearsome looking, living so nearby, that we feared it might begin to stalk us."

Ekkehard blinked several times in quick succession, as if her words didn't quite make sense to him. Then, with a shrug, he sent Milo forward to fling the lamp onto the corpse from a safe distance.

Flames exploded from the body. Useless, still hanging about hoping to glean a few more feathers, got singed and skipped back, yelping like a hurt dog.

"Are you sure you're all right?" Ermanrich demanded of Ivar for the fourth time.

Ivar could only shrug. Sigfrid knelt at a safe distance from the bonfire and began to pray, lips moving although no intelligible sound could come out. He was still weeping.

The fire roared, and as feathers crisped and evaporated in the heat, Ivar began to see shapes in the flames: a multitude of honey-colored doves borne upward by the smoke; lions pacing into an unseen distance, sleek and pale; silvery roes leaping away as up invisible stair-steps of rock, vanishing into the heavens; salamanders delighting in the flames, their bright bodies more red than coals and their eyes sparking blue fire.

"I think we made a terrible mistake," he whispered.

Beyond the fire, where the rejoicing hadn't slackened and no one seemed aware of these strange emanations except as a heady cloud of incense wafting heavenward, an argument erupted as violently as had the fire out of the great bird.

"You're lying to us, you old bladder!" Wichman towered over the old woman who had first spoken to them, threatening her with a bloody-knuckled fist. "I know you hid your daughters. You admit yourself that it was a lie that the beast ate any of them. I saw some of them running into the woods."

"Leave them alone," said Ekkehard suddenly. He was still sitting on the ground, Milo, Baldwin and Udo hovering behind him as his servingmen agonized over how to get the bloodied mail shirt off without aggravating his injured shoulders. "What right have you to molest them?"

"The right of a commander who just lost a soldier to defend these miserable vermin!"

"I grieve for Lord Altfrid, too, but that's no reason to rape their daughters in exchange."

Wichman snorted, throwing his arms out and taking a big step to one side. He had a way of flinging his body into any space nearby when he was in a foul mood, the way a person took up room to show that he could. He wiped blood from his nose. "Now here's a change of heart from the randy little boy who was never happier than when groping his sluts in Gent. Or are you happy enough with your pretty attendant Baldwin? If he's not sword enough for you, I can loan you Eddo here, for he'll probe the canals of quite any creature, human, animal, or otherwise."

"Don't mock me," said Ekkehard in a low voice. "And don't molest these people." He had gone white along the jaw, but at least blood wasn't dripping anymore. The wind was blowing the inebriant smoke from the beast's pyre directly into his face, although he didn't seem to notice.

Wichman had, of course, stepped wisely out of the heaviest stream of smoke. "How do you mean to stop me? I have fifteen experienced men to your fourteen half-grown boys. We could chop you into pieces and go on our way without breaking a sweat."

"And pork the village girls besides," added Thruster enthusiastically. "Did they really *hide* them from us? Mean of them!"

"My father—" began Ekkehard, almost squeaking with anger.

"Ai, God!" cried Wichman, clapping a hand to his head in the familiar, mocking way. "What will dear Uncle Henry do to me? I'm kin. And he needs my mother's support, doesn't he? So just shut up, little Cousin, and go back to your novices and your prayers, or have you forgotten that you're a monk, not a soldier?"

"Then do it," said Ekkehard quietly. Sitting, he looked like a child vainly attempting to bully a roaring giant. Yet as the smoke poured off the pyre, it seemed to pool around his body. For an instant, Ivar thought he saw the golden shadow of the dead bird rising, wings outstretched, from the battered shoulders of the prince.

With a grimace, and some help from his companions, Ekkehard got to his feet. Even standing he was entirely outmatched by his brawny cousin, a big, stout, experienced fighter, survivor of the second battle of Gent, leader of that troop of reckless young men who, outnumbered and outmatched, had fought hit-and-run engagements against Bloodheart's Eika raiders for half a year. Ivar had heard all the glorious stories. So had Ekkehard, and his admiration for his cousin had become both embarrassing and a nuisance to Wichman.

But something had changed.

"Do it," repeated Ekkehard. "Just be sure my father knows who killed me, and who terrorized these helpless villagers. They've got no lady or lord to avenge them, to call out a feud on their behalf, to get repayment for any damages you do them. They've only got the pledge of the king that they are under his protection." He turned then to address the villagers. To their credit, they hadn't fled; they'd only slunk back like dogs about to be whipped who knew that bars hemmed them in with their captor. "Keep your daughters hidden," he said to them before turning back to defy his cousin. "Now what will you do? Kill them one by one until they bring out their daughters? Don't they have enough sheep to satisfy you and your companions?"

Wichman slugged him.

He fell, thrashing a little like the bird had as it died in the stream. His wounded arms fluttered, then stilled. With eyes rolled up in his head, he lay there limply.

Baldwin lunged for Wichman, and then there was a gasp of fighting, Ekkehard's boys throwing themselves against Wichman's men. Ivar would have leaped in, but Ermanrich restrained him and it was over in moments in any case. Half of Ekkehard's boys had blackening eyes and the rest purpling cheeks, most of them now held at arm's length like puppets.

"Let them go," said Wichman with disgust. "Bring me my horse," he called to his groom. He spat at the feet of the crone before mounting. The horse sidestepped, trying to get away from the pyre, and he yanked its head round. "Let's go," he said to his companions. "We can find better lodging than this. Get Altfrid's ring so we can return it to his sister."

They thundered off through the woods, making for the main road. Strangely, after their departure, the sun came out from its veil of clouds. The fire roared on, oblivious. Glittering stags poured out of the burning corpse, running in the sweet smoke until their shapes were lost in the light of the sun.

In the morning, Ekkehard still couldn't move his arms well enough to ride, but he looked remarkably cheerful as the villagers fussed over him. He'd been given the best bed in the hamlet, roomy enough for three and, according to Baldwin, not more infested than usual with fleas. The householder had strewn the floor with tansy to keep away vermin, and rushes had been brought in plenty to make soft bedding for Ekkehard's companions and servants.

But Sigfrid was missing.

They found him at the pyre. By the golden sheen of soot on his hair and nose and the state of his robe, they deduced he had snuck out sometime late in the evening after everyone else had gone to sleep and prayed all night beside the pyre. Seeing Ivar and Ermanrich, he grabbed a stick and scratched writing into the ashes.

"The Feast Day of St. Mercurius the Changeable," read Ermanrich, who still had an easier time reading than did Ivar. "No doubt accounting for Prince Ekkehard's noble behavior yesterday." He took the stick from Sigfrid and poked at the coals still smoldering in the pyre. No smoke rose, but a low mist of ashes seemed to hang about the coals as though blown up by some vast creature exhaling below. The pyre still gave off heat. It smelled now like a vast grave of flowers, a hundred rich scents tangled into one.

"Euw!" Ermanrich leaped back, dropping the stick.

Within the bright embrace of the coals, a gleaming red-gold worm writhed.

Startled, Sigfrid flung out his hands to hold Ivar and Ermanrich back. He actually tried to speak—normally he never forgot about his missing tongue—but he was so excited now, trembling, mobile face working, that he made the most pathetic noises until, finally, he grabbed the stick and tried to write something in the ashes. But a hard wind came up and they had to jump back as the pyre swirled up in a cloud of golden ash, spinning, then settled.

The glowing worm had vanished.

Sigfrid began to weep.

"It was a sign," said Ermanrich portentously. "But was it the Enemy, or God?"

Sigfrid, looking ecstatic more than grief-stricken, flung himself down onto his knees and began to pray again. They could not budge him, and there he prayed for the rest of the day while villagers came and went to exclaim over the remains of the beast, although none dared touch the coals. Indeed, as the day progressed, the coals seemed to glow more hotly. But maybe that was only Ivar's imagination, his own weak flesh reacting as, emboldened by Wichman's departure, the village's young women crept back. Nervous at first, like pigs knowing that one of their kind has been slaughtered, they grew bolder when none of the young men in Ekkehard's party molested them.

"Perhaps our preaching has finally reached Prince Ekkehard's heart," Ivar said to Ermanrich that evening as they feasted on roast chicken flavored with mustard, honey cakes, greens, and a very coarse dark bread that he had to soak in ale to make edible.

"I don't know," said Ermanrich, looking doubtful. "It was very sudden."

Ekkehard's arms still hurt him too much to move, although otherwise they seemed to be healing well. He allowed Baldwin to feed him, and had further charmed the villagers by drinking out of the wooden cup, engraved with a swan, offered to him by a village elder.

"I pray you, my lord prince," said Baldwin, smiling prettily, "let me take something out to our companion, Sigfrid, for otherwise I'm afraid he won't eat."

"Pray do so," said Ekkehard, who like everyone admired Sigfrid for his humble devotion to God and the ease with which he shed sincere tears. But then, the noble expression shattered briefly, twisting into something else. "But don't take *him*," he said, waving toward the far end of the table where Ivar and Ermanrich sat. "Take the fat one."

Ivar flushed. Ermanrich rose, leaning to whisper in his ear. "He's just jealous of you because Baldwin loves you. Don't mind it, Ivar."

But he did mind it. He finished his meal in silence, shunned by the others now that Ermanrich and Baldwin were gone. They all despised him because Prince Ekkehard despised him, and yet hadn't the blessed Daisan forgiven his enemies? Hadn't He reminded his followers that we who live in flesh are all weak and subject to temptation? Each person certainly was glad when she acted rightly, and yet the body, born into the tainted world, often did not walk hand in hand with the unstained soul.

It was so hard to be good all the time.

It was so hard that night when he woke up from an uncomfortably vivid dream of Liath, and it took him a moment, panting to ease himself, to realize he'd been jostled by a foot. In the warm late spring night both shutters and door had been left open, and by the light of a nearly full moon he saw the pale shape of a woman dressed only in her undershift ease down onto the bed shared by Ekkehard, Baldwin, and Milo. Milo was a heavy sleeper under any circumstance, and Ekkehard had been dosed with juice of poppy because the pain as he shifted in his sleep made it difficult for him to rest.

But Baldwin was awake.

"My lord prince!" she whispered. "Your Highness—!" She lay a hand on Baldwin's naked chest.

"I'm not the prince," he murmured, although he did not attempt to remove her hand. "That is Prince Ekkehard, beside me."

"But you're so beautiful, my lord. Like an angel." She reached inside the neck of her tunic. For an instant Ivar saw the pale expanse of her skin as she drew the cloth aside, and he had to close his eyes, he was so flushed everywhere and still aching from the dream that he thought he might lose himself entirely.

"I got me a feather, my lord" she was whispering. "An angel feather."

He couldn't help but look. She hadn't exposed herself but rather a golden feather whose mellow glow set Baldwin's handsome features alight and made the girl seem the prettiest he'd ever seen, dark hair, a small nose, a mole on her right cheek that moved as she smiled. "I knew it were a sign. I've had so many strange dreams ever since I saw them lights in the old stone circle, before the beast come. I dreamed that I'd be visited by an angel. So did Rodlinda and Gisela and Agnes, and she's even been married since last autumn. Isn't that you, my lord? Aren't you the angel? Didn't God send you to come in unto us and give us a revelation?"

Ivar had remained chaste since the day of his revelation, but God surely knew it hadn't been easy.

"Ah!" Baldwin's exhalation made him sound more pleased than surprised as the young woman, not waiting for his answer, moved down over him.

Ivar rolled up and away from snoring Ermanrich, who wouldn't have woken up if a herd of stampeding horses had thundered past, and scrambled outside before he did that which would brand him forever or at least give Ekkehard another thing to make fun of him for. Mercifully, the moon's light allowed him to trudge out of the village through orchard and wood until he reached the pyre, although he stepped on more stickers than he could count and his face and arms got scratched up by low-hanging branches.

Sigfrid had fallen asleep and some kindly soul had thought to drop a ragged blanket over him. His thin fox-face, in repose, was so innocent and sweet that at once Ivar's doubts and desires evaporated and he could kneel with a clear heart. He didn't know why, but he thought it important that someone pray beside the pyre of that brilliant creature which had killed nothing more than food for itself until it had been attacked by lustful men misled by fearful ones. Certainly it had frightened the villagers who, so they'd said, had come across the eviscerated corpses of deer, but wasn't it natural for such creatures to feast on meat? Unlike humankind, animals had no liberty to change what they were and how they acted. Even a creature molded by God needed to eat. It hadn't truly harmed anyone, and maybe it never would have.

Yet perhaps those visions he'd seen rising from the smoke off the pyre had been hallucinations, visions sent by the Enemy. Maybe it was only a matter of time before the beast would have begun preying on the villagers and their livestock. But he doubted it. He had been driven by fear and lust, too; by his own actions, he had helped to kill it.

He wasn't sure of the time. Unlike Sigfrid and Ermanrich, he hadn't learned how to chart by the rising and setting of stars when to begin Vigils, but when he heard a distant cockcrow, he began to sing, chanting the night prayer.

"Why do the wicked prosper, Lady,
while the pure of heart suffer torments on this earth?
Why do they who wear violence as their robe and talk nothing
*   but malice*
live in glorious wealth, untouched by trouble?"

Aurora came as he sang the Benedictus, and Sigfrid stirred and woke, kneeling to pray beside him although, of course, he could utter no words. They saw it long before anyone came to find them: a tiny red-gold fledgling bird fluttering among still-glowing coals. As the light rose, it buried itself deep among the ashes.

At midmorning Milo came to fetch them, looking angry that he had had to make the trip and a little nervous as he examined the still glowing pyre from a safe distance. "Prince Ekkehard wants you," he called. "Isn't that thing out yet? Why do you keep praying out here? It's dead, isn't it?"

Back at the village, Baldwin looked utterly exhausted, as if he hadn't slept at all. He couldn't stop yawning, and perhaps the prince would have noticed something wrong, but he was still woozy, recovering from the poppy juice.

"Perhaps Brother Sigfrid can explain it," Ekkehard was saying as they came in.

Certain members of the village had gathered, come to complain about dreams and disturbances that had plagued them since the mysterious arrival of the beast.

"In truth, good Brother," said the old crone who seemed appointed as their spokeswoman, "we thought these visions would go away once the beast was dead, but it in't any different now.

Worse, maybe. What does God mean by this? Have we done aught wrong? Are we being punished?"

Ermanrich had grown adept at communicating with Sigfrid, with or without writing, and Sigfrid was so far ahead of them all in his understanding and interpretation of God's will that they had tacitly agreed to defer to him on matters of doctrine and scripture.

"What is a soul?" Sigfrid asked, although Ermanrich spoke for him. "It is all that we are, and yet we cannot live on this earth without a body. The blessed Daisan wore a mortal body that was inhabited by an immortal soul, for God so loved the world that She gave to us Her only son, that He should take upon himself the measure of our sins. So He came before the Empress Thaisannia, she of the mask, and He would not bow down before her, for He knew that only God is worthy of worship. The empress had Him flayed, as they did to criminals in those days, and His heart was cut out and thrown onto the ground where it was torn into a hundred pieces by the dogs, for are we not ourselves the dogs, who unthinkingly devour God's treasures in the course of our growling and fighting?"

Baldwin was trying not to yawn again. The villagers present were beginning to look nervous.

Prince Ekkehard was actually able to bend one arm at the elbow so he could rub his nose with the back of a hand. "I think that's enough for now," he said.

"I pray you, believe us!" cried Ermanrich, loud enough that a number of people including some of Ekkehard's other companions jumped. "His blood washed away our sins!"

Sigfrid tugged on Ermanrich's robes and made a complicated signal of signs and grunts, sweeping rushes aside so he could trace letters into the dirt floor of the longhouse.

"Oh!" said Ermanrich, startled enough that for the first time he looked anxious. "Are you sure—Prince Ekkehard said—" Sigfrid nodded his head emphatically. "Uh, well," continued Ermanrich, stuttering only a little. He glanced once at Sigfrid, his good-natured face drawn down in a frown, but Sigfrid's expression was as fixed as adamant stone. "My good Brother Sigfrid says that you who have no faith in the truth of our words will see a miracle at dawn tomorrow, and then you will believe."

Ekkehard called them aside after the villagers had straggled out to spread the news. "What are you talking about? I don't want to lose the goodwill of these villagers by having you babble on and scare them! Baldwin!" Obviously the poppy juice was wearing off, but his arms had more flex and movement in them than they'd had the day before, and he submitted to having his bare shoulders bathed in pine oil water as he scolded Baldwin. "What if we reach my sister and she sends us all home because of your ranting? Ai, God! Nay, leave off!" he snapped at the servant who was probing the bruises on his shoulders. "I will ride out tomorrow. I can ride well enough, I'm much better. Lord protect me! All night I dreamed of naked succubi sighing and moaning beside me in the bed until I thought I'd go mad. I made a promise not to touch any of their daughters, and I don't want to look bad now, not after I made Wichman look so bad in front of them, but we've got to get out of here."

"Truly spoken, Your Highness," said Ivar with a nasty glance at Baldwin.

"Let us go pray at the beast's pyre, my lord prince," said Baldwin. "The villagers stay away from it now, and we'll be at peace."

Ekkehard regarded Ivar with suspicion, as if he'd used sleight of hand to tempt Baldwin away from his rightful lord, but because he wanted to avoid trouble he agreed. Ten of the young men in Ekkehard's company accompanied them back to the pyre.

"This is a change of heart," muttered Ivar as they trod along the path. "I haven't seen you praying much the last few months. Too busy kissing the feet of my lord prince."

"Is this how I'm thanked?" retorted Baldwin. "With your petty grumpiness? Haven't I been protecting you all this time? Didn't I save us from Judith? God help me but I hope you can return the favor, for I can't take another night like the one I just suffered through! They kept sneaking in through the window, one after the next, raving about angels and revelations." He shuddered, but not even a grimace could mar his perfect features. Walking this close to him, Ivar smelled oil of jessamine lingering on his skin, A sprig of dried lavender was caught in his brilliant hair, and Ivar plucked it out and crushed it between his fingers. A faint scent burst, then dissipated.

"God protect us," exclaimed Milo, who was walking at the front. Where the pyre lapped the stream, steam boiled up, and all the ashes and coals were hidden by the churning mist. A scent like flowers distilled to incense permeated the air. A whispery crackling came from the shroud of mist, melding with the babble of water over the stones and the curdling hiss of steam.

"I—I don't like it here," said Milo, taking several steps back, but Baldwin marched right up as close as he could stand and plopped down on his knees.

"Nothing could be worse than what I endured last night!" he proclaimed. "I would rather die than go through that again." Sigfrid nudged him, and he added hastily: "Although of course I know that God protects us. We are meant to be here." He grabbed Sigfrid by the sleeve and jerked him closer, lowering his voice. "Aren't we?"

In this way, somewhat anxiously, the second day passed. Sometimes villagers came to look in on them, as if to make sure they weren't getting up to any mischief, but mostly they were left alone although once or twice Ivar thought he heard giggling at the edge of the distant wood, far enough away that, when he looked back, he only saw pale flashes moving among the trees, dogs or goats, or poor Baldwin's tormentors.

Baldwin prayed more beautifully than anyone, and he could lead them at prayers as long as Ermanrich prompted him.

> *"They who wander far from God are lost,*
> *and they are destroyed, who forsake Her.*
> *But if I desire nothing on earth,*
> *then God shall be my refuge forever."*

In this way, twilight came, and Prince Ekkehard joined them at dusk as they sang the service of Vespers, all of them joining in. Their voices blended sweetly, light tenors and strong ones, and a few deeper voices that still cracked sometimes.

"It stinks in that village," said Ekkehard as the time of silence came upon them, although this night the moon was full and merry. "I'd rather sleep out here. Isn't the fire warm?"

The fire was warm, and it hadn't ceased bubbling in that odd way, but no one else seemed to think anything weird was going on. Ivar felt torn in two: frightened and yet unable to slink away because deep in some unlikely core of his being he could not shake the feeling that something very strange and wonderful was about to happen.

He slept as the moon swept upward to midnight. The crowing of a cock woke him. He lay on the dew-dampened ground with his cheek smashed against a hummock of cold earth and a piece of grass half stuck up his nose. Something was crawling on his face, and he cursed and flicked at it before he pushed up, hoping to get the kink out of his neck.

Nearby, Sigfrid was singing the Benedictus Domina, except Sigfrid couldn't sing anymore, and yet Ivar recognized that voice; he had sung beside Sigfrid so often in Quedlinhame that the other boy's sweet tenor had become his lifeline in the worst of his despair.

Sigfrid was singing, and weeping with joy, and as the auroral dawn breathed the first light and color into the heavy air Ivar saw that the mist had cleared to reveal the pyre grown to a monstrous height, golden-red coals like a thousand gathered stones heaped up upon each other until they rose higher than a man. Ekkehard, coming awake, stumbled up, arms pinwheeling as though he'd forgotten that he'd been injured, and staggered backward, and so did the others, but they ran up against the villagers, who had come in a throng to stare. Now even some of these ventured forward crying out that their toothache had vanished or their lameness been healed. Sigfrid sang with arms lifted toward the heavens, and Ermanrich, who was quite overcome but eminently practical, dragged him bodily back as the pyre heaved and shifted like a creature coming awake. Baldwin knelt so fixedly with hands clasped in prayer that Ivar thought he'd gone into a trance. He dashed forward to shake him, to wake him up, to warn him.

The rising edge of the sun glinted beyond the tumulus where the old stone ruins lay like the shattered and gargantuan crown of a long-dead queen. Day broke free from night.

The pyre opened. A cloud of fragrance burst over them. Flowers showered down around them, insubstantial petals vanishing as soon as they touched the earth.

It unfolded, wings unfurling, and the great beast rose as glorious as the day after a long, black, and hopeless night. It trumpeted. The sound rang from the heavens down to the Earth and back again, echoing on and on and on until Ivar knew that it wasn't an echo at all but an answer.

"The phoenix," cried Sigfrid. "It is the sign of the blessed Daisan, who rose from death to become Life for us all."

It took flight and rose so swiftly into the heavens that the last star winking into oblivion as the sun spilled light everywhere might have been the last flash of its being seen from mortal Earth.

When it was gone, Prince Ekkehard cried out in astonishment and all the villagers exclaimed in surprise and awe: the hurts of every soul there had miraculously vanished.

"You have witnessed the power of the Son and the Mother," said Sigfrid, who alone among them seemed unamazed. His faith had never wavered. "Thus you are healed."

But Ivar knew that its beauty had scarred him forever.

4

"DO not be so impatient. This is only a minor setback. We have over five years to train her to fulfill her part, more than enough time. You are allowing your natural distaste for her conduct to overshadow your reason, Brother. All will unfold by our design."

"So you say. But there have been far too many surprises and setbacks up to now."

Sanglant had to concentrate on staking down the log walkway, swinging his mallet at the same rhythmic pace he had been using before Severus and Anne had emerged from the tower and begun walking toward him. He didn't want them to suspect he was listening. After ten months, they still hadn't figured out how good his hearing was.

"It is true that she must be brought to see what folly it is to be bound by earthly desires. I hope that her confinement and illness have shown her the senselessness of indulging in carnal pleasure."

"We must be rid of that—that brute!"

"Cautiously, Brother. I have tested his strengths in many ways, and I am afraid that the geas his mother set on him is stronger than our magic."

"You mean you can't kill him."

"I cannot. But I have certain ideas. We still hold the strongest piece. We must only wait until we can use it against him."

"You will never persuade her to turn on both husband and child!"

"We shall see, Brother. Let us speak of other things."

They had been strolling down the new walkway all this while and now Sanglant stepped aside to let them pass.

"A good day to you, Prince Sanglant," said Anne to him as they cut around the portion he was staking into place. Brother Severus grunted out something that might have been a greeting.

"Good day," he said, resting the mallet over one shoulder. He had a wild urge to slam the wooden sledge into their smug faces, and for an instant the desire seemed blindingly clever, but he dismissed it as quickly. No doubt Anne protected herself, and anyway, he would hardly maintain Liath's good opinion if he murdered her mother.

Even if she had just admitted to being the person who had tried to kill *him*.

"Will Liath be attending the noon meal?" asked Anne pleasantly, pausing just out of his reach. She could, he reflected, as easily have walked down the path to ask Liath that question herself. But she did not.

"Nay, I think not." He jiggled a log with one foot; he had almost the entire walkway laid between tower and hall. He and Heribert had set the walkway over the worst muddy bits first as the spring rains ground the pathways into sludge, so that Severus and Anne did not even get their slippers dirty as they skirted this last missing section. "She'll eat her meal at our cottage." Then he smiled.

Anne's hound growled at him, sensing his insincerity, perhaps. He had left his Eika dog staked down near Liath, a habit he had fallen into these last two months since the birth of Blessing.

"Very well," said Anne, and she and Severus stepped up onto the other portion of the walkway and continued on. Sister Zoë stood just outside the door to the hall, pretending not to watch. Sanglant admired her from this distance, lush curves suggested by the drape of her robe, and she turned suddenly and vanished into the hall. He laughed, and one of the servants pinched him on the thigh, as if to scold him.

"Hush," he said to it, still chuckling. "I've worked enough this morning. Surely I can amuse myself in such a harmless fashion." But it had already flitted away toward the hall where, no doubt, it would be called upon to serve or clean. He smelled freshly-baked bread and realized then how hungry he was. The walkway could wait. Shifting the mallet to drape across both shoulders, he jumped over the logs and strode back along the winding path, through budding grapes and orchards green with leaves and young fruit, that led to his wife and child.

He heard her before he saw her.

"Nay, nay, of course he did the only thing he could. I can't help but envy her, that she can nurse my daughter and I can't."

He came into sight of the hut to see Liath reclining on the couch Heribert had built for her so that she could lie outside and study in the books that Meriam and Venia brought for her. Heribert sat at the foot of the couch. He had been carving a rattle out of cherrywood, but knife and carving lay still in his hands as he and Liath watched Jerna nursing the baby under the shade of an apple tree.

It was truly an odd sight: he could see the bark of the tree through Jerna's translucent body, and although she seemed to have no substance but air and water, she could still hold the baby for short periods of time, enough to nurse it, before it slipped through her pale body as through a thick pudding and sank softly to the ground.

"What do you think her milk is made of?" whispered Liath, but Heribert could only shrug.

"Blessing grows," he said, as if that were enough. And it was enough.

Liath looked up and saw Sanglant. She got a silly grin on her face; swung her legs off the couch, and levered herself up by clinging to the curling seashell back so painstakingly carved by Heribert out of maple. "No, no," she called. "I'll come to you."

It wasn't far, no more than one hundred steps, but he had to grit his teeth to stop himself from running to help her. She was still so weak, as if all her strength had been drained from her, poured out into the child. She couldn't even light a candlewick. But she could walk a hundred paces and only have to lean on him a little as they walked back together. The warmth of her body against him set off all kinds of sensations, but he carefully eased her back onto the couch, patted the dog, and went to wash his hands and face in cold water at the trough by the door.

By the time he returned, a procession of servants had brought trays of food up from the hall: ale, bread, soft cheese flavored with dill, and a pottage of rye meal flavored with salt and cream. She moved aside so that he could sit beside her, and on the whole they ate silently. He was still stewing over the conversation he'd overheard earlier. How had he overlooked that it might have been Anne all along, trying to kill him? She was the obvious choice.

Did Anne truly mean to set Liath against both him and the baby? And how did she mean to accomplish that?

"You're thoughtful today, my lord prince," said Heribert.

"Ah, but today is the feast day of St. Mercurius the Changeable," retorted Liath, "and many stranger things have happened on this day."

Becoming an invalid had released an unlikely store of humor from some recess deep in Liath's being. She wasn't always very funny, but he always felt obliged to laugh because he didn't want to hurt her feelings, and in any case, it was charming to see her try, who had been so unremittingly serious before.

"It is a strange day," he agreed. "For once I'm heartily sick of work."

"I wish we could go somewhere. I don't think I've ever stayed so long in one place as we have here, except for Heart's Rest, and Qurtubah. I'm used to being on the move. It's beautiful here, truly, but sometimes I feel like a prisoner."

Under the tree Blessing finished nursing and as she squirmed, needing to be burped, she began her slow sink through Jerna's arms and body. Heribert leaped up and ran to fetch her.

"We *are* prisoners," Liath added.

"Hush," said Sanglant, laying a hand over hers. "Come, my love, you're just tired of the view. We'll go to the old cottage up—"

Heribert returned and sat down at his place on the couch, mulishly reluctant to give up the baby. He was making stupid faces at her, exaggerated eyes and grins, cooing and ooing, because Blessing had just started to smile, and it was truly astounding the lengths to which the three of them would go to coax one of those sudden half startled smiles out of the tiny infant.

"I don't know if I can walk that far," said Liath, but she bit her lip, looking up through the orchard and toward the slopes, as if she'd like to tackle it.

"Then you can ride Resuelto."

It was as easy to coax her as it was to coax a smile from Blessing, who was as yet a remarkably easygoing baby. They finished their meal and started up the path with the dog running point. Liath walked as far as she could, and when she faltered among the dogwood, Sanglant simply swung her up onto the back of Resuelto. Heribert had refused to give up Blessing, and Jerna trailed somewhat behind, nervous of Liath as she always was. The path was strewn with flowers and a layer of decaying pine needles. Here and there they passed stumps of trees he had chopped down.

"Ai, Lady," murmured Liath. "Is it terrible of me to wish there was somewhere else to study? Rosvita suggested the convent of St. Valeria, but I think I'm ruined for that now." She laughed as she looked at him in a way that made his skin flush. An invalidish wife made the marriage bed an uncomfortable place, at least for a man who, before Gent, had never needed to practice self-denial. "Imagine the king's schola if mathematici were among those welcome to get an education there!"

"Hush," he murmured, still thinking about the manifold comforts of the marriage bed. "If there are servants about, they'll carry your words to them below."

They came past the birch grove to the high clearing and the barrier of cliff and fallen boulders. Summer flowers had sprung up among the spring primroses and snowdrops. It was still difficult to tell the seasons in a valley where any apple tree bore bud, flower, and fully ripened fruit on every branch. But with Liath he had learned to watch the wheel of the stars, and he knew that summer was almost upon them. Out in the world beyond, the campaign season had begun. Did Henry fight in the east? Had he marched south to Aosta, or was he stalled in the north haggling with or threatening recalcitrant nobles? Had Eika attacked again, or had their defeat at Gent weakened them so badly that it would be a generation before they struck the northern coasts with the same fury they had under Bloodheart?

Remarkably, he could think of Bloodheart now without an unwanted growl slipping from him. He hadn't had a nightmare for two months. He helped Liath off Resuelto. She was so tired, and she dozed off as he settled her down on the pallet in the old hut that they'd made comfortable months ago, the only place they could escape the watchful eyes of Anne's servants. He had certain vivid memories of those days.

"I haven't been up here much" said Heribert, poking around.

"Ah! Liath's scribbling." He displayed a parchment covered with diagrams and equations, then set it aside to pick up an old, cracked leather sole, turning it over to see if he could find a craftsman's mark. He had Blessing tucked into one elbow. She, too, had fallen asleep, and Sanglant took her and settled her tenderly in the crook of Liath's elbow. Liath murmured something, shifting position to pillow the baby against her. With her eyes shut and her lips brushing Blessing's thick black hair, you could almost see a resemblance, but the baby's face was still too unformed.

"Liath's stronger," said Heribert softly, glancing back to make sure that Jerna hadn't followed them inside. "How much longer will you keep her innocent of that which you've discovered?"

"Lord help me, Brother, but I've only confided in you because I can't stand not to talk!" He grinned to take the sting out of the words. "But as long as we have no way free of this place, and she's still this weak, I choose this way of protecting her. Even if it makes me no better than Sister Anne."

Heribert grunted good-naturedly. "A damning comparison, my friend. Yet if she doesn't know the secret of the stones, then how can we run?"

"I would think that if I were them, then that would be the last thing I would teach her. It's an odd thing in her, that she's wise in some ways and so ignorant in others."

"I don't suppose everyone has had your wide experience of life, my lord prince."

He said it jestingly, but Sanglant shuddered. "Nor would I wish it on them."

"Hush," said Heribert, echoing Sanglant's own admonition to Liath, and for an instant Sanglant thought the cleric was comforting him. Then, looking at the cant of his head, he realized Heribert was listening.

Jerna was singing. But it wasn't a song, it wasn't even really a tune but more like the brook's voice.

He slipped outside, Heribert right behind him.

He didn't see her at first, only water slipping over the huge wall of boulders that blocked one edge of the meadow. Heribert tugged on his sleeve and drew him forward, pointing, face flushed and sweating with excitement.

She was singing her way into the rock fall, not gouging a path but opening one that had lain closed and invisible where the brook cut down through the rock.

He waited only long enough to stake down the dog on a long lead by the cottage door before he followed her into the rock fall. Heribert dogged him, clipping his heels once, once grasping at his salamander sword belt when he slipped on a slope of pebbles. But the path was obvious and clearly marked, once you knew you were on it, winding up beside the brook through a spill of boulders as big as cottages and skirting the edge of ragged cliff faces until it speared up a narrow defile and ended on a ledge that looked down into another place. Jerna would come no farther than the last tumble of stones, but Sanglant walked all the way out until the wheel-rutted path turned into a thin trail more like a goat's path. He didn't see any goats although two little gray birds flitted along a nearby rock face, probing in crevices with their slender bills. It was almost a different season here: snow still covered half the hillside although here and there, on the sunniest slopes, gorse bloomed. He took a few steps farther on, kicking snow off the path, and came to rest on an outcropping from which he could view the vista beyond.

Below, a road wound through a steep-sided pass bounded by cliffs and shadowed by three monumentally high peaks that gleamed in the sun. Mist shrouded the highest peak, but the others rose stark and clear against the blue vault of sky, so white that their glare hurt his eyes.

"God preserve us," whispered Heribert, coming up beside him. "This is St. Barnaria's Pass."

"The Alfar Mountains!" breathed Sanglant. "I've never seen them except their foothills in the north. I've never ridden them, though I've heard tales." He was astounded by the high peaks. He had seen them before, of course, from Verna: one had a distinctive crook, as though the summit had slipped slightly to one side. But from this angle, they seemed just so much more massive, and he hadn't before appreciated the vast sheer face of the big middle mountain plunging down to the steep defile that cut into the land below, marking a pass. The road struck straight through the pass, engineered out of stone. Farther along, partially hidden by the thrusting shoulder of a ridge, he saw a cluster of buildings that resembled a monastery and was probably some kind of traveler's hostel.

And indeed he saw travelers on the road, a retinue fit for a grand lady or a nervous merchant hauling spices and silks from the east: a half dozen wagons and a troop of some thirty mounted soldiers and perhaps as many on foot. They were coming from the south in a line that had gotten rather strung out along the way, in part because heavy snow still blocked portions of the road and the wagons were having a hard time getting through. Now, the vanguard turned in to the hostel, and several tiny figures emerged from one of the buildings to greet them.

A banner opened in the breeze, revealing the lion, eagle, and dragon of Wendar. "Lord and Lady!" He heard his own voice tremble as he examined the riders making their way below. "It's Theophanu. Ai, God, look there! It's Captain Fulk and his men."

He had learned to make quick decisions. In battle, how swiftly and resolutely you moved often meant the difference between victory and defeat.

"This may be our only chance," he said, "for it's clear they've hidden the path and we can't come through without Jerna's aid. You go on, Heribert. I have to go back to get Liath and Blessing."

"What do you mean?"

One thing he loved about a troop of good soldiers was that once they trusted you, they knew better than to ask stupid questions. "This is our chance to escape. You descend now, go to Theophanu, and tell her that I'm coming. If we're pursued, we may have to fight."

"But—but I can't go! I'm an outlaw! I'm under censure by the church."

"I don't care what you've done in the past, Heribert. You've been a good friend to me, and I trust you. Throw yourself on Theophanu's mercy. Tell her that I sent you and that I mean for you to reside under her protection, no matter what. Give her—" But he had nothing to give, not even a ring, nothing that she would know was incontrovertibly his, that he would never give up except in death. He had nothing, except their life together as children. "Remind her of the time we saved the robin's eggs from Margrave Judith's cat, and got that bastard Hugh a whipping for almost letting the cat drown." He shoved Heribert forward. "Go!"

No soldier had ever resisted that tone. Even a cleric might find his feet moving before his mind had fully agreed.

Heribert stumbled down the path, fetched up in a drift of snow, arms waving like those of a jellyfish, slave to the currents he was caught up in. "I hate to leave you, my lord prince," he called, looking as if he meant to turn around and come back.

"Heribert," he shouted, almost beside himself, knowing when action was needed and talking of no use, "if it's true about the Lost Ones, that they're to return in an avalanche of fire and blood, then King Henry needs to know! He needs to know that my daughter is the great-great-grandchild of Taillefer! Damn it! Just use your wits. Go!"

Maybe Henry wouldn't believe such an outrageous story, but it didn't matter. Sanglant knew an opportunity when he saw one. He waited only long enough to see Heribert stagger on down the path. Then he turned and sped back up into the rocks. Jerna followed at his shoulder, agitated, plucking at him as if to haul him back, but he was in too much of a hurry to heed her now. He knew what burned in his heart: he was restless; he had recovered. His entire life he had lived as movement, striking when his enemy's line was weak, training new Dragons, hunting, whoring—in all honesty he could scarcely call it anything else—riding from one skirmish to the next to protect his father's kingdom. He wasn't used to inaction, and it felt now as if he had finally woken up from a long, long sleep.

"Liath!" he cried as he slipped out from the hidden crevice with Jerna whimpering behind him, and burst into the meadow. Flowers bloomed in such profusion that the meadow seemed more like a garden, a peaceful paradise.

Except for the ugly stench of blood.

His Eika dog lay by the cottage, throat cut. Green-copper blood soaked into the grass.

Anne was waiting for him, standing patiently by the door with her hands clasped before her exactly in the manner of those of her namesake, St. Anne the Peaceful, whose image he had seen painted on one pier of Taillefer's chapel in Autun. Her hound sat beside her, scratched up around the muzzle, skin stained with copperish fluid, but otherwise unharmed. It stiffened, growling when it saw Sanglant, but Anne stilled it with a touch on its head.

"Brother Heribert will have to take his chances," she said, "but I was rather hoping you might run, too."

He used a word so crude that at first he thought she hadn't understood him, until she spoke.

"Wicked there are in plenty, but you are right in your conclusions. The daimone acted under my orders. You will not find that path again. I had not counted on your loyalty to wife and child, although perhaps it should not surprise me. Dogs often go to the death protecting their own."

He was too angry at his own mistake to do more than gesture toward the dead Eika dog, his last and most faithful follower.

"It would not let us pass. Sister Zoë overcame her abhorrence and carried Blessing down to the tower. Brother Severus led down the horse. Liath still lies asleep inside, since none of us have the brute strength to carry her and she would slip right through the servants' arms." She stepped aside so that he could pass by her, and he tried to draw his sword, but the servants swarmed about him and so clotted the air about his wrist that he could not move it up or down. "She is not meant for that world, Prince Sanglant. Did we neglect to tell you that she has been excommunicated and outlawed by a council presided over by your own father? Nay? That she has dwelt here and learned more of the secrets of the mathematici would only seal her fate. In Darre, they execute mathematici. Go then, leave us. I will still let you depart, alone. It is better this way."

Never let it be said that he did not fight until the last breath, or that he abandoned his own.

He needed to say nothing. They both knew it was war.

He walked past her, into the cottage, to get his wife, and with Anne at his heels and Jerna trailing skittishly behind, he returned mute and furious to Verna.

5

THE chapel at Autun commissioned by Taillefer and built by his craftsmen was the most beautiful building Hanna had ever seen, eight huge pillars separating eight vaults, each arch made of alternating blocks of light and dark stone. On the second level, slender columns rose higher yet, with a third tier of columns above them, illuminated by tall windows. Behind this grandiose octagon lay the ambulatory where hangers-on and servants like Hanna waited, able to see into the central space where the regnant might conduct his ceremonies or wait to be admitted to the apse beyond the eastern vault, where the altar lay.

Taillefer's tomb lay at the center, under the dome. The huge stone coffin was topped by a lifelike effigy, a stone portrait that despite his legendary craftsmen did not quite rival the effigy of Lavastine at Lavas Church. But jewels encrusted his stone robes, formed into stylized roses, and he held in his marble hands a gold crown with seven points, each point set with a gem: a gleaming pearl, lapis lazuli, pale sapphire, carnelian, ruby, emerald, and banded orange-brown sardonyx. A crowd of saints painted onto the stocky piers watched over him, each one so distinctive that Hanna felt that she knew them all, like old and familiar relatives.

But almost everyone else was not observing the saints or the crown but rather the scene unfolding on the dais that held Taillefer's remains.

"No!" Tallia had flung herself at her uncle's feet and was now clutching his ankles with her bony hands. "I beg you, Uncle, if you love me at all, do not leave me here with my mother." Her sobs echoed liquidly in the chapel.

If the scene had not been so embarrassing, Hanna would have laughed outright at the expression on Henry's face. He rarely showed his true feelings so nakedly. "I pray you, Constance," he said to his sister, who reigned as biscop and as duke, "remove her from my sight, if you will. I tender her into your care."

Biscop Constance had the reserve of a woman who is at peace with God and well aware that she also lies blameless in the eyes of the regnant. If she was as disgusted with Tallia as was Henry, Hanna could not tell from the smooth tenor of her face.

"Tallia," she said, pressing a hand onto the girl's thin shoulder, "you must control yourself. You will stay under my care here. That your mother bides here as well is also through her own choosing. As I hear it, you cast aside a vocation at Quedlinhame and then a respectable marriage. Now you will stay at Autun until we see what is to be done with you."

"Pray do not give me into my mother's keeping!" Tallia would not relinquish her grip on Henry's feet, nor did her hoarse sobs quiet. Hanna hoped devoutly that Alain was not one of those Lions on guard duty right now, so that he would be spared this humiliating scene.

Henry had some trouble keeping his balance with Tallia dragging at him like an anchor, but he was able to signal to his servants, and they moved to open the great doors. He clenched one hand and squared his shoulders, as if bracing for a blow.

From where Hanna stood, she could not see the doors pushed open, but a wind blew in from outside and on its sharp summer breath followed an entourage of richly clad servants and noble companions with the jewel of their party glittering in their midst in tawny velvet robes ornamented with gold-embroidered sleeves. Her dark hair was shot through with silver, although she was still robust—she had been born out of a sturdy line. She wore the gold torque of royal kinship at her neck, and she strode forward with no more than a perfunctory nod for the biscop who was her jailer.

"My God. Can this truly be my offspring lying here on the floor like the lowest sniveling beggar? The years have not improved her." She turned to regard her brother with a sudden half smile. "Well, Henry, I hear my stepmother is dead, and I'm sorry for it, for she never treated me ill even if she did push her own children forward to take what was rightfully mine. You look tired, Brother. I hear we are to feast together tonight." Tallia had broken out into fresh screams, as if she were being knifed to death. She rolled herself so hard against Henry's legs that he almost fell over. "Oh, God," continued Sabella, signing to the nearest of her servants. "Can we not be rid of this wailing?"

The mask of stone had concealed Henry's true face again. He said nothing, moved not at all, as certain brawny and unexpectedly attractive young men among Sabella's retinue hurried forward and pried Tallia off her uncle before carrying her, still sobbing and writhing, away.

"Let us pray," said Henry in the silence that followed, "that my blessed mother may rest in the peace she deserves, and that we may all be reconciled as God—and she—would wish."

Biscop Constance bowed her head and lifted her hands as in prayer. "For it was sung in the city of Queen Salomae the Wise, 'let there be peace among sisters and brothers.'" She looked at Henry in a way that suggested to Hanna that she and her brother had had a long conversation about this meeting. "Come." She opened a hand to indicate that they should move forward. "Let us pray."

It was Luciasmass, the first day of summer, and therefore a feast was laid out in the biscop's hall. Hanna had almost become accustomed to the splendor of royal feasts, but even so, Biscop Constance's table had the grandeur and sumptuousness of a feast set out in heaven. White linens swathed the tables, and at every place lay a folded knee covering—a table napkin embroidered with grapevines in green and purple. No person there did not sit on a cushioned bench, or eat off platters of gold or silver or brass, according to her station, that had been polished to such a high gloss that they could also have served as mirrors. Noble girls poured wine for the king and his royal siblings through delicate sieve spoons. A swan, decorated with its own feathers, was brought forward on a gold plate so heavy that it took two men to carry it. Haunches of beef still steaming from the spit were carried to the lower tables, and outside the hall chicken and pork were served to those who could not enter. On midsummer's long afternoon they had no need of candles to light their merrymaking, but fully three harpists traded songs or joined together, not that their music could often be heard above the noise of the feasters or the throngs of petitioners who were led forward at intervals to entreat the king.

Hanna waited behind the king's chair with Hathui and in this way was able to gain a bite of the coveted swan, dark meat swimming in a sauce so pungent that she had to shut her eyes as she savored it. The flavor was so overwhelming that she didn't hear him come in among the newest crowd of arrivals, only heard the king make a terse comment, and then his familiar, grave voice, a man never afraid to speak before the regnant.

"I left Princess Theophanu in Aosta, Your Majesty. She was then whole and healthy, and she had arrived safely with most of her retinue intact after a tremendously difficult journey through the mountains. But as I reported to her myself, Queen Adelheid at that time lay under siege in the city of Vennaci. An Aostan warlord calling himself Lord John Ironhead has been determined to wed her since the news of her young husband's death."

It was indeed Wolfhere, as hale and hearty as ever if that were possible. He saw her standing beside Hathui, and Hanna could have sworn he winked. She was always surprised by how pleased she was to see him.

Henry grunted irritably before he took a sip of wine. "You know nothing more?" He swirled the dregs, staring into the cup like a conjureman of the old religion who could read fortunes from such leavings. "Damned stubborn child," he muttered so softly that only his attendant Eagles and, perhaps, his sister Constance could hear him. "If he had obeyed me and gone—" But he trailed off, then held out his cup so that it could be refilled.

Sabella, at his left, regarded the Eagle who knelt before Henry with a quizzical eye, rather like a woman who wonders if the dancing bear can also talk. "I've heard news of this Ironhead from one of my clerics, who was educated in Aosta," she said. "It's rumored he murdered his nobly-born half brother and married the widow. But if he's pursuing Queen Adelheid, the woman must be dead. Or retired to the convent."

If Wolfhere was surprised to see Sabella feasting at table with her brother, he did not show it. He only inclined his head in agreement. "I met Lord John, Your Highness. I expect that retirement to a convent would be a merciful release from his attentions for a woman of noble breeding."

Sabella snorted, looking well entertained.

"There is other news," added Wolfhere. "While I was still in Karrone after crossing the mountains, we heard news that Ironhead had pursued Queen Adelheid and Princess Theophanu into the hills northwest of Vennaci. They took refuge at a small convent in the Capardian wilderness. Since then, I have heard nothing more."

While Henry mulled over this troubling news, Hanna was given leave to take Wolfhere outside and see that he was fed.

"Why didn't you stay with them?" she asked.

"I had other duties, as you know, Hanna, and other messages to deliver. How fares it with you?"

She sat with him and told him of her adventures while he picked clean half a chicken that was only slightly charred from too much roasting, then washed it down with bread and ale.

"What do you think these dreams mean?" she concluded. "Are they true visions, or false ones?"

"I cannot tell you. An indigestion in your stomach might cause them. Or it may be you have picked up a strange destiny. I have caught a stone in my shoe now and again, and once it was a beautiful agate that I polished and hung on a chain." He smiled as at a very old memory. "Nay, I cannot say. I know little of the Eastern tribes." He chuckled. "I met Prince Bayan in earlier days. Who would have thought Princess Sapientia would have liked him so well?"

"Who would have thought," muttered Hanna, "that she would have liked him better than Father Hugh? Do you know where Liath is, Wolfhere?"

"Somewhere safe, I should hope," he replied smoothly. " It would go ill for her to return to a court where she would face trial on the charge of sorcery."

Since Wolfhere was always surprising her, it took her a moment to respond. "How can you know what happened at the Council of Autun? I only learned of it ten days ago when I joined the king's progress."

The summer evening had a drowsy light to it, not quite day and not quite night. "You have seen enough, Hanna," he said at last. "I can trust you with the Eagle's sight."

"What is the Eagle's sight?" she demanded, but she already had her suspicions.

"Meet me tomorrow at cockcrow out beyond the Lions' encampment." He would say no more.

In Taillefer's chapel the clerics were singing Vigils as she made her way past stables and palace to the field where three hundreds of Lions had set up their campground, with small tents and larger pavilions, wagons placed in a corral, and a dirt arena roped off for training.

Some few Lions were up and about. As commoners and field soldiers, they marched with few servants, and part of their duties were to take care of themselves like the Dariyan legionnaires of old who, it was said, dug their own earthen forts each night when they were on campaign and moreover did not scorn doing so.

She could not pass the sentries without looking for her old friends, but as it happened, she found Ingo out by the wagons with a piece of sausage in his hand and a kitten hissing at him from behind a wagon wheel.

"Friend!" she called just as the kitten scratched, and he yelped, dropping the bit of sausage. The kitten scampered into a mound of straw lying heaped up along the axle. "Now that's a dangerous foe," she said, crouching beside him. "I beg pardon for startling you. It looks like a hard-fought battle."

He sucked on his scratched finger. "Poor things. Their dam was run over by one of the water wagons yesterday and we've tried to coax them out, but they won't come near even to take a bit of meat."

The waning quarter moon hung low at the trees. The stars were fading as dawn grew around them.

"Skittish," said Hanna. "So my dam always said, that you can't shove a child among strangers and expect it to sing and dance." He smiled. Picking up the sausage, he held it out again and clucked under his tongue, hoping to tease out the kittens. She heard their sharp and almost laughable hisses from their hiding place in the straw. "I haven't seen your new recruit at the palace," she added.

Ingo shrugged without taking his eyes off the straw, which had a pronounced wiggle and slip to it; briefly, a gray tail peeped through, then vanished. "Thiadbold's captain of our company now," he said, "and he's decided to keep him busy here in the camp for the time being. No need to make him suffer more than he has already, poor lad. After all he went through, he hasn't a bad word to say of anyone."

"She turned on him," said Hanna in a low voice. "But perhaps he was a bad husband."

"Hush, friend," said Ingo suddenly. He rose, and she shifted to see a tall figure coming down the line of wagons with a shovel resting on his shoulder and two huge dogs walking at his heels. He stumbled to a halt just before them and almost tripped. The dogs sat down as polite as you please, without a noise. But she saw who they were now, and she couldn't help rising to face them, though they made not one threatening sound or movement.

"I beg your pardon, Ingo," said Alain. "I didn't see you." He saw Hanna, too, and offered a polite greeting. Obviously he didn't know who she was, and she wasn't about to remind him of Liath, whom he might associate with happier days. He gestured toward the wagon. "Are we moving out today? I didn't hear any orders."

"Nay, not today. It's those kittens—"

"Ah." He, too, seemed to know about the kittens. He knelt

by the wheel, setting the shovel down, and examined the now-motionless heap of straw.

This close to the shovel, Hanna could smell the pungent aroma of the pits and see bits of dirt and stickier substances clinging to the spade's edge. He had been on nightsoil duty, an odd chore for a man who had not ten days ago walked among the great princes of the realm. But if the labor annoyed him, she could see no trace of resentment on his face; he had an interesting profile, clean, a little sharp because of the cut of his nose. His dark hair was growing out raggedly and had been caught back with a leather string. At this moment, he stared so intently at the straw that she wondered if he had forgotten she and Ingo crouched beside him. Slowly he extended a hand; he made the slightest whistling noise under his breath, hardly a sound at all, but the straw wiggled and shuddered and a tiny pink nose peeped out, then a second, beside it.

His hand did not move, nor had he taken the sausage from Ingo. The gray kitten slipped out of the straw and tottered skittishly forward, sniffed his fingers, then with its little pink tongue began to lick. A second shadow, more motley than gray, staggered out beside the first, followed by a third.

Hanna was afraid to move. Ingo seemed frozen with amazement, sausage dangling limp from his fingers. The hounds watched, eerily silent. One settled down to lick a paw.

After the kittens had licked Alain's fingers, he turned his hand over slowly and stroked them until tiny purrs rumbled. Still moving cautiously, he scooped them up against his chest, where they settled down, faces hidden.

"I'll take them to Cook," he murmured. "Maybe they'll take some cream." He gestured with a foot toward the shovel. "I'll come back—"

"Nay, comrade," said Ingo. "I'll take the shovel to its place."

"Thank you," said Alain, and with his burden and his disquieting attendants, he walked on down the line of wagons and vanished into camp.

"Well," said Hanna. "What do you make of that?"

"He's a strange one, in truth," said Ingo, staring after Alain with a pensive expression. "Not disrespectful or arrogant, considering what he was. Nor is he humble and groveling either. You'd think he'd always been a Lion, really. Yet when I saw him sit among the lords, I never doubted he belonged there. And those hounds. Fierce as lions 'round anyone else but him, and with him they might as well be lambs."

"I thought the hounds belonged to the Lavas counts! Didn't they stay with Lord Geoffrey?"

"Nay, they're here in camp. I don't know if they followed him or if Lord Geoffrey turned them out. Still, it's very odd."

She left him there, thinking it odd herself, but she was late, and Wolfhere was waiting out beyond the sentries where a campfire burned. He was just feeding it another log when he saw her and indicated that she should sit down opposite him.

"I had hoped Hathui could come as well, but she must stay beside the king."

"He trusts and respects her."

"As he should," retorted Wolfhere, but then he smiled his wolf's grin, sharp, deadly, and oddly reassuring. "I've a trick to teach you. We call it Eagle's Sight. It's a way of seeing long distances through fire."

Hanna laughed at such an absurd claim.

"Yet you believe me, don't you?" he observed. "With proper training, many Eagles can learn to see through fire any person we have observed closely enough that we can form their likeness in our minds. In time, you may learn to hear voices within the flames as well, but that won't happen at first. And I must warn you that some people simply are blind. If that proves so for you, Hanna, then think no worse of yourself."

"Only envy those who aren't blind!"

"Here, now. Look into the fire. See nothing, not even the flames. No, *truly* see nothing. Expect nothing. See what lies beyond the flames, not my hands or the trees or the camp, but that stillness which lies at the heart of all things. That stillness links all of us, and through it as through a window we can see."

She sat as still as she could, just staring.

"Good," he whispered. Clearly he felt something she did not. She felt only the heat of the flames and yet a taste of some other pulse, another thread that drew her toward the wasp sting in her heart. Shadows quivered in the flames, and for an instant she thought she saw the profile of the Kerayit princess. "Tell me who you see," he murmured.

"Liath," she whispered. "I want to see Liath."

And she saw something truly, not flames, not shadows, but

a wall, like a veil of fire. "Is that the Chamber of Light? Ai, God. Is she dead?"

"Or only hidden from us," he replied so calmly that her fears dissolved. "You're fast to catch on to this, Hanna. I begin to think your dreams are true dreams, and that some portion of your soul has already opened to these teachings."

"But I don't *see* anything!" Frustrated, she wiped a hand over her eyes, which stung from the smoke. "Ai, Lady! Isn't this sorcery? Am I imperiling my immortal soul by doing this?"

He sat back, relaxing. "Nay, child. This skill you use for the sake of the king. With Eagle's Sight you can gather intelligence hidden by distance or through intrigue. When you travel, you can find the king's progress more easily if you know where he's traveling."

She chuckled. "Rather than track him always two days behind! No wonder you arrive so quickly, and with so few detours."

"Have you seen enough? The sun is rising, and we've our duties to attend to."

"And no doubt look a little crazy staring into the fire like this. But—may I try one more time? What about Prince Sanglant? Surely if he's with Liath, then I would at least know where Liath is."

He simply lifted a hand, as if he hadn't the energy to dissuade her. Yet as the fire burned and snapped, she saw nothing, and she began to think that he was only humoring her, that she'd never seen anything at all in the flames.

"Well, then, one last time," she said, because Mistress Birta's daughter wasn't one to give up so easily. "I tell you truly, Wolfhere, I've always wondered what became of Biscop Antonia and Brother Heribert, if they really did survive that avalanche. Lady knows I got to know their faces well enough. Poor Heribert. He seemed harmless enough. I always wondered why he was so loyal to her."

At first she thought it was smoke, a wet branch caught in the middle of the fire. But the shadow spread and grew form, and Wolfhere made a little noise, almost inaudible, what a mouse might utter when the cat sprang upon it.

"We dare not delay any longer," says a woman whose silhouette is regal and whose voice is cool and measured. It is a familiar voice, but through the agency of flame Hanna cannot

quite make out the secret of its timbre. "We left Novomo before we were certain the pass was open because we got word that Ironhead was marching north to take Adelheid into custody. He styles himself king of Aosta now."

Was that hiss the flames, or Wolfhere?

A supplicant kneels before the great lady. "He meant to follow me at once, Your Highness. If he did not, then he was held against his will."

More shapes cluster beyond the flames yet somehow still in them; they are like the shadows of buildings seen beyond a palisade, and one among them speaks. "We found nothing, Your Highness. The goat track runs out on the hillside, and the cliffs are too steep to climb. Either he is lying to save his own skin—"

"Or there is more magic loose than we have ever suspected," says the regal woman. *"After everything we have seen, I think we must believe the latter. Nay, I am convinced this man was with my brother. Can you not tell me more, Brother Heribert?"*

Is this a true vision, or a false one? Hanna dared not speak for fear that her voice would scatter the shadows. Was it truly Brother Heribert? Where had he been hiding all this time?

"I can say no more except that he was alive and healthy when I left him. I fear to say any more, Your Highness. Some words are better left unspoken."

"It's a thin reed to build a bridge on," says the man in the distant shadows.

"Once more, where is my brother?" she asks.

"If he did not follow, then he could not follow," insists Heribert. *"There are powers you do not comprehend—"* He seems afraid to say more.

"What, then, do you suggest, Brother?" She sounds slightly exasperated, and Hanna begins to believe that the curve of her shoulders isn't natural, it's a cape, some item of clothing common to travelers; the regal woman is simply ready to leave and is only waiting to receive, or to give, the final word.

"What he said himself. Go to the king, as you mean to do in any case."

"King Henry himself sealed the document that ordered you to be censured and taken before the skopos. Dare you to go before him now, knowing what might await you?"

"I trust you to protect me, Your Highness. Prince Sanglant said you would."

"Ai!" She sounds pained and amused together. *"So I am bound by his word, damn him."* That shadow within the shadow, the slash of her mouth, is a smile. *"You would risk this for him?"*

"Who would not?" he asks, sounding honestly surprised, and her laughter in answer is sharp. *"There is one other thing, Your Highness. I pray you, may I speak to you privately?"*

She gestures, but not all the shadows recede. *"Trust you this man, Princess?"* asks her counselor.

"I trust my brother, Captain Fulk," she answers, *"and so do you."* As flames shift and leap Hanna now sees only two shadows wavering in the fire.

When Heribert speaks again, at first she can scarcely hear him. *"He has a child."*

"A child! By the Eagle?"

"What mean you, the Eagle?"

"The woman called Liathano."

"Yes, by Liath. He believes that Liath, and thus his daughter, is descended from—"

Dirt flew in her face. Wolfhere had leaped to his feet and kicked ashes and earth over the fire, and it guttered as she coughed and spat. But he was already leaving, striding away with his shoulders set so tensely that she almost feared to run after him.

But she had too many questions. She had seen too much to fear him now. And she was still spitting dirt and hot ashes from her lips.

"Wolfhere!" She ran, and although he did not quicken his pace, she was panting hard by the time she caught him. "Why did you do that? Wasn't that Princess Theophanu? Why is Brother Heribert with her, and why is he speaking of Prince Sanglant as though they were old companions? Did he truly mean that Liath and Sanglant had a child together? Is what I saw true, or only a vision sent from the Enemy?"

"Your time with Liath marked you," said Wolfhere harshly. And then, with an agony that did not show in his expression: "Have I misjudged her so completely? Has she changed so much?"

"But—"

He turned on her with an expression more fitting for a man who has just seen Death riding down the road in his direction. "Go to Hathui and serve her and the Eagles well. But don't ask me any more questions, for I cannot and will not answer them. You have a good heart, and I like you. Stay away from that which you can't comprehend."

He would say no more, although she followed him like a lost puppy, still asking questions. He did not even acknowledge her, only went to the stables and commandeered a horse although he hadn't the king's permission to leave. He would not answer her, he just left, riding out of Autun without looking back.

After the noon meal Henry called Hanna before him in the private garden of the biscop's palace. "Hathui says that you witnessed the departure of Wolfhere."

"I did, Your Majesty."

"He left without permission from me, or orders from any of my stewards or chamberlains."

She looked first at Hathui, but the other woman only lifted her chin, a signal Hanna could not interpret. After all, she was the King's Eagle. It was to him she owed her loyalty, wasn't it? "So he did, Your Majesty. But I know not where he was bound."

"Hathui?"

"I do not know either, Your Majesty," Hathui replied with obvious reluctance.

He slapped his leg hard enough that the sound made Hanna jump. "I knew he would betray himself some day." He seemed exultant. "The faithful Eagle abandons his post. So be it. I place him under the regnant's ban. If he is seen again by any woman or man loyal to me, let him be taken into custody and brought before me in chains, for desertion." He turned that pitiless lightning gaze on Hanna. "Know you what brought about his flight? Fear not, Daughter. I can see you are innocent of his treachery."

She could not lie. She saw in an instant that he comprehended the whole of her guilt.

She bowed her head in a vain attempt to gather her thoughts. Bricks paved the walkway she knelt on, set in a lozenge pattern that repeated itself on and on and on around the square path that enclosed a central gazebo. When she looked up again, the king had leaned forward from the cushioned bench on which he sat, balancing himself with an elbow on one knee.

"Go on," he said, although she had not yet said anything.

"You know of that skill called the Eagle's Sight?" she asked.

No flicker of surprise or distaste marred his expression. He remained masked with dignity. "My father told me certain things known only to the heir. Indeed, it was Wolfhere who brought the trick of the Eagle's Sight to your company. Did you know that?" She did not, and he must have recognized it from her expression because he went on. "For that and many other things my father honored Wolfhere and made him his boon companion. But I know otherwise. What did you see?"

"This, Your Majesty. First, a woman I believe was Princess Theophanu, interviewing a man who called himself Brother Heribert. That same Heribert, I believe, who was sent to Darre with Biscop Antonia and who vanished with her in the avalanche that I myself witnessed. I was curious what might have become of them—" But she broke off, struggling back to the warp of the tale. The king remained silent, listening. "The princess said that Lord John Ironhead was marching in pursuit of Adelheid, and that he had been crowned king of Aosta." Henry grunted, like a man kicked in the stomach, but said nothing. "Brother Heribert told the princess that he had shortly before been with Prince Sanglant—" Now she had his attention fully, and she didn't like it. "But that the prince was somehow prevented from following him. Heribert said that the prince would want him to travel on to you, Your Majesty. He had a child—"

"Brother Heribert had a child?"

"Nay, Your Majesty, forgive me. Brother Heribert said that Prince Sanglant had had a child by Liath." She clenched her jaw, waiting.

Henry narrowed his eyes to slits and shook his head, as when the child who claims to be too clumsy to hunt comes home with the first boar of the season. "God help me for having sired such a stubborn son. If I could get Adelheid for him, then there would only be Ironhead to drive out, and the child he needs to prove his fitness is already born." After a moment, he remembered her. It was terrible to be focused under that gaze. She had never realized his eyes were such a complex shade of brown, veined with yellow and an incandescent leaf-green. "What other news can you bring me of my son? Where is he?"

"I do not know, Your Majesty. I saw no landmarks, nor do I know whether they spoke indoors or out. But Heribert said one thing more. He said that Liath, and the child, were descended from—"

A gate opened, and Biscop Constance emerged into the garden, saw her brother, and began to walk toward them.

"Descended from—?" Henry glanced up, saw Constance, and lifted a hand to wave her over. Then he looked back at Hanna.

"That was the end, Your Majesty. I heard nothing more. I am not sure that Wolfhere didn't kick the fire out to conceal the rest."

Henry said nothing, only sat back and fingered the gold torque he wore, symbol of his royal kinship and right to rule. Here at his ease in the noonday garden he wore no royal robes; in truth, Hanna had rarely seen him robed and crowned in the regnant's dignity. He wore the dress common to every Wendish noble, a richly-embroidered tunic, leggings, sandals, and the various handsome rings worn by any great prince of the realm. One of these he drew off now and gave to Hanna.

She gaped at it: an oiled and polished emerald of a pale and almost milky green, set in thick gold band studded with tiny blood-red garnets.

"What news, brother?" asked Biscop Constance, sitting down beside him without asking his leave. "You have that certain smile on your face. I think the cats did not get the cream today."

"I had thought it might be prudent to travel to Wayland, but instead I have been visited with a blessing in the person of this Eagle. She will ride back to Sapientia with two hundreds of Lions and fifty cavalry to fight in the east. But I will ride south to seek out Theophanu."

"South to Aosta? Do you think that wise, Brother? You would do better to make your peace with Conrad in Wayland before you begin any grand enterprises."

But he had put on the mask of stone, and Hanna had never seen anyone—even his powerful sisters—argue with him when he was in this mood. "I believe that many unexpected things will come of this. Indeed, I am sure of it."

XIII
THE INVISIBLE TIDE

1

PERHAPS it was a blessing, after all, that he be allowed to march away from the memories that afflicted him. Walking for hours a day in the summer had a certain soothing rhythm, balm to the heart, and at night he never had any trouble sleeping once he had gotten camp pitched and pits dug and eaten a meal of flat bread and beans, all made heartier with ale or sweetened vinegar. The king kept his milites strong by feeding them well, and their pace was brisk enough that only the most determined camp followers could straggle along.

Still, it broke his heart to see them: peddlers hawking their wares; beggars holding out gourd cups in hope of a scrap of bread or thin soup; youths hoping to join the famous Lions or just gain a bit of experience fixing wheels or grooming the cart horses; women and boys come to trade favors for food or a trinket. Sometimes a Lion would even shelter a sweetheart on the long march, although that was against the rules. The captains were strict: as long as no one shirked chores or fell behind, they would look the other way.

The cavalry were another story, of course. They moved both faster and more slowly, helped and hindered by their fine horses and their little entourages, a groom, a servant, a concubine, and a camp-boy for the least of them and rather more servants for the greater.

He was digging out the night pits with Folquin when he saw her for the second time, a pale figure in dirty novice's robes kneeling before a pair of beggars who had swung into the procession three nights before: a brawny man with the face of a frightened child and his companion, a wizened man who had no feet. "Look there." He nudged Folquin with the butt of his shovel. "Do you see her?" She had poured water into a cup and was offering it to the crippled man.

Folquin had lost his only other tunic at dice last night, and he was in an irritable mood today, jabbing at the dirt with angry grunts. "Huh?" he said, looking up abruptly.

"That woman—" But she was already gone, slipped away into the whores' makeshift encampment. At this time of the evening, various of the cavalrymen, unencumbered by any work except riding to war, were out strolling in twos or threes, looking for trouble, or a bit of pleasure, or some combination of the two.

"Do you fancy one of them, then?" asked Folquin. "I thought—" Sorrow growled softly, and Folquin struck himself on the head. He was a good soul, if a little reckless, and easy to get along with. "I beg your pardon. It's nothing to jest about."

"Nay, don't mind it." Alain patted Sorrow on the head reprovingly, and he settled down again beside Rage. "It wasn't your fault. But I could swear I know her. And if it's who I think it is, she's got no business traveling with the army."

"Who do you think it is?"

"My wi—" He bit off the word, stabbed by the old shame. "Nay, I must be mistaken."

"Here, I tell you what," said Folquin hastily. "I'll take your first hour of watch and you can go looking for her. Then you'll know whether you're mistaken." He got a good spadeful of dirt and tossed it above the ditch. "I always hate it when I can't stop thinking over something that might be, or might not have been. If only I hadn't rolled a deuce!"

Alain had to laugh. "If only you hadn't rolled at all."

"Nay, leave off, I beg you," cried Folquin, leaning on his shovel and grinning, "you won't be lecturing me as Ingo did, will you?"

"Nay, not as Ingo did. In my very own way, I'm sure. Didn't your own aunt weave that tunic for you?"

Folquin groaned, pounding his head against the shovel's haft. "Ai, God! Have mercy! Ingo calling me a shameless gambler was bad enough. Now this! My poor aunt. How can I ever face her now? She'll know how careless I was with the things she. gifted me with."

"And sweated over."

Alain had discovered that Folquin's adventurous heart concealed a very real devotion to his distant family, the same ones he'd abandoned for the life of a King's Lion. He was always collecting pretty ribands and little luxurious household items, like a wooden sieve-spoon that was a copy of the silver and gold ones used by noble ladies in the great halls, for his younger sisters; he had friends enough among the Eagles that on occasion one of them would deliver a package made up of such items to his village, if they happened to pass that way.

Now as a bit of rain spattered over them, warm and refreshing, he saw that Folquin truly looked remorseful. "It's true, isn't it? I risked something that I'd no right to wager on, for it was like she gave me a piece of her heart when she gifted me with that tunic."

"Here, now," said Alain quickly, "you lost it to Dedi in third cohort, didn't you? Maybe we can offer to take some of his duties in exchange. I don't know what Ingo would say, for he's enough responsibilities, but I wouldn't mind taking a turn at Dedi's privy digging for a night. If you and Stephen and Leo did as well, and explained the matter to Dedi, too, then why shouldn't he be willing to return the tunic?"

Folquin straightened up and stared at him for a moment in the most uncomfortable way. He had curly hair, cropped short. He tugged on it now, a habitual gesture, before turning back to his digging. "I'd be grateful," he said in a low voice. "And I meant what I said about you looking for that woman tonight, if you've a mind to. I'll take your watch."

By the time they had eaten their night's meal, the day had passed into that long hazy twilight that in summer lingers on and on. For some reason it was a loud evening at the whores' encampment, a straggle of tents, shelters, and awkward lean-tos made of canvas roped to trees that rose and fell each night as the army marched east. Perhaps the cooling rains had given a second wind to the cavalrymen. A bard played while three women danced for an appreciative audience. In the shadows, items changed hands, and hands sought under skirts for that which was hidden. The bounty in breasts was more evident than the bounty in almsgiving, for there were more beggars than usual, too, children with palsied hands, thin women in torn skirts and mended, filthy tunics, withered old men shoved out of the way by robust young lords who were seeking release from that boredom which is the burden of the well-fed. Alain had forgotten to set food aside as he sometimes did, and the sight of so much suffering chafed. But there was always suffering in the world. Rage and Sorrow padded beside him, and he never minded their presence. On a night like this, in such surroundings, it kept the peddlers and the whores away. He really didn't want to have a woman leaning up against him, offering him the very thing Tallia had denied him for so long. Surely some good must come out of the promise he had kept to her; he had never done violence to the oath she had made, even if he couldn't help but look on the women now and wonder what it would be like to take that which they offered more freely than Tallia had.

But all things came with a price.

Rage whined, slewing her head round as she caught a sound, or a scent, that he couldn't yet hear. He didn't see the one he was looking for. Surely he had only imagined her earlier.

He heard the noises coming from a dense thicket beyond a broad stream. At first he thought that frenzied grunting was a rootling pig. When he heard low, hard male laughter, he realized he was hearing a desperate and one-sided struggle. He didn't hesitate, thought no more of getting his feet wet than of thrusting aside the leafy branches with his forearms and stumbling into a dome of low-hanging leaves and branches where two men hunkered over to watch a third wrestle on the ground with a woman in a dirty robe who was trying to scramble away. It was her, grunting hopelessly. It was them, laughing.

A moment later, he realized who she was.

Leaves dragged on his hair as he crashed forward. Under the dome of leaves, it was darker, as if a shroud had been drawn over the sun. Forest litter smothered the footfalls of his boots. The hounds pushed through the thicket behind him. The men turned.

"Ho! Dietrich, we have company!"

"Leave us be!" the one on the ground snarled.

One of his comrades, clearly drunk, giggled. "Nay, let him join in. If she won't take coin then she'll take what she gets, eh? More than enough for four."

He didn't try to fight them. They were three, and he only one, but he shoved through the dome of vegetation around them, getting his face and hands all scratched up, and grabbed hold of the woman's wrist. Alain dragged her backward while she fought half against him and half against the man still groping for her thighs, his own tunic hiked up to his hips to expose a vast fleshy expanse. He had wits enough to pull her out into the woodland, not to the stream where her predicament would become a public scene to be laughed over.

The three men followed him, thrashing and swearing, and he shoved the young woman behind him and waited for them. They weren't all taller than he was, but they had the muscular arms and proud faces of noble sons accustomed to privilege. They rushed him like three bulls, but he stood his ground and raised one hand, pitching his voice to carry. He knew how to do it now, because he had once been a lord mightier than they. And he had Rage and Sorrow at his side.

"How dare you molest this holy woman!"

The words brought them up short, or perhaps the hounds did, standing silent and massive with muzzles pulled back to reveal their teeth and their great bodies poised for attack.

"Look at the size of those dogs," muttered the first. "Where's my damned sword?" He had to grope a little—overcompensating for drink—but he found the hilt and drew the blade.

The second flexed his knuckles and then clenched his hands, grinning at the prospect of a fight. He cast around and found a stick, beat it twice on the ground to test its heft.

Yet with the hounds at his side, Alain felt no fear. It might even be possible that these young lordlings could beat him, scar him and best him, even pitted against the hounds, but that would be a minor crime compared to their assault on *her*.

"What manner of men are you, who would assault a holy woman sworn to the church—"

"And found consorting with the whores!" cried the man who'd been on the ground. He finished hitching up his belt, drew his knife, and fingered it menacingly. "Get out of our way, Lion. You've no right to be interfering with us. And I want no trouble with those hounds. If she's your paramour, I'll pay you for damages, but there is no whore-woman who'll say nay to me in that fashion and get away with it. By God, I'd be shamed before my comrades!"

"You'll be shamed before God!" said Alain, low and furious. "What manner of parent raised you to think that your pride matters more than this innocent woman's fear? That your lust matters more than her charity? *She* has cast aside every luxury and every privilege to minister to the poor, who are God's creatures as much as we are. What have you cast aside? You cannot even walk one step without dragging your own vainglory with you, as if God made this world solely for you to take your pleasure in it. You cannot even take in one breath of air without filling your heart with wrath because you have forgotten that compassion should rule in our hearts, not self-love. You are an empty shell, pumping and groaning in the night, and long before you take the last step off into the Abyss you will find that you wander on this earth no better than a rotting corpse because all that is good in you will have fled and all that is thoughtless and bestial will have eaten you alive."

For some reason, the three men had fallen back, and as he took a step toward them, they fell to their knees.

"The blessed Daisan taught us that good is natural to humankind, but that evil is the work of the Enemy. In whose camp do you intend to muster? Choose your place now."

He was actually shaking, he was so angry. And he did not know, nor did he care, how they meant to respond. When they began to weep and beg his forgiveness, he was surprised enough that he could not think of one word to say to them, and in the end they staggered up and stumbled off back to their camp, still hanging on each other, trembling and moaning.

"My lord."

In his fury, he had forgotten her. Now he turned. She was kneeling, shawl torn from her head, hair half tumbling down her shoulders. Her robe was stained with dirt and vegetation, and she had gotten leaner in the face, but she still had the habit of blinking at him, marmotlike, a helpless animal needing shelter.

"Lady Hathumod." He extended a hand to help her up, but she shrank away from him, or from the hounds, who had come up on either side of her. Standing, their heads came level to hers where she knelt. "Pray tell me you haven't been injured."

"Nothing more than scratches, my lord."

"You shouldn't be here. How are you keeping yourself? Surely not—"

"Nay, my lord," she said, gaze dropping, suddenly embarrassed. She had lost her slippers or worn them out: her bare feet, untangled from the robe, were blistered and bloody.

"I pray you, forgive me. Of course you were not. But then how are you living? I saw you a few days ago, and then again tonight, bringing water to the beggars. Who is keeping you?" He knew she could not be keeping herself. How could a noble-woman's daughter survive outside the hall or the cloister unless like some young noble ladies she chose to ride to war with her brothers?

"The whores keep me, my lord. There's no churchwoman who preaches the word to them, or sings mass for them, or blesses them. They are as eager as any soul to hear the good news. Isn't it good news to them that the blessed Daisan took upon his own body our pains and our sins, and in this way brought Life to all humankind? Isn't it a comfort to them, who know no other way of life but sinning? Shouldn't we minister to the sick and the afflicted before we give our substance to those who live in comfort, my lord?"

"I beg you," he said, because the words were as painful as a knife cut, "do not call me by a title I can no longer claim."

She pressed hands to her forehead but did not answer.

"You can't travel with the army, Lady Hathumod. It isn't right. We'll come to a convent, and I'm sure they'll take in a young woman of your birth and education and good sense."

"God have mercy, my lord." She swayed forward, clung to his hand. "Do not make me leave you."

Was it possible that she loved him in the same hopeless way that he loved Tallia? Or was she merely clinging to someone familiar in a world that must seem strange to her, severed from the noble way of life she had become accustomed to? Either way, he owed her gentleness.

He helped her rise and walked with her back into camp. She showed him the tent where she slept. They had to wait there a few moments until a blowsy woman emerged and, behind her, a Lion from the third cohort who was straightening his tunic, a man Alain vaguely recognized but didn't know. He greeted Alain without embarrassment and walked away, whistling. The whore took a swig of cider and looked Alain over.

She wasn't a pretty woman, but she had the knack of letting the neck of her shift hang low over her breasts, and she knew how to set hand to hip and jut out her leg just so, to suggest goods for sale in the market.

Was this how his mother had looked? Or had she still retained some flower of innocence blooming somehow in the mire of her life? Henri had always said she was beautiful. How would his mother have looked had she lived on, with all the beauty hardened out of her like sap squeezed from a young tree? Was beauty doomed to wither where its goodness was not nurtured? Could beauty only arise out of innocence and purity? Or was it a quality entirely unrelated to anything but the accident of its presence in the world?

"I pray you," he said to the whore. "I just saved Sister Hathumod from being raped. They'd dragged her into the bushes—"

"That would be Lord Dietrich," said the whore, looking Hathumod over with a resigned sigh, probing at her ribs and abdomen while Hathumod stood with head bowed. The young novice was ashamed, or humiliated, or uncaring; he couldn't tell which. "He's gone through every woman in the train, and he's looking for fresher prey."

"Is there anything that can be done to protect her?"

She had a smile no more scornful than that of those hard-eyed noblewomen who oversaw extensive estates and flogged their servants when they were angry. "From the lords?" She laughed. "You Lions are more honest than them. We're lucky if they give us food after they've taken what they want." With a practiced touch, she hooked fingers up between Hathumod's thighs and felt at her groin. Alain looked away quickly, ashamed on Hathumod's behalf, but Hathumod only gasped, shuddering, hands hiding her face. She didn't even protest. The whore sniffed her fingers, then shook her head as she addressed Alain. "No harm done, this time. But there's not much we can do for her, friend. She's a bit touched in the head, thinks she's a noble lady's get, and while I grant you she's well spoken, I don't see any retinue following at her heels. She hasn't a clue how to take care of herself. She brings us nothing to eat for she's no way of getting food and no possessions to trade. We've been feeding her in exchange for her preaching, for truly she's got no other skills. She can't even mend a tear in a skirt."

He knew a bargainer when he saw one. He had watched Aunt Bel haggle on market day many times. "I'll see what extra food I can bring. But I've no coin. I'm new to the Lions, and we're only paid in coin twice a year."

"Umm," she said, looking him over again in a considering way. "New to the Lions, indeed. You've got nice shoulders, my friend. But nice shoulders don't make dinner."

In that instant, he hated Geoffrey for impoverishing him. It had been within his power, before, to aid the poor and the helpless. Now he had little enough himself, and *he* felt helpless. "On the nights when I haven't duties in camp I'll do what I can to help you, bring in firewood, hunt a little. Gather berries when they're ripe."

Someone had bitten the whore's lower lip, and the wound hadn't yet healed. She played at the wound with her tongue as she eyed him with professional interest. "You're a good-looking lad, and well spoken. I've a young cousin at my old village of Felsinhame. She's looking for a husband. She'd not mind one who was away for months at a time, if he was a good lad otherwise." Seeing something in his expression, she hurried on. "She's not like me, a horrible sinner, an old slut." She said the word harshly, and for an instant he glimpsed an angry memory deep within her, rooted in her face. "She's not like me. She's a good girl."

"I'm not looking for a wife," he said softly as, behind him, Hathumod whimpered and finally began to cry.

"Did you find her?" Folquin asked when, at midnight, Alain arrived at his sentry post somewhat farther downstream on the same brook that he had splashed over to rescue Lady Hathumod.

"Ai, God, so I did," said Alain, feeling so weary that he wanted to lie down and let the grass grow over him so that he wouldn't have to care what happened to poor Hathumod and all the other suffering, lost souls. Yet someone had to care. "She's—" But Hathumod's secrets weren't his to divulge. "She shouldn't be here."

"Nor should any of them be here," said Folquin. "I knew a boy once, my mother's cousin's cousin's son. He was just too pretty, that boy, and he found out that there were those men who would give him anything they had if he'd act the girl for them. So maybe he liked getting it or maybe he liked getting the trinkets or maybe he just liked jerking them on that rope. I'll never know. He got killed in a knife fight, poor stupid boy." He went off then, to get his rest.

Alain stroked Sorrow's ears absently. They'd been on the march for ten days and had camped this night somewhere in Fesse or Saony, he wasn't sure. He didn't know the lay of the land here. Captain Thiadbold, Ingo, and the older Lions in first cohort had marched this way before; they recognized the landmarks and the estates, the names of villages and the courses of rivers. They'd crossed one ford that had once been a ferry crossing, and been forced to detour around a second ford that was now a high-cut, eroded bank too steep to pull the wagons up. Summer woodland made their march pleasant, delightfully uneventful except for the usual injuries: a foot run over by a wheel, a man kicked in the thigh by a horse, two fistfights, and one knifing over a village woman. Here in central Wendar, King Henry's reign was marked by tranquillity and enough to eat.

But he was not tranquil as he stood watch on the verge of the silent woodland, a tangle of young trees at the edge and older ones farther in, massive and brooding with only stars to light them, an ancient forest not yet fallen before the axes of humankind. They had passed a village earlier in the day, but now only the straight track led before them, striking straight as an arrow's flight into the forest. Here and there on the track stones showed through, scoured with lichen, dark with moss, an old line of march built by another people. Had Dariyan generals once marched their armies through this forest?

He stood on that track now, stones felt as an unyielding surface under the soles of his sandals. A few steps in front of him the half-concealed track crossed the stream at an old ford. He heard it more than saw it in the darkness where the water sang over the stones. Such a crossing point made a good sentry post, so Ingo had theorized.

Frogs chorused and fell silent. A single splash spread ripples of sound into the night, then stilled. Off to his right he saw the figure of another sentry pacing nervously at the edge of a particularly aggressive stand of oak that thrust out into the meadow in which they'd set up camp. He recognized the stout shoulders of Leo, Folquin's tent-mate. A twig snapped. An owl hooted. The stars blazed, a multitude of glorious lights. He sensed nothing unusual in the night, although a wind was coming up from the southeast. This past day they had marched through open woodland and meadows. Now dense forest lay ahead, a good long day of it, so Ingo said, before they came to the Veser River Valley and its string of forts and fortified towns and villages. East past the Veser there would be more forts and more fortifications, built in the reign of King Arnulf the Elder as protection against the depredations of the Rederii and Helvitii tribesmen who, until twenty years ago, had raided every winter. Now they were Daisanites and quiet plowmen, working in peace side by side with their Wendish overlords. But in recent years, according to the nightly gossip at the campfires, Quman tribesmen had raided far into the interior of Saony, lightning bolts that struck, sizzled, and vanished. Farther east, past the Oder River, their group would enter the marchlands and from that point on they would always have to be on their guard.

War. Was this war different in kind than the terrible duel between Henry and Sabella, brother against sister? Would it be easier to fight an enemy who was so unlike and so savage? Yet even against the inhuman Eika, he had learned that he could not kill.

He had ben too stunned to remember that fact the day he had lost Lavas County and taken service in the king's Lions.

What would the Lions do when they found out he couldn't fight?

What would he do if the Lady of Battles had forsaken him?

Rage whined, nosing his fingers, and he chuckled a little under his breath. What did it matter? He would march into battle at the side of the others, because that was the loyalty they owed each to the other and to the king. If he died, then at least he would be at peace, and if he lived, he would be no worse off than he was now.

No worse off, as long as he didn't think about Lavastine and Tallia. As long as he just kept walking each day, talking each day, working and eating and sleeping as though another Alain who had never known any life but this one inhabited his body, that empty shell, scoured and scalded by the lie that had ruined Lavastine's hopes. For he had no doubt that God was punishing him for the lie. And yet, given the choice again with Lavastine at his last breath, he would do it again, over and over again, every time, just to hear that beloved voice say: *Done well.*

Sorrow nipped at him, and he began to weep, but he struggled against it. He rubbed his face hard with the back of a hand, obliterating the tears. He knew where weeping would lead. He had to keep walking without looking back.

Ai, God. The innocent boy dreaming in Osna village would have given anything to march among the Lions, bent eastward toward adventure and the glory of righteous war.

Ai, God. That innocent boy *had* given everything: the only home and family he knew, the only woman he loved, the father who had loved him and died at peace because he had given everything he had into the hands of the heir he trusted.

All in ruins.

He sank to his knees, had to support himself on the ground with his spear fallen to the track beside him as he fought against the sobs that welled up in his chest. He could not weep. He must not weep. But he was drowning, swimming in grief, lost as the waves swamped him. Bodies jostled against him as though to lift him out of the tide

as he looks over the shoulder of Namms Dale's new chieftain. There were few sons of the old chief left to choose from, after the conflagration visited upon Namms Dale by Nokvi, but Stronghand has been patient in gathering up a stray ship here and a pack of warriors there: Now one of Namms Dale's surviving children has risen to take the staff of leadership. He has given himself the name Grimstroke and, like Bloodheart, he has chosen to observe the death magic ceremony.

Like Bloodheart, he has called his underlings together to witness his ceremony, to give notice that he does not fear death and treachery because treachery will rebound with greater force upon any person who dares to assassinate him.

But in truth, only one who fears death and doubts his own strength resorts to the death magic spell. Bloodheart revenged himself in this way upon the man who brought about his death. But the curse is a sign of weakness, not of strength. Bloodheart, after all, is still dead.

Stronghand watches as Grimstroke extrudes a claw and unhooks a tiny jar carved out of granite. Only stone can contain the venom of the ice-wyrms. The delicate granite lid falls back, and at once Hakonin's hall is permeated with the scent of the only death a RockChild fears. Only a single grain of silvery venom lies in the jar, but it alone is enough poison.

The Namms Dale priest shakes a rattle and tosses a handful of herbs into the air. The herbs drift down onto the altar where corpse and jar lie side by side. The dead hatchling is no bigger than a man's hand, and as white as roe. One pinch of a claw would slice it in half. It reeks of salt and seawater.

Only through killing does a hatchling become a RockChild instead of remaining forever a dog. In each nest, some of the blind hatchlings turn upon the others while most merely escape to live their short lives in the dog pack, the unthinking brothers of those who walk and plan. It is mind that separates a son from a dog, thinking that makes one a person and another simply a beast. In the nests of the Mothers, it is that first blind, groping kill that makes a mind flower.

And when the nests burst open and the hatchlings stumble out, corpses remain behind, caught in the ragged membrane. They soak there in brine, untended, unobserved, undecayed—

—unless a new chieftain fears death enough to risk the trek to the lair of the ice-wyrms, so that he can weave the death magic: the dead hand that will stalk the one who killed him and bring about the murderer's death as recompense, a death for a death.

The priest lights incense, and the scent of it is so sweet that it stings, but it does not vanquish the smell of the grain of venom. With pincers forged of iron, Grimstroke lifts the grain from the jar and gently deposits it into the gaping, unformed mouth of the tiny corpse.

There is silence in the hall as Grimstroke's underlings wait and watch. But there are other chieftains in the hall, from other tribes, whom Stronghand has called together to witness the rebirth of the Namms Dale chieftainship. It is his way of overturning Nokvi's victory, of calling notice that he, Stronghand, will say who lives and who dies, who will flower and who will merely bark at his heels like a dog. Yet he needs these same allies to defeat Nokvi. And they need him. Alone, they will be sucked one by one into Nokvi's jaws to become puppets dancing to the tune of human magic. They all know what transpired when Rikin's tribe raided Moerin, that the Alban sorcerers ensorcelled their own human brothers to charge as berserkers into

a battle they could not win. Perhaps some even hoped Stronghand would die there, caught in Nokvi's trap, but he did not.
They know now that Nokvi's alliance with the Alban tree sorcerers threatens them all, and that they have no protection against
Nokvi's magic unless they join with Rikin.

The dead hatchling shows no change as the venom dissolves
into its lifeless body.

"You carry the curse," says Grimstroke suddenly, claw still
extruded, a lingering threat or something simply forgotten.

"I do not," says Stronghand, and he pitches his voice so that
it carries to all of the gathered chieftains: eight tribes have sent
representatives, have come, as the humans say, when he called.
He is not sure it will be enough.

"I do not carry the curse," he repeats. "I did not weave the
death magic spell when I took Rikin's standard for my own hand.
Any of my rivals who is strong enough and cunning enough to
kill me is welcome to his victory."

Grimstroke laughs. He is beholden to Stronghand for his chieftainship, and because he knows it and resents it, his gratitude,
like old fish, stinks a little. "I will gladly walk behind you until
your shoulders bow under the weight of your arrogance. Then
I'll kill you and take your place."

Stronghand grins, baring his teeth as humans do to show fel-
low-feeling. "Then we understand each other," he says, although
the words are meant for all of them.

The priest croaks out a garbled phrase and shrinks back from
the altar. Like all priests, who prolong their lives by unnatural
means, he fears anything that smells of death.

The chest of keeping is brought and opened beside the dead-
white hatchling that still lies limp on the altar. The late summer
sun spills in through the western doorway, pouring light down
the central aisle and veining the dark wood altar with its amber
glow.

The little corpse shudders, stirs, and comes to life, out of
death, for that is the other legacy of the ice-wyrm's venom, that
it can bring life out of death or death out of life, the horror that
is both and neither.

Priest-words are spoken that seal it, the dead hand, to the
life of its killer, and Grimstroke claps shut the lid and shuts the
corpse inside the box that will hold it now and until he dies.

*   *   *

Alain screamed, trapped in darkness.

But it wasn't his voice he heard.

He heard the scream again, a shriek, a frantic call for help. A horn stuttered, wavered, and sputtered out. From the camp, he heard answering shouts made faint by a wind rushing in his ears like a tempest, and as he came fully to himself he found himself kneeling on the ground, braced on his hands. Water gurgled past his fingers, and as he stared at the water, he realized that he had shifted forward during his lapse until his hands fetched up in the stream, pressing against the moss-covered stone track.

The stream was running the wrong way.

Sandaled feet stopped in mid-stream right in front of him. From this vantage, all Alain could see was leather winding up muscular calves. An obsidian spearpoint slid into view, drifting in front of his nose. Although there was no moon, there was light enough to see clearly the man standing before him: as Alain looked up from calf to thigh to a torso fitted with a cuirass ornamented with strange, curling beasts, he knew with a chill that it was no *man.*

A white half cloak was clasped at the figure's shoulders.

He looked up into a beardless face more bronze than pale, with deep, old eyes under a sweep of black hair tied up in a topknot and adorned with an owl feather. The spearpoint remained fixed before Alain's nose.

At this instant, Alain became aware of two things: the tense murmur of men gathering to fight in the brush behind him, and the silence of the hounds, who sat alert but unmoving at his feet.

"I do not kill you only because the sacred ones attend you," said the prince. Alain recognized him now, but it was not at all clear that this prince of a lost people recognized Alain. "Move off the road. Let us pass."

From behind, Alain heard Thiadbold's strong voice. "Roll away, Alain, and we'll loose a volley. There are more behind him, a host of them. My God."

Was it starlight alone that lit them, or an unnatural light that flowed with them like witchfire? Cautiously, Alain straightened until he knelt, upright, before the prince. His knees pressed hard into paving stone. Behind the prince, the procession trailed off down the path into the forest, a host he could not count because he could not see them all. They all had that wonderful, disturbing consistency to them, more shade than real and yet real enough. Their weapons looked as deadly as his own spear, which lay as a dark spar in the grass. They looked deadly enough to kill, these shades, bows and spears held ready by grim-faced soldiers, both female and male and yet manifestly not human men and women. Light rose from them in the same way that steam rises from a boiling pot. The old track gleamed as well, a silvery thread piercing the land east to west.

"What are you?" asked Alain. "Are you Dariyan?"

"I know not this tribe," answered the prince. "Stand aside."

"If we stand aside, will you go on your way without harming us?" asked Alain, not moving from the path.

"Let us shoot, Alain! Move aside!" cried Captain Thiadbold, and by the stillness of the prince's face and the unblinking regard of those soldiers closest to him, Alain realized that the prince and his followers could not hear Thiadbold's voice.

"Nay, Captain," said Alain. "Let them pass in peace. Their fight is not with us."

"Are there others with you?" demanded the prince.

A shade-woman crowding behind the prince hissed, raised her bow, and drew down on something behind Alain's head just as he heard grass rustle behind him and Thiadbold's voice, much closer now. "They're spread thin," said the captain. "Use cover to give you room to shoot."

"I'm standing up," said Alain, and with infinite care he did so, moving as slowly as he could to make sure no one would be startled. He was careful to keep his feet on the old track. "I beg you, Captain Thiadbold. Call your men back. Let them pass in peace. They have no quarrel with us." He lifted a hand, palm up and open in the sign of peace. "Where is Liathano, my lord prince?"

"She is walking the spheres," said the prince, eyes widening with elegant astonishment. "How is it you know of her? Yet there is something familiar about you—"

"Go on your way in peace, I pray you," said Alain. "I swear on my God, the Two who dwell in Unity. Swear on your own god, and we will step back. We will not molest you. There is no war between us."

The shade-woman standing behind the prince spat on the ground. "There is always war between us!"

"Nay, be not impatient," said the prince, setting his spear haft down on the path. "We have our own troubles. This *ijkia'pe* tells the truth. They are fully of the world. We need not fight them."

"Not now," said the woman, "but if the tide washes us back to shore, then it is better if there are less of them."

"Nay, reckless one. Or have you forgotten the army of *shanaret'zeri* which pursues us?" He lifted his spear and shook it. Bells, tied to the base, rang softly. "So be it, *ijkia'pe*. I swear by He-Who-Burns that as long as you touch no one of us, we will touch no one of you. But I will stand here beside you while my people pass, and my spear will pierce your heart if you have lied to me."

Alain stepped back from the path. "So be it. Captain Thiadbold, I pray you, tell the men to stand down. Let these people pass, and there will be no fighting."

A woman's voice, very human, spoke. He thought it might be that of the blonde Eagle who rode with them. "Listen to him, comrade. I think he sees more than we do."

"Stand down," said Thiadbold. "Let no man attack, by my order."

The command passed down through the gathered Lions, an echo of the whisper of the shadowy procession as it moved on. The prince stood aside to wait beside Alain, although he kept his feet upon the stones, and now the shade-woman led the way, striding forward with her bow taut before her. She, too, wore a cuirass of gleaming bronze, but she had no sword, only an ugly obsidian dagger strapped to her thigh.

"God have mercy," swore Thiadbold. By the sound of his voice, he seemed to be standing a few steps behind Alain. "I've never seen a woman that beautiful. I'd die happy if she plunged her dagger into my heart at the moment of release."

The wind had come up, as if blown off the march itself, the procession winding by. They walked two abreast, with their unearthly bronze-complexioned faces and their strange garb, more beads and feathers than Alain had ever seen. Only a few wore metal, whether armor or decoration. All their weapons were of stone except for their arrows, which looked like slender, arm-length darts whittled out of bone. Not one man among them had a beard. Not one woman did not carry a bow. There were a few children, preciously guarded in the middle of the long line, naked bronze-skinned babies or long-limbed, silent youngsters with eyes as bright as stars. Every soul among them wore jade in an ear. Their passage was like the wind, and as Alain watched, he realized that in fact their feet didn't quite truly tread on the ground. No grass bent. No dirt stirred.

They weren't really here, not as he was.

Some man was crying in fear among the human crowd, babbling about a procession of shades come to haunt the waking world.

"Where do you come from?" Alain asked softly as the last dozen strode by, as silent as corpses, eyes alert although in truth they didn't really seem to see him. "Where are you going?"

"We were caught between one place and the next when the world changed. We were swept out to sea where the ground always shifts beneath our feet. But I feel the tide turning. It is coming back in. As the reckless one said, mayhap the tide will wash us back onto the earth again. Then we will have our revenge."

The prince swung into line behind the last of his soldiers.

Light rimmed the horizon. A cock crowed. The thin pinch of the last waning crescent moon floated just above the trees, fading into the dawn.

They vanished.

Had Alain been slugged in the stomach, he wouldn't have felt any more like the wind had been knocked right out of him. The stream flowed past, gurgling over the stones, and now it ran the same way it had last night, northeast, into the forest. Or perhaps he had only been dreaming it, before.

"What was that?" demanded Thiadbold as everyone began to talk at once.

"Captain! Captain!" A man came running. "It's Leo. He was sentry out by the forest. It's elfshot, Captain! He's terrible shot through with fever."

Alain went to the forest's edge with Captain Thiadbold, the blonde Eagle, and a nervous crowd of Lions, who promptly spread out in pairs to search among the trees. Dawn made them bold. There was no trace on the narrow track that any party, much less one of a hundred or more people, had passed over it during the night.

Leo was a man who didn't say much, and then usually only to swear. He was shaking now, a hand clasped over his right shoulder, but the rash had already spread up his exposed throat.

Sweat ran from his neck and forehead. His eyes had the glaze of shock.

"Nay, nay," he was mumbling, trying to push away someone in front of him who didn't exist. "Nay, nay. Be quiet now or they'll hear you coming."

"Get his mail off so we can see the wound," said Thiadbold. He still wore his helm, covering his red hair, but Alain could just see the scarred ear where the leather ear flaps had been pulled askew. "I thought it was a dream," the captain went on, looking at Alain. "That's why I went along with what you said. That, and what Hanna said—" He gestured toward the Eagle, who had evidently scrambled up so quickly from her bed that she hadn't belted up her tunic. "You sounded so sure of yourself—" He shook his head, frowning. Not quite suspicious, but looking as if he were sorry that he'd ever agreed to take on Henry's new recruit.

"Many of us have seen strange things in these days," said the Eagle. "Strange things in strange times."

Her words produced a flood of anxious commentary from the assembled Lions, broken only when Leo screamed as three of his fellows pinioned him and pulled his mail coat up over his shoulders. Then, thrashing, he rolled on the ground like a madman.

"Hush," said Alain, stepping forward and pressing him down by one shoulder. "God will help you if you will only be still."

Leo moaned, spittle running from his mouth, then fainted.

There was no sign of any arrow in his shoulder nor, when Alain probed with his fingers at the little hole pierced in Leo's shoulder, did he find a point or shaft broken off in the skin. But it was festering. Angry red lines already lanced from the wound, and his skin was rashing and blistering all around it. Alain set his mouth to the wound and sucked, spat, sucked again, spat again, until his jaws ached.

"Waybread and prayer for elfshot," said Alain. "That's what my Aunt Bel always said."

"A poultice of wormwood to draw out the poison," added the Eagle, but she gestured toward Thiadbold. "Your healer may know other charms."

"I've never seen so strange a sight," said Thiadbold. "Not once in my ten years as a Lion." He wasn't looking at Leo at all, but at Alain. "You were speaking to them, but I couldn't

hear a word they said. They were only shades. Shadows of the
Lost Ones. How could you speak to them, who are ghosts? What
manner of man are you?"

Folquin and Ingo shoved their way through the crowd of
Lions. "Here, Alain," said Folquin too heartily, but he reached
down to grasp one of Leo's legs. "Let's carry him back to camp."

"We can rig a place on one of the wagons," said Ingo, drawing Thiadbold aside. "It won't take much time. We won't lose
much on the march. I'd just as soon be through this forest before twilight."

In this way, they moved on. Folquin and Stephen jested with
Alain and with the men around them as the day passed swiftly,
a steady march under the canopy of the forest. By evening they
cleared the thickest portion of the wood and, from a ridgetop
lookout, could see the Veser River a half day's march beyond.
Incredibly, Leo was recovering and he ate so much at supper
that they joked they'd all have to fast. No one mentioned Alain's
part in the incident, or at least not within his hearing.

Yet Alain was so tired he was dizzy, and he couldn't eat. He
bundled up his bread and cheese and eased away from the fire.
He found Hathumod easily enough, sitting in the last twilight
trying to mend a torn skirt, squinting at the needle. As he came
up beside her, coughing softly to let her know of his approach,
she started, jabbed the needle into her fingers, and cried out.

"I beg your pardon, Lady Hathumod," he said. "I didn't mean
to startle you."

"Nay, my lord," she said in a soft voice. Blood welled up on
her forefinger, and without thinking she lifted the finger to her
mouth to suck. She had gotten thinner. He wondered if she ever
had enough to eat or if, like Tallia, she chose to fast.

He held out the bread and cheese. "You must eat this, Lady
Hathumod, for you must keep up your strength. You can't fast
and also march all day. Truly, I don't begrudge these beggars
their share, but I haven't enough to feed them all."

She looked at him strangely. "Of course there will be enough,
my lord, if it comes from your hands."

It was impossible to argue with someone who talked like that.
He wondered how many beggars she had really seen before running off in the wake of the Lions. Did she cherish an innocent
belief that Lady Fortune smiled equally kindly on every soul,

here on this earth? Was her faith more pure than his, or only more naive?

He left her, because he couldn't bear the calm zealotry of her expression. He wandered up on the ridgetop, stumbling on rocks because he couldn't see his feet well. Up on the ridge, he felt the open land to his left, falling eastward into mystery, the uncharted land that is every footstep into the future. He felt the forest off to his right, a restless, breathing beast that had much to say in the wind of night and many secrets to hide. Had the prince and his followers been marching into the forest, or out of it? He couldn't now remember. Maybe it had been a dream.

But there was a flavor in the air tonight, something new that he hadn't tasted there before. At times the world seems to shift and invert: inside turns out, and outside turns in; dreams become waking, and waking becomes a dream.

Crickets thrummed. An owl hooted.

When he closed his eyes he could see Stronghand riding the waves, his ship turning as the tide turned, heading out to sea.

Something was going to happen. He would gather ships and allies, and he would drive Nokvi to a final confrontation in which one would emerge the winner, and the other would be thrown into the sea.

A watchfire burned in the distance, marking Namms Dale's new hall, so freshly built that the timbers still wept pitch and the aroma of pine was as heavy as incense. He was dizzy tonight, or perhaps it was only the veil of time opening and closing like bellows pumped by vast hands. Had dream become waking, and waking turned into dream?

The water chopped against the hull as the rowers set to. Stronghand shifted as they hit a swell, rode it, and plunged forward into the sound. A single lantern blazed at the stem, held aloft on a post. He knew the waters well, here. They would beach at a sand spit out in the sound and there he and his favored advisers—four warriors of his own tribe, two from Hakonin, and two human slaves—would take council, where the merfolk could send an emissary: a place between sea and land where neither held the advantage.

It washed him again, an invisible tide that overturned all things that lay in its path. He knelt on the deck to steady himself as the lantern swayed, back and forth, back and forth *and he is walking down through the camp where the Lions, still jumpy from their dawn encounter with the shades of the Lost Ones, have come to find entertainment among the whores. Lamp oil burns aplenty tonight; lanterns seemingly as numerous as the stars sway from branches. He smells venison roasting.*

There, beside the fire where a raggedly-dressed boy turns a haunch of venison on a spit, he sees Hathumod holding what must be her only possession: a battered and smudged copy of the Holy Verses. Folk have gathered at the fire, mostly beggars and hangers-on but a few Lions also, but he is alert tonight, he knows the tide is turning and that anything might happen. Because he is alert he sees them coming, Lord Dietrich and his two cronies, big, broad bodies pushing arrogantly through the crowd as they make their way toward their prey and then, abruptly, sit down at the front, taking precedence over the others.

He moves forward quickly. "Are they bothering you?" he asks her, catching Hathumod by the sleeve before she can step forward into the firelight.

"Nay, my lord," she says, and her surprise is the surprise of the guileless child who is asked if she has ever laid an offering before her grandmother's gods. "They've done as you said. They've chosen their place. They've come to hear the teaching."

2

IN the evening light, the stones looked like shrouded clerics standing watchfully at the top of the slope. Waiting for what? Since the fiasco at the old cottage, she and Sanglant had searched many times among the boulders in the high meadow but had found no path. Jerna still nursed Blessing, but her voice was gone; stolen, perhaps, or closed off by Anne's magic, who had used the daimone to lure Sanglant away and then made sure she could not be used in that way again.

As Liath waited for the first stars to wink into life above, she spun through her fingers the gold feather she had received from the old Aoi sorcerer. There was a secret hidden in the stones, and it was being concealed from her by the very people who claimed to be her teachers: everything was shrouded, not just the stones. She hugged the sleeping Blessing against her chest, kissed her black hair. Her little soft, round body was easy to hold and easy to cradle. She had a habit of sucking on two fingers as she drowsed off. Now, fast asleep, her tiny mouth had relaxed enough that the equally tiny and perfect and somewhat chubby little fingers lay tucked between her cheek and Liath's shoulder.

Her braid stirred. Wisps of loose hair fluttered on her neck. Was that a rising breeze, or the touch of one of the servants? Had Jerna followed her? She didn't look.

The stone crown at Verna was not a true circle but rather more of a slightly flattened oval. That it drew in the power of the rising and setting stars, the angles of the planets each to the other as they traveled through the ecliptic, seemed obvious to her: that was the art of the mathematici. At first she had examined the circle from within, standing at the central stone and sighting outward, but no reasonable line of sight presented itself. It seemed impossible to weave the alignments of the stars from inside the circle, like trying to draw the shuttle through the warp when you yourself were within the loom and the threads, not standing outside it.

That observation, of course, had made all the difference.

She heard footsteps and now she did turn, tucking the feather between tunic and breast so it lay concealed.

He had his tunic off his shoulders, gathered by his belt at his hips so that his chest and back were bare. With his ax balanced along his shoulders, he looked a tempting sight. He swung down the ax, kissed her, then the baby, then pressed against her as if to kiss her again. The sheen of sweat on his body must have been cooling rapidly as the night breeze rose; surely he was cold, or perhaps he just didn't notice. She was trembling, but not from cold. She touched a finger to his lips and just so slightly pushed him back.

"Ai, God," he said, sounding frustrated.

Yet surely he was no more frustrated than she was. They had already done things they ought not to have done, not with the situation as desperate as it was. She could not risk getting pregnant again, not now.

"This isn't a natural platform," she said, indicating the level ground beneath her feet. She stood downslope from the stones, which from this angle lay to the west. From this angle, she looked *up* at the stone crown. "From this angle, the stones become the loom and I become the weaver. Before it didn't make sense that the stones weren't a true circle, but look—" She tucked Blessing more tightly into the crook of her left arm and, pulling the gold feather out again, used it to point. "Because of the flattened circle, those two stones, the left edge of the nearer one and the right edge of the farther one, make a line of sight that lines up with that notch in the ridge. There. Do you see it?"

He was silent for a long time. Then he moved up behind her onto the level shelf of ground, which was not more than two strides square. He was careful not to touch her, but she felt him nevertheless. He might as well have been making love with her, his presence lay so heavily on her, but that was her own desire speaking through her body. He understood the risks, too. He was the one who, when she had finally recovered her strength, had pointed out that a second pregnancy and labor might be as debilitating as the first and that to be completely sure that she was strong enough to escape at a moment's notice, they must make sure she did not get pregnant.

At moments like this, she wondered if it were a sin to hate the woman who had brought her here and thrown her in a cage only slightly less repressive than the one Hugh had shut her in. Yet was it truly less confining just because the hand that held her had a softer touch?

"They betrayed me," she went on, lowering her voice, knowing that the servants could be anywhere, could be listening and would be listening. There were no secrets in this valley from the one who ruled over it. But she went on anyway because anger left burning inside will only blacken the heart. "I thought this would be a place where I could study in peace, but it isn't true. I'm nothing but a tool to them. Now I learn that my own mother has tried to kill you, and I can't trust any of them with Blessing, because they might try to kill her as well. I can't trust any of them at all. They all lied to me."

"I lied to you, too. I didn't tell you what I suspected and later knew."

"Nay." She shook her head emphatically. "You can't compare yourself to them. You did it to protect me. You waited until I was strong enough to act. I don't doubt you meant it for the best." She tried to be better than she was, but she couldn't keep the irritation out of her voice. Then she laughed bitterly. "Surrounded on all sides by villains. Even the trees might hear our whispers and give away our secrets."

Because he stood behind her, she couldn't see his expression but she felt him shift and God help her she almost turned at that moment; she wanted to set down the baby and have done with caution. But she could not. As Sanglant had so bluntly phrased it, a second pregnancy might kill her.

"I do see it," he said suddenly, then added, "the line of sight."

It was a timely reprieve. "A star should rise in that notch. If I'm right, then its thread of starlight brings the crown to life. Once the magic is alive within the stones, then the other stars and planets, and the moon, can be woven into the crown so that it makes—well, I don't know. It's the gateway we came through to get here. It's a way of moving from one crown to another."

"Then if you can weave the starlight through this crown, we can leave. Can't we?"

She smiled wryly. "It's never that simple, is it? First of all, this crown is limited because the mountains cut off the horizon. There's a narrower band of sky than there would be on a plain, or on a hill, for instance. Second of all, I don't know how old these stones are. They might have been raised in the last twenty years. They might be perfectly aligned to the stars as we now see them. But if they were constructed by the Aoi, if they're that old, then because of the precession of the equinoxes it would have been other stars rising at that notch at this day and time of year, other threads of light laying the weft into the shed than the ones that rise in these days at this time. The stars change more than the mountains do."

He was shaking his head again, fiddling with the ax as he did when he grew impatient with her explanations. Maybe battle seemed more straightforward than astronomy. "But you said they're fixed stars—"

"Nay, nay," she said, chuckling. Hadn't she explained this before? "They're fixed in relationship to each other. But, for instance, look there—" Standing to the west of the stone crown they gazed east, of course, and along the eastern ridge a few faint stars could now be seen blooming as twilight faded to dusk. Again she used the feather to point. "That's the Penitent rising in the east. In truth, a bit to the northeast. There aren't any really bright stars rising at this time of night, this time of year, but the Crown of Stars—you know, the little cluster of seven stars—will rise later, although I don't think it will rise, just there, in the notch." He said nothing, just set the ax down with a thud. He seemed discontent, with life, with imprisonment, with her answer. She pointed overhead. "See there, above us. The summer evening sky is the Queen's sky. There she rides, and there are her Staff and Sword and Crown. And those three bright stars—"

"Are the Sapphire, the Diamond, and the Citrine. I remember that much."

"But because the wheel of the heavens slips backward bit by bit over the years, if we had stood here in the time of the Aoi two thousand and more years ago, the summer evening sky would have been—Well."

She had to think about it. Blessing stirred, fussing in her arms, and she rocked from side to side as she calculated.

She had worked so hard to regain her strength in these two months after the shock of Heribert's escape and the sudden bald revelation that Anne wanted to kill Sanglant and even Blessing. The magi claimed that Liath was not their prisoner but rather their colleague, but that was, as the old Dariyan orators might have said, just splitting hairs. They had stolen from her the one thing she had come here for: to learn unencumbered by anything but pure knowledge. They didn't truly care about pure knowledge at all, that was the frightening thing. It was war. Sanglant had said so, and he was right. He knew war when he saw it.

And yet, if it wasn't for their hatred of Sanglant, might she not have joined willingly in their cause? If the Aoi return would cause a cataclysm that would rip apart the Earth, if sea became the mountains and the mountains became the sea, then wasn't it right to stop the Aoi before they wreaked such monumental destruction?

They might be wrong about Sanglant and right about the obligation laid upon them.

But how could she know?

"The Sisters," she said as the wheel of the heavens shifted in her mind's eye, turning through the centuries. For this alone she loved the stars: They were eternal and silent, uninvolved in the tide of conflict that continually racked the earth. "I think the Sisters would have been rising, and the Guivre would have been at zenith. Different stars would have different influence. If it's true the Aoi built these stone crowns as a loom for magic, then the threads they were using would have been entirely different in each season than the threads made by the stars today."

"But the Sisters still rise more or less in the same position, don't they?" he objected. "Just at a different time of year. Or a different time of night."

"It's more complicated than that. All things change over time, even the heavens, but unless we had an unbroken chain of recorded observations reaching from their time into ours, we can only trust what we see with our own eyes. The rest is computation."

"And it's all very interesting, I'm sure," he replied, a little exasperated, "but can you open a gate in the stones or not?"

"Ai," she said on a sigh. "It should be possible. But I wouldn't know where we'd end up. There had to be some system to the placement of the crowns. I've seen more than two dozen with my own eyes, scattered all over these lands, as far north as Heyetrop and as far south as the deserts west of Kartiako. I've heard of more. The Lion's Claw woven at rising in spring might take you to one place, and the Lion's Claw woven at setting in winter might take you somewhere else. Did you know there's another shelf like to this one on the other side of the crown? So that you can sight into the west, to the setting of the stars."

"And north and south as well, I suppose."

"No, stars don't rise and set to the north and south, but it's probable that here or at other crowns you could, say, measure the southern limits of moonrise and moonset. The moon has a cycle of a little over eighteen years according to—"

"Liath, I beg you. Listen to what I'm saying. Does it matter where we end up as long as we're free?"

She brushed Blessing's hair with her lips. The baby had such a clean smell, fresh and warm. She was an astonishing gift to come from the simple act of two bodies joining, a blessing indeed. Sanglant set a hand on Liath's shoulder and caressed her neck with a thumb.

"I brought something for you," he said. "You wouldn't wear it before. You said it was wrong for you to wear it, but I knew it was meant for you. I knew it was meant for you long before I understood why."

"What if she's lying?" said Liath as she touched her own

throat. But he was already moving to slip the gold torque of royal kinship around her neck. It felt like a slave's collar, as heavy as anything Hugh had ever bound her with.

"Of course she's Taillefer's granddaughter. She isn't lying, Liath, and you don't truly believe she is."

"I saw his tomb at the chapel in Autun," she said softly. "I prayed there with my father, once. I remember staring at his effigy and wondering how craftsmen could render any face so perfectly in stone. Da was weeping. I don't know why. I suppose I'll never know why. He holds a seven-pointed crown in his hand. The cleric in attendance said it was the emperor's crown, the one he wore when he went abroad in his royal dignity, and that each gem represented one of the wandering stars. It marked his right to rule, that Emperor Taillefer ruled Earth just as God ruled in the heavens, that he had their imprimatur. But Da said that the crown was a funeral gift from Biscop Tallia, Taillefer's favorite daughter. He said that she meant it to represent the seven spheres that the emperor's soul would have to traverse to reach the Chamber of Light."

The torque weighed hard on her neck. The two gold knobs dug into her collarbone. It still didn't feel right. "It's strange. I remember text so easily. But faces don't always stay clear in my mind. When I think back, I just can't see his carved face clearly enough to know if I resemble him."

She gave in to it then, leaned back against him, and let him put his arms around her and the baby. They stood there for a long time, watching the stars.

3

WANDERING down the path of doubt was a slippery slope that always ended in the mire. Antonia, formerly Biscop of Mainni and now masquerading under the name Sister Venia where she lived among a nest of mathematici, had no inclination to be trapped in the mud.

They hadn't wanted Heribert among them all along, although

his manners and elegant bearing—if a little smirched by his months attending the dog-prince—were certainly the jewel of this altogether detestable place. Although she shuddered to contemplate it, the hall he had crafted with his hands and the aid of the servants and Prince Sanglant was such a vast improvement over the decrepit tower that had been the main building when they had arrived that she could not understand why they were so eager to rid themselves of him, since he alone had made of this valley a fitting residence for noble persons of their rank and accomplishment.

Or perhaps they hadn't cared about him one way or the other. Like the savage Eika dog they'd killed to get to the baby, he had just been in the way at the wrong time.

So she had listened to the various explanations, none proffered with as much self-righteous anger as that of the prince, who truly was not able to temper his emotions. Perhaps it was true that Sister Anne's cool recital *ought* to have carried more weight. Reason always triumphed over base emotion.

But Prince Sanglant had recklessly told her other things as well, and rather than doubt she had decided that perhaps she didn't really support the goals of the Seven Sleepers. Perhaps she didn't see any need to save earth from the disaster that, they claimed, would soon be visited upon it.

After all, why shouldn't the world suffer in a cataclysm brought on by the Lost Ones? There were wicked in plenty, and God had never before shied away from punishment. If some innocents died together with the damned, then so be it: They would die secure in the knowledge that death was only a passageway leading to the blessed Chamber of Light, where they would reside for eternity in the peace of God's all encompassing light.

Perhaps Heribert was better off out in the world, as long as he had the protection of someone more powerful than himself. Perhaps she had learned as much as it was worth learning, here at Verna. Perhaps it was time for her to venture back into the world and see what she could make of it, now that she had mastered so many new skills.

She knelt at the altar, a simple wooden box carved out of cherrywood and polished to a handsome sheen. Over Severus' protests, Heribert had added various ornaments, grape leaves signifying God's bounty at every corner and edge and elaborate roses, for purity, on each side. She liked to admire them as she prayed, because they reminded her that God didn't condemn luxury, the little fine details that made life more elegant, but rather *luxuria*, the wanton desire for carnal and earthly things.

"'Open to me the gates of victory,'" she prayed. "'In Your service I have suffered reproach. I pray you then, redeem me, and rebuke my enemies.'"

It was the twentieth day of Aogoste, the feast day of St. Guillaime of Benne who had chastised the wicked king Tarquin the Proud of Floretia and then when King Tarquin would not institute laws according to Guillaime's wishes—and the will of God, of course—brought down a great flood upon Floretia that washed every soul in it out to sea. Including himself—thus had he gained his martyr's crown, and her respect, although she would have gotten out of the city before calling down God's wrath. The city had never recovered and, according to Heribert, still lay in ruins.

She heard voices outside and, with some effort, got to her feet. It was harder to get up and down these days. She was getting old, and therefore had less time in which to improve the world. When she left the chapel, she was surprised to see Brother Marcus walking beside Sister Anne on the plank walkway, speaking so intently to her that he didn't at first notice her or the other figure passing by: Prince Sanglant. These days, the prince normally did not walk among the lower buildings; he kept to himself, with his daughter and wife up at his hut or working in the meadows or woodland on the upper slopes. But a burst of summer storms had dislodged a wooden shingle on the roof of the hall, and he had, he had said, too much respect for Heribert's hard work to let it go to ruin.

Brother Marcus looked up abruptly and saw the prince, and he stopped short and gaped as if he expected to see a slavering pack of wolves come howling out of the air around him. "Will he bite?" he demanded of Anne.

"Walk on, Brother," said Anne. "We are in no danger."

Sometimes, Antonia reflected, allies walked right into your camp and declared themselves.

"Truly, Prince Sanglant," she said, coming up beside him when Anne and Marcus had vanished into the tower, "there have been many unexpected comings and goings. Yet I wonder that those who most wish to depart remain behind."

"Why do you wonder?" He had Blessing with him, swaddled in a linen band and resting at his back in much the same way, she supposed, he carried his broadsword during wartime. The infant was not allowed in the magi's tower, so when Liath took her lessons or met with the others, he had perforce to carry the baby with him. After all, now that Heribert was gone and the guard dog dead, there was no one else he could trust to watch over her.

"It is no wonder you are suspicious of me," she said, "so I will offer you a confidence, so that you can understand that I am also imperfect, and not your enemy. Heribert is not my nephew. He is my son."

She had surprised him. That was good.

"He kept your secret," he said.

"He is an obedient son." *Had been*, at least, until the magi here at Verna corrupted him. Truly, they had a lot to answer for.

"Why tell me now?" he asked, but she only gestured to the air.

"Nay," he said, "There are no servants near us now. There is no one to hear except for me."

It was true he had an uncanny way of knowing when the servants gathered nearby and when they were absent. Nor would it be to his advantage to offer any more knowledge to Anne than what Anne already knew. "Trust is a complicated thing. Some have said that either you trust completely, or never trust at all. As one who has studied the Holy Verses at some length, I can see there is a great deal of truth to that. Either we trust in God, or we do not. Either we abide by Their laws, trusting that They hold us in Their hands, or we do not. There is no bridge between faith and apostasy. But in earthly matters we are all stained with darkness, even the best of us. All but the blessed Daisan, of course, for how else could he have been lifted bodily up to the Chamber of Light if any taint of the Enemy had touched him? He alone among humankind was entirely of God."

"Isn't that a heresy?" he said, almost laughing, and it angered her that he would make light of her wisdom and experience in this way. It angered her, until she remembered that he was not wicked: like the beasts, he simply lacked understanding.

"Nay, child," she said, "the heresy mistakenly teaches that the blessed Daisan partook of both a mortal and an immortal soul, that he was both human and divine. This cannot be, of course. God did not allow Their messenger to be sacrificed, as some heretics claim. It is on this very point that the true church, in Darre, broke off with the Arethousans three hundred years ago, because the Arethousan patriarch was in error—" She had lost him. He had that same blank look in his gaze as the cattle chewing their cud in the field.

With some men, one had to interact on the most basic terms. She tickled the baby under its chin. "Such a precious burden," she said, and saw him soften. Like most men, he suffered from an excess of sentiment. She recognized it, of course, because of her own weak affection for Heribert. In some ways she admired Anne's ability to disregard sentiment with her own daughter when, in the cold, clear light of day, she had to make hard choices. Antonia had never been able to use Heribert as ruthlessly as Anne used Liath. "My son trusted you, Prince Sanglant," she said now. "So do I."

"Sister Venia!" Zoë called to her from the door of the tower, and she had to leave him.

"He is useful," Anne was saying when Antonia crossed the threshold and came into the tower chamber. Anne stood at the head of the table. Severus sat to her right, and next to him sat Brother Marcus, then Sister Zoë. To Anne's left, Sister Meriam sat with hands folded. She was so small and bent that she almost looked like a child sitting at table. Liath sat next to Meriam. Anne saw Antonia enter and gestured toward the empty bench beside Liath. "That we can eat and sleep in the comfort of the hall is due in part to his efforts."

"It seems strange," said Brother Marcus, but his lips quirked. "Yet there must be some satisfaction in setting the child of our enemy to work like a common laborer, to benefit ourselves. Perhaps it is a sign."

Antonia sat down next to Liath, who was mute, picking at the edge of the table with a finger while she stared at the wall. A book lay closed before her; its ivory cover had been cleverly carved in miniature to show the famous episode of St. Valeria confounding the pagan astrologers in the city of Saïs the Younger. A few days ago Liath had begun wearing the gold torque, symbol of her royal kinship; her dark complexion set off the rich gold sheen more beautifully, really, than did Anne's pale, fair skin. And although it was lowering to think that Sanglant had stumbled on the secret of Anne's descent before she had, Antonia was not one to throw away information just because it came from an unlikely quarter. Indeed, what Antonia found most interesting was that not one of the other magi had ever commented upon Anne's breeding, or Liath's sudden adoption of the torque.

"You have come precipitously from Darre," said Anne to Marcus. "Tell us your news, Brother."

"Darre is not the place it was," he said, glancing toward Liath as if he weren't sure whether she ought to be there or not. Perhaps *he* found the gold torque gleaming at her neck disconcerting, but like the rest of them, he did not mention it. "There is a new power at work in Darre. That is why I dared not risk speaking through fire."

"What can you mean, Brother?" demanded Zoë. "Surely you aren't suggesting that some other person might without our tutelage have learned to listen through fire or travel within the crowns?"

"The veils grow thin," said Anne. "Other creatures walk abroad in this time. Brother Marcus, I commend your caution."

"Any man must walk cautiously in the presbyter's hall. I learned that years ago." He was sitting across from Liath, and he reached across the table to draw the ivory-covered book to him. He opened it and idly turned the pages, but he wasn't looking at the text, only considering. Anne watched him. Liath said nothing. "Queen Adelheid fled Darre when her husband died and the last of her male relatives were killed in the south. No sooner had she run than Lord John Ironhead rode after her. His origins are questionable, to say the least. It is commonly known that he is the bastard son of a nobleman put into service in his guards. He rose to captain and steward, slew his own half brother when that man came into the title, and married his widow, taking upon himself the title of Lord of Sabina. Ironhead besieged Queen Adelheid at Vennaci. Soon after this, Princess Theophanu together with a small army of Wendish soldiers came south over the mountains. They claimed to be on a peaceful mission to Darre to bring certain petitions from King Henry to the notice of the skopos. Ironhead of course assumed that they, too, were after Adelheid, and he attacked Vennaci. Adelheid and Theophanu vanished in the wilderness and were rumored to be dead. Ironhead returned to Darre with Adelheid's treasure and a new adviser, a Wendish churchman who had, so we heard in the presbyter's hall, been sent south to stand trial for sorcery. Yet as soon as Ironhead came to Darre, Mother Clementia crowned Lord John king of Aosta. I believe that this churchman bound a daimone and that he now controls the skopos through its agency."

"Can this be true?" demanded Severus. "How could he have learned of the binding of daimones? I traveled extensively in my youth from monastery to monastery to erase every reference to sorcery and the art of mathematici that I could find."

Brother Marcus was enjoying himself. He closed the book and lifted a finger, as if to enjoin patience. "When spring came, a new rumor infected the city. Queen Adelheid had reappeared in the north, and some claimed that sorcery had aided her in her flight from King John. Some claimed that stone crowns had been seen gleaming with starlight and moonlight."

Even Liath looked up, gaze made sharp by surprise. Severus grunted with annoyance. Zoë clapped a hand to her ample bosom, looking shocked. Meriam's smile was thin and unreadable. Anne simply waited for Marcus to go on.

Brother Marcus suffered the failing of pride, and he was proud of himself now. Yet the sin of pride was not the worst failing a woman or man could have, reflected Antonia; not as long as she, or he, was right.

"He has Bernard's book," he said, and then sat back to enjoy the reactions this statement caused. Antonia, too, was free to study her companions because she had no idea what "Bernard's book" was or why it mattered.

"Nay!" said Severus. "I thought it was burned."

"The servant brought no report of the book," cried Zoë. "Under such constraints, it couldn't lie!"

"Can Bernard actually have had the power to conceal it and pass it on?" asked Meriam. But she seemed intrigued more than angry.

"Go on," said Anne without expression. She alone seemed unsurprised. But then, Anne never seemed surprised. But then, Anne never seemed surprised. Yet neither did Liath seem surprised.

"Well, Bernard's book. What was I to do? I made an effort to recover it, but, alas, I failed. He was more alert to magic than I had supposed. I underestimated him because it seemed obvious to me that he was working sorcery far beyond his understanding of the art. He was more cunning than I thought."

Liath's lips moved, forming a word or a name, but she made no sound.

Marcus drew out a scroll from his sleeve and displayed it almost in the way a boy teases his little sister with a toy she badly wants. "But I did manage to grab this before I had to retreat. I have no idea where he found it, but I think you'll agree that it is of great interest to us." With a flourish, he untied the ribbon that bound it closed, and unrolled it on the table, holding down the curling edges with his hands. Everyone leaned to see.

"I beg you," he said tartly when Liath touched it, "have a care! It's ancient."

"It's papyrus," she said. "It isn't parchment at all."

The strange markings on the page confused Antonia at first; then, just as Meriam spoke, she too recognized it for what it was. "It is a map," said Meriam softly. "These hatchings are meant as mountains, I think. Here is a river. These are meant, I think, as trees."

It was a map, but nothing like those ancient navigator's instruments drawn by the Arethousans or by the Dariyans in the time of their empire. Besides obscure symbols at the border of the map, probably meant to represent heavenly bodies or certain heathen gods, there were seven main places marked on the pale sheet, six at equidistant points on the outside, almost in a circle, and one in the center ringed by what appeared to be mountains. Each of the seven places was made up of seven objects, ragged, arrowlike angles, surrounded by markings that seemed to indicate mountains, or a river, or a valley, or a forest, or the sea. It was hard to tell, and age had obscured some of the map.

"Those represent stone crowns." Severus actually sounded amazed. "I'm sure of it!"

Marcus smiled slyly and let the scroll roll back up. He tied the ribbon back on, and handed the scroll to Anne. "It looks as if my theory is the correct one." If his smugness was meant to wound Severus, it evidently worked. The older man looked annoyed and sat back with a grunt.

"Interesting news," said Anne, although neither her tone nor her expression changed. She placed the scroll on the table. Liath stared at it fixedly; she seemed to want to pick it up, to study it again, but she did not. She only waited. "What shall we do about Darre?"

Marcus waved a hand dismissively. "Mother Clementia is old and weak. She is no threat to us. Whether Ironhead or the old

Adeline house rules in Aosta matters nothing to me, and I do not believe it should change our plans."

"Who rules always matters," said Meriam softly.

"That book is a danger to everything I worked so painstakingly to conceal," muttered Severus.

"I have worked for many years," cried Zoë, affronted, "and still I can only assist in the weaving of the gateways because of their complexity. I remain the sixth part of the dragon, and truly I am content with my position, I don't mean to suggest otherwise. But it seems impossible to me that an untrained man can through his own efforts open a gateway! With no help!"

"No help but Bernard's book," said Anne. "In the right hands, it would be a powerful goad as well as a powerful aid to one who has strength of will and a promising intelligence."

"Or the ability to lie convincingly," retorted Zoë.

"What do you say, Liath?"

Unlike Sanglant, Liath had learned how to control her expression; the feelings she carried in her heart did not show on her face. She was opaque. Not remote, like Anne, but veiled. "I have nothing to say." Yet it seemed a trifle hotter in the chamber.

Lady Above! This entire episode made plain what was wrong with these people. The Chamber of Light was a long way away. God hadn't put people on Earth so that they could twiddle their thumbs while waiting for death to claim them. This time on Earth was a test. And God had chosen certain, more righteous souls to make sure that all of humankind followed God's teachings, whether they liked it or not. Like cattle, they must be herded, or else the wolves—the minions of the Enemy—would eat humankind alive.

"Should we kill him?" asked Marcus.

Anne smiled coolly. She turned with deliberate calm to Liath. "Should we kill him, Liathano? You have some acquaintance with this man, I believe. I would value your opinion."

"Who are we to judge who shall be killed and who shall live?" replied Liath in a low voice, but now Antonia heard real anger beneath that opaque facade.

If Anne was offended by this reproof, she did not show it.

"Is it necessary to kill a person who may prove valuable to us later?" asked Meriam.

"When is it necessary to kill?" asked Anne. "We must only

act in such a drastic way when there is no other choice, when there would be more dire consequences in letting a dangerous person live than in bringing death to him." The armillary sphere set on the shelf behind Anne spun suddenly, although there was no breeze. The planets shifted position and slowed, settling into a new configuration. "But Sister Venia has not yet spoken."

"I think," said Antonia carefully, "that the strength of your reactions is founded on a history and an association that I know nothing of. I joined you only recently. These names mean little to me. I am still young in the art." And increasingly curious. A man had been moving in court circles in Wendar with an interest in sorcery. It was a shame she hadn't found him first. "Who is this Wendish churchman sent to stand trial for sorcery? From what lineage does he spring? Who is this Bernard whose book you all speak of? Where is he now?"

"Bernard is dead," said Liath. "He was killed by a daimone. Someone had been hunting him for a long time."

The celestial globe sitting on the shelf beside the armillary sphere began to glow suddenly, the painted pinpricks on its surface—representing stars—brightening as if a flame, or one of the servants, had somehow wriggled inside. A ripple of light twined along one of the beams overhead, and the smell of charred wood scented the air. Outside, leaves rattled as a stiff wind shook them, then stilled. The gust shifted the door, which stood ajar.

Liath rose suddenly, as stiff as a dog which has scented danger. Carefully, she swung a leg over the bench, extricating herself, and as deliberately walked over to the door. "You killed him," she said. The sun's light limned her, made her even seem to glow a little, yet for all her taut anger, her expression was unreadable. The veil had fallen to reveal the monotone face and voice of anger overridden by shock.

It was unusual to see Anne stricken with more emotion than the adversary she faced. Her mouth tightened. Her hands closed over nothing, except, perhaps, memory. "He stole you from us. He almost ruined you in the years he had you in his keeping. He almost rendered you unfit, as we can see this day, as we have seen every day since you joined us. I did what had to be done. When you see the necessity of that, Liath, I will know we have finally undone the damage Bernard did to you."

"He loved you," whispered Liath. "He was your *husband.*

Didn't you care for him at all? Didn't those oaths mean anything to you?"

"We cannot let affection, or hatred, cloud our judgment. We must be strong enough to kill the ones who stand in our way. We are all only tools in Their hands, and our lives are meaningless except as we act as the instruments of Their will."

"My God," said Liath, and she walked out.

There was silence, of a kind. The light in the celestial globe dimmed and winked out.

"Who was Bernard?" repeated Antonia.

"He was once one of us. He stole Liathano from us when she was only eight years old, and you can see what the years under his care wrought of her. That was eleven years ago. We have a great deal of work to do to make her into the vessel through which our plans can be fulfilled, our work completed, and Earth rescued from its terrible fate."

"Indeed," said Severus primly, "she was brought into this world precisely because she is, given what she is, the only one who has any hope of killing Prince Sanglant. 'No disease known to you will touch him, nor will any wound inflicted by any creature male or female cause his death.' She is the only one who can stop them."

"But why would he steal her? Didn't he understand the whole?" As a mother herself, Antonia found Anne's cold-blooded statements startling, although one had to admire her single-mindedness. But wasn't it a little unnatural for a woman to be so willing to sacrifice her only child? How many noblewomen, and poor ones, too, had come to make confession at the altar in the great cathedral of Mainni, begging God to give them a child? She had lost count. Indeed, for a long time Antonia had wondered if the one sin, the one slip that had led to Heribert's birth, hadn't been God's way of allowing her to understand their desire. For as the blessed Daisan had said: "The road to purification arises out of conception and birth."

"Bernard was misguided," said Anne sternly. "He loved the world too well."

Marcus sighed loudly, pulling the ivory-covered book back toward himself and tapping on the filigree with impatient fingers. "Have we done with this scene?" he asked. "I am reminded of the theater in Darre, which is quite the rage these days now that Ironhead has taken the throne and is quite eager to investigate the charms of every stage dancer who strikes his fancy, which seems to be most of them. But I have other news. I found Lavrentia, just where Brother Lupus said she would be."

Anne turned and walked to the shelf. She reached toward the spinning armillary sphere, and its turning metal bands stilled abruptly. Without turning back, so that her face was hidden, she asked, "She is truly still alive?"

"She is Mother at the convent of St. Ekatarina."

"Brother Lupus was misled," said Anne quietly.

"Nay," said Marcus. "He was baldly lied to those many years ago. She must have grown suspicious. She must have taken refuge there, and the nun who was then mother of the convent must have taken her in and sent the message that she had died. I call that lying, myself."

"Forty years ago," muttered Severus. "It is a long time to live concealed from us."

"Have you ever visited the convent of St. Ekatarina, Brother?" asked Marcus, not a little sarcastically.

"Nay, I have not. I will thank you not to take that tone with me, Brother."

"Then I will only say that it is an isolated place and very difficult to gain access to. What are we going to do about her? Is she a danger to us?"

Anne did turn now. Whatever expression she had turned away to hide had vanished. She looked as cool and collected as ever. "Did she seem to you a danger?"

"She seemed evasive. She is called Mother Obligatia now, but I did not see her face. I had nothing to judge her by except her voice, and she sounded old and frail, not robust."

"Voices can be deceptive. We were misled once. There is more here than meets the eye."

Truly, thought Antonia, there was far more here than met the eye. Sister Anne did not have all of Earth under her control, although after a year or more at Verna one might begin to think so. Who was Lavrentia? Why was she important enough to be discussed in such terms? But she had already asked enough questions. She did not want to draw any suspicion that she might be less loyal to their cause than she appeared on the surface. Mercifully, Zoë did not fear to speak her mind.

"Who is this Lavrentia, and this Mother Obligatia, or whatever you call her?" she demanded. "I've never heard of her. Of what interest is she to us?"

Even Marcus remained silent, watching Sister Anne.

"She was the woman who gave birth to me."

"Your mother!" cried Zoë, looking amazed at the revelation, or perhaps only amazed that a woman like Anne had actually *had* a mother.

"Nay. She was not my mother except that it was in her womb that I was conceived and nurtured, her womb from which I was expelled. I never saw her." Anne lifted the armillary sphere. It was large for her to carry alone, but the ripples that marked the servants helped her, blowing the air beneath her hands to give her lift. She set it down heavily, and the whole table shuddered under its weight. Erekes spun lightly. Mok shifted a finger's breadth, and the bright halo of the Sun shook but did not move. "The woman whom I consider my mother is the one who raised me. It is her influence that guided what I have become."

Antonia could puzzle out most of the rest, but a few questions remained unanswered. "Was this Lavrentia the daughter of Emperor Taillefer, or his daughter-in-law?" And if she had been related only by marriage, then how had Queen Radegundis hidden her son?

Anne merely looked at her, then spun Aturna. The mechanism was ponderous on the outermost sphere, and the planet of wisdom moved only a short way. "It is true that I am the daughter of Emperor Taillefer's son. But he and Lavrentia form the lesser part of my lineage. I was raised by a woman named Clothilde, and it was she who tutored me in the arts of the mathematici, just as she herself was tutored by Biscop Tallia. First and foremost, it is to Biscop Tallia that I claim kinship. In truth, the biscop was my aunt, but in every other way I think of her as the woman who created me. She is the mother who gave birth to all of us, the Seven Sleepers, the ones who, in the last hundred years, have labored to prevent this catastrophe."

So Liath, and so Sanglant: two children born out of enemy camps. If the Seven Sleepers prepared for cataclysm on Earth, then surely the Aoi were making their own plans—wherever they might be, concealed in the aether. Why else go to the trouble to travel through the veils that separated one sphere from the next? Why else send one of their women to Earth to make a child bred half out of humankind and half out of Aoi?

Once, she had supported Sabella's claim because she believed in it. But Sabella was under the care of Biscop Constance in Autun now. She held no grudge against Sabella for her failed attempt at the throne; God had chosen to lend Their support in another place. And perhaps They had chosen otherwise because, like the angels and the daimones, They could see both into the past and into the future. They had seen this day coming.

And she knew just how to take advantage of it.

4

LIATH returned unexpectedly. Sanglant had just settled Blessing into Jerna's embrace. The infant was a silent, efficient eater; she would latch on and suckle, and when she was done, she was done. She had the heft to show for it, all pudgy arms and legs, but sometimes he wondered exactly what kind of nourishment she was imbibing, and why she seemed to be growing so fast.

Better not to think too much about that. When a man extended a hand to you when you were drowning, you didn't stop to ask him his rank and breeding, or if he had leprosy.

"Sanglant."

He heard it as a whisper. By the time he got up and came round the side of their hut, she was just reaching the door. She saw him, grasped him by the elbow. She was in the grip of such an overpowering emotion that her skin almost burned him. He put a hand to her forehead, to draw it off, but she only caught his other arm and gazed at him fiercely.

"Are any of the servants near?"

He listened. Whistled. "Nay, none but Jerna. She's nursing the baby."

She dropped her voice to a whisper anyway. "There are four goats with kids down by the stock shed. We'll need one of them. As long as Sister Anne's sorcery binds this valley, Jerna won't be able to leave."

"I've never heard you refer to her as 'Sister Anne' before. What's amiss, Liath?"

She leaned into him as if to embrace him—dangerous enough in itself—but she spoke so softly into his ear that even a servant dancing on the wind nearby would not have been able to overhear. "We will leave tonight."

"What's amiss, Liath?" he repeated. It was a windless day, remarkably so, and yet, from this angle of the valley he could see trees swaying down by the tower and hall. Up here, on the middle slope, it was quiet.

Hidden behind the hut, Blessing began to wail. Liath bolted, but he caught her and passed her up, came around the side of the hut to see the tree where Jerna usually settled when it was time for a feeding. Jerna was gone. Blessing lay tumbled on the ground, screaming, linen swaddling bands a little unwound as though she'd hit the ground and rolled. He caught her up and held her against his chest, and she quieted almost at once. Then, in the way of babies, to whom past and future seem equally meaningless, she began to coo and smile.

"Ai, Lady," said Liath, coming up beside him. She put out her arms. He laid Blessing in them, and the little girl babbled sweetly as Liath stood there with tears running down her face. "She killed him."

The wind down by the lower buildings had picked up. He could actually hear its rustle and murmur now, and yet it wasn't climbing the slope as would a natural wind. Were they all thrashing and moaning in an eddy centered about Anne? Was all of this, inevitably, about Anne?

"She killed Da."

"Ah." That exhausted his eloquence. What else could he possibly say? *I can't believe she would do such a thing?* But he could believe it. That was the problem.

"Da was running from her all along. From them, from the magi. Why did he steal me from them? What did he know that would make him do something so drastic? He must have known they would pursue him. He must have thought it was worth the risk. Why didn't he tell me what he knew? Why didn't he tell me?"

"Sit down," said Sanglant, and she sat. Shock had made a puppet of her. "Who can we look to for aid?"

She laughed bitterly. "No one. None of them."

"But Sister Venia seems discontent. She wasn't happy that Sister Anne let Heribert go."

"She is better than the others, in some ways. She doesn't treat me as if I'm diseased just because I have a child and a husband. I like Sister Meriam, but I don't believe she will help us if helping us means going against Sister Anne. Ai, Lady. I let them lull me. They taught me only what they wanted me to know, and I listened to their promises and sat by passively all these months while they threw me the crumbs. Just enough. Just enough to keep me content, like a cow never looking past the fence."

The low rumble of a distant avalanche shuddered the air, but when he gazed up at the high ridges and peaks that hemmed them in, he saw no telltale rise of dust, no plume of white haze. A moment later he heard a sharp crack, like distant thunder, but there were no clouds today except for the plumes that often were tethered at the highest peaks.

"Something has distracted them," he said, watching wind whip tree branches into a frenzy below. It remained calm and windless here, not two hundred strides above the little storm. "In the chest there should still be that little pouch of sheep's gut. We can use that to feed Blessing. I'm sure she'll take goat's milk now. There's a small sack of barley and some beans hanging from the rafters. There's fennel and mint, already dried—"

"We've got chestnuts, too."

He nodded. "When you've filled the packs and saddlebags, hide them in the chest. I don't believe the servants can find it there. I only ever saw one of them able to move into wood, and I haven't seen him since Heribert left."

"I pray he's well," murmured Liath.

"As God wills. No need to touch my armor. I'll put it on tonight. I'll go down now to the shed and bring up one of the goats. I'll bring up Resuelto."

She nodded, began to get to her feet.

"Can you open the gate, Liath?"

Poised to rise with the baby held tight against her shoulder, she looked at him. Her hair seemed to actually spark, in that instant, and he thought the grass at her feet might burst into flame. But she controlled herself. "If Hugh can do it," she said in a soft, furious voice, "then so can I."

*   *   *

He wondered where Jerna had gone, and why she had departed so precipitously. She had never abandoned Blessing before. Someone or something had called her away. Judging by the disturbance in the trees in the lower part of the valley, he guessed it was Anne.

Resuelto was eager enough to come with him; the gray gelding always looked forward to their daily rides. The goat was less eager, but he got hold of her kid and she followed meekly enough, although she had a tendency to try to butt him from the rear and she kept pulling away from the path to nip at any delectable flower or weed.

He had buried the dog along the path, just below their hut, as a reminder to Anne and the others that he hadn't forgotten their treachery. After two months, all the grass and wildflowers had withered on the mound that marked the burial, leaving only dirt and dead things. In a sour kind of way he liked the look of it; at times, chafing at the elegant bonds that held him, the barren little tumulus matched his mood.

He was still fuming. As soon as Jerna had sung open the concealed pathway up in the high meadow, he should have thrown Liath over Resuelto and taken them all out, not just Heribert, but he had chosen caution. Maybe he had been right to be cautious: it *had* been a trap, after all. But it galled to know they had been so close to escape.

And yet, how far would they have gotten before Sister Anne sent her servants after them? He knew how Liath's father had died, and while he didn't fear for himself, or even Liath, he wasn't sure that he could protect Blessing.

· He went so deep into this sort of fruitless musing that he actually tied up Resuelto and the goat to opposite ends of the post by the trough before he realized that Liath was talking to someone, inside the hut. He halted, hearing Blessing fuss a little, and there was a silence. Perhaps she had only been talking to herself.

"Nay," Liath said with anger, "you're too kindhearted a soul to trust a man like Hugh of Austra."

"Is he a dangerous man, then, set loose in Darre?"

"With Da's book, and a daimone at his command? He is."

"But a clever one, evidently."

Liath grunted. Sanglant dipped a hand in the cold water of the trough, and waited. "Hugh told me once that you could only hate what you could also love. But you can never trust him.

Never, ever." Sanglant had never heard her speak with such passionate and almost gleeful fury. "If that had been Hugh who was here when I was ill, he would have sat beside my bed and read aloud to me, and reminded me that Sanglant can't read. Hugh would have knelt beside me as I measured the angle of rising or plotted the course of the moon through the zodiac, and he would have mentioned just so elegantly that Sanglant has learned some of the names of the constellations and stars, enough to navigate the night sky, but it doesn't truly engage him. That he doesn't have the passion for knowledge. Not like I do. Not like Hugh does."

"Not all of us are granted that particular passion," said Venia soothingly, as if nervous of Liath's anger. "I must confess that I find the computus to be tedious beyond measure. All those long strings of calculations! But I can see that for a woman who loved them, it would be easy to feel affection for a person who could love them in his turn."

"That isn't what I meant at all." Then she let out such a drawn-out, tense sigh that Sanglant only came to himself when he felt the goat chewing at the hem of his tunic. He shoved it back and stepped away. "I don't wear a slave's collar anymore. I don't have to. *And I never will again.* Don't trust Hugh of Austra because he'll twist every word you utter and warp every thought that passes through your mind to his own use. He has to live with his hand clutched at the throat of any creature he wants to possess."

Sister Venia made no answer. Perhaps it would have been more prudent to remain outside, but truth be told, he was too stung by the unflattering comparison made between him and Hugh. He stepped over the threshold to see Sister Venia holding the baby while Liath stood with one foot up on the chest and her gaze turned away from both of them.

"Ah," said Venia. "Prince Sanglant."

"What are you thinking of with that grim look on your face?" Sanglant asked his wife.

She didn't look at him. "Freedom," she said, and for an instant he thought he heard the cold arrogance of Anne in her tone. Then she shook free of it and turned to indicate their visitor. "Sister Venia has come, as you see. She says that the council broke up with much disagreement on all sides, and that the servants are in a frenzy."

Venia smiled compassionately. "You are in a difficult situation. I took advantage of the servants' confusion to speak with you. But I dare not remain long."

Sanglant sighed. "Are you here to propose something?"

"Nay, Prince Sanglant. Only to make a point." She clucked at the baby for a moment, and Blessing smiled and reached for the shiny gold Circle of Unity that hung at her breast. Venia flicked the jewelry briskly away. "It seems to me that the Aoi in their distant home plotted to create Prince Sanglant for their own purposes. It seems that Sister Anne and her cabal plotted to make Liath—Princess Liathano—for their own purposes. But why succumb to their plans? Why simply fight them without any vision of your own?" She waited, letting the baby grab her forefinger. They tussled gently. Blessing chortled.

"Go on," said Sanglant.

Venia shrugged as if to make light of her own words. "What do I see here in this common hut, locked away in a mountain valley? I see Emperor Taillefer's great-granddaughter, of legitimate issue, wed to the favorite son of King Henry, the most powerful regnant in the western realms, and who is also quite likely born out of a royal line of his mother's people, the very ones, we have heard, who seek to rule in their own right when they return. Yet neither of you have experience in these matters. Princess Liathano was born into a magi's villa, and then, it appears, spent much of her life as a fugitive. Prince Sanglant was raised as a fighter, not a courtier. Because of this, you haven't seen how you can mold the situation to your own advantage."

Liath remained silent, watching neither Venia nor Sanglant but the grain of wood on the lid of the chest, as if she expected it to writhe into life at any moment.

"Go on," said Sanglant.

"If a great cataclysm is coming, then those who survive it will be in chaos. They will need strong leadership. Separately, I am sure you stand as powerful pieces in this great game being waged above our heads. Together, you could be more powerful still." Then she smiled modestly, holding out the baby. "I believe she is wet."

She left, and left them in silence.

"Why did you speak of Hugh with her?" asked Sanglant.

She looked him straight in the eye as if challenging him to

object to anything she had said, as if she knew he'd been listening. "He was being discussed by the others because of his activities in Darre. He was sent to the palace of the skopos to stand trial for sorcery, but instead he seems to have bound the skopos to his will by means of a daimone, and thrown his power behind a man called John Ironhead, who has been crowned king of Aosta."

"What news of Queen Adelheid?"

"Dead. Fled. No one knows. Or they won't say. Sister Venia felt at a disadvantage during the discussion because she didn't know anything about Hugh."

"So she came to you."

"She might have felt I would have fewer compunctions about telling her what I knew."

"She might have wanted to curry favor," he pointed out. But he was too proud to let her know how much he'd overheard. Did it really bother her that much that he couldn't read?

"What do I care about her currying favor?" demanded Liath. "I was upset, and she listened. How can it matter what I said now? Tomorrow we won't be here."

"But what she said—" he began, and she turned on him with as much anger as he'd ever seen in her.

"Rule as emperor and empress with the dogs all going for our throats? *Never.*"

"But, Liath," he began, coaxingly, seeing what an uncertain and difficult temper she was in, "what Sister Venia says is true. We have to look farther than our own escape, our own well-being. Many more people than you and I and Blessing will be swept up in this tide, when it floods in. If we have any power to protect them, then isn't it right that we act?"

But she only started to laugh. "You'd better change her," she said. "Jerna brought down some fresh moss from the slopes this morning. You're dripping."

He had to laugh, too. In his passion, he'd not noticed. "Ai, God," he said, feeling the dampness seep over his hands. "I suppose it would be wise to remember the old saying: 'One task at a time.'"

Blessing began to fuss. As he stepped to the door, Liath sat down on the edge of the bed and, stylus pressing into wax, began to make diagrams.

5

THEY met the outriders at midday, a party made up of soldiers and stewards who were riding ahead to the palace of Angenheim to alert its steward to expect the arrival of the king, his retinue, and his army on the morrow. Since Adelheid's party had just sheltered for three nights in the manifold comforts of Angenheim, Rosvita would happily have turned 'round right then and followed the king's party back to the palace, to await Henry's coming.

"If we wait for King Henry at Angenheim, we can make ready for the meeting," she explained to the queen and the princess. "And he will have word of our presence."

Adelheid refused to consider this course of action. "We will ride on to meet the king." Belatedly, she turned to Theophanu. "What do you think, Cousin?"

Theophanu did not glance at Rosvita. Once, before the escape from St. Ekatarina, the princess would have sought Rosvita's opinion, even acquiesced to her judgment. But no longer. "Let us ride on," said Theophanu. "I would rather see my father this night than ride back the way we came and not see him until to-morrow."

Rosvita missed the understanding they had once shared. Now Theophanu was more likely to turn to quiet Brother Heribert, who rode next to her like a favored adviser. After her passionate accusation of Hugh, it was puzzling to see Theophanu develop such a close friendship with a man who had been accused of sorcery and implicated with Biscop Antonia. But Theophanu and Heribert both trusted, and remembered, their link to Prince Sanglant. In a way, Sanglant bound them. It saddened Rosvita to think that because of the choice she had made, because of the trust Theophanu had given into her hands when they were confronted with Hugh at the convent, she had lost Theophanu's confidence. Indeed, in dark moments, she wondered if Theophanu felt that she had actually in some manner betrayed her.

She wondered if she had betrayed herself and her own principles for the sake of her implacable curiosity, because it was obvious that Theophanu hated not the thought of magic, but the thought of any kind of alliance with Hugh.

"It will be good to ride among the schola again," said Fortunatus softly as their retinue started forward. Adelheid and Theophanu rode at the forefront, with their noble companions and their clerics around them. The servants and wagons—all of their supplies and many of their horses had been a gift from Lady Lavinia at Novomo—followed, with Captain Fulk and his soldiers bringing up the rear.

"You have missed Amabilia, have you not, Brother?"

"I even miss poor Constantine." Crossing the Alfar Mountains had restored some of his humor, although he was still slender, a little pinch-faced: He was not a man suited to leanness, and with the weight had gone that seemingly inexhaustible supply of joviality. "I confess to you that I still cannot understand all that lisping and slurring of our Aostan comrades. And while I have scarcely encountered a more polished vessel than Brother Heribert, I am not sure he trusts us, or if we should trust him, knowing what he was once accused of."

"He speaks of it freely enough," she said, feeling obliged to come to Heribert's defense if only because she admired his brilliant command of fully five languages. "But I understand your meaning well enough, Brother. We shall be back among our own soon. I also have missed the schola." And it was true, she thought, a little surprised: She had missed the genial companionship of other churchwomen and men, the books, the documents, the ink-stained fingers, and, not least, the company of the king himself. She had missed Henry.

Did Henry, too, mistrust her? Was that why he had sent her to Aosta? Or had he sent her away because of her involvement with the accusations against Hugh only because, at that time, he had needed to placate Margrave Judith?

Soon she would find out.

Soon enough they rode over a stout bridge crossing a tributary of the Malnin River. They rode under the canopy of forest for a while before emerging into the cultivated lands that surrounded the city of Wertburg. Summer fields lay rich around them, ripe for harvest. They wound their way up a rise and, before them, saw the king's banner flying from the biscop's palace in the city lying to their north.

A flush had come to Adelheid's cheeks. Theophanu looked pale. Fortunatus sighed deeply in the way of a man who has finally come home.

With a shout, Captain Fulk and his soldiers burst into song: "*In honor of the king, I sing.*"

Amazingly, as they rode down and passed through the gates of Wertburg, Rosvita found herself weeping.

They rode, truly, as a rather bedraggled expedition, much depleted in number and without the dazzling magnificence due a queen. But as they passed down the dirt streets, townsfolk gathered on plank walkways to stare, and by the time they reached the biscop's palace, they had a substantial escort trailing behind them, folk who were curious to see what this meeting would bring.

King Henry was holding court in the great hall. The throng of petitioners crowding the doors parted to let Adelheid through, and she strode forward into the hall with Theophanu at her right side and two servingwomen to her left carrying the only portion of the queen's treasure that had survived her flight. Rosvita and the other clerics stuck close behind them, followed by the rest of their noble companions. Captain Fulk and the soldiers remained outside.

She saw him, first, seated on his throne and listening patiently to a group of petitioners. His trusted Eagle stood behind him, and at intervals he would beckon to her and she would lean down and murmur a comment into his ear. He seemed lost in thought, somewhat distracted from the complaints and entreaties brought before him. He had lines on his face that hadn't been there before, and he looked tired, drawn out, and worn of spirit.

She still had tears, and she let them fall. At that moment, she comprehended the heart of the exile who at last has come home. Hadn't his courtiers been taking care of him? How had he fallen into such a careworn state?

Hathui saw their party at once, and she got his attention, whispered urgently in his ear.

Surprised, he rose.

The petitioners shrank back, like water parting before the stem of a proud ship. Adelheid had little enough, a rich gown that had stood up remarkably well on their travels, rings and

necklaces fit for her station, black hair that had come partially
undone to lap her shoulders and frame her pretty face, but most
importantly she had youth, and intensity, and a determined, rap-
turous expression.

Henry took a step forward. He had the kind of stunned look
on his face that afflicts very young men who have seen a beautiful woman smile at them for the first time. But he had been
king for almost twenty years; he knew how to collect himself.

"Word was brought me that your party had been sighted," he
said, "but I did not expect to see you so soon, Daughter." He
extended a hand, brought Theophanu to him, and allowed her to
kiss him on either cheek. "Bring a chair," he said to his stewards. "One for my left hand." He indicated to Theophanu that
she should sit there, but it was obvious that he was having a
difficult time keeping his gaze off Adelheid. "And one for my
right."

"King Henry," she said, in greeting. "Well met."

"Queen Adelheid. You are welcome in my kingdom. I pray
you, sit beside me and rest."

She gestured to her servants to open the little chests they carried. "Truly, after such a journey in desperate circumstances, I
cannot rest until I am sure of your intentions. See what I have
brought." Her voice rang easily throughout the hall. Clasps were
opened; oiled hinges wheeled. A servingwoman knelt and uncoiled cloth from the objects nestled in the first chest: two burnished gold crowns set with rubies. "These are the queen's crown
and the king's crown of Aosta," she went on, "which I have rescued from the grasp of John Ironhead. I have with me also all
that I could salvage: the tribute lists, the royal insignia, the seals,
the scepter, and the royal cup of the Adeline line, and the robe
of the blessed Daisan which we have kept in our treasure for a
hundred years. These things I have brought to you, for surely
you have heard by now that I was driven from my throne by
one unworthy to hold it. I am in need of your aid, Henry."

She paused to look once around the hall, as if gauging her
audience, as if measuring them. The last of the combs holding
up her hair, already jogged loose, slipped out and fell to the
floor just as her hair tumbled down in a sensuous fall. A servant bent to retrieve the comb, but Henry reached it first, picked
it up, and with a sudden and quite startling smile presented it

to Adelheid as if it were a precious jewel rather than a simple ivory comb.

Their hands touched.

Only Rosvita and the servingwomen stood close enough to hear Adelheid's hoarse whisper. "You are everything I expected you would be."

Ai, Lady! What man was proof against a young, passionate, and pretty woman who held in her possession the crowns of the realm he had so long desired? Not Henry.

The comb dropped unheeded to the floor as he clasped her hands tightly. "Come," he said, and it was possible that his voice was a little unsteady. "Sit beside me."

This time Adelheid did not hesitate. She sat beside him in a chair only somewhat less finely carved than his own, and Theophanu sat as well, to his left. Seated, Henry saw Rosvita and beckoned her forward.

"Sister Rosvita! My most valued adviser!" He clasped her hands as she knelt before him. As always, the sheer force of his approval staggered her. Was it possible that she had subsisted so many months without it? Only now, separated from him for so long, did she truly realize how much she loved him. "I knew that if I entrusted you with this task, you would succeed. You have brought me a great treasure."

"Your Majesty," she said, for once at a loss for words.

But she had been trained in a hard school, she knew the court, and she knew what traps and pits to avoid. Theophanu sat so still that she might have been posing as the image of the queen in an ancient fresco. Rosvita knew when to be prudent, and when to be frank. She used the business of bending to pick up the comb to give herself a few moments to find the right words. It was, after all, no simple ivory comb but rather one fit for a queen: studded with pearls and tiny opals and carved in the shape of a leopard. When she straightened, comb in hand, she spoke.

"Indeed, Your Majesty, it is your daughter, Princess Theophanu, who should receive all credit for any success this expedition has had."

"Nay, do not say so!" cried Adelheid. "My cousin Theophanu has been a strong companion to me in this crisis, but Sister Rosvita's wisdom led us to escape. We are all beholden to her for her steadiness and firm counsel."

He laughed. "We must celebrate this meeting with a feast,"

he said, and as he gestured stewards scurried off to begin preparations.

But Adelheid frowned, ever so slightly, and she leaned toward him so that her shoulder brushed his. She wore a delicate perfume, musk of roses distilled from some sun-drenched Aostan garden. "Why not a wedding feast?" she declared boldly.

At once, whispers swept the hall as her question was relayed to those, in the back, who couldn't hear. Rosvita could not help herself, it was such a brilliant flanking maneuver that she heard herself chuckle before she knew she meant to do so. Henry rarely looked startled, but he did so now. Yet he did not look displeased.

"I bring news," said Theophanu, stirring in her seat like a woman who cannot find a comfortable place, "of my brother Sanglant."

"Ah," said Henry with a small smile. "Sanglant. He placed a hand over Adelheid's smaller one. His hand rested on hers lightly, but firmly, and he seemed overtaken by some kind of sea change, a lightening of expression, a shift of perspective. Once, Rosvita had understood the shores of his ambition, but Adelheid had swept in, bearing with her an invisible tide that had altered the landscape. "We have also heard news of Sanglant, and I believe that you have with you in your retinue one who can reveal much more to us."

It was Theophanu's turn to look startled. "So I do, Father," she said obediently.

"Well," he said, reading reluctance in her otherwise placid expression, "now is not the time. Still, there remains the matter of Sanglant. Both Villam and Judith have ridden east to rally their marchlanders against the Quman threat. If there is war in the east and war coming in Aosta, then certainly we must hope to convince Sanglant to return to court." This comment scarcely caused a ripple, given the swells that had passed through the crowd before. Henry turned to regard Rosvita with his most compelling gaze. "But I can make no decision without consulting the best of my counselors. What do you advise, Sister? How am I to respond to Adelheid's proposal?"

Curiously, it was Hathui, standing behind the king's chair, who lifted her chin to show support, or to suggest an answer. The hall lay as silent as any hall could be with fully three or four hundred people crammed inside, all sweating and struggling to get close enough to hear what would come next.

In that silence of coughs and shifting feet, a distantly shouted question floating in from outdoors, and the whine of some poor dog crushed in the crowd, Rosvita remembered Theophanu's words at the convent of St. Ekatarina, the ones the princess had spoken when she thought Rosvita was still asleep: *"What good is my high birth if our lord father marries again and sires younger children whom he loves more and sets above me? Why should I serve them, when I came before them? Is that not why the angels rebelled?"*

Rosvita was fond of Theophanu, truly. She had sympathy for the difficult position that Theophanu had, all these years, handled with dignity and calm. She even admired Theophanu's cool loyalty to her elder brother, Sanglant, and the constant, uncomplaining service she had given her father.

But Rosvita was Henry's loyal servant first and foremost—after God, of course. Henry would always come first in her heart, and as his trusted counselor she had also to take into account what would benefit the kingdom as well the man himself. She stepped forward to offer him the ivory comb.

"You are still young, Your Majesty." She needed to say nothing more. Like her, he was not more than forty-three years old.

He smiled brilliantly, and indeed he looked five years younger in that moment, as if Adelheid had brought in her train a spell of youth which she now spun over him. He brought the comb to his lips and kissed it gently, then turned over Adelheid's hand and placed the comb in it, folding her fingers over it and sealing her grasp with his own hand, cupped over hers. She sat back with a sharp, satisfied, and vehement smile.

"Send ahead to Angenheim," said Henry to his stewards and to every soul waiting in the hall. "Tell them to make ready for a wedding feast fitting for the marriage of a queen to a king!"

6

ZACHARIAS woke at sunrise. He ached all over from sleeping all night. Kansi-a-lari sat cross-legged in the shallow pit, arms raised to greet the sun. She was singing in her own language, and when she had finished, she bent to bathe her face in the pool of still water that had collected in the shallow pit over the night. With beads of water slipping down her chin, she swung to look at him.

"Now we descend," she said.

"Will we cross the sea flat again?" he asked, shuddering. This time they might not be so lucky. This time the tide might come in while they walked, vulnerable, over the sands, and sweep them away.

She smiled enigmatically and indicated the water, as if suggesting he, too, bathe his face in preparation for the ordeal ahead. "The cosmos is like wood much eaten by insects. It is riddled with holes and passages through which people can travel. Some holes are natural. Some are built with magic in long-ago times. That is why we come to churendo, the palace of coils. Here the three worlds meet. Here we can descend the spiral path and the gate will open to that place where now he is hidden."

"Your son," murmured Zacharias. She didn't look old enough to have an adult son, and yet she didn't look young either. She said nothing, only waited, and at last he crawled forward cautiously and dipped fingers in the pool of water. It was cool and, when he splashed it on his face, it stung, a little briny. But it seemed harmless enough.

He had saved out water for the horse, and he let it take the precious liquid out of his cupped hands as Kansi-a-lari readied her pack and pouch, straightened her skin skirt, and hoisted her spear. It was a cool morning, without the bite of winter. Fog bound them on all sides; he couldn't see the distant shore nor could he see the sea at the base of the island, although he heard it as a steady sigh and murmur.

"Is it really spring?" he asked. "Could we have traveled so far in one night?"

She examined him in silence, then untied one of the ribbons fastened just below the obsidian point of her spear and trailed it like a snake across the surface of the brackish pool. "We are the—what do you call them? To move he boat, what you use to pull at the waves?"

"Oars?"

"We are the oars. We stir the waves of the deep pool, like so." She drew the ribbon along the surface in a circle that crossed its starting point, became another circle, and wound back to the beginning. "We have far to travel on the coils of air and earth." The ribbon dripped as she lifted it from the water. "In the palace of coils you can leave behind where you are doubting in your heart." She let the ribbon fall back into the pool and it lay there on the surface, twining slowly to an unseen current. She tapped her breastbone. "Throw where you are doubting into the pool. Then it will stay here while you descend."

He had so many doubts, but none of them were things he could hold in his hand. And yet hadn't his grandmother always said that a wildflower was a good enough sacrifice to the old gods as long as it was given with a true heart? He had seen strange things. Maybe it was time to throw his doubts away.

He reached for the leather thong inside his robe and pulled out the wooden Circle of Unity which his father had carved for him long ago. Pulling it off, he held it out. "I have seen many things I never knew existed. I will walk the path of truth, not blind tradition. I will keep my eyes open."

He dropped the Circle into the pool. It vanished with a plop, and as the waters closed over it, it dragged down the ribbon with it until both disappeared. The pool lay smooth and still, but he could see nothing below the surface.

"Come," she said.

He took the horse's reins and walked after her through the corbeled archway. The stone lionesses seemed to curl down to sniff at him, their massive shadows as heavy on his back as if they pushed at him with furled claws, but surely that was only his imagination. The path cut sharply to the right and they began to descend deocil.

After three steps he felt dizzy; he doubted. They had ascended deocil. The path had cut right to enter the plaza, hadn't it? How could they descend in like manner? It was as if the path were leading them forward, not backward, as if they were walking toward a place that didn't yet exist, rather than returning to the place where they had started.

He began to shake. His skin felt like a thousand spiders were crawling on it, and he was so tense he could scarcely get one foot in front of the next. Only the steady plod of the horse dragged him along, only the taut line of Kansi-a-lari's back moving before him drew him in her wake. It was hard to focus, but there was light burning ahead so blinding in its blue-white radiance that he struggled to reach it even when her hand stayed him, even when her sharp whisper hissed out a curse—or a prayer.

"Grandmother," he cried, staggering forward toward the light.

The Aoi woman cried out. She jerked him back just as the gate flared and bright wings of light unfolded, so pitiless in their brightness that his face burned as though fire scorched him. A fulgurant arm reached for him as if to drag him through the blinding gate, or haul itself out. He cried out and flung himself sideways, and Kansi-a-lari caught him and yanked him to safety.

He screamed, and then he was running and panting and, finally, falling. He knelt there with grit on his knees while the horse nosed his back. He smelled scorched cloth and felt the sting of a burn along his back and on his cheeks.

"Come," she said, and he heard fear in her voice although she had never seemed afraid before. "The veils are thinning. We must go on."

It wasn't easy to flounder after her, and yet although the burning gate was lost along the curve of the wall, he was afraid to stay behind. What if they had followed him? What if they touched him again and he was burned to ash? She walked with a stride that never faltered, never doubted; she had thrown it all into the pool and truly left it behind. Had he?

"Pale Hunter," he breathed, steadying himself with a hand on the horse's reins. It plodded stolidly along beside him, flicking one of its ears impatiently. "Give me strength. In the name of my grandmother, lend me some of your power now." Was that the wind, or the breath of the Moon? Was it night now, or day? A cooling wind breathed across his neck, and his aches lessened. The path sloped steadily downward.

She had gotten so far ahead of him that she was already leav-

ing the malachite gate when he first caught sight of it around
the opening bend in the path. Had she paused there? Had she
spoken again to the voice that had called her "cousin?" He was
bolder, now. Hadn't he, too, cast away his doubts? Either the
old gods would protect him, or they would not, and she had
never warned him against this gate whose multicolored bands of
green made him think of meadows cut by the spring fields sown
by his people, in the land of his birth.

He paused to catch his breath before the malachite gateway,
and pressed a hand against the cool, gleaming stone.

*There is a silver-gold ribbon running through the heavens,
twisting and turning through the spheres until he cannot tell one
side of the ribbon from the other, or if it even has two sides at
all but only one infinite gleaming surface without end, ever-dying
and ever-living. The cosmos streams around him, great billowing clouds of black dust, bright flocks of blue-white stars so brilliant that they can only be the birthing ground of angels, vast
expanses of void so intense that he feels an abyss yawning at
his feet, a huge spiral wheel of stars spinning in an awesome
silence that might be the future or the past or merely the prayer
of the gods. Yet the planets and the Moon and the Sun still chart
their interminable course, he hears the chiming sweet melody of
the wheeling heavens, and he reaches out to touch it because it
is so beautiful. But his hand cannot pass through the gate. The
green stone dims and fades, and he sees on the silver-gold pathway winding through the heavens the shape of an island whose
size he cannot comprehend; it could be as small as his hand or
as large as Earth because the universe has no boundaries he
can make sense of, he can neither measure nor span its girth.*

*Seeing the island far, he sees it as suddenly near, as though
he were briefly an angel, set free to wing his way through the
churning heavens. It is a dry land, green fading to brown fading to dust. There is no rain. The animals are dying. The corn
no longer sprouts.*

There are no children.

The horse nudged him, hard, and he lost his balance and
stumbled to one side, hand slipping off the stone. The vision
was gone. He stood alone on the dusty path with marble walls
rising high on each side. He had never felt more alone in his

life and yet with solitude came a kind of freedom. He had given away his past freely, tossed it into the deep tidal pool of mortality where all things are lost in time. He could stand here forever, if he chose, and himself turn to dust to be walked on some day by another pair of feet. But the palace of coils touched all three worlds, the world beneath, the world above, and the world between, and so he too had touched them. He had thrown away his doubts. He could walk on without fear.

"Come, friend," he said to the horse, giving a tug to the reins. It followed him as he set off, down, himself following Kansi-a-lari although he had long since lost sight of her.

When he came to the fifth gate with its luminescent and faintly perilous glow of palest violet, he did not falter; he walked past without trying to look beyond it. She had warned him before, he had been attacked when he'd ignored her, and he wasn't fool enough to ignore her warning a second time.

Although he walked steadily, and his back no longer hurt, he did not see her when he came to the fourth gate. The lustrous amber surface called to him as though it had a voice of its own. He could not resist it, could not help but stroke its burnished surface, almost oily under his palm. He saw.

A boy on the cusp of manhood lies asleep in a cave full of treasure, attended by six sleeping companions. But there is something swelling and shifting in the darkness of the cave, like a malignant beast coming awake.

He hurried on, unwilling to see more. The horse dragged him along, eager to go forward—or else it had smelled fresh water. The walls curved away before them and, in an infinity of time that lasted no more than an instant, he saw her on the path before him where the azure gate rested, set into the high, pale walls.

She had paused, hesitated, a hand raised but held cautiously no more than a finger's breadth beyond the ice-pale blue stone. He came up beside her, although she said nothing nor even appeared to notice that he was there. Beyond the gate, the sea boiled and lashed under a cloudy sky, torn by storm. Foam sprayed the rock walls, and he could not see the shore because of the white spray and the low clouds and the surging sea.

"Who is there?" she asked, and as she laid her palm against the pale blue stone, he pressed his against the gate next to hers.

Banners fly outside a fine wood hall. Ranks of young men wait restlessly, talking among themselves, handling their spears as grooms walk among the horses tightening the girths of saddles and making a last examination of hooves. A few wagons are still being loaded with royal treasure: mantles and rich vestments; thin bars of gold and silver wrapped in linen; small iron chests full of minted coins; gold and silver plate and utensils worthy of a king; tents sewn out of a heavy imperial cloth more deeply purple than violets. A chest heavy with royal regalia and crowns. As the sun rises, the full moon sets. The grass grows high beyond the hall, and the trees are dense with leaves.

The doors of the hall are flung open and the king strides out, escorting a pretty young woman half his age who has the bearing of a queen. He laughs delightedly at something she says. His courtiers swirl around them like the tidal currents, some in, some out. A servant lifts a mantle woven of a plain gray weave and swings it open over her shoulders, but his attention is caught by the Eagle badge at her shoulder. It is his sister, and as the cape swirls and settles around her torso, he is spun by that motion

into the gray surge and slap of waves against the hull of a lean, long ship. He swims in the salty seawater and heads bob around him but they have faces so inhuman that he shudders, stroking away. They have eels for hair and no true noses, only slits for breathing and their teeth glitter with menace. But as he turns and dives, tail slapping the surface, he realizes he is one of them, coursing alongside the ships toward some unknowable destination. The sky is dark without even stars to mark their course. A light flares from the stem of the foremost ship, a signal echoed on a distant, unseen shore

that he watches as a rider escorted by three men bearing torches dismounts outside a large pavilion of white cloth. The torches spit and hiss in the drizzle. Rain wets the ground, and grass squelches under the messenger's feet as he pulls off his hat, loose fitting and curled to a point at the top, before stepping out of the rain and into the shelter of a striped awning that makes a sheltered entranceway for the pavilion. A tall bronze tripod stands under the awning. A bowl of thick glass sits on the tripod, and a candle burns inside the bowl with a muted, cloudy light. After a moment, a burly man staggers out of the pavilion, tying up the strings of baggy trousers.

The messenger kneels. "My lord prince. A large host under Prince Bulkezu has attacked the garrison at Matthiaburg and won a victory. There was much slaughter. Lord Rodulf of Varingia and his companions fell or were taken prisoner. Rederii scouts reported that at least ten of their headless corpses were seen stuck on pikes outside the Quman camp."

"How know they these are the corpses of Rodulf and his companions?" demands the prince. He gestures to one of his servingmen, who brings him a cup of wine.

"By their arms and armor, my lord prince."

He sips at his wine consideringly. He has well muscled shoulders and a bit of a paunch around the middle. The curtain leading into the interior of the pavilion stirs, and a small, black-haired woman looks out. She is dressed in nothing more than a gorgeously embroidered blanket which she has wrapped around herself.

"What news?" she asks.

"The Quman are on the move." He spits suddenly, a faint purplish stain flowering on the carpet. "Again we must retreat. Them we cannot engage with the troops we have now. We must have reinforcements from your father!"

"No word from Margrave Judith?" she asks. "The Quman will be in her territory soon."

"No word," he says softly. "But north we must ride along the Oder River. There hope we to meet up with her forces. Then we can to attack."

The woman steps out into the soft lamplight. The blanket she holds so tightly glitters, gold thread tracing antelopes and bounding lions no bigger than her hands. She, too, has well-muscled shoulders, compellingly white, and the prince rests a hand caressingly on one of them. A wind sighs along the cloth face of the pavilion. Bells sewn to the fringe of the awning chime in a hundred light and ever-changing voices.

Bells chimed, and Zacharias started back, flailing a little as he got his balance.

"The tide comes in," she said. She shook her spear a second time, an incantation of bells that echoed along the narrow path.

The high stone walls seemed to sing back in answer to their song, but as the sound faded, she merely began walking again, downward as the spiral steepened and small stair-steps became evident in the path.

He shook himself out of inaction and followed her, but she seemed already so far below him, a thousand leagues away through a substance as murky as the glass bowl that had sheltered the single burning candle. Mist cloaked the sky, and he only knew the sun's position by a whitening glare of haze above.

The next gate shone with a pale iron gleam not unlike the mist that lay dense along the top of the stone walls. Beyond the gate lay a cover of fog so thick that it might have been a host of sheep gathered together, blotting out the earth and sea beneath. Oddly, he could see a few stars overhead and a quarter moon sliding in and out of wispy clouds.

He was so tired suddenly, and very thirsty. He leaned into the wall, bracing himself, unwilling to see any more visions, but his fingers slid anyway along the slick wall and he touched the iron gate and saw beyond it.

A woman sits in a chair carved with guivres. She wears the gold torque of royal kinship at her throat and a coronet on her brow. Her hair runs to silver, and her face is lined with old angers and frustrations. A girlish young woman with hair the color of wheat kneels before her, trembling. She wears only an undershirt, the linen cloth woven so fine that he can see the shape of her body beneath. She is very thin.

"Constance has gone on progress through her duchy," says the seated woman with a tone no less iron than the gleaming gate. "You could have ridden with her, but you chose to remain here."

"She promised me—" sobs the kneeling woman.

"I made no promises to you. I have my allies, and they have their price. You threw away one husband, Tallia. Now you will do as I bid you. Let that be the end of it." She rises from her chair. "Gerhard," she calls to one of the guards. "I will walk in the garden now. Let our guest enter."

The guards standing at the door move aside to admit a man. He walks into the room with the kind of effortless force of a thunderhead. He isn't particularly tall but his broad shoulders and his somewhat bow-legged swagger suggest a man who has fought in many battles and ridden a long way to get here.

"Duke Conrad," says the silver-haired woman, greeting him with a nod. "I have met the terms of our agreement." She gestures toward the sobbing young woman, who has clasped her hands in prayer. "I've cleaned her up a bit, although I can't imagine why any man would find her appetizing." Without waiting for an answer, perhaps even finding the entire transaction distasteful, she walks out of the chamber.

The young woman walks on her knees until she can rest her clasped hands on the ornate altar set against one wall. "I pray you, Cousin." Her thin body heaves as she moans. "I have sworn myself to God's service as a pure vessel, a bride to the blessed Daisan, the Redeemer, who sits enthroned in Heaven beside his Mother, She who is God and Mercy and Judgment, She who gave breath to the Holy Word. I beg you, do not pollute me here on Earth for mere earthly gain."

As she speaks, he walks around her in a slow circle in the way of a thirsty man eyeing a particularly noxious pool of slime he must decide whether or not to drink from. "Have you done?" he asks when she falls silent, staring at him with huge eyes more hollow than bright.

She flings herself facedown on the floor. "I am at your mercy," she cries, face pressed to the carpets. "Do you mean to defile what has been made holy by God's touch?"

"Ai, God," he says in disgust. He is oddly shadowed, a trick of the light, perhaps, or else his complexion is much darker than that of most Wendish folk. Standing above her groveling form, he surveys her with a prim frown quite at odds with the sheathed energy with which he holds himself. "If only my dear Eadgifu hadn't died," he says as the girl snivels at his feet. "She was a real woman. What I would give for one more tumble in bed with her!"

"Lust is the handmaiden of the Enemy," she sobs.

"I beg you," he puts in, "pray do not delude yourself into thinking that you stir one grain of lust in me, Lady Tallia. It is your lineage I desire, not your person. Doubly descended from the throne of Wendar and the throne of Varre, and with so little to show for it! I would rather have my Eadgifu back. But God have made Their will manifest, and now we will be wed."

"Did not the blessed Daisan enjoin us to cleanse ourselves of the stain of darkness that contaminates us here on Earth?"

"So he did." He laughs, but he is not very amused. *"I believe he preached that the road to purification lies through conception and birth."*

"Nay," she cries, as he kneels beside her and sets a hand on her side, rolling her over. She scuttles back out of his reach. *"That is the lie. You are mistaken in believing the error."* She fetches up, panting, against the heavy chair in which the elder woman had sat earlier. She opens her hands as though to reveal a sign, but it is only her palms, marked by pus and weeping sores. *"Don't you know of the blessed Daisan's sacrifice and redemption? I am no more worthy than any other vessel, and yet God has chosen me—"*

"Nay, your mother and I have chosen you. Good God. Get your servants to wash your hands properly after we're through. Come now. Let's get this over with." He grabs her by an armpit and tugs her up toward the canopied bed, *"Ai, Lady! You smell like sour milk. Don't you ever wash?"* He sits her on the bed, not ungently, but she falls back bonelessly and lies limp on the feather mattress as he begins to disrobe, quickly and without any amorous words or passionate glances. *"Get you pregnant I must, so get you pregnant I will."*

When he is down to almost nothing, she begins to sob violently. She bolts from the bed, trying to find somewhere to hide, but there is quite obviously nowhere to hide. She runs to the door and pounds on it, but her bony fists make scarcely any sound, and the heavy door is shut tight. No one answers.

Zacharias recoiled. He could not bear more of it. It was too horrible.

"This is not the mating ceremony I remember," said Kansia-lari with cool disdain, and as he reflexively wiped his hand on his robe, he realized that she was still watching the scene unfold through the gate, her eyes narrowing, then widening; her mouth parted on an exhaled breath as she drew back swiftly. Then she chuckled. "Nay, that is not as I remember it. Maybe the years have changed human kin. They do such violence to each other." She shivered, as if a spider had crawled up her spine or the Enemy's fingers touched her at the base of the neck.

"Let us go on. Now I worry. Now I know I did not leave all my doubts behind. Why have they hidden my son?"

It was hard going as they set off again. He felt as though he were walking through a huge vat of mud. Soon he was taking two breaths for every step, and then three, and then four. Only the horse seemed unaffected, even a little impatient.

He got a rhythm going—step, breathe and breathe and breathe and breathe, step, breathe and breathe and breathe and breathe— and he would not have stopped as the path curled away to reveal the second gate worn thin, a pale pink rose incised with faint letters and incomprehensible sigils. But she stopped. Her eyes flared as she set a palm against the stone of the gate. He saw, first, the quiet sea below and, for a miracle, the distant shore lying clean and clear under a night sky. Stars blazed. He saw no moon.

Then, because he could barely stand, he, too, leaned against the gate. The pale stone warmed his skin.

He smells burning fennel, and as his eyes adjust to night he sees two figures standing in darkness on the slope of a hill crowned with stones. One holds aloft a tightly-wrapped stick of herbs that smolders. His shoulders are strangely humped, and he holds a sword in one hand. Behind him, waiting patiently, stands a silent, strong warhorse, reins hanging loose over its head to trail on the ground. A shield is fixed to the saddle. A leadline attached to the saddle slithers and whips, and a moment later he sees a goat pulling restlessly against the resolute warhorse, which stands firm.

The second figure, armed with a short sword and a bow, kneels and with an arrow's shaft begins to trace a diagram in the dirt. The shaft has neither point nor fletching, but a gold feather that glows with a feeble light is bound to one end. The figure stands, sighting with that shaft toward the eastern horizon which, oddly enough, lies above her. By the curve of her body under her tunic he sees she is female, tall enough but not as tall as her companion, who by the breadth of his malformed shoulders must be male. It is too dark to make out features or expressions.

Trees begin to sway. Leaves toss in a rising wind.

Where a notch cuts the bulge of a mountain, a bright yellowish star appears. The woman chants and with the shaft and the rippling gold feather bound to its end, she seems to draw down that light until it tangles in the stone circle, weaving through the standing stones a pattern of faint light not unlike those sigils inscribed into the stone gate before him. She uses the shaft like a weaver's shuttle as she sights on the brilliant light of the evening star, now sinking down on the horizon of high hills almost opposite that of the rising yellow star. This light she draws into the stone as well, and where the two lights meet, one malevolently yellow and the other as bright as an angel's gaze, a thin archway of light forms between two of the standing stones.

"Hurry," *she says to her companion, and with his free hand he grabs the reins of the horse. His cloak parts to reveal a good, strong mail coat underneath. A baby begins to cry. His shoulders quiver and shift, and little arms bat aside the corner of cape thrown over it: He is carrying an infant strapped to his back in place of his long sword. The goat bleats, tugging against the leadline as though it is itself being hauled backward by an invisible ebb tide.*

But there is a tide, drawing his gaze away from the scene by the stones and into the darkness, down into the valley below where a stone tower stands watch over a handsome timber hall. A stream burbles gaily past, and all is quiet; too quiet. In the stone tower, three figures sit deep in meditation, strange diagrams mark the table before them, and a silvery light gleams from the wood grain along the outline of those diagrams, a stylized rose, a sword, a crown, a staff, and others he has no time to decipher because the tide has dragged his body outward to the livestock pens beyond the tower where shadows have smothered even the light of the stars. From these shadows he can hear the whispers of the malcontent.

"I am against it. It is rash to kill him now, when he could serve us in other ways if we are only patient."

"Nay, Sister. You are reluctant only because you do not comprehend the whole. We are all that protects humankind from the Lost Ones. You are either with us, or against us, and if you are against us, Sister Venia, then I have been instructed by Sister Anne to kill you."

"Very well."

He hears the panicked bleat of a goat just as he sees, as its echo, the flash of a knife. Night half conceals the gruesome sac-

rifice: a frowning woman cuts open the thrashing goat, which is held down by a man in cleric's robes. She thrusts a hand inside its ribs as blood pumps out over her arm. She gropes, tugs, and pulls out its still beating heart. Somehow, horribly, the goat is still alive.

"Light the lamp," she says, and it is done. The glow of the lamp lends a slippery unreality to the scene as the goat bleats weakly and the heart beats liquidly in her hand. She begins to chant.

A smell rises all around, like the breath of the forge, leaching somehow even through the iron gate that seals him away from the vision. Hairs rise on the nape of his neck, and his hands tingle as he is drawn on a wave of shadows in the grip of the tidal current that flows up the hill and back to the man and the woman and the growing archway of light that now manifests within the stone circle.

Abruptly, light flares from stone to stone, a cascade of brilliance, a patterned web like to one of the diagrams he glimpsed in the tower room below. The woman throws up a hand to shade her eyes, but it is too late. They are discovered. Figures pour out of the darkness, but he cannot tell what are shades and what are real, which are doubts and which are solid human forms. One of them cuts through the light-woven gateway with a polished black staff, and the threads unravel and fray into nothing as the man takes a cautious step backward, shoulder bumping up against the steady horse, and raises his sword.

"Hurry," said Kansi-a-lari. Her breath came in short bursts. Sweat had broken, streaming, on her brow. She hooked her spear haft between his body and the rose gate, and·he now realized that he was flattened against it all along the length of his body, as if suction held him there. The haft pressed into his ribs, broke him free, and he stumbled back.

"Hurry," she repeated. As she turned to run down the path between the high walls, she was already getting her bow ready, and she drew out the first of the arrows fletched with griffin feathers, whose touch dissolves magic.

He had to run to keep up. The tide dragged against him, but the horse, and her urgency, pulled him forward against the flow.

Then the ebony gate shone before him. Through its glamour, he saw the sea lapping at its base, a white-capped storm surge.

The path gleamed underneath his feet, rimed with a frostlike gleam. He knelt, entirely out of breath, and even with both hands to brace himself on the ground, he could barely hold himself up.

"*Grandson.*" Her voice shook through the earth.

But he had no time to answer her. Kansi-a-lari had already cut one of her palms and smeared the blood over the black stone. She cut his palm in the same manner, with more haste than care. As he swiped his bleeding hand over the stone she nicked the horse on the shoulder and wiped its blood there, too, dark smears soaking into the slick obsidianlike surface. Sweating now, grunting with desperation and anger, she laid both hands against the ebony gate. She spoke one word.

The gate swung open on silent hinges. Water poured in to swallow their feet, and he followed her across the threshold into the maelstrom.

XIV
THE SOUND OF
THEIR WINGS

1

HANNA had just about had enough rain for one summer, and she was one of the lucky ones: riding, her feet weren't perpetually damp. Unlike half the Lions, she didn't have foot rot. In the woodlands, low ground shone with a sheet of shallow water, ponds that bred mosquitoes so persistent and numerous that every soul in their party scratched constantly. They were plagued by spiders. Any helmet left on the ground would soon swarm with the nasty creatures; any tent, unrolled and set up, would rain spiders from its ceiling all night. By Aogoste they had lost all the whores and beggars.

At the fortress of Machteburg, dysentery hit their ranks. Lady Fortune still marched with them: only one Lion died, although the disease devastated the camp followers and at least a dozen of the cavalry's servants had to be buried by the roadside. They lost ten days before Captain Thiadbold and Lord Dietrich proclaimed them ready to march on. They were ferried across the Oder River on barges, and then they headed east on a grassy track. A dozen stubborn camp followers boasting two handcarts between them plodded in their wake. She couldn't understand why they would follow the Lions into the wilderness where nothing awaited them except war. But perhaps those dozen souls had nothing to go back to, and no place else to go.

It was still raining.

Three abysmally slow days of marching later, on a soggy summer's day in early afternoon, they came to a village of ten longhouses and a dozen more pit-houses and sheds. Ringed by an inner palisade and ditch, the village lay at a crossroads and was prosperous enough to boast a tiny church built just beyond the inner ditch. A second ditch surrounded the gardens, fields, and a half-dozen corrals, and within this second ditch a fair number of folk labored. But as soon as they caught sight of the host approaching, they hoisted their tools and ran to the safety of the palisade even though they all could see the Wendish banner that marked this as an army marching under King Henry's personal seal.

Thiadbold halted his Lions beyond the outer ditch and sent Hanna in with an escort of a dozen Lions. The cavalry was content to disperse in the surrounding meadowland so that their horses could graze.

The gate remained stubbornly closed as they approached. "Nay, you cannot come in," said the young man keeping watch there, peering down at them from a square wooden tower. "I pray you, we've had enough trouble. I'm under orders not to let in any armed men." He spoke Wendish with an accent, hissing his "p"s and "t"s. "But the Eagle, now. She can come in with her news."

Ingo was with her. "As like they're bandits themselves in this town," he grumbled. "I don't know if we can trust them."

"Nay, I'll go," said Hanna. "They're only being cautious. Why would they harm me with an army of two hundreds of Lions and thirty cavalry outside?"

Ingo and the others moved back, the pedestrian gate was opened, and she walked through into the village. It stank because most of their livestock had been driven inside. There were a few gardens, and a fair number of dirty children underfoot. A stream muddied by the summer rains, or by sewage, ran down a narrow canal with reinforced stone walls. There was a well at the center of the village; a pair of young villagers, one girl and one boy, stood guard over the stone housing, monitoring the flow of buckets. A child appeared, wiped its runny nose, and beckoned to her. She followed it to the longhouse that lay closest to the well. Three men and three women waited for her, seated at a huge wooden table much pitted with knife scars and burns. It had one leg freshly fixed on, of a lighter shade than the others. They greeted her politely. After she sat, a girl dressed in a remarkably clean linen gown brought her a fine strong mead.

"We meant no offense by closing our gates," said the scarred woman who acted as spokeswoman for the council. The scars looked recent, two slashes on her chin. "Not that we don't trust the king's milites, mind you, but we've had trouble recently with armed bands. Better to be safe. War's coming, they say." The council members nodded. The girl brought a fresh pitcher of mead and refilled cups all the way around the table.

"What kind of armed bands?" asked Hanna. Some of the words the woman used were unfamiliar, and her accent was a bit odd, although once she got used to the hissing it was easy enough to understand. "Bandits? Barbarians?"

"We've Salavii neighbors, it's true, but it's not them we're worried about now. Just four days ago a wild group of young men come from the west claiming to be noble sons of Saony. There was trouble, and it weren't pleasant. They did that to three of the girls here in town that isn't right, begging your pardon, Eagle, and one of our lads got knifed in the bargain. But Lady Fortune smiled on us. Just when things were about to get ugly, Margrave Judith rode up with a host, why, surely as large as yours and perhaps larger, for she had more horses and riding men. She turned them out with a sharp word!" The others at the table nodded as they, too, remembered the incident. "But the damage was done. Poor young Hilde hung herself at the old oak tree two nights ago, and there's some who want to cut it down because of evil spirits. It's the place where our old mothers used to leave offerings to The Fat One—" Here, at a sharp gesture from one of her comrades, she smiled nervously and gestured to the servant to bring forward bread. "But that's none of your worry, Eagle."

"Of course it is my worry," said Hanna. "If bandits are plaguing you, or even noblewomen's sons, then King Henry will wish to be told of it."

"What can he do?" asked one of the men bitterly. "The leader of them wild boys claimed to be the king's nephew. What *will* he do? We are nothing to the king."

"It's true that you're no blood kin of the king's, friend. But you live under his protection, and if he lets wild young men, even his nephew, take what they want and harry as they will among those folk who look to the king for protection, then he might as well hand the whole of his treasure over and set aside his crown. The king does not tolerate disobedience, even from his nephews. I've seen civil war, my friends, and I know that King Henry will not tolerate any behavior that cuts into his authority. No more would you let your own young children run roughshod through your house, overturning the tables and throwing the apples out to rot."

They nodded, seeing the wisdom in this answer.

"What was his name, who was leader of that warband?" But they didn't know, or wouldn't answer. They were still afraid. The bread steamed when she broke it open. "Well, then, what of Margrave Judith? Did she say where she was marching? What road did she take when she left here?"

"East and south, she said," explained the scarred woman. "She was going at the summons of the king's daughter, so we heard. That's how we know war's coming. There's been fighting. Some say the *wing-men* are coming. We've spoken of building a second palisade. Is it true they cut off people's heads?"

It took Hanna a moment to figure out who the *wing-men* were. "I've heard that story," she said cautiously, not wanting to scare them. And yet, what chance did this village have against a host of Quman warriors? They had built a stout palisade and a good steep-sided ditch further fortified by stakes at the bottom, but there weren't all that many of them. "I rode with Princess Sapientia and Prince Bayan, her husband. They defeated a host of Quman, but it was only an advance force."

"Should we abandon our homes and go west?" demanded the man who had spoken before.

"Nay, Ernust," retorted the scarred woman. "If we leave, then those damned Salavii tribesmen will just move in and take our village, and never give it back!"

They all began to argue with a passion that showed they had quarreled over this point many times in the last few days. At last the scarred woman pounded her cup on the table until the rest fell silent. She turned to Hanna.

"What do you advise, Eagle?"

They looked at her expectantly, and she thought she had never been offered a heavier burden than the one implicit in their gazes. She didn't know how much weight they would give her opinion, and yet any words she said now might make the difference between life and death for them.

"The Quman move swiftly," she said at last. "If you're caught on the road, you'll all be slaughtered. The rains have been bad enough that the roads are terrible in any case. It took us three days to get this far from the fortress of Machteburg, and you'll find no closer refuge than that. I think you're better off building a second palisade hard up against the ditch, and bracing for a siege. If your Salavii neighbors are good Daisanites, you might try to ally with them to protect yourselves—"

But that was more objectionable even than the thought of dying at Quman hands. True, the Salavii had converted ten or even twenty years ago, and they weren't particularly belligerent even as more Wendish settlers moved into what had once been exclusively Salavii territory—their Wendish overlords saw to that—but everyone knew that they were dark, dirty, different. Their daughters were whores and their sons rams. They talked a funny language and were too stupid to learn Wendish. They couldn't be trusted. Worst of all, when the church had finally sent a deacon to minister to the region, she had established her parish by the Salavii village instead of in the perfectly fine little church they had built here in expectation of her coming, and she walked here on Hefensdays and LadysDays to lead Mass and preach a sermon. It was a terrible insult.

Hanna had a fair idea that it was wise of the deacon to stay closest by those of her flock who were most likely to stray. But she wasn't about to tell these people that, not when their anger roiled in the longhouse as acrid as smoke from the hearth fire.

"I pray you, friends," she began, raising her hands for silence. "These are difficult times, and we must pray to God to give us guidance. But if there is nothing further I can do to help you, then we must march on so that we can join up with the host of Princess Sapientia. If Margrave Judith has joined them with a host as well, then perhaps the Quman need never reach your village at all, and you can get on with your harvest."

"If there is a harvest with all this rain," the talkative Ernust began. "We haven't had more than ten days of sun this summer—"

The distant blare of a horn drowned out the rest of his complaint. The startled servant girl dropped the pitcher, and it hit the corner of the table, cracked, and spilled crockery and fragrant mead all over the packed earth floor. Every head turned toward the sound.

Hanna was already on her feet and headed toward the door when the others began talking, calling to her, begging to know what the horn symbolized.

"It's the call to arms," said Hanna, and then she got outside and ran toward the gate.

"What are they talking about now?" Ivar reined up next to Baldwin, who had for the first time in the two days since they'd left the fortress of Machteburg fallen back from his favored position riding beside Prince Ekkehard. Right now, the prince was conferring with the captain of his new escort, a dozen light cavalrymen who had agreed to ride with him as far as Prince Bayan's encampment, which according to the last report lay somewhere to the east.

"I think they're agreeing that there's nothing worse than trailing an army," said Baldwin.

"It would be worse *not* to be trailing an army," retorted Ivar. "The enemy could be anywhere out here, so they said at Machteburg."

Ermanrich, mounted on a sway-backed gelding which had seen better days, only snorted. "We won't be trailing them for long from the looks of it."

They all expected to see the Lion standard appear around every bend. The manure that dotted the track was still warm. Fresh wagon ruts had made treacherous ridges and valleys in the muddy road, a trap for horse's hooves. A few isolated fields and the well-worn trail suggested that a village was near, and Ivar hoped against hope that the army that marched just ahead of them had stopped there, even though it was just past midday. He surveyed the gloomy landscape, the unkempt strips of fields lying to the south, the mucky road that stretched east toward war and adventure and, perhaps, freedom. To the north lay woodland, thin but dark under the gray clouds. The branches of the trees rattled in a gentle drizzle.

"Imagine, Ivar," Ermanrich said, "you were to enter the monastery of St. Walaricus that lies somewhere out here in these Godforsaken lands. But I suppose that the missionaries who bring the word of truth are the favorites of God, not the forsaken ones."

"We should remain out here after the war is over," suggested Sigfrid. It was still startling to hear his voice. "Maybe this is where we're meant to preach."

Baldwin replied, but Ivar didn't really hear him. Something held his gaze on that strip of northern woodland, something about the way distant branches shifted as the wind died and the drizzle let up. The others began to move on, but he held his mount up short and stared into the woods.

There it was again. Branches moved. A pale form flashed beyond a thicket.

"Ivar, what is it?" Baldwin called back to him.

"Wait," he replied in a low voice. First Ermanrich, then Baldwin, then Sigfrid reined their horses aside. They, too, looked into the wood. Surely they were as nervous as he was.

Leaving the fortress of Machteburg and crossing the Oder River had made the adventure of war and righteous preaching seem a little less golden. Yet when he closed his eyes, he could still see the phoenix, rising, and he knew in his heart that he had to find that splendid creature again, that in the cloud of its being he would find truth, and peace. If he breathed enough of that magical smoke, surely he would stop dreaming of Liath. What shifted among the trees wasn't golden, but for an instant he thought it was another great bird, caught in the forest.

Then he realized his error.

Sigfrid gave a croak of dismay and alarm, then recalled he could speak: "God have mercy!"

"There!" cried Ermanrich. "To the left of the wide oak."

"Oh, shit," murmured Baldwin.

The wings had the high sweep of a vulture's and the same cold white underside. But it moved swiftly, negotiating the trees not with great flaps but at a canter. Other wings appeared behind trees or rising from gullies or over hillocks. Maybe they would have been visible all along had he thought to look. Or maybe they were cleverer than the troop of half-grown boys and the untried escort who had crossed the Oder River with the idea that adventure lay beyond it.

His heart pounded so furiously that he couldn't speak. Maybe there was a reason adventure always sounded so good in the safety of a hall, with a bard singing to those who had survived.

Baldwin's voice rose high and sharp with the alarm. "To arms, to arms! They're coming from the woods!"

Ahead of them on the road, Prince Ekkehard hoisted his lance, only to have his arm restrained by the older man who was captain of the escort. "Those are Quman raiders! I pray you, my lord prince, let us ride hard ahead in hope of meeting with Captain Thiadbold. He has fully two hundreds of Lions—"

"But there can't be more than a dozen of them!" cried Ekkehard.

The words of the captain had already been heard by more than Ivar. A few of the company began to move rapidly down the road. By this time Ivar could see a score of Quman riders approaching through the woods.

"Thank God we left the wagons at Machteburg in exchange for more horses," said Ermanrich as he kicked Ivar in the thigh. "Ride, you idiot! They'll run you down if you sit there gaping!"

"Ride, my lord prince!" cried the captain.

Ekkehard hesitated, as if contemplating the nobility of such action.

But the captain was a man of experience, and he knew how to deal with hotheaded young charges. "Follow me!" he cried, and the entire company lurched forward. Ivar needed no more urging. That faint memory of the phoenix, glimpsed through the trees, vanished as soon as he saw their hideous forms clearly: winged like demons but riding stout ponies, they had flat, featureless faces, broad bulky bodies, and skin leprous with huge square scales.

As they reached a gallop, mud kicked up off the hoofs, flung through the air. Ivar turned in the saddle to see the first of the Quman clearing the woods. They, too, broke into a gallop in pursuit. Maybe it was better not to look behind. Ivar resolutely focused ahead, until a sound, as of an arrow whistling at his back, made him duck low to his horse. Had they already caught up to him? He was the last man in line.

He had been issued a spear at Machteburg, and he swung around now, almost overbalancing himself. There was no rider

at his heels. It was nothing but the sound of their wings singing
a song of the battle to come.

He heard a shout as they thundered round a broad bend in
the road. Ahead he glimpsed a Lion starting forward, spear raised,
and a cavalryman swinging up onto his horse. Another Lion let
forth the shout "To arms!" and a horn rang out, three sharp tones.
Ekkehard's company had already pounded past the first line of
soldiers. The grooms and servants rode on toward the safety of
the main force of Lions, who had broken their march on the
outside of a ditch that surrounded gardens, fields, and an inner
palisade marking a fortified village.

One by one, Ekkehard and his soldiers turned their mounts
to face back the way they had come; Ivar grabbed his shield off
the saddle, bracing his spear on his boot. Another half-dozen
riders in heavier armor had joined them by the time all of Ekkehard's fighting company was poised to face the Quman. As they
came riding hard down the road, the Quman dropped their lances,
and in that moment as their line solidified, the whistling of those
wings was the only sound in the entire universe.

"At them!"

Ivar wasn't sure where the command came from, but it was
firm. He started forward with the others, a whoop forced out of
his lungs from fear and exhilaration.

Ai, God! He'd never been in battle before. Hadn't he dreamed
of this? Hadn't he wanted to run away with Liath and go join
the Dragons? Join any noble lady's warband so he could escape
the monotony of his life as Count Harl's youngest child in the
quiet backwater of the north country? Hadn't certain noble fraters
and even abbots fought on God's behalf in just this way?

He was terrified and thrilled and on fire, and he didn't hesitate. There wasn't time to make it to a full gallop before the
first lance broke upon the first shield. Like a pot dropping down
a flight of stone steps, the crash rang as warrior after warrior
crushed into a foe.

Ivar held his shield tight over his cheek and chest, and leaned
into his spear. The blow was like the wallop of a smith's hammer, and he felt his mount slide between his knees as he was
propelled backward over his saddle. A lance had struck his helmet, but he knew he wasn't dead as his back slammed into the
ground. His horse bolted, and where that body had once sheltered him he now saw the wings of his foe silhouetted against

the clouds. Yet between one frightened blink and the next, Lion shields passed over him as stout infantrymen leaped across his body, a heavy line of shouting men who themselves charged in good order at the stopped Quman line.

One of them, decorated with captain's silks and protected by the shield line held fast before him, wielded a great hooked spear with which he yanked rider after rider from their seat. Ivar barely had time to scramble crablike backward before ten of the Quman had fallen prey to the Lions, and a few others been struck down in their charge. The remaining dozen winged riders turned and fled back toward the wood.

"Hold fast the line!" cried the Lion in captain's silks, and his command was echoed first by Ekkehard's captain, then by Ekkehard himself, and then by a latecomer, a nobleman wearing the heavy armor of shock cavalry who had just ridden up. One nervous horseman trotted forward a few paces in pursuit of the fleeing Quman only to rein back his horse when an arrow skittered at his feet.

Ivar struggled to his feet. His left elbow hurt terribly, and his hips ached. Baldwin appeared at his side, shaking him by the arm.

"Ivar! Ivar! Can you speak?"

"Ai! Don't pull my arm off! I'm fine. I think I took the worst of it on my behind." He hitched up his light chain mail coat and rubbed himself there, wincing.

"Udo's dead," said Baldwin as the others assessed the damage and a heavy line of sentries were posted along the forest verge. A party emerged from the shadow of the palisade and hurried toward them. Ivar allowed Baldwin to drag him over to poor Udo, who lay dead as dead on the ground. A lance had passed through the neck of his horse and then through his unarmored belly. The sight made Ivar queasy.

Prince Ekkehard knelt beside Udo, shedding a few noble tears. "Take his ring, Milo. We'll return it to his sister."

"He doesn't have a sister," hissed Milo, struggling to get the ring off Udo's limp hand.

Ekkehard shook himself, glancing 'round quickly as if to make sure that his mistake hadn't been noticed. His gaze flicked over Ivar, who wasn't important enough to count. "Well, we'll return it to his kin, as is proper."

"My lord prince." The Lion captain approached, prudently

going down on one knee. "I did not know you were marching
east to the war—" He was an experienced man, clearly, and obviously one who knew the king's court well. Ivar could almost
watch him think, sorting information and deciding that it might
be wiser not to mention that he, perhaps, knew that Prince Ekkehard had been sent to Gent to become a monk. "I pray you, my
lord prince. If you will lead our army, then we will all march
in more safety until we reach your sister's host."

Ekkehard rose with dignity. "That would be well," he agreed.
"But what are these creatures who have attacked us? Are they
monsters, or men?"

They had leisure to examine the dead while the rest of the
army fell into marching order and a hasty burial was arranged
for Udo. Apparently at least three men, out foraging with their
horses, had not returned, and a party of twenty men went out
searching for them.

The flat, demon faces and terrible wings and scaly bodies of
the Quman were only ornament. The wings, crushed where the
men had fallen in death, looked pathetic now; the feathers that
had whistled so frighteningly were shredded, fragile. The flat
expressionless faces were only bronze masks attached to helms.
The Quman wore a strange kind of armor, leather scales reinforced by metal scales, each one about the width and length of
three fingers held together. Yet underneath they were almost as
human as he was: young men's faces, olive-skinned, with narrow eyes and yellowing teeth. One was still alive, thrashing a
little. A Lion cut his throat, and his blood was as red as any
blood Ivar had ever seen.

Thank God it wasn't his own blood. He had survived.

"Ivar! What are you doing here? Why aren't you with Margrave Judith?" Hanna stared down at him from her mount. She
wore her Eagle's cape jauntily, and the kind of daunting frown
that comes right before a scolding.

Ai, God! Would he never be found worthy? "God has called
us to a greater destiny!" he retorted, and he would have gone
on, but Ermanrich rushed up and grabbed him by the arm.

"My lord prince will happily leave you standing here like an
idiot, Ivar. Get moving!"

Hanna watched him go and then rode off to her own place
in the host. His was in the train of the prince, but their trials

weren't done because they arrived at the head of the host to find Ekkehard and Baldwin engaged in a quiet but fierce argument.

"I won't go!" cried Baldwin.

"You will go!"

"I won't go! Did you hear what they said? Margrave Judith is just a few days ahead of us. She'll be at your sister's camp. It won't just be me she'll be mad at, you know."

"I'm not afraid of Margrave Judith!"

"You should be! After she's whipped me and killed me, she might ask for *you* for her next husband!"

"Ride on your own way, then!" cried Ekkehard, flinging an arm wide to display the empty roads that departed these crossroads and vanished into silent woodland. "You won't fare so well against the Quman raiders by yourself, will you?"

Ivar pressed his horse forward through the throng and fetched up at Baldwin's side. "Baldwin," he said in a low voice, "Prince Ekkehard is right. It's death to us to remain behind."

"I'd rather be dead than return to her bed," muttered Baldwin, pouting a little. But even when he pouted, he did it beautifully.

"Anything could happen," said Ivar. "We're armed, and we're all at war. We haven't met up with Margrave Judith yet, it's true, and things might go ill if she discovers us. But after what I've just seen, I'm not leaving this army!"

For the first time, Ekkehard nodded at him in approval. Baldwin, still pouting, sighed heavily and shrugged, to show that he gave in. "But we'll regret it," he said ominously. "You'll see."

Hanna hung back in the rearguard as the army marched out. She had never expected to see Ivar again, and yet here he was, with Prince Ekkehard instead of Margrave Judith.

This whole day seemed tainted. She shivered, although it wasn't really cold despite the intermittent drizzle. The baggage train lurched down the road that arrowed east into woodland, and just behind the baggage wagons walked those last stubborn dozen souls, the camp followers, and their two laden carts, which they took turns pulling. Half of the first cohort marched in good order at the rear, and for once they did not let the camp followers straggle behind. She saw Alain in that final rank, but he didn't notice her. He was watching the woods, and she wondered if he had struck a blow in the fight or if he, like most of the Lions, had simply witnessed that brief skirmish. He was a lord, wasn't he? Had *been* a lord, at least, and she had heard much of his victory at Gent when, with a small force, he'd held a lightly fortified hill against a swarm of Eika. He knew how to fight already. No wonder King Henry had offered him service in the Lions, although in truth she was surprised that the king hadn't offered to fit him out more nobly, perhaps even to offer him service in the Dragons. But Henry's mind was closed to her. She couldn't understand why he did what he did. Meanwhile, they still had uncounted days to march before they met up with Sapientia. Did more Quman roam these woodlands, waiting to strike at any passing retinue? Her back prickled, and she swung her horse into step with the rear guard so that she would not be the last person in line.

As they came to a bend in the road that cut off their view of the village, she glanced back, and perhaps it was only the darkening clouds or perhaps it was a shadow over her eyes, sowing fear and doubt and premonition.

Carts and wagons emerged from the palisade, laden with hastily packed clothing and chests and barrels, overflowing with crates of chickens and baskets of turnips. The villagers had panicked. As the Lions marched east on the trail of Margrave Judith and the host of Princess Sapientia, Hanna stared as the villagers began their flight westward toward the fortress of Machteburg, all strung out with their crying, clinging children and such weapons as villagers had: pitchforks, spears, shovels. They only paused to spit on the corpses of the dead Quman.

She rode toward them, shouting: "Stay in your village. You'll be attacked on your way west. Don't go."

But they wouldn't listen.

She had already lost sight of the rearguard in the forest. She had her own duty. She'd done what she could here.

She turned her horse and rode east down the now-empty road. The drizzle only made it worse because every drip, every snap of a water-logged branch, made her start round, ready for those dozen Quman who had escaped to come whistling down on her and cut her to pieces. Cut her head off and blacken it and burn it until it became one of those horrible little shriveled heads. She'd noticed that the raiders they'd met didn't carry heads at

their belts. Didn't that mean they were young men who hadn't
made their first kill yet? Wouldn't that make them more dangerous, because they were desperate to prove themselves?

She heard a shout, and abruptly relaxed as she came round
a corner to see a dozen Lions waiting on the road, her old comrades Ingo, Folquin, Stephen, and Leo among them.

Ingo had a good grip on his spear and shield, so he used a
lift of his chin to indicate the road behind her. "Alain noticed
you'd fallen behind. Did you see aught?"

"Only those poor fool villagers. They're running west to
Machteburg."

"Ai, God," said Ingo. "No doubt they'll run right into those
raiders. Poor souls. But we can't wait for them. Come, lads."
They turned to follow the army.

As Hanna made her way up through their ranks, knowing that
she ought to ride in the vanguard, she overheard Alain speaking to Folquin.

"Poor souls," he said softly. "I pray that God protect them
until this war is over and peace returns."

They camped that night within sight of the Salavii village. A
rough palisade protected the village, which boasted more houses
than that of the Wendish settlement, but while the Wendish built
longhouses, the Salavii favored smaller, rounder homes with
curved roofs whose low eaves made storage shelters around each
house. They looked poorer, hadn't as much livestock but seemed
overflowing with little black-haired, pale-complected children
who stared at the soldiers and had to be dragged inside the log
palisade by their more cautious older siblings.

The deacon came to greet them. She had bare feet, was astoundingly filthy, had lost her two front teeth, and needed a cane
despite her youth, but was otherwise cheerful. "What do you
recommend, Eagle?" she asked after she had made an awkward
courtesy to Prince Ekkehard and Lord Dietrich. She had come
from the west and had no discernible accent. Two Salavii men
trailed behind her, one young and one quite old.

"Your Wendish neighbors have fled," said Hanna. "I would
recommend you take these folk to the other village, which is
better fortified."

"They won't want to go," she explained. "They don't trust
the Wendish settlers."

"If they trust you, then you must persuade them, Deacon. We fought a Quman raiding party hours ago. There will be others. Brace for it here if you will, or find stronger shelter if there are other fortified settlements nearby. War may yet be averted, but it is better to be ready for anything."

"Wise words, Eagle. I will do what I can."

The rain slackened finally. She sought out Prince Ekkehard's tent, looking for Ivar, and found him at prayer· with the others. The frailest of their number led them, a thin-faced and very young man with a persuasively sweet voice. Every word seemed fraught with a deeper meaning, one she couldn't understand, but she understood that it made her terribly uncomfortable.

"We pray you, Lady, watch over us as you watched over Your Son—"

The words thrilled through her with a kind of horror. But she waited stubbornly until they finished, and Ivar, seeing her, rose and came out to speak with her.

She was so disturbed that it came in a flood. "You're still in-volved in that heresy. And you've corrupted Prince Ekkehard. Why aren't you with Margrave·Judith? Or in a monastery? Don't you understand what a dangerous path you're treading?"

"It isn't a heresy, Hanna." He had changed. He rested a hand lightly on her arm and spoke with the same persuasive fervor as had his frail friend, although his voice hadn't the same music in it. "It's truth. You didn't see the miracle of the phoenix. If you had, you'd not wonder why Prince Ekkehard prays with us now when he only tolerated us before."

"What kind of miracle?" she asked, although she did not like to do so: this new Ivar made her nervous. Once, like a climb-ing rose, he had grown luxuriantly and with spontaneity. Now, he seemed like a vine trained to a fretwork that some other per-son had constructed.

"A miracle of healing—" Then he caught sight of the ring, and his expression changed again. "But what's this? Has some great lord seduced you with the wealth of worldly goods?"

"The king gave me this as a reward for my service!" she re-torted, furious. "How dare you accuse me—"

"It's what Liath did!" he cried. Then, perhaps hearing that name, Margrave Judith's pretty husband called to him, and Ivar hesitated only a moment before walking away with a curt farewell. Had they grown so far apart? Was their old closeness so quickly ripped into nothing? She walked away, agitated and disturbed, nor did the warm night promise anything better. No matter where she lay down her blanket, dampness seeped through as soon as she settled her weight onto it. She didn't sleep well, and when she lay awake, she twisted the emerald ring round and round on her finger.

At dawn, as they made ready to leave, the deacon came to them again with her two Salavii companions.

"There's been word," she said, translating as the old man spoke in a harsh, impenetrable language. "An army has been sighted east of here carrying the Wendish banner. These people will retreat to an old hill fort north of here. There they'll hope to weather the storm. But he'll lend you the boy to guide you to the other army, if you'll swear by God and to my satisfaction that you'll not harm the lad and that you'll release him as soon as you've met the scouts of the other army. As I said," she added when the old man was done talking, "they don't trust the Wendish."

The deal was done, and certain objects changed hands: the young man came to stand nervously beside Hanna's horse, and Captain Thiadbold saw fit to reward the old Salavii man for these services with a good wool tunic, linen leggings, and a pair of boots—they had belonged to the Lion who died of dysentery, and no one wanted to wear them because of the agony in which he'd died.

The Salavii lad was skittish. He would not accept food or drink from them, nor did he speak a single word for the rest of the day as he led them first east, then south down a narrower track, and then northeast along a broad but shallow stream running through woodland and meadows. In late afternoon they were challenged by half a dozen mounted scouts, and by the time Hanna had established that they had, indeed, met up with Princess Sapientia's army, the lad was gone, vanished into the ash and aspen that lined the stream, which she now saw was only a tributary of a larger river.

At the confluence of stream and river, where the river itself curled around a small hill, Bayan had set up camp with his usual keen eye and cunning. To the north lay denser forest, mostly oak and pine, and to the west and south scattered woodland and grass. To the east, hills rose in a steep escarpment, and the rise which Bayan had chosen seemed like the last straggler, or first

scout, of that army of hills. Some ancient people had built a
structure on this hill, worn now into low earthen ramparts that
crowned the height. It reminded her of a fort gone to ruin, the
kind of place where people and livestock could defend themselves against an enemy. There might have been some tumbled
stones there as well, but from this distance, and angle, it was
hard to make out. Bayan—for she'd no doubt that Bayan had
overseen the placement of the encampment—had pitched the
royal pavilion on the hill itself where one rampart, like a curling finger, gave it shelter. The wagon in which his mother traveled rested about ten strides away, hard up against a curve in
the rampart. Was the Kerayit princess still with the old woman?
Or were Hanna's dreams true dreams?

Now she would find out.

The rest of the encampment straggled down from that central point in rings, each ring of tents protected by fresh ditches,
none particularly deep but enough to break up a cavalry charge.
Riding at the van, she could see the doubled sentries as well as
restless scouts roaming in pairs and half dozens on horseback.
Woodland covered the western vista; to the east, woods followed
the river's valley where it cut a wide pass into the hills. The
camp was ready for war. On high alert, men napped in their
armor with their spears lying as close beside them as might
lovers. Many of the horses remained saddled, and the rest were
being groomed or watered. To the northwest, riders oversaw the
foraging of perhaps forty or fifty horses in the open woodland.

Half the camp came out to welcome them. Hanna wasn't sure
she'd ever seen so many soldiers assembled in one place before,
except at the battle of the Elmark Valley, near the town of Kas-
sel, when Henry had defeated Sabella. Princess Sapientia's banner stirred in the breeze. There were other banners as well at
tents and pavilions only somewhat less grand than that of the
princess, but she only recognized one of them: the leaping panther of Margrave Judith.

As they came into camp, the army split into factions according
to a complicated and confusing maneuver which she couldn't
follow, but in the end she approached the royal pavilion in the
company of Prince Ekkehard, Lord Dietrich, who led the cavalry sent by King Henry, and Captain Thiadbold, representing
the Lions.

The princess sat at her ease beneath the awning of her pavilion, eating a plum as she watched her husband roll dice with a young Wendish nobleman and a flamboyantly dressed Ungrian who boasted mustachios so long that he had tied them back behind his neck to keep them out of the way of his game. Brother Breschius stood quietly in attendance, and it was he who delicately interrupted the game, although by this time Sapientia had risen, seeing Ekkehard or, perhaps, Hanna. Maybe it wouldn't be such a joyous reunion.

Bayan hadn't forgotten her. He leaped up enthusiastically. "The snow woman to us returns!"

"You have come from my father," said Sapientia, more coolly, glancing at her husband with the sudden pinched mouth common to those who distrust their intimates. "And who is this? *Ekkehard?*"

"Sister! Aren't you glad to see me?" He dismounted and came forward, not waiting for permission. She embraced him in a sisterly fashion, kissing him on either cheek. He was taller than Sapientia, but she had gotten a little stouter in the past months, broader in the shoulders, and set against his youthful slimness she looked quite able to out arm wrestle him, should they set to it.

"God help us, little Cousin," said the young nobleman who had been playing at dice with Bayan, "I thought for sure you'd be eaten alive by the Quman."

"No thanks to you, Wichman!" retorted Ekkehard, and for a moment they looked ready to come to blows, but Bayan stepped neatly between them.

"God have blessed us," he exclaimed. "New troops to us come. With this number, we can meet the Quman."

Tallies were quickly made, but Sapientia's humor did not improve. "Two hundreds of Lions? Thirty heavy cavalry and no more than two score inexperienced light? And Ekkehard with twelve untried boys and a few servants? Is this all my father could spare, Eagle? Didn't you tell him how urgent our situation is here?"

"I relayed your message faithfully, Your Highness," said Hanna.

"Come now, wife," said Bayan, interceding. "The lioness must not upon the Eagle pounce who is the messenger only." He seemed amused by his own wordplay and laughed heartily. "Also the margrave's forces we have, and so this is more than what before we had, is it not?"

"So it is," agreed Sapientia grudgingly as he caressed her shoulder. "But where is my father? I thought he would understand how grave our situation is and ride here himself. Where is he, Eagle?"

"Riding south to Aosta, Your Highness."

"Aosta! Always Aosta!" She flung the plum, which narrowly missed striking one of her attendants and instead rolled off into the dirt. "Why is he wasting his substance in Aosta when the real threat is here? He hasn't—" She broke off. But a moment of stillness exhausted her resources. "There hasn't been word of Sanglant, has there?"

Hesitation is always fatal.

"I knew it!" cried Sapientia in cold triumph. "Tell me what you've heard—!"

"I know nothing official, Your Highness. But it has come to the king's attention—" She had no chance to finish. Her cautious recital was interrupted by the arrival of Margrave Judith with a retinue of servants and companions at her back. The margrave was, manifestly, in a cold anger.

"Is it true that Prince Ekkehard has arrived among us? By God, so it is. Where is he?"

"Ekkehard is here," said Sapientia, although it was obvious to everyone else that Judith knew exactly where Ekkehard was.

To give him credit, he did not shrink away from her. "He wants a divorce," he said as calmly as any lad of fifteen or so years could to a furious, formidable, and armed woman old enough to be his grandmother.

Someone in her crowd of followers tittered and was hushed.

"A divorce is within my right to obtain, not his. He has no grounds for divorce, nor has his family power enough to abrogate our agreement. Nor can the marriage be annulled since I recall quite vividly that it was consummated. So the marriage remains binding. Where is he?"

Ekkehard was not a king's son for nothing. "I swore that I would protect him. If I give him up to you, then I cannot count myself an honorable man."

"You are not even a man, Prince Ekkehard. You are only a very foolish boy."

"You can't talk to me like that!"

"Of course I can. I am sure your father feels affection for you, but you are only the third of his three healthy, and adult, children. Princess Sapientia is all but crowned as his heir. You are not necessary to your father's rule. I am. And I want my husband back."

The one called Wichman broke into snorting laughter. "Ai, Lord! Now you're reaping what you've sowed, little Cousin. Which one of those delightful boys is the missing bridegroom? Nay, it all comes clear now, it must be the angel. Not one of the others would have been missed, ugly little rats. Although I fear that Baldwin can scarcely be called an angel now since who knows how many have shared his favors."

Margrave Judith was generous with her anger. "I recall, Lord Wichman, that your reckless behavior caused problems at Gent. Do not forget that your mother and I are old friends. Pray do not forget either that while a king's third son may be of minor utility to him, a duchess' superfluous sons are even less valuable than that."

"Come now, Cousins," said Bayan. He set a deceptively light hand on Wichman's shoulder, more like that of a doting uncle, but steered him nevertheless away from Margrave Judith. "Arguing among ourselves we must not." He swore in his own language and said something hurriedly to Brother Breschius.

"Prince Bayan reminds us that this is not the time to argue," said Breschius with the amiable smile of the accomplished courtier. "We have a war to fight, and none of us knows when it may come to a fight—"

Perhaps God had a sense of humor, except, of course, that war was only amusing in the odd detail, never in the naked face of battle.

"Make way!" guards shouted, and scouts rode up in that instant.

"Prince Bayan! Your Highness!" Two men flung themselves to their knees before their commander. "News of Prince Bulkezu! His outriders have been sighted not an hour's ride east of here, coming down along the river valley."

"Ale for these men," said Bayan.

The news spread from the royal pavilion as though carried by a plague of flies, lighting everywhere. Hanna could almost see it wash through the camp as men bolted up from their naps or huddled in groups or hastily threw saddles over their mounts. Bayan remained calm.

"Where do we fight them?" asked Judith.

"Surely we won't retreat *again*?" cried Sapientia.

Bayan took his time. He asked many and more detailed questions while the army made ready below. He interviewed the two scouts thoroughly, and when a second pair came galloping up, he had ale brought for them as well. They had seen the van of the Quman army, a terrible, whistling many-headed beast swarming over the ground along the northern bank of the river. One of their number had fallen to Quman arrows, and they had themselves been slightly wounded and only barely escaped capture.

"We must hold our ground here," he said at last, speaking in Ungrian and letting Breschius translate. He could not afford to be misunderstood. "This hill fort gives us strength. But, in addition, if their numbers are overwhelming, we can hold the ground to the northwest and retreat that way, across the river. They will hesitate because they are superstitious about crossing water. Also, this summit will give my mother the sight necessary to aid us."

Everyone glanced nervously toward the small wagon. Two slaves waited, cross-legged, beside the steps, one a pale handsome man with an iron bracelet closed tightly on his left arm and the other a very tall, lean man whose skin had the blue-black color of ink. Not even Liath had skin so dark. Did the Kerayit princess wait inside? Hanna caught Brother Breschius' eye then, and he smiled encouragingly at her, but at this moment he could say nothing.

Bayan made a sharp gesture and the guards leaped to attention as one among their number blew into a ram's horn.

The call to arms blazed, and all activity in the camp came to a halt as everyone paused to look up at the hill, toward the royal pavilion. Bayan took Sapientia's hand and they stepped forward so that they could be seen by most of the army. A great shout rose up, and then every man and woman there made ready for battle.

The call to arms came unexpectedly, because it was late afternoon, only a few hours until dark. In all the great poems battle

was joined at dawn, with the first glint of the rising sun splintering off the spears or swords of the enemy as they closed.

But this wasn't a poem.

Ekkehard's boys huddled together at the base of the hill, lead-
erless, confused, unsure what to do, while Prince Ekkehard himself still remained at the royal pavilion.

"I say we bolt north, while everyone is confused," Baldwin
was muttering. "No one will notice we're gone. Then we can
cut back west to that village."

Ivar checked his saddle girth for the third time. "God Above,
Baldwin! It would be dishonorable to desert Prince Ekkehard
now. They'll call us cowards."

"What do I care what they call us?" demanded Baldwin. His
spear lay on the ground, rolling as he caught a foot on it and
almost tripped. "I just want to get out of here before she finds
me!"

"How will we escape alone? We'll more likely just get ourselves killed, and if we're dead, we can't preach the True Word."

"Why should God honor us with Her Truth if we act like
base cowards?" said Sigfrid. He looked so frail and ridiculous
with a spear clutched in both hands. He wasn't strong enough
to wear a mail coat, so he rode unarmored.

"Just so!" said Ivar. "We have to stay, Baldwin. At least until
the battle is over. Then I'll do whatever you say."

Baldwin's expression worked its way through about ten emotions, each of them equally pleasant to look upon. Ivar felt a
sudden, stabbing moment of pity for him, doomed by his beautiful face to be nothing more than a mirror in which other people would see their own desires and dreams.

"Ivar! Sigfrid! Baldwin! Look who I found! It's a miracle!"

Ermanrich stumbled out of the confusion of soldiers forming into units or running off on unknowable errands, of a troop
of cavalry riding out past them and wagons pulling back to the
river's edge where, in pairs, they were being hauled over to the
far shore. Weaving like a drunken man, he seemed oblivious to
the army making ready for battle. He was clutching the wrist of
a very filthy young woman who, like him, was weeping what
were apparently tears of joy.

"It's Hathumod!" Ermanrich cried, and it was a good thing
he identified her, for otherwise Ivar would never have recognized Ermanrich's robust cousin in this thin, ragged woman. She

looked more like a beggar, even had a red sore under one nostril and untrimmed, dirty fingernails.

"Lady Hathumod!" Sigfrid looked astonished. "You were sent away from Quedlinhame with Lady Tallia. Is she here as well, the holy one who revealed the truth to us all?"

"Oh, God," cried Baldwin, grabbing Ivar's arm so hard that Ivar yelped. "It's her. It's *her*."

Suddenly, armed and glorious, Margrave Judith descended the hill at the head of her cavalry, a massive force boasting more than one hundred and fifty heavily armored riding men. To her left, her captain carried the margrave's helm tucked under one arm, and her banner bearer rode at her right hand, banner haft braced on his boot and the banner unfurling as they rode to the plain where battle would be joined.

Baldwin shrank behind Ivar, but it was already too late. Perhaps she had discovered their position by asking where Ekkehard's party rested. Perhaps she could simply smell him, the panther who has fed once upon the flesh of a delicate yearling buck and means to finish him off.

"Ai, Lady!" cried Ermanrich. "Milo's still holding the prince's banner up! You idiot! We were supposed to be hiding."

But it was already too late. Maybe they had been foolish to think they could escape her.

She lifted a hand, and her entire host clattered to a halt behind her as she turned her panther's gaze on her prey. Baldwin fell to his knees with hands clasped at his chest and gaze lifted to the heavens as though he entreated God to bring down such a storm of wrath as would protect him from her notice.

The great ram's horn blared again, sharp and urgent.

"The Quman! To arms! To arms!"

Cries and shouts burst like thunder all through camp and, distantly, Ivar heard a faint, fine whistling noise that sent shudders through his body. He hadn't imagined the sound of their wings could carry so far.

"You will be punished for your disobedience, Baldwin," said Margrave Judith, her mouth set in a satisfied line. "Do not think you will escape me." But she took her helmet out of her captain's hands and settled it on her head. With that, her banner raised high to stream behind, she and her cavalry moved forward toward the battleground.

Ekkehard's boys were mounting, making ready to ride out.

Ermanrich grabbed Sigfrid, whose frail figure and slight body made him seem like a boy even among such a company of very young men. "Sigfrid." He found Hathumod's hand and tightened her grip around Sigfrid's frail wrist. "Go with my cousin. She knows where the baggage train is. You have to stay there." Then he surveyed the others belligerently. "He's just not fit for combat. You all know it's true! He wasn't made for this kind of war. Go on, Sigfrid!" He gave both Sigfrid and the sniveling Hathumod a shove. "Go on!" They hurried off. He wiped away tears as he swung up onto his own horse, grunted at the strain of hitting the saddle hard and, belatedly, grabbed the spear and shield he'd forgotten on the ground, which a groom handed up to him.

"Go with God, young lords," said the groom, who like many of the other servants was falling back to the baggage train.

To their relief, Prince Ekkehard rode up to the company, mounted on a bay gelding. He looked bright and lively, wearing chain mail and a polished conical helm with a bronze nasal. He had unsheathed his sword and waved it enthusiastically. "We are to take up a position on the right flank, along the north bank of the river."

Ivar stood in his stirrups, trying to get a view of the line. The Wendish cavalry stretched across the plain in front of the hill. The Lions formed a line midway up the hill; they were flanked by other infantry. According to Ekkehard, Bayan's and Sapientia's heavy horse waited in reserve hidden between the hill and the river, while more lightly-armed horsemen guarded the northern flank of the hill, keeping the ford clear. Bayan himself stood with Sapientia at the top of the hill, visible to most of the army. As Ivar settled back into his saddle, both Bayan's and Sapientia's banners were lifted high, once, twice, and the third time held there, upraised.

Ivar felt a cool breeze pass through his hair, and it grew in strength until he had to shelter his eyes with a hand in order to keep looking up at the hill. It was a northwest wind, blowing hard toward the southeast, where the Quman approached. On the wings of that wind, the banner of Prince Bayan leaped as if it had suddenly sprung to life, and crisply snapped, so loud that Ivar thought he could hear it whip-sharp even from this distance. Through the gray clouds, a single wide ray of light shone down upon that banner and its simple device, a two-headed eagle, and upon the prince, standing in full battle gear while a groom held the reins of his horse.

All up and down the line men murmured as the column of light shone, trembled, and faded as a cloud covered the sun. Surely they had just seen a divine omen. God marched with them. Ekkehard chivvied his companions up through the loosely-spaced line of light cavalry so that they could reach the front. As Ivar came to the first rank of men armed in light mail hauberks, spears, and shields, he heard Baldwin gasp beside him. The Quman line ran like a sinewy fence over the nearest hill and down into the river valley. The contours of the land were accentuated by the long line of horsemen, which covered at least three of the visible hills.

There was only one banner in the entire Quman host, and it sagged dark and still on the center hill, a black round of cloth marked by three white slashes. The Quman waited a full two bow shots from the Wendish host. They made no move. The entire host simply sat there on their horses, their wings still. How many birds had died to make so many wings?

As Ivar scanned their line, he began to see a pattern to it. Their heavy cavalry massed in the center and left, with light troops on their right. The lighter troops had lances fixed upright along their high-backed saddles, and they held their bows at ready. The heavy troops held lance and shield. All of the riders had wings and several, spread randomly among the host, had wings that glinted as brightly as if the sun were upon them, yet no sunlight fell in the east. The Quman army was shrouded by low-hanging, dark clouds.

"There!" said Baldwin, pointing. Beside the sagging banner waited one rider without wings. Because of this, he didn't have the spreading breadth of the other riders, but even at this distance his presence and his posture left no doubt in Ivar's mind that this wingless rider was the fearsome Prince Bulkezu.

"What happened to his wings?" muttered Milo. His spear, with Ekkehard's battle banner affixed just below the lugs, dipped as he shifted in the saddle. No one answered.

Both armies waited, soldiers staring across the gap in a disconcerting silence. Their nervous mounts snorted, flicking ears, stamping hooves. Horn blasts rang out at intervals, two sharp blasts that reminded the Wendish forces to hold.

Yet after every blast a flood of obscenities flowed from Lord

Wichman's mouth. He waited impatiently with his band just to the left of Ekkehard's position.

"He thinks he knows so much," said Ekkehard. "But Prince Bayan knows better. If he sends this line to the attack, then we'd be wrapped around by the Quman flanks and they could cut us off from the ford, and from our stoutly defended hill."

"Will we sit out here until sunset?" Ivar demanded. The hour was late, and with the heavy cloud cover dusk would come sooner than usual. "I can't believe the Quman would attack a defended hill at night."

"Then we can sneak across the river and fight another day," muttered Baldwin.

"Nay," said Ekkehard boldly. "God have given us a sign. This day will not end without a battle, and God will show Their Hand by choosing a victor."

"Look there!" cried Ermanrich, who rode to the right of Milo.

In unison, three Quman riders rode forward from their line, one from each flank and one from the center. Each rider carried three spears. When they had crossed a third of the distance between the armies, each man planted a spear in the ground. Red pennants hung limply from these planted spears.

Halfway between the armies, the riders each thrust a second spear into the ground. Still they cantered forward. Soldiers shifted restlessly in the Wendish line, but at that moment, as if Prince Bayan sensed their disquiet, the horns rang out again, the two sharp blasts ordering the hold.

But not everyone was listening. Lord Wichman broke free of the line and galloped toward the nearest rider, who still bore his third spear. The Quman man, in answer, lowered his lance to the charge while his two distant companions brought up their horses a sling's throw away from the Wendish line and planted their third lances hard into the ground, like an insult.

Wichman and his Quman opponent met at a charge. A shout rose up from the Wendish host just as wild ululations rang from the Quman. The Quman's spear glanced from Wichman's shield, while his own spearpoint, wavering, missed the rider's head. But the haft of Wichman's spear, striking the rider's faceplate, staggered the Quman. He flipped off the right side of his horse, with his right leg still caught in the stirrup and his wings dragging and disintegrating in the dirt, the wood frame splintering and feathers flying everywhere.

The Quman pony continued to run as Wichman wheeled about and gave chase. The Quman warrior lost both helm and spear as he was dragged through the grass toward the Wendish line, his arms flailing as he struggled to get hold of his saddle. Wichman shrieked in frustration as the Wendish line, where Margrave Judith's banner flew, parted to admit the spooked pony. A cry of triumph erupted as the line quickly closed again. Moments later, the head of the hapless rider decorated a lance. Wichman's oath could be heard all along the line, and at once a roar of laughter erupted from the Wendish line as every man there relaxed, sure now that a great victory was at hand.

Wichman turned his horse to face the Quman host, as if contemplating pursuit of the other two riders, who were returning to their own side, but at that moment, beside the Quman commander, pennants rose and fell in a complicated scheme and the enemy line advanced smoothly and with an unnatural silence, no battle cries, nothing but the steady sound of hooves.

As they reached the first red lance, a hail of arrows rained on the left flank of the Wendish. Horses screamed, but from his position on the far right, Ivar couldn't see how much damage was done there. The Quman continued at a trot, and at the second red pennant a new flight of arrows fell into the Wendish forces even as the Quman riders made the transition to a canter, gaining power and speed. Yet as the Quman line approached the third lance, the sky above them suddenly turned as black as smoke, and a stab of white light struck amidst the Quman archers. A resounding clap of thunder boomed, and for several breaths Ivar could hear nothing, no screams, no horns, no hooves even as he watched the Quman line reach the third lance at a gallop. Another thick hail of arrows blackened the air before falling furiously into the Wendish ranks. The first thing Ivar heard as the ringing in his ears faded was the horrible whistle of a thousand streaming wings.

Horns rang out from the old ring fort where Bayan and Sapientia watched the unfolding battle, staccato blasts that signaled the charge. The Wendish cavalry jolted forward, gaining speed, to meet the oncoming assault. Ivar lowered his spear as he gained momentum, got his weight forward, tucked his spear under his arm. The Quman line loomed close ahead, but because of the looseness of their lines, he faced no enemy. To his left, a Quman rider bore down on Baldwin; to his right, another winged rider fixed his lance toward Milo.

Ivar had hardly any time to think, much less choose. He struck to his left. The Quman rider batted Ivar's spear thrust aside with his own square shield just as Baldwin caught him high in the chest with the point of his own spear. One of them went flying, and Ivar wheeled around to his right just as Milo's riderless horse collided with him. Staggered, Ivar kicked his horse back toward the safety of his own line even though all lay in chaos around him, lines hopelessly mixed together. On the ground in front of him Milo lay dead, a shattered lance protruding from his open mouth.

For too long the gruesome sight of Milo held his gaze. He felt the sword strike more than saw it, parried it with his spear, felt the blow catch and hang there, and then, oddly, his spear fell from his hand. He hadn't lost his grip, and as he panicked, driving forward to try to reach the clot of riders massing around Ekkehard, he saw blood oozing from the stumps where two of his fingers had been only moments before.

It was an oddly unaffecting sight. He grabbed for his long knife, the only weapon left to him, and was pleased to note that his hand still functioned. The Quman with the sword had vanished into the melee. Ivar closed on another Quman rider from behind and, unable to reach the rider through the wooden contraption that was the frame of his wings, he drove his knife deep into the ribs of the pony. He twisted the knife hard around and yanked it free as he passed, and then he was beyond it, using his shield to slam a Quman rider to his left, trying to get by.

There, to his right, the banner of Ekkehard wavered in the hands of one of the escorts from Machteburg. The prince himself struck wildly around with his long sword as three Quman drove down on him. The wing feathers of one of the riders shone like metal, a hard, unpleasant glitter as though he wore at his back a hundred steel knives. Wielding an ax, Baldwin joined Ekkehard, striking down a Quman as he did. But the metal-winged Quman hit Baldwin at a charge, his lance shattering on the jaw of Baldwin's mount. The horse stumbled and fell; Baldwin vanished. The rider, barely slowing, drew his sword, and with two Quman flanking him he made for Ekkehard.

"To the prince!" cried the standard-bearer.

Ivar kicked his mount forward into the fray. He blindsided

one of the flank riders, a stunning crash that sent both men and both horses to the ground. Ivar groped for his knife, lost in the trampled grass. A blow struck him in the side of his helm, and he parried, caught the arm instinctively as a gloved fist trimmed with metal knuckles swung at him again. With all his weight, he drove the man's elbow to the ground, held the wrist down while wrenching the arm over, driving the man's shoulder into the churned grass and then, with another twist, straining the arm until it cracked.

The Quman rider's metal faceplate muffled his scream. Ivar hooked his fingers into the eyeholes of the mask and tried to twist the head around, but instead the man's helmet gave way and slipped free, throwing Ivar off-balance. Pushing off with his unbroken arm, the Quman rolled free. He was young, younger than Ivar, and his face was perfect, as pretty as that of a maiden. Long silken black hair tumbled down over his shoulders. With his left hand, the Quman drew a knife and lunged at Ivar. Without thinking, Ivar struck him across the face with the helmet, knocking him back, and then again Ivar struck, and again and again, and with each blow those beautiful youthful features were scarred and mangled until that face was merely a red smear in the mud.

Breathing raggedly, Ivar looked desperately around for help. Ekkehard's banner lay on the churned grass; like a shroud, it covered the man who had borne it, a silent corpse among so many others. But Prince Ekkehard still rode. Two of his men defended the prince against the attack of the metal-winged Quman rider, who cut them down like so many sheep and pressed for the kill. Ekkehard drove in wildly, cutting around to the man's side, but the wings turned his sword and themselves cut his mail to ribbons. He fell back, wounded, and the winged rider pulled his horse around, ready to deliver the deathblow.

Ivar rose from his knees to run to Ekkehard's aid, but he was too far away. His legs weighed like logs. He would never reach Ekkehard in time.

A roar like a lion bellowing rang from behind the Quman warrior. Wichman charged the rider. They clashed, Wichman raining blow after blow with his heavy sword. The Quman parried and struck in answer, and the two circled and traded blows, neither gaining the advantage. Ivar could hear Wichman's half-crazed laughter, a true berserker's fit.

"Watch out!"

Ivar dove to the shelter of the dead man he'd just killed as a sword cut over his head. Baldwin appeared, ax in hand. "Here." Baldwin thrust a spear into his crippled hand.

"The Prince is down," cried Ivar, but they couldn't aid Ekkehard; they could only aid themselves. The rider who had just passed them wheeled and turned, coming back. Ivar thrust ineffectually at him as he dodged aside. Baldwin nicked the horse's rump with the ax. The man pulled up some distance away from them and turned again, but as Baldwin and Ivar set for him, he calmly sheathed his sword and, without taking his eyes from them, reached behind his back and drew a strung bow. Another lightly armed rider drew up beside him and, seeing the sport at hand, nocked an arrow. Behind him, a third closed in to join his comrades.

"Run!"

Had he cried out, or had Baldwin? They bolted for the hill. He waited for arrows to pierce his back. Shot like a wounded boar! It wasn't the way he had expected to die.

The sky exploded again with a blinding flash, and the air shook with thunder. Stinging rain lashed the ground. Horses reared in fright, although the soldiers focused on battle—those who weren't thrown or already lying dead or wounded—continued on heedless of the weather. Ivar risked a backward glance, and of the men who had meant to shoot him, he saw one rider thrown and the other two struggling to control their mounts.

With a gasp of thanksgiving, he and Baldwin reached the hill and scrambled up onto a curling rampart of earth where two Lions stood, steadfast and still untouched by the battle. The rain had stopped as suddenly as it had begun.

"Well done, young lords, you carried yourselves well out there," said one of the Lions jovially as he helped Ivar up the muddied slope.

"But Prince Ekkehard has fallen." Baldwin was weeping. "We left him out there!"

"Nay, nay, fear not, you've not broken your oaths. One of Lord Wichman's men pulled the young prince from the battle. I think he yet lives."

Their blithe words infuriated Ivar. He felt dizzy, and sick, and hopeless. "Why do you just stand here watching?" he cried. "Why haven't you marched onto the field to bring us victory?"

The older of them snorted. "The battle will come to us soon enough, alas. But if we left this hill, we would be more like to wheat among a harvest of horsemen."

"And where would fancy young nobles like you have to run when their horses are lost and their comrades dead, if not for our station here on this hill?" asked the other, and though the words were spoken in a merry tone, they stung as badly as did his wounded hand.

An arrow struck earth between the Lions. "Go on now, lads," said the elder. "There's a ford on the other side. If you hurry, you can get there in time." Arrows peppered the ground around them as a group of Quman riders closed on the hill but held back, reluctant to attempt a mounted assault up those steep banks.

Halfway up the hill, shielding themselves behind yet another low rampart, Ivar and Baldwin stopped to look back. The mounted archers had closed to within a dozen paces of the slope and were shooting arrows at the two Lions, who slowly skidded up the hill on their behinds, covering their bodies with their large shields. Both seemed wounded in their legs; he hadn't noticed that before. Arrows glanced off their helms and stuck in the woven front of their shields, dangling and bouncing with each movement.

A horseman urged his horse up the slope, but it slipped onto its side, and rider and horse washed down the slope in a slide of mud. Far over to the left, where the slope was less steep, a knot of Lions had formed into a square of shields that bristled with spears. In tight formation, they slowly retreated toward the top of the hill. Now and again a rash rider drove toward them to strike a blow, but always their spears drove the attacker off. As Ivar watched, a rider was hooked and dragged behind the shields. His corpse appeared a moment later, left behind as the wall of shields steadily backed up the hill.

Baldwin was panting, holding his side. "There's too many of them," he said hoarsely.

It was true enough. The Quman gathered at the base of the hill fort like a swelling tide. Only when the metal-winged Quman rode in among them did they begin to disperse, riding away toward the river.

"They're going for the ford." Baldwin had gone very pale, and he could barely speak through his labored breathing. "We'll be cut off."

"Then we'd better hurry if we want to escape." Ivar's hand throbbed, and he stared at it absently as Baldwin rose to a half crouch. Blood oozed from the severed flesh. He really should bind it, but he couldn't think of what to use to stop the bleeding.

"Come on, Ivar!" Baldwin's voice cracked with fear. "Let's go that way." They lost all sight of the battlefield as they moved around the west side of the hill where the cold, muddy ramparts made a maze of their path.

"God be praised! My friends!" Ermanrich slid out from a screen of brush, causing Baldwin to yelp. Ivar merely staggered. "What are you laggards doing hiding up here?"

"Ermanrich!" They pounded each other on the back, wept a few tears, and then started all around, looking for the enemy. The clash of arms still rang ominously, muted now and again by the rumble of distant thunder.

"What happened to you?" Baldwin demanded. "I never saw you again after the first charge."

"My shield was cut in two. I lost my spear. When my horse was struck out from under me, I decided perhaps God hadn't meant for me to be a warrior. So I ran."

"Very brave, dear Ermanrich," said Ivar.

"I see I called it quits two fingers ahead of you. Let me see that." Ermanrich's tunic was shredded and he easily ripped off a strip of wool and bound Ivar's hand tightly. "It's swelling. Does it hurt?"

Ivar shook his head, feeling more and more numb. "Yes. No. Little darts of pain up my fingers—I mean, where my fingers were. Nothing else. And it aches."

They kept moving and as they came around the narrow end of the hill they saw a large force of Quman moving round just inside the river's bend. About fifty heavy horse riding under Princess Sapientia's banner moved south to meet them. The weight of her lead riders simply pressed the Quman toward the river as though they were herding cattle, and yet every one of those lightly armored Quman riders chose to face sword and shield rather than try to swim to safety.

The weight of the melee was all to Sapientia's advantage. Killing as they went, the heavy cavalry drove the Quman back along the river's bank until the metal-winged warrior appeared again, rallying his troops into a counter charge. The two massed lines of horse clashed on the narrow strip of flood plain, but already twilight dimmed the scene as sword and armor and shield clanged like the echo of some great smithy. A horn call rang, one short, one long. Then it repeated.

"That's the call to retreat!" cried Baldwin. "Ai, God! We're going to be abandoned here! The Quman will walk up this hill tonight and cut us down one by one!"

Ermanrich tugged him on, and they ran from rampart to rampart, those strange curling earthworks that wrapped the slope more like decoration than fortification. As dusk lowered, Ivar saw Sapientia escorted from the field by her husband as fully half her company fought on, screening her retreat.

"Young lords, give me a hand, I pray you." The voice was low, almost lost under the din of battle and the growing peals of thunder. In the shadow of an earthen mound, the Lion who had shielded their first retreat lay with blood running from a dozen shallow wounds. He had a hand closed over the boiled-leather jacket of his comrade and was trying to tug him down from the exposed rim of the earthen dike—he and his comrade had evidently retreated by another route, only to intersect them here. A misting rain began to fall.

"We can't wait!" whispered Baldwin, but Ermanrich had already surveyed the situation.

"Nay," he said. "The princess' forces have drawn off those who were climbing the fort before. They won't pursue us right now."

Baldwin was shaking. "But they might be swarming up the other side of the hill. They'll drop down on us from above."

"Then we'll be dead," said Ivar. "I thought you said you'd rather be dead than go to Margrave Judith's bed again. You might just get your wish!"

"But I don't want to die!" wailed Baldwin. Ermanrich slapped him, and he sniffled, wiping his nose, and then, as if nothing had happened, he jumped forward, grabbed the silent Lion's leg, and helped tug him down from the rampart.

They moved on around the hill, sliding in wet ground until their knees and hands dropped mud. The mist turned to drizzle and steadied into rain as they by turns tugged and pushed the unconscious Lion through the moss and the mud while his wounded fellow staggered behind. As they rounded the southwestern turn of the hill fort, they saw the ford lying dim below

them in the ragged glow of a full moon now and then veiled by
cloud. Somehow, although it still rained where they crouched,
the ford lay full in the moonlight, and Ivar could see that the
front of rain quite simply ceased about twenty paces in front of
a semicircle of Lions whose locked shields made a barrier behind which horsemen and infantry forded the river to the safety
of the north shore. As though they were the gates of a refuge,
the shields opened to admit stragglers who came pelting in alone
or in small, beleaguered groups, and then closed again to meet
the erratic charges of the furious Quman, who could not break
the strong shield wall. Across the river, the army wound away
into the woodland in remarkably good formation. The baggage
train was long gone, but a single small wagon more like a little house on wheels sat beside the shore, and for an instant Ivar
thought he saw its beaded window shiver and sway as someone
pressed aside the hanging to look out.

At a stone's toss from the wagon, he saw a pale-haired figure in an Eagle's cloak standing beside her horse. Hanna was
safe across the river.

Off to the east, thunder still rolled, distant now, as if the
storm had passed them by. Below, they could see the Quman
pressing Sapientia's troops backward toward the ford.

"We'll never make it," said Ermanrich. "We're cut off."

"Nay, lads" said the old Lion. "Don't wait for us. If you run
for it—"

"Can't run—" gasped Baldwin.

"Are you hurt?" demanded Ivar.

"No. Just—can't run anymore."

"Look there," said Ermanrich. "There's a bit of a fosse up
ahead. We'll hide there and then make a run for the ford in the
middle of the night."

"The Quman will post a guard," said Baldwin. "They'll kill
anyone they find. We'll never make it."

"Now here's a lad who believes in God's grace," said the old
Lion with a rattling laugh.

"It's true," added Baldwin philosophically, "that death will
free me from my wife."

"At least Sigfrid and Hathumod are safe," said Ermanrich.
"And we might be as well, if we don't despair. That's a sin, you
know."

Ivar knew it was a sin, but his hand was really hurting now

and he just wanted to lie down and rest. But he pressed on with the others toward a ditch lush with reeds and bushes, sheltered from the river by the steep, almost clifflike slope of the hill and by two stark ramparts, their faces slick with mud and, curiously, shale. Hauling the unconscious Lion gave him something to concentrate on as first Ermanrich and then the old Lion slid into the shelter of the ditch. Ivar and Baldwin shoved the unconscious man over the lip, and he tumbled down into a hand's height of water. Ermanrich quickly got his face free of water, although even the rough jostling hadn't woken him. Maybe he was already dead.

Behind them, up at the height of the hill, a thin light began to glow.

"Ai, God!" whispered Baldwin. "Look! It's the Quman, coming with torches to search us out!" He flung himself down into the ditch, and Ivar slipped and slid in his wake, so utterly filthy by now that another layer of mud seemed to make no difference. The rain had slackened and the clouds on this side of the hill had pressed southward, leaving them with the waxy light of a full moon and that eerie, lambent glow from the crown of the hill.

Bounded on one side by the earthen dike, the ditch had become a pool because of the steep precipice on its other side where a stream of water coursed down the cliff face. The falling water had exposed two boulders capped by a lintel stone embedded in the hillside, which were mostly hidden by a thick layer of moss, now shredded and hanging in wet tendrils over the great stones as water trickled through.

Ivar cupped his hands and drank, and the cold water cleared his head for the first time since he had lost his fingers.

"This must have been the spring or cistern for the old fort," he said as he traced an ornate carving still visible beneath the moss on one of the stones: a human figure wearing the antlers of a stag. He pushed away the hanging moss. "Look!" Baldwin slithered up beside him. A tunnel lanced away into darkness, into the hill. Without waiting, Ivar slipped behind the green curtain. It was narrowly cut, but he could squeeze through. Inside lay black as black, and water lapped at his knees, but it seemed safe enough. "Baldwin!"

Ripples stirred at his knees, and then Baldwin brushed up beside him. "Ivar? Is that you, Ivar?"

"Of course it's me! I heard a rumor that the Quman fear water. Maybe we can hide here, unless it gets too deep." He probed ahead with one foot but the unseen bed of the pool seemed solid enough, a few pebbles that rolled under his boots, nothing more. No chasms. He plunged his arm into the black water and found a stone to toss ahead. The plop rang hollowly, then faded. He heard a drip drip drip—and a sudden scuffling, like rats.

"What was that?" hissed Baldwin, grabbing Ivar's arm at the elbow.

"Ow, you're pinching me!"

Then they heard it, a wordless groan like the voice of the dead, an incomprehensible babble.

"Oh, God." Ivar clutched Baldwin in turn. "It's a barrow. We've walked into a burial pit and now we'll be cursed!"

"Iss i-it you?" The voice was unfamiliar, high and light and oddly distorted by the stone and the dripping water. "Iss i-it Ermanrich-ch'ss friendss?"

"L-Lady Hathumod?" stammered Baldwin.

"Ai, t-thank the Lady!" They couldn't see her, but her voice was clear, if faint, blurred by stone and echoes. "Poor Ssigfrid wass wounded in the arm and we got losst, and—and I prayed to God to show me a ssign. And then we fell in here. But it'ss dry here, and I think the tunnel goess farther into the hill, but I was too afraid to go o-on."

"Now what do we do?" muttered Baldwin.

Because of the cold shock of the water, he could think again. His hand throbbed like fire, but he knew what they had to do, even if it meant the risk of awakening the ghost of some ancient, shrouded queen.

"Let's get the others, and then we'll go as deep as we can into the hill. The Quman will never dare follow us through this water. After a day or two they'll go away, and we can come out."

"Just like that?" asked Baldwin, disbelieving or awestruck.

"Just like that," promised Ivar.

2

THE fleet gathered north of Hakonin, in the bay known as Vashinga, and from there they sailed north around the promontory of Skagin and on past the Kefrey Islands, known also as the Goat Brothers. A few ships put in for provisions where various small villages of fisherfolk nestled in the inlets, and there they fetched up barrels of dried herring and slaughtered what goats they could catch.

But Stronghand kept his gaze on sterner prey. His scouts brought him news of Nokvi's fleet, and when they sailed into the great bay of Kjalmarsfjord, they found their enemy anchored in the gray-green waters. A reef complicated their approach, and furthermore Nokvi had positioned his ships between two small rocky islands called Little Goat and Big Serpent.

No matter. Nokvi only had seventy-four ships in his fleet. He still believed that the magic of the Alban tree sorcerers would bring him victory.

From the afterdeck of his ship, Stronghand surveyed his own fleet spread like wings out to either side: fully ninety-eight longships and a score of attendant skiffs for fishing the wounded out of the water. In their wake ran the rippling currents that marked the host of the merfolk, come to feed. Their backs skimmed the surface, glittering, graceful curves that vanished into the deeps as they sounded. A wind had come up from the south, chopping the waters into white froth. It blew hot and damp, and in the south clouds rolled up over the headland.

All along the line of his fleet, sails were furled. Oars chopped at the sea as they formed into battle array: the ships of Hakonin and Jatharin on the northern wing, those of Vitningsey and the Ringarin in the southern wing. Stronghand placed himself with the Rikin ships in the center, with Namms Dale ships to his left and his newest allies, Skuma, Raufirit, and Isa to his right where he could keep an eye on them.

He ordered the masts laid down. Hide drums beat a rhythm for the stroke, and the fleet rowed forward.

"Stronghand." Tenth Son of the Fifth Litter gestured toward the sky at their backs. Rain-laden clouds followed them, and streaks of gray mist tied the clouds to the sea. "It is ill fortune to attack under a dark sky."

"That is the work of the tree sorcerers. It will hinder us less than it will hinder the chieftain they seek to aid. Their magic is nothing more than a shadow beneath the midday sun."

His ship cut the water deep, prow dipping low at each swell. His craftsmen had hammered iron plates at the stem of his ship and bearded the prow with iron spikes. As the storm closed, a strong wind came up from the south, pressing them toward Nokvi's line. At the center of his fleet Nokvi had ordered his warriors to lash together groups of ships into greater platforms, little islands for fighting. His lighter ships he had spread to his flanks, for mobility, and at his rear bobbed a few rounder boats with unfurled sails and uncanny masts, still green and bearing leaves. In these vessels, the Alban tree sorcerers would watch the battle and ply their trade.

But it would avail them nothing. Indeed, he has already seen Nokvi's downfall in the magic Nokvi relies upon for aid.

As the fleets closed, Stronghand hoisted his standard, and the Hakonin ships and the Vitningsey ships swung in to strike Nokvi's flanks. At once, fighting surged fiercely from deck to deck, and as it spread, he raised his standard again for the second flank attack to commence, more ships swinging even wider to grind hulls against their enemy and sweep the ships clean. His center he held steady, shipmen gently backing their oars to hold their distance just beyond an arrow's flight. But he could hear Nokvi's men calling out taunts and insults. Yet neither did Nokvi order the advance; he had already readied his ships, oars pulled in, hawsers tight. He waited for the storm.

At his back, Stronghand felt the wind rise.

On the left flank, one of Isa's ships ground up upon the reef, and a Vitningsey ship drifted aimlessly toward Big Serpent island, cleared of its crew. But some of Nokvi's ships were floundering, too; one had caught fire, and another had but a dozen men defending the afterdeck.

The wind blew with greater strength now. The deck rocked

gently under him, a reminder of the sea's power. Hakonin's ships had driven hard into Nokvi's flank.

Stronghand signaled, and the cauldrons were readied as his warriors rose with a great shout, eager to plunge into the fight. Black streams of smoke rose from the center of Nokvi's fleet; he, too, planned to use fire. Cables snaked out from ship to ship, lashing together those which would strike head-on into Nokvi's center. His own dragon-prowed ship he kept just to the rear of the foremost Rikin platform, three ships abreast.

To the north and south, Nokvi's ships were floundering under the weight of superior numbers, many floating without a crew, empty but for corpses. Of his own fleet, one of Raufirit's ships had capsized and a Ringarin ship lay in flames.

The wind at their backs grew to a gale. Seawater slapped the side, and foam sprayed his face. He lifted his standard for the final time as the first sheets of rain lashed down over them.

His fleet closed. Shields locked, men braced themselves. As the two fleets neared, Nokvi's warriors swarmed to the fore of their ships. The strongest of them loosed their arrows, but wind had reached such a pitch by now that not one flight came close to Rikin's platforms before the arrows were spun harmlessly into the water. His own warriors shot flight after flight, as steady as the rain. Missiles struck across the length of the enemy ships, passing well over the wall of shields that ran back from each stem.

The heavy clouds swept in, and the day darkened as the first of the great platforms ground together, and the real fighting began in the middle of a violent storm. Yet it affected his own men less than Nokvi's. It was Nokvi's men who had to fight facing into the storm. Their vision was battered by the squall. They could barely stand up against the screaming wind while his own ships drove again and again hard against the wooden walls of their enemy and his soldiers cast stones across the gap, as plentiful as hail.

The cauldrons of pitch swung wildly, spilled smoke and hot pitch down shields and into the sea, where it sizzled and died. In this wind, fire gained him little. But it gained Nokvi less. He saw Nokvi at last, standing on the raised afterdeck of his ship, a brawny RockChild with a golden cast of skin, pure as the skeins of a SwiftDaughter's woven skirts. He wore a multicolored girdle of silver, gold, copper, and tin, a magnificent pat-

tern that echoed the intertwined circles painted onto his chest.
Was it possible that he had taken the gods of the humans as
well as their magic?

Stronghand touched the wooden Circle that rested against his
chest, drew his finger around it in the remembered gesture. *It is
well to know your enemy, even to learn from him, but foolish
to believe that he is right. With such an admission, you have
only seeded the ground for your own destruction. As Nokvi had
done, all unknowing.*

Now, at last, Stronghand gave Namms Dale's chieftain, Grimstroke, the longed-for signal. To Grimstroke he had offered the
privilege of revenge.

They laid their ships broadside. Spikes cracked the boards of
Nokvi's ship, and all along the line ships crashed, but the creaks
and groans of wood strained to their utmost was soon covered
by the cries of the RockChildren who leaped the gap and set
about themselves. Grimstroke pressed forward with the strongest
of his men, those who had been absent when Nokvi and his Moerin brothers attacked Namms Dale and burned alive the war
leader and his followers in their own hall. Fury was a great goad.
Grimstroke flowered with it, such that none could stand before
him. He used a wooden club lined with stone blades, and as it
fell first at his right and then at his left, he crushed shield and
helm, arm and skull.

But when Nokvi saw Grimstroke clearing the deck as he
plowed forward, striking to each side, he himself leaped forward
with his spear. As Grimstroke raised his club to strike again,
Nokvi struck a handsome blow, swift and sure: he caught Namms
Dale's chieftain in the throat. But as he fell, Grimstroke swung
one last time, with his dying strength, and his club caught Nokvi's
right hand at the wrist and severed it with such force that hand
and spear flew over the railing and into the sea. Then, with a
gush of blood, Grimstroke ceased to move.

All but the rear of Nokvi's ship had been cleared. Running
forward from the afterdeck, Stronghand saw in the battle all
round him that victory was at hand. Other ships fought on, but
they would yield or run as soon as they saw their leader fallen.

He let his warriors clear the way before him. He had no illusions about his prowess in battle; he was not a great warrior,
nor had he ever wanted to be.

He wanted to be king over all the RockChildren. Not even Bloodheart had gained that much power.

"Kill them all but Nokvi," he cried, and his good strong Rikin brothers made quick work of the last of Nokvi's fine Moerin host until only Nokvi stood, lashing out with a dagger while spears prodded him back.

Stepping up between his troops, Stronghand thrust with his spear at Nokvi's chest with all his might. The thrust pinned Nokvi's good arm to the rudder, and he roared furiously, helplessly, as Stronghand took an ax from one of his brothers and cut off Nokvi's other hand.

His warriors cheered, and from the afterdeck he saw the battle die, as the wind died.

He wrenched the spear out of the rudder, and swiftly, with the haft, upended the spitting and flailing Nokvi until he lay helpless, bent backward over the railing. The sea boiled at the aft of the ship where the merfolk gathered, slick backs churning the bloody waters.

"Let none of the clans stand against me," he cried, "or they shall serve me as Moerin's chief serves me today!"

He flipped Nokvi over the side.

Yet as Nokvi struggled against the grip of the merfolk, and as abruptly sank, as the wind died and the rain let up so abruptly that he knew no natural weather could account for it, he sprang to the stern of the ship and clambered as high as he could, searching for the boats of the Alban tree sorcerers. A fog shrouded the northern entrance to the bay, as though the clouds that had swept up from the south had passed over the battle only to sink into the ocean. He saw a glimpse of a green, flowering mast vanishing into the mist.

Had the Alban tree sorcerers betrayed Nokvi as a way to destroy Nokvi, or had they only deserted him when it became obvious he would lose?

He ran back to his own ship, which rested on the waves free of the hawsers that bound the other ships together, and with Tenth Son of the Fifth Litter steering he set himself to the oars with his brothers as they chased the Alban boats into the fog.

Truly, they had speed and strength that would allow them to catch the Alban boats, but despite his standard fixed at the stem of the ship just below the dragon's prow, they were lost almost at once in the dense fog. He left the oars to stand at the stem

so he could peer into the mist that fell silent around them until
he wondered if they had left Earth entirely. Yet he could still
smell the remains of battle. He smelled a colony of petrels on
an offshore cliff, and heard the shrill cries of a flock of fulmars
gathering by the now-distant ships to feed on the scraps left by
the merfolk. The oars beat the water. The sea soughed against
an unseen shoreline.

He leaned forward into the fog. Was that a flash of light?
Was that movement? Mist streamed against his face, chilling and
moist, and it became so oddly silent that he thought he could
hear the clash of another battle down such a distance that he
knew he was dreaming. He knew he was dreaming of Alain,
even as he felt the sea foam spit on his hands and the clammy
touch of fog curl around his throat.

*The Lions stay on the hill. Below, Prince Bayan has arrayed
the cavalry to face the winged Quman riders, a host so numerous that they seem more like a flood overtaking the eastern hills.
Like a flood, they charge into the Wendish and Ungrian line. He
thinks he has never heard anything as horrible as the sound of
their wings. Nothing, at least, since Tallia repudiated him.*

*Below, battle is joined on the flanks. A bolt of lightning strikes
in the midst of the Quman archers, but after a swirl of confusion, they right themselves and fight on.*

*He can only wait and watch: soon the wounded and unhorsed
cavalry will seek safety among the Lions, and although he stands
in safety now, he knows it is illusion: safety is ephemeral. Lady
Fortune only waits to spin her wheel.*

He wonders at his own bitterness.

*"There!" cries Folquin. "There's their standard, but is that
their commander? Why does the rest of their host proudly wear
wings and yet he wears none?"*

"Pride," suggests Ingo.

*"Humility?" Stephen is youngest among them, still hesitant
to speak his mind.*

*Leo laughs. "Nay, princes are not humble, Stephen. Haven't
you learned that yet?"*

*Then they look at him, and he sees by their expression that
they are remembering what he once was. They are remembering the argument he had with Captain Thiadbold when the captain ordered him to chain his hounds to the baggage train so*

that they wouldn't follow him into the battle; they are remembering, perhaps, the moment during that argument that he forgot himself and acted like a count, not a common Lion whose mother was a whore and whose fate lay in the hands of the king.

The hounds went with the baggage wagons.

"Look," he says now. *The clouds race in out of the east like seagulls flocking to shore before a storm.* *"There'll be rain soon."*

"God help them," says Ingo. *They know what rain will do to a field churned by horses.*

Alain can see no pattern to the battle, only movement boiling in eddies and tides that swell and ebb across the shifting line of melee. Banners jerk from one spot to another, like a boat in choppy seas. Sometimes they fall. Sometimes they rise again in another man's hands.

Folquin gasps and points again. *"He's moving."*

Prince Bulkezu's standard raises high. A howl rises with it, the first voiced sound he has heard from the Quman, who ride silent into war and into death except for their wings. As the wingless prince rides into the battle, horns ring out from the Wendish side.

Prince Bulkezu leads his charge at the center of the Wendish line, straight at the banner of Austra and Olsatia. Margrave Judith and her troops lurch forward to meet the enemy charge. So numerous are they that Alain feels the rumble of hooves shuddering the earth itself. Or perhaps that is only the distant roll of thunder as black clouds sweep in over the hills and the eastern horizon is sheeted in rain.

The heavily armored Wendish horse press eagerly through the Quman line, and soon enough the Lions roar with triumph as Margrave Judith, her banner bobbing beside her, bears down on the Quman standard. Wind lifts her banner until it streams out in glory. The Quman standard only bells outward, hooked to its poles at all four corners. The wingless prince is driven back, and back, by the force of their press, and around Alain the Lions break into a fervent hymn as if their voices will spur their comrades on.

"Blessed are God, who trained our hands for war."

But they are only another sound lost in the din of battle. The margrave's lance glances off the head of the wingless prince, spinning his helm, and as Judith closes, throwing away her lance, he knocks his helm free and a rush of black hair tumbles loose down his shoulders. Her sword strikes true, down on his unprotected head.

But the blow never lands.

A rider plunges forward between them on a horse as white as untouched snow. A battered round shield catches the blow, and its wielder simply shifts and counters with a single smooth blow that takes off Judith's head from her shoulders.

The Austran banner falls next, cut in two, to be trampled into the ground. The wingless prince, freed of his helmet and with his hair so shining a black that it seems a silken banner in its own right, sets to work with his sword.

And she rides at his right hand, as she once rode at Alain's.

All along, Alain believed the Lady of Battles would appear again to him. He had not feared standing to battle because he knew she would be there, as she always had been before.

And she is there. But this time, she rides at the right hand of the enemy. Has she forsaken him? Was it all a lie? Is that her rose, burning at his chest, or only fear in a panicking heart?

The Wendish center collapses utterly as Judith's followers flee the field.

Alone on the hill, the Lions are left exposed.

"Come, friends!" cries Captain Thiadbold, moving along the line. "We'll pull back toward the ford in good order. Keep your shields in position. Cavalry can't break us as long as we keep our shield wall strong."

As the battle dissolves into a hundred melees, the wingless prince leads a charge against the Lions stationed on the hill. Bulkezu swings to the left first, along the southwest flank of the hill fort, but finding it too steep for horses he circles back. The main force of Lions has already reached the summit and started down the northern side of the hill, out of sight. The first cohort stands the rear guard, and Alain keeps step with his comrades as they retreat up the hill after their fellows. The slope below them has a shallow enough pitch that riders can press upward, even with dirt ground to mud by boots and this morning's rain. Yet the ramparts slow their passage. The Lions, on foot, have the advantage here. Nevertheless, he is fiercely glad that Rage and Sorrow are not with him. Here, he cannot protect them.

They make it to the hilltop. Weather and time have worn the

ramparts down to hummocks. In the center of the central ring of earth lies a jumble of fallen stones, and Thiadbold pulls the last cohort into the stones just as Quman riders find their way through the maze of ramparts and burst onto the summit. Spear thrusts thunk on shields. Swords chip at metal rims. But the wall holds.

They retreat through the stones. Alain sees nothing but riders pressing before him. He simply hangs on. His only prayer now is that he hold his place in line, that he not slip at the wrong moment, that his is not the shield that offers the first, and killing, gap. The others strike when a strike is offered. He can only grip his shield and pray. He is useless, but he strives to do his part as best he can so as not to break faith with his comrades.

He has already broken an oath to the family who raised him. He has already lied to a dying man and, by breaking trust with him, lost the very thing that man had given him in trust. He has already lost the only woman he has ever loved.

At least here and now, he can serve the Lady of Battles as he once swore to do.

Then he sees her, a woman of middle age in a coat of mail patched with newer rings of iron. Her sword is nothing fancy, only hard, good metal, made for killing. She wears no helm because she needs no helm.

The Lady of Battles has come to him at last.

But she is still fighting for the other side.

"Hold your line!" cries Thiadbold, striking with his hooked spear at the Quman just to the right of the Lady. With an effortless swing, she drives his spear away from the warrior beside her. Yet still no Quman sword or spear can shatter the shield wall.

She sees Alain.

She raises her sword and then it falls, cleaving his shield into two parts that hang together by only splinters of wood. The shield wall is breached. Now everyone will die.

But not if he sacrifices himself.

He plunges forward so that they can close ranks behind him. Faintly, he hears his name called, but they are not fools. Thiadbold's voice rings out again: "Close the gap! Hold your line!"

For a moment, he knows triumph. Then she stabs him through, just below the ribs. His mail parts like butter before her sword.

Blood seeps through his tabard as he collapses, stunned, and falls:

"But I swore to serve you," *he whispers, astonished, because he really never thought that this of all things would happen to him. He never thought that he would be the one to die on the battlefield.*

"So you have." *Her voice, low and deep as a church bell, rings in his head.* "Many serve me by dealing death. The rest serve me by suffering death. This is the heart of war."

She rides on as the battle flows forward, abandoning him.

A hoof crushes his left hand as a Quman warrior rides over him; he is kicked in the cheek by the trailing leg of another horse. His helmet, strap severed, rolls off.

The tide of battle passes over him. A man moans in agony nearby. Rain spits gently on his exposed cheek. Everything seems much darker now, and for a while he thinks his vision is fading, but then he realizes that the sun is setting; it really is getting darker. A fire has been lit under his ribs, and he thinks maybe it will burn him clean out from the inside. He understands now why it is easy for some men to lie down and die. But he still hears that poor man crying in agony. Reaching, he drags himself over the wings of a fallen Quman rider. He slides over the bloodied body and falls, facedown, in the mud, but with a grunt he pushes up again to his hands and knees, and the misting rain washes his vision clear. There, eye-to-eye, face-to-face, he stares at a dead Lion. He knows the man, but he can't remember his name. It doesn't really seem to matter now because what is a body without a soul? What animated the dead man once is now fled. As his own soul soon will fly. Yet he crawls on because he just can't bear to hear that other man suffering.

He finds a Quman rider writhing on the ground with little swipes and pumps of his limbs, all he can manage as he whimpers, poor soul. A deep cut through his abdomen has spilled his intestines over the ground, and he has been trampled as well.

Ai, God, why does suffering plague humankind? When will it end?

Distantly, he hears the ring of battle, lost over the northern slope of the hill fort. Isn't this the heart of war?

The Quman sees him, then, sees him staring. Their gazes meet. Maybe on the field of battle every soldier shares an un-

derstanding. A dagger lies between them. The man moans words. It is a plea, surely. It is a prayer.

Alain grasps the dagger and with all his strength lunges forward to cut the unresisting man's throat so that he can have a merciful death, if this can be called mercy. Then he falls back, exhausted.

Now he has dealt death. Now he will suffer death. In this way, he has served the Lady of Battles. He gropes at his chest but hasn't the strength to pull out the little pouch that hides the rose. He hasn't anything anymore, nothing that counts, no family, no comrades, no promises that bind him. He is alone now in death as he came alone into life, torn out of a dying woman.

The misting rain turns heavier, soaking the ground. Dusk veils them, but the moon has risen. Yet how can he see the moon when clouds cover the sky? In the tumble of fallen stones, a pale light glows steadily brighter.

Probably he should just lie down now and accept death, but something nags him, pushing him onward. He struggles toward the source of the light. He thinks that when he fought up here before that the stones all lay fallen in, torn down by human hands long ago or simply by the tidal forces of time and weather. Yet one stone stands now at the center of the ruin. It casts a faint bluish light, a ripple like water up and down its length. When he reaches it, he claws his way up its rough surface, bracing himself so that he can stand and see.

Below, the last knot of Lions has made it to the ford. He recognizes Thiadbold's red hair; somehow the captain has lost his helm. Prince Bayan and his cavalry cross the river. Farther to the north, Alain sees the army retreating in good order. At the ford, where some fifty Lions, all that remains of the first cohort, hold their position, the Quman close in.

Upriver, a lower wave crests the bank and slides out onto the plain like a probing finger. Prince Bayan calls out, and the Lions retreat step by step into the shallow ford: There is rash and sentimental Folquin, quiet Stephen, brawny Leo, and fair-minded Ingo. The boldest of the Quman riders press their horses to the shore and even forward a few steps into the water.

The river is rising. A swell of water spills into the Quman line, scattering their horses, and they pull back superstitiously as the Lions retreat in good order across the current and, at last, make it safely to the far shore. As soon as their unit clears the water, a flood roars downstream, borne out of the eastern hills. The river becomes impassable. He thinks maybe he sees creatures in the waves, spinning and twirling as they ride the foam, but he knows any visions he has now can't be trusted.

Pain stabs in his body. He coughs, and an agony like ripping claws tears through his chest. A warm liquid trickles down his lips, and he tastes blood. The world is silent except for the gurgle of his own breathing and the distant roar of the flooding river.

Then, distinctly, he hears a bark. The blue fire flickering along the stone caresses his back. Oddly, it soothes him and sharpens his hearing. He hears another bark, and they tumble up against him, tails beating his body until the pain of their whip-hard tails slapping against him makes his head spin, but he is already spinning. Sorrow licks his hands and Rage leaps right up, a huge paw on either side of his slumped shoulders, and licks his face with that wonderful slobbery tongue.

And he weeps, because he doesn't want to leave them.

It isn't fair to leave them here alone in the world.

Light flares. Cold fire smothers him, and with a sickening wrench he feels the ground jerked one way while he falls the other. . . .

Gone.

Just like that, the link had shattered.

Sunlight glared down on the water. Stronghand had to shade his eyes in order to see. To his left, a little island swarmed with a raucous colony of petrels. Water slapped the ship as they hit the swells off the open sea, rounding the cape that protected the inner bay leading into Kjalmarsfjord. The Alban boats had vanished onto the empty sea.

Still, the tree sorcerers hadn't truly escaped him. Once he had mopped up the last minor resistance among the clans and brought all the tribes and chieftains to acclaim his kingship, he would strike farther afield. All the RockChildren would follow him then, and none among humankind would be able to stop them.

In the ship, his men roared in triumph, and he heard a distant echo from the inlet behind them, where his allies and tribe brothers celebrated.

Today he had won a great victory.

Yet all he felt was grief.

3

DEFEAT tasted oddly sweet. Anne had found them out, and yet for the first time in two years he stood whole, ready for battle, sword raised and a good sturdy horse at his back. For the first time, he saw more than potential in the woman he had married; he saw power manifest. She was more than incomprehensible calculations and annoying, repetitive questions and late night sojourns under the silent stars during which she sometimes seemed more interested in measuring the altitudes of stars than in, well, measuring him. She had earned the sword of power which is true sorcery, something you could *use*.

If they could just get out of this together—

Anne swung her staff away from the unraveling archway of light and pointed it, like an empress' scepter, at Liath. When she spoke, it was with the tone of a regnant, with equal parts severity and mercy. "Liathano, I know you think that I killed your father, but I swear this to be true, you were not conceived of a carnal bond between Bernard and myself. Such a bloodline would be too weak for the path before you." Liath, struggling stubbornly to reweave the patterns and angles of starlight within the stones, faltered as Anne went on. "Your family is not what you believe it is. Your enmity toward me is misplaced. Bernard had no right to steal you. He took what was not his to shape. Surely you see that destiny is upon us. Time is short. Let us not waste it bickering when our combined powers are all that can save this world from ruin."

From a distance he heard the faint, frantic bleating of a goat, a sound that faded into the stuttering grunts of a dying animal. Bells rang, far off at first and then closer, yet they sounded no more loudly in his ears. Three steps in front of him, Liath swung wildly with the arrowshaft as shadows poured like water down over them from the stone circle, tangling the last shimmering lines of her spell like a dark wind that shatters a dew-laden spiderweb.

"We're leaving Verna," said Liath.

"That I cannot allow. Verna is where you must weave your part when the day comes. Here lies the center of it all. Can you not understand, child?" In the midst of the shadows Anne stood, radiant not because she shone with any brilliance of her own but merely because the shadows sliding past her were so utterly black that their blackness limned her form.

Liath cursed under her breath as the sparking, fading lines of her spell tangled, like beheaded snakes, into knots perceptible now only because of the trail of mist left by their threads writhing against the unearthly blackness that swelled everywhere, consuming the heavens and the Earth. But her voice, in reply, was strong. "I am leaving with my husband and child."

"Ai, God!" continued Anne. "I tried to aid you, to prevent this ill conception, this child. Don't you see, Liathano? Prince Sanglant has used you in a most devious way. He tried to kill you by getting a child on you, and look how close he came to succeeding! Only your strength saved you. You are deceived in him. He does not truly love you. He only wants you and the child to gain victory for his own people. When you are free from his influence, you will finally see clearly your duty to God and humankind."

"I don't believe you." Liath took one step toward Anne but seemed to fetch up against an unseen resistance, like a wall of air. Slowly, as against a heavy weight, she lifted her right hand, probing with the shaft; she narrowed her eyes. The gold feather gleamed.

The hem of Anne's robes caught on fire. Startled, Anne took a step back. Air swirled around her until it became a whirlwind, and the fire snuffed out.

"You remain under his spell," said Anne harshly. "So I am left with no choice. 'Nor will any wound inflicted by any creature male or female cause his death.' Let God forgive us for trafficking with such evil creatures, but our cause is just." She raised both arms. "Let the *galla* come and consume him and the child."

Bells tolled at his back, a throb that shuddered up through his feet. The stench of the forge boiled up the hill. The bitter scent made his skin tingle, as after the strike of lightning.

The goat tied to Resuelto's saddle, or its kid, made a sound so horrible that he actually shuddered, whipping around to brace for an attack. Blessing wailed as though something had bitten her.

They were surrounded.

These weren't Anne's captive daimones, feathery creatures formed out of air and water. Blessing's wails turned to infant howls of pain and he felt a stinging, nasty burn pouring over his shoulders and a stab like razor-edged tusks goring his neck.

He lunged toward Anne, thrusting with his sword.

Shadows closed before and behind him, great columns of darkness shuddering and swaying in an unseen wind. They pressed against him, bodiless demons smothering him in their handless grasp. Their voice was the muttering of bells, and they whispered his name.

"Sanglant. Come to us, and you will find peace."

With all his might he pushed his shoulder hard into a shadow, thrusting the sword farther in, but the creature did not yield. Where his arm lay against it, a thousand needles of ice penetrated armor and flesh. Blood rose in pinpricks on his exposed hand, and he felt the warmth of drawn blood sting all along the length of his arm. He recoiled, only to press backward into a burning cold that impaled his back. Blessing screamed, the terror of a tiny child who can only know pain but nothing of its cause. He struck wildly to either side, to free himself, but his sword cut harmlessly through streaming shadow. He twisted, trying to keep his daughter out of their grip.

But he was surrounded. Their huge forms towered over him, bending until he could no longer see the sky. The air swelled with stinging heat until he could barely breathe. Their touch scoured his head until he licked blood from his lips. Blood dribbling from gashes in his scalp and face trickled into his eyes, obscuring his vision. Mail did not protect him. Their bodiless touch reached right through his armor and rent his flesh. Blessing screamed and screamed.

"Call them off," cried Liath from somewhere a long way away. He could see her because even through the black substance of their bodies, she shone. The shaft, cast aside, shone as well: the gold feather burned against the blackness and gave him light to see by. She had drawn her bow. She nocked an arrow, brushed a finger over the point—and the haft began to burn, flames licking up and down the length of it. She drew, sighted, and held there one instant as the *galla* swirled around her but did not close on her. He could no longer see Anne for blackness, but Liath could. Liath could hear Blessing's screams. She loosed the arrow.

Blazing, it flew. And stopped, dead in the air, held aloft by the *galla* or by Anne's daimones, he could not know. Distantly, although truly it could be no more than a few paces from him, he heard Resuelto bolt and clatter away into the trees.

"I'll never aid you!" cried Liath. "Let them go free."

"I will let them go free when you pledge your service to the Seven Sleepers," said Anne coolly.

He heard it as a lie and knew Anne would never allow him to live. But he had no breath in his lungs to tell Liath so. Ai, God, were the creatures even now tearing Blessing to pieces on his back?

How had he come to be on his knees? He tried to lift his sword, to beat them off, but he no longer had any strength in his arms, and his vision was blurring.

Blessing's screams continued unabated, a horrible counterpoint to the knell that throbbed in his ears and obliterated every other sensation until his head boomed with their voices, or maybe that was only his own dying pulse plangent in his ears.

"With us you will find peace, Sanglant."

The air hissed and spun around him. An arrow buried itself in the ground between his hands, and suddenly, winking free of darkness, he saw unshrouded sky above and twinkling stars. A second arrow struck the ground just beyond his left hand, spitting dirt, and another *galla* vanished, winked out with a sizzle.

These weren't Liath's arrows. With that odd narrow concentration given to a man in battle, he saw them clearly: shafts of an unknown wood and fletched with a metal hard feather that he knew at once, with a shiver of misgiving. A griffin's feather.

A third arrow struck off to his right, and he could see its trail, a faint smear of blue cutting through the fell creatures that attacked him. A fourth arrow skittered over the ground, sparks glittering in its wake. It had a slick stone point, ragged and deadly.

A dull blue haze streamed from the center of the stone circle, like steam boiling out of a kettle. He saw through it to another place: a massive rampart, huge marble walls, and an ebony gate already half open. A woman emerged from that gate with bow drawn, and she had only taken one step before she shot again. He ducked instinctively, but the arrow flew over his head and he heard the sizzle of another *galla* banished from the sphere of Earth.

In her wake he smelled the heavy scent of the sea, could even feel the salty sea air on his lips; in her wake, a man leading a laden pony stumbled out into the stone circle. Arrows sang from her bow, and with each shaft sparks sprayed and glittered in the air and *galla* flicked out of existence.

He got to his feet and was rewarded by a sudden indignant squall from Blessing; she still lived. But already Anne's voice rang through the darkness. Surprised by an unexpected enemy, she was not yet defeated. Like a general, she mustered her forces and called up reserves—or perhaps her reserves had only just arrived, called down from the higher spheres. Those who served her at Verna had the delicacy of air and the fluidity of water. These who came at her command at the height of battle had a harsher aspect: human-shaped yet faceless, with wings as pale as glass. They, too, had a voice of bells, a throbbing bass vibrato that made the air ring. They streamed like a wild wind and flung themselves at Anne's enemy with the howling breath of a gale. Their tenuous bodies dissolved to become the tempest.

Into such a wind, the woman could not shoot. But the man at her back grabbed an arrow out of the quiver and, holding it up by the point, he swung it in a circle around himself so that the griffin fletching tracked blue sparks in an arc.

Galla swarmed up around him; Blessing wailed again, and as he fought to move forward, to get out from under them, he saw what damage the griffin feathers did: they harmed the daimones not at all, but in some way they severed the bond that Anne had used to bind her servants to Earth. One by one, daimones darted away into the heavens, to vanish into the night sky. Freed from Anne.

That was what these intruders were here for: to free him from Anne.

He recognized the woman now; he had seen her in his dreams. Wind still battered her, but she, too, had taken an arrow and with it in her hand, head thrust into the wind and her hair streaming back like a banner behind her, she cut a way toward him. With each swipe more daimones tumbled free of the cord that bound them to Anne's spells. It seemed to him that many of Anne's servants flung themselves willingly into the whirlwind of their fellows as if in attack—and in defeat—they sought liberty.

He sheathed his sword and scrabbled for the arrows that had struck earth beside him. The griffin fletching cut into his palms, but he heeded it not. Let it not be said that he did not fight until his last breath. With stone-tipped arrows as his only weapon, he laid about himself furiously. The *galla* drew back, yet they did not flee. Could such creatures even know fear? Did cutting their earthly form cause them pain? Sundered, would their spirits drift endlessly like that of a fallen warrior who has lost his faith? They throbbed and swarmed around him, held back by the threat of griffin's feathers, nothing more than that. It took all his will not to lunge into them, only to hold them at bay. He could not expose Blessing to their touch again.

A pale form slid into the circle he had drawn around himself, the length of his reach with the arrows. He began to lash out; caught himself as he recognized her fluid figure. It was Jerna, writhing, her aetherical mouth twisting and distorting as she tried to communicate with him even as another force seemed to drag her away.

He struck, then, into her pale torso. A silver ribbon shredded into filaments and vanished, and at once Jerna flung herself on him. She coiled, all soothing coolness, over his shoulders and around the crying baby. Blessing's sobs hiccuped to a stop, and for a moment, with the *galla* still hanging back, he had the unexpected leisure to survey the battlefield.

For a moment.

Anne stood by one of the stones, staff raised; daimones crowded her, their light forms throwing her stern figure into relief. He couldn't see Liath, only a cloak of utter darkness where she had stood, as if the *galla* had consumed her entire being. Off to his right, Resuelto had halted at the trees, whose branches whipped and slashed in the gale. The *galla* had only retreated out of range of the griffin feathers. That stench of forge iron was the scent of blood taken from a thousand thousand victims; they were hunters, and they had not given up on their prey.

Distantly, he heard the thunder of an avalanche. Then the storm howled in, out of nowhere. The tempest drove him to his knees as the *galla* shuddered under those impossibly strong winds. The gale raged in his face until he could hear nothing and feel nothing but its scream. He could not even lift his head.

The winds blew dirt into his gritted teeth, choked him with clots
of dirt from the ground itself as though under Anne's command
the daïmones meant to strip the Earth down to its bones. Not
even the *galla* could advance into the maelstrom.

"Liath!" he cried, but he couldn't hear his own voice above
the screaming wind.

And she called fire.

Fire blossomed like wings over Liath's head. The host of
galla who had enveloped her were obliterated in the blaze, and
he saw her in that instant: caught in the blaze, bow raised and
drawn down on Anne, her expression so focused that she seemed
unaware of anything else in the world. She seemed unaware that
her fire had caught in the stones, leaped the gap as a great forest fire leaps from tree to tree like the hand of God. The blue
haze that outlined those shrouded and half-seen marble walls,
that traced the contours of the ebony gate through which the intruders had reached them, ignited into a scorching white blast
of heat that singed his hair although he knelt many paces away.

"Sharatanga protect us!" The voice sounded unexpectedly
loud, at his ear. A strong hand grabbed his arm and tugged him
up. He looked into eyes as sharply green as emeralds: like his
daughter's eyes. Like his own eyes. "What manner of creature
is she? Run, Son! Run! She is calling them through! No one can
survive where they walk!"

High above, the stars themselves seemed to uncoil whips of
light, like fiery arms reaching out. The bowl of the sky itself
seemed to bulge downward, as if something were trying to get
through. And then it found the gateway that had already been
opened.

It flowered out of the ebony gate, a spirit with wings of flame
and eyes as brilliant as knives. It had a form, of a kind, vast
and terrible. Where its feet touched the earth, streams of fire
raced away, igniting the grass. Where its gaze touched the great
crowns of trees, the lush summer foliage simply *whoofed* into
sheets of fire, like a sequence of torches set alight, and birds
burst from the woods in a flurry of wings and flocked in panic
toward the cliffs.

Impossibly, others crowded behind it, pressing out through
the gateway into the tiny valley that seemed far too small to
hold them all. The air became torrid, blushed with a golden haze
rising off their coruscating bodies. The swarming *galla* simply

flicked out of existence as if sucked away into a neighboring room. In their terror, the mules kicked over the corral gate and bolted.

Below, the timber hall burst into flame. He had a moment to grieve for Heribert's fine creation before he heard screams, livestock panicking, the wails of the airy servants still caught by Anne's bonds. The sheds kindled. Cattle and goats and pigs scattered into the darkness. Two human figures stumbled after them.

Incredibly, the tower went up in flames. Even the stone burned, and as he watched, two figures flung themselves from its confines, clutching their precious books to their chests. The luster of this incandescent fire shone even onto the towering cliffs around them, until he realized with horror that this was no reflection of the conflagration but only a continuation of it.

Even the mountains burned.

"Run, Son!" She yanked him on, but he dragged her to a halt. Standing, he was a good head taller. Her pony shoved against him, and reflexively he caught hold of its halter to hold it in place. Of her human servant there was no sign.

"Liath!" he cried, because he couldn't see her in the face of their brilliance. He drew in air to call out again, but the heat of it scalded his lungs and he could not utter one word.

As they pressed forward, they cast from side to side, searching, and he realized that, here on Earth, they were blind. But they were not mute.

Their voice struck like a thunderclap.

"Where is the child?"

Then they found her.

Their wings unfurled in pitiless splendor as they launched themselves toward the heavens. The sound of their wings reverberated off the high mountain walls, a great, booming flood's roar, and the night brightened until it shone with the heat of the noontide sun. He had to shut his eyes, had to shield them with a hand because even through his eyelids the light burned.

Then faded.

He opened his eyes to devastation. Fires smoldered and embers gleamed. Blackened trees cracked and shattered, branches dissolving into ash. He groped at his back, found Blessing's beloved mat of curly hair. She stirred at his touch. A little hand closed on his finger, and she babbled something.

Ai, God. Still alive.

Jerna's sweet breath tickled his hand, soothing his skin.

As he stood there, catching his breath, he saw dawn's light rime the eastern slopes. Somehow, the night had passed them by.

"Sanglant." The hand that closed on his hand was still cool, slightly moist, as though she was coated with a sheen of water. Her voice was a stranger's voice and yet entirely familiar. Was this truly his mother, who stood before him dressed in nothing but a ragged skin skirt and bold painted patterns marking her otherwise naked skin? "I did not know they had made such an ancient and dangerous enemy. Let us go."

He let go of the pony's halter and staggered forward, slipping on ash. Even the ground had been parched and blackened. Alone of all things in this valley, the stone circle stood untouched. Of the marble walls and ebony gate he saw no sign. A single figure lay crumpled at the base of one of the stones: Anne.

Liath was gone.

Maybe he had known from the first instant he had seen them breach the gate and emerge into this world, which could not contain them. He had sensed it before, but now he finally, truly, understood what essence lived inside Liath, like a second being trapped within her skin.

Fire.

"Sanglant, we must go."

He looked at her bleakly. "Where do you intend to take me?" he demanded. "Why should I trust you? How do I know you didn't bring those creatures through to attack us and steal my wife?"

She sized him up rather like a lady examines a stallion she will buy as long as its temperament proves suitable. "I beg your pardon, Son. There should be affection between us, but there is none."

"You abandoned me." He hadn't known he was so bitter. He hadn't known until this moment how much he resented her for what she had done.

But she took no offense at his anger. "I abandoned you because I had to. Because you had to build the bridge between our kind and humankind."

"A bridge, or a sword?"

"What can you mean?"

"Isn't it your intention to conquer humankind once you return to Earth from your refuge?"

She cocked her head to one side, regarding him quizzically. "This I do not understand. Not by our own will did we leave Earth."

With a great sighing gasp, the timber hall collapsed in on itself. Ash and smoke poured up from its rubble into the sky, teased and torn by daimones as they fluttered round the ruined valley. Were they free, making sport of their old prison, or were these the ones not yet unbound from Anne's spell? Anne herself, lying by the stone, groaned and stirred. Below, a hound barked, and he saw its black shape come loping up the hill.

"Her I do not wish to battle again," said his mother. She flicked soot from her mouth, spat, and scented the air, almost like a dog might. "My servant is of no more use to me."

"Is he dead? Should we bury him?" But he, too, watched Anne suspiciously, and in truth, a good captain knows that at times one must retreat in good order even when it means leaving the dead behind.

"Let us go," she repeated, as if in echo of his own thought. "Time grows short. Can you take me to *Henri*?" Although she spoke understandable Wendish, she still said his father's name in the Salian way, with an unvoiced "h" and a short, garbled "ri".

He whistled, and good Resuelto, miraculously unharmed although a trifle singed, trotted nervously over to him, the poor goat hobbling in his wake. He untangled her back legs from the leadline, although she bleated most accusingly and tried to chew on his arm. Her kid was gone, consumed by the *galla*. "I know a path out of the valley that should be open now, unless you want to leave the way you entered. Through the stones."

"Where they did walk, the old paths will be twisted by their fire into a new maze." Hoisting her spear, she shook it, and the bells tied to its base tinkled merrily. "That gate is closed to us."

"Ai, Lady," he murmured as he took Resuelto's reins and soothed the agitated horse, then offered the reins to her.

"Nay, I walk. I lead this small horse." Cautiously, she touched Blessing on the head. Jerna slid away, twining onto Resuelto's neck. "So fecund is the human blood," she murmured, as if to herself. Then she turned and gestured toward the woodland. The air still had a smoky color, almost purplish with dawn. Small animals skittered through the ashy remains, and as they started up the path, leading the two horses, he saw tiny animals digging out from the debris, frantic squirrels and bewildered mice, chittering or silent as was their nature.

"Who is she, the woman they took?" his mother asked.

But he could only shake his head, too choked with rage and sorrow to speak.

4

SHE could not see. She could not hear. Yet she was neither deaf nor blind, only drowning in a wash of such brilliance and overwhelming sound that it had all become a flood, one note, one tone, one absence of color that was pure light. She wasn't sure she was actually breathing, or that there was any air, and yet she wasn't dead either. Oddly enough, she also wasn't afraid. For the first time in years, she understood that there was nothing to fear. The grain of her bow lay comfortably against her palm, gripped tight. The tip of her sheathed short sword, Lucian's friend, grazed her thigh. Her quiver of arrows weighed on her back even as a shift in her position caused the leather straps to press against her collarbone, shifting the gold torque that lay heavily at her throat. A stray curl of hair tickled an ear.

Blue winked.

An instant or a thousand years later she saw it again: the blue flash of the lapis lazuli ring that Alain had given her. Somewhere, where her hand flailed at the tip of her nose or a hundred leagues away from the rest of her body, the ring found purchase and sparked color, a thread her vision could follow.

They were rising. She had a direction now. Her wings beat steadily in time with the others, the sound of their wings as variegated as the voice of a great river. But she didn't have wings. They were carrying her. They had lifted her with them as they sprang to the heavens.

They had named her "*child*."

In the seven-gated city of memory, in the tower of her heart, at the center of her being, rested a chamber set with five doors. Four faced the cardinal directions, north, east, south, and west. Da had taught her all this, the secrets of memory. With his tutoring, she had constructed the room in her mind. But the fifth door, set impossibly in the center of the room, he had built; through the keyhole she could see only fire, which he had locked away even from her.

Now she knew why.

Whose child was she?

Above her, blue flickered again, and as she reached with one hand to touch the other, she saw not the lapis lazuli ring but a tenuous curtain roiling the air, rimmed by blue-white flame whose outline had the same contours as the burning stone she had seen on Earth. Was this another gateway? Was the burning stone only one of many passages from one sphere to the next, from one plane of existence to another?

How was she to pass through, if she could not walk or ride?

They said, *"Fly, child."* And let her go.

But she didn't have any wings.

She plunged. The air was suddenly too thin to breathe. Flailing, she managed only not to drop her precious bow. And for that moment, as she fell, she saw the world laid out below her, a dense black carpet of earth with only the barest pale limning of receding sunlight far to the west where ocean surged restlessly at the edge of her vision. Yet against the vast carpet of land, far below, seven crowns gleamed, seven crowns with seven blazing points each, a central crown and six surrounding it, flung far from that center as though the central crown marked the axle and the other six glittering points along a wheel's rim. She recognized it at once: it was Emperor Taillefer's crown of stars writ large across the breadth of the land, encompassing many kingdoms and uncounted leagues. It was the great wheel, the true crown of stars. The ancient map she had seen at Verna made sense now: seven crowns in seven locations. Was this wheel the loom by which the Aoi had woven their immense and cataclysmic working two thousand seven hundred years ago?

At that moment, sucking in air that didn't give her enough substance to breathe, she also realized that she was going to die.

. Then the glorious creatures blazed around her again.

"She is too heavy to cross into the higher spheres."

"She is not all of the same substance as are we."

"She has no wings."

They gathered her into them, and at their touch she knew an intense joy unlike anything she had ever experienced. They blazed with pure fire, fierce and bright, and the door that Da had locked against her was consumed in that flame. As it opened, she saw for the first time into her innermost heart, the core of her being:

Fire.

Not as fierce as theirs, truly, but of the same substance, impossibly intermingled with her human flesh.

Whose child was she?

They reached the shimmering curtain of light, and she passed through it as through a waterfall, waves of light pouring down over her. Yet she was no longer rising. She seemed caught in the eddy, and they had begun to fade as if they flew on and she remained behind.

"Wait!" she cried. But they had already moved beyond her reach, wings thrumming as one voice caught on the smooth shell where a higher sphere overlapped a lower:

"Follow us."

There are spirits burning in the air with wings of flame and eyes as brilliant as knives. They move on the winds that blow far above the sphere of the Moon, and now and again their gaze falls like the strike of lightning to the Earth below, where it sears anything it touches. Their bodies are the breath of the Sun coalesced into mind and will.

She cannot follow them, and her heart breaks.

Yet as the light of their passing faded, she began to search around herself, found herself walking through endless twisting halls that, scoured and scalded by their passage, glowed with a faint blue luminescence. She was inside the vision made by fire, which is the crossroads between the worlds. She had to find her way home.

But she didn't even know where home was.

There! A boy slept with six companions, heads pillowed on stone, bodies resting on a rich hoard of treasure.

There! Misshapen creatures crawled through tunnels, trapped there by the element of earth that coursed through their blood.

There! A dying man slumped against the burning stone, two great hounds nudging him and licking him as though these attentions would bring him back to life. He stirred, and she recognized him with horror and grief: It was Alain.

She leaped for him, but she misjudged the currents in this place. They swept her into the stone, through the gateway, and she could only grab for him as she passed by. Her hand caught on a mailed shoulder—

He sees a woman clothed in cold fire, and her fiery touch hauls him ruthlessly sideways until he falls free and slams into the ground. He lies there for an interminable time, in a stupor, so washed in pain that he is blind. Then the tongues lick him again, driving him, always driving him to live.

Weeping, he staggers up, not truly able to stand because the wound has pierced so deep, but their great shoulders give him support. He still stands in the hill fort, but even numbed by pain he sees that he is no longer where he once was. It is absolutely silent. No bodies litter the ground, dashed and broken. No horns ring, nor do men cry out in pain, nor does the flooding river's roar overpower the rumbling of distant thunder. The sun rises in the east to reveal a clear and pleasant day.

Impressive ramparts twine down the hill, some of them freshly dug. Where a low mist kisses the low-lying ground still half in shadow below, he sees a river winding through a sparse woodland of pine and beech, only the river does not follow the same course as the river he crossed this morning. It is a different river in the same place. Yet why, then, does the hill fort look so new? Why, at the crown of the hill fort, do all seven stones stand upright where moments ago they all lay fallen in a lichen-swamped heap?

No blue-fire stone burns in the middle of the circle. Instead, within the ring of stones he sees a sward, hacked down so that grass bobs raggedly at various heights. Cowslip and yellow dewcup give scattered color to the grass. Pale purple-white flax flowers ring the squat upright stones. Mist veils the farthest reaches of the hilltop and twines around the more distant of the standing stones.

On a low, flat stone situated in the center of the circle stands a huge bronze cauldron incised with birds: herons and ducks, ravens and cranes. From its rim hang rings, each one linked to a second ring, from which dangles a bronze leaf. He can smell that the cauldron is filled with water. The pure scent of it teases his lips and nostrils. Truly he no longer has any reason to live. He doesn't even know where he is anymore. It would be better just to lie down and die peacefully here, to lay aside his anger at the injustice of his fortune, lay aside his grief at what he's lost and what he failed to do. Yet his legs move anyway. With a hand on either hound to support his weight, he staggers forward toward the cauldron because he has an idea that one sip of that water will heal him, even though he wants to die because the pain is so bad, both the physical pain and the pain of anger and grief. Yet those same feet keep taking their stumbling, weak steps because he can't even despair enough to fall down and die. He wonders if it is possible to love life too well.

Yet why would the world be so beautiful if it wasn't meant to be lived in and loved?

It seems to him that a woman moves toward him. As she emerges from the mist in the gap between two stones he sees that she isn't truly a woman at all. She has long black hair that falls to her waist and a complexion the creamy rich color of polished antlers. Her eyes don't look right; the pupils are sharp, not round, and her ears aren't round either, they pull into a point tufted with dark hair. Where her waist slopes to her hips, her body changes to become a mare's body, sleek and black like her hair.

She is the most beautiful creature he has ever seen.

She comes to a halt before the cauldron, dips her hands in, and lifts them. Water trickles down between her fingers.

"Do you want to live?" Her voice is a melody. "If you want to live, you must give me everything you carry with you. Then you may taste the water of life."

He wants to live. But it is so hard to give up what he has carried for so long.

Yet his hands move anyway because he thirsts for that water. The promise of water is like an infusion of woundwort and poppy, giving him strength to cast aside his belt and boots, to struggle out of his mail coat and tabard. The entire left side of his wool tunic is soaked in blood, but he peels it off and discards it with his leggings so that he kneels naked now beside the cauldron while the hounds lick the seeping blood off his side. Pain and the agony of thirst have numbed him, he can barely feel their tongues or the terrible aching pressure under his ribs.

"Yet you have not given me everything," she says, and he

sees that it is so. He hasn't given her the pouch. It hangs at his neck as heavy as lead. It is so hard to lift his arms, to dip his head, to pull it free. The pouch gapes open, string unwound, and the rose, wilting now, falls beside the stained nail onto the ground.

"Yet you have not given me everything," she says. "Two things you carry with you yet."

He knows the last burdens he carries, but they are not objects he can pass from hand to hand. "How can I give them to you?" he asks, gasping as blood leaks from his wound faster than Rage and Sorrow can lick it clean. Blood trickles from his lower lip, bubbling in time to his breathing. "How can I give you the oath my foster father made, that I forswore? How can I give you the lie I spoke to Lavastine because I wanted him to die at peace?"

"Now they are mine," she says. She sidesteps in the graceful way of horses.

Where she stood, he sees a young woman kneeling in an attitude of intent meditation, so still that she surely must have been there all along even though it is manifestly impossible for two creatures to inhabit the same space at the same time. The young woman does not seem to see him or even hear the conversation, and she is dressed quite strangely, in a tightly-fitted cowskin bodice with sleeves cut to the elbows and an embroidered neck, and a string skirt whose corded lengths reveal her thighs. Copper armbands incised with the heads of deer bind her wrists, and a gorgeous broad bronze waistband ornamented with linked spirals and hatched, hammered edges covers her midriff. She wears a necklace of amber beads and a gold headdress decorated with finely incised spirals and two curling, gold antlers. In one hand she holds a polished obsidian mirror fixed to a handle of wood carved in the shape of a stag. Her expression is pensive, but it is the contrast between eyes drowned in sadness and a generous mouth that seems ready to smile given the least provocation that makes her handsome.

Then the centaur woman moves between him and the cauldron, so he can no longer see her. He can barely cant his neck back to look up into her face. A bubble of blood swells and pops in his nose as his lungs draw sustenance out of his heart. His vision fades, comes into focus again, and he sways. Her body looms, not because she is as big as the warhorses that carry

*Wendish lords into battle but because he realizes now that she
is not mortal in the same way he is.*

*She holds out her cupped hands and brings them to his lips.
He sucks, and the water slides down his throat like nectar.*

*Like nectar, it spreads its essence quickly. He no longer feels
any pain in his ribs, and the shock of healing is so profound
that he falls forward in a daze. Oddly, he feels the prick of the
rose on his right cheek, where his skin presses into the earth.
The hounds nose him, then settle down contentedly on either
side of his prone body. He is so tired.*

But he is alive.

*Then he hears movement, and a moment later a woman's
voice gasps out surprise and a hand touches his naked back with
the kind of stroke reserved for a lover.*

*"Here is the husband I have promised you, Adica," says the
centaur-woman. "He comes from the world beyond."*

*"Did he come from the land of the dead?" This new voice,
eminently human and close by his ear, is low, a little ragged,
not musical but rather the voice of a woman who is courageous
enough to walk open-eyed into the arms of death.*

*"Truly it was to the land of the dead that he was walking.
But now he is here."*

*Her hand rests pleasingly on the curve of his right shoulder,
as if she is about to turn him over to see what he looks like.
But when she speaks, her voice breaks a little on the words.
"Will he stay with me until my death, Holy One?"*

"He will stay with you until your death."

—and then she had lost him and tumbled free, landing hard
on her knees with the wind knocked out of her lungs. Her bow
lay beside her on the sandy ground. Branches rattled in a dry
wind, and a gold feather drifted down through the air to catch
in her hand. Coughing, she got to her feet.

"Well," said the old Aoi sorcerer, letting the half-twined rope
fall to the ground as he stood. "This time you have surprised
me."

"I didn't expect to come here," she admitted. She had to lean
with hands braced on her thighs, catching her breath. Catching
the sobs that shook her. She wanted to weep, but that was one
of the lessons that Da had taught her, that she'd learned so well

that it had become habit: *"If you're crying, you can't hear them coming up behind you."*

Ai, God. There was nothing she could do for Alain. But she had to be strong enough to find Sanglant and Blessing; she had to be strong enough to come to their aid. She rose, letting her breath out with a shudder, tucked the feather away, and brushed dirt from the knees of her leggings and from her palms. She checked herself reflexively for her possessions: bow, quiver, sword, dagger, cloak, Alain's ring, the torque Sanglant had given her. Of Blessing she had nothing but the link of shared blood.

"I meant to leave Verna," she continued, still stunned by the departure of the creatures who had meant to take her with them. "But I didn't know I'd end up here."

"Yet you are here."

"I am here," she agreed, "But—" But still she hesitated.

"You are still bound to the other world," he said, not dismayed, not irritated, not cheerful. Simply stating what was true.

"I am still bound to the other world." Without thinking, she set her hand against the blue-white fire of the stone, and she looked inside.

He leans back against the rock face and lets the glorious heat of the sun warm him. They came clear of the valley an hour or so after dawn and, with the birds singing around him and his mother walking beside him, he understands he is free for now of Sister Anne and her threats and her war. Yet how can he be free from that war knowing what he has learned, that his mother's people mean to return to Earth from whatever place they have been hiding, or exiled? True, his mother desires to go to Henry. But what will she tell him? And what will he say to his father? Whose story can he believe? On whose side will he muster?

He opens his eyes. Resuelto and the pony crop at what grass they can find upon the hillside. Below, smoke curls up from the cookhouse of the hostel below, and he sees robed figures hastening about. The monks are agitated today. Even the bees are agitated, swarming around flowers but not landing to sip nectar.

His mother crouches to one side of the path, spearpoint driven into the ground by her feet. With her forearms braced on her knees, she intently watches Jerna, who is suckling Blessing. The sight clearly fascinates her, although he isn't sure why it ought to. Before he begged her to clothe herself in Liath's spare tunic, it was obvious that the women of the Lost Ones are built no differently than human women in certain regards.

Ai, God. Where is Liath now? He listens, but he cannot hear her.

He dreams that she calls to him across the gulf of the heavens.

"Sanglant," she says. "Beloved."

Blessing pulls her head back from Jerna's breast and babbles, batting at the air as if to grab something only she can see. But he sees and hears nothing.

"You are weeping, child," the old man said as he rested a companionable hand on her shoulder.

"So I am," she agreed. But this time she let the tears fall.

"Truly, there is more to you than even I first saw." He regarded the burning stone with a frown as light flickered along its length and began to die. "I can only see through the gateways using the power of blood. Yet you can simply look, and thereby see."

Startled, she turned on him. "I thought you were a great sorcerer. Can't you teach me everything I need to know?"

He smiled at her and walked away, but he was only going to sit on his bench of rock. He picked up the rope and began to twist the strands against his thigh.

"In the end, only one person can teach you everything you need to know, and that is your own self. If you wish to learn with me, you must be patient. Now." He gestured toward the burning stone. "You must make your choice—there, or here. The gateway is closing."

The flames flickered lower until they rippled like a sheen of water trembling along the surface of the stone.

She was still weeping, gentle tears that slid down her cheeks. "Ai, Lady! What must I do? How can I leave them?"

Yet she had known all along that it might come to this. She could never regret the choice she had made before and, knowing what she had known then, she would make the same choice again: to return to Sanglant.

But she knew a lot more now.

Now she knew who her enemies were. This decision had been made when Anne had tried to set her against Sanglant, when Anne had proved herself willing to let her own granddaughter die. This decision had been made when Brother Marcus had told them that Hugh had worked the sorcery of the crowns. This decision had been made when Anne had admitted that she had herself bound and commanded the daimone that had murdered Da. This decision had been made in that first glorious instant when *they* had emerged through the gate and called her "*child*."

"I'm no use to him or to anyone until I master my own power," she said softly. "They thought I should have wings, and if that's true, then I have to find them—or find out what they meant and what they are."

She crossed to the old sorcerer, set down her weapons, and sat at his feet. Without a word, he handed her strands of flax and, saying nothing more, resumed twisting flax fiber into rope against his thigh. She waited for a moment, expecting him—like Severus—to begin lecturing her. But he did not. He simply twisted flax into rope, humming a little under his breath.

Behind her, the burning stone flickered, faded, and the last glint of blue fire died into the stone until it was only a dark pillar, mute and as solid as rock. Slowly, clumsily, and with many false starts, she began to twist the slender, single strands into a stronger cord.

EPILOGUE

ON that morning some time after dawn, as he crawled out from the shelter of the stone that had shielded him and thus saved his life, Zacharias met a dragon. The creature stretched from one side of the valley to the other. Where its lashing, golden tail seemed to touch a mountaintop, plumes of snow and ice streamed off the summit, whipped free. Its great head huffed and blew beyond the ridge that bounded the valley to the southeast. Sparks rained from its nostrils like so many falling stars. Its belly had the color of sulfur and each claw, tipped with gleaming steel, was as big as a house. Its golden scales lay so close-knit, one overlapping the next, that they appeared like rank upon rank of glittering, impenetrable shield wall. It hung there for fully an hour, or perhaps more, while Zacharias knelt in awe and terror and watched the shimmering undulations of its belly and the clouds of ice billowing off the peak.

Then, with a clap like thunder, it flew up into the heavens and vanished in a wink of light.

After a while, he staggered out of the stone circle and found a stream, where he washed his face and soothed his reddened hands. Two goats wandered haplessly beyond the blackened reeds at the shoreline, and he was too much his grandmother's grandson to leave them there alone. He used his rope belt as a tether.

About that time he noticed the ruined tower and hall below, and he realized that other people moved in the valley. He hid in the trees and watched for a while as two men and three women salvaged what they could from the wreckage. They seemed rather at a loss, as if they were unfamiliar with fetching and carrying, sorting and binding.

He saw no reason to trust them, not after everything that had transpired. He faded back into the woods. In time, and with the help of the goats, he made his way to a meadow high up on the northwestern slope. Here he found several precious items in an old cottage that graced one side of the clearing: rope, an old leather sole, a small cook pot, hazelnuts and withered elderberries stored in a gourd, and a torn scrap of parchment with numbers and diagrams written on it. He wasn't really able to read or write or cipher. The biscop of Machteburg had ordained him as a frater because his capacious memory had never failed him: under examination, he had recalled flawlessly the various services with which churchmen ministered to believers and the stout declarations with which he was enjoined to convert the heathen.

But although he couldn't really decipher it, he sat for a while studying that page in the shelter of the cottage while the goats tore up blackberry bushes and nettles outside. Someone had drawn circles and orbits, and stars in clusters like to the constellations his grandmother had traced for him in the sky: the Hunting Hound, the Stag, the Randy Goat, and the Rabbit. The church mothers had given the constellations other names, and yet all of these wise women and men had passed down certain immutable truths: that five stars wandered in the heavens through a band of stars known as the world dragon, that the Sun and the Moon walked northward and southward in winter and summer, that the passage of the year and the time of the night could be measured by the turning wheel of the stars.

Here in this valley where Kansi-a-lari had brought him, someone had wondered and dreamed about the vast cosmos and the workings of the heavens. Perhaps her son was the scholar, or perhaps it was the beautiful woman he had seen first in his vision at the palace of coils and then in a moment of shining glory before she was enveloped by the fiery daimones and transported by their wings up into the heavens. Possibly the clerical figures he had seen down by the tower were the scholars, but he could not trust them after they had tried to kill him. And anyway, why would they hide this scrap up here when they had been given a fine tower and hall below in which to write and contemplate in comfort?

No doubt he ought not to linger so long. He didn't know what those people down there intended now, in the face of such absolute ruin. He tucked the scrap into the pot, yanked the goats away from their feasting, and found a neat, clearly-marked path leading up through a field of boulders. It took him over the ridgetop and into the arms of three skittish monks.

They spoke Wendish poorly, and although he knew enough Dariyan to quote the liturgy fluently and at length, he had a hard time understanding their babbling explanation of mountains catching fire and portents seen in the sky. He tried to dissuade them from exploring down the path into the valley, but he failed. Apparently they had not until this day known the valley existed although the monastic hostel which they tended had been built over fifty years before by a previous generation of brothers.

They pointed out the hostel to him. Because by this time it was afternoon, and he hadn't eaten for three days, he made his way down a narrow path more suitable to the goats and onto a remarkably well-preserved old stone road that passed the monastery gates. The gatekeeper was either laconic or too stunned to speak after the events of the previous night. The man simply waved Zacharias through, and with some effort, because he was by now quite light-headed, he left his goats in the care of the flustered stablemaster and found his way to the hostel. There he gratefully collapsed while the brother guestmaster brought him a bowl of steaming hot pulse porridge topped by a pat of exquisite butter.

"These are strange times," said the guestmaster when Zacharias had finished his meal and washed down the porridge with a cup of very bold wine. He spoke a number of languages well enough, Wendish among them.

"Are there other guests here today?"

"Nay, none have asked shelter of us today, Brother, although I heard that a man and a woman were seen on the road an hour after dawn. But I think poor Brother Cunradus is seeing things again, for he said they weren't of human face though they were dressed in human clothing. The man was even armed, riding a warhorse, but he had a terrible hunched back, like a demon."

"Ah," said Zacharias carefully. "I'd hope not to meet such a pair, myself. Did they go south or north?"

"North, so he said. From where have you come, Brother?" He gestured, and his young assistant filled Zacharias' cup.

"From the east."

"Where did you lay up last night? Did you see the great fire along the mountains? Did you see the dragon.? As it says in the *Revelation* of St. Johanna, 'Woe to all who stand beside earth and sea, for when the dragon comes, there may be but little time.'"

At once, Zacharias realized his dilemma. What was he to tell this man? Ought he to be honest, or prudent? Might they not bundle him up and send him south to stand trial before the skopos as an accessory to foul sorcery if they knew everything he had done, and thought? Yet no longer could he justify the hypocrisy of pretending to agree. "Do you believe that the dragon is only a portent of some great disaster?"

The guestmaster gave him an odd look. "Truly, what else could these visions mean?"

"Did you not see how it left the air near us by flying up into the heavens and then vanishing? Surely this is not a portent. Surely we merely saw a living creature not accustomed to the confines of Earth who somehow yesterday made its way down through the spheres because of the great disturbances in the heavens. There are gateways through the spheres through which corporeal creatures can travel—"

The guestmaster stood up so suddenly that his bench went flying over. "What manner of heresy is this? The church mothers teach that only our incorporeal souls can travel up and down the ladder of the spheres."

"It isn't so!" objected Zacharias. "They may have believed it was so, but they didn't know everything. If the old wisdom is incomplete or even wrong, why shouldn't we bury it with reverence and grant pride of place to what we discover to be true?"

"Are you repudiating the wisdom of the church mothers? Do you claim to have been granted wisdom that they were denied?"

"I have seen a vision of the cosmos! In it I saw many miraculous things, but I saw no Chamber of Light but rather a great creature so vast that it had neither beginning nor end. And I thought then that we are too small to encompass God. We cannot name God, or gods of any kind. Such a cosmos is ineffable, unknowable. But we are not helpless in the face of glory. Perhaps we can come to understand how a dragon can descend and ascend so that we can hope to do so in time. We can learn why the stars turn in a wheel as they do, or why—"

"You are raving," said the guestmaster coldly. "I see that our good Father Lentfridus foretold rightly this morning at Prime when he said that these portents signaled disorder and disaster.

He will deal with you, because I cannot. Come, Wigo, you have been polluted."

He left the room without another word, and the poor young assistant, all goggly eyes and frightened "o" of a mouth, hurried after him.

Well. Some things didn't change after all. As among the Quman, it was his wretched and ready tongue that got him into trouble. But he could not regret his passionate words. They only confirmed the aim that had been taking shape in his mind since the first moment he saw the dragon.

He had lost his manhood and his honor, been humiliated and shamed. He had lost his simple faith in the Unities and because of that he had no desire to return to the home where he had first pledged fealty to that faith.

But he had gained something else: a new vision of the cosmos, not as a place where God in Unity reign in splendor from a fixed, static throne or where his grandmother's gods gather in the sacrifices and mete out gifts and punishments accordingly, but a cosmos where all these things are true and yet none of them are, a place altogether more magnificent, more numinous, and more mysterious than he had ever imagined.

And he wasn't the only person trying to come to grips with new things. At least one other person in this world was scribbling on parchment, and he recognized in those markings questions rather than answers. Although Kansi-a-lari had abandoned him, either because she thought he was dead or because she had no further use for him, he knew he had to go after her not for her sake, but because of her son. Her son would know who had written on the scrap of parchment.

He had a good idea that he ought not to wait for the guestmaster to return with the abbot, who would no doubt descend with all the wrath of an offended lord and the heavy weapons of orthodoxy at his right hand. His grandmother had always enjoined him to be practical. So he gathered his sparse belongings and departed by way of the stables. With the goats as his stubborn and rather truculent companions and a hearty meal in his stomach, he struck north along the old stone road, following the prince.

KATE ELLIOTT
Crown of Stars

"An entirely captivating affair"—*Publishers Weekly*

In a world where bloody conflicts rage and
sorcery holds sway both human and other-
than-human forces vie for supremacy. In
this land, Alain, a young man seeking the
destiny promised him by the Lady of
Battles, and Liath, a young woman gifted
with a power that can alter history, are
swept up in a world-shaking conflict for the
survival of humanity.

KING'S DRAGON	0-88677-771-2
PRINCE OF DOGS	0-88677-816-6
THE BURNING STONE	0-88677-815-8
CHILD OF FLAME	0-88677-892-1
THE GATHERING STORM	0-7564-0132-1
IN THE RUINS	0-7564-0268-9
CROWN OF STARS	0-7564-0326-X

To Order Call: 1-800-788-6262
www.dawbooks.com

DAW 14

The Golden Key
Melanie Rawn
Jennifer Roberson
Kate Elliott

In the duchy of Tira Verte fine art is prized above all things. But not even the Grand Duke knows just how powerful the art of the Grijalva family is. For thanks to a genetic fluke certain males of their bloodline are born with a frightening talent: the ability to use their paintings to cast magical spells which alter things in the real world. Their secret magic formula, known as the Golden Key, permits Gifted sons to vastly improve the fortunes of their family. Still, the Grijalvas are fairly circumspect until two talents come into their powers: Sario, a boy who will learn to use his Gift to make himself virtually immortal; and Saavedra, a girl who may be the first woman ever to have the Gift. Sario's personal ambitions and thwarted love for his cousin will lead to a generations-spanning plot to seize control of the duchy.

0-88677-899-9

To Order Call: 1-800-788-6262

www.dawbooks.com

DAW 34

Melanie Rawn

"Rawn's talent for lush descriptions and complex characterizations provides a broad range of drama, intrigue, romance and adventure."
—*Library Journal*

EXILES
THE RUINS OF AMBRAI	0-88677-668-6
THE MAGEBORN TRAITOR	0-88677-731-3

DRAGON PRINCE
DRAGON PRINCE	0-88677-450-0
THE STAR SCROLL	0-88677-349-0
SUNRUNNER'S FIRE	0-88677-403-9

DRAGON STAR
STRONGHOLD	0-88677-482-9
THE DRAGON TOKEN	0-88677-542-6
SKYBOWL	0-88677-595-7

To Order Call: 1-800-788-6262
www.dawbooks.com